THE BIG BAD CITY

ALSO BY EVAN HUNTER

NOVELS

The Blackboard Jungle (1954) Second Ending (1956) Strangers When We Meet (1958) A Matter of Conviction (1959) Mothers and Daughters (1961) Buddwing (1964) The Paper Dragon (1966) A Horse's Head (1967) Last Summer (1968) Sons (1969) Nobody Knew They Were There (1971) Every Little Crook and Nanny (1972) Come Winter (1973) Streets of Gold (1974) The Chisholms (1976) Love, Dad (1981) Far from the Sea (1983) Lizzie (1985) Criminal Conversation (1994) Privileged Conversation (1996) Candyland (2001)

SHORT STORY COLLECTIONS

Happy New Year, Herbie (1963) The Easter Man (1972)

CHILDREN'S BOOKS

Find the Feathered Serpent (1952) The Remarkable Harry (1959) The Wonderful Button (1961) Me and Mr. Stenner (1976)

SCREENPLAYS

Strangers When We Meet (1959) The Birds (1962) Fuzz (1972) Walk Proud (1979)

TELEPLAYS

The Chisholms (1979) The Legend of Walks Far Woman (1980) Dream West (1986)

ALSO BY ED McBAIN

THE 87TH PRECINCT NOVELS

Cop Hater* • The Mugger • The Pusher (1956) The Con Man • Killer's Choice (1957) Killer's Payoff • Killer's Wedge • Lady Killer (1958) Til Death • King's Ransom (1959) Give the Boys a Great Big Hand • The Heckler • See Them Die (1960) Lady, Lady, I Did It! (1961) The Empty Hours • Like Love (1962) Ten Plus One (1963) Ax (1964) He Who Hesitates • Doll (1965) Eighty Million Eyes (1966) Fuzz (1968) Shotgun (1969) Jigsaw (1970) Hail, Hail, the Gang's All Here (1971) Sadie When She Died • Let's Hear It for the Deaf Man (1972) Hail to the Chief (1973) Bread (1974) Blood Relatives (1975) So Long As You Both Shall Live (1976) Long Time, No See (1977) Calypso (1979) Ghosts (1980) Heat (1981) Ice (1983) Lightning (1984) Eight Black Horses (1985) Poison • Tricks (1987) Lullaby* (1989) Vespers* (1990) Widows* (1991) Kiss (1992) Mischief (1993) And All Through the House (1994) Romance (1995) Nocturne (1997) The Big Bad City* (1999) The Last Dance* (2000)

THE MATTHEW HOPE NOVELS

Goldilocks (1978) Rumpelstiltskin (1981) Beauty & the Beast (1982) Jack & the Beanstalk (1984) Snow White & Rose Red (1985) Cinderella (1986) Puss in Boots (1987) The House That Jack Built (1988) Three Blind Mice (1990) Mary, Mary (1993) There Was a Little Girl (1994) Gladly the Cross-Eyed Bear (1996) The Last Best Hope (1998)

OTHER NOVELS

The Sentries (1965) Where There's Smoke • Doors (1975) Guns (1976) Another Part of the City (1986) Downtown (1991) Candyland (2001)

*Available in paperback from POCKET BOOKS

ED McBAIN

LULLABY

VESPERS

WIDOWS

THREE CLASSIC NOVELS OF THE 87TH PRECINCT

POCKET BOOKS
New York   London   Toronto   Sydney   Singapore

An *Original* Publication of POCKET BOOKS

 POCKET BOOKS, a division of Simon & Schuster, Inc.
1230 Avenue of the Americas, New York, NY 10020

Introduction copyright © 2001 by HUI Corporation
Lullaby copyright © 1989 by HUI Corporation
Vespers copyright © 1990 by HUI Corporation
Widows copyright © 1991 by HUI Corporation

These titles were previously published individually.

ISBN: 0-7394-2512-9

THE CITY IN THESE PAGES IS IMAGINARY. THE PEOPLE,
THE PLACES ARE ALL FICTITIOUS. ONLY THE POLICE ROUTINE
IS BASED ON ESTABLISHED INVESTIGATORY TECHNIQUE.

Contents

Introduction

In suggesting that we package *Lullaby, Vespers,* and *Widows* in one volume, I recall thinking that these three novels were of a piece, a seamless trilogy that marked a particularly dark time in the annals of the 87th Precinct. Whether or not this coincided with a somewhat bleak era in the history of New York City is a matter for conjecture. Isola, of course, is not New York—regarding which a note of explanation may be necessary.

When Pocket Books, Inc. first approached me about doing a mystery series back in 1955, I told them I felt the only valid people to investigate crimes were cops. Not private eyes, not attorneys, not rabbis or priests, certainly not cats, or little old ladies who belonged to the garden club and solved murder mysteries in their spare time—but cops. C-O-P-S, cops. I told them I wanted to write realistically about cops in New York City. Cops with wives or husbands, boyfriends or girlfriends, families, flaws, even head colds. They gave me a contract for three books—"to see how it goes"—and I started researching and writing the books. The only difference between what I'd discussed and what finally came out of the typewriter was the substitution of a mythical city for New York.

I did this for several very practical reasons, least of which was trying to keep up with the constantly changing rules and regulations of the NYPD. More important, cops needed to know names, addresses, and telephone numbers. If I used a real city, I was risking the possibility of innumerable lawsuits. Isola is fictitious. So are the people and places in it. (The phone numbers, too.) Happily, the mythical city turned out to be a creative plus. I could invent geographical locations that did not exist, and I could invent histories for those places. I could have fun. Anyway, whenever you read a novel set in, let's say Denver, Colorado, and the writer tells you there's a gigantic tower in the center of that city, how would you know whether that tower really exists if you'd never been there? I've never been to Iowa or Idaho; for me, either of those places is only as real as the writer makes it.

For me, Isola is *very* real.

Even so, New York was undeniably going through some bad times during 1989, 1990, and 1991 when these three novels were written. It was a time of random crimes, perps killing victims they didn't even know. It was a time of enormous anger, otherwise polite individuals flaring up in outraged indignation if you happened to brush against them on the street or—God forbid!—snatched a taxicab they thought they'd hailed. It was a time when pedestrians constantly checked their perimeters to make certain they were not about to be ambushed. It was a time when citizens began to distrust, and law enforcement officers began to despair.

It is no accident that the crimes in this trilogy are particularly uncivilized. They seem to speak of a resurgence of, if not evil—which is, after all, a theological concept—then certainly mercilessness. You do not kill an infant. You do not kill a priest. But more than that, in these three novels even the men and women of the Eight-Seven seem to be in extraordinary peril. Civilization, you know, is premised on laws we've constructed and enforced over the centuries. When we break those laws, we threaten the very fabric of society itself. And when the people authorized to enforce those laws are themselves the ones being threatened, the danger is multiplied exponentially. It is as if the last bastions of civilization are under assault. It is as if, finally, we are facing anarchy.

However . . .

Doomsday ain't quite here yet, folks.

All is not lost.

Despite the dark tone of these novels, there is still decency and honor and dedication, and there is humor (I hope) and there is love (I most certainly hope) and there is a promise of better times ahead.

Enjoy.

ED McBAIN
Weston, Connecticut

LULLABY

This is for Julian and Dorothy Pace

Flynn doorstep and tell them their sixteen-year-old daughter was dead. And forevermore, the first of every year would be for the Flynns an anniversary of death.

Meyer had handled the questioning of the Hoddings. Carella figured it was his turn. He knocked on the door again. Knocked long and hard this time.

"Who *is* it?"

A man's voice. Somewhat frightened. Four o'clock in the morning, somebody banging down his door.

"Police," Carella said, and wondered if in that single word he had not already broken the news to Annie Flynn's parents.

"What do you want?"

"Mr. Flynn?"

"Yes, what is it? Hold up your badge. Let me see your badge."

Carella took out the small leather case containing his shield and his ID card. He held it up to the peephole in the door.

"Could you open the door, please, Mr. Flynn?" he asked.

"Just a minute," Flynn said.

The detectives waited. Sounds. A city dweller's security system coming undone. The bar of a Fox lock clattering to the floor. A chain rattling free. Oiled tumblers clicking, falling. The door opened wide.

"Yes?"

A man in his mid-forties was standing there in striped pajamas and tousled hair.

"Mr. Flynn?"

"Yes?"

"Detective Carella, Eighty-Seventh Squad," Carella said, and showed the shield and the ID card again. Blue enamel on gold. Detective/Second Grade etched into the metal. 714-5632 under that. Detective/Second Grade Stephen Louis Carella typed onto the card, and then the serial number again, and a picture of Carella when his hair was shorter. Flynn carefully studied the shield and the card. Playing for time, Carella thought. He knows this is going to be bad. It's four o'clock in the morning, his baby-sitting daughter isn't home yet, he knows this is about her. Or maybe not. Four A.M. wasn't so terribly late for New Year's Eve—which it still was for some people.

At last he looked up.

"Yes?" he said again.

And with that single word, identical to all the yesses he'd already said, Carella knew for certain that the man already knew, the man was bracing himself for the words he knew would come, using the "Yes?" as a shield to protect himself from the horror of those words, to deflect those words, to render them harmless.

"Mr. Flynn . . ."

"What is it, Harry?"

A woman appeared behind him in the small entryway. The detectives had not yet entered the apartment. They stood outside the door, the cold air of the hallway enveloping them. In that instant, the doorsill seemed to Carella a boundary between life and death, the two detectives bearing the chill news of bloody murder, the man and the woman warm from sleep awaiting whatever dread thing had come to them in the middle of the night. The woman had one hand to her mouth. A classic pose. A movie pose. "What is it, Harry?" and the hand went up to her mouth. No lipstick on that mouth. Hair as red as her dead daughter's. Green eyes. Flynn, indeed. A Maggie or a Molly, the Flynn standing there behind her husband, long robe over long nightgown, hand to her mouth, wanting to know what it was. Carella had to tell them what it was.

"May we come in?" he asked gently.

The squadroom at a quarter past five on New Year's morning looked much as it did on any other day of the year. Dark green metal filing cabinets against apple green walls. The paint on the walls flaking and chipping. A water leak causing a small bulge in the ceiling. Cigarette-scarred wooden desks. A water cooler in one corner of the room. A sink with a mirror over it. Duty chart hanging on the wall just inside the wooden slatted rail divider that separated the squadroom from the long corridor outside. A sense of dimness in spite of the naked hanging light bulbs. An empty detention cage. Big, white-faced clock throwing minutes into the empty hours of the night. At one of the desks, Detective/Third Grade Hal Willis was typing furiously.

"Don't bother me," he said the moment they came into the room and before anyone had said a word to him.

Willis was the shortest man on the squad. Curly black hair. Brown eyes. Hunched over the machine like an organ grinder's monkey, he pounded at the keys as if he'd been taught a new and satisfying trick. Battering the machine into submission. Both fists flying. The reports Willis submitted were no masterpieces, but he didn't realize that. He would have made a good lawyer; his English composition qualified him for writing contracts no one could understand.

Neither Carella nor Meyer bothered him.

They had business of their own.

They had learned little of substance from either the Hoddings or the Flynns; they would question them again later, when the shock and subsequent numbness had worn off. But they had been able to garner from them some definite times that pinpointed Annie Flynn's whereabouts and activities while she was *not* being murdered. Starting with all the negatives, they hoped one day they might get lucky enough to fill in the positives that would lead to the killer. Cops sometimes got lucky, Harold.

Meyer sat behind the typewriter.

Carella sat on the edge of the desk.

"Quiet, you two," Willis called from across the room.

Neither of them had yet said a word to him.

"Eight P.M.," Carella said. "Annie Flynn leaves her apartment at 1124 North Sykes . . ."

Meyer began typing.

". . . arrives Hodding apartment, 967 Grover Avenue, at eight-fifteen P.M."

He waited, watching as Meyer typed.

"Okay," Meyer said.

"Eight-thirty P.M. Hoddings leave Annie alone with the baby . . ."

Meyer kept typing.

A cold gray dawn was breaking to the east.

He had shared bacon and eggs with Eileen in an all-night diner on Leland and Pike and then had jokingly but hopefully asked, "Your place or mine?" to which she had given him a look that said, "Please, Bert, not while I'm eating," which was the sort of look she always gave him these days whenever he suggested sex.

Ever since she'd blown away that lunatic last October, Eileen had sworn off sex and decoy work. Not necessarily in that order. She had also told Kling—who, she guessed, was still her Significant Other, more or less—that she planned to leave police work as soon as she could find another job that might make use of her many-splendored talents, like for example being able to disarm rapists in the wink of an eye or put away serial killers with a single shot. Or, to be more accurate, *six* shots, the capacity of her service revolver, the first one in his chest, the next one in his shoulder, the third one in his back, and the others along the length of his spine as he lay already dead on the bed. I gave you a chance, she'd said over and over again, I gave you a chance, blood erupting on either side of his spine, I gave you a chance.

"Now *I* want a chance," she'd told Kling.

He hoped she didn't mean it. He could not imagine her as a private ticket, tailing wayward husbands in some imitation city, of which there were many in the U.S. of A. He could not imagine her doing square-shield work in a department store somewhere in the boonies, collaring shoplifters and pickpockets. I'm quitting the force, she'd told him. Quitting this city, too. This fucking city.

Tonight, they'd left the diner and he'd gone up to her apartment for another cup of coffee, greet the new year. Kissed her demurely on the cheek. Happy New Year, Eileen. Happy New Year, Bert. A sadness in her eyes. For what had been. For the Eileen who'd been his lover. For the Eileen who'd been a fearless cop before the city and the system burned it out of her. Ah, Jesus, he'd thought and had to turn his head away so she wouldn't see the sudden tears flooding his eyes. Still dark outside when he'd left the apartment. But as he'd driven home through silent deserted streets, a thin line of light appeared in the sky in the towers to the east.

He turned the corner onto Concord.

Oh, shit, he thought, I don't need this.

There were four men on the street corner.

Three huge black men and a small Puerto Rican.

The streetlamp was still on over their heads. They struggled silently in the morngloam, natural light mingling with artificial, the three black men wielding baseball bats, the little Puerto Rican trying to defend himself with nothing but his hands. Blood spattered up onto the brick wall behind him. This was in earnest.

Kling yanked up the hand brake and came out of the car at a run, hand going for his gun, rules and regs racing through his mind, felony in progress, substantial reason to unholster the piece. "Police officer," he shouted, "freeze!"

Nobody froze.

A bat came spinning out of the half-light, moving like a helicopter blade, horizontal on the air, twirling straight for his head. He threw himself flat to the pavement, a mistake. As he rolled over and brought the gun into firing position, one of the black men kicked him in the head. In the dizziness, he thought Hold on. In the dizziness, he thought Shoot. Blurred figures. Someone screaming. Shoot, he thought. And fired. One of them fell to the pavement. Someone else kicked him again. He fired again. Knew he was okay by the book, piece as a defensive weapon, tasted blood in his mouth, not a means of apprehension, lip bleeding, how the hell, almost choked on something, a tooth, Jesus, and fired again, blindly this time, angrily, and scrambled to his feet as one of the men swung a baseball bat for his head.

He took a step to the side, the thick end of the bat coming within an inch of his nose, and then he squeezed the trigger again, going for the money, catching the batter too high, five inches above the heart, spinning him around with a slug in the shoulder that sent him staggering back toward the blood-spattered brick wall of the building where the third black man was busily beating the shit out of the little Puerto Rican, swinging the bat at him again and again, long-ball practice here on the corner of Concord and Dow.

"Put it down!" Kling shouted, but his words this morning were having very little positive effect, because all the man seemed intent on doing was finishing off the little Puerto Rican who was already so bloody he looked like a sodden bundle of rags lying on the sidewalk. "You dumb *fuck!*" Kling shouted. "Put it *down!*"

The man turned.

Saw the gun. Saw the big blond guy with the gun. Saw the look in his eyes, knew the man and the gun were both on the thin edge of explosion. He dropped the bat.

"Hey, cool it, man," he said.

"Cool *shit!*" Kling said, and threw him against the wall, and tossed him, and then handcuffed his hands behind his back.

He knelt to where the little Puerto Rican was lying on the sidewalk, bleeding from a dozen wounds.

"I'll get an ambulance," he said.

"*Gracias por nada,*" the Puerto Rican said.

Which in Spanish meant, "Thanks for nothing."

2

A RECONSTRUCTED TIMETABLE can only be verified by the one person who cannot possibly verify it: the corpse.

It appeared, however, that Annie Flynn had left her home on North Sykes, seven and a half blocks from the Hodding apartment, at eight o'clock and had taken a Grover Avenue bus (she'd told this to the Hoddings) down to Twelfth Street, arriving there at eight-fifteen. The Hoddings had left for their party at eight-thirty sharp, taking a cab to their friends' apartment only four blocks downtown on Grover; Mrs. Hodding said she hadn't wanted to walk even such a short distance because of the high heels and the long gown.

From eight-thirty P.M. until approximately twenty minutes past midnight neither the Hoddings nor the Flynns had talked to Annie. As was usual on New Year's Eve, all circuits were busy after midnight and it took Annie's father a while to get through to her. Both he and his wife wished her a happy new year and then chatted with her for five minutes or so. Hodding was trying to reach his home at about that same time. Kept getting a busy signal. It was around twelve-thirty when finally he got through. He ascertained that the baby was okay, wished Annie a happy new year, and then hung up. It was certain, then, that she was still alive at twelve-thirty in the morning. She was not alive at two-thirty, when the Hoddings came back to the apartment. There was no way of knowing whether Annie Flynn—as was often the case with sitters—had made or received any other calls on the night of her murder. The telephone company did not keep records of local calls. Period.

It was now ten minutes past eight.

Meyer and Carella had been relieved officially at a quarter to, but this was a homicide and the first twenty-four hours were the most

important. So once again they put on their overcoats, and their muf-
flers, and their gloves, and they went back to the Hodding building,
this time to knock on doors. This was the tedious part. No cop liked
this part. No cop liked getting shot at, either, but given the choice
many cops would have preferred a good old-fashioned chase to the sort
of legwork that required asking the same questions over and over
again.

With only one exception, each and every resident of 967 Grover
Avenue wanted to know whether it was necessary to be asking these
questions so early in the morning. Didn't they know this was New
Year's Day? Didn't they realize that a lot of people had been up late the
night before? What was so important that it couldn't wait till later in
the day? With only one exception, everyone in the building was
shocked to learn that the Hodding baby and her sitter had been murdered last night. This was such a good neighborhood, they could
understand if something like this had happened farther uptown, but
here? With a doorman and everything? With only one exception, everyone the detectives interviewed had neither heard nor seen anything
strange or unusual between the hours of twelve-thirty and two-thirty
last night. Many of them hadn't even been *home* during those hours.
Many of them had gone to sleep shortly after midnight. The one
exception—

"You're a little late, aren't you?" the man said at once.

"What do you mean?" Meyer said.

"The big show was last night," his wife said. "We had the whole
damn police department here."

"Well, two uniformed cops and a detective," the man said.

As opposed to all the other tenants in pajamas and robes, the
Ungers—for such was the name on their doorbell—were fully dressed
and ready to take their morning walk in the park, *despite* what had
happened last night. What had happened last night . . .

"We were robbed last night is what happened," the wife said.

Her name was Shirley Unger. She was a good-looking brunette in
her late twenties, wearing a gray sweatshirt with a University of Michi-
gan seal on it, gray sweat pants to match, red Reeboks. Hair springing
from her head like a tangle of weeds. Red sweatband on her forehead.
Luminous brown eyes. A Carly Simon mouth. She knew she was gorgeous. She played to the cops like a stripper on a runway.

"We got home at about one-thirty," she said. "The robber was just
going out the window. In the TV room. Actually a second bedroom."

She rolled her eyes when she said the word "bedroom," as though there'd been something licentious about a burglar going out the window. She seemed to be enjoying the thrill of all this criminal activity, although—like most honest citizens—she confused burglary with robbery. To your honest citizen, somebody stole something from you, it was robbery. Any cheap thief on the street knew the difference between burglary and robbery. Any garden-variety crook could reel off the penal-code numbers for each crime, the maximum prison terms. Just like a cop. In this business, you needed a scorecard to tell which player was which.

"We called the police right away," Unger said.

"They were here in three minutes flat," Shirley said. "Two cops in uniform and a detective. A little short guy with curly hair."

Willis, they both thought.

"Detective Willis?" Carella asked.

"Yes," Shirley said. "That's the one."

"Must have picked it up on the car radio," Meyer said.

Carella nodded.

A police department was a big organization. There were close to twenty-eight thousand cops in this city. Even in the same squadroom, you didn't always get a chance to cross-check one case against another. Willis had probably been making a routine run of the sector when he'd caught the 10-21. Burglary Past. Figured he'd run on over, save the responding blues the trouble of calling it back to the precinct. The report Willis had been typing so furiously when Meyer and Carella got back to the squadroom may have been on the Unger burglary. They hadn't told him they'd caught a double homicide at 967 Grover. He hadn't told them he'd caught a burglary at the same address. Nobody asked and nobody offered. Sometimes you had to go the long way around the mulberry bush.

"So what's this?" Shirley asked. "The follow-up?"

They told her what this was.

She did not seem terribly impressed. She was more interested in whether the police were going to get back the emerald ring her husband Charlie had bought for her eight years ago on their honeymoon in Calle di Volpe, Italy, on the island of Sardinia. She was also interested in whether the police were going to get back the new VCR Charlie had bought her for Christmas this year. "Well, *last* year already, am I right?" she said and smiled a radiant smile that said I would love to kiss your pectorals. She also wanted to know how long this was going to take because she wanted to go out for her walk and she was beginning to get hot here in the apartment, dressed for the outside as she was.

Carella told her that any questions regarding the burglary would have to be answered by Detective Willis, but that he and his partner wanted to know a little more about this man they'd seen going out the window . . .

"Yes, onto the fire escape," Shirley said.

. . . because the burglary here in the Unger apartment on the sixth floor of the building might have been related somehow to the double homicide downstairs on the fourth floor.

"Oh," Shirley said.

"Yes," Meyer said.

"Then would you mind if I took off˙my sweatshirt?" she asked. "Because, really, it *is* very warm in here."

Without waiting for their permission, which she didn't need anyway, she pulled the U-Mich sweatshirt over her head, revealing fat red suspenders and a flimsy white cotton T-shirt. She was not wearing a bra under the T-shirt. She smiled modestly.

"You say this was around one-thirty?" Carella said. "When you came into the apartment?"

"Yes," Shirley said shyly. Now that she was half-naked, she was playing a novitiate nun at a cloister in the mountains of Switzerland. Her husband was still wearing a ski parka. He had begun to perspire visibly, but he did not take off the parka. Perhaps he figured he could inspire the detectives to cut this short if he did not remove the parka. Let them know he wanted to get the hell out of here, go take his walk in the park. Subtly hint to them that he didn't give a flying fuck about the baby who'd got snuffed in the apartment downstairs. *Or* her babysitter, either. What were they going to do about getting back his camel hair coat that had been bought at Ralph Lauren for eleven hundred bucks was what *he* wanted to know.

"And you say the burglar was in the bedroom, going out the window . . ."

"Yes. The robber," Shirley said. "With my VCR under his arm."

"What did he look like?" Meyer asked. "Did you get a good look at him?"

"Oh, yes," Shirley said. "He turned to look back at us."

"As we came into the bedroom," Unger said.

Carella had already taken out his pad.

"Was he white?" he asked. "Black? Hispanic? Orient . . . ?"

"White."

"How old?"

"Eighteen, nineteen."

"Color of his hair?"

"Blond."

"Eyes?"

"I don't know."

"Neither do I."

"How tall was he?"

"That's difficult to say. He was all hunched over, you know, going out the window onto the fire escape."

"Can you guess at his weight?"

"He was very thin."

"Well, he was wearing black," Shirley said. "Black makes a person look thinner."

"Even so, he was thin," Unger said.

"Was he clean-shaven? Or did he have a beard, a mustache . . . ?"

"A mustache."

"A small mustache."

"Well, a *scraggly* mustache. He was just a kid, you know."

"Like it was just growing in."

"You know the kind of mustache a kid has? Like fuzzy?"

"That's the kind of mustache this was."

"When you say he was wearing black . . ."

"A black leather jacket," Unger said.

"Black slacks."

"And sneakers."

"White sneakers."

"And my coat," Unger said.

"Your what?"

"My camel hair coat Shirley bought for me at Ralph Lauren for eleven hundred bucks."

Must be some coat, Meyer thought.

Carella was thinking the same thing. The first *car* he'd owned had cost eleven hundred bucks.

"What color was the coat?" Meyer asked.

"I told you. Camel hair. Tan."

"And he was wearing this over the black leather jacket . . ."

"Yes."

"And the black slacks . . ."

"Yes, and the white sneakers."

"Any hat?" Meyer asked.

"No."

"Did you say anything to him?"

"Yes, I yelled 'Take off my coat, you fucking crook!'"

"Did *he* say anything to you?"

"Yes."

"What did he say?"

"He said, 'If you call the cops, I'll come back!'"

"Very scary," Shirley said.

"Because he was pointing a gun at us," Unger said.

"He had a gun?" Carella said.

"Yeah, he pulled a gun out of his pocket."

"Very scary," Shirley said again.

"So I called the police right away," Unger said, and nodded for emphasis.

"Do you think he'll be back?" Shirley asked.

Carella didn't know what she was playing now.

Maybe the expectant rape victim.

"I don't think so," he said.

"Did Detective Willis examine that fire escape?" Meyer asked.

"Yes, he did."

"Would you know if he found anything out there?"

"Nothing belonging to *us,* that's for sure," Shirley said.

Detective Hal Willis was in bed with a former hooker when the telephone rang at ten minutes past twelve that afternoon. He was sleeping soundly, but the phone woke him up and he grabbed for the receiver at once. Every time the phone rang, Willis thought the call would be from some police inspector in Buenos Aires, telling him they had traced a murder to the city here and were planning to extradite a woman named Marilyn Hollis. Every time the phone rang, even if he was asleep, Willis began sweating. He began sweating now.

Not many cops on the squad knew that Marilyn Hollis had done marijuana time in a Mexican prison or that she'd been a hooker in B.A. Willis knew, of course. Lieutenant Byrnes knew. And Carella knew. The only cop who knew that Marilyn had murdered her Argentine pimp was Willis.

"Willis," he said.

"Hal, it's Steve."

"Yes, Steve," he said, relieved.

"You got a minute?"

"Sure."

"This burglary you caught last night . . ."

"Yeah."

Beside him, Marilyn grunted and rolled over.

"We're working a double homicide in the same building."

"Oh boy," Willis said.

"Occurred sometime between twelve-thirty and two-thirty."

"Mine was at one-thirty," Willis said.

"So the Ungers told us."

"How'd you like her tits?" Willis asked.

Beside him, Marilyn rammed her elbow into his ribs.

"I didn't notice," Carella said.

"Ha!" Willis said.

"The Ungers told us you were poking around on . . ."

"Who's us?"

"Me and Meyer. Poking around on the fire escape."

"Yeah."

"Did you find anything?"

"A vial of crack."

"So what else is new?"

"Plus there looked like a lot of grimy prints on the windowsill, where he was working with a jimmy to get in. I called in for the van, but nobody showed. This was only a two-bit burglary, Steve. On New Year's Eve, no less."

"If it's linked to a homicide . . ."

"Oh, sure, they'll dust the whole damn city for you. *Two* homicides, no less."

"You mind if I give them a call?"

"Please do. We bust the burglar, I'll have an excuse to go see Shirley again."

Marilyn gave him another poke.

"Did you file your report yet?" Carella asked.

"It's probably still sitting on Pete's desk."

"Mind if I have a look at it?"

"Go right ahead. Let me know what happens, okay? I bust a big burglary, I'll maybe make Second Grade."

"Don't hold your breath," Carella said.

"Talk to you," Willis said, and hung up.

*   *   *

In this city, if your apartment got burglarized, the police sometimes sent around a team of technicians to see what they could find by way of latent fingerprints. This was if the burglary involved big bucks. A dozen fur coats, negotiable securities, expensive jewelry, cash, like that. In smaller burglaries, which most of them were, the technicians never showed. This was not negligence. Close to a hundred and twenty-five thousand burglaries had been committed in this city during the preceding year, and there were only one lieutenant, six sergeants and sixty-three detectives in the Crime Scene Unit. Moreover, these people were more urgently needed in cases of homicide, arson, and rape.

So your average responding uniformed police officer would tell the burglary victim that a detective would be handling the case, and that they could expect a visit from him within the next day or so. Which was normally true unless the detective's case load was backed up clear to China, in which event the victim wouldn't be getting a visit from him until sometimes a week, ten days, even two weeks after the burglary. The detective would then take a list of what was stolen and he would tell the victim, quite honestly, that unless they caught the perpetrator in the act of committing another burglary or else trying to pawn the stuff he'd stolen here, there wasn't much chance they'd ever find him *or* their goods. And then the detective would sigh for the dear, dead days when cops used to have respect for burglars.

Ah, yes, there once was a time when burglars were considered the gentlemen of the crime profession. But that was then and this was now. Nowadays, most burglars were junkie burglars. Your more experienced junkie burglars usually jimmied open a window, the way the Unger burglar had done, because they knew that nothing woke up neighbors like the sound of breaking glass. Your beginning junkie burglars didn't give a shit. *Whap,* smash the window with a brick wrapped in a dish towel, knock out the shards of glass with a hammer, go in, get out, and then run to your friendly neighborhood fence (who was most often your dope dealer as well) and pick up your ten cents on the dollar for what you'd stolen. Only the most inexperienced burglar went to a pawnshop to get rid of his loot. Even a twelve-year-old kid just starting to do crack knew that cops sent out lists of stolen goods to every pawnshop in the city. To take your stuff to a pawnshop, you had to be either very dumb or else so strung out you couldn't wait another minute. Either that, or you were visiting from Mars.

So the chances of the Crime Scene Unit showing up at the Unger apartment were very slight, when one considered that the only items stolen were an emerald ring purchased in Italy for the sum of $2000, which gave you some idea of the quality of the emerald; a VCR that had cost $249 on sale at Sears; and an admittedly expensive cloth coat which was, nonetheless, merely a cloth coat. In a city crawling with addicts of every color and stripe, in a city that was the nation's drug capital, the dollar amount of your average burglary haul fell somewhat lower than what had been stolen from the Ungers, but this was still nothing to go shouting in the streets about and nobody down at the lab was about to dispatch the van for a garden-variety *burglary*, for Christ's sake, when people were getting killed all *over* the place, for Christ's sake!

Until Carella called in to say they had a double homicide and that one of the victims was a six-month-old baby.

In the private sector, if a CEO asked for an immediate report on something which in his business would have been the equivalent of a homicide, that report would have been on his desk in the morning. All two hundred and twenty pages of it. Otherwise, heads would have rolled. But this was not the private sector. This was civil service work. Considering, then, that New Year's Day was a Sunday and that the holiday was officially celebrated on a Monday, Carella and Meyer were hoping that by the end of the week—maybe—they'd have some urgently needed information from the Latent Print Unit. If one of the forty-three examiners assigned to that unit could come up with a match on the prints the Crime Scene boys had lifted from the Unger windowsill; if they could further match the prints on the handle of the Flynn murder weapon with prints in the Identification Section's files, everybody could go to Lake Como for a vacation.

On Tuesday morning, the third day of the New Year, they had a long talk with Annie Flynn's parents. Harry Flynn worked as a stockbroker for a firm all the way downtown in the Old City; the walls of the Flynn apartment were covered with oils he painted in whatever spare time he managed to salvage from his rigorous routine. His wife—neither a Molly nor a Maggie but a Helen instead—was secretary to the president of a firm in the garment district; she mentioned the name of the clothing line, but neither of the detectives was familiar with it. This was now ten o'clock in the morning. The Flynns were dressed to go to the funeral home. He was wearing a dark suit, a white shirt, and a black tie. His wife was wearing a simple black dress, low-heeled black pumps, and dark glasses.

The detectives did not yet know where to hang their hats.

The Flynns came up with a possible peg.

"Scott Handler," Flynn said.

"Her boyfriend," Mrs. Flynn said.

"Used to be, anyway."

"Until Thanksgiving."

"Broke off with him when he came down for the Thanksgiving weekend."

"The long weekend they had in Thanksgiving."

"Broke off with him then."

"Came down from where?" Carella asked.

"Maine. He goes to a private school in Maine."

"How old is he?" Meyer asked.

"Eighteen," Mrs. Flynn said. "He's a senior at the Prentiss Academy in Caribou, Maine. Right up there near the Canadian border."

"They'd been going together since she was fifteen," Flynn said.

"And you say she broke off with him in November?"

"Yes. Told me she was going to do it," Mrs. Flynn said. "Told me she'd outgrown him. Can you imagine that? Sixteen years old, she'd outgrown somebody." Mrs. Flynn shook her head. Her husband put his hand on her arm, comforting her.

"Called the house day and night," Mrs. Flynn said. "Used to burst into tears whenever I told him she didn't want to talk to him. Spent hours talking to me instead. This was long distance from Maine, mind you. Wanted to know what he'd done wrong. Kept asking me if he'd done something. I really felt sorry for him."

"He came by again just before Christmas," Flynn said.

"Home for the holidays."

"Caught Annie here in the apartment, she was the one who answered the door."

"We were in the back room, watching television."

"Started begging her to tell him what he'd done wrong. Same thing he'd kept asking my wife on the phone. What'd I do wrong? What'd I do wrong? Over and over again."

"Annie told him it was over and done with . . ."

"Said she didn't want him to come here ever again . . ."

"Said she wanted nothing further to do with him."

"That's when he raised his voice."

"Began hollering."

"Wanted to know if some other guy was involved."

"We were in the back room, listening to all this."

"Couldn't hear what Annie said."

"But *he* said . . ."

"Scott."

"He said, 'Who is it?' "

"And then Annie said something else . . ."

"Couldn't quite make it out, her back, must've been to us . . ."

"And he yelled, 'Whoever it is, I'll *kill* him!' "

"Tell them what else he said, Harry."

"He said, 'I'll kill you both!' "

"Those exact words?" Carella asked.

"Those exact words."

"Do you know his address?" Meyer asked.

Scott Handler's mother was a woman in her late forties, elegantly dressed at eleven-thirty that Tuesday morning, ready to leave for a meeting with clients for whom she was decorating an apartment. She looked a lot like Glenn Close in *Fatal Attraction.* Meyer thought that in this day and age, he would not like to be any woman who looked like the lady in that movie. If Meyer had been a woman with naturally curly blonde hair, he'd have paid a fortune to have it straightened and dyed black just so he wouldn't have to look like the woman in that movie. Luckily, he was bald and didn't look like her in the slightest. On the other hand, Mrs. Handler had a problem. Right down to a somewhat chilling smile.

"My son left for Maine early this morning," she said.

"Went back to school, did he?" Meyer asked.

"Yes," Mrs. Handler said, and smiled that slightly psychotic, hair-raising smile, although Meyer did not have any hair.

"The Prentiss Academy," Carella said.

"Yes."

"In Caribou, Maine."

"Yes. Why do you want to see him? Does this have something to do with the little Irish girl?"

"Who do you mean?" Meyer asked innocently.

"The one who got killed on New Year's Eve. He broke off with her months ago, you know."

"Yes, we know," Carella said.

"If their relationship is why you came here."

"We just wanted to ask him some questions."

"About where he was on New Year's Eve, I'd imagine."

The chilling smile again.

"Do you *know* where he was?" Carella asked.

"Here. We had a big party. Scott was here."

"All night?"

"All night."

"What time did the party start?"

"Nine."

"And ended?"

She hesitated. Merely an instant's pause, but both detectives caught it. They guessed she was trying to remember if she'd read anything about the time of Annie Flynn's death. She hadn't because that was one of the little secrets the detectives were keeping to themselves. But the hesitation told them that her son had *not* been at the party all night long. If he'd been there at *all*. Finally, she chose what they figured she thought was a safe time to be saying goodbye to the old year.

"Four in the morning," she said.

"A late one," Meyer said, and smiled.

"Not very," she said, and shrugged, and returned the smile.

"Well, thank you very much," Carella said.

"Yes," she said, and looked at her watch.

On Wednesday morning, the fourth day of January, both murder victims were buried.

The detectives did not attend either of the funerals.

The detectives were on extension phones to the Prentiss Academy in Caribou, Maine, talking to an English professor named Tucker Lowery, who was Scott Handler's advisor. They would have preferred talking to Scott himself; that, after all, was why they had placed the long distance call. Both men were wearing sweaters under their jackets. It was very cold here in the city, but even colder in Caribou, Maine. Professor Lowery informed them at once that it was thirty degrees below zero up there. Fahrenheit. And still snowing hard. Carella imagined he could hear the wind blowing. He decided that if his son ever wanted to go to the Prentiss Academy, he would advise him to choose a school on the dark side of the moon. His daughter, too. If Prentiss ever began admitting females. Who, being the more sensible sex, probably would not want to go anyplace where it got to be thirty degrees below zero.

"I don't know where he is," Lowery said. "He's not due back until the ninth. Next Monday."

"Let me understand this," Carella said.

"Yes?" Lowery said.

Carella imagined a tweedy-looking man with a pleasant, bearded face and merry brown eyes. A man who was finding this somewhat amusing, two big-city detectives on extension telephones calling all the way up there to Maine.

"Are you saying that classes won't resume until next Monday?" Carella said.

"That's right," Lowery said.

"His mother told us he'd gone back to school," Meyer said.

"Scott's mother?"

"Yes. We saw her yesterday morning, she told us her son had already gone back to school."

"She was mistaken," Lowery said.

Or lying, Carella thought.

The Puerto Rican's name was José Herrera.

There were tubes sticking out of his nose and mouth and bandages covering most of his face. One of his arms was in a cast. Kling was there at the hospital to try to learn when Herrera would be released. He had come here upon the advice of Arthur Brown, one of the black detectives on the squad.

Brown had said, "Bert, you have shot two men, both of them black. Now every time a cop in this city shoots a black man, you got deep shit. A cop can shoot seventeen honest Chinese merchants sitting in the park minding their own business, no one will even raise an eyebrow. That same cop sees a black man coming out of a bank with a .357 Magnum in his fist, he just stole fifty thousand dollars in cash and he shot the teller and four other people besides, your cop better not shoot that man or there's going to be an outcry. All kinds of accusations, racial discrimination, police brutality, you name it. Now, Bert, I would love to see what would happen if one day I *myself* shot a black man, I would love to see how *that* particular dilemma would be resolved in this city. In the meantime, my friend, you had best get over to that hospital and talk to the man whose brains were getting beat out on that street corner. Get him to back up your word that you were following departmental guidelines for drawing and firing your pistol. That is my advice."

"Go fuck yourself," Herrera told Kling.

The words came out from under the bandages, somewhat muffled, but nonetheless distinct.

Kling blinked.

"I saved your life," he said.

"Who asked you to save it?" Herrera said.

"Those men were . . ."

"Those men are gonna kill me anyways," Herrera said. "All you done . . ."

"I almost got killed *myself!*" Kling said, beginning to get angry. "I lost a goddamn *tooth!*"

"So next time don't butt in."

Kling blinked again.

"That's what I get, huh?" he said. "That's the thanks I get. I save a man's goddamn life . . ."

"You know how much pain I got here?" Herrera asked. "If you'da let them kill me, I wouldn't have no pain now. It's all your fault."

"*My* fault?"

"You, you, who you think? I get outta this hospital, they'll kill me the next minute. Only this time I hope you ain't there. This time I hope they finish the job."

"Nobody's gonna kill you," Kling said. "Only one of them's out on bail . . ."

"How many does it take? You don't know these people," Herrera said. "You got no idea how they operate."

"Tell me all about it."

"Sure. Big fuckin' brave cop, knows everything there is to know. You don't know shit. These people are gonna *kill* me, you understand that?"

"Why?"

"Go ask *them.* You're the big hero, go talk to who you busted. They'll tell you."

"Since I'm here, why don't you just save me the time?" Kling said.

"Go fuck yourself," Herrera said again.

3

THE LATENT PRINT UNIT reported back on Thursday morning. That very same morning, Meyer and Carella received reports from both the police lab and the Medical Examiner's Office. This had to be some kind of record. The Hat Trick, for sure. Every other detective on the squad was astonished and envious. Cotton Hawes, who was himself working a burglary, asked if he could use the Hodding-Flynn murders as an excuse to get the lab to do some work for *him*. Hawes looked furiously angry when he asked this question, perhaps because he was a huge man with fiery red hair except for a white streak over his left temple where once he'd been knifed. The streak made him look even more furious, like a vengeful bride of Frankenstein. Unintimidated, Willis told him to go find his *own* double murder.

The lab reported that the tool marks found on the fire-escape window and sill in the sixth-floor Unger apartment did not match the tool marks found on the fire-escape window and sill in the fourth-floor Hodding apartment.

The lab reported that the cord attached to the mobile discovered on the floor in the baby's bedroom matched a cord fastened to a hook in the ceiling over the baby's crib. This suggested that the mobile had been torn loose from the ceiling. The mobile was made of tubular metal painted red and blue. It emitted a chime-like sound when one section of it struck any other section. There were no fingerprints on any section of the mobile.

The lab reported that the hairs vacuumed from Annie Flynn's body and clothes were foreign pubic hairs.

The Medical Examiner's Office reported finding fresh seminal fluid in Annie Flynn's vaginal contents.

Had she been resisting rape?

They had not, until this moment and despite the girl's torn blouse, considered the possibility that this might be a rape-murder. But . . .

The M.E.'s report went on to note that within a few minutes after female orgasm, spermatozoa normally was spread throughout the somewhat alkaline cavities in the uterus and fallopian tubes. The spermatozoic spread at the time of the Flynn autopsy—begun half an hour after the body reached the morgue—had been well-advanced, indicated not only penetration but orgasm as well. Absent orgasm, as was normal in most rape cases, the spread often took as long as six hours. The M.E. was not conclusively ruling out rape. He was merely pointing out that the girl had apparently achieved orgasm. The report further noted that semen samples had been sent to the laboratory for identification and group-typing in the event of later comparison with isoagglutination groups in the blood of the accused—God willing, Meyer thought.

The Latent Print Unit reported that Annie Flynn's fingerprints were the only good ones found on the handle of the knife that had killed her. There were foreign prints as well, but these were too smudged to be useful in a search. Regarding the burglary in the Unger apartment, the unit had done what was called a *cold* search. No suspect's prints against which to compare. No names to check. Nothing but the latents lifted from the Unger window and sill. Find out who had left them there. A cold search on the local level could sometimes take weeks. On the state level, it often took months. Carella had once asked the FBI to do a cold search for him, and they had not come back to him until a year later, after the case had already gone to trial. But on this fifth day of January, the LPU reported that the latents on the Unger window and sill had been left there by a man named Martin Proctor—alias Snake Proctor, alias Mr. Sniff, alias Doctor Proctor—who had a record going back to when he was twelve years old and first arrested for breaking into a candy store in Calm's Point. His B-sheet, as supplied by the Identification Section, filled in the rest.

At the time of his first arrest, Proctor belonged to a street gang called The Red Onions, comprised of daring young bandits between the ages of eleven and fourteen, all of them with an apparent craving for chocolate. Snake (as Proctor was then known) had been elected to break into the candy store and steal a carton containing a full gross of Hershey bars—with almonds, the president of The Red Onions S.A.C. had specified. The S.A.C. stood for Social and Athletic Club, a euphemism most street gangs affected.

The cop on the beat had caught him coming out of the back of the store. Snake had grinned and said, "Hi, want a Hershey bar?" The arresting officer had not found this comical. The judge, however, thought Snake's casual remark indicated a good sense of humor, which he felt was the prime requisite for making a worthwhile contribution to society. He let Snake off with a warning.

First mistake.

Six months later, Snake . . .

He was called Snake, by the way, because there was a python tattooed on his left biceps, beneath which, lettered in blue, were the words LIVE FREE OR DIE, the motto for the state of New Hampshire, though by all indications he had never been there.

Six months later, Snake was arrested for a jewelry store smash-and-grab and this time the judge was a lady who frowned upon such activities even if they netted only a pair of eighteen-karat-gold wedding bands and a digital wristwatch selling for $42.95. Snake, a juvenile offender, was sent to a juvenile detention facility upstate, from which he was released at the age of fourteen. By then, he had learned how to do cocaine, which for a price was readily available at the facility, and had acquired the name "Mr. Sniff," which was a *nick*name as opposed to the earlier "Snake," which had been a *street* name. The new name was apparently premised on Mr. Sniff's insatiable need for sucking up into his nostrils however much cocaine he could purchase or steal.

Drugs and stealing go together like bagels and lox.

Your white collar drug users may not necessarily be thieves, but down in the streets, baby, your user is a hundred times out of a hundred stealing to support his habit.

Over the years, Proctor managed to avoid imprisonment again until he was nineteen years old and got caught red-handed inside somebody's house in the nighttime. Burglary One, for sure, in that the dwelling was also occupied and Proctor threatened the person with a gun, little knowing the house was wired with a silent alarm, and all of a sudden two cops were on him with guns bigger than his own, so goodbye, Charlie. A Class B felony this time. State penitentiary this time. Big time this time. The D.A. flatly refused to let Proctor cop a plea— well, why the hell should he? They had the man cold. But the court sentenced him to only half the max, and he'd been paroled from Castleview two years ago, after having served a third of his term.

The name "Doctor Proctor" had been acquired in prison.

Proctor had a habit as long as the Pacific Coast Highway. Every thief in the world knew that Castleview was as tight as a virgin's asshole. You wanted to cure a dope habit, you got yourself sent to Castleview because, man, there was no way of getting even a shred of grass inside there. Unless you were Doctor Proctor.

No one knew how he did it.

It had to be some kind of miracle.

But if you were hurting, baby, Doctor Proctor could fix you. If you needed what you needed, Doctor Proctor could get it for you. Always ready to help a friend in need, that was Doctor Proctor. A confirmed junkie, and a prison dope dealer. But none of that mattered. He had a *title* now, which was better than either a nickname *or* a street name. Doctor Proctor. Who for the past two years had been on the streets again. Apparently doing burglaries again. Or perhaps worse.

His mug shot showed a round clean-shaven face, dark eyes, short blond hair.

The Ungers had described him as thin and blond and growing a mustache.

The date of birth on his records made him twenty-four last October.

The Ungers had said he was eighteen, nineteen.

The last address his parole officer had for him was 1146 Park Street, in Calm's Point. But he had long ago violated parole, probably figuring if he was going to go back to work at his old trade it certainly didn't pay to waste time with parole-officer appointments. If a man was going to break parole by stealing, then why check in with the P.O.? If he got caught stealing, he'd go back to prison anyway. Besides, he wasn't going to *get* caught.

No criminal ever thinks he's going to get caught. Only the *other* guy gets caught. Even criminals who've already been caught and sent to prison believe they won't get caught the next time. The reason they got caught the first time was they made a little mistake. The next time, they wouldn't make any mistakes. They would never get caught again. They would never do time again.

It never occurred to a criminal that a sure way to avoid doing time was to find an honest job. But why should a man take a job paying $3.95 an hour when he could go into a grocery store with a gun and steal four thousand dollars from the cash register! Four fucking thousand dollars! For ten minutes' work! Unless he got caught. If he got caught, he'd be sent up for thirty years, and when you divided the four grand by thirty, you got two hundred a year. And when you broke that down to a forty-hour week for every week in the year, you saw that the man had earned a bit more than six cents an hour for his big holdup.

Terrific.

He marches in there with a big macho gun in his big macho fist, and he scares the shit out of Mom and Pop behind the counter, and he never once thinks, not for a minute, that what he's doing is betting thirty years against that money in the cash register—which, by the way, might turn out to be *four* dollars instead of four *thousand*.

Smart.

But who says criminals have to be brilliant?

And, anyway, he's not going to get caught.

But even if he does get caught, even if he does make another teeny-weeny little tiny mistake the second time around, and even if the judge throws the book at him because now he's a habitual criminal, he can do the time standing on his head, right? The Castleview Penitentiary S.A.C. Lots of old buddies from the street in there. Hey, Jase! How ya doin', Blood? Lift a lot of weights in there. Shoot the shit in the Yard. Get some fish in the gym to suck your cock, your buddies standing watch and then taking their turns. Send away for correspondence courses can make you a lawyer or a judge. Shit, man, you can do the time with one hand tied behind your back.

The signs tacked up in every police precinct in this city read:

> If you can't do the
> TIME—
> Don't do the
> CRIME!

Criminals laughed at those signs.

Those signs were for amateurs.

Martin Proctor had been to prison and enjoyed it very much, thanks, and he was out again, and had at least burglarized one apartment on New Year's Eve, and perhaps done something more serious than that. But the cops had an address for him. And when you had an address, that was where you started. And sometimes you got lucky.

1146 Park was in a section of Calm's Point that had once been middle-class Jewish, had gone from there to middle-class Hispanic, and was now an area of mostly abandoned tenements sparsely populated by junkies of every persuasion and color. Nobody in the building had ever heard of anyone named Proctor—Martin, Snake, Mr. Sniff or even Doctor.

Sometimes you got lucky, but not too often.

"I should be in Florida right this minute," Fats Donner said. He was talking to Hal Willis. Willis had dealt with him on many a previous occasion. Willis did not like him at all. Neither did any of the cops on the Eight-Seven. That was because Donner had a penchant for young girls. In the ten- or eleven-year-old age bracket; for Donner these days, twelve was a little long in the tooth. Willis was here only because he'd worked with Donner more often than had any other cop on the squad. Donner, being such an expert ear, might have heard something about Proctor's recent whereabouts, no?

"No," Donner said.

"Think," Willis said.

"I already thought. I don't know anybody named Martin Proctor."

Donner was a giant of a man, fat in the plural, fat in the extreme, Fats for sure, an obese hulk who sat in a faded blue bathrobe, his complexion as pale as the January sky outside, his fat hairless legs resting on a hassock, one obscenely plump hand plucking dates from a basket on the end table beside his easy chair, the hand moving to his mouth, his thick lips sucking the meat off the pit. Standing beside him, Willis—who was short by any standards—looked almost tiny.

"Doctor Proctor," he said.

"No," Donner said.

"Mr. Sniff."

"Four hundred people named Mr. Sniff in this city, you kidding?"

"Snake."

"*Eight* hundred Snakes. Give me something easy like Rambo."

He smiled. He was making a joke. Rambo was another popular name. A piece of date clung to his front upper teeth, making it look as if one of them was missing. Willis really hated being in his presence.

"It's your burglary," Carella had told him.

"You've worked with him before," Meyer had said.

And was working with him again now.

Or trying to.

"You think you can listen around?" he asked.

"No," Donner said. "I think I can go to Florida. It's too fucking cold here now."

"It's cold in Florida, too," Willis said. "But it can get hot both places."

"Oh, look, Maude," Donner said to the air, "here comes the rubber hose."

They both knew that the only reason an informer cooperated with the police was that the police had something on him that they were willing to forget temporarily. In Donner's case, the something wasn't child abuse. No cop in this city was willing to forget child abuse, even temporarily. Dope, yes. Murder, sometimes. But child abuse, never. There was a criminal adage to the effect that the only thing you couldn't fix in this city was a short-eyes rap.

The main thing the police had on Donner was the long-ago murder of a pimp. The way the police looked at it, the city was better off without pimps in general, but this did not mean that they could condone murder. Oh, no. They had the goods on Donner and could have sent him to prison for a good long time. Where there were no girls, by the way. Young or otherwise. But the cops chose to work this one six ways from the middle. They didn't give a damn that the city had lost another pimp. And they wouldn't have minded sending Donner up for the crime. But they figured there were other ways to make him pay for what he'd done.

A tacit deal was struck, no handshakes sealing the bargain—you did not shake hands with murderers and especially not with child abusers—not a single word spoken, but from that day forward Donner knew he was in the vest pocket of any cop who wanted him, and the cops knew that Donner for all his bullshit would deliver or else.

Willis merely looked at him.

"You got a picture of him?" Donner asked.

This is the way it worked.

A hearing-impaired person like Teddy Carella—who'd been deaf since birth and who had never uttered a single word in her entire life—had finally and reluctantly been convinced by her husband to purchase and have installed one of these newfangled gadgets that had only been on the market for the past God knew how long. The gadget she'd resisted all this time—

Listen, I'm an old-fashioned girl, she'd signed with her hands and mimed with her face.

—was called a Telecommunication Device for the Deaf and was known in the trade as a TDD.

It looked like a typewriter that had married a telephone and given birth to a character display and an adding machine. When the TDD was in use, a telephone rested at the very top of the unit, where two soft, molded cups were shaped to fit the handset. Between these was a roll of paper some two and a quarter inches wide, upon which printed messages appeared in uppercase type. Beneath this, and running horizontally across the face of the unit, was the display line. Twenty-character display. Blue-green vacuum fluorescent illumination. Half-inch character height. Angled so it could be read from above. Just under the display screen was a forty-five key, four-row keyboard with almost the same lettering layout as on a typewriter.

State of the art was not yet able to translate voice to type or vice versa. This would have made things simple indeed for any hearing- or speech-impaired person in the world. But, listen, it was simple enough the way it was. In the Carella house, there was a TDD on the kitchen counter under the wall phone. On Carella's desk at the office, there was an identical TDD alongside *his* phone. Either of the telephones could be used for normal use, but when Teddy—or any other hearing-impaired person, for that matter—wished to make a call, she first turned the TDD power switch on, placed the handset of her phone onto the acoustic cups, waited for the steady red light that told her she had a dial tone, and then dialed the number she wanted. A slow-flashing red light on the unit told her the phone was ringing. A fast-flashing red light told her the line was busy.

Whenever the phone on Carella's desk rang, he picked up and said "Eighty-seventh Squad, Carella." If the call was from a hearing, speaking person, the conversation continued as it normally would. But if this was Teddy calling—as it was at three o'clock that afternoon, while Willis was mildly intimidating Fats Donner—Carella would hear beeping that sounded like a very rapid diddle-ee-dee. This was caused by Teddy repeatedly hitting the space bar on her machine to let the person on the other end know this was a hearing-impaired caller.

If Carella had been calling *her,* a master ring-signal jacketed to the telephone line and linked to remote receivers throughout the house would flash lamps in several different rooms, letting Teddy know the phone was ringing. A similar device told her when someone was ringing the doorbell. But meanwhile, back at the Eight-Seven Corral, when Carella heard that rapid beeping—as he did now—he immediately knew it was Teddy calling, and he cradled the handset of his phone onto the TDD, and switched on the power, and by golly Moses, what you got was two people talking!

Or, to be more exact, two people typing.

HI HON, he typed, GA.

The words appeared on both his display line and the one Teddy was watching at her kitchen counter all the way up in Riverhead. It was magic. Moreover, a printer on each machine simultaneously printed out the message on the roll of paper. GA was the abbreviation for Go Ahead. On many TDD units—as was the case with theirs—a separate GA key was on the right-hand side of the keyboard. To save time, TDD users often abbreviated commonly used words or expressions.

Teddy typed HI SWEETIE HV U GOT A MIN GA.

Carella typed FOR U I HV HRS GA.

RMBR BERT/EILEEN TONITE, Teddy typed, GA.

Carella typed YES 8 O'CLOCK GA.

PLS WEAR TIES, Teddy typed, GA.

They continued talking for the next several moments. When Carella pulled the printout from the machine later, the twenty-character lines looked like this:

```
HI HON GA HI SWEETIE
HV U GOT A MIN GA FO
R U I HV HRS GA RMBR
BERT/EILEEN TONITE G
A YES 8 O'CLOCK GA PL
S WEAR TIES GA I'LL
TELL BERT HV TO GO N
OW SEE YOU LTR LUV Y
OU SK LUV YOU TOO SK
SK
```

The letters SK were also on a separate key. SK meant Signing Off.

They were both smiling.

Peter Hodding hadn't gone back to work yet.

"I don't think I could stand looking into people's eyes," he told Carella. "Knowing they know what happened. I had a hard enough time at the funeral."

Carella listened.

The sky outside was darkening rapidly, but the Hoddings had not yet turned on the lights. The room was succumbing to shadows. They sat on the living room couch opposite Carella. Hodding was wearing jeans, a white button-down shirt, a cardigan sweater. His wife Gayle was wearing a wide skirt, a bulky sweater, brown boots.

"He'll go back on Monday," she said.

"Maybe," Hodding said.

"We have to go on," she said, as if to herself.

"I wonder if you can tell me," Carella said, "whether Annie Flynn ever mentioned a boy named Scott Handler."

"Gayle?" Hodding said.

"No, she never mentioned anyone by that name."

"Not to me, either," Hodding said.

Carella nodded.

He and Meyer were eager to talk to the Handler boy—if they could find him. But where the hell was he? And why had he fled? Carella did not tell the Hoddings that they'd been looking for the boy for the past two days. There was no sense in building false hopes and even less sense in implicating someone before they'd even talked to him.

Gayle Hodding was telling him how strange life was.

"You make plans, you . . ."

She shook her head.

Carella waited. He was very good at waiting. He sometimes felt that ninety percent of detective work was waiting and listening. The other ten percent was luck or coincidence.

"I quit college in my junior year," she said, "oh, this was seven, eight years ago, I went into modeling."

"She was a very good model," Hodding said.

Carella was thinking she still had the good cheekbones, the slender figure. He wondered if she knew Augusta Kling, Bert's former wife. He did not ask her if she did.

"Anyway," she said, "about a year and a half ago, I decided to go back to school. Last September a year ago. How long is that, Peter?"

"Sixteen months."

"Yes," she said, "sixteen months. And I was about to enroll for the new semester in September when the agency called and my whole life changed again."

"The modeling agency?" Carella said.

"No, no, the adoption agency."

He looked at her.

"Susan was adopted," she said.

"I'd better put some lights on in here," Hodding said.

He'd had to come down from the roof.

Security in the building, he knew this, twenty-four-hour doorman, elevator operator, no way to get in unobserved through the front door. You had to do gymnastics. Go up on the roof of the connecting building, no security there after midnight, go right on up in the elevator, break the lock on the roof door, cross the roof and climb over the parapet to the building you wanted, 967 Grover.

Down the fire escapes.

Past windows where you could see people still partying, having a good time. He'd ducked low on each landing, sidling past the lighted windows. Counting the floors. Eighteen floors in the building, he knew which window he wanted, a long way down.

Fourth-floor rear.

He'd eased the window open.

The baby's bedroom.

He knew this.

Dark except for a shaft of light spilling through the open doorway from somewhere else in the apartment. The living room. Silence. He could hear the baby's soft, gentle breathing. Two o'clock in the morning. The baby asleep.

The master bedroom was at the other end of the apartment.

He knew this.

In the middle, separating the sleeping wings, were the kitchen, the dining room, and the living room.

He leaned in over the crib.

Everything changed in the next several seconds.

In the next several seconds, the baby was screaming.

And a voice came from the living room.

"Who is it?"

Silence.

"Who's there?"

More silence.

And suddenly there she was. Standing there. Standing in the door to the baby's room, a knife in her hand.

He had to go for the knife.

4

OSTENSIBLY, Kling was eating and enjoying the cannelloni on his plate while listening to Carella tell him about the several approaches he and Meyer were taking to the Hodding-Flynn murders. But he caught only snatches of what Carella was telling him. His mind and his ears were on what Eileen was saying to Teddy.

He had never heard her so bitter.

They sat on opposite sides of the round table.

Eileen with her red hair and her green eyes, blazing now, her hands flying all over the place as the words tumbled from her mouth.

Teddy listening, her head cocked to one side, dark hair falling over one cheek, brown eyes open wide and intently watching Eileen's mouth.

". . . find this Handler kid," Carella was saying, "then maybe we can . . ."

"And your cop comes home at last," Eileen said, "and he's watching television after a long, hard day of dealing with a wide variety of victimizers, and he sees a news broadcast about the rioting in this or that prison wherever in the United States, and the convicts are saying the food's terrible and there aren't enough television sets and the equipment in the gymnasium is obsolete, and the cells are overcrowded, and you know what that cop *thinks*, Teddy?"

From the corner of his eye, Kling saw Teddy shake her head.

". . . cause why would he have run if he hasn't got something to hide?" Carella asked. "On the other hand . . ."

"That cop sits there shaking his head," Eileen said, "because *he* knows how to rid the streets of crime, man, *he* knows how to make sure the guy he arrested two years ago isn't out there again right this minute doing the same damn thing all over again, *he* knows *exactly* how to get kids thinking that serving up burgers at a drive-in is more attractive than a life of criminal adventure—and, by the way, the answer isn't Just Say No. That's bullshit, Teddy, Just Say No. That lays the guilt trip on the *victim,* don't you see? If only you'd have said No, why then you wouldn't have got addicted to heroin, and you wouldn't have been molested by some weirdo in the street . . .

Here it comes, Kling thought.

". . . and you wouldn't have been raped or murdered, either. All you have to do is just say no. Have a little willpower and nobody'll hurt you. Where the hell does Mrs. Reagan live? On the moon? Did she think the streets of America were in Disneyland? Did she think all it ever came to was politely saying No, thank you, I've already had some, thank you? I'm telling you, Teddy, someone should have just curtsied and said no to *her,* told her that cute little slogan of hers *sucked,* lady, that just isn't the way it is."

Teddy Carella sat there listening, wide-eyed.

Knowing.

Realizing that Eileen was talking about her *own* rape. The time she'd got cut. The time she'd said *Yes.* Because if she'd have said No, he'd have cut her again. Just say no, my ass.

"Every cop in this city knows how to keep criminals off the street," Eileen said. "You want to know the answer?"

And now she had Carella's attention, too.

He turned to her, fork in mid-air.

"Make the time impossible to do," Eileen said. "Make *all* time *hard* time. Make it back-breaking time and mind-numbing time. Make it senseless, wasted time. Make it the kind of time where you carry a two-hundred-pound boulder from point A to point B and then back to point A again, over and over again, all day long, day in and day out, with no parole, Charlie."

"No parole?" Carella said, and raised his eyebrows.

"Ever," Eileen said flatly. "You catch the time, you *do* the time. And it's hard, mean time. You want to be hard and mean? Good. Do your hard, mean time. We're not here to teach you an honest job. There are plenty of honest jobs, you should've found one *before* you got busted. We're here to tell you it doesn't pay to do what you did, what*ever* you did. You wouldn't be here if you hadn't done something uncivilized, and so we're going to treat you like the barbarian you are."

"I'm not sure that would . . ."

But Eileen was just gathering steam, and she cut Carella off mid-sentence.

"You want to go out and do another crime after you've served your time? Good, go do it. But don't let us catch you. Because if we catch you for the same crime again, or a different crime, what*ever* crime you do, why, the next time you're going to do even *harder* time. You are going to come out of that prison and you are going to tell all your pals on the street that it doesn't pay to do whatever illegal thing they're thinking of doing. Because there's nothing funny or easy about the kind of time you're going to do in any slammer in the country, you are going to do hard, hard time, mister. You are going to carry this ten-thousand-pound rock back and forth all day long, and then you are going to eat food you wouldn't give a *dog* to eat, and there'll be no television, and no radio, and no gym to work out in, and you can't have visitors and you're not allowed to write letters or make phone calls, all you can do is carry that goddamn rock back and forth and eat that rotten food and sleep in a cell on a bed without a mattress and a toilet bowl without a seat. And then maybe you'll learn. Maybe once and for all you'll *learn*."

She nodded for emphasis.

Her eyes were shooting green laser beams.

Carella knew better than to say anything.

"There isn't a cop in this city who wouldn't make prison something to *dread*," she said.

Carella said nothing.

"Mention the word prison, criminals all over this city would start shaking. Mention the word prison, every criminal in the United States would just say *no*, Mrs. Reagan! No! Not *me!* Please! Do it to Julia! Please!"

She looked at Carella and Kling.

Daring either of them to say a word.

And then she turned to Teddy, and her voice lowered almost to a whisper.

"If cops had their way," she said.

There were tears in her eyes.

On her doorstep Eileen said, "I'm sorry."

"That's okay," Kling said.

"I spoiled it for everyone," she said.

"The food was lousy anyway," he said.

Somewhere in the building, a baby began crying.

"I think we ought to stop seeing each other," she said.

"I don't think that's such a good idea."

The baby kept crying. Kling wished someone would go pick it up. Or change its diaper. Or feed it. Or do whatever the hell needed to be done to it.

"I went to see somebody at Pizzaz," Eileen said.

He looked at her, surprised. Pizzaz was the way the cops in this city pronounced PSAS, which initials stood for the department's Psychological Services and Aid Section. Calling it Pizzaz gave it a trendy sound. Made it sound like the In thing to do. Took the curse off psychiatric assistance, which no cop liked to admit he needed. Psychiatric assistance often led to a cop losing his gun, something he dreaded. Take away a cop's gun, you were putting him out to pasture. The Tom-Tom Squad. Indians with bows and arrows, no guns.

"Uh-huh," Kling said.

"Saw a woman named Karin Lefkowitz."

"Uh-huh."

"She's a psychologist. There's a pecking order, you know."

"Yes."

"I'll be seeing her twice a week. Whenever she can fit me in."

"Okay."

"Which is why I thought you and I . . ."

"No."

"Just until I get my act together again."

"Did *she* suggest this?"

He was already beginning to hate Karin Lefkowitz.

"No. It's entirely my idea."

"Well, it's a lousy idea."

"I don't think so."

"I do."

Eileen sighed.

"I wish somebody would pick up that fucking baby," Kling said.

"So," Eileen said, and reached into her bag for her key. He could see the butt of her revolver in the bag. Still a cop. But she didn't think so.

"So what I'd like to do," she said, "if it's okay with you . . ."

"No, it's not okay with me."

"Well, I'm really sorry about that, Bert, but this is *my* life we're talking about here."

"It's my life, too."

"You're not drowning," she said.

She put her key into the latch.

"So . . . let me call you when I'm ready, okay?" she said.

"Eileen . . ."

She turned the key.

"Good night, Bert," she said, and went into the apartment. And closed the door behind her. He heard the lock being turned, the tumblers falling with a small oiled click. He stood in the hallway for several moments, looking at the closed door and the numerals 304 on it. A screw in the 4 was loose. It hung slightly askew.

He went downstairs.

The night was very cold.

He looked at his watch. Ten minutes to ten. He wasn't due at the squadroom until a quarter to twelve.

"What I think you should do," Lorraine said, "is go to the police."

"No," he said.

"Before *they* come to you."

"No."

"Because, Scott, it looks very bad this way. It really does."

Lorraine Greer was twenty-seven years old. She had long black hair and a complexion as pale as moonstone. She claimed she had violet-colored eyes like Elizabeth Taylor's, but she knew they were really only a sort of bluish-gray. She affected very dark lipstick that looked like dried blood on her lips. She had good breasts and good legs, and she wore funky clothes that revealed them to good advantage. The colors she favored were red and yellow and green. She dressed like a tree just starting to turn in the fall. She figured this leggy, busty, somewhat tatterdemalion look would immediately identify her once she became a rock star.

Her father, who was an accountant, told her there were *thousands* of busty, leggy girls in this country. *Millions* of them all over the world. All of them dressed in rags. All of them thinking they could be rock stars if only they got a break. Her father told her to become a legal secretary. Legal secretaries made good money, he said. Lorraine told him she was going to be a rock star. She'd never had any formal musical training, that was true, but he had to admit she had a good singing voice and besides she'd written hundreds of songs. The lyrics to them, anyway. Usually she worked with a partner who put music to her words. She was writing songs all the time, with this or that partner. She knew the songs were good. Even her father thought some of the songs were pretty good, maybe.

Years ago, she'd been Scott Handler's baby-sitter.

She'd been fifteen, he'd been six. That was the age difference between them. Nine years. She used to sing him to sleep with lullabies she herself wrote. The lyrics, anyway. At that time her partner used to be a girl she knew from high school. Sylvia Antonelli, who when she was nineteen years old married a man who owned a plumbing supply house. Sylvia now had three children and two fur coats and she lived in a big Tudor-style house. She never wrote songs anymore.

Lorraine's partner nowadays was a woman who'd been in *Chorus Line*. On Broadway, not one of the road companies. She'd played the Puerto Rican girl, whatever her name was, the one who sang about the teacher at Music and Art. Be a snowflake, remember? Gonzalez? Something like that. She wrote beautiful music. She wasn't Puerto Rican, she was in fact Jewish. Very dark. Black hair, brown eyes, she could pass easily for Puerto Rican, Lorraine could visualize her in the part. She had also played one of Tevye's daughters in a dinner-theater production of *Fiddler*. In Florida someplace. But her heart was in writing songs, not in singing or dancing. She was the one who'd told Lorraine she was robbing the cradle here. Starting up with a kid nine years younger than she was. Lorraine had merely shrugged. This was only last week.

He'd come to her a few days after Christmas.

She was living in an apartment downtown in the Quarter. Her father paid the rent, but he kept warning her that pretty soon he'd turn off the money tap. She knew he didn't mean it; she was the apple of his eye. She'd once written a song, in fact, called "Apple of My Eye," which she'd dedicated to her father. Rebecca—that was her new partner's name, Rebecca Simms, née Saperstein—had written a beautiful tune to go with Lorraine's lyrics.

> *Apple of my eye . . .*
> *Lovely child of yesterday . . .*
> *Little sleepy eye.*
>
> *Hear my lullaby . . .*
> *Sleepy girl as bright as May . . .*
> *Little lullaby.*

And so on.

The song brought tears to Lorraine's eyes whenever she sang it. Rebecca thought it was one of their better efforts, though her personal favorite was a feminist song they'd written called "Burn," in which Joan of Arc was the central metaphor. Rebecca wore her dark hair in a whiffle cut. Sometimes, Lorraine wondered if she was gay. She'd seemed inordinately angry about Scott moving in.

Lorraine hadn't expected to go to bed with Scott.

He'd just shown up on her doorstep, his eyes all red, his face white, she'd thought at first it was from the cold outside. He told her he'd got her address from her father, who'd remembered when she used to baby-sit for him, and she'd said Oh sure, that's okay, come on in, how are you? She hadn't seen him now in it must have been three, four years. Since he'd gone off to school in Maine. He'd looked like a kid then. Pimply-faced, lanky, you know. Now he looked like . . . well . . . a man. She was really surprised by how handsome he'd turned out. But of course he was still a kid.

He told her he remembered how he used to tell her everything when she used to sit for him, how he used to trust her more than he had his own parents.

She said, "Well, that's very nice of you, Scott."

"I mean it," he said.

"Thank you, that's very nice of you."

She was wearing a short red skirt with red tights and yellow leg warmers. Short, soft, black leather boots. She was wearing a green blouse, no bra. She was sitting on the couch, long legs tucked under her. She had offered him a drink, which he'd accepted. Apple brandy. Which was all she had in the house. He was on his third snifterful. The snifters were a birthday gift from Rebecca. This was the twenty-eighth day of December. It was very cold outside. Wind rattled the windows in the small apartment. She was remembering how she used to take him to the toilet in his Dr. Denton's. Hold his little penis while he peed. Sometimes he had a little hard-on. Six years old, he'd have a little hard-on, he'd piss all over the toilet tank, sometimes the wall. She was remembering this fondly.

He told her this girl he'd been going with had suddenly ended their relationship. She thought this was cute, his using a very grown-up word like relationship. But, of course, he was eighteen. Eighteen was a man. At eighteen, you could vote. When he was home for Thanksgiving, he said. Some Thanksgiving present, huh? She wondered if people exchanged gifts for Thanksgiving. Maybe the Indians and the Pilgrims had. She wondered if there was an idea for a song in that. He was telling her the girl had made it final last week. He'd gone over to see her the minute he'd got home for the Christmas break. She'd told him she never wanted to see him again. He'd been crying for the past week, well, actually nine days now. She hoped he didn't think he was a baby, coming here like this. And then he started crying again.

She'd held him in her arms.

The way she'd done when he was six and she was fifteen and he woke up crying in the middle of the night.

She'd kissed the top of his head.

Comforting him.

And next thing she knew . . .

Well, one thing just sort of led to another.

His hands were all over her.

Under the short red skirt, down the front of the green silk blouse.

Christmas colors.

Falling away under his rough, manly hands.

That was on the twenty-eighth.

He'd been living here since. Today was the sixth of January. Not five minutes ago, he'd told her what he'd said to Annie the last time he'd seen her. Annie Flynn, that was the girl's name. About killing them both. Annie and her new boyfriend, whoever he was. And now someone had *really* killed Annie and he was afraid the police might think it was him.

"Which is why you have to go to them," she said.

"No," he said.

Nibbling at his lower lip. Handsome as the devil. She got damp just looking at him. Wanted him desperately, just looking at him. She wondered if he knew what effect he had on her.

"Unless, of course, you *did* kill her," she said.

"No, no," he said.

He wasn't looking at her.

"*Did* you?" she asked again.

"I told you no."

But he still wasn't looking at her.

She went to him.

Twisted her hand in his hair. Pulled his head back.

"Tell me the truth," she said.

"I didn't kill her," he said.

She brought her mouth down to his. God, such sweet lips. She kissed him fiercely.

And wondered if he was telling the truth.

Somehow, the idea was exciting.

That maybe he *had* killed that girl.

José Herrera was sitting on a bench in the second-floor corridor when Kling came in that night. Head still bandaged, face still puffy and bruised, right arm in a cast.

"Buenas noches," he said, and grinned like one of the Mexican bandits in *Treasure of the Sierra Madre*. Kling wanted to go hide the silver.

"You waiting for *me?*" Kling asked.

"Who else?" Herrera said. Still grinning. Kling wanted to punch him right in the mouth—for the way he was grinning, for the way he'd behaved at the hospital the other day. Finish off what those black guys had started. He went to the railing, opened the gate, and walked into the squadroom. Herrera came in behind him.

Kling went to his desk and sat.

Herrera came over and took a chair alongside the desk.

"My head still hurts," he said.

"Good," Kling said.

Herrera clucked his tongue.

"What do you want here?" Kling asked.

"They let me out this afternoon," Herrera said. "I think they let me out too soon, I may sue them."

"Good, go sue them."

"I think I may have a good case. My head still hurts."

Kling glanced at a Ballistics report he had requested on a shooting that had taken place during the four-to-midnight on Christmas Eve. A family dispute. Man shot his own brother on Christmas Eve.

"I decided to help you," Herrera said.

"Thanks, I don't need your help," Kling said.

"You told me at the hospital . . ."

"That was then, this is now."

"I can get you a big drug bust," Herrera said, lowering his voice conspiratorially, glancing over to where Andy Parker was on the telephone at his own desk.

"I don't *want* a big drug bust," Kling said.

"These guys who were trying to dust me? I'll bet you thought they were just regular niggers, am I right? Wrong. They were Jamaicans."

"So?"

"You familiar with Jamaican posses?"

"Yes," Kling said.

"You are?"

"Yes."

The Jamaican gangs called themselves posses, God knew why, since traditionally a posse was a group of people deputized by a sheriff to assist in *preserving* the public peace. Kling figured a little bit of Orwellian doublethink was in play here. If War was Peace, then surely Bad Guys could be Good Guys and a Gang could be a Posse, no? The Jamaicans couldn't even pronounce the word correctly. Rhyming it with Lassie, they called it passee. Then again, when they wanted to say "man," they said "mon." Either way, mon, they would break your head as soon as look at you. Which they had successfully but not fatally done to Herrera.

And now he was ready to blow the whistle.

Or so it seemed.

"We're talking here a posse that's maybe the biggest one in America," he said.

"Right here in our own little precinct, huh?" Kling said.

"Bigger than Spangler."

"Uh-huh."

"Bigger than Waterhouse."

"Uh-huh."

"You know Shower?"

"I know Shower."

"Bigger even than Shower," Herrera said. "I'm talking about dope, white slavery, and gun-running. Which this posse is muscling in on all over the city."

"Uh-huh," Kling said.

"I'm talking about a big dope deal about to go down."

"Really? Where?"

"Right here in this precinct."

"So what's this big posse called?"

"Not so fast," Herrera said.

"If you've got something to tell me, tell me," Kling said. "You're the one who came here, I didn't come knocking on your door."

"You're the one who wanted me to back your story about . . ."

"That's a thing of the past. They're convinced downtown that I acted within the . . ."

"Anyway, it don't matter. You owe me."

Kling looked at him.

"*I* owe *you?*" he said.

"Correct."

"For what?"

"For saving my life."

"*I* owe *you* for saving *your* life?"

"Is what I said."

"I think those baseball bats scrambled your brains, Herrera. If I'm hearing you correctly . . ."

"You're hearing me. You owe me."

"What do I owe you?"

"Protection. And I'm not gonna let you forget it."

"Why don't you take a walk?" Kling said, and picked up the Ballistics report.

"I ain't even talking cultures," Herrera said.

"That's good, 'cause I'm not even listening."

"Where if you save a person's life, you are responsible for that person's life forever."

"And which cultures might those be?" Kling asked.

"Certain Asian cultures."

"Like which?"

"Or North American Indian, I'm not sure."

"Uh-huh," Kling said. "But not Hispanic."

"No, not Hispanic."

"You're just muscling in on these cultures, correct? The way this Jamaican posse is muscling in on dope and prosti . . ."

"I told you I *ain't* talking cultures here."

"Then what the fuck *are* you talking, Herrera? You're wasting my time here."

"I'm talking human decency and responsibility," Herrera said.

"Oh, dear God, spare me," Kling said, and rolled his eyes heavenward.

"Because if you hadn't stopped them Jakies . . ."

"Jakies?"

"Them Jamaicans."

Kling had never heard this expression before. He had the feeling Herrera had just made it up. The way he'd made up his cockamamie Asian or North American Indian cultures that held a man responsible for saving another man's life.

"If you'd have let them Jakies kill me," Herrera said, "then I wouldn't have to be worrying they would kill me now."

"Makes perfect sense," Kling said, shaking his head.

"Of course it makes sense."

"Of course."

"This way I'll probably have a nervous breakdown. Waiting for them to kill me all over again. You want me to have a nervous breakdown?"

"I think you already had one," Kling said.

"You want them Jakies to kill me?" Herrera asked.

"No," Kling said honestly. If he'd wanted them to kill Herrera, he'd have let them do it the first time around. Instead of getting a tooth knocked out of his mouth. Which he still hadn't gone to the dentist to see about.

"Good, I'm glad you realize you owe me," Herrera said.

Kling was neither a Buddhist monk nor a Hindu priest nor an Indian shaman; he didn't think he owed Herrera a goddamn thing.

But if a strong Jamaican posse really *was* about to do a big dope deal right here in the precinct . . .

"Let's say I do offer you protection," he said.

5

THE ORIENTAL GANGS in this city had difficulty pronouncing his name, which was Lewis Randolph Hamilton. Too many L's and too many R's. The Hispanic gangs called him *Luis El Martillo*. Which meant Louie the Hammer. This did not mean that his weapon was a hammer. Hamilton was strapped with a .357 Magnum, which he used liberally and indiscriminately. It was said that he had personally committed twenty-three murders during his several years in the States. The Italian gangs called him *Il Camaleonte*, which meant The Chameleon. That was because hardly anyone knew what he looked like. Or at least what he looked like *now*.

There were Miami P.D. mug shots of Hamilton wearing his hair in an exaggerated Afro, mustache on his upper lip. There were Houston P.D. pictures of Hamilton wearing his hair in Rastafarian style, so that he looked like a male Medusa. There were N.Y.P.D. pictures of him with his hair cut extremely short, hugging his skull like a woolly black cap. There were L.A.P.D. pictures of him with a thick beard. But here in this city, there were no police photographs of Lewis Randolph Hamilton. That was because he'd never been arrested here. He'd killed eight people here, and the underworld knew this, and the police suspected it, but Hamilton was like smoke. In Jamaica, as a matter of fact, he had for a number of years been called Smoke, a name premised on his ability to drift away and vanish without a trace.

Hamilton's posse was into everything.

Prostitution. Exclusively Mafia in the recent dead past, increasingly Chinese ever since a pair of lovely sisters named Tina and Toni Pao moved from Hong Kong to San Francisco and began smuggling in girls from Taiwan via Guatemala and Mexico, their operation expanding eastward across the United States until it was now fully entrenched and—because of its local-tong and overseas-triad connections—virtually untouchable here in this city. Hamilton had discovered the enormous profits to be made in peddling ass on carefully selected, police-protected street corners. Nothing high-class here. No Mayflower Madam shit. Just a horde of young, drug-addicted girls standing out in the cold wearing nothing but *Penthouse* lingerie.

Gun-running. The Hispanics were very big on this. Maybe because, like cab drivers coming back from the airport, they didn't like to ride deadhead. Bring up a load of Colombian coke, you didn't want that ship going back empty. So you filled it with guns—high-powered handguns, automatic rifles, machine guns—which you then sold at an enormous profit in the Caribbean. Hamilton already knew how to bring up the dope. He was now learning—way too damn fast to suit the Hispanics—how to send down stolen guns.

And, of course, drugs.

Unless a gang—*any* gang, any nationality, any color—dealt drugs, then it wasn't a gang, it was a ladies' sewing circle. Hamilton's posse was heavily into dope. With enough weaponry to invade Beirut.

All of this was why the slants, the spics and the wops wanted him dusted.

Which amused Hamilton. All those contracts out on him. If they didn't know what he looked like, how could they reach him? Unless one of his own people turned, there wasn't no way anybody could be out there squatting for him. All highly amusing. Their dumb gang shit. Contracts. What was he, a kid playing in the mud outside a shack? The concept of a Hollywood hood with a broken nose looking high and low for him made him laugh.

But not today.

Today he wasn't laughing.

Today he was annoyed by the way three of his people had mishandled the José Herrera thing.

"Why baseball bats?" he asked.

The word "bats" sounded like "bots."

Very melodious. Heavy bass voice rumbling up out of his chest. Bots. Why baseball bots?

A reasonable question.

Only one of the three was standing there in front of him. The other two were in the hospital. But even if the cop hadn't jammed them, they'd have been denied bail. Assaulting a police officer? Terrific. The one who'd been sprung looked shamefaced. Six feet three inches tall, weighing in at two hundred and twelve pounds, big hands hanging at his sides, he looked like a schoolboy about to be birched. Like back in Kingston when he'd been a kid.

Hamilton sat there patiently and expectantly.

At an even six feet, he was smaller than the man he was addressing. But he emanated even in his reasonableness a sense of terrible menace.

He turned to the man sitting beside him on the couch.

"Isaac?" he said. "Why baseball bats?"

The other man shrugged. Isaac Walker, his confidant and body-guard—not that he needed one. A confidant, yes. It could get lonely at the top. But a bodyguard? Wasn't anyone ever going to take out Lewis Randolph Hamilton. *Ever.*

Isaac shook his head. He was agreeing that baseball bats were ridiculous. Baseball bats were for spics out to break a man's legs. For chasing after a man's woman. Very big thing with the spics, their women. There were women attached to the posse, of course. Camp followers. There when you needed them. But nobody was going to get into a shootout over a mere cunt. Big macho thing with the spic gangs, though. Even the Colombians, who you thought would have more sense, all the fuckin' green involved in their operation. Mess with a spic's woman, it wasn't maybe as serious as messin' with his shit, but it was serious enough. Break the man's legs so he couldn't chase no more. But who had given these three the order to use baseball bats on Herrera?

"Who told you baseball bats, man?" Hamilton asked.

It came out "Who tole you baseball bots, mon?"

"James."

Like a kid telling on his best friend.

James. Who was now at Buenavista Hospital where they had dug the cop's bullet out of his shoulder. At the hospital, James had whispered to Isaac that he'd knocked out one of the cop's teeth. He'd sounded proud of it. Isaac had thought he was a fucking dope, messing with a cop to begin with. A cop showed, they should have split, saved Herrera for another day. Which they were having to do anyway. Jump up and down on a cop? Had to be fucking crazy. James. Who, it now turned out, had told them to go after Herrera with baseball bats.

"James told you this?"

Hamilton speaking.

"Yes, Lewis. It was James for certain."

The Jamaican lilt of his words.

Andrew Fields was his name. Giant of a man. He could have broken Hamilton in half with his bare hands, torn him limb from limb, the way he'd done other people without batting an eyelash. But there was deference in his voice. When he said "Lewis," it somehow sounded like "sir."

"Told you to use baseball bats on the man?" Hamilton asked.

"Yes, Lewis."

"When I specifically said I wanted the man put to sleep?"

"That message did come down, Lewis."

"But you used baseball bats *anyway,*" Hamilton said.

Andrew was hoping he believed him. He didn't want Hamilton thinking that he himself, or even Herbert, had been acting on their own initiative. Had somehow taken it in their heads that the way to do the little spic was with ball bats. Herbert had been the third man on the hunting party. The one who'd thrown his bat at the cop. The first one the cop had shot. He'd had nothing at all to do with deciding on the ball bats. James had made that decision. Maybe because the person they were about to do was a spic and spics understood baseball bats. But if the whole idea was to put the man to sleep, then what difference did it make *how* they did it? Was he later going to remember in his grave that it was a gun or a knife or three ball bats had done him? James's reasoning on this had eluded Andrew. But in a posse, as in any kind of business, there were levels of command. The man had said ball bats, so ball bats it had been.

"Was it James's notion to merely *harm* the man?" Hamilton asked.

"I think to box him," Andrew said.

"Not just to break a few bones, eh?"

"He told us you wanted the man boxed, Lewis."

"Then why baseball bats?" Hamilton asked reasonably, and spread his hands before him, and lifted his shoulders and his eyebrows questioningly. "If we are looking to put this man in a box in a hole in the ground, why take the long way home, Andrew, why take the dusty road by the sea, do you understand what I'm asking? Why not short and sweet, *adiós, amigo,* you fuck with us, you kiss your sister goodbye? Am I making my point?"

"Yes, Lewis."

"Did James have an explanation? Did he say I want to use bats for this or that reason?"

"He didn't offer no reason, Lewis."

"Oh my my my," Hamilton said, and sighed, and shook his head, and looked to Isaac for possible guidance.

"Shall I go to the hospital and ask him?" Isaac said.

"No, no. The man's been denied bail, there's a policeman outside his door. No, no. Time enough to talk to him later, Isaac."

Hamilton smiled.

The smile was chilling.

Andrew suddenly did not want to be James. It seemed to Andrew that the best thing that could happen to James was to be sent away for a long, long time. Where Hamilton could not get to him. Although Andrew couldn't think of a single prison in the United States that Hamilton could not reach into. Andrew didn't know why Hamilton had wanted the little spic killed, nobody had told him that. But he knew James had fucked up badly and the spic was still out there walking around.

"Andrew?"

"Yes, Lewis."

"I'm very troubled by this."

"Yes, Lewis."

"I send three men to do *one* little spic . . ."

"Yes, Lewis."

". . . a man who could have been blown away with a fucking twenty-*two* . . ."

Those eyes.

Blazing.

"But instead the three of you decide to use . . ."

"It was James who . . ."

"I don't *give* a fuck who! The job wasn't done!"

Silence.

Andrew lowered his eyes.

"Do I have to go do this myself?" Hamilton asked.

"No, Lewis. You still want the job done, I can do it."

"I want the job done."

"Fine then."

"No mistakes this time."

"No mistakes."

"We are not trying to win the World Series, Andrew."

A smile.

"I know, Lewis."

"Go sing the man his lullaby," Hamilton said.

* * *

The social worker who had handled the adoption for the Hoddings was a woman named Martha Henley. She had been working for the Cooper-Anderson Agency, a private adoption agency, for the past fourteen years now. In her late sixties, a trifle stout, wearing a dark brown suit, low-heeled walking shoes, and gold-rimmed eyeglasses that demanded to be called spectacles, she warmly greeted the detectives at ten o'clock that Monday morning, and offered them seats on easy chairs facing her desk. A bleak wintry sky edged with skyscrapers filled the corner windows of her office. She told them at once that she loved children. She told them that nothing brought her greater happiness than to find the right home for a child needing adoption. They believed her. They had told her on the telephone why they wanted to see her. Now she wanted to know why they felt information about the adoption of Susan Hodding was important to their case.

"Only in that it's another possible avenue," Meyer said.

"In what way?"

"We're investigating *two* possibilities at the moment," Carella said. "The first is that the murders may have been felony murders—murders that occurred during the commission of another crime. In this case, a burglary. Or a rape. Or both."

"And the second possibility?"

She was making notes on a lined yellow pad, using an old-fashioned fountain pen with a gold nib. She was left-handed, Meyer noticed. Wrote with her hand twisted around peculiarly. Meyer figured she'd been growing up when schoolteachers were still trying to change all left-handers into right-handers. He imagined this had something to do with Good vs. Evil, the right hand of God vs. the sinister left hand of the Devil. All bullshit, he thought. Those exercises at changing a person's handedness had in many cases led to stuttering and a whole carload of learning disabilities. Carella was still talking. Mrs. Henley was still writing.

". . . who wanted the *sitter* dead, the Flynn girl. In which case, the murder of the infant was a side-effect, if you will, an offshoot of the other murder. That's the second possibility."

"Yes," she said.

"But there's a third possibility as well," Carella said.

"Which is?"

"That the murderer wanted the *baby* dead."

"A six-month-old child? That's difficult to . . ."

"Admittedly, but . . ."

"Yes, I know. In this city . . ."

She let the sentence trail.

"So," Carella said, "the reason we're here . . ."

"You're here because if the baby *was* the primary target . . ."

"Yes . . ."

". . . you'll need to know as much about the adoption as possible."

"Yes."

"Where shall I begin?" she asked.

The Hoddings had first come to her a bit more than a year ago, on the recommendation of their lawyer. They'd been trying to conceive ever since Mrs. Hodding . . .

"She used to be a model, you know," Mrs. Henley said.

"Yes."

. . . quit modeling some three or four years back. But although they'd assiduously followed their physician's directions, their efforts merely proved fruitless and bitterly disappointing, and they had ultimately decided to seek legal assistance in finding a reputable adoption agency.

Those were Mrs. Henley's exact words. She had a rather flowery way of speaking, Carella noticed, as old-fashioned as her gold-nibbed fountain pen and her gold-rimmed spectacles.

"Their lawyer recommended us," she said, and nodded as if in agreement with the lawyer's good taste. "Mortimer Kaplan," she said, "of Greenfield, Gelfman, Kaplan, Schuster and Holt. A very good firm. We did all the home studies, obtained all the necessary references, prepared the Hoddings in advance for the sort of baby that might realistically turn up . . ."

"What do you mean?" Carella asked.

"Well, many of them want what we call a Gerber Baby, do you know? Blue eyes and blonde hair, cute little smile, chubby little hands. But not all babies look like that. We get all sorts of babies put up for adoption. We place all of them."

"*All* of them?" Meyer said.

"All of them. We've placed babies born with handicaps. We've even placed babies born with AIDS. There are a great many decent, caring people out there, I'm happy to say."

Carella nodded.

"Anyway," she said, "to cut a long story short, in July of last year I telephoned the Hoddings to say we had a newborn infant for them to look at. Well, not quite newborn. The baby at that time was two weeks old. That's the initial grace period we give the birth parents. Two weeks. Agency policy is to place the infant in a foster home, give the birth parents an opportunity to change their minds about adoption, if that's what they wish. At the end of the two weeks, they can either reclaim the baby or else sign a legal surrender that transfers custody to the agency. In this case, I had little doubt that the mother—this was the only birth parent involved—would allow the adoption to proceed. In any event, I called the Hoddings and asked them to come see the baby. A little girl. They were—as I'd expected—thoroughly enchanted with her. A beautiful baby, truly. A storybook child, a little princess. Well, a Gerber Baby. I gave them all the facts about her . . ."

"What facts would those be, Mrs. Henley?"

"Background information about the birth mother and birth father— in this case, not much was known about him—medical, religious, educational, all that. Hospital record on the infant. Hospital record on the birth mother. And so on. Everything they needed to know. The foster mother and I spent about twenty minutes with the Hoddings and little Susan . . . that was the name we'd given her here at the agency, Susan; the mother hadn't cared to name her. The Hoddings, as I'm sure they told you, still don't know the birth mother's name. It's here on record at the agency, of course, but the court records of the adoption are sealed and so is the original birth certificate. At any rate, as I say, the Hoddings loved the child on sight and agreed to take her home for the ninety-day trial period."

"This was when, Mrs. Henley?"

"Early in August. That's when they took Susan home with them. Little Susan."

Mrs. Henley shook her head.

"And now this," she said.

Now this, Carella thought.

"When did the actual adoption take place?" he asked.

"Early in December."

"Who was the child's natural mother?" he asked.

"I'll have the records sent in," Mrs. Henley said, and pressed a button on her telephone console. "Debbie," she said, "would you bring in the Hodding file, please? Mr. and Mrs. Peter Hodding. Thank you," she said, and released the button. "This won't take a moment," she said, looking up at the detectives again.

A knock sounded on the door five minutes later.

"Yes, come in," Mrs. Henley said.

A dark-haired girl wearing a long skirt and a ruffled white blouse came in carrying a manila folder. She put the folder on Mrs. Henley's desk . . .

"Ah, thank you, Debbie."

. . . turned, smiled at Carella, and then walked out again. Mrs. Henley was already riffling through the papers in the folder.

"Yes, here we are," she said. "But you know, gentlemen, I really can't release this information without . . ."

"Of course," Carella said. "You've been very kind, Mrs. Henley, and we don't want to place you or the agency in jeopardy. We'll be back in a little while with a court order."

The birth mother's name was Joyce Chapman.

Last June, when she'd first gone to the agency, she'd given her address as 748 North Orange, apartment 41.

"The Three-Two," Meyer said. "Down near Hopscotch."

Carella nodded.

On the Cooper-Anderson background information form, she had listed her age as nineteen, her height as five feet ten inches, her weight as one hundred and fifty-two pounds . . .

COLOR OF HAIR:	Blonde.
COLOR OF EYES:	Green.
COMPLEXION:	Fair.
BEST FEATURE:	Pretty eyes.
PERSONALITY:	Cheerful.
NATIONALITY:	American.
ETHNIC ORIGIN:	Scotch-Irish.
RELIGION:	Catholic.
EDUCATION:	High-school degree.
	One year college.
WORK EXPERIENCE	
& OCCUPATION:	None.
TALENTS OR HOBBIES:	Tennis, scuba diving.
HEALTH HISTORY	
ILLNESSES:	Measles, whooping
	cough, etc.
ALLERGIES:	None.
OPERATIONS:	None.

No, she had never been confined to any mental institution . . .
No, she was not addicted to any controlled substance . . .
No, she was not an alcoholic . . .
And No, she had never been arrested for a felony or sentenced to imprisonment in a state penal institution.

Among the papers released by the court order was an agreement Joyce had signed shortly after the baby was born. It read:

AGREEMENT WITH
THE COOPER-ANDERSON AGENCY

I, Joyce Chapman, do hereby consent to the release of my child, Female Baby C, to a representative of the Cooper-Anderson Agency and do hereby direct the proper officers of the St. Agnes Hospital to permit the removal of said child by a representative of the Cooper-Anderson Agency.

I hereby authorize the Cooper-Anderson Agency to consent on my behalf to any medical, surgical or dental services which in the opinion of the doctor or doctors selected by the Cooper-Anderson Agency are deemed necessary for the well-being of said child. I further agree to the testing of said child for exposure to the human immunodeficiency virus (HIV) which can cause AIDS, and any other necessary and related tests. The Cooper-Anderson Agency will inform me of the test results.

I hereby agree to plan for my child with the Cooper-Anderson Agency and to keep the Agency informed at all times of my address and whereabouts until such time as final plans have been completed with the Agency for adoption, or until (or unless) I should decide to take said child back into my care and custody.

Dated this . . .

And so on.

Joyce had also sworn and subscribed to—before a notary public—a document that read:

AFFIDAVIT OF NATURAL MOTHER
CONCERNING
INTEREST OF ALLEGED NATURAL FATHER

Before me, the undersigned authority, personally appeared Joyce Chapman, who, being first duly sworn, deposes and says:

1. That she is the natural mother of: Female Baby C.

2. That the natural father of said child is: UNKNOWN. Residence: UNKNOWN

3. That the natural father has never contributed to or provided said child with support in a repetitive and customary manner, nor has he shown any other tangible sign of interest in said child.

4. Due to the aforesaid statements, it is affiant's belief that the natural father has no interest in said child and would not have any objection to the adoption of said child.

Signature: *Joyce Chapman*
Affiant

And yet another document that read:

The Cooper-Anderson Agency wishes to advise each parent who releases a child for adoption that at some time in the future your child may wish to know your name and whereabouts. The Agency will not release this information without your consent, unless required by law to do so.

To help your child in the future, the Agency asks you to keep us advised of any health problems which may develop with you or your family which could later affect your child.

I would_____ I would not__*X*__ want to be notified if my child wishes to contact me at a later date.

I do not_____ wish at this time to make a decision on this matter.

I understand that my decision may be changed at any time in the future by writing to the Agency.

Signed: *Joyce Chapman*

"Let's go see her," Carella said.

748 North Orange was in the area of the city that sounded like a Chamber of Commerce promo for a small Florida town. Narrow, twisting little streets with names like Lime, Hibiscus, Pelican, Manatee and Heron lay cheek by jowl with similarly narrow streets like Goedkoop, Keulen, Sprenkels and Visser, which had been named by the Dutch when you and I were young, Maggie.

The center of the Three-Two was in Scotch Meadows Park, which opened at its westernmost end onto Hopper Street, hence the ellipsis "Hopscotch" for the now-voguish area where many of the city's artists and photographers had taken up residence. Orange Street itself was hardly voguish. Too far uptown to be Lower Platform, too far downtown to be Hopscotch, it meandered almost to the Straits of Napoli and Chinatown on its eastern end and then veered sharply north to run into the warehouses hugging the River Harb. 748 North was in a building that used to be a shoe factory, was later a warehouse for the storage of heavy machinery, and was now divided into lofts occupied not by artists—as were those in the Quarter and in Hopscotch—but by people who called themselves actors, playwrights, musicians and dancers. Most of these people were students. The *real* actors, playwrights, musicians and dancers lived farther uptown in a recently renovated neighborhood near the theater district, but don't get confused, Harold.

The young woman who answered the door to apartment 41 was named Angela Quist.

The detectives told her they were investigating a homicide and asked if they could talk to Joyce Chapman.

She told them Joyce didn't live there anymore, and then said that she herself was on the way out. She was wearing a loden coat, blue jeans, boots, and a red wool cap pulled down over her ears. She told them she was really in a hurry, class started at one, and she didn't want to be late. But she took off her coat and hat and said she could give them a few minutes if they really made it fast. They sat in a small living room hung with framed Picasso prints.

Angela Quist was an actress.

Who lived in a loft.

But Angela Quist was in reality a waitress who took an acting course once a week on her day off, and her loft was a twelve-by-twenty space sectioned off with plasterboard partitions from a dozen similar small spaces on the floor.

It did, however, have a high ceiling.

And Angela did, in fact, have a beautifully sculpted face with high cheekbones, an aristocratic nose, a generous mouth and eyes like star sapphires. And her hair was the color of honey and her voice sounded silken and soft, and who said Cinderella *couldn't* go to the ball and live in a palace?

She had known Joyce Chapman in Seattle, Washington, where they'd both grown up.

Went to high school with her.

They'd both come to this city after graduation, Angela to seek a career in the theater, Joyce to study writing at Ramsey U.

"With Parker Harrison," Angela said.

Carella said nothing.

"The poet," Angela said. "And novelist."

Carella felt he was supposed to say, "Oh, *yes,* of course! Parker Harrison!"

Instead, he cleared his throat.

"He's *quite* famous," Angela said.

Meyer cleared his throat, too.

"It's very difficult to get accepted for his course," Angela said.

"But apparently he accepted Joyce," Carella said.

"Oh, yes. Well, she's marvelously talented, you know."

"And is she still studying with him?" Meyer asked.

"Joyce? Well, no."

"What's she doing now?" Carella asked.

"I really don't know," Angela said.

"Do you know where she's living?"

"Yes."

"Can you give us her address?"

"Well, sure. But . . . I mean, if this has to do with something that happened *here* . . ."

"Yes, it . . ."

". . . in this city, I don't see how my giving you Joyce's address is going to help you."

"What do you mean, Miss Quist?"

"Well, she's in Seattle. So . . ."

The detectives looked at each other.

"I mean, she went back there shortly after the baby was born. Well, actually, as soon as the baby was placed."

"Uh-huh. That would've been in August sometime."

"Around the fifteenth, I think it was. Well, the baby was born in July . . ."

"Yes."

"And I think arrangements were made right away for . . ."

"Yes."

"So as soon as she was clear . . ."

"Clear?"

"Well, she didn't want to be saddled with a baby, you know. I mean, she's only nineteen. We talked about it a lot. She's Catholic, so abortion was out of the question, but she certainly didn't want to *keep* the baby. I mean, Joyce is *enormously* talented. She's got a tremendous future ahead of her, she never even once considered keeping the baby."

"Did she consider marriage?" Meyer asked.

"Well, I don't think this was that kind of relationship."

"What do you mean?"

"I mean, she picked him up in a bar. A merchant seaman. He was on his way to the Persian Gulf. He doesn't even know he's a father."

"What's his name?"

"I don't know."

"Does Joyce know?"

"I guess so. I mean, this was an *extremely* casual encounter, believe me."

"Uh-huh," Meyer said.

"I think she was stoned, in fact. I mean, I was here asleep when she came in with him. Usually we, well, we made arrangements if we planned to be with someone, you know."

"Uh-huh."

"Asked the other person to spend the night someplace else, you know."

"Uh-huh."

"So there'd be some privacy."

"Uh-huh. But she just came home with this sailor . . ."

"Yeah. Well." Angela shrugged. "She's a little impetuous sometimes, Joyce. But she's very talented, so you know." She shrugged again.

"She can be forgiven her little oddities," Meyer said.

Angela looked at him as if suspecting sarcasm.

"What'd he look like?" Carella asked.

"I have no idea. I told you. I was asleep when they got here, and still asleep when he left the next morning."

"And you say she was enrolled in this man's course . . ."

"Yes. Parker Harrison."

"Then why'd she go back to Seattle?"

"Her father's sick."

"Uh-huh."

"Dying, in fact. He owns a big lumber company out there. Chapman Lumber."

"Uh-huh."

"Cancer of the liver. I've been meaning to call her, see how he's coming along."

"When's the last time you spoke to her?" Meyer asked.

"She called from Seattle on New Year's Eve."

The detectives looked at each other.

"She was in Seattle at that time?" Carella asked.

"Yes. That's where she called from. Seattle. To wish me a happy new year."

"Could we have the number there, please?" Meyer asked.

"Sure, let me get it," Angela said. "But what's this homicide got to do with Joyce?"

"Her baby got killed," Carella said.

The two men were in a diner on Longacre and Dale.

This was now one-thirty in the afternoon, but they were just having breakfast. One of the men was eating buttered French toast over which he'd poured syrup. The other man was eating eggs over easy with sausage and home fries. Both men were drinking coffee.

This was a little early for either one of them to be up and around. One-thirty? Very early when you had a night job. Usually, their separate days didn't start till two, three in the afternoon. Roll out of bed, have a cup of coffee in the apartment, make a few calls, see who wanted to meet you for a bite, take your time showering and getting silked up, have your first meal of the day maybe around four, four-thirty.

"You sure got enough syrup on that," the one eating the eggs said.

"I like it wet."

"Tell me about it."

The man eating the French toast looked at the other man's plate. "What you're eating there is enough cholesterol to give you six heart attacks," he said. "The eggs. There's more cholesterol in a single egg than there is in a whole steak."

"Who told you that?"

"It's true."

"So who cares?"

"So it could kill you, cholesterol."

"So what do you think they make French toast with?"

"What do you mean?"

"French toast, French toast, what you're eating there all covered with syrup. French toast. What do you think they make it with?"

"They make it with bread."

"And what else?"

"They fry the bread."

"*Before* they fry the bread."

"What do you mean?"

"I mean what do they *dip* it in?"

"I don't know. What *do* they dip it in?"

"Eggs."

"No, they don't."

"Yes, they do."

"Are you tryina tell me there's eggs in this?"

"What do you *think* that stuff is?"

"What stuff?"

"All over the toast. Both sides of the toast."

"I thought it was what they fried it in."

"No, that's the eggs, is what it is. I'm surprised you don't know that."

"How'm I supposed to know that? I never cooked French toast in my life."

"So now you're gonna have a heart attack. All that cholesterol."

"No, I'm not."

"Sure you are. There's more cholesterol in a single egg . . ."

"Yeah, yeah . . ."

". . . than there is in a whole steak, isn't that what you said?"

"Let me eat in peace, okay?"

They ate in silence for several moments.

"What'd you do last night?" the one eating the eggs asked. He had lowered his voice. They were sitting in a booth at the far end of the diner, with only one other person in the place, a man in a booth near the door, but he had lowered his voice nonetheless. The man sitting across from him soaked up some syrup with a piece of the toast and brought it dripping to his mouth. He chewed for a while, licked his lips, and said, "A supermarket." He had lowered his voice, too.

"Where?"

"In Riverhead. A lay-in job. I worked it with Sammy Pedicini, you remember him?"

"Sure, how is he?"

"He's fine. It was his job, he called me up on it."

"What'd you get?"

"There was only two grand in the safe. I figure this was like to put in the cash registers in the morning, get them started, you know. I'll tell you the truth, I wouldn'ta took the job if I knew Sammy was talkin' a grand apiece. I wasted the whole fuckin' night in there. First I had to knock out the alarm so I could let him in, and then we spent I don't know how long on the safe, it was one of those old boxes with a lead spindle shaft, a real pain in the ass. With the locknuts away from the shaft, you know the kind? For two lousy grand! We got through it had to be four in the morning. I told Sammy he ever calls me again with a dog like that one, I'll piss on his leg. How about you?"

"I done a private house in Calm's Point. I was watching it the past week, I figured the family was away on a trip."

"You go in alone or what?"

"How long you know me to ask a question like that? Of course I went in alone."

"What'd you come away with?"

"A couple of nice coats."

"The one you're wearing?"

"No, no, I got this one New Year's Eve. This is a Ralph Lauren coat, it's worth eleven hundred bucks."

"It don't look like eleven bills, Doc, I gotta tell you the truth."

"That's what it costs, go check it out. It's camel hair."

"I believe you. I'm just saying it don't look the money."

"There's a Ralph Lauren on Jefferson, go in and price the coat."

"I told you I believe you, Doc. It's just that a cloth coat . . ."

"These two I got last night are furs."

"What kind?"

"A raccoon . . ."

"Which ain't worth shit. I don't waste time with raccoons no more. What was the other one?"

"A red fox."

"That's a nice fur, red fox."

"Yeah."

"You said Calm's Point, huh? Where you got the coats?"

"Yeah, the furs. Not the one I'm wearing."

"You oughta be careful, Calm's Point."

"What do you mean?"

"According to Sammy, anyway."

"Why? What's the matter with Calm's Point?"

"There were cops came around your old building."

His voice lower now.

"What are you talkin' about?"

His voice lowering, too.

"According to Sammy. Park Street, am I right?"

"Yeah?"

"His girlfriend lives on Park. She told him some cops came around lookin' for you."

"What the fuck are you saying?"

"This is according to Sammy."

"He said some cops were *looking* for me?"

Both men virtually whispering now.

"Yeah, is what his girlfriend told him. She lives in an apartment with two other hookers, she said some detectives . . ."

"When was this?"

"Last night. While Sammy was workin' the spindle, it took *forever* with that fuckin' . . ."

"I mean when did they come around *looking* for me?"

"Coupla days ago? You gotta ask Sammy. I think he said Friday. Give him a call, he'll tell you."

"Did his girlfriend say *why* they were looking for me?"

"This is all secondhand, Doc. The cops weren't questioning *her,* they were talking to people in your old building."

"On Park?"

"Yeah."

"1146 Park?"

"Whatever. But when the cops were gone, she wandered over, you know . . ."

"Yeah?"

"And asked what the fuck was happening. So this guy in the building says they were lookin' for you."

"For me."

"Yeah."

"Why?"

"To ask you some questions."

"About what?"

"I don't know, Doc," he said, and smiled. "You done something bad lately?"

6

CARELLA PLACED THE call at two o'clock his time.

The receptionist who answered the phone at Chapman Lumber in Seattle was surprised to be receiving a call from a detective in the east. Carella told her that he was trying to locate Joyce Chapman, and the receptionist asked him to hold, please. Another woman came onto the line.

"Yes, may I help you?" she asked.

Carella explained all over again who he was and why he was calling. He had tried the number he'd been given for Miss Chapman . . .

"What did you wish to talk to Miss Chapman about?" the woman asked.

"Who am I talking to, please?" Carella said.

"Mr. Chapman's secretary. He's been in the hospital . . ."

"Yes, I know."

"So if you can tell *me* what . . ."

"I don't want to talk to Mr. Chapman," Carella said. "I have some business with his daughter. But the number I have for her doesn't seem to be a working number . . ."

"Yes, what sort of business?"

"What did you say your name was, ma'am?"

"*Miss*. Ogilvy. Miss Pearl Ogilvy."

Figures, Carella thought.

"Miss Ogilvy," he said, "I'm investigating a double homicide here, and I'd like very much to talk to Joyce Chapman. If you have any knowledge of her whereabouts, you'd save me the trouble of calling the Seattle police, who, I'm sure . . ."

"Miss Chapman has been staying at the Pines."

"Is that a hotel there in Seattle?"

"No, it's Mr. Chapman's home. The Pines."

"I see. Do I have the correct number there?" he asked, and read off the number Angela Quist had given him.

"No, the last digit is a nine," Miss Ogilvy said, "not a five."

"Thank you very much," Carella said.

"Not at all," Miss Ogilvy said, and hung up.

Carella pressed the receiver rest on his phone, got a fresh dial tone, dialed the 206 area code again, and then the number, with a nine this time. The phone on the other end kept ringing.

And ringing.

He was about to give up when—

"Hello?"

A muffled, sleep-raveled voice.

"Miss Chapman?"

"Mmmm."

"Hello?"

"Mmmm."

"This is Detective Carella of the 87th Precinct, I'm calling from . . ."

"Who?"

"I'm sorry if I'm waking you up," he said, "is this Joyce Chapman?"

"Yes, what time is it?"

"A little after eleven your time."

"Who did you say this was?"

"Detective Carella, I'm calling from Isola, Miss Chapman, we're investigating a double homicide here, I wonder if . . ."

"A *what?*"

"A double homicide."

"Jesus."

"We spoke earlier today to a woman named Angela Quist . . ."

"Angie? Is she involved in a murder?"

"No, Miss Chapman. We talked to her because she was the person we found at the last address we had for you."

"For *me?*"

"Yes."

"The last address you had for *me?*"

"Yes."

"What've *I* got to do with a homicide? And where'd you get my last address?"

"From the Cooper-Anderson Agency," Carella said.

There was a long silence on the line.

"Who got killed?" Joyce finally said. "Mike?"

"Who do you mean?" Carella asked.

"Mike. The baby's father. Did somebody kill him?"

"Mike who?" Carella said.

There was another silence. Then:

"Is he dead or isn't he?"

"He may be, for all I know," Carella said. "But he's not one of the victims in the case we're investigating."

"Then what is he? A suspect?"

"Not if he was on a ship in the Persian Gulf on New Year's Eve. May I have his last name, please?"

"How'd you know he was a sailor?"

"A merchant seaman," Carella said.

"Same thing."

"Not quite. Miss Quist mentioned it."

"Is she the one who told you I'd put the baby up for adoption?"

"No."

"Then how'd you know about Cooper-Anderson?"

"The baby's adoptive parents told us."

"And Cooper-Anderson gave you my *name*? That's a fucking violation of ..."

"Miss Chapman, it was your baby who got killed."

He thought he heard a small sharp gasp on the other end of the line. He waited.

"She is not my baby," Joyce said at last.

"Not legally perhaps ..."

"Not emotionally, either. I gave birth to her, Mr. Carella, is that your name?"

"Yes, Carella."

"That was the extent of my involvement with her."

"I see. But she is nonetheless dead."

"I'm sorry to hear that. Why are you calling me, Mr. Carella?"

"Miss Chapman, we know you were in Seattle on New Year's Eve ..."

"Is that when she was killed?"

"Yes."

"Who else was killed? You said a double ..."

"Her baby-sitter. A young girl named Annie Flynn. Does the name mean anything to you?"

"No."

"Miss Chapman, can you tell me the father's full name?"

"Why do you want to know? If you think he's the one who . . ."

"We don't think anything yet. We're merely trying to . . ."

"He didn't even know I was pregnant. I was with him on a Saturday night, and he sailed the next day."

"Where'd you meet him, Miss Chapman?"

"At a disco called Lang's. Down in the Quarter."

"Yes, I know the place. And you took him back to the Orange Street apartment?"

"Yes."

"And spent the night with him?"

"Yes."

"Did you see him again after that?"

"No. I told you. He sailed the next day."

"For the Persian Gulf."

"To pick up Kuwaiti oil. At least, that's what he told me. It may have been bullshit. Some guys try to impress girls by saying they do dangerous work."

"Do you know if he's still in the Persian Gulf?"

"The last time I saw him was at eight o'clock on the morning of October eighteenth, fifteen months ago."

"You keep track of time nicely," Carella said.

"So would you if you gave birth nine months after you kissed somebody goodbye."

"Then Susan was conceived that . . ."

"Is that what they named her?"

"Susan, yes."

"Susan," she repeated.

"Yes."

"Susan," she said again.

He waited.

Nothing more came.

"That weekend," Carella concluded.

"Yes," she said.

"What's his last name?" Carella asked. "The father."

"I don't know," Joyce said.

Carella raised his eyebrows.

"You don't know his last name," he repeated.

"I do not know his last name."

"He didn't tell you his . . ."

"Sue me," she said.

Carella nodded to the squadroom wall.

"What'd he look like?" he asked.

"Tall, dark hair, blue eyes, who knows?"

"Uh-huh," he said.

"I'm not promiscuous," she said.

"Okay," he said.

"I was stoned."

"Okay."

"We were having a good time, I asked him to come home with me."

"Okay. Was he white, black, Hispanic . . . ?"

"White."

"And he never mentioned his last name?"

"Never."

"And you never asked."

"Who cared?"

"Okay. Did he tell you what ship he was on?"

Silence.

"Miss Chapman?"

"Yes, I'm thinking."

He waited.

"A tanker."

"Yes?"

"Do they name them after generals?"

"I guess they can."

"The General Something?"

"Maybe."

"Putnam? Or Putney? The General Putney? Could that be a tanker?"

"I can check it out."

"But how could he have killed her?" Joyce asked. "He didn't even know she existed."

"Well, we *would* like to talk to him, if we can find him," Carella said. "Miss Chapman, does the name Scott Handler mean anything to you?"

"No."

"He isn't anyone you might have known?"

"No."

"Or might have met somewhere even casually?"

"Like at a *disco?*" she said, her voice turning suddenly hard and mean. "I told you, Mr. Carella, I'm not promiscuous."

"No one said you were, Miss Chapman."

"You stressed the word 'casually' . . ."

"I didn't intend to."

"But you did! How the hell am I supposed to know who this Scott Hampton . . ."

"Handler."

"Who*ever* the fuck, how am I supposed to know him?"

"I was only asking if his name sounded . . ."

"No, you wanted to know if I'd met him *casually* . . ."

"Yes, but I . . ."

"The way I'd met *Mike!*"

Carella sighed.

"I don't know him," Joyce said.

"Okay," he said.

There was a long awkward silence.

"Listen," she said.

"Yes?"

"If you . . . if you find who . . . who . . . who killed . . ."

It was hard for her to say it. It seemed as if she would never say it. But at last the name formed on her lips and came over the telephone wires like a whisper.

"Susan," she said. "If you find who killed Susan . . ."

Her voice caught.

"Let me know, okay?" she said, and hung up.

Eileen was taking her measure.

This was only the second time she'd seen the woman, and she wasn't sure she'd be seeing her again. Like a cop studying a suspect, she scrutinized Karin Lefkowitz.

Big-city Jewish-girl looks. Barbra Streisand, but prettier. Brown hair cut in a flying wedge. A sharp intelligence in her blue eyes. Good legs, she probably looked terrific in heels, but she was wearing Reeboks. A dark blue business suit—and Reeboks. Eileen liked what she saw.

"So," Karin said. "Shall we begin with the rape?"

Straight for the jugular.

Eileen liked that, too—she guessed.

"It's not the rape I want to talk about," she said.

"Okay."

"I mean, that's not why I'm here. The rape."

"Okay."

"The rape was a long time ago. I've learned to live with it."

"Good. So what *did* you want to discuss?"

"As I told you last week . . . I want to quit the force."

"But not because you were raped."

"The rape has nothing to do with it." Eileen crossed her legs. Uncrossed them again. "I killed a man."

"So you told me."

"That's why I want to quit."

"Because you killed a man in the line of duty."

"Yes. I don't want to have to kill anyone else. Ever again."

"Okay."

"I think that's reasonable."

"Uh-huh."

Eileen looked at her.

"What are we supposed to do here?" she asked.

"What would you like to do?" Karin asked.

"Well, first off," Eileen said, "I'd like you to understand I'm a cop."

"Uh-huh."

"A Detective/Second Grade . . ."

"Uh-huh."

". . . who knows a little bit about interrogation."

"Uh-huh."

"As for example answering questions with questions to get a suspect talking."

"Uh-huh," Karin said, and smiled.

Eileen did not smile back.

"So when I ask you what we're supposed to do here, I don't like you asking me what I'd like to do here. You're the trained person, you're the one who's supposed to *know* how to proceed here."

"Okay," Karin said.

"And by the way I know the Uh-Huh-Okay routine, too," Eileen said. "You got yourself a suspect? Good. Just keep him talking, just okay and uh-huh him to death."

"But you're not a suspect," Karin said, and smiled.

"What I'm saying . . ."

"I understand what you're saying. You'd appreciate my treating you like the professional you are."

"Yes."

"Good. I will. If you'll extend the same courtesy to me."

Eileen looked at her again.

"So," Karin said. "You want to quit the force."

"Yes."

"And that's why you're here."

"Yes."

"Why?" Karin asked.

"I just told you. I want to . . ."

"Yes, quit the force. But that doesn't tell me why you're here. If you want to quit the force, why did you come to see me?"

"Because I was talking to Sam Grossman at the lab . . ."

"Yes, Captain Grossman."

"Yes, and I was telling him I forget what now, something about, I don't remember, I guess looking for a job in some other line of work, and we got to talking, and he asked me if I knew about Pizzaz, and I said I did, and he suggested that I give Dr. Lefkowitz a call, she might be able to help me with this problem I seemed to have."

"And what is this problem you seem to have?"

"I just told you. I want to quit the force."

"So why don't you?"

"Well, that's the problem. Every time I'm about to hand in my resignation, well, I . . . I can't seem to do it."

"Uh-huh. Have you actually written a resignation letter?"

"No. Not yet."

"Uh-huh. And this shooting occurrence took place when?"

"This *killing* occurrence, you mean. I *killed* a man, Dr. Lefko . . . what am I supposed to *call* you, anyway?"

"What would you like to call me?"

"You're doing it again," Eileen said.

"Sorry, but it's habit."

Eileen sighed.

"I'd still like to know what I should call you," she said.

"Are you uncomfortable with Dr. Lefkowitz?"

"Yes."

"Why?"

"I don't know why. Do you plan to call me Detective Burke?"

"I don't know what I plan to call you. What would you like me to . . . ?"

"I don't think this is going to work," Eileen said.

"Why not?"

"Because I realize you've got to ask a question every time I ask a question, but that's the same game we play with any cheap thief off the street."

"Yes, but this isn't a game here," Karin said.

Their eyes met.

"The same way questioning a thief isn't a game," Karin said.

Eileen kept looking at her.

"So maybe you should concentrate less on my technique and more on our getting comfortable with each other."

"Maybe."

"That is, if you can overlook my clumsiness."

Karin smiled.

Eileen smiled, too.

"So," Karin said. "What would you like me to call you?"

"Eileen."

"And what would *you* like to call *me?*"

"What would *you* like me to call you?" Eileen said.

Karin burst out laughing.

"Karin, okay?" she said.

"Karin, okay," Eileen said.

"Will you be comfortable with that?"

"Yes."

"Good. Can we get to work now?"

"Yes."

"All right, when did you kill this man?"

"On Halloween night."

"This past Halloween?"

"Yes."

"Less than three months ago."

"Two months and nine days," Eileen said.

"Where did it happen?"

"In a rented room in the Canal Zone."

"On the docks?"

"Yes."

"Over in Calm's Point?"

"Yes."

"The Seven-Two?"

"That's the precinct, yes. But I was working with Annie Rawles out of Rape. It gets complicated. Homicide called her in, and she contacted me because they needed a decoy." Eileen shrugged. "I'm supposed to be a good decoy."

"Are you?"

"No."

"Then why'd Annie call you in?"

"I was then."

"A good decoy."

"Yes. But I'm not anymore."

"Is that why you want to quit the force?"

"Well, if I can't do the job right, I might as well quit, no?" She shrugged again. "That's the way I look at it, anyway."

"Uh-huh. What was this man's name?"

"The one I killed?"

"Yes. Why? Who did you think I meant?"

"I thought you meant the one I killed. That's what we were talking about, wasn't it? Halloween night?"

"Yes."

"His name was Robert Wilson. Well, Bobby. He called himself Bobby."

"Why did you kill him, Eileen?"

"Because he was coming at me with a knife."

"Uh-huh."

"He'd already killed three hookers here in this city."

"Nice person."

"He was, actually. I mean . . . this sounds stupid, I know . . ."

"Go on."

"Well, I had to keep reminding myself I was dealing with a killer. A man who'd killed three women. One of them only sixteen years old. They showed me pictures up the Seven-Two, he'd really done a job on them. I'm talking genital mutilation. So I knew this, I knew he was very danger-ous but he seemed *charming*. I know that's crazy."

"Uh-huh."

"Kept telling jokes."

"Uh-huh."

"Very *funny* jokes. It was strange. I was sitting there with a killer, and I was *laughing*. It really was strange."

"What did he look like?"

"Bobby? He was blond. Six-two, six-three, in there. Two hundred pounds or so, well, a bit over. Maybe two-ten, fifteen. A big man. With a tattoo near his right thumb. A blue heart outlined in red."

"Anything in it?"

"What do you mean?"

"The heart. Any lettering in it?"

"Oh. No. Nothing. I thought that was strange, too."

"At the time?"

"No. Later on. When I thought about it. A heart without a name in it. Usually there's a name, isn't there?" Eileen shrugged. "All the thieves I've dealt with, if they've got a heart tattoo, there's always a name in it. But not him. Strange."

"So let me understand this. He was telling jokes while you were in this rented room with him?"

"No, earlier. In the bar. They planted me in a bar. In hooker's threads. Because . . ."

"Because the previous three victims were hookers."

"Yes. And he hit on me in the bar, and I had to get him out of there so he could make his move. So we went to this rented room."

"Where he came at you with a knife and you had to shoot him."

"Yes."

"Where were your backups?"

"I lost them. But that's another story."

"Let me hear it?"

"Well," Eileen said, and sighed. "My S.O. thought I needed a little help on the job. So he . . ."

"What's *his* name?"

"Kling. Bert Kling. He's a detective up in the Eight-Seven."

"Do you think of him as that?"

"As what? A detective?"

"No, your Significant Other."

"Yes. Well, I did."

"Not any longer?"

"I told him I didn't want to see him for a while."

"Why'd you do that?"

"I figured while I was trying to sort things out . . ."

"Uh-huh."

". . . it might be best if we didn't see each other."

"When did this happen?"

"Well, I told him Friday night."

"How'd he take it?"

"He didn't like it very much."

"What'd he say?"

"First he said he didn't think it was such a good idea, and then he said it was a lousy idea. He also wanted to know whether you were the one who'd suggested it."

"And what'd you tell him?"

"I said it was my own idea." Eileen paused, and then said, "*Would* you have suggested it?"

"I really couldn't say at this point."

"But do you think it's a good idea? Until I get myself straightened out?"

"How long have you known him?" Karin asked.

"Quite a while now. I was doing a job for the Eight-Seven, and we met up there. A laundromat. This guy was holding up laundromats. They planted me like a lady with a basket full of dirty laundry."

"Did you catch him?"

"Oh, yeah."

"And this was when?"

"A long time ago. I sometimes feel I've known Bert forever."

"Does he love you?"

"Oh, yes."

"And do you love him?"

Eileen thought about this.

"I guess so," she said at last.

"I'm assuming you've been intimate . . ."

"Oh, sure. Ever since . . . well, I had another job shortly after the laundromat, some guy who was raping nurses in the park outside Worth Memorial. The Chinatown Precinct, you know?"

"Uh-huh. Did you catch him, too?"

"Oh, yeah."

"Then you *must* have been very good."

"Well, I was okay, I guess. But that was then."

"But you were saying . . ."

"Only that when it was over, the thing in the park, I went up to Bert's place and we, you know."

"And that was the start of it."

"Yes."

"And you've been intimate since."

"Yes. Well, no."

"No?"

"Not since . . ."

Eileen shook her head.

"Not since when?"

"Halloween," Eileen said. "But *that's* another story, too."

"Maybe they're all the same story," Karin said.

Andrew Fields was waiting outside José Herrera's apartment building when he came downstairs at three o'clock that Tuesday afternoon. It was a cold, gray shitty day like the ones you always got in January in this city. In Jamaica, you never got days like this. Never. It was always sunny and bright in Jamaica. Even when it rained it was a different kind of rain than you got here in this shitty city. There were times when Fields was sorry he'd ever left Jamaica except for the money. Here there was money. In Jamaica, you wiped your ass on last year's newspaper.

Herrera was wearing his overcoat like a cloak, thrown over his shoulders, unbuttoned to accommodate the cast on his left arm. Fields wondered what he had on under the coat. A sweater with only one sleeve? After he shot him, he would take a look under the coat, see what he was wearing. He would also steal the wristwatch he saw glinting on Herrera's left wrist, which looked like gold from this distance, but which may have been only junk. Lots of spics wore fake jewelry.

Fields planned to approach Herrera soon as he found an opportunity, fall into step beside him, tell him in English—if the fuckin' spic *understood* English—that this was a gun here in Fields's pocket and that he should walk very nice and quiet with him and keep walking till they came to 704 Crosley, which was an abandoned building in this lovely spic neighborhood Herrera lived in. Fields planned to walk him up to the third floor of that building and shoot him in the back of the head. Very clean, very simple. No fuss, no muss.

Herrera stood on the front stoop, looking up and down the street.

Playing it like a cool television gangster.

Only ten thousand blacks in his immediate vicinity, so the dumb spic was trying to pick his exterminator from the bunch.

Fields smiled.

On New Year's Day, when they'd gone after him with the baseball bats, they were wearing jeans and leather jackets, boots, red woolen watch caps, they'd looked like some kind of street gang. Today, Fields was dressed like a banker. Dark suit and overcoat, black shoes, pearl gray stetson, black muffler. Briefcase in his left hand. So his right hand could be on the piece in his coat pocket when he caught up with Herrera and advised him that they were about to take a healthful little morning walk.

Herrera, apparently satisfied that no one on the street was life-threatening, came down the steps in front of the building, and then stopped to talk to an old man standing near a fire in a sawed-off gasoline drum. It took Fields a minute to figure out what Herrera wanted. He was showing the old man the package of cigarettes he had just taken from his coat pocket. He was asking the old man to light a cigarette for him. The old man nodded in comprehension, took the matchbook Herrera handed him, struck several matches unsuccessfully against the wind, finally got one going, and held it to the tip of the cigarette dangling from Herrera's mouth.

Enjoy it, Fields thought.

It'll be your last one, man.

Herrera thanked the old man, retrieved his matchbook, and put it in the same pocket with his cigarettes. He looked up and down the street again. It'll be a terrible shame if nobody assassinates this dude, Fields thought, seeing as he's looking for it so bad.

Herrera was in motion now.

So was Fields.

Following behind him at a safe distance, waiting for a good time to make his approach, didn't want too many people around, wanted the street populated enough to provide cover, but not so crowded that anyone brushing by could hear what he was telling Herrera. They had come maybe five, six blocks when Fields saw up ahead a nice break in the sidewalk traffic. Two, three people in Herrera's immediate orbit, moving in the same direction, half a dozen more up ahead, walking toward him. Time to move on the man.

He stepped out smoothly and quickly, planning to come up fast on Herrera's left, the side with the bad arm and also the side closest to the gun in the right-hand pocket of his coat. He was half a dozen paces behind him when Herrera suddenly veered in toward a door on his right. Fields stopped dead. The little spic was going into a bar. The name of the bar was *Las Palmas*. Fields peeked in through the plate glass window.

The big blond cop who'd done all the shooting on New Year's Day was sitting at the bar.

Herrera took the stool alongside his.

Felice Handler was standing against a zebra-striped wall. With her frizzied blonde hair and her amber eyes, she looked somewhat like a healthy lioness posing against the hides of a herd she had stalked, killed and eaten. The other walls in the apartment's den were black. As she had already mentioned, Mrs. Handler was an interior decorator.

Workmen were still trotting through the apartment as Meyer and Mrs. Handler talked. It made their conversation difficult. He suspected she welcomed the interruptions; he was there, after all, to ask further questions about her son. For Mrs. Handler, everything else took precedence over the business of bloody murder. Did the wallpaper with the tiny floral pattern go in the master bedroom or the second bedroom? Which wall in the master bedroom got the floor-to-ceiling mirror? (Meyer knew the answer to that one.) Where did the gold metallic paper with the purple flecks go? Would she like to see a dipstick sample of the red for the ceiling in the study? Did the rocket ship paper go in the nursery? What was this roll of yellow paper that wasn't indicated anywhere on the floor plan? Where should they put it? (Meyer had an answer to that one, too.)

"Mrs. Handler," he said at last, his patience virtually exhausted, "I know it's important that you give all these people the answers they're . . ."

"Yes, it is," she said.

"I realize that," he said. "But we have a lot of people waiting for answers, too."

"Oh?"

One eyebrow raised. Her expression saying *What in the world could possibly* be more important than what I'm doing here?

"Yes," he said. "So, you know, I'd hate to have to get a subpoena just to *talk* to you, but . . ."

He let the sentence trail.

She looked at him.

Was he really about to subpoena her?

Amber eyes flashing with intelligence.

Considering whether to tell him to go ahead and get his goddamn subpoena if *that's* how he wanted to be.

Instead, the smile from *Fatal Attraction*.

"I do apologize," she said, "I know you must be getting a lot of pressure. The case is all over everything, isn't it?"

He wished he could have said that the pressure from upstairs had nothing to do with his eagerness to solve the case. But this wasn't entirely true. Television and the tabloids were having a holiday with this one. A six-month-old baby? Murdered in her crib? If a baby wasn't safe from the maniacs in this city, then who was?

The calls to Lieutenant Byrnes had started on the morning the story broke. First a captain from Headquarters Division downtown. Then the Chief of Detectives. Then Howard Brill, one of the Deputy Police Commissioners, and then the First Dep himself, and finally the Commissioner, all of them politely inquiring as to whether Byrnes felt the investigating detectives were making reasonable headway or did he think Homicide should enter the case in something more than an advisory capacity? Or perhaps Special Forces? Just checking, of course, please let them know if the squad needed any help. Meaning please let them know if his men were ready to admit to failure before they'd even done the preliminary legwork.

"Do you think we could step out into the hall?" Meyer said. "For ten minutes, okay? Without your people bothering us? That's all I ask."

"Certainly," she said, and looked at her watch. "It's time for a cigarette break, anyway."

They went out into the corridor, and walked down to the end of it, where there was an emergency exit. Mrs. Handler shook a cigarette free from a package of Pall Malls, and offered the package to Meyer. He had smoked Pall Malls for years. The familiar red package filled him with craving. He shook his head. And watched as she lighted her cigarette. And inhaled. And exhaled in deep satisfaction. Chinese torture.

"Mrs. Handler," he said, "you know, of course, that your son's not back at school yet."

"No, I didn't know."

"I called Prentiss this morning, shortly before I spoke to you."

"I see. And now you want to know if I've heard from him."

"Have you?"

"No."

"When we spoke to you last Tuesday . . ."

"Yes."

"You said your son had left for Maine early that morning . . ."

"Yes."

"But of course he hadn't."

"I didn't know that at the time."

"He told you he was going back to school."

"Yes."

"Mrs. Handler, do you have a school calendar?"

"What do you mean?"

"Didn't you know that classes would not resume until the ninth?"

"Yes, I knew that."

"But you didn't think it odd that your son was going back on the *third*. Almost a full week before he was *due* back."

"Scott is a very good student. He was working on a difficult science project and he wanted to get back early."

"Then you saw nothing odd about . . ."

"Nothing. He's a graduating senior. The top colleges look favorably on student initiative."

"So when he said he was going back . . ."

"I had no reason to believe he did *not* go back."

She inhaled and exhaled smoke every two or three sentences. Meyer was getting a nicotine fix just standing beside her.

"And do you find it odd that he isn't there at the school now? The day *after* classes started again?"

"Yes, I find it odd."

"But you don't seem very concerned," Meyer said.

"I'm not. He's a big boy now. He knows how to take care of himself."

"Where do you think he might be, Mrs. Handler?"

"I have no idea."

"He hasn't called you . . ."

"No."

"Or written to you."

"No."

"But you're not concerned."

"As I told you . . ."

"Yes, he's a big boy now. Mrs. Handler, let's talk about New Year's Eve."

"Why?"

"Because your son had a relationship with one of the victims, Mrs. Handler, and now we can't find him. So I'd like to know what he was doing on New Year's Eve."

"I already told you . . ."

"Yes, you had a party that started at nine o'clock . . ."

"Yes."

". . . and ended at four in the morning."

"That's an approximate time."

"And your son was there all night long."

"Yes."

"Are you sure about that?"

"I'm positive."

"I suppose the other guests at the party would be willing to corroborate . . ."

"I have no idea whether anyone else noticed Scott's comings or goings. He's my son, I'm the one who . . ."

"*Were* there comings and goings?"

"What do you mean?"

She dropped her cigarette to the floor and ground it out under her sole. Then she opened her handbag, reached for the package of Pall Malls again, shook one free, and lighted it. A delaying tactic, Meyer figured. She'd already made her first mistake, and she knew it. But so did he.

"You said he was there all night long, Mrs. Handler."

"Yes, he was."

"Well, when he's home, he *lives* with you, doesn't he?"

"Yes?"

Cautious now. The lioness sniffing the air.

"So he didn't have to *come* to the party, did he? He was already *there*, wasn't he?"

"Yes?"

"And he didn't have to *go* anywhere after the party, did he? Since, again, he was already where he lived. So what did you mean by his comings and goings?"

"That was merely a figure of speech," she said.

"Oh? Which one? Simile? Meta . . . ?"

"Listen, you," she said, and hurled the cigarette down like a gauntlet.

"Yes, Mrs. Handler?"

Her eyes were blazing again.

"Don't get smart with me, okay?"

She stepped on the cigarette, ground it out.

And looked challengingly into his eyes.

Taxpayer to civil servant.

Meyer figured it was time to take off the gloves.

"I'll need a guest list," he said.

"Why?"

"Because I want to know if everyone at that party will swear that your son was there all night long. While a six-month-old baby and her sixteen-year-old sitter were getting *killed*, Mrs. Handler. If you want me to go get a court order, I will. We can make it easier by you just giving me, right here and now, the names, addresses and telephone numbers of everyone who was there. What do you say? You want to save us both a lot of time? Or do you want to protect your son right into becoming the prime suspect in this thing?"

"I don't know where he is," Mrs. Handler said.

"That wasn't my question," Meyer said.

"And I don't know where he went that night."

Meyer pounced.

"Then he *did* leave the party."

"Yes."

"What time?"

"About . . ."

She hesitated. Trying to remember when the murders had taken place. Covering her son's tracks again. Counting on the faulty and perhaps drunken memories of whoever had seen him putting on his coat and hat and—

"Okay, forget it," Meyer said. "I'll go get my subpoena while you work up that guest list. I just want you to know you're not helping your son one damn bit, Mrs. Handler. I'll see you later."

He was starting for the elevator when she said, "Just a minute, please."

7

THEY FOUND COLBY STROTHERS at two o'clock on Wednesday afternoon, the eleventh day of January. He was sitting on a stone bench in the Matisse Wing of the Jarrett Museum of Modern Art on Jefferson Avenue, making a pencil sketch of the huge Matisse painting that hung on the white wall in front of him. For several moments, so intent was he on what he was drawing, he didn't even know the detectives were standing there. When finally he looked up, it was with a surprised look on his face.

"Mr. Strothers?" Meyer asked.

He looked pretty much the way Felice Handler had described him. Nineteen years old, with startlingly blue eyes, a cleft chin, a shock of dark brown hair falling over his forehead. He had the strapping build of a football player but apparently the soul of an artist, too: Strothers was a freshman at the Granger Institute, one of the city's more prestigious art schools.

"Detective Meyer, 87th Squad," Meyer said, and showed his shield and ID card. "My partner, Detective Carella."

Strothers blinked.

Mrs. Handler had directed Meyer to the Granger Institute. He had gone there this morning and spoken to someone in the Registrar's Office, who had passed him on to the head of the Art Department, who had told him that Strothers would be at the Jarrett that afternoon. Now Meyer and Carella stood with a Matisse at their backs and a puzzled art student directly in front of them, looking up at them from a stone bench and probably wondering if it was against the law to sketch in a privately owned museum.

"Want to come someplace where we can talk?" Meyer asked.

"Why? What'd I do?" Strothers said.

"Nothing. We want to ask you some questions," Carella said.

"About what?"

"About Scott Handler."

"What'd *he* do?"

"Can we go outside in the garden?"

"In *this* weather?"

"Or the cafeteria. Take your choice."

"Or we can sit right here," Meyer said. "It's up to you."

Strothers kept looking at them.

"What do you say?" Carella asked.

"Let's go to the cafeteria," Strothers said.

They walked like three old buddies through corridors lined with Picassos and Van Goghs and Chagalls and Gauguins. They followed the signs past the glass wall overlooking a sculpture garden dominated by a magnificent Chamberlain, and then up the escalator to the second floor and the newly installed Syd Solomon exhibition, and on up to the third floor where the signs led them past the museum's movie theater (which was currently running a Hitchcock retrospective that included *The Birds*) and finally into the cafeteria itself, only mildly busy at ten minutes past two in the afternoon.

"Would you like some coffee?" Carella asked.

"Sure," Strothers said tentatively. He looked as if he was wondering whether they would dare use a rubber hose on him in a public place.

"What do you take in it?"

"Sugar and a little cream."

"Meyer?"

"Black."

Carella went to the counter. Meyer and Strothers sat at the table. Meyer smiled at him, trying to put him at ease. Strothers did not smile back. Carella returned, transferred the coffee cups and spoons from the tray to the table, and then sat with them.

"So," Meyer said, and smiled again.

"Tell us where you were on New Year's Eve," Carella said.

"I thought this was about Scott."

"It is. Were you with him?"

"Yes."

"Where?"

"At his house. His folks gave a party. Scott invited me."

"What time did you get there?"

"What'd Scott do?"

"Nothing. Have you talked to him lately?"

"No."

"What time did you get to the party?"

"About nine-thirty, ten o'clock."

"Alone."

"No, I had a girl with me."

"What's *her* name?"

"Why?"

"Mr. Strothers, this is a routine questioning, all we . . ."

"Well, thank you, but I'd like to know why you're . . ."

"We're trying to pinpoint Scott Handler's whereabouts on New Year's Eve," Meyer said.

"So why do you need my girlfriend's name? If this is about Scott, why . . . ?"

"Only because she would have been another witness," Carella said.

"A witness to what?"

"To where Scott Handler was at what time."

"What time are you trying to pinpoint?" Strothers asked.

Carella noticed that he still hadn't given them his girlfriend's name. He guessed he admired that. He wondered now if he should level with the kid. Tell him they were interested in knowing where Handler was between twelve-thirty, when Annie Flynn received her last phone call, and two-thirty that same morning—when the Hoddings came into their apartment to find her dead. His eyes met Meyer's briefly. Meyer nodded with his eyelids. A blink. Go ahead, risk it.

"We're investigating a double homicide," Carella said. "One of the victims is a girl Scott Handler knew. We're trying to establish his whereabouts between twelve-thirty and two-thirty in the morning."

"On New Year's Eve," Strothers said.

"Yes. Well, New Year's *Day*, actually."

"Right. So this is pretty serious, huh?"

"Yes, it's pretty serious."

"But if those times are critical . . ."

"They are."

"Then Scott isn't your man."

"Why do you say that, Mr. Strothers?"

"Because I know where he was during those hours, and it wasn't out killing anybody."

"Where was he?"

"With me. And my girl. And his girl."

"Do you want to tell us their names?"

"Isn't my word good enough?"

"Sure," Carella said. "But if two other people can swear to it, your friend would . . ."

"Who says he's my friend?"

"I thought . . ."

"I hardly know him. I met him at a gallery opening around Thanksgiving. He was down from Maine, he goes to a private school up there."

"Uh-huh."

"He'd just broken up with some girl, he was really . . ."

He stopped dead.

There was sudden understanding in his eyes.

"Yes?" Meyer said.

"Is that who got killed?"

The detectives waited.

"The girl who dumped him?"

"What'd he tell you about her?"

"Only that she'd shown him the door. It couldn't have been too serious a thing, he seemed to be over it by New Year's Eve."

"Had you seen him at any time between Thanksgiving and . . ."

"No. I told you. We met at this opening, and then him and me and my girl went to a party afterward. At this loft an artist friend of mine has down in the Quarter. Scott seemed very down, so we asked him to come along. Then he called me just before New Year's Eve, told me there was going to be a party at his house, could I come and bring Doro . . ."

He cut himself short.

"Is that your girlfriend's name?" Carella asked. "Dorothy?"

"Yes."

"Dorothy what?"

"I'd like to leave her out of this, if that's okay with you," Strothers said.

"Sure," Carella said. "So you got to this party at about nine-thirty, ten o'clock . . ."

"The pits," Strothers said. "If he'd told me we were gonna be the only young people there . . . I mean, everybody there was thirty, forty years old!"

Meyer's expression said nothing.

"How long did you stay there?" Carella asked.

"We left a little after midnight."

"You and Dorothy, and Scott and his girlfriend."

"No, his girl wasn't there. That's where we *went*. To *her* place."

"She wasn't at the Handler party?"

"No."

"Any idea why not?"

"Well, she's older than Scott, maybe he wasn't too keen on having his mother meet her."

"How *much* older?" Meyer said.

"Well, she's pretty old," Strothers said.

"Like what?" Meyer asked. "Thirty? Forty?"

His expression still said nothing.

"Close to it, that's for sure. She's got to be at least twenty-seven, twenty-eight."

"What's *her* name?" Carella asked.

"Lorraine."

"Lorraine what?"

"Greer."

"Her address?"

"I don't know. Someplace down in the Quarter. We went by taxi from Scott's apartment."

"But you don't remember the address?"

"No, I'm sorry."

"What does she do, do you know?"

"She's a waitress. Wants to be a rock star."

Strothers shrugged elaborately, rolled his eyes, and then grimaced, making it abundantly clear what he thought her chances were.

"What time did you get to her place?" Meyer asked.

"Maybe a quarter to one? Something like that."

"You left Scott's apartment at a little past midnight . . ."

"Around twenty after."

"And you got downtown at about a quarter to one."

"Yes."

"And what time did you leave Miss Greer's apartment?"

"A little after five. Some of the people were already having breakfast."

Meyer asked the big one.

"Was Scott Handler with you all that time?"

"Yes."

"You're positive about that?"

"Well . . ."

"What is it, Mr. Strothers?"

"Well . . . we were together when we left his apartment, of course . . ."

"Of course."

"And we were together when we got to Lorraine's place . . ."

"Yes?"

"But it was sort of a big party there, you know . . ."

"Did you lose track of him, is that it?"

"Well, Dorothy and I sort of drifted off, you know . . ."

"Uh-huh."

"So we were sort of . . . well . . . *out* of it, you know, for maybe . . . well, an hour or so."

"By *out* of it . . ."

"In the bedroom, actually."

"Uh-huh. From when to when?"

"Well, I'd say maybe from around one o'clock to maybe two-thirty or so."

"So then you don't really know for *sure* that Scott Handler was there all that time."

"Well, he was there when we went in the bedroom and he was there when we came out, so I've got to assume . . ."

"There at one o'clock, and there at two-thirty."

"Well, a little later than that, maybe."

"Like what?"

"Like maybe three."

"Uh-huh."

"Or even three-thirty. I guess."

"So, actually, you were *out* of it for two and a half hours."

"Well, yeah. I guess."

Which would have given Handler plenty of time to have run back uptown.

"You said she's a waitress," Meyer said.

"Scott's girlfriend? Yeah."

"Did she mention where she works?"

Lewis Randolph Hamilton was pacing the floor.

"You hear this?" he asked Isaac.

Isaac had heard it. Fields had just told them both.

"You're sure it's the same cop?" Hamilton asked.

"The same," Fields said. "The one shot Herbert and James and was ready to shoot me, too, I hadn't lain down the bat."

"Together in this bar, huh?"

"*Las Palmas.* On Walker."

"Sitting together in this bar, talking like old friends."

"Like brothers," Fields said.

"Now what do you suppose little Joey was telling the man?" Hamilton said.

Isaac looked at him meaningfully.

Hamilton walked to Fields and threw his arm around his shoulder.

"Thank you, Andrew," he said. "You were wise to back off when you did. Forget little Joey for a while, okay? Forget little José for now."

Fields looked at him, puzzled.

"You don't want him done?" he asked.

"Well, now, Andrew, how can you get *near* him, man? With fuzz growing on him? No less fuzz that has looked you in the eye and knows you?"

Fields was suddenly concerned. Was Hamilton blaming him somehow? Was Hamilton saying he had fucked up? The way James had with the ball bats?

"They didn't see me, Lewis," he said. "Neither one of them. Not the spic nor the cop neither."

"Good," Hamilton said.

"So if you still want me to dust him . . ."

"But what has he already told the cop?" Hamilton asked.

A fairy tale.

Kling was almost embarrassed to report it to the lieutenant.

This was the story according to Herrera:

A ship was coming in on the twenty-third of January. A Monday night. Scandinavian registry, but she was coming up from Colombia. There would be a hundred kilos of cocaine aboard that ship. Normal purchase price would have been fifteen to twenty-five thousand a key, but since the posse was taking delivery on the full shipment, the price was a mere ten grand per. A kilo was two point two pounds, ask any kid on the block. A million dollars in cash would be exchanged for two hundred twenty pounds of cocaine. That was a lot of coke, friend. That was a great big mountain of nose dust. On the street, that huge pile of flake would be worth twelve and a half million bucks.

So far it sounded within the realm of reason. The normal return on a drug investment was five to one. The return here would be twelve and a half to one. So, okay, the stuff was being discounted.

But this was where the brothers Grimm came in.

According to Herrera, the posse had made arrangements for the cocaine to be delivered to an address right here in the city, which address he didn't know as yet, but which he would find out for Kling if Kling made sure the posse didn't kill him in the next few days. The million dollars was supposed to be turned over at that time, after the customary testing and tasting. That was where Kling and his raiders would come in, busting up the joint and confiscating the haul—as soon as Herrera found out where delivery would take place, of course.

"Of course," Kling said.

He was wondering what was in this for Herrera.

He didn't ask him as yet.

He asked him instead what the name of this posse was.

Herrera said again that it was bigger than Shower or Spangler, bigger even than the Tel Aviv posse, which was a strange name for a gang run by Jakies, but it happened to be real nonetheless. As a side excursion, Herrera told Kling that the way the Jakies decided to call their gangs "posses" was from watching spaghetti Westerns down there in the Caribbean, which were a very popular form of entertainment down there, the Westerns. Kling thought that was very interesting, if true. He still wanted to know the name of the posse.

"I don't know the name of this posse," Herrera said.

"You don't."

"I do not," Herrera said.

"These guys want to kill you, but you don't know who they are."

"I know the people you arrested were trying to kill me."

"Did you know those people *before* they tried killing you?"

"Yes," Herrera said. "But not who they were."

And here the fairy tale began to grow and grow like Jack's beanstalk. Or Pinocchio's nose.

According to Herrera, he'd been sitting in this very same bar, *Las Palmas,* where he and Kling were sitting at the time of the tale, in one of the booths there across the room, when he overheard a discussion among three black men sitting in the adjoining booth.

"Uh-huh," Kling said.

"These three men were talking about the shipment I just told you about."

"Talking all the figures and everything."

"Yes."

"The hundred kilos . . ."

"Yes."

"The discounted price . . ."

"Yes, all of that."

"And the date of delivery. All the details."

"Yes. Except where. I don't know where yet."

"You overheard all this."

"Yes."

"They were talking about a shipment of cocaine, and they were talking loud enough for you to hear them."

"Yes."

"Uh-huh," Kling said.

But, according to Herrera, they must have seen him when he was leaving the bar, and they must have figured he'd been listening to everything they'd said, so they probably asked the bartender later who he was, and that was how come they'd tried to kill him on New Year's Eve.

"Because you knew about the shipment."

"Yes."

"And, of course, you could identify these men."

"Of course."

"Whose names you didn't know."

"That's true, I didn't know their names."

"James Marshall, and Andrew Fields and . . ."

"Well, yes, I know the names *now*. But then, I didn't know the names."

"You didn't."

"I did not."

"So why were they worried about you? You didn't know who they were, you didn't know where delivery would be made, why should they be worried about you?"

"Ah-ha," Herrera said.

"Yeah, ah-ha, tell me," Kling said.

"I knew the delivery date."

"Uh-huh."

"And how much cocaine would be on the ship."

"Uh-huh. What's the name of the ship?"

"I don't know. Swedish registry. Or Danish."

"Or maybe Finnish."

"Maybe."

"So they got very worried, these three guys in this posse—they *did* mention a posse, huh? When you were listening to them?"

"Oh, yes. The posse this, the posse that."

"But not the *name* of the posse."

"No, not the name."

"Too bad, huh?"

"Well, that I can find out."

"The way you can find out where delivery's gonna take place, huh?"

"Exactly."

"How?" Kling asked. "These guys are trying to kill you, how do you plan to find out where they're gonna take delivery of this shit?"

"Ah-ha," Herrera said.

This was some fairy tale.

According to Herrera, he had a cousin who was a house painter in Bethtown, and this man's wife cleaned house for a Jamaican whose brother was prominent in posse circles, who in fact reputedly belonged to the Reema posse, which wasn't the posse in question here. Herrera knew that if his cousin's wife, who was his cousin-in-law, asked a few discreet questions about the person—Herrera himself—who'd almost got killed on New Year's Eve, she could find out in three minutes flat the name of the posse the three assassins belonged to. And once she told Herrera the name, the rest would be easy.

"How do you know this isn't the Reema posse?" Kling asked.

"What?" Herrera said.

"You said the Reema posse was not the posse in question."

"Oh. I know that because my cousin's wife *already* asked some questions, and it wasn't this posse that tried to do me."

"So once you learn the name of the posse in question, why is the rest going to be easy?"

"Because I have connections," Herrera said.

"Uh-huh," Kling said.

"Who know such things."

"What things?"

"Posse business."

"Uh-huh."

Kling looked at him.

Herrera ordered another Corona and lime.

Kling said, "So what's in this for you, José?"

"Satisfaction," Herrera said.

"Ahhh," Kling said, "satisfaction."

"And, of course . . . protection. You owe it to me."

Here we go with the owing again, Kling thought.

"You saved my life," Herrera said.

Kling was wondering if there was even the tiniest shred of truth in anything Herrera had told him.

The Steamboat Cafe was in a newly created mall-like complex directly on the River Dix. South and west of the midtown area, Portside had been designed with an adult trade in mind. Three restaurants ranging from medium-priced to expensive to *very* expensive. A dozen better shops. But, alas, the teenagers who discovered the area weren't interested in eating at good restaurants or buying anything in up-scale shops. They were interested only in meeting other teenagers. Portside was a good place to do that. Day and night, teenagers began flocking there from all over the city. In no time at all, thousands of them were wandering through the beautifully landscaped area, congregating on the benches, holding hands on the walks, necking under the trees on the cantilevered riverside platforms.

In this city, adults did not like teenagers.

So the adults stopped going to Portside.

And all the boutiques, and the bookshop, and the florist, and the jewelry stores were replaced by shops selling T-shirts, and earrings, and blue jeans and records and sneakers. The *very* expensive restaurant closed in six months' time, to be replaced by a disco called Spike. The merely expensive restaurant also closed; it was now a thriving McDonald's. The Steamboat Cafe, the medium-priced restaurant, had managed to survive only because it actually *was* a transformed steamboat floating there on the river and docked alongside one of the platforms. Teenagers loved novelty.

According to Colby Strothers, Lorraine Greer worked as a waitress at the Steamboat Cafe.

The detectives got there at twenty minutes past four.

The manager told them the girls on the day shift would be leaving as soon as they set the tables, filled the sugar bowls and salt and pepper shakers, made sure there was enough ketchup out, generally got things ready for the next shift. That was part of the job, he explained. Getting everything ready for the next shift. He pointed out a tall young woman standing at the silverware tray.

"That's Lorraine Greer," he said.

Long black hair, pale complexion, bluish-gray eyes that opened wide when the detectives identified themselves.

"Miss Greer," Carella said, "we're trying to locate someone we think you know."

"Who's that?" she asked. She was scooping up knives, forks and spoons from the silverware tray. Dropping them into a basket that had a napkin spread inside it. "Don't make me lose count," she said. Meyer figured she was multiplying the number of her tables by the place settings for each table, counting out how many of each utensil she would need.

"Scott Handler," Carella said.

"Don't know him," she said. "Sorry."

She swung the basket off the stand bearing the silverware tray, and began walking across the restaurant. The detectives followed her. The floor—the *deck*—rolled with the motion of the river. Carella was trying to figure why Strothers might have lied to them. He couldn't think of a single reason.

"Miss Greer," he said, "we feel reasonably certain you know Mr. Handler."

"Oh? And what gives you that impression?"

Fork on the folded napkin to the left of the plate. On the right, she placed a knife, a tablespoon, a teaspoon, in that order. Working her way around the table. Six place settings. Eyes on what she was doing.

"We talked to a young man named Colby Strothers . . ."

"Don't know him, either. Sorry."

River traffic moving past the steamboat's windows. A tugboat. A pleasure craft. A fireboat. Lorraine's eyes sideswiped the entrance door amidships. Both detectives caught the glance.

"Mr. Strothers told us . . ."

"I'm sorry, but I don't know either of those people."

Eyes checking out the door again.

But this time . . .

Something flashing in those eyes.

Both detectives turned immediately.

The young man standing in the doorway was perhaps six feet two inches tall, with blond hair, broad shoulders, and a narrow waist. He was wearing a red team jacket with ribbed cuffs and waistband, brown leather gloves, brown trousers, brown loafers. He took one look at them standing there with Lorraine, and immediately turned and went out again.

"Handler!" Carella shouted, and both detectives started for the door. Handler—if that's who he was—had already crossed the gangplank and was on the dock when they came out running. "Police!" Carella shouted, but that didn't stop him. He almost knocked over a teenybopper eating a hamburger, kept running for the streetside entrance to the area, and reached the sidewalk as Carella and Meyer came pounding up some twenty yards behind him. Handler—if that's who he was—then made a left turn and headed downtown, paralleling the river.

The streetlights were already on, it was that time of day when the city hovered between dusk and true darkness. A tugboat hooted on the river, an ambulance siren raced through the city somewhere blocks away, and then there was a sudden hush into which Carella again shouted, "Police!" and the word shattered the brief stillness, the city noises all came back again, the sounds of voices and machines, the sound of Handler's shoes slapping against the pavement ahead—if that's who he was.

Carella did not like chasing people. Neither did Meyer. That was for the movies. In the movies, they filmed a chase in forty takes that were later edited to look like one unbroken take where the hero cop is running like an Olympics gold-medal track star and the thief is running like the guy who won only the bronze. In real life, you did it all in one take. You went pounding along the sidewalk after a guy who was fifteen to twenty years younger than you were, and in far better physical condition, and you hoped that his red team jacket wasn't for track or basketball. In real life, the calves of your legs began to ache and your chest caught fire as you chased after someone you knew you'd possibly never catch, watching the back of that disappearing red jacket, barely able to make out the white lettering on it, *The Prentiss Academy,* which in the gloom and with your thirty-something-eyes you couldn't have deciphered at all if you weren't already familiar with it. In real life, you watched the beacon of that red jacket moving further and further—

"We're losing him!" Carella shouted.

But then suddenly, Harold, in this city of miracle and coincidence, a police car came cruising up the street from the opposite direction, and Handler—if that's who he was—spotted the car, and made an immediate hundred-and-eighty-degree turn and began running diagonally across the traffic. Toward them. On the other side of the street. Running for the corner, where he undoubtedly planned to turn north. They anticipated his route, though, and came racing for the same corner, Carella getting there an instant before he did, Meyer getting there an instant later, so that they had him boxed between them. He saw the guns in their hands. He stopped dead. Everyone was out of breath. White puffs of vapor blossomed on the air.

"Scott Handler?" Carella said.

That's who he was.

The two women were white hookers of a better grade than those Hamilton's people placed on the street every day of the week. Hamilton had in fact ordered these two from a lady named Rosalie Purchase, which happened to be her real name. Rosalie was a dame in her sixties whose call-girl operation had survived the inroads of the Mafia, the Chinese, and now the Jamaican and "other exotic punks," as she defiantly called them. Rosalie dealt in quality flesh. Which might have accounted for her survival. In a day and age when two-buck whores were turning vague tricks for holier-than-thou ministers in cheap roadside motels, it was nice to know that if a *real* sinner wanted a racehorse, Rosalie Purchase was there to provide one.

Rosalie wore hats as a trademark.

On the street, in the house, in restaurants, even in church.

The cops called her Rosalie the Hat.

Or alternately Rosalie the Hot, despite the fact that she had never personally performed even the slightest sexual service for any one of her clients. If, in fact, she *had* any clients. For a lady who'd been openly running a whore house for a good many years now, it was amazing how little the police had on her. For all the police could prove, Rosalie might just as easily have been a milliner. Nobody could understand why she had never been busted. Nobody could understand why a wire had never been installed on her telephone. There were rumors, of course. Hey, listen, there are rumors in any business.

Some people in the department knew for a fact that Rosalie had grown up in East Riverhead at the same time Michael Fallon was coming along, and that as teenagers they'd been madly in love with each other. It was also true that Rosalie later moved to San Antonio, Texas, after Fallon ditched her to marry a girl named Peggy Shea. The rest, however, was all surmise.

Was it true, for example, that poor, brokenhearted Rosalie had learned how to run a cathouse out there in the Wild West? Was it true that the reason she'd never been busted in this city was that she'd become Fallon's mistress the moment she came back here to make her fortune and buy a lot of hats? Was it true that she was *still* Fallon's mistress? In which case, this might have explained why she'd never been busted, since Michael Fallon happened to be Chief of Detectives.

All this was whispered around the water coolers down at Headquarters.

The two girls were named Cassie and Lane.

These were not their real names. They were both from West Germany, and their real names were Klara Schildkraut and Lottchen Schmidt, but here in the land of opportunity they were Cassie Cole and Lane Thomas. They were both in their early twenties, both blond, both wearing ankle-strapped spike-heeled slippers and teddies—Cassie's was red and Lane's was black—and both stoned out of their minds on cocaine and champagne. So were Hamilton and Isaac.

This was a nice little sundown party here in the penthouse Hamilton owned on Grover Park North. This was also a little business meeting here on the twenty-first floor, but there was nothing Hamilton liked better than mixing business with pleasure. The two girls had been trained by Rosalie Purchase to dispense pleasure by the cartload. Isaac was dispensing a little pleasure himself, by way of refilling the girls' glasses and heaping fresh mounds of very good coke onto their mirrors. The girls sniffed with their legs widespread, the better to see you, my dear. In the west, the sun was almost completely gone, its dying stain visible only peripherally through the apartment's south-facing windows.

The two girls spoke with heavy German accents.

"This is very good shit here," Cassie said.

It sounded like, "Das ist vehr gut schidt hier."

"We have connections," Hamilton said, and winked at Isaac.

Both of them were all silked out for the girls. Hamilton was wearing green silk pajamas and a yellow silk robe and black velvet slippers with what looked like the crest of the king of the Belgians on the instep. He looked like Eddie Murphy playing Hugh Hefner. Isaac was wearing a red silk, V-necked, short-sleeved top over what looked like red silk Bermuda shorts. He was barefooted. He was wearing eyeglasses. He looked like a trained monkey with an enormous hard-on.

"Come do me here, sweetheart," he said to Lane.

Lane was busy snorting a mountain of coke. With her free hand, she reached down to unsnap the crotch of her black teddy. Snorting, she began stroking herself. Isaac watched her working her own lips.

"But why do you feel the cop takes precedence?" he asked.

"For what Herrera may have told him," Hamilton said.

"But what does the little spic *know?*"

"Naughty, naughty," Cassie said, at last raising her head from the mirror. Rosalie had taught her that calling Hispanics spics was a no-no in this business where so many of her customers were Colombian dealers up from Miami.

"You finished with that shit?" Hamilton asked.

"For now," Cassie said, grinning.

Oh my, she was stoned. Oh my, these two niggers had glorious shit here.

"Then come do me," Hamilton said.

"Oh, yeah," she said.

It sounded like, "Ach, ja."

She went to him, and settled down on the carpet between his knees, making herself comfortable. The strap of the teddy fell off her right shoulder. She was about to put it back when Hamilton said, "Leave it."

"Okay," she said, and lowered the strap completely, pulling the front of the teddy down over her right breast. Hamilton cupped her breast in his hand. He began kneading it, almost absentmindedly. The nipple actually stiffened, she was that stoned.

"He likes tits," she said to Lane.

Lane was on Isaac's lap now, facing him, straddling him. Both her breasts were in his hands.

"He does, too," she said.

They were talking German now, which Rosalie had warned them against ever doing in the presence of customers. Customers didn't like to think they were being discussed in a foreign language. But in this case it was okay because now Hamilton and Isaac fell into a Jamaican Creole patois neither of the girls could understand. So Cassie and Lane chitchatted back and forth in German like hausfraus gossiping over the back fence except that one had Hamilton in her mouth and the other was riding Isaac hell-bent for leather. Hamilton looked down at Cassie's bobbing blonde head and sipped at his champagne and sang out the riffs of the patois to Isaac who sipped his champagne and then told Lane in perfectly understandable English to turn around the other way, which she did at once, commenting to Cassie in German that if he tried any backdoor stuff all bets were off, this was getting to be a dirty party.

Dirty in more ways than one.

Isaac and Hamilton were discussing murder.

Hamilton was saying that if José Herrera, in gratitude or for whatever reason imaginable, had told the blond cop anything at all about
their operation, why then they were *both* dangerous, the cop more so
than Herrera. In which case, the cop had to be dusted very quickly. To
silence him if he hadn't yet discussed the posse with anyone else in the
department. Or, if he had already shared the information, to dust him
as a warning to the others.

"We have to make a statement, man," Hamilton said in the patois.

Let the police know that where millions of dollars were at stake, no
one could be allowed to interfere.

"Especially not with all the money we're paying them," Isaac said in
the patois.

"Was his name in the newspaper?" Hamilton asked.

"I'll find it."

Lane was standing in front of him, her legs widespread, bent over,
hands on her thighs, looking straight at Hamilton while Isaac pumped
her from behind. There was a blank expression on her face. Hamilton
suddenly desired her fiercely.

"Come here," he said.

"Me?"

"No, Adolf Hitler," he said, making a joke.

Lane was twenty-two years old. She had only vaguely heard of Adolf
Hitler. But she knew who the boss was here. She eased Isaac out of her,
giving him a promising backward glance, head turned over her shoulder. Smiling, then, she licked her lips the way Rosalie had taught her
and walked the way Rosalie had taught her to where Hamilton was on
the couch with Cassie.

Isaac knew better than to complain.

He poured himself another glass of champagne and watched as the
two girls began working Hamilton.

In the patois, Hamilton said, "I'll take the cop out myself."

"Why?"

"Because none of them knows what I look like," Hamilton said, and
smiled. In English, he said to the girls, "Yeah, good, I like that."

"He likes it," Lane said in German.

"I'll *bet* he likes it," Cassie said in German.

"And then we take out the spic," Hamilton said in the patois. "For
what he stole from us."

"You finish him off," Lane said in German.

"Ick," Cassie said in English.

* * *

Carella talked to Lorraine in the Interrogation Room.

Meyer talked to Scott in the squadroom.

Lorraine thought she was playing to a packed house at the London Palladium. A star at last. All this attention focused on her. There were probably a hundred other cops in the next room, behind that fake mirror on the wall. She had seen a lot of movies and she knew all about two-way mirrors. Actually, no one was watching her and Carella through the admittedly two-way mirror, but Lorraine didn't know this, and she was doing a star turn, anyway. Big performance here at the old station house. Give the cops the show of their lives. Cop, as the case actually happened to be.

On the other hand, Scott thought he was talking to his priest.

He guessed Meyer was Jewish, but this was a confessional scene anyway.

All contrite and weepy.

Waiting for Meyer to dispense penance.

"I didn't kill her," Scott said.

"Did someone accuse you?" Meyer asked.

He *almost* said, "Did someone accuse you, my son?"

With his bald head, and in Scott's abject presence, he felt like a tonsured monk. He felt like making the sign of the cross on the air and saying "Dominus vobiscum."

Instead, he said, "Why'd you run?"

"I was scared."

"Why?"

"Because I knew exactly what you'd be thinking."

"And what was that?"

Stopping himself before he added, "My son?"

"That I'd done it," Scott said. "Because she bounced me."

"Do you want to tell me where you were on New Year's Eve?"

"He was with *me*," Lorraine said.

She was on her feet, facing both Carella and the mirror behind which the Police Commissioner and the Chief of Detectives and all the high-ranking departmental brass were undoubtedly standing, watching her performance. She had changed out of the waitressing costume and into her street clothes before leaving the Steamboat Cafe. Short denim skirt, red sweater, red tights, short black boots with a cuff turned down above the ankle. She was strutting for Carella and everybody behind the mirror. Carella knew that she knew she possessed long and spectacularly beautiful legs.

"From what time to what time?" he asked.

He was sitting on the opposite side of the long table that ran the vertical length of the room. The mirror was behind him.

"He got to the party at around twelve-thirty," Lorraine said.

Strothers had said a quarter to one.

"Was he there all night?" Carella asked.

"All night, yes," Scott said.

"Until when?"

"Well, I spent the *night* there. I mean, I slept over. With Lorraine."

That'll be another fifty Hail Marys, Meyer thought.

"I've been staying there," Scott said. "With Lorraine. When I found out about the murder . . ."

"How'd you find out?"

"On television."

Nobody reads the newspapers anymore, Meyer thought.

"I figured I'd . . . I knew you'd think I did it. Because her parents would've mentioned the argument we had. And what I said. And I knew . . ."

"What was it you said?"

"That he was going to kill her," Lorraine said.

"Uh-huh," Carella said.

"Her and her new boyfriend both."

"Uh-huh. And this is what he told you that day he came to your apartment?"

"No, no. This was later. When he came to the apartment, she'd just broken up with him. A few days earlier."

"This was . . . ?"

"Three days after Christmas. When he came to me. Because I used to be his baby-sitter. And he could tell me anything."

"And he told you Annie Flynn had broken up with him."

"Yes."

"But he didn't mention the death threats."

"Well, I wouldn't call them death threats."

"What would you call them, Miss Greer?"

"Well, would *you* call them death threats?" she said, looking directly into the mirror behind Carella and above his head.

"Yes, I would call them death threats," Carella said. "When a person threatens to kill someone, we call that a death threat."

"Well, he didn't mean he'd *actually* kill them."

"That was just an expression," Scott said.

"That you'd kill her and her new boyfriend."

"Yes. I was angry, I just . . . I was just saying anything that came to my mind. Because I was angry, and hurt and . . . do you understand what I'm telling you?"

Yes, my son.

"Yes, I understand," Meyer said. "What I *don't* understand is why you thought it was better to hide instead of . . ."

"He was scared," Lorraine said. "He figured her parents would tell you what he'd said, and you'd get him up here and wring a confession out of him. I don't mean *beat* a confession out of him. I mean *outsmart* him, get him to say things he didn't really *want* to say. Don't you go to the movies?"

"Sometimes," Carella said. "When did he tell you all this?"

"Last Friday. I advised him to turn himself in."

"Uh-huh."

"Otherwise you'd think he killed her."

"And what'd he say?"

"He said he *didn't* kill her."

"Then why wouldn't he come in?"

"I told you. He was scared."

"I don't see why. He had a perfect alibi."

"Sure, alibis," she said to the mirror, dismissing the possibility of an innocent man being able to protect himself from a roomful of clever, aggressive cops. Like the ones behind the mirror.

"Well, he *does* have an alibi, doesn't he?" Carella said.

She looked at him. Was *he* starting to get clever?

"You said he was with you all night . . ."

"That's right."

Flatly. Challengingly. You don't like the idea of my sleeping with a nineteen-year-old kid? Tough. Rock stars can do whatever they want to do.

"Didn't leave the apartment at any time, is that right?"

"He was there all night long. We had breakfast around five, five-thirty. Then everyone left, and we went to bed."

"So there you are," Carella said.

* * *

"...scrambled eggs and bacon, coffee, hot rolls. I guess everybody cleared out by seven, seven-thirty. Then Lorraine and I went to bed."

Meyer nodded.

"Tell me about this new boyfriend," he said.

"Huh?"

"Annie's new boyfriend. The one you said you were going to kill."

"I told you, that was just an ex . . ."

"Yes, I know. But did she say who he was?"

"She said I was crazy."

"Meaning what?"

"I guess . . . well, meaning there *wasn't* anyone else."

"And did you believe that?"

"No."

His eyes met Meyer's.

"I think she dropped me because of another guy."

New apartment building and all, he'd had to present himself in the sales office as somebody looking to buy. So he could get floor plans. He knew which apartment the Hoddings were in, he'd got that from the directory in the lobby the first time he'd gone to the building. Doorman said Yes, sir, can I help you? Told him he was looking for the sales office, which it turned out was on the third floor in an apartment that had been furnished as a model. One of the bigger apartments, the salesperson said it was going for $850,000, because of the parkside view. Same apartment higher up in the building—there were eighteen stories in all—went for a million-six. There were less expensive apartments without a view of the park, all of them facing the side street, and these started at five and a quarter, it wasn't cheap living in this part of the city, the salesperson told him.

He'd asked for floor plans of the different apartments being sold. Each apartment had a name. Like ordering from a menu. There was the Cosmopolitan and the Urbanite and the Excel and the Luxor and the most expensive of them all, the Tower Suite, which shared the entire eighteenth floor of the building with an identical apartment flipflopped. The building on the right was also only eighteen stories high, and there were height restrictions built into the zoning, so there was no question of ever being overshadowed. And, of course, on the left there was the side street.

He'd gathered up the floor plans for all the different apartments and then asked for a plan showing the location of the apartments on each floor. He knew the Hoddings were in apartment 4A. All of the A apartments were Urbanites.

So he had the floor plan right there in his hand.

Knew exactly where the fire escapes were.

Knew exactly how to get in.

Exactly how to get to her.

The salesperson thought she had a live one.

8

DANNY GIMP WAS OFFENDED.

"How come you went to Donner?" he asked.

The two men were sitting on a bench facing the ice-skating rink that had been named after Louis Weiss, the noted mountain climber. In this city, it was common knowledge that no mountain in the world was too high for Weiss to assail. With the help of his faithful shleppers—faithful *sherpas*—and with a god-given sense of humor and a ready smile, Weiss continued climbing to ever loftier heights, suffering frostbite of the nose only once. It was perhaps in memory of this single mishap in the Himalayas that an ice-skating rather than a roller-skating rink had been named after him. On occasional Saturdays, Weiss himself could be seen gliding over the ice, cheerfully asking children not to scatter candy bar wrappers on his rink. He was not there this Saturday.

It was already the fourteenth day of January.

Exactly two weeks since the murders were committed.

Eight days since Hal Willis had first contacted Fats Donner.

Now Danny Gimp wanted to know why.

Carella said, "How do you know we went to Donner?"

"My *job* is listening," Danny said, even more offended. "I really am upset, Steve. Truly."

"He has a short-eyes history," Carella said.

"That is no reason to have gone to him."

"If a baby and a sixteen-year-old are the victims, it's a very *good* reason."

"This is a very big case, Steve, it's all over the papers, you can't turn on your TV without seeing something about it."

"I know," Carella said wearily.

"So instead of giving me a shot at a whammer, you give it to Donner. I can't understand that, Steve, I really can't."

"Also," Carella said lamely, "it may be linked to a burglary Willis is working. So he went to Donner. Because he's worked with him before. Willis."

Danny looked at him.

"Okay," Carella said.

"I mean, you know, Steve . . ."

"I said okay."

Both men fell silent. On the rink, children of all ages flashed by in a rainbow of color. A young girl who thought she was Katarina Witt leaped into the air, did a triple jump, beamed happily in mid-air, and fell on her ass. Without embarrassment, she got up, skated off, and tried another jump—a double this time.

"Does it hurt when it's cold like this?" Danny asked.

Carella knew instantly what he was talking about.

" 'Cause the leg does," Danny said. "From when *I* got shot."

This was a lie. Danny had never been shot. He limped because he'd had polio as a child. But pretending he'd been wounded in a big gang shootout gave him a certain cachet he considered essential to the business of informing. Carella was willing to forgive the lie. The first time he himself got shot, Danny came to the hospital to see him. This was unusual for an informer. Carella guessed he actually liked Danny. Gray and grizzled and looking chubbier than he actually was because of the layers of clothing he was wearing, Danny sat on the bench and watched the skaters. He and Carella might have been old friends sitting in the park on a wintry day, remembering good times they had shared, complaining about small physical ailments like a leg that hurt when the temperature dropped.

" 'Cause I heard you got shot again," Danny said.

"Yeah," Carella said.

"On Halloween, I heard."

"That's right."

"So I was wondering if it hurts when it gets cold like this."

"A little."

"You got to stop getting shot," Danny said.

"I know."

"That can be a bad failing for a cop."

"I know."

"So be more careful."

"I will."

"And give me a call every now and then when you got a whammer. Instead of *I* have to call *you* and beg for a meeting here in the park where I'm freezing my ass off."

"The park was your idea," Carella said.

"Sure, all I need is to get spotted in a bar someplace, talking to a cop. Especially one who gets himself shot every other weekend. You're starting to be like that other guy you got up there, what's his name?"

"O'Brien."

"O'Brien, right. He's got a reputation for that, ain't he? Getting himself shot every time he gets out of bed in the morning."

"He's been shot a fair amount of times," Carella said drily.

"So what're you trying to do? Break his record?"

Carella suddenly realized that Danny was truly concerned.

"I'll be careful," he said gently.

"Please do," Danny said. "Now tell me who you're looking for."

"A man named Proctor."

"The Doctor?"

"You know him?"

"I know the name. He ain't into murder, Steve. He's a two-bit burglar and a sometime-dealer."

"We're thinking maybe a felony murder."

"Well, maybe," Danny said dubiously.

"Because we know he did a burglary in the same building on the night of the murders. If he was doing *another* one, and the sitter surprised him . . ."

"Well, sure, then you got your felony murder."

"Because he used a knife."

"Yeah, I saw that on television."

"A weapon of convenience."

"Yeah."

"Which could happen if a person is surprised. He grabs a knife from the rack . . ."

"He don't have to be surprised to do that."

"Well, nobody goes in *planning* to use what he finds on the spot."

"I suppose," Danny said, and shrugged. "Proctor, Proctor, where did I hear something about him lately? Did he just get out?"

"Two years ago."

"Did he break parole or something?"

"Yes. Where'd you hear that?"

"Shmuck breaks parole it's all over the street. Captain Invincible, right? Nobody can touch him. But that's not it. I mean, this was something new. Where the hell did I hear it?"

The men fell silent again.

Danny was thinking furiously.

Carella was waiting.

There were two figure skaters out on the ice now. They floated like sugar plum fairies among the children churning furiously around them. An ice hockey game, strictly against the rules, was in its formative stages, two rosy-cheeked boys choosing up sides while half a dozen others circled them.

"They always picked me last," Danny said.

He never misses a trick, Carella thought.

"Because of the leg."

"They picked me last, too," Carella said.

This was a lie. He'd always been a fairly good athlete.

"Who you think has the better legs? The one in blue or the one in red?"

Carella looked out over the ice.

"The one in red," he said.

"Really. You know what I call those kind of legs? I call them Chinese legs."

"Why?"

"I don't know why. It's the kind of legs Chinese girls have. Did you ever make it with a Chinese girl?"

"Never."

"That's the kind of legs they got. My money's on the one in blue."

"Okay," Carella said.

"Salzeech his own, huh?" Danny said, and smiled.

Carella smiled, too.

"That's a pun," Danny explained.

"I know."

"You know the expression 'To each his own'?"

"Yes."

"That's the pun," Danny explained. "The Italians say *salsiccia*, which means sausage. Salzeech for short. I ain't Italian, but you ought to know that."

"I do know it."

"So that's the pun. Salzeech his own."

"I got it already, Danny."

"So how come you didn't bust out laughing?" he said, and smiled again.

Carella smiled with him.

They fell silent again.

Danny was still thinking.

"It'll come to me," he said at last.

The man sitting at Kling's desk was obviously Jamaican.

One of the Jakies, as Herrera had labeled them. As if this city needed more ethnic labels than it already had.

His speech rolled from his tongue like the sea nudging the shores of his native island.

He was telling Kling that his wife had threatened to kill him.

He was asking Kling to come back to the apartment with him, to warn his wife—whose name was Imogene—not to say such things to him anymore. And especially not to *do* such things, if that was what she really planned to do. Which he strongly believed was her plan since she had recently purchased from a street vendor a .22-caliber pistol for sixteen dollars and change.

The man talking to Kling said his name was Dudley Archibald.

He was, Kling supposed, in his early thirties, with a very dark complexion, soulful brown eyes, and a thin-lipped mouth. He wore his hair in a modified Afro. He was dressed conservatively in a tan suit that appeared a bit tropical for the frigid temperatures outside. You told somebody in the Caribbean that it was cold up here, he nodded knowingly, figured all he had to do was pack a sweater. Like for when it got a bit chilly at night in the islands. Just like that. Sure. Came up here, immediately froze to death. Tan tropical suit with the temperature outside at twenty-one degrees Fahrenheit and the squadroom windows rimed with ice.

Archibald told Kling he was a postal worker. This was his day off. Saturday. He'd come up here on his day off because he was truly worried that his wife Imogene would take it in her mind to use that pistol one of these days.

"I would appreciate it, sir," he said, "if you came home with me and told her that wouldn't be such a good idea, sir."

"You know," Kling said, "people sometimes say things they don't really . . ."

"Yes, sir, but she bought a pistol, sir."

"Even so."

"I don't think you would want my murder on your head, sir."

Kling looked at him.

What the hell *was* this?

First Herrera, now Archibald. Telling Kling if he didn't take care of them, their murders would be on his head.

"How'd you happen to come to me?" he asked.

He really wanted to say Of all the detectives on this squad, why the fuck did you pick me?

"You did a burglary in the neighborhood," Archibald said.

Kling realized he wasn't suggesting that Kling had *committed* a burglary. He was merely saying that Kling had *investigated* one. Of several hundred, Kling imagined. In this precinct, burglaries were as common as jaywalking.

"Which one?" he asked.

"I forget her name," Archibald said. "A fat lady."

"Uh-huh."

"She said you were very good."

"Uh-huh."

"So I asked the sergeant downstairs for you. Gloria Something?"

"Well," Kling said, and shrugged.

"Gloria, I think."

"Well, in any event, Mr. Archibald, I don't think it would be appropriate for me to come to your home and to intrude on what doesn't even appear to be a family dispute as yet. I would suggest . . ."

"A pistol *is* a family dispute," Archibald said. "If she has threatened to kill me with it."

"Did she use those exact words? I'm going to kill you?"

"She said she would shoot me with the pistol. A .22-caliber pistol."

"Was this during an argument?"

"No, it was calmly. Over breakfast."

"When?"

"Every day this week."

"Every day."

"Yes."

Kling sighed.

"She keeps the pistol in the bread box," Archibald said.

"I see."

"In the kitchen."

"Uh-huh."

"She probably plans to shoot me while we're eating."

Kling sighed again.

"I can't come with you . . ."

"Then my murder . . ."

". . . just now," Kling said. "I've got a showdown to run, some women are coming in at one o'clock." He looked at his watch. "I should be done around two, two-thirty. I can maybe get over there around three. Will your wife be home then?"

"Yes, sir. Thank you, sir."

"Where do you live?"

"337 South Eustis. Apartment 44."

"You make sure your wife's there, okay? I'll come by and talk to her. Does she have a license for that pistol?"

Archibald looked as if he suddenly realized he'd bought more trouble than he'd bargained for.

"No, sir," he said. "But I don't want to . . ."

"Gives me a reason to take the gun away from her, right?" Kling said, and smiled.

Archibald did not return the smile.

"Relax, nobody's going to hurt her," Kling said.

"Thank you, sir," Archibald said.

"I'll see you at three," Kling said.

It never occurred to him that in this city certain types of Jamaicans sometimes shot policemen.

There were times when the irony of the situation amused Teddy.

She was deaf. She had been born deaf. She had never heard a human voice, an animal's cry, the shriek of machinery, the rustle of a fallen leaf. She had never spoken a word in her life. A woman like Teddy used to be called a "deaf mute." A label. Intended to be descriptive and perhaps kind. "Dummy" would have been the cruel word. Now she was called "hearing-impaired." Progress. Another label. She was, after all, merely Teddy Carella.

What sometimes amused her was that this deaf mute, this hearing-impaired person, this *dummy* was in fact such a good listener.

Eileen Burke apparently understood this.

Perhaps she'd understood it all along, or perhaps she'd only reached her understanding last Friday night, when during dinner she had seized upon Teddy as a sympathetic ear.

"I've always thought of you as my best friend," she said now, surprising Teddy. Their relationship had, at best, been a casual one. Dinner out with their respective men, an occasional movie, a football game, a private party, a big police affair. But best friend? Strong words. Teddy was a woman who chose her words carefully. Perhaps because her flying fingers could only accommodate so few of them in a single burst. Best friend? She wondered.

"I wouldn't tell this to anyone else," Eileen said. "I've been seeing a shrink, Teddy. I go twice a . . ."

She hesitated.

There was a puzzled expression on Teddy's face.

One of the words had thrown her.

Eileen thought back for a moment, and then said, "Shrink," exaggerating the word on her lips. Then, to nail it down, she said, "Psychologist."

Teddy nodded.

"I go to her twice a week."

Without saying a word, merely by slightly raising her eyebrows and opening her eyes a trifle wider, Teddy said—and Eileen understood—a multitude of things.

And?

How's it going?

Tell me more.

"I think she's going to be okay," Eileen said. "I mean, I don't know yet. It bothers me that she's younger than I am . . ."

Teddy began signing.

And caught herself.

But she used her hands, anyway, signaling Eileen to go on, to elaborate, to tell her exactly . . .

"Twenty-six or -seven," Eileen said.

Teddy pulled a face.

"Yeah," Eileen said, "that's just it. She seems like a kid to me, too."

The restaurant was crowded with Saturday shoppers taking a break away from the Hall Avenue department stores. Eileen was wearing jeans, a bulky green sweater, and brown boots. A dark blue car coat was draped over the back of her chair. Her service revolver was in her shoulder bag, on the floor under the table. Teddy had taken the subway in from Riverhead. She, too, was dressed for a casual afternoon in the city. Jeans, a yellow turtleneck with a tan cardigan over it, Adidas jogging shoes. A black ski parka was draped over the back of her chair. Her small handbag was on the table. At a nearby table, two women noticed that she was using her hands a lot, making exaggerated facial expressions. One of them whispered, "She's deaf and

dumb," another quaint label Teddy would have found offensive had
she heard it. She did not hear it because she was too busy talking and
listening.

Eileen was telling her that she'd stopped seeing Kling.

"Because I don't think he understands what I'm trying to do here."

Teddy watched her intently.

"Or how much . . . how . . . you know . . . I don't think he . . . he's a
man, Teddy, I don't think any man in the world can really understand
what . . . how . . . you know . . . the effect that something like . . . like
what happened . . . how traumatic it can be to a woman."

Teddy was still watching her.

Dark brown eyes luminous in her face.

Listening.

Waiting.

"Rape, I mean," Eileen said.

Teddy nodded.

"That I was raped."

Tears suddenly sprang to Eileen's eyes.

Teddy reached across the table, took her hands in her own.

"So . . . so you . . . I figure if I have to cope with *his* goddamn feelings while I'm trying to understand my own . . . I mean, it's just too
much to handle, Teddy."

Teddy nodded. She squeezed Eileen's hands.

"I mean, I can't worry about his . . . his . . . you know . . . *his* sensi-
tivity, he's not the one who got raped. Aw, shit, I don't know, maybe I
did the wrong thing. But don't *I* count, Teddy? Isn't it important that I
. . . aw, shit," she said again, and reached down into her bag for the
package of Kleenex tissues alongside her gun.

"Excuse me," a man said, "are you all right?"

He was standing alongside the table. Tall. Brown eyes. Dark hair.
Craggy good looks. Perhaps thirty-seven, thirty-eight years old. Wearing a brown overcoat and brown gloves. Obviously just leaving the
restaurant. Obviously concerned about Eileen's tears.

"I'm fine," she said to him, turning her head away, drying her eyes.

He leaned over the table. Gloved hands on the table.

"Are you sure?" he said. "If there's any way I can help . . ."

"No, thank you, that's very nice of you," Eileen said, "but I'm okay,
really. Thank you."

"As long as you're all right," he said, and smiled, and turned swiftly
from the table and began walking toward—

"Hey!" Eileen yelled and shoved back her chair, knocking it over. "Hey, you!"

She was on her feet and running, shoving past a waitress carrying a trayload of sandwiches, throwing open the front door and racing after the man, who made an immediate right turn on the sidewalk outside. Teddy could not hear Eileen shouting, "Police, stop!" but she did see the man as he came past the restaurant's plate glass window, and she did see Eileen come up fast behind him, both of them running, and she saw Eileen leap at the man in a headlong tackle that sent something flying out of his gloved hand, and only then did she realize that the something was a woman's handbag, and the handbag was hers.

They went down in a jumble of arms and legs, Eileen and the man, rolling over on the sidewalk, Eileen on top now, her right arm coming up, no gun in her hand, her gun was still in her shoulder bag on the floor under the table. Her right fist was bunched. It came down hard on the side of the man's neck. The man stiffened as if a nerve had been struck. A uniformed cop was suddenly on the scene, trying to break them apart, Eileen screaming she was on the job, which Teddy did not hear but which she guessed the officer understood because all at once his gun was in his hand and he was cuffing the man on the sidewalk and having a nice friendly chat with Eileen who just kept nodding at him impatiently.

She picked up Teddy's handbag from where it lay beside the handcuffed man. The cop wanted the bag. Eileen was telling him no, shaking her head. The conversation seemed to get very heated. Eileen began using her hands, the bag in one hand, both hands waving around in the air. Finally, she turned away from the cop, the bag still in her hand, and started back for the restaurant, automatically shooing away the crowd that had gathered outside, a holdover from the days when she herself had been a uniformed cop.

She came back to the table.

"How do you *like* that guy?" she said, shaking her head in amazement.

Teddy nodded.

She was thinking how strong Eileen had been, how brave and—

But Eileen, noticing everyone looking at her, flushed a red the color of her hair, and said in embarrassment, "Could we get out of here, please?"

And to Teddy she suddenly seemed like a little girl standing in front of a mirror in her mother's dress and shoes.

* * *

In Calm's Point, there was a Jamaican neighborhood called Camp Kingston. In Riverhead, the Jamaican section was called Little Kingston. In other parts of the city, there was a Kingston North and even a Kingston Gulch, though how that name had originated was anyone's guess. Here in the Eight-Seven, the Jamaican section ran for several blocks from Culver Avenue to the River Harb, where what was still officially called Beaudoin Bluff was now familiarly called Kingston Heights. In any of these neighborhoods, whenever a cop broke up a street fight and asked the participants where they were from, the proud answer was "Kingston." Not a single Jamaican in this city was from Montego Bay or Savannala-Mar or Port Antonio. Every Jamaican in this city came from Kingston. The *capital,* man. The same way every Frenchman in the world came from Paris. *Mais je suis* Parisien, *monsieur!* The raised eyebrow. The indignant tone. Kingston, mon, where you tink?

Kling had not been in this part of the precinct since it was Puerto Rican. Before that, it had been Italian. And before that, Irish. And if you went back far enough, Dutch and Indian. But there was no sense of history in these streets. There was merely a feeling of a transient population inhabiting a decaying slum. The buildings were uniformly gray here, even though there was red brick beneath the ageless soot. The streets had been only partially cleared of snow; in this neighborhood—as was the case in most of the city's ghettos—garbage collection, snow clearance, pothole repair, and most other municipal services were provided at a rather leisurely pace. The streets here looked dirty at any time of the year, but particularly so during the winter months. Perhaps because of the soiled snow. Or perhaps because it was so goddamn cold. In the summer months, for all its poverty, a slum looked extravagantly alive. During the winter, the deserted streets, the vain bonfires in vacant lots, the wind sweeping through narrow gray canyons, only exaggerated the ghetto's meanness. Here is poverty, the ghetto said. Here is dope. Here is crime. Here is only the thinnest thread of hope.

The mayor seemed not to know that the snow up here hadn't been cleared yet.

Perhaps because he rarely went to dinner in the 87th Precinct.

337 South Eustis Street was in a line of tenements on a street that dropped swiftly toward the river. There was ice out there today. The sky over the high rises in the next state glowered with clouds threatening more snow. Kling walked with his head ducked against the fierce

wind that blew in over the choppy gray water. He was thinking that what he'd hated most as a patrolman was a family dispute, and here he was a detective about to march into somebody's house to settle a marital problem. Call used to come in over the radio, 10-64, Family Dispute, a non-crime incident, and the dispatcher would almost always tag it with "See the lady," because it was usually the wife who'd called 911 to say her husband was batting her around the apartment. Today, he was about to see the man; it was Dudley Archibald who'd made the complaint about his wife Imogene.

He entered the building.

The stench of urine.

He wondered if there was a building in the entire 87th Precinct that did not stink of piss in the entrance hallway.

Broken mailboxes. Jimmied for the welfare, Social Security or Medicare checks.

A naked light bulb overhead. Miraculously unbroken and unscrewed; victimizers normally preferred waiting in the dark.

An inner door with a missing doorknob. Stolen for the brass. You unscrewed enough brass doorknobs, you sold them to the junkman, you picked up the five bucks you needed for your vial of crack.

Kling put his palm flat against the door, a foot and a half above the hole left by the missing doorknob, shoved the door open, came into the ground-floor vestibule, and began climbing.

Cooking smells.

Alien.

Exotic.

Tile floors on the landings. Cracked, chipped, faded, worn. But tile nonetheless. From a time when the city's North Side was flourishing and apartments here were at a premium.

Television sets going behind every door. The afternoon soaps. A generation of immigrants learning all about America from its daytime serials.

Apartment 44, Archibald had told him.

He kept climbing.

The tile on the fourth-floor landing had been ripped up and replaced with a tin floor. Kling wondered why. The staircase wound up for another flight, dead-ending at a metal door painted red and leading to the roof. Four apartments here on the fourth floor. Forty-one, two, three, and four, count 'em. No light here on the landing. He could barely make out the numeral forty-four on the door at the far end of the hall. Not a sound coming from behind that door. He stood in the near-darkness, listening. And then, because he was a cop, he put his ear to the wood and listened more intently.

Nothing.

He looked at his watch. Squinted in the gloom. Ten minutes past three. He'd told Archibald he'd be here at three.

He knocked.

And the shots came.

He threw himself instinctively to the floor.

His gun was already in his hand.

There were two bullet holes in the door.

He waited. He was breathing very hard. The only sound in the hall-way. His breathing. Harsh, ragged. Those two holes in the door right at about the level of where his head had been. His heart was pounding. He waited. His mind raced with possibilities. He'd been set up. Come talk to my wife, mon, she bought herself a .22-caliber pistol, and she has threatened to shoot me with it. Come help me, mon. A woman named Gloria told me about you. You did a burglary for her. A fat lady. Set the cop up because he's been talking to a man who knows that a huge shipment of cocaine will be coming into the city nine days from now. Kill the cop here in Kingston Heights where life is cheap and where those holes in the door did not look as if they'd been drilled by a mere—

Bam, bam, bam, three more shots in rapid succession and more wood splintering out of the door, showering onto the air like shrapnel.

And Archibald's voice.

"You crazy, woman?"

Kling was on his feet.

He kicked at the door where the lock was fastened, followed the door into the room as it sprang open, gun fanning the room, eyes following the gun, eyes swinging with the gun to where a skinny woman the color of whole-wheat bread stood near the kitchen sink opposite the door. She was wearing only a pink slip. A substantial-looking piece was in her right hand, a thirty-eight at least, the hand sagging with the weight of it, and Dudley Archibald over there on Kling's left, five shots gone now, Archibald balancing on his feet like a boxer trying to decide which way to duck when the next punch came.

Kling wished he knew how many bullets were in that gun, but he didn't.

There were thirty-eights with five-shot capacities.

There were also thirty-eights with nine-shot capacities.

"Hey, Imogene," he said softly.

The woman turned toward him. Gray-green eyes. Slitted. The big gun shaking in her tiny fist. The big gun shaking but pointed at his chest.

"Why don't you put down the gun?" he said.

"*Kill* the bastard," she said.

"No, you don't want to do that," Kling said. "Come on. Let me have the gun, okay?"

Jesus, don't shoot me, he thought.

"I told you," Archibald said.

"Just stay out of this," Kling said. He did not turn to look at him. His eyes were on Imogene. His eyes were on her eyes.

"Put down the gun, okay?" he said.

"No."

"Why not? You don't want to get yourself in trouble, do you?"

"I'm in trouble already," she said.

"Nah, what trouble?" Kling said. "Little family argument? Come on, don't make things worse than they are. Just let me have the gun, nobody's going to hurt you, okay?"

He was telling the truth.

But he was also lying.

He did not plan on hurting her. Not physically. Not he himself.

But neither he nor the police department were about to forget a lady with a gun. And the criminal justice system *would* hurt her. As sure as he was standing there trying to talk her out of firing that gun again.

"What do you say, Imogene?"

"Who tole you my name?"

"He did. Put the gun there on the table, okay? Come on, you're gonna hurt yourself with that thing."

"I'm gonna hurt *him*," she said, and swung the gun from Kling toward her husband.

"Hey, *no!*" Kling said at once.

The gun swung back again.

One of us is gonna get it, he thought.

"You're scaring hell out of me," he said.

She looked at him.

"You really are. Are you gonna shoot me?"

"I'm gonna shoot *him!*" she said, and again the gun swung onto her husband.

"And then what? I'm a police officer, Imogene. If you shoot this man, I can't just let you walk out of this apartment. So you'll have to shoot me, too, am I right? Is that what you want to do? Shoot me?"

"No, but . . ."

"Then come on, let's quit this, okay? Just give me the gun, and . . ."

"No!"

She shouted the word.

It cracked into the apartment like another pistol shot. Archibald winced. So did Kling. He had the sudden feeling that his watch had stopped. The gun was pointed at him again. He was drenched in sweat. Nineteen degrees out there, he was covered with sweat.

He did not want to shoot this woman.

But if she turned that gun toward her husband again, he would make his move.

Please don't let me shoot you, he thought.

"Imogene," he said, very softly.

The gun was trained on his chest. The gray-green eyes watching.

"Please don't let me hurt you," he said.

Watching.

"Please put the gun down on the table."

Watching, watching.

"Please, Imogene."

He waited for what seemed forever.

First she nodded.

He waited.

She kept nodding.

Then she walked to the table, and looked down at the table top, and looked at the gun in her hand as if first discovering it, and then she nodded again, and looked at Kling, and put the gun on the table. He walked to the table slowly, picked up the gun, slipped it into his coat pocket, and said, "Thank you."

He was putting the handcuffs on her when Archibald, safe now, shouted, "Bitch!"

Kling made the phone call from the super's apartment downstairs.

People had gathered in the hallway. They all knew there'd been shooting on the fourth floor. Some of them seemed disappointed that no one had been killed. In a neighborhood where violence was commonplace, a shooting without a corpse was like scrambled eggs without onions. It would have been nice, in fact, if the cop had been killed.

Not many people in this neighborhood liked cops. Some of the people in the hallway began jeering Kling as he led Imogene out.

At that moment, he didn't feel very good about himself, anyway. He was thinking that the system would wring Imogene out like a dirty dishcloth. Ninety-six pounds if she weighed a nickel, the system would destroy her. Not twenty minutes ago, all he'd been thinking about was his own skin. Heard shots, figured they were meant for him. Ambush for the big detective. A genuine family dispute erupting into a lady-with-a-gun situation, and all he could think at the time was that someone had set him up. Maybe he deserved to be jeered.

They came out of the building into the bitter cold.

Imogene in handcuffs.

Archibald on one side of her, looking penitent now that it was all over, Kling on the other side, holding her elbow, guiding her toward the patrol car at the curb.

He did not notice a tall, thin black man standing in a doorway across the street.

The man was watching him.

The man was Lewis Randolph Hamilton.

9

IT WAS FAT OLLIE WEEKS who came up with the lead on Doctor Martin Proctor.

Fat Ollie was not an informer; he was a detective working out of the Eight-Three. Fat Ollie was not as fat as Fats Donner; hence Ollie's obesity was in the singular whereas Donner's was in the plural. The men did have two things in common, however: they were both very good listeners and nobody liked either one of them. Nobody liked Fats Donner because his sexual preferences ran to prepubescent girls. Nobody liked Fat Ollie because he was a bigot. Moreover, he was that rare sort of bigot who hated everyone.

The cops of the Eight-Seven still remembered Roger Havilland, who'd been an Ollie Weeks sort of person before he got thrown through a plate glass window to his final reward. No one—well, hardly anyone—wished such a dire fate would befall Ollie, but they did wish he would bathe every now and again. On a fair day with a brisk wind, you could smell Ollie clear across Grover Park.

On Monday morning, the sixteenth day of January, Ollie walked into the Eight-Seven's squadroom as if he owned the joint. Pushed his way familiarly through the slatted rail divider, his beer barrel belly preceding him as surely as did his stench, wearing only a sports jacket over his open-collared shirt, despite the frigid temperature outside. His cheeks were rosy red, and he was puffing like a man actively seeking a heart attack. He walked directly to where Carella was typing at his desk, clapped him on the shoulder, and said, "Hey, Steve-a-rino, how you been?"

Carella winced.

"Hello, Ollie," he said unenthusiastically.

"So you're looking for the Doctor, huh?" Ollie said, and put his finger to the side of his nose like a Mafia sage. "You come to the right person."

Carella hoped Ollie didn't mean what he thought Ollie meant.

"Martin Proctor," Ollie said. "Sounds like a Jew, don't he? The Martin, I mean. You ever heard of anybody named Martin who wasn't a Jew?"

"Yes, Martin Sheen," Carella said.

"He's *worse* than a Jew," Ollie said, "he's a fuckin' Mexican. His son's name is Emilio Estevez, so where does he come off usin' an American name like Sheen? There was this bishop in New York, his name was Sheen, wasn't it? So who's this fuckin' Mexican using a Jewish first name and an Irish last name?"

Carella was suddenly sorry he'd brought it up.

But Ollie was just gathering steam.

"You get these fuckin' immigrants, they change their names so nobody can tell they're foreigners. Who do they think they're kiddin'? Guy writes a book, he's a fuckin' wop, he puts an American name on the book, everybody knows he's really a wop, anyway. Everybody says You know what his real name is? His real name ain't Lance Bigelow, it's Luigi Mangiacavallo. Everybody knows this. Behind his back, they laugh at him. They say Good morning, Lance, how are you? Or Good evening, Mr. Bigelow, your table is ready. But who's he kidding? They all know he's only a wop."

"Like me," Carella said.

"That's true," Ollie said, "but you're okay otherwise."

Carella sighed.

"Anyway, you got me off the track with your fuckin' Martin Sheen," Ollie said. "You want what I got on Proctor, or you want to talk about Mexicans who put makeup on their faces to earn a living?"

Carella sighed again.

He did not for a moment doubt that Ollie Weeks had a line on Martin Proctor. But he did not want favors from Ollie. Favors had to be paid back. Favors owed to a bigot were double-edged favors. However good a cop Ollie Weeks was—and the sad truth was that he happened to be a very good cop—Carella did not want to owe him, did not want Ollie to come back later to say the note he'd signed was due. But a six-month-old baby and her sitter had been murdered.

"What've you got?" he asked.

"Ah yes, the man is interested," Ollie said, doing his world-famous W. C. Fields imitation.

Carella looked at him.

"Very definitely interested, ah yes," Ollie said, still doing Fields. "Let us say for the sake of argument that there is a certain lady who frequents a bar, ah yes, in the Eighty-Third Precinct, which some of us mere mortals call home, ah yes. Let us further say that this lady has on occasion in the past dispensed certain favors and information to certain detectives in this fair city who have looked the other way while the lady was plying her trade, do I make my point, sir?"

Carella nodded.

Weeks was banging a hooker in the Eight-Three.

"What's her name?" he asked.

"Ah yes, her name. Which, may I say, sir, is none of your fucking business, ah yes."

"Could you please drop the Fields imitation?" Carella said.

"You knew it was him, huh?" Ollie said, pleased. "I also do Ronald Reagan."

"Don't," Carella said.

"I do Ronald Reagan after they cut off his legs."

"What about this hooker?"

"Who said she was a hooker?"

"Gee, for some reason I thought she was a hooker."

"Whatever she may be, let us say she got to talking the other night . . ."

"When?"

"Saturday night."

"And?"

"And seeing as I am a law enforcement officer, and seeing as how we were sharing a few intimate moments together . . ."

"Get to it, Ollie."

"The lady inquired as to whether I knew why the police were looking for Martin the Doctor. This was like a strange situation, Steve. Usually, *I'm* the one pumping *her*. But there we were . . ."

His sex life, no less, Carella thought.

". . . both of us naked as niggers in the jungle, and *she's* the one tryin'a get information outa *me*. Can you see how peculiar that was?"

Carella waited.

But Ollie hadn't intended the question rhetorically.

"Do you see how peculiar that was?" he repeated.

"Yes," Carella said. "Very peculiar."

"I mean, she is riding me bareback like a fuckin' Indian on a pony and she wants to know why the cops are lookin' for Proctor, who I don't know from a hole in the wall."

"So?"

"So I get outa bed afterward, and I go wipe my dick on the drapes . . . do you know that joke?"

"No."

"It's what a Jewish guy does to get his wife excited after he comes. He wipes his dick on the drapes, you get it? To get his wife excited. Because Jewish girls . . ."

"I get it," Carella said.

"I didn't *really* wipe my dick on the drapes," Ollie said. "I mean, I know I'm a fuckin' slob but I'm not *that* big a slob."

"What *did* you use?" Carella asked. "Your tie?"

"That's very funny," Ollie said, but he didn't laugh. "Anyway, while she's squatting over a basin rinsing herself out, she tells me this friend of hers is a friend of Proctor's, and he was wonderin' why the cops were snoopin' around Proctor's old address, lookin' for him. And if I knew anything about it, she would appreciate it if I would tell her, seeing as we were old friends and all. So she could pass the information on to her friend. Who I guess, but she didn't say, would then pass it on to Proctor, saving his ass from whatever terrible thing we had in mind for him, the cops. I told her I would sniff around."

"So where is he?"

"Proctor? One thing at a time. Don't you want to hear what a brilliant detective I am?"

"No."

"Okay, then I won't tell you how I went to this spic snitch named Francisco Palacios, who is also known as The Gaucho, or sometimes The Cowboy, and who runs a little store that sells in the front medicinal herbs, dream books, religious statues, numbers books, tarot cards and such, but in the back French ticklers, open-crotch panties, vibrators, dildoes, benwa balls and the like, not that this is against the law. I won't tell you how The Cowboy mentioned to me that another stoolie named Donner had been in asking about this very same Doctor Proctor who it seems the boys of the Eight-Seven have been inquiring about. I won't tell you how it occurs to me that perhaps it was somebody from up here who was nosing around 1146 Park Street, which was Proctor's last known address, who according to The Cowboy he has busted parole and is being very cautious, anyway. I will not tell you all this, Steve-arino," Ollie said, and grinned.

"What will you tell me?"

"Not where Proctor is, 'cause I don't know."

"Terrific," Carella said. "So what are you doing up here?"

"My friend? This lady I was telling you about?"

"Yeah?"

"I know *her* friend's name."

Eileen hadn't said a word for the past twenty minutes.

Just kept sitting there staring at Karin.

Karin hadn't said anything either.

It was a staring contest.

Eileen looked at her watch.

"Yes?" Karin said.

"Nothing."

"You can leave whenever you want to," Karin said. "This isn't violin lessons."

"I didn't think it was."

"What I mean is . . ."

"Yes, I . . ."

"No one's forcing you to do this."

"I'm here of my own free will, I know."

"Exactly."

"But that doesn't . . ."

Eileen caught herself, shook her head.

"Doesn't what?"

"Doesn't mean I don't know you're sitting there waiting to *pounce* on whatever I might say."

"Is that what you think?"

Eileen said nothing.

"That I'm waiting to pounce on you?"

"That's your job, isn't it? To take whatever I say and make a federal case out of it?"

"I never thought of my job as . . ."

"Let's not get into *your* job, okay? The reason I'm here is I want to quit *my* job. And so far I haven't had any help in that direction."

"Well, we've only seen each other . . ."

"So how long does it take to write a resignation letter?"

"Is that what you want me to help you with? A resignation letter?"

"You *know* what I . . ."

"But I don't know."

"I want to *quit,* damn it! And I can't seem to do it."

"Maybe you don't want to quit."

"I do."

"All right."

"You know I do."

"Yes, that's what you told me."

"Yes. And it's true."

"You want to quit because you killed a man."

"Yes."

"And you're afraid if you stay on the job . . ."

"I'll be forced into another situation, yes, where I'll have to use the gun again."

"Have to fire the gun again."

"Yes."

"Kill again."

"Yes."

"You're afraid of that."

"Yes."

"What else are you afraid of?"

"What do you want me to say?"

"Whatever you're thinking. Whatever you're feeling."

"I know what you'd *like* me to say."

"And what's that?"

"I know *exactly* what you'd like me to say."

"Tell me."

"You'd like me to say rape."

"Uh-huh."

"You'd like me to say I'm afraid of getting raped again . . ."

"Are you?"

". . . that I want to quit before some son of a bitch rapes me again."

"Is that how you feel?"

Eileen did not answer.

For the remaining five minutes of the hour, she sat there staring at Karin.

At last, Karin smiled and said, "I'm sorry, our time is up. I'll see you on Thursday, okay?"

Eileen nodded, slung her shoulder bag, and went to the door. At the door, she hesitated with her hand on the knob. Then she turned and said, "I am. Afraid of that, too."

And turned again and went out.

Sammy Pedicini was used to talking to cops. Whenever a burglary went down in this city, the cops paid Sammy a little visit, asked him all kinds of questions. Sammy always told them the same thing. Whatever it was they were investigating, it wasn't Sammy who did it. Sammy had taken a fall ten years ago, and now he was outside again, and he had learned his lesson.

"Whatever this is," Sammy told Carella now, "I didn't do it."

Carella nodded.

"I learned my lesson up at Castleview, I been clean since."

Meyer nodded, too.

"I play saxophone in a band called Larry Foster's Rhythm Kings," Sammy said. "We play for these sixty-year-old farts who were kids back in the Forties. They're very good dancers, those old farts. All the old Glenn Miller stuff, Harry James, Charlie Spivak, Claude Thornhill. We have all the arrangements. We get a lot of jobs, you'd be surprised. I learned how to play the sax in stir."

"You must be pretty good at it," Meyer said. "To earn your living at it."

"Which, if that's supposed to be sarcastic, happens to be true. I *do* earn my living playing saxophone."

"Just what I said," Meyer said.

"But what you *meant* is I'm still doing burglaries on the side. Which ain't true."

"Did I say that?" Meyer asked. He turned to Carella. "Steve, did I say that?"

"I didn't hear you say that," Carella said. "We're looking for Martin Proctor. Do you know where he is?"

"Is he a musician?" Sammy asked. "What does he play?"

"The E-flat jimmy," Meyer said.

"He's a burglar," Carella said. "Like you."

"Me, I'm a saxophone player. What Proctor is, I don't know, because I don't know the man."

"But your girlfriend knows him, doesn't she?"

"What girlfriend?"

"Your girlfriend who's a hooker and who was asking a detective we know why the police were snooping around Proctor's old address."

"Gee, this is news to me. I'll tell you the truth, I wish my girlfriend *was* a hooker. Teach me a few tricks, huh?" Sammy said, and laughed. Nervously.

"Proctor did a job on New Year's Eve," Carella said, "in a building on Grover. Two murders were also done in that same building, the same night."

Sammy let out a long, low whistle.

"Yeah," Carella said.

"So where is he?" Meyer asked.

"If I don't know the man, how can I tell you where he is?"

"We're going to bust your girlfriend," Carella said.

"What for?"

"For prostitution. We're going to get her name from this detective we know, and we're going to haul her ass off the street and ask *her* about Martin Proctor. And we'll keep busting her until . . ."

"Oh, you mean *Martin* Proctor. I thought you said *Marvin* Proctor."

"Where?" Meyer said.

Hamilton followed Kling from the station house on Grover Avenue to the subway station three blocks away, and then boarded the downtown train with him. Stood right at the man's elbow. Bertram A. Kling. Detective/Third Grade. Isaac had got the information from the court records. Isaac was very good at gathering information. He was, however, somewhat dim when it came to comprehending the complexities of high-level business arrangements. Which was why Hamilton had not told him about the telephone call last month from Carlos Ortega in Miami. Or the necessity of employing a fool like José Herrera, who had turned out to be a fucking crook as well. Isaac would not have understood. But, giving the devil his due, he had done well on the cop. Bertram A. Kling. Who had testified at the arraignments of Herbert Trent, James Marshall, and Andrew Fields. Bertram A. Kling. Who did not know that the man standing next to him hanging on a subway strap was Lewis Randolph Hamilton, who would kill him the moment he could do it conveniently and vanish like smoke.

There were perhaps forty blacks on the subway car.

This was good for Hamilton.

Even if there were recent pictures of him in this city's police files—which he knew there were not—but even if there were, a white cop like Kling wouldn't have recognized him, anyway. Kling—with his blond hair and his peachfuzz appearance—looked like the kind of white cop who thought all black criminals looked alike. Only thing that was different on the mug shots was the numbers. Otherwise, they all looked like gorillas. He had heard too many white cops say this. Actually, it would give him great pleasure to kill Kling.

He liked killing people.

Blowing them away with the big mother Magnum.

He particularly liked killing cops.

He had killed two cops in L.A. They were still looking for him out there. Black man with a beard. Gorilla with a beard. He didn't have a beard, anymore, he'd shaved in Houston before the posse took that big shipment coming up via Mexico. Wore his hair Rastafarian down there in Houston.

Hamilton hated cops.

Not even knowing Kling, he hated him. And would have enjoyed killing him even if Herrera hadn't told him a goddamn thing. Which was possible, after all, because how could Herrera have learned anything about the Tsu shipment coming up next Monday? When not even Isaac knew as yet.

Hamilton stood by Kling's side on the subway, a black man invisible among other black men, and smiled when he wondered how many people on this train even imagined that he and the big blond man were both wearing guns.

Kling got off the train at Brogan Square, and came up out of the tunnel into a day that was still cold but beginning to turn a bit sunny. He had called Karin Lefkowitz first, to make an appointment with her, and now he hurried along High Street to her office in what used to be the Headquarters Building. Linked to the Criminal Courts Building by a third-floor passageway through which prisoners going to court could be moved, the old gray building looked like a Siamese twin to the one beside it. He came up the low flat steps out front, entered through the huge bronze doors, showed his identification to a uniformed cop sitting behind a desk in the marbled ground-floor corridor, and then took the elevator up to the fifth floor. A sign hand-lettered PSAS indicated by way of a pointing arrow that the office was to the right. He followed the corridor, spotted another sign and yet a third one, and then found a door with a glass paneled top, lettered with the words Psychological Services and Aid Section.

He looked at his watch.

Five minutes to two.

He opened the door and went in.

There was a small waiting room. A closed door opposite the entrance door. Two easy chairs, a lamp, a coat rack with two coats on it, several back-issues of *People* magazine. Kling hung up his coat, sat in one of the chairs and picked up a copy with Michael Jackson on the cover. In a few moments, a portly man with the telltale veined and bulbous nose of a heavy drinker came through the inner door, went to the rack, took his coat from it, and left without saying a word to Kling. He looked like a thousand sergeants Kling had known. A moment after that, a woman came through that same door.

"Detective Kling?" she said.

"Yes."

He got to his feet.

"I'm Karin Lefkowitz. Won't you come in, please?"

Short brown hair, blue eyes. Wearing a gray dress, with pearls and Reeboks. Twenty-six or -seven, he guessed. Nice smile.

He followed her into her office. Same size as the waiting room. A wooden desk. A chair behind it. A chair in front of it. Several framed degrees on the wall. A framed picture of the police commissioner. Another framed picture of the mayor.

"Please," she said, and indicated the chair in front of the desk.

Kling sat.

Karin went to the chair behind the desk.

"Your call surprised me," she said. "Did you know that Eileen was here this morning?"

"No."

"I thought she may have . . ."

"No, she doesn't know I called. It was entirely my idea."

"I see."

She studied him. She looked like the kind of woman who should be wearing glasses. He wondered if she had contacts on. Her eyes looked so very blue. Sometimes contacts did that.

"What was it you wanted to discuss?" she said.

"Has Eileen told you that we've stopped seeing each other?"

"Yes."

"And?"

"And what?"

"What do you think about it?"

"Mr. Kling, before we go any further . . ."

"Confidentiality, I know. But this is different."

"How?"

"I'm not asking you to divulge anything Eileen may have told you in confidence. I'm asking *your* opinion on . . ."

"Ah, I see. *My* opinion. But a very thin line, wouldn't you say?"

"No, I wouldn't. I want to know whether this . . . well, separation is the only thing I can call it . . . whether you think it's a good idea."

"And what if I told you that whatever is good for Eileen is a good idea?"

"Do you think this separation is good for Eileen?"

Karin smiled.

"Please," she said.

"I'm not asking you to do anything behind Eileen's . . ."

"Oh? Aren't you?"

"Miss Lefkowitz . . . I need your help."

"Yes?"

"I . . . I really want to be with Eileen. While she's going through this. I think that her wanting to . . . to . . . stay apart isn't natural. What I wish . . ."

"No."

Kling looked at her.

"No, I will not advise her to resume your relationship unless that is what she herself wishes."

"Miss Lefkowitz . . ."

"Period," Karin said.

Hamilton saw him coming down the steps of the old Headquarters Building, walking at a rapid clip like a man who was angry about something. Blond hair blowing in the sudden fierce wind. Hamilton hated this city. You never knew from one minute to the next in this city what was going to happen with the weather. The sun was shining very bright now, but the wind was too strong. Newspapers rattling along the curbs, people walking with their heads ducked, coattails flapping. He fell in behind Kling, no chance of a shot at him here in this crowded downtown area, courthouses everywhere around them, cops moving in and out of them like cockroaches, Christ, he was walking fast.

Hamilton hurried to keep up.

Where the hell was he going, anyway?

He'd already passed the entrance to the subway.

So where was he headed?

The pocket park was an oasis of solitude and quiet here in the city that normally paid only lip service to such perquisites of civilization. Kling knew the park because on days when he'd had to testify in one case or another, he'd buy himself a sandwich in the deli on Jackson, and then come here on the lunch break. Sit on one of the benches, eat his sandwich in the sunshine, think about anything but a defense attorney wagging his finger and wanting to know if he'd *really* observed the letter of the law while making his arrest.

The park was virtually deserted today.

Too windy for idlers, he guessed.

Set between two office buildings on Jackson, the space was a long rectangle with a brick wall at its far end. A thin fall of water cascaded over the top of this wall, washing down over the brick, even in the dead of winter; Kling guessed the water was heated. The park was dotted with trees, a dozen of them in all, with benches under them.

Only one of the benches was occupied as Kling came in off the street.

A woman reading a book.

The sounds of the streetside traffic suddenly vanished, to be replaced by the sound of the water gently running down the brick wall.

Kling took a seat on a bench facing the wall.

His back was to the park entrance.

In a little while, the woman looked at her watch, got up, and left.

Hamilton couldn't believe it!

There he was, sitting alone in the park, his back to the entrance, no one in the place but Bertram A. Kling!

This was going to be too simple. He almost regretted the sheer simplicity of it. Walk up behind the man, put a bullet in the back of his head, gangland style. They might even think the Mafia had done it. This was delicious. He could not wait to tell Isaac about it.

He checked the street, eyes swinging right, then left.

And moved swiftly into the park.

The Magnum was in the right-hand pocket of his overcoat.

Patches of snow on the ground.

Water rolling down the brick wall at the far end.

The park silent otherwise.

Ten feet away from him now.

Careful, careful.

The gun came out of his pocket.

Kling saw the shadow first.

Suddenly joining his own shadow on the ground in front of him.

He turned at once.

And saw the gun.

And threw himself headlong off the bench and onto the ground just as the first shot boomed onto the air, and rolled over, and reached in under his overcoat for the gun holstered on the left side of his belt, another shot, and sat upright with the gun in both hands and fired at once, three shots in succession at the tall black man in the long gray coat who was running out of the park.

Kling ran after him.

There were only three hundred and sixty-four black men on the street outside the park.

But none of them looked like the man who'd just tried to kill him.

Martin Proctor had just come out of the shower and was drying himself when the knock sounded on his door.

He wrapped the towel around his waist, and went out into the living room.

"Who is it?" he asked.

"Police," Meyer said. "Want to open the door, please?"

Proctor did not want to open the door.

"Yeah, just a second," he said. "I just got out of the shower. Let me put on some clothes."

He went into the bedroom, took a pair of undershorts from the top drawer, slipped them on, and then hastily put on a pair of blue corduroy trousers, a blue turtleneck sweater, a pair of blue woolen socks, and a pair of black, seventy-five-dollar French and Shriner shoes with some kind of synthetic soles that gripped like rubber.

From outside the apartment door, he heard the same cop asking, "Mr. Proctor? You going to open this door for us?"

"Yeah, I'll be with you in a minute," he yelled and went to the closet and took from a hanger the eleven-hundred-dollar Ralph Lauren camel hair coat he had stolen on New Year's Eve, and then he went to his dresser and took from the same top drawer containing his undershorts and handkerchiefs a .22-caliber High Standard Sentinel Snub he had stolen last year sometime from a guy who also had a stamp collection, and then he yelled to the door, "Just putting on my shoes, be there in a second," and went out the window.

He came down the fire escape skillfully, not for nothing was he a deft burglar with the courage of a lion tamer and the dexterity of a high wire performer. There was no way he was going to have any kind of discussion with any representative of the law, not when he was looking at a renewed stretch in the slammer for breaking parole. So he came down those fire-escape ladders as fast as he knew how, which was *damn* fast, because he knew that the cop in the hallway would be kicking in the door if he hadn't already done it, and him and his partner, they always traveled in pairs, would be in that apartment in a flash, and the minute they went in the bedroom—

"Hello, Proctor," the man said.

The man was looking up at him from the ground just below the first-floor fire escape. The man had a gun in one hand and a police shield in the other.

"Detective Carella," he said.

Proctor almost reached for the gun in the pocket of the coat.

"Just lower the ladder and come on down," Carella said.

"I didn't do anything," Proctor said.

He was still debating whether he should go for the gun.

"Nobody said you did. Come on down."

Proctor stood undecided.

"My partner's up there above you," Carella said. "You're sand-wiched."

Proctor's hand inched toward the coat pocket.

"If that's a gun in there," Carella said, "you're a dead man."

Proctor suddenly agreed with him.

He lowered the ladder and came on down.

10

THE Q & A BEGAN in Lieutenant Byrnes's office that Monday evening at ten minutes past six. Present were the lieutenant, Detectives Carella and Meyer, Martin Proctor, a lawyer named Ralph Angelini who'd been requested by Proctor, and a stenographer from the Clerical Office, as backup to the tape recorder. The detectives did not know as yet whether Proctor had asked for a lawyer because he was facing a return trip to Castleview on the parole violation, or whether he knew that the subject about to be discussed was murder. Twice.

The lawyer was Proctor's very own and not someone supplied by Legal Aid.

A nice young man in his late twenties.

Carella knew that even thieves and murderers were entitled to legal representation. The thing he couldn't understand was why honest young men like Ralph Angelini *chose* to defend thieves and murderers.

For the tape, the lieutenant identified everyone present, and then advised Proctor of his rights under Miranda-Escobedo, elicited from him his name and present address, and turned the actual questioning over to his detectives.

Carella asked all of the questions.

Proctor and his lawyer took turns answering them.

It went like this:

Q: Mr. Proctor, we have here a report from the . . .
A: Just a minute, please. May I ask up front what this is in reference to?
Q: Yes, Mr. Angelini. It is in reference to a burglary committed on New Year's Eve in the apartment of Mr. and Mrs. Charles Unger at 967 Grover Avenue, here in Isola, sir.

A: Very well, go ahead.

Q: Thank you. Mr. Proctor, we have here a report from the Detective Bureau's Latent Print Unit . . .

A: *Your* police department?

Q: Yes, Mr. Angelini.

A: Go ahead then.

Q: A report on latent fingerprints retrieved from a window and sill in the Unger apartment, and those . . .

A: Retrieved by whom?

Q: Retrieved by the Crime Scene Unit. Now Mr. Proctor, the fingerprints retrieved from the Unger window and sill match your fingerprints on file downtown. Can you tell me . . . ?

A: Do you have a copy of that LPU report?

Q: Yes, Mr. Angelini, I have it right here.

A: May I see it, please?

Q: Yes, sir. And may I say, sir, that in this Q and A so far, your client has not been allowed to give a single answer to any of the questions I've put. Pete, I think maybe we ought to call the D.A., get somebody here who can cope with Mr. Angelini, because I sure as hell can't. And I'd like that left on the record, please.

A: I believe I have every right asking to see a report purporting to . . .

Q: You know damn well I wouldn't *say* we had a report if we *didn't* have one!

A: Very well then, let's get on with this.

Q: You think maybe your client can answer a few questions now?

A: I said let's get on with it.

Q: Thank you. Mr. Proctor, how did your fingerprints get on that window and sill?

A: Is it okay to answer that?

A: (from Mr. Angelini) Yes, go ahead. Answer it.

A: (from Mr. Proctor) I don't know how they got there.

Q: You don't, huh?

A: It's a total mystery to me.

Q: No idea how they got on that window and sill just off the spare bedroom fire escape.

A: None at all.

Q: You don't think you may have left them there?

A: Excuse me, Mr. Carella, but . . .

Q: Jee-sus *Christ!*

A: I beg your pardon, but . . .

Q: Mr. Angelini, you are perfectly within your rights to ask us to stop this questioning at any time. Without prejudice to your client. Just say, "That's enough, no more," you don't even have to give us an explanation. That's Miranda-Escobedo, Mr. Angelini, that's how we protect the rights of citizens in this country of ours. Now, if that's what you want to do, please do it. You realize, of course, that on the strength of the LPU report, the D.A. will undoubtedly ask for a burglary indictment, which he'll undoubtedly get. But I think you should know there's a more serious charge we're considering here. And . . .

A: Are you referring to the parole violation?

Q: No, sir, I'm not.

A: Then what charge are you . . . ?

Q: Homicide, sir. Two counts of homicide.

A: (from Mr. Proctor) What?

A: (from Mr. Angelini) Be quiet, Martin.

A: (from Mr. Proctor) No, just a second. What do you mean homicide? You mean murder? Did somebody get murdered?

A: (from Mr. Angelini) Martin, I think . . .

A: (from Mr. Proctor) Is that what you're trying to hang on me here? Murder?

Q: Mr. Angelini, if we could proceed with the questioning in an orderly manner . . .

A: I wasn't aware that this Q and A would concern itself with homicide.

Q: Now you are aware of it, sir.

A: I'm not sure my client should answer any further questions. I'd like to consult with him.

Q: Please do.

(Questioning resumed at 6:22 P.M. aforesaid date)

Q: Mr. Proctor, I'd like to get back to those fingerprints we found in the Unger apartment.

A: I'll answer any questions about the alleged burglary, but I won't go near whatever you plan to ask about homicide.

Q: Is that what Mr. Angelini advised you?

A: That is what he advised me.

Q: All right. Did you leave those fingerprints on the Unger window and sill?

A: I did not.

Q: Were you surprised in the Unger apartment by Mr. and Mrs. Unger at approximately one-thirty A.M. on the first of January?

A: I was home in bed at that time.

Q: For the record, I would like to say that we have a sworn statement from Mr. and Mrs. Unger to the effect that . . .

A: May I see that statement, please?

Q: Yes, Mr. Angelini. I didn't plan to read it into the record, I merely . . .

A: I would like to see it.

Q: I wanted to explain the content so that your client . . .

A: Just let me see it, okay, Mr. Carella?

Q: Okay, sure, Mr. Angelini.

A: Thank you.

   (Questioning resumed at 6:27 P.M. aforesaid date)

Q: Do I now have your permission to summarize the content of that statement for your client and for the tape?

A: (inaudible)

Q: Sir?

A: I said go ahead, go ahead.

Q: Thank you. Mr. Proctor, the Ungers have made a statement to the effect that at one-thirty A.M. on the first of January, they entered their spare bedroom . . . what they use as a TV room . . . and surprised a young man going out the window onto the fire escape. They described him as having blond hair . . . excuse me, but what color is your hair?

A: Blond.

Q: And they said he was thin. Would you describe yourself as thin?

A: Wiry.

Q: Is that thin?

A: It's slender and muscular.

Q: But not thin.

A: He's answered the question, Mr. Carella.

Q: They also said he had a mustache that was just growing in. Would it be fair to say that you have a new mustache?

A: It's pretty new, yes.

Q: And they said that the young man pointed a gun at them and threatened he would be back if they called the police. I show you this gun, Mr. Proctor, a High Standard Sentinel Snub, .22-caliber Long Rifle revolver, and ask if it was in the pocket of your overcoat when you were arrested this afternoon.

A: It was.

Q: Is it your gun?

A: No. I don't know how it got in my pocket.

Q: Mr. Proctor, when you were arrested tonight, were you wearing a camel hair coat containing a Ralph Lauren label?

A: I was.

Q: Is this the coat?

A: That's the coat.

Q: Where did you get this coat?

A: I bought it.

Q: Where?

A: At Ralph Lauren.

Q: Mr. Angelini, we have a list of goods stolen from the Unger apartment on the morning of January first—I'm showing you the list right this minute before you ask for it—and one of the items on that list is a Ralph Lauren camel hair overcoat valued at eleven hundred dollars. I wish to inform your client that the Ungers in their statement said the man going out their window was wearing the camel hair coat described in the list of stolen goods. Mr. Proctor, do you still claim you were not in the Unger apartment that night?

A: I was home in bed.

Q: Mr. Proctor, the Ungers said that the man going out their bedroom window was also wearing a black leather jacket, black slacks and white sneakers. I show you this black leather jacket, these black slacks, and these white sneakers and ask you if these articles of clothing were found in your closet this afternoon at the time of your arrest.

A: They were.

Q: I also show you this emerald ring which was found in your apartment at the time of your arrest, and I refer you again to the list of goods stolen from the Unger apartment. An emerald ring and a Kenwood VCR are on that list. Mr. Proctor, would you now like to tell me again that you were not, in fact, in the Unger apartment at the time and on the night in question, and that you did not, in fact . . .

A: I would like to talk to my lawyer, please.

Q: Please do, Mr. Proctor.

(Questioning resumed at 6:45 P.M. aforesaid date)

A: In answer to your question, yes, I was in the Unger apartment that night.

Q: Thank you. Did you commit a burglary in that apartment on the night in question?

A: I was in the apartment. Whether that's burglary or whatever, it isn't for me to say.

Q: How did you enter the apartment?

A: I came down from the roof.

Q: How?

A: Down the fire escapes.

Q: And how did you get into the apartment?

A: By way of the fire escape.

Q: Outside the spare bedroom window?

A: Yes.

Q: Did you jimmy the window?

A: Yes.

Q: How did you leave the apartment?

A: The same way.

Q: The Unger apartment is on the sixth floor, isn't that so?

A: I don't know what floor it's on. I just came down from the roof and when I saw an apartment looked empty, I went in.

Q: And this happened to be the Unger apartment.

A: I didn't know whose apartment it was.

Q: Well, the apartment where you stole the Ralph Lauren coat and the Kenwood VCR and the . . .

A: Well . . .

Q: That apartment.

A: I guess.

Q: Which was the Unger apartment.

A: If you say so.

Q: Now when you went out of this sixth-floor window onto the fire escape, did you then go up to the roof or down to the street?

A: Down to the street.

Q: Down the ladders, floor by floor . . .

A: Yes.

Q: To the street.

A: Yes.

Q: Did you stop in any other apartment on your way down to the street?

A: No.

Q: Are you sure?

A: I'm positive. Oh, I get it.

Q: What do you get, Mr. Proctor?

A: Somebody was killed in that building, right? So you think I done the sixth-floor burglary and then topped it off with a murder, right?

Q: You tell me.

A: Don't be ridiculous. I never killed anybody in my entire life.

Q: Tell me what you did, minute by minute, after you left the Unger apartment at one-thirty A.M.

A: Really, Mr. Carella, you can't expect him to remember minute by *minute* what he . . .

Q: I think he knows what I'm looking for, Mr. Angelini.

A: As long as it's clear that you don't mean minute by minute *literally*.

Q: As close as he can remember.

A: May I ask on my client's behalf, is he correct in assuming that a homicide was committed in that building on the night of the burglary?

Q: *Two* homicides, Mr. Angelini.

A: What are you pursuing here, Mr. Carella?

Q: Let me level with you. Your client . . .

A: (from Mr. Proctor) Go hide the silver, Ralph.

Q: Well, I'm happy for a little levity here . . .

A: (from Mr. Proctor) You either laugh or you cry, am I right?

Q: I'm glad you have a sense of humor.

A: One thing you develop in the slammer is a good sense of humor.

Q: I'm happy to hear that, but I don't think there's anything funny about a dead six-month-old baby.

A: (from Mr. Angelini) So *that's* the case.

Q: That's the case.

A: Maybe we ought to pack up and go home, Martin.

Q: Well, Mr. Proctor isn't going anywhere, as you know. If you mean you'd like him to quit answering my questions, fine. But as I was about to say . . .

A: Give me one good reason why I should permit him to continue.

Q: Because if he didn't kill that baby and her sitter . . .

A: He didn't. Flatly and unequivocally.

Q: Before you even ask him, huh?

A: My client is not a murderer. Period.

Q: Well, I'm glad you're so certain of that, Mr. Angelini. But as I was saying, I wish you'd permit your client to convince *us* he's clean. We're looking for a place to hang our hats, that's the truth. Two people are dead, and we've got your client in the building doing a felony. So let him convince us he didn't do a couple of murders, too. Is that reasonable? That way we go with the burglary and the parole violation and we call it a day, okay?

A: I wish we were talking only parole violation here.

Q: There's no way we can lose the burglary. Forget it.

A: I was merely thinking out loud. You understand what I'm saying, don't you?

Q: You're asking me what's in it for you. The D.A. might want to bargain on the burglary charge, that's up to him. But it won't just disappear, believe me. We're looking at a Burglary One here. Two people in the apartment while he was doing the . . .

A: Not while he was in there. He was already out the window.

Q: He spoke to them. Threatened them, in fact. Pointed a gun at them and . . .

A: The gun is your contention.

Q: Mr. Angelini, we've got an occupied dwelling at nighttime, and a threat with a gun. I don't know what else you think we need for Burglary One, but . . .

A: Okay, let's say you do have a Burg One. How can the D.A. help us?

Q: You'd have to discuss that with him.

A: I'd be looking for a B and E.

Q: You'd be looking low.

A: Would he go for Burg Two?

Q: I can't make deals for the D.A. All I can tell him is that Mr. Proctor was exceedingly cooperative in answering whatever questions we put to him about the double homicide committed in that building. Which is of prime importance to a lot of people in this city, as I'm sure you must realize. On the other hand . . .

A: Tell him what he wants to know, Martin.

A: (from Mr. Proctor) I forgot the question.

Q: Minute by minute. Starting with one-thirty when you went out on that fire escape.

Minute by minute, he had come down the fire escapes until he reached the one outside the first-floor window, and then he had lowered the ladder there to the cement area in the backyard, and had gone down it and jumped the four, five feet to the ground, and then he'd come around the side of the building carrying the VCR under his arm and wearing the camel hair coat with the emerald ring in one of the pockets. He'd walked up to Culver and dumped the VCR right away, sold it to a receiver in a bar named The Bald Eagle, which was still open as this must have been a little before two in the morning by now.

"Better nail it down closer," Carella advised.

"Okay, a movie was just starting on the bar TV. A Joan Crawford movie. Black-and-white. I don't know the name of it, I don't know the channel. Whatever time the movie went on, that's what time I got to the bar."

"And sold the VCR . . ."

"To a fence who gave me forty-two bucks for it. I also . . ."

"His name," Carella said.

"Why?"

"He's your alibi."

"Jerry Macklin," Proctor said at once.

He'd also showed Macklin the emerald ring, and Macklin had offered him three bills for it, which Proctor told him to shove up his ass because he knew the ring was worth at least a couple of grand. Macklin offered him fifty for the coat he was wearing, but Proctor liked the coat and figured he'd keep it. So he'd headed out, still wearing the coat with the ring in the pocket, looking for somebody he could score a coupla vials off . . .

"What time did you leave The Bald Eagle?" Meyer asked.

"Exact?"

"Close as you can get it."

"I can tell you what scene was on in the movie, is all," Proctor said. "I didn't look at a clock or anything."

"What scene was on?"

"She was coming out a fancy building."

"Who?"

"Joan Crawford. With an awning."

"Okay, then what?"

Proctor had gone out of the bar and cruised Glitter Park, which was the street name for the center-island park on Culver between Glendon and Ritter, where he'd run across . . .

"Oh, wait a minute," he said, "I can pin the time down closer. 'Cause this guy I made the buy from, he told me he had to be uptown a quarter to three, and he looked at his watch and said it was already two-twenty. So you got to figure it took me five minutes to walk from the Eagle to Glitter, so that puts me leaving the bar a quarter after two."

"And his name?" Carella said.

"Hey, come on, you got me doin' a snitch on half the people I know."

"Suit yourself," Meyer said.

"Okay, his name is Fletcher Gaines, but you don't have to mention the crack, do you? You can just ask was I with him at twenty after two."

"So according to you," Meyer said, "you . . ."

"Can you do that for me, please? 'Cause I'm cooperating here with you, ain't I?"

"Does this guy deliver all the way upstate?" Meyer asked.

"What do you mean?"

"You broke parole, Proctor. You're heading back to Castleview to see all your old buddies again. You don't have to worry about where your next vial's coming from."

"Yeah, I didn't think of that," Proctor said.

"But let's try to nail this down, okay?" Meyer said. "You were in the Unger apartment at one-thirty . . ."

"Just *leaving* at one-thirty . . ."

"And you came down the fire escapes . . ."

"Right."

"No stops on the way down . . ."

"Right."

"No detours . . ."

"Right."

"And you walked to The Bald Eagle on Culver and . . . *where'd* you say it is?"

"All the way up near Saint Paul's."

"Why'd you go all the way up there?"

" 'Cause I knew Jerry'd be there."

"Jerry Macklin."

"Yeah."

"Your fence."

"Yeah. Who I knew would take at least the VCR off my hands. So I could buy some vials to tide me over, you know?"

"You walked all the way up there, huh?"

"Yeah, I walked."

"That's a long walk, cold night like that."

"I like the cold."

"And you got there just as the Joan Crawford movie was coming on."

"A few minutes before. We were just beginning to talk price when it went on. It musta gone on about two o'clock, don't you think? I mean, they start them on the hour, don't they?"

"Usually. And you left there at a quarter after."

"Yeah."

"And took another little walk. This time to Glitter."

"Well, that wasn't too far. Five minutes is all."

"You like walking, huh?"

"As a matter of fact, I do."

"So if all this is true . . ."

"Oh, it's true."

"Then you can pretty much account for your time between one-thirty and a quarter past two. Provided Macklin and Gaines back your story."

"Unless you scare them with shit about receiving stolen goods and dealing controlled substances, they should back my story, yes. Look, I'm going back to jail, anyway, I got no reason to lie to you."

Except maybe a couple of dead bodies, Carella thought.

They found Macklin at a little past nine that night.

He corroborated everything Proctor had said.

He even remembered the name of the Joan Crawford movie that had gone on at two in the morning.

And he remembered looking up at the clock when Proctor left the Eagle; he'd been invited to a New Year's Eve party, and he was wondering if it'd still be going at this hour. Which was a quarter past two in the morning.

It took them a while longer to find Fletcher Gaines.

Gaines was a black man living all the way uptown in Diamondback.

When finally they caught up with him at five minutes to ten that Monday night, he told them he was clean and asked them if they weren't just a wee bit off their own turf. They told him they weren't looking for a drug bust, which news Gaines treated with a skeptically raised eyebrow. All they wanted to know was about New Year's Eve. Did he at any time on New Year's Eve run into a person named Martin Proctor?

No mention of time.

No mention of place.

Gaines said he had run into Proctor in Glitter Park sometime that night, but he couldn't remember what time it had been.

They asked him if he could pinpoint that a bit closer.

Gaines figured his man Proctor was looking for a net.

No way to lie for him, though, because he didn't know what time Gaines needed covered.

So he told them he wasn't sure he could be more exact.

They told him that was a shame, and started to walk off.

He said, "Hey, wait a minute, it just come to me. I looked at my watch and it was twenty minutes after two exact, is that of any help to you?"

They thanked him and went back downtown—to their own turf.

*   *   *

Visiting hours at the hospital were eight to ten.

The old man was in what was called the Cancer Care Unit, he'd been there since the third of July, when they'd discovered a malignancy in his liver. Bit more than six months now. A person would've thought he'd be dead by now. Cancer of the liver? Supposed to be fatal and fast.

They visited him every night.

Two dutiful daughters.

Got there at a little before eight, came out of the hospital at a little after ten. Said their goodbyes in the parking lot, went to their separate cars. Joyce was driving the old man's car now. Big brown Mercedes. Living in the big house all alone. Went back to Seattle in August, soon as she found out the old man was going to die. Visited him in the hospital every night. A person could've set his watch by her comings and goings. Melissa was driving the old blue station wagon. Waddled like a duck, Melissa did.

It was foggy tonight.

Big surprise. Fog in Seattle. Like London in all those Jack the Ripper movies. Or those creepy werewolf movies. Only this was Seattle. If you didn't get fog here in January, then you got rain, take your choice, that's all there was. In this city, rain was only thicker fog. You wanted to get rich in Seattle, all you had to do was start an umbrella factory. But he figured the fog was good for what he had to do tonight.

The gun was a Smith & Wesson Model 59, which was a nine-millimeter double-action automatic pistol. Same as the 39 except that it had a fourteen-shot magazine instead of an eight. Otherwise, you couldn't tell the two apart: bit more than seven inches long overall, with a four-inch barrel, a blued finish and a checkered walnut stock. It looked something like an army Colt .45. He'd bought it on the street for two hundred bucks. You could get anything you wanted on the street these days. He planned to drop the gun in the Sound after he used it tonight, goodbye, darling. Even if they found it, they'd never be able to trace it. A gun bought on the street? No way they could link it to him.

He'd had the gun sent to Seattle. Just sent it UPS second-day air. Carried it all wrapped and sealed to one of those post-office alternatives that sent things by Federal Express and UPS, even wrapped things for you if you asked them to, though he wasn't about to have them wrap a *gun* for him. Told the girl who weighed it that it was a toy truck. The weight, with the packing and all, had come to twenty-eight pounds. She'd marked on the shipping label TOY TRUCK and asked if he wanted to insure it for more than the already covered hundred bucks. He'd said, no, it had only cost him twenty-five. That easy to send a gun. This was a democracy. He hated to think what *real* criminals were getting away with.

There she came.

Down the hospital steps.

Wearing a yellow rain slicker and black boots, made her look like a fisherman. Melissa was wearing a black cloth coat, kerchief on her head. Fifteen years older than Joyce. Prettier, too. Usually. Right now, she was pregnant as a goose.

Two of them walking toward the parking lot now.

He ducked down behind the wheel of the car.

Fog swirling in around the car, enclosing him.

Watched the yellow rain slicker. A beacon. Joyce in the slicker, bright yellow in the gray of the fog. Melissa's black coat swallowed by the gray, a vanishing act. A car door slamming. Another one. Headlights coming on. The old blue station wagon roared into life. Melissa pulled the car out into the fan of her own headlights, made a right turn, heading for the exit.

He waited.

Joyce started the Benz.

New car, the old man had bought it a month before he'd learned about the cancer. You could hardly hear the engine when it started. The headlights came on. He started his own car.

The Mercedes began moving.

He gave it a respectable lead, and then began following it.

The house sat on four acres of choice land overlooking the water, a big gray Victorian mansion that had been kept in immaculate repair over the years since it was built. You couldn't find too many houses like this one nowadays, not here in the state of Washington, nor hardly anywhere else. You had to figure the house alone would bring twenty, thirty million dollars. That wasn't counting the furnishings. God alone knew what all those antiques were worth. Stuff the old lady had brought from Europe when she was still alive. And her jewelry? Had to be a fortune in there. The paintings, too. The old man had been a big collector before he got sick, the art in there had to be worth millions. The old Silver Cloud in the garage, the new Benz, the thirty-eight-foot Grand Banks sitting there at the dock, those were only frosting on the cake.

He parked the car in a stand of pines just to the north of the service road. Went in through the woods, walked well past the house and then approached it from the water side. Huge lawn sloping down to the water. Fog rolling in, you couldn't even see the boat at the dock no less the opposite shore. Lights burning in the upstairs bedroom of the house. The shade was up, he saw her move past the window. Wearing only a short nightgown. House was so naturally well protected by water and woods, not another house within shouting distance, she probably figured she could run around naked if she wanted to.

He could feel the weight of the gun in the pocket of his coat.

He was left-handed.

The gun was in the left-hand pocket.

He could remember movies where they caught the killer because he was left-handed. Left-handed people did things differently. Pulled matches off on the wrong side of the matchbook. Well, wrong side for *right*-handed people. That was the old chestnut, the matchbook. More left-handed killers got caught because they didn't see all those movies with the missing matches on the left side of the matchbook. Another thing was ink stains on the edge of the palm, near the pinky. In this country we wrote from left to right and the pen *followed* a right-handed person's hand, whereas the opposite was true for a left-handed person. A left-handed person *trailed* his hand over what he'd already written. Live and learn. If you were left-handed and you'd just finished writing a ransom note in red ink, it was best not to let the police see the edge of your palm near the pinky because there'd surely be red ink on it.

He smiled in the darkness.

Wondered if he should wait till she was asleep. Go in, shoot her in the head. Empty the gun in her, make it look like some lunatic did it. Maybe smash a few priceless vases afterward. Cops'd think somebody went berserk in there.

In a little while, the upstairs bedroom light went out.

He waited in the dark in the fog.

In her dream, the wind was rattling palm fronds on some Caribbean island and there was the sound of surf crashing in against the shore. In her dream, she was a famous writer sitting in a little thatched hut, an old black Smith-Corona typewriter on a table in front of her, a little window open to a crescent-shaped beach and rows and rows of palms lining an endless shore. The sky was incredibly blue behind the palms.

In the distance there were low, green-covered mountains. She searched the sky and the mountains for inspiration.

In her dream, she reached idly for a ripe yellow banana in a pale blue bowl on a shelf near the open window. Beautifully shaped bowl. Bunch of bananas in it. She pulled a banana from the bunch. And peeled it down to where her hand was holding it. And brought it to her lips. And put it in her mouth. And was biting down on it when suddenly it turned cold and hard.

Her eyes popped wide open.

The barrel of a gun was in her mouth.

A man was standing beside the bed. Black hat pulled low on his forehead. Black silk handkerchief covering his nose and his mouth. Only his eyes showed. Pinpoints of light glowing in them, reflections from the night light in the wall socket across the room.

He said, "Shhhhh."

The gun in his left hand.

"Shhhhh."

The gun in her mouth.

"Shhhhh, Joyce."

He knew her name.

She thought, How does he know my name?

He said, "Your baby is dead, Joyce."

His voice a whisper.

"Susan is dead," he said. "She died on New Year's Eve."

All whispers sounded alike, but there was something about the cadence, the rhythm, the slow, steady spacing of his words that sounded familiar. Did she know him?

"Are you sorry you gave the baby away?" he said.

She wondered if she should say Yes. Nod. Let him know she was sorry, yes. The gun in her mouth. Wondered if that was the answer he was looking for. She would give him any answer he wanted, provided it was the right answer. She was not at all sorry that she had given the baby away, had never for a moment regretted her decision, was sorry now that the baby was dead, yes, but only because she'd have been sorry about the death of *any* infant. But if he wanted her to say—

"I killed the baby," he said.

Oh Jesus, she thought.

"Your baby," he said.

Oh Jesus, who *are* you? she thought.

"And now I'm going to kill *you*," he said.

She shook her head.

He was holding the gun loosely, allowing it to follow the motion of her head. Her saliva flowed around the barrel of the gun. There was a metallic taste in her mouth. The barrel was slippery with spit.

"Yes," he said.

And turned her head so that she was facing him.

Used the gun to turn her head.

A steady pressure on the gun in her mouth, turning her head so that the left side of her face was on the pillow, his arm straight out, his hand and the gun perpendicular to the bed.

She began to whimper.

Small whimpering sounds around the barrel of the gun.

She tried to say Please around the barrel of the gun. Her tongue found the hole in the barrel of the gun, and pushed out against it as if to nudge it gently and unnoticed from her mouth. The barrel clicked against her teeth. She thought at first that he had moved the gun because he'd discovered she was trying to expel it from her mouth. But she realized all at once that the reverse was true. The gun was steady in her mouth; it was her trembling jaw that was causing her teeth to click against the barrel.

"Well . . ." he said.

Almost sadly. And paused. As if trying to think of something else to say before he pulled the trigger. And in that split second, she knew that unless she herself said something brilliantly convincing, unless she spit that gun barrel out of her mouth and pleaded an eloquent—

The first shot took off the back of her head.

11

THE PERSON CARELLA SPOKE TO at the Coast Guard's Ship Movement Office was named Lieutenant Phillip Forbes. Carella told him he was trying to locate a ship.

"Yes, sir, which ship would that be, sir?" Forbes said.

"I don't know exactly," Carella said. "But I'll tell you what I *do* know, and maybe you can take it from there."

"Who did you say this was, sir?"

"Detective Carella, 87th Squad."

"Yes, sir. And this is in regard to?"

"A ship. Actually a person *on* that ship. If we can locate the ship."

"Yes, sir. And you feel this ship may be in port here, is that it?"

"I don't know where it is. That's one of the things I'd like to find out."

"Yes, sir, may I have the name of the ship, please?"

"The General Something. *Are* there ships called the General This or the General That?"

"I can think of at least fifty of them off the top of my head, sir."

"Military vessels or what?"

"No, sir, they can be tankers, freighters, passenger ships, whatever. There're a lot of Generals out there on the ocean."

"How about a General Something that would have been here fifteen months ago?"

"Sir?"

"Do you keep records going back that far?"

"Yes, sir, we do."

"This would've been October a year ago."

"Do you mean October of last year?"

"No, the year before that. Can you check it for me?"

"What is it you want to know, exactly, sir?"

"We have good reason to believe that a ship named the General Something was here in port fifteen months ago. Would you have any record of . . . ?"

"Yes, sir, all ships planning to enter the port must notify us at least twelve hours in advance of arrival."

"*All* ships?"

"Yes, sir, foreign or American. Arrangements for docking are usually made through the ship's agent, who contracts for a berth. Or the owner-operator can do it. Or sometimes the person who chartered the ship. But we also get captains who'll radio ahead to us."

"What information do they give you?"

"Sir?"

"When they notify you. What do they tell you?"

"Oh. The name of the ship, its nationality, the tonnage. Its cargo. Where it's been. Where it's going when it leaves here. How long it plans to be here. Where it'll be while in port."

"Do they usually dock right here in the city?"

"Some of them do, yes, sir. The passenger ships. But not too much of anything else, anymore. There're plenty of berths, you know, the port covers a lot of territory. All the way from Hangman's Rock to John's River."

"If a ship *did* dock here in the city, where would that be?"

"The Canal Zone, most likely. Nothing on the North Side, anymore. It'd be the Canal Zone, over in Calm's Point. Well, the Calm's Point Canal is its right name. That's the only place I can think of where they'd dock. But more than likely—well, this wouldn't be a passenger ship, would it?"

"No."

"Then most likely it'd head for Port Euphemia, over in the next state."

"But you said there *would* be a record . . ."

"Yes, sir, in the Amber files."

"Amber?"

"Amber, yes, sir. That's what the tracking system is called. Amber. Anytime a ship notifies us that it's coming in, all that information I told you about goes right into the computer."

"Do you have access to that computer, Lieutenant? To the Amber files?"

"I do."

"Could you kick up an October eighteenth departure . . ."

"This wasn't *last* October, am I right?"

"October a year ago. See what you've got on a tanker named the General Something-or-Other. Possibly the General Putnam. Or a General Putney. Leaving for the Persian Gulf."

"Take me a minute, sir, if you'd like to hang on."

"I'd like to hang on," Carella said.

When Forbes came back on the line, he said, "I've got two Generals departing on the eighteenth of October that year, sir. Neither of them are tankers. And neither of them are either a Putney or a Putnam."

"What are they?"

"Freighters, both of them."

"And they're called?"

"One of them's the *General Roy Edwin Dean* and the other's the *General Edward Lazarus Kalin.*"

"Which one of them was heading for the Persian Gulf?"

"Neither one, sir. The *Dean* was bound for Australia. The *Kalin* was headed for England."

"Terrific," Carella said, and sighed heavily. Either Joyce Chapman's seaman had been lying in his teeth, or else she'd been too stoned to remember *anything* about him. "Well, Lieutenant," he said, "thank you very . . ."

"But you might want to run down there yourself," Forbes said.

Carella guessed he meant Australia.

"The Canal Zone," Forbes said. "The *Dean*'s in now. I know you're looking for a Putney or a Putnam but maybe your information . . ."

"Have you got a berth number?" Carella asked.

The Calm's Point Canal.

The police had long ago dubbed it the Canal Zone, and the label had seeped into the city's general vocabulary. For the citizens who had never seen it, the name conjured a patch of torrid tropicana right here in the frigid north, a glimpse of exotic Panama—which they had also never seen. The only thing Hispanic about the Zone was the nationality of many of the hookers parading their wares for seamen off the ships or men cruising by in automobiles on their way home from work. Much of the trade was, in fact, mobile. A car would pull up to any one of the corners on Canalside, and the driver would lean over and roll down his window, and one of the scantily dressed girls would saunter over, and they'd negotiate a price. If they both agreed they had a viable deal, the girl would get in the car, and the trick would drive around the block a couple of times while she showed him what an expert could accomplish in all of five minutes.

There were some thirty-odd berths on each side of the canal, occupied at any time of the year because docking space was scarce anywhere in this city. The *General Roy Edwin Dean* was in berth number twenty-seven on the eastern side of the canal. A sturdy, responsible-looking vessel that had weathered many a storm and always found its way back to safe harbor, it sat squarely on the water, bobbing on a mild chop that rolled in off the River Dix and the open water beyond.

Meyer and Carella had not called ahead; the truth was, they didn't know *how* to make a phone call to a ship. Lieutenant Forbes had given Carella the number of the berth, and he and Meyer simply showed up at five minutes past one that Wednesday afternoon. A fierce wind was blowing in off the water. Whitecaps crested as far as the eye could see. Carella wondered why some men felt they *had* to go down to the seas again, the lonely sea and the sky. Meyer was wondering why he'd forgotten to wear his hat on a day like today. There was a gangplank. Carella looked at Meyer. Meyer shrugged. They climbed to the deck of the ship.

Not a soul in sight.

"Hello?" Carella shouted.

Not a soul, not a sound.

Except for the wind banging something metallic against something else metallic.

A door beckoned. Well, a hatchway, Carella guessed you called it.

Darkness beyond it.

Carella poked his head inside.

"Hello?" he said again.

There was a staircase going up. Well, a ladder.

They climbed it. Kept climbing till they reached a small house on top of the ship. Well, a cabin. There was a man in the cabin. He was sitting on a stool behind a counter, looking at a map. A chart. Listen, the hell with it, Carella thought.

"Yes?" the man said.

"Detective Carella, my partner Detective Meyer," Carella said, and showed his shield.

The man nodded.

"We're investigating a double homicide . . ."

The man whistled.

He was, Carella guessed, in his late fifties, wearing a heavy black jacket and a peaked black cap. His sideburns were brown, but his beard had come in white, and he sat on his stool like a salty-dog Santa Claus, dark eyebrows raised now as his low whistle trailed and expired.

"May I ask who we're talking to, sir?" Carella said.

"Stewart Webster," he said, "captain of the *Dean*."

The men shook hands. Webster had a firm grip. His eyes were brown, sharp with intelligence. "How can I help you?" he asked.

"Well, we're not sure you can," Carella said. "But we figured it was worth a shot. We're looking for a ship we have as the General Putnam or the General Putney . . ."

"That's a long way from Dean," Webster said.

"Yeah," Carella said, and nodded. "Supposed to have departed for the Persian Gulf on the eighteenth of October, a year and three months ago."

"Well, I'm pretty sure we were in these parts around then . . ."

"But didn't you leave on that day?"

"I'd have to check the log. It would have been on or near that date. But, gentlemen . . ."

"We know," Meyer said. "You went to Australia."

"Haven't been anywhere *near* the Middle East since Reagan got those marines killed in Beirut. We were there when it happened. The owner cabled us to load our cargo and haul ass out. Afraid he'd lose his ship."

"We've also got a seaman named Mike," Carella said.

Webster looked at him.

"If that's his name," Meyer said.

Webster looked at *him*.

"We know," Carella said. "It's not much to go on."

"But it's all we have," Meyer said.

"Mike," Webster said.

"No last name," Carella said.

"Presumably on the *Dean*," Webster said.

"Or a ship with a General in its name."

"Well, let's take a look at the roster, see if we've got any Mikes," Webster said.

"Michael, I guess it would be," Meyer said.

There were no Michaels in the crew.

There was, however, a Michel.

Michel Fournier.

"Is he French?" Carella asked.

"I have no idea," Webster said. "Do you want me to pull his file?"

"If it's no trouble."

"We'll have to go down to the purser's office," Webster said.

They followed him down a different ladder from the one they'd climbed earlier, walked through several dark passageways, and came to a door that Webster opened with a key. The compartment resembled Alf Miscolo's clerical office back at the Eight-Seven. There was even the aroma of coffee on the air. Webster went to a row of filing cabinets—gray rather than the green in Miscolo's space—found the one he wanted, opened the drawer, began thumbing through folders, and then yanked one of them out.

"Here he is," he said, and handed the folder to Carella.

Michel Fournier.

Born in Canada, the province of Quebec.

When he'd shipped on, three years ago, he'd given his address as Portland, Maine.

No address here in the city.

"Was he with you in that time period we're talking about?" Carella asked.

"If he shipped on three years ago and his folder's still here in the active file, then yes, he was with us fifteen months ago, and he's still with us now."

"You mean he's aboard ship now?"

"No, no. The crew went ashore the moment we docked."

"Which was when?"

"Two days ago."

"When are they due back?"

"We won't be sailing again till early next month."

"Any idea where Fournier might be?"

"I'm sorry. I don't even know the man."

"Where does he sleep aboard ship?"

"Well, let's see, there ought to be a quarters-assignment chart someplace around here," Webster said, and began opening drawers in his purser's desk.

Fournier's quarters were in the forward compartment on B deck. His bunk was in a tier of three, folded up against the bulkhead now. Foot lockers ran along the deck under the bunks. All of the lockers were padlocked.

"This one is Fournier's," Webster said.

"What do we do?" Meyer asked. "Another goddamn court order?"

"If we want to see what's in there," Carella said.

"Think we'll even get it?"

Webster was standing there, but the men were thinking out loud.

"It'd have to include permission to bust open that lock."

"Boy, I don't know, Steve. Wouldn't she have mentioned a French accent? If the guy's French . . ."

"Canadian," Carella said.

"Yeah, but Quebec."

"We're close to downtown, you know. Right over the bridge."

"Kill the whole damn afternoon," Meyer said.

"And he may deny it, anyway."

"Yeah."

"So what do you think?"

"I don't know, what do *you* think?"

"I think the judge'll kick us out on our asses."

"Me, too."

"On the other hand, he may grant the warrant."

"I doubt it."

"Me, too. But *if* he does, we may find something in the locker."

"Or we may find only dirty socks and underwear."

"So what do you think?"

"Will we need a cop from Safe, Loft & Truck?"

"What do you mean?"

"If we get the search warrant. I mean, how the hell else are we going to open that lock? Those guys have tools can get into anything. They're the best burglars in this city."

"Mr. Webster," Carella said, "was your ship here in port on New Year's Eve?"

"Yes, it was," Webster said.

"Did the crew go ashore?"

"Well, certainly. New Year's Eve? Of course."

"We'd better go get that warrant," Carella said.

If the case had not concerned the murder of a six-month-old baby, the supreme court magistrate to whom the detectives presented their affidavit might not have felt they had probable cause for a search warrant. But the judge read newspapers, too. And he watched television. And he knew this was the Baby Susan case. He also knew it was the Annie

Flynn case, but somehow the sitter's murder wasn't quite as shocking. In this city, sixteen-year-old girls got stabbed or raped or both every day of the week. But smothering an infant?

They went back to the ship with their search warrant and a pair of bolt cutters.

They were not bad burglars themselves.

It took them three minutes to cut through the lock.

They did indeed find a lot of dirty socks and underwear in Michel Fournier's foot locker.

But they also found a letter a girl in this city had written to him only last month.

The letter had a return address on it.

Herrera was trying to explain to his girlfriend why there was a uniformed cop on the front stoop downstairs. Consuelo didn't understand a word of it. It had something to do with the police department owing him protection because a detective had saved his life, which made no sense at all. She sometimes thought Herrera was a little crazy, which she also found tremendously exciting. And confusing. All she could gather was that a policeman followed Herrera everywhere he went, to make sure nobody tried to kill him again. She hadn't realized he was so important.

But now he was telling her that he had rented another apartment and that they would be moving there. Temporarily. He would be losing the cop, and they would be moving into this new apartment for just a little while. Until he settled some business matters, and then they would go to Spain. Live on the Costa Brava. Consuelo had never been to the Costa Brava, but it sounded nice.

"When will we leave for Spain?" she asked, testing him. This was Lenny asking George to tell about the rabbits again. She hadn't believed Herrera's story the first time around, but he sure made it sound better every time he told it. He told her now that he'd already booked the flight and would be picking up the tickets very soon. First-class seats for both of them. Get out of this city where no one would ever find him again. Not the Chinks, not the Jakies, and not the cops, either.

"The Jakies?" she said.

"That's what they call them," he said.

Consuelo figured he probably knew.

She had never realized he was so smart.

He was, in fact, even smarter than he himself had realized he was.

Street smart.

Which didn't only mean knowing how to kick the shit out of somebody. It also meant learning what was about to go down and figuring how to take advantage of it. For yourself. Playing for number one. Stepping out quicker than the other guy. Which came naturally if you grew up in these streets. Which the Jakies hadn't done, and which the Chinks hadn't done, either. Now maybe the streets of downtown Kingston or downtown Hong Kong were as mean as the streets here in this city, but Herrera doubted it. So whereas these small-town hoods could move in with their money and their muscle, there was something about this city that would always and forever elude them because they had not been born into this city, it was not in their *blood* the way it was in Herrera's.

This was *not* their city.

Fucking foreigners.

This was *his* city.

And he knew the stink of rotten fish, all right.

Had caught that stink the minute Hamilton approached him with the deal. Thought Uh-oh, why is he coming to me? Not coming to him in person, not going to where Herrera lived, but sending someone to get him. This was three days before Christmas. The deal was going down on the twenty-seventh. A simple dope buy, Hamilton explained. Very small. Fifty dollars for three kilos of cocaine. Close to seventeen grand a key. Hamilton needed someone to deliver the cash and pick up the stuff for him.

So why me? Herrera wondered.

All the while Hamilton talked, Herrera was thinking This is bullshit, the man *wants* something from me. But what can it be?

Why is he asking *me* to pick up this cocaine for him?

Why doesn't he send one of his own people?

"You'll be carrying the money in a briefcase," Hamilton said.

Fifty fucking K! Herrera thought.

"This is the address."

He's trusting me with all that cash.

Never met me in his life, trusting me with all that money. Suppose I split with it? Straight to Spindledrift, I get on an airplane to Calcutta. Or else the coke. I give them the money in the briefcase, I pack the three keys, I disappear from the face of the—

"Don't get any ideas," Hamilton said.

But Herrera figured that was for show; the fish stink was very strong now.

"My people will be waiting for you downstairs," Hamilton said.

Then why don't you send your people *upstairs?* Herrera wondered.

Why send me instead? Who you never met in your life.

"You're probably wondering why I came to you," Hamilton said.

Now why would I be wondering such a thing, Herrera thought.

"You worked for Arthur Chang some years ago, didn't you?" Hamilton said.

Herrera never admitted having worked for anyone at any time. To anybody. He said nothing.

"We need a man who understands the Chinese mentality," Hamilton said.

The word sounded so pretty on his Jamaican tongue.

"Men-tahl-ee-tee."

But why? Herrera wondered.

"Why?" he asked.

"The men making delivery are Chinese," Hamilton said.

Herrera looked at him.

This was the lie. He knew this was the lie, but he didn't yet know *what* the lie was. He knew only that he saw the lie sitting in Hamilton's eyes on Hamilton's impassive face, and the lie had something to do with Chinese making the delivery.

"Which Chinese?" he asked.

"That is for me to know, man," Hamilton said, and smiled.

"Sure," Herrera said.

"So do you think you might be interested?"

"You haven't yet mentioned how much this is worth to you."

"I thought ten dollars," Hamilton said.

Which was very fucking high.

High by about eight.

Especially high when you figured he could just as easily send someone on his payroll.

So why such rich bait?

It suddenly occurred to Herrera that this fucking Jakie was buying a fall guy.

"Ten sounds about right," he said.

The return address on the flap of the envelope was 336 North Eames.

The woman had signed her letter *Julie.*

The mailboxes downstairs showed a J. Endicott in apartment 21. They climbed the steps to the second floor, stood outside the door listening for a moment, and then knocked. This was now a quarter to seven in the evening. Even if Julie had a job, she should be—

"Who is it?"

A woman's voice.

"Police," Carella said.

"Police?"

Utter astonishment.

"Miss Endicott?" Carella said.

"Yes?"

The voice closer to the door now. Suspicion replacing the surprise. In this city all kinds of lunatics knocked on your door pretending they were somebody else.

"I'm Detective Carella, 87th Squad, I wonder if you could open the door for me."

"Why? What's the matter?"

"Routine inquiry, Miss. Could you open the door, please?"

The door opened just a crack, restrained by a night chain.

An eye appeared in the crack. Part of a face.

"Let me see your badge, please."

He held up his shield and ID card.

"What's this about?" she asked.

"Is this your handwriting?" he asked, and held up the letter so that the envelope flap showed.

"Where'd you get that?" she asked.

"Did you write this?"

"Yes, but . . ."

"May we come in, please?"

"Just a second," she said.

The door closed. There was the rattle of the chain coming off. The door opened again. She was, Carella guessed, in her mid-twenties, a woman of medium height with long blonde hair and brown eyes. She had the look about her of someone who had just got home from work, still wearing a skirt and blouse, but she'd loosened her hair and undone the stock tie on the blouse, and she was barefoot.

"Julie Endicott?" Carella said.

"Yes?"

She closed the door behind them.

They were in a small entrance foyer. Tiny kitchen to the right. Living room straight ahead. In the living room, a young man sat on a sofa upholstered in a nubby blue fabric. There was a coffee table in front of the sofa, two drinks in tall glasses on it. A pair of medium-heeled women's shoes were on the floor under the coffee table. The young man was wearing jeans and a V-necked sweater. His shoes were under the coffee table, too. Carella figured they'd interrupted a bit of fore-play. Lady home from work, boyfriend or husband waiting to mix the drinks. She lets down her hair, they kick off their shoes, he starts fiddling with her blouse, knock, knock, it's the cops.

The young man looked up at them as they came in.

He was white.

Tall.

With dark hair and blue eyes.

Joyce Chapman's vague description of . . .

"Michel Fournier?" Carella asked.

His eyes opened wide. He looked at Julie. Julie shrugged, shook her head.

"Are you Michel Fournier?" Carella said.

"Yes?"

"Few questions we'd like to ask you."

"Questions?" he said, and looked at Julie again. Julie shrugged again.

"Privately," Carella said. He was thinking down the line. Thinking alibi. If Julie Endicott turned out to be Fournier's alibi, he'd want to question her separately later on.

"Is there anything you have to do?" he asked her.

"What?"

"Take a shower, watch the TV news . . ."

"Oh," she said. "Sure."

She went through the living room and opened a door opposite the couch. A glimpse of bed beyond. The door closed.

"We know the *Dean* was in port on New Year's Eve," Carella said. Straight for the jugular. "We know the crew went ashore. Where'd *you* go, Mike?"

First-name basis. Reduce him at once to an inferior status. An old cop trick that usually worked. Except when you were talking to a professional thief who thought you were calling him Frankie because you liked him.

"New Year's Eve," Meyer said.

"Where, Mike?"

"Why do you want to know?"

"Do you know a girl named Joyce Chapman?"

"No. Joyce Chapman. No. Who's Joyce Chapman?"

"Think back to October," Carella said.

"I was nowhere *near* this city in October."

"We're talking about October a year ago."

"What? How do you expect me to remember . . . ?"

"A disco named Lang's. Down in the Quarter."

"So?"

"Do you remember it?"

"I think so. What's . . . ?"

"A girl named Joyce Chapman. You did some dope together . . ."

"No, no."

"Yes, yes, this isn't a drug bust, Mike."

"Look, I really don't remember anyone named Joyce Chapman."

"Blonde hair," Meyer said.

"Like your friend Julie," Carella said.

"I like blondes," Fournier said, and shrugged.

"Green eyes," Meyer said.

"Pretty eyes."

"Her best feature."

"You went back to her apartment on North Orange . . ."

"No, I don't re . . ."

"She had a roommate."

"Asleep when you came in . . ."

"Still asleep when you left early the next morning."

"Angela Quist."

"I don't know her, either."

"Okay, let's talk about New Year's Eve."

"A year ago? If you expect . . ."

"No, Mike, the one just past."

"Where'd you go and what'd you do?"

"I was with Julie. I stay here with Julie whenever the *Dean*'s in port."

"How long have you known her?"

"I don't know, it must be six, seven months."

"She came after Joyce, huh?"

"I'm telling you I don't know anybody named . . ."

"Wants to be a writer," Meyer said.

"She was studying writing here in the city."

"Her father owns a lumber company out west."

"Oh," Fournier said.

Recognition.

"You got her now?" Carella said.

"Yeah. I think. A little tattoo on her ass?"

Nobody had mentioned a tattoo to them.

"Like a little bird? On the right cheek?"

"Picasso prints on the wall over the couch," Meyer said. "In the apartment on Orange."

"Like some kind of modern stuff?" Fournier said.

"Yeah, like some kind of modern stuff," Meyer said.

"I think I remember her. That was some night."

"Apparently," Carella said. "Ever try to get in touch with her again?"

"No. I'll tell you the truth, I didn't even remember her name."

"Never saw her again after that night, huh?"

"Never."

"Tell us about New Year's Eve, Mike."

"I already told you. I was with Julie. Did something *happen* to this girl? Is that why you're asking me all these questions?"

"You were here on New Year's Eve, is that it?"

"Here? No. I didn't say here."

"Then where?"

"We went out."

"Where?"

"To a party. One of Julie's friends. A girl named Sarah."

"Sarah what?"

"I don't remember. Ask Julie."

"You're not too good on names, are you, Mike?"

"All right, you want to tell me what happened to this girl?"

"Who said anything happened to her?"

"You come here, you bang down the door . . ."

"Nobody banged down the door, Mike."

"I mean, what the hell *is* this?"

The outraged citizen now. Guilty or innocent, they all became outraged at some point in the questioning. Or at least *expressed* outrage. People of Italian descent, guilty or innocent, always pulled the *"Conesce chi son'io?"* line. Indignantly. Roughly translated as "Do you realize who I am?" You could be talking to a street cleaner, he came on like the governor of the state. "Do you realize who I am?" Fournier was doing the same high-horse bit now. "What the hell *is* this?" Outrage on his face and in his blue eyes. The innocent bystander, falsely accused. But they still didn't know where he'd been on New Year's Eve while Susan and her sitter were getting killed.

"What time did you leave here?" Meyer asked.

"Around ten. Ask Julie."

"And got home when?"

"Around four."

"Where were you between twelve-thirty and two-thirty?"

"Still at the party."

"What time did you leave there?"

"Around two-thirty, three."

"Which?"

"In there. Closer to three, I guess."

"And went where?"

"Came straight back here."

"How?"

"On the subway."

"From where?"

"Riverhead. The party was all the way up in Riverhead. Something happened to this girl, am I right?"

"No."

"Then what happened?"

"Her daughter got killed," Carella said, and watched his eyes.

"I didn't know she had a kid," Fournier said.

"She didn't."

Still watching the eyes.

"You just said . . ."

"Not when you knew her. The baby was six months old."

Both detectives watching his eyes now.

"The baby was yours," Carella said.

He looked first at Carella and then at Meyer. Meyer nodded. In the kitchen, a water tap was dripping. Fournier was silent for a long time. When he spoke again, it was stop and go. A sentence, a silence, another sentence, another silence.

"I didn't know that," he said.

"I'm sorry," he said.

"I wish I'd known," he said.

"Will you tell her how sorry I am?" he said.

"Do you know where I can reach her?" he said.

The detectives said nothing.

"Or maybe you can give her the number here," he said. "If you talk to her. If she'd like to call me or anything."

In the kitchen, the water tap dripped steadily.

"You don't know how sorry I am," he said.

And then:

"What was the baby's name?"

"Susan," Meyer said.

"That's my mother's name," he said. "Well, Suzanne."

There was another long silence.

"I wish I'd known," he said again.

"Mr. Fournier," Carella said, "we'd like to talk to Miss Endicott now."

"Sure," Fournier said. "I really wish I could . . ."

And let the sentence trail.

Julie Endicott told them that on New Year's Eve they had left the apartment here at a little past ten o'clock. They had gone to a party at the home of a friend named Sarah Epstein, who lived at 7133 Washington Boulevard in Riverhead, apartment 36. Julie Endicott went on to say that they had stayed at the party until ten minutes to three, had walked the two blocks to the subway station on Washington and Knowles, and had got back to the apartment here at a few minutes after four. They had gone straight to bed. Mike Fournier had been with her all night long. He had never left her side all night long.

"Did you want Sarah's phone number?" she asked. "In case you plan to call her?"

"Yes, please," Carella said.

Sarah Epstein corroborated everything they'd been told.

They were back to square one.

12

CARELLA PLACED THE CALL to Seattle on Thursday morning, at a little after nine Pacific time. He tried the number for the Pines, and got no answer. He then called the Chapman Lumber Company, and spoke to the same woman he'd spoken to nine days ago. *Pearl Ogilvy*, his notes read. *Miss*. He explained that he had a message for Joyce Chapman, and couldn't reach her at the house. He wondered if she might pass the message on to her.

"Just tell her that Mike Fournier would like to talk to her. His number here is . . ."

"Mr. Carella? Excuse me, but . . ."

There was a sudden silence on the line.

"Miss Ogilvy?" Carella said, puzzled.

"Sir . . . I'm sorry, but . . . Joyce is dead."

"What?"

"Yes, sir."

"What?"

"She was murdered, sir."

"When?"

"Monday night."

Carella realized he was frowning. He also realized he was shocked. He had not been shocked in a long, long time. Why the murder of Joyce Chapman should now have such an effect on him . . .

"Tell me what happened," he said.

"Well, sir, maybe you ought to talk to her sister. She was out here when it happened."

"Could I have her number, please?"

"I don't have her number back east, but I'm sure it's in the phone book."

"Where would that be, Miss Ogilvy? Back east where?"

"Why, right where you're calling from," she said.

"Here? She lives here in this city?"

"Yes, sir. She came out because Mr. Chapman was so sick and all, and everybody was expecting him to die. Instead, it was poor Joyce who . . ."

Her voice caught.

"And she's back here now?" Carella asked.

"Yes, sir, they flew home yesterday, her and her husband. Right after the funeral."

"Which part of the city, would you know?"

"Does Calm's Point sound right? Is there a Calm's Point?"

"Yes, there is," Carella said. "Can you tell me what her married name is?"

"Hammond. Melissa Hammond. Well, it'd probably be under Richard Hammond."

"Thank you," Carella said.

"Not at all," she said, and hung up.

Carella immediately dialed Seattle Directory Assistance, asked for the Seattle P.D. and looked up at the clock. 9:15 A.M. their time. If it worked the way it did here, the day shift would have been in for an hour and a half already. He dialed the number. Identified himself. Asked to talk to someone in Homicide. A sergeant told him he was just passing through with some papers, heard the phone ringing, picked it up. Didn't seem to be anyone up here at the moment, could he have someone get back? Carella told him he was trying to reach whoever was handling the Chapman case. Joyce Chapman. The Monday night murder. He said it was urgent. The sergeant gave his solemn word.

The man who called back at one o'clock Carella's time identified himself as Jamie Bonnem. He said he and his partner were working the Chapman case. He wanted to know what Carella's interest was.

"Her daughter was murdered here on New Year's Eve," Carella said.

"Didn't know she was married," Bonnem said.

Sort of a Western drawl. Carella didn't know they talked that way in Seattle. Maybe he was from someplace else.

"She was single, but that's another story," he said. "Can you tell me what happened out there?"

Bonnem told him what had happened.

Killed in her own bed.

Pistol in her mouth.

Two shots fired.

Gun was a Smith & Wesson 59.

"That's a nine-millimeter auto," Bonnem said. "We recovered both bullets and one of the cartridge cases. We figure the killer picked up the other one, couldn't find the one he left behind. He couldn't do anything about the bullets 'cause they were buried in the wall behind the bed."

"Anything else involved?" Carella asked.

"What do you mean?"

"Was she raped?"

"No."

"What've you got so far?"

"Nothing but the ballistics make. What've you got?"

Carella told him what he had.

"So we've *both* got nothing, right?" Bonnem said.

"He asks for protection, and then he disappears on me," Kling said.

He had the floor.

The detectives were gathered in Lieutenant Byrnes's office for the weekly Thursday afternoon meeting. The meetings were the lieutenant's idea. They took place at three-thirty every Thursday, catching the off-going day shift and the on-coming night shift. This way, he hoped for input from eight detectives, all of them airing their various cases. If he ended up with six of them in his office, what with vacations and people out sick, he considered himself lucky. The lieutenant called these meetings his Thursday Afternoon Think Tank. Detective Andy Parker called them the Thursday Afternoon Stink Tank.

There were only five detectives with Byrnes that afternoon. O'Brien and Fujiwara were on stakeout and had relieved on post. Hawes was out interviewing a burglary victim. Parker wished he could have thought up some good excuse to miss the meeting. He hated these fucking meetings. He didn't like hanging around late if his shift happened to be the one getting relieved, and he didn't like coming in early if he was the one about to do the relieving. Anyway, he had enough problems with his own case load without having to listen to somebody else's troubles. Who *gave* a damn what was happening with Kling and this Herrera character? Not Parker.

He sat in a straight-backed chair, looking out the window. He was willing to bet anyone in the room that it would start snowing again any minute. He wondered if that blue parka was still downstairs in his locker. He was glad he hadn't shaved this morning. A two-day growth of beard kept you warm when it was snowing. He was wearing rumpled gray flannel trousers, unpolished black shoes, a Harris tweed sport jacket with a stain on the right sleeve, and a white shirt with the collar open, no tie. He looked like one of the city's homeless who had wandered into a warm place for the afternoon.

"Maybe he only needed cover till they turned off the heat," Brown suggested.

He was wearing a dress shirt and tie, the trousers and vest to a suit; he'd been in court all day, testifying on an assault case. His jacket was draped over the back of his chair. He was a huge man, his complexion the color of his name, a frown on his face as he tried to work through Kling's problem with him. The frown came out as a scowl.

"Okay, Artie," Kling said, "but why would the posse suddenly quit? Two weeks ago, three weeks, whenever it was, they tried to kill the man. So all at once all bets are off?"

"Maybe the color of blue scared them," Carella said.

"What'd you have on him?" Willis asked. "A round-the-clock?"

"No, sun-to-sun," Kling said.

"All we could afford," Byrnes said. "The man's small time."

He sat behind his desk in his shirt sleeves, a man of medium height with a compact bullet head and no-nonsense blue eyes. It was too damn hot in this room. Something wrong with the damn thermostat. He'd have to call Maintenance.

"Don't forget the one who came after me," Kling said.

"You think that's connected, huh?" Brown said.

"Had to be," Carella said.

"You get a make on him?"

"Nothing."

"What you got here," Parker said, turning from the window, "is a two-bit courier who gave you a story so you'd put some blues on him, and you fell for it hook, line and sinker. So now he disappears, and you're surprised."

"He told me a big buy was coming down, Andy."

"Sure, when?"

"Next Monday night."

"Where?"

"He didn't know where yet."

"Sure, you know when he's gonna know? *Never* is when he's gonna know. 'Cause there ain't no buy. He conned you into laying some badges on him till the heat cooled, Artie's right. Now he don't need you anymore, it's goodbye and good luck."

"Maybe," Kling said.

"Why would he have lied?" Byrnes asked.

"To get the blue muscle," Parker said.

"Then why didn't he lie bigger?" Carella said.

"What do you mean?"

"Give Bert the time, the place, the works. Why the slow tease?"

The room went silent.

"Which is why I figure he's really trying to find out," Kling said.

"Why?" Parker said.

"So we can make the bust."

"Why?" Parker said.

"So we'll put away the people who tried to kill him."

Parker shrugged.

"That's a reason," Byrnes said.

"Bust up the posse," Brown said.

"Herrera walks away safe," Meyer said.

"But something's missing," Carella said. "Why'd they want him dead in the first place?"

"Ah-ha," Parker said.

The men looked at each other. Nobody seemed to know the answer.

"So what's next?" Parker asked. "I want to go home."

Brown scowled at him.

"You're scaring me to death, Artie," Parker said. "Can we get on with this, Loot?"

Byrnes scowled at him, too.

Parker sighed like a saint with arrows in him.

"This double on New Year's Eve," Carella said. "The baby's mother was killed Monday night, in Seattle. It may be linked, we don't know. I'll be seeing her sister later today."

"The sister lives here?" Byrnes asked.

"Yeah. In Calm's Point."

"They're originally from Seattle," Meyer explained.

"So have you got any meat at all?" Parker asked impatiently.

"Not yet. According to the timetable . . ."

"Yeah, yeah, timetables," Parker said, dismissing them as worthless.

"Let him talk," Willis said.

"You get six different timetables from six different people," Parker said. "Makes it look like the person got killed six different times of day."

"Just let the man *talk*," Willis said.

"It's ten after four already," Parker said.

"The way we've got it," Carella said, "the sitter was still alive at twelve-thirty in the morning. The parents got home at two-thirty and found her and the baby dead. The father had been drinking, but he was cold sober when we got there."

"The girl was raped and stabbed," Meyer said.

"The baby was smothered with a pillow," Carella said.

"What was it in Seattle?" Brown asked.

"A gun."

"Mmm.

"How do you know she was still alive at twelve-thirty?" Kling asked.

"You want to look at this?" Carella said, and handed him the timetable he and Meyer had worked up.

"Twelve-twenty A.M.," Kling said, reading out loud. "Harry Flynn calls to wish Annie a happy new year."

"The sitter's father?" Willis asked.

"Yeah," Meyer said.

"Twelve-thirty A.M.," Kling read. "Peter Hodding calls to check on the baby . . ."

"Peter *who*?" Parker said.

"The baby's father."

"His name is Peter *Hard-On*?"

"Hodding."

"How would you like to go through life with a name like Peter Hard-On?" Parker asked, laughing.

"He tells the sitter they'll be home in a little while, asks if everything's okay."

"Peter Hard-On," Parker said, still laughing.

"*Was* everything okay?" Byrnes asked.

"According to Hodding, she sounded fine."

"No strain, no forced conversation, nobody there with her?"

"He said she sounded natural."

"And this was at twelve-thirty, huh?" Willis asked.

"Yeah. According to Hodding."

"Who'd had a little to drink, huh?" Brown said.

"Well, a *lot* to drink, actually," Meyer said.

"So there's your problem," Parker said. "One end of your timetable is based on what a fuckin' *drunk* told you."

Carella looked at him.

"Am I right?" he asked.

"Maybe," Carella said.

"So can we go home now?"

It broke her heart sometimes, this city.

On a day like today, with the storm clouds beginning to gather over the river, gray and rolling in over the gray rolling water, the certain smell of snow on the air . . .

On a day like today, she remembered being a little girl in this city.

Remembered the playground this city had been, winter, summer, spring and fall. The street games changing with the changing seasons. A children's camp all year round. In the wintertime, on a day like today, all the kids would do their little magic dance in the street, praying that the snow would come soon, praying there'd be no school tomorrow, there'd be snow forts instead and snowball fights, the girls shrieking in terror and glee as the boys chased them through narrow canyons turned suddenly white. Eileen giggling, her cheeks red, her eyes flashing, bundled in a heavy parka, a woolen pom-pommed hat pulled down over her ears, her red hair tucked up under it because she was ashamed of her hair back then, made her look too Irish, whatever that was, too much the Mick, her mother used to say, We're American, you know, we didn't just get off the boat.

She loved this city.

For what it had inspired in her.

The need to compete, the need to excel in order to survive, a city of gutter rats, her father had said with pride in his voice. Michael Burke. They called him Pops on the beat, because his hair was prematurely white, he'd looked like his own grandfather when he was still only twenty-six. Pops Burke. Shot to death when she was still a little girl. A liquor store holdup. The Commissioner had come to his funeral. He told Eileen her father was a very brave man. They gave her mother a folded American flag.

Her Uncle Matt was a cop, too. She'd loved him to death, loved the stories he told her about leprechauns and faeries, stories he'd heard from his mother who'd heard them from hers and on back through the generations, back to a time when Ireland was everywhere green and covered with a gentle mist, a time when blood was not upon the land. Her uncle's favorite toast was "Here's to golden days and purple nights," an expression he'd heard repeated again and again on a radio show. Recently, Eileen had heard Hal Willis's new girlfriend using the same expression. Maybe *her* uncle had listened to the same radio comic.

Chances were, though, that Marilyn's uncle hadn't been killed in a bar while he was off duty and drinking his favorite drink and making his favorite toast, here's to golden days and purple nights indeed. Not when the color of the day is red, the color of the day is shotgun red, Uncle Matt drawing his service revolver as the holdup man came in, red plaid kerchief over his face, blew him off the barstool and later took fifty-two dollars and thirty-six cents from the cash register. Uncle Matt dead on the floor in a pool of his own blood. Another folded American flag for the family. The shooting took place in the old Hundred and Tenth in Riverhead. They used to call it The Valley of Death, after the Tennyson poem about into the Valley of Death rode the six hundred. How this applied to the Hundred and Tenth, God alone knew; the lexicon of cops was often obscure in origin.

She wondered if she should tell Karin Lefkowitz that the main reason she'd joined the force was so that someday she could catch that son of a bitch with the red plaid kerchief over his face, rip off that kerchief, and look him dead in the eye before she blew him away. Her Uncle Matt was the reason. Not her father who'd been killed when she was still too young to have really known him. Her Uncle Matt.

Who still brought tears to her eyes whenever she thought of him and his leprechauns and faeries.

This city . . .

It . . .

It taught you how to do something better than you'd ever done anything else in your life. Taught you how to be the *best* at it. Which was what she'd been. The best decoy cop in this city. Never mind modesty, she'd been the best, yes. She'd done her job with the sense of pride her father had instilled in her and the sense of humor her uncle had encouraged, never letting it get to her, balancing its risks and its rewards, eagerly approaching each new assignment as if it were an adventure, secure in the knowledge that she was a professional among professionals.

Until, of course, the city took it all away from her.

You either owned this city or you didn't.

Once upon a time, when she was good, she owned it.

And now she owned nothing.

Not even herself.

She took a deep breath and climbed the low flat steps in front of the old Headquarters Building, and went through one of the big bronze doorways, and wondered what she should tell Karin Lefkowitz today.

Carella did not get to the Hammond apartment in Calm's Point until almost ten o'clock that night. He had phoned ahead and learned from Melissa Hammond that her husband usually got home from the office at seven, seven-thirty, but since he'd been away from work for almost a week now and since there was a lot of catching up to do, he might not be home until much later. Carella asked if she thought eight would be okay for him to stop by, and she told him they'd be having dinner as soon as her husband got home, so if he could make it a bit later . . .

It was five minutes to ten when he knocked on the door.

He'd been on the job since a quarter to eight that morning.

Before he'd left the office, he'd called a woman named Chastity Kerr, who'd given the party the Hoddings had attended on New Year's Eve. He'd made an appointment to see her at ten tomorrow morning. So if he got out of here by eleven, he'd be home by midnight. Have a snack with Teddy before they went to bed, wake up early in the morning so he could have breakfast with the twins before they caught their seven-thirty school bus, leave for the office at eight, catch up on the reports he hadn't got to yesterday *or* today, and then go see Mrs. Kerr. Just thinking about it made him more tired than he actually was.

The Hammonds were still at the dinner table, lingering over coffee, when he arrived. Melissa Hammond, a very attractive, pregnant blonde with the same green eyes her sister had listed as "Best Feature" on the Cooper-Anderson background form, asked Carella if he'd care for a cup. "I grind the beans myself," she said. He thanked her, and accepted the chair her husband offered. Richard Hammond—his wife called him "Dick"—was a tall, good-looking man with dark hair and dark eyes. Carella guessed that he was in his late thirties, his wife a few years younger. He had obviously changed from the clothes he'd worn to work this morning, unless his law office was a lot more casual than the ones Carella was accustomed to. Hammond worked for the firm of Lasser, Bending, Merola and Ross. He was wearing jeans, a sweat shirt with a Washington State University seal on it, and loafers without socks. He offered Carella a cigar, which Carella declined.

Melissa poured coffee for him.

Carella said, "I'm glad you agreed to see me."

"We're eager to help in any way possible," Melissa said.

"We were just sitting here talking about it," Hammond said.

"The coincidence," Melissa said.

"Of this baby getting killed."

"Joyce's baby, yes," Carella said and nodded.

"Well, you don't know that for sure," Hammond said.

"Yes, we do," Carella said, surprised.

"Well," Hammond said, and looked at his wife.

"I'm not sure I understand," Carella said.

"It's just that this *baby,*" Melissa said, and looked at her husband.

"You see," he said, "this is the first we're hearing of it. When you called Melissa earlier today and told her Joyce's murder might be linked to the death of her *baby* . . ."

"I mean, as far as I knew, Joyce never *had* a baby."

"But she did," Carella said.

"Well, that's your contention," Hammond said.

Carella looked at them both.

"Uh . . . look," he said. "It might be easier for all of us if we simply accept as fact . . ."

"I assume you have substantiating . . ."

"Yes, Mr. Hammond, I do."

"That my sister-in-law gave birth to . . ."

"A baby girl, yes, sir. Last July. At St. Agnes Hospital here in the city. And signed it over for adoption to the Cooper-Anderson Agency, also here in the city."

"You have papers showing . . . ?"

"Copies of the papers, yes."

"And you know for a fact that this baby who was murdered on . . . ?"

"Yes, was your sister-in-law's baby. Adopted by Mr. and Mrs. Peter Hodding, yes."

Hammond nodded.

"Well," he said, and sighed.

"This is certainly news to us," Melissa said.

"You didn't know your sister had this baby?"

"No."

"Did you know she was pregnant?"

"No."

"Never even suspected she might be?"

"Never."

"How often did you see her?"

"Oh, on and off," Melissa said.

"Every few months or so," Hammond said.

"Even though you lived here in the same city, huh?" Carella said.

"Well, we didn't move here till last January," Hammond said.

"And, anyway, we were never very close," Melissa said.

"When would you say you'd seen her last?"

"Well, in Seattle. All the while we were in Seattle. I saw her the night she was killed, in fact. We were at the hospital together."

"I meant before then."

"Well, we flew out together. When it looked as if my father might . . ."

"What I'm trying to ask . . . your sister gave birth in July. When did you see her *before* that?"

"Oh."

"Well, let's see, when was it?" Hammond said.

"We moved here last January . . ."

"So it must've been . . ."

"My birthday, wasn't it?" Melissa said.

"I think so, yes. The party here."

"Yes."

"And when was that?" Carella asked.

"February twelfth."

"March, April, May, June, July," Carella said, counting on his fingers. "That would've made her four months pregnant."

"You'd never have known, I can tell you that," Hammond said.

"Well, lots of women carry small," Melissa said.

"And she was a big woman, don't forget. Five-ten . . ."

"Big-boned . . ."

"And she always wore this Annie Hall sort of clothing."

"Layered," Melissa said. "So it's entirely possible we'd have missed it."

"Her being pregnant," Hammond said.

"She never confided it to you, huh?" Carella asked.

"No."

"Didn't come to see you when she found out . . . ?"

"No. I wish she would have."

"Melissa *always* wished they were closer."

"Well, there's the age difference, you know," Melissa said. "I'm thirty-four, my sister was only nineteen. That's a fifteen-year difference. I was already a teenager when she was born."

"It's a shame because . . . well . . . now there's no changing it. Joyce is dead."

"Yes," Carella said, and nodded. "Tell me, did she ever mention any-one named Michel Fournier? Mike Fournier?"

"No," Melissa said. "At least not to me. Dick? Did she ever . . ."

"No, not to me, either," Hammond said. "Is he the father?"

"Yes," Carella said.

"I figured."

"But she never mentioned him, huh?"

"No. Well, if we didn't know she was pregnant . . ."

"I thought maybe in passing. Without mentioning that she was preg-nant, do you know what I mean? Just discussing him as someone she'd met, or knew, or . . ."

"No," Melissa said, shaking her head. "Dick?"

"No," he said. "I'm sorry."

"Did she have any boyfriends back in Seattle?" Carella asked.

"Well, no one recent," Melissa said. "She moved here right after high school, you know . . ."

"Graduated early . . ."

"She was only seventeen . . ."

"She was very smart . . ."

"Wanted to be a writer . . ."

"You should see some of her poetry."

"She was studying here with a very important man."

"So she came east . . . when?" Carella asked. "June? July?"

"It would've been two years come July."

"And we came here in January," Melissa said. "Dick had a good job offer . . ."

"I'd been practicing out there, but this was too good to refuse," Hammond said.

"So when you got here in January . . ."

"Yes, toward the end of . . ."

". . . your sister was already pregnant," Carella said.

"Was she?" Melissa said.

"Yes. She would've been three months pregnant," Carella said. "Did you look her up when you got here?"

"Yes, of course."

"But you didn't notice she was pregnant."

"No. Well, I wasn't looking for anything like that. And, anyway, what'd you say it was? Three months?"

"Three, yes."

"Yes," Melissa said. "So she wouldn't have been showing, would she? At least, not so *I* could notice."

"All the Chapman women carry small," Hammond said. "Melissa's eight months pregnant now, but you'd never guess it."

Carella had the good grace not to look at her belly.

"Who was Joyce's most recent boyfriend?" he asked. "Out there in Seattle?"

"I guess it would have been Eddie," Melissa said.

"She was seeing a lot of him in high school."

"Eddie Gillette."

"Pretty serious?" Carella asked.

"Well, high school stuff," Hammond said. "You know."

"Have the Seattle police talked to him?"

"I really couldn't say."

"Didn't mention his name as a possible suspect or anything, did they?"

"Didn't mention *anyone's* name."

"They're pretty much scratching their heads out there," Melissa said.

"A thing like this . . . it's not too common out there," Hammond said.

"Well, people get *killed*," Melissa said.

"Yes, but not like here," Hammond said. "Is what I meant."

"Big bad city, huh?" Carella said, and smiled.

"Well, it is, you know," Hammond said, and returned the smile.

"What sort of law do you practice?" Carella asked.

"*Not* criminal," Hammond said. "The firm I'm with now specializes in corporate law."

"And out there in Seattle?"

"General law. I had my own practice."

"He was his own boss out there," Melissa said, and smiled somewhat ruefully.

"Yes, but the opportunities were limited," Hammond said. "You make certain trade-offs in life. We may go back one day, Lissie, who knows?"

"Time we go back, there'll be no family there anymore," she said.

"Her father's very ill, you know," Hammond said.

"Yes," Carella said.

"Never rains but it pours," Melissa said, and sighed heavily.

Carella looked at his watch.

"I don't want to keep you any longer," he said. "Thanks very much for your time, I appreciate it."

"Not at all," Hammond said.

He walked Carella into the entry foyer, took his overcoat from the closet there, and helped him on with it. Carella thanked him again for his time, called "Good night" to Melissa, who was clearing the dining room table, and then went out into the hallway and took the elevator down to the street.

It was just beginning to snow.

13

CHASTITY KERR was the sort of big-boned person Melissa had said her sister was. Tall, sturdy but not fat, she gave the impression of a woman capable of handling any physical task a man could, only better. Blonde and suntanned—she explained that she and her husband had just come back from two weeks at Curtain Bluff on Antigua—she offered Carella a cup of coffee and then sat with him at a small table in the kitchen alcove overlooking Grover Park.

It was still snowing outside.

"Two days ago, I was lying under a palm tree sipping a frozen daiquiri," she said. "Look at this, willya?"

Carella looked at it.

It did not make him happy.

The plows wouldn't come out until the snow stopped, and it showed no sign of doing that.

"Mrs. Kerr," he said, "the reason I'm here . . ."

"Chastity, please," she said. "If you have a name like Chastity, you either use it a lot, or else you ignore it or change it. My sisters and I *use* our names, I think to spite our father, who chose them. I should tell you that there are four girls in our family, and they're named, in order, Verity, Piety, Chastity—that's me—and guess what he named the fourth one?"

"Sneezy," Carella said.

"No. Generosity. Can you believe he had the *temerity?*"

Carella smiled. "Anyway, Mrs. Kerr," he said, "what I'm . . ."

"Chastity, please."

"Well, what I'm trying to do, I'd like to pinpoint the time Peter Hodding called home on New Year's Eve. To talk to the murdered girl."

"Oh, my, New Year's Eve," Chastity said, and rolled her eyes.

"Yes, I know."

"Not a night when one normally tracks comings and goings, is it?"

"Not normally."

"What time did he give you?"

"Well, I'd rather you told me."

"Big rush for the phone," Chastity said. "I know I tried to get through to my sister in Chicago shortly after midnight, but all circuits were busy. I don't think *any*one was getting through to *any*where. At least, that's my recollection."

"When do you think Mr. Hodding placed his call?"

"I'm trying to remember."

Carella waited.

Chastity was thinking furiously.

"He was in the guest bedroom," she said, nodding, "that's right."

"Mr. Hodding?"

"Yes, he was using the extension in there."

"And this was when?"

"Well, that's what I'm trying to do, place the time. I know he told her he'd been trying to reach her, but the line was busy."

"Told who?"

"The sitter. When he finally got through."

"Told her the *line* had been busy? Or the circuits?"

"I'm sure he said the line."

"That would've been her father calling."

"Well, I don't know what you're talking about, so I can't really comment."

"I'm thinking out loud," Carella said. "How'd you happen to hear this conversation?"

"I was in the room next door. Checking on my daughter. I have an eight-year-old daughter. The door between the rooms was open, and I . . . well, there you are."

"Where?" Carella said, and smiled.

"I'd just got through to my sister, and she'd given me a hassle about not calling sooner. Said it was a tradition to call at midnight, and that was half an hour ago. And I went in to check Jennifer right after that. So it must've been a little past twelve-thirty."

"When you overheard Peter Hodding on the telephone."

"Yes."

"How much of the conversation did you hear?"

"Well, all of it, I suppose. From the beginning. From when he said, 'Annie . . .'"

"Then this definitely *was* the call to the sitter."

"Oh, yes. No question. 'Annie, it's me,' he said, and went on from there."

"'Annie, it's me.'"

"Yes."

"Not, 'Annie, it's Mr. Hodding'?"

"No, 'Annie, it's me.' I guess she knew his voice."

"Yes. Then what?"

"Then he said he'd been trying to get through but the line was busy . . ."

"Uh-huh."

"And then he asked how the baby was, little Susan."

"Yes."

"God, every time I think of what happened," Chastity said, and shook her head.

"Yes," Carella said. "Then what?"

"He told her they'd be home in a little while."

"A little while," Carella repeated.

"Yes."

"But they didn't leave until sometime between two and two-thirty."

"Yes. Well, I didn't look at the clock, but it was around that time."

"So that would've been at least an hour and a half later."

"Are you thinking out loud again?"

"Yes. If he called home around twelve-thirty, it would've been an hour and a half later when he and his wife left the party."

"That's what it would've been," Chastity said.

"But he told Annie he'd be home in a little while."

"Well, I didn't hear him say *exactly* that."

"What *did* you hear him say?"

"Just 'In a little while.'"

"Only those words?"

"Yes."

"'In a little while.'"

"Yes. She must have asked when they'd be home."

"Yes, I would guess so."

"Would you like more coffee?"

"Yes, please."

She got up, moved to the coffee-making machine, picked up the pot, carried it back to the table, and freshened Carella's cup. The snow kept coming down outside.

"Thank you," Carella said. "Why do you suppose he told the sitter they'd be home in a little while when actually they didn't leave until . . . ?"

"Well, he'd had a little to drink, you know."

"So I understand."

"I thought he was going to be sick, as a matter of fact."

"Uh-huh."

"Gayle was mad as hell. Told him she didn't enjoy the company of a drunken pig. Those were her exact words."

"This was when?"

"Actually, I think he was already drunk when he called home."

"Why do you say that?"

"Well, you know the way drunks sound. The way their speech gets? That's how he sounded."

"So when he made that call at twelve-thirty, he sounded drunk. While he was talking to Annie."

"Yes. *Very* drunk."

"How'd the conversation end?"

"Goodbye, so long, I'll see you, like that."

"And when did the argument with his wife occur?"

"Shortly after that. He'd spilled a drink on someone, and Gayle told him she was never going anyplace with him again . . . well, I told you what she said, except it was the company of a *fucking* drunken pig. Was what she said, actually."

"Pretty angry with him, huh?"

"Furious."

"But they stayed at the party, anyway, till sometime around two in the . . ."

"Well, *she* did."

"What do you mean?" Carella asked at once.

"Gayle stayed."

"I thought they left together at . . ."

"Yes, that was later. After he came back from his walk."

"What walk?"

"He went down for some air."

"When?"

"After Gayle tore into him."

"Are you saying he left the party?"

"Yes. Said he needed some air."

"Said he was going down for a walk?"

"Well, I assume he was. He put on his overcoat. He didn't just go stand out in the hall, if that's what you mean."

"What time was this?"

"It must've been around one o'clock."

"Mrs. Kerr . . ."

"Chastity. Please."

"Chastity . . . what time did Peter Hodding come back from his walk?"

"At two o'clock. I know because I was in the hallway saying goodbye to some of my guests when the elevator doors opened and Peter stepped out."

"How do you know it was two o'clock?"

"Because I was asking these people why they were leaving so early, and the man said, 'It's already two,' and that's when the elevator doors opened and Peter stepped out."

"Did he look as if he'd been outdoors?"

"Oh, yes. His cheeks all ruddy, his hair all blown. Yes, very definitely."

"Was he sober?"

"He was sober," Chastity said.

Francisco Palacios was surprised to see Bert Kling.

"Does this have to do with Proctor again?" he asked.

"No," Kling said.

"Because I had two fat guys in here asking about Proctor," Palacios said. "First one was an obnoxious snitch named Fats Donner, you know him?"

"I know him."

"He digs Mary Jane shoes and white cotton panties. Second one was a fat cop from the Eight-Three, his name is Weeks. You know him, too?"

"I know him, too," Kling said.

"*He* digs a hooker works in his precinct. I gave Weeks the name of her boyfriend plays saxophone. But I don't know where Proctor is. I told Weeks, and I'm telling you the same. How come he's so hot all at once, this two-bit little jerk?"

"We already found him," Kling said.

"Thank God. 'Cause I don't know where he is, anyway."

"I'm looking for a guy named Herrera."

"Give me a hard one, why don't you? You know how many Herreras we got in this city?"

"Are they all named José Domingo?"

"Most of them," Palacios said.

"This one did work for the Yellow Paper Gang some years back."

"What kind of work?"

"Dope. Which is what he's into right now."

"Who isn't?" Palacios said, and shrugged.

"Which is the next thing I want to know."

"Uh-huh."

"There's a big shipment coming in next week," Kling said. "I'd like details."

"You're hot stuff," Palacios said, shaking his head. "You give me a common name like Smith or Jones in Spanish, and you tell me there's a big shipment coming in next week, which there's a big shipment coming in *every* week in this city, and you expect me to help you."

"A hundred kilos of cocaine," Kling said.

"Uh-huh."

"Coming in on the twenty-third."

"Okay."

"By ship."

"Okay."

"Scandinavian registry."

"Uh-huh."

"Coming up from Colombia."

"Got it."

"The coke's going for ten grand per."

"A bargain."

"Earmarked for a Jamaican posse."

"Which one?"

"*Not* Reema."

"That leaves plenty others."

"I know. But a million bucks'll be changing hands, Cowboy. There's got to be somebody whispering about it."

"A million bucks is not so much nowadays," Palacios said. "I hear stories about twenty-, thirty-million-dollar dope deals, they're commonplace."

"I wish you'd tell *me* some of these stories," Kling said.

"My point is, a million-dollar deal nowadays you don't have people wetting their pants. It won't be easy getting a line on something like this."

"That's why I came to you, Cowboy," Kling said.

"Yeah, bullshit," Palacios said.

"Because I know you like the hard ones."

"Bullshit, bullshit," Palacios said, but he was grinning.

The doorman at 967 Grover Avenue was a roly-poly little person wearing a green uniform with gold trim. He looked like a general in a banana republic army. The people in the building knew him only as Al the Doorman, but his full name was Albert Eugene Di Stefano, and he was proud of the fact that he used to be one of the doormen at the Plaza Hotel in New York City. He immediately told Carella that he'd once given the N.Y.P.D. valuable information that had helped them crack a case involving some guy who was breaking into rooms at the Plaza and walking off into Central Park with bags full of jewelry. He would be happy to help Carella now in solving this terrible crime he was investigating. He knew all about the fourth-floor murders. Everybody in the building knew about them.

It so happened that he had, in fact, been working the midnight to eight A.M. shift on New Year's Eve, which he happened to pull because he'd drawn the deuce of clubs instead of the three of diamonds or the four of hearts. That was how the three doormen here at the building had decided who would work this particular shift on New Year's Eve, it being not what you would call a choice shift. He had drawn the lowest card, and he'd got stuck with it. So, yes, he was on that night. But he didn't see anyone suspicious coming in or going out of the building, if that was what Carella wanted to know.

"Do you know Mr. Hodding personally?" Carella asked.

"Oh, yes. A very nice man. I suggest a lot of commercials to him, he's a copywriter at an advertising agency. I told him one time I had a good idea for a Hertz commercial. The car rental people, you know? I thought they could show an airport with a lot of people waiting on lines at all these other car rental counters, but this guy goes right up to the Hertz counter, and he's walking off with a car key in ten seconds flat, and as he's passing all those people still waiting on the other lines, he busts out laughing and he says, 'I only laugh when it's Hertz.' They could even have a jingle that goes 'I *own*-lee *laugh* when it's *Hertz*, bom-bom.' Mr. Hodding told me his agency don't represent Hertz. So I gave him . . ."

"Do you know what he looks like? Mr. Hodding?"

"Oh, sure. I gave him this other idea for a Blue Nun commercial, this is a wine, you know, it's got a picture of a little blue nun on the label, well it's *called* Blue Nun. I told him the headline they should use on their commercial is 'Make a little Blue Nun a habit.' They could have a jingle that goes 'Make a *litt*-el *Blue* Nun a *ha*-bit.' Mr. Hodding told me his agency don't represent Blue Nun. So I gave him . . ."

"Would you recognize Mr. Hodding, for example, if he walked up the street right this minute?"

"Oh, sure. I gave him this other idea for a Chrysler Le Baron commercial. We see this World War I German fighter pilot with the white scarf, you know, and the goggles . . ."

"Did you see him at any time on New Year's Eve?"

"Who?"

"Mr. Hodding."

"As a matter of fact, I did, yes."

"When would that have been?"

"Around one o'clock. Well, a little after one. Ten after one, a quarter after, around then."

"Where did you see him?"

"Well, *here*," Di Stefano said, sounding surprised. "This is where I *was*. Remember when I told you I caught the low card? Which was how come I . . ."

"You saw him here in this building sometime between one and one-fifteen, is that correct?"

"Not only *saw* him, but also *spoke* to him. Which is the irony of it, you know? He comes here to check on the baby . . ."

"Is that what he said? That he was going to check on the baby?"

"Yes. So he's up there a half-hour, and right after he leaves there's this terrible thing happens. I mean, he must've missed the killer by what? Ten, fifteen minutes? Something like that?"

"You saw him when he came downstairs again?"

"Yes. Came right off the elevator. I was watching TV in this little room we got over there," he said, pointing, "we can see the whole lobby from it if we leave the door open."

"What time was this? When he came down?"

"I told you. It must've been around a quarter to two."

"Did he say anything to you?"

"He told me everything was okay. I told him it never hurts to check.
He said That's right, Al, and off he went."

"Did he seem sober?"

"Oh, yes."

"Sober when he got here?"

"Sober when he got here, sober when he left."

"Any blood on his clothing?"

"Blood?"

"Or his hands?"

"Blood?" Di Stefano said, appalled. "Mr. Hodding? Blood? No, sir.
No blood at all. No, sir!"

"Were you still here when he came home with Mrs. Hodding?"

"I was here all night. Till eight in the morning."

"And what time was that? When they got home?"

"Around two-thirty. Well, a little before."

"Okay," Carella said. "Thanks a lot."

"Don't you want to hear the Le Baron commercial?" Di Stefano
asked.

She could not get Eileen Burke out of her mind.

"My wife says I drink too much," the detective was telling her. "Her
father was a drunk, so she thinks anybody has a few drinks, *he's* a
drunk, too. She says I get dopey after a few drinks. It makes me want to
punch her out. It's her goddamn upbringing, you can't grow up in a
house with a drunk and not start thinking anybody takes a sip of elder-
berry wine is a fuckin' alcoholic.

"We were out last night with two other couples. I had the day shift,
we're investigating this murder, somebody sawed off this woman's head
and dropped it in a toilet bowl at the bus terminal. That is what I was
dealing with all day yesterday. A fuckin' woman's *head* floating in a toilet
bowl. From eight-thirty in the morning till six at night when I finally got
outta that fuckin' squadroom. So I get home, we live in Bethtown, we got
this garden apartment there near the bridge, I pour myself a Dewar's in a
tall glass with ice and soda, I'm watching the news and drinking my drink
and eating some peanuts and she comes in and says 'Do me a favor, don't
drink so much tonight.' I coulda busted her fuckin' nose right then and
there. She's already decided I'm a drunk, I drink too much, don't drink
so much tonight, meaning I drink too much *every* night. Which I don't.

"I had a fuckin' heart attack last April, I can't *eat* what I want to eat,
I have to walk two fuckin' miles every morning before I go to work, I

used to smoke two packs of cigarettes a day and now I can't smoke any at all, and she's giving me no, no, no concerning a couple of drinks I allow myself when I get home after a head floating in a toilet bowl. Two fucking drinks! Was all I had before we left the house! So we meet these two other couples at this Chinese restaurant on Potter, one of the guys is an assistant D.A., the other one's a computer analyst, their wives I don't know what they do. We're sharing, you know, the way you're supposed to when you're eating Chinks, and we order a bottle of wine goes around the table once and it's empty. Well, there's six people there, you know. So we order another bottle of wine, and that makes two glasses of wine I have, which is what everybody at that table had, *including* my fuckin' Carry Nation wife with her hatchet.

"Now it's ten-thirty, and we're leaving the restaurant, all of us together, and she takes her keys out of her bag and says so everybody can hear it, '*I'll* drive, Frank.' So I say 'Why?' and she says 'Because I don't trust you.' The assistant D.A. laughs, this is a guy I work with, we call him in whenever we got real meat, make sure the case'll stick, you know, he's laughing at what my wife says. A guy I *work* with. The other guy, the computer analyst, he picks up on it, he says, 'I hope you've got the day off tomorrow, Frank.' Like they're all taking the cue from Cheryl, that's her name, my wife, and making Frank the big drunk who can't drive a car and who maybe can't even walk a straight *line* to the fuckin' car.

"On the way home, I tell her I don't want to start an argument, I'm tired, I worked a long hard day, that fuckin' head in the toilet bowl. She tells me I didn't work harder than any of the other men at the table, and I say 'What do you mean?' and she says 'You know what I mean,' and I say 'Are you saying I drank more than Charlie or Phil, are you saying I'm drunk?' and she says 'Did I say you're drunk?' and all at once I want to break every fuckin' bone in her body. All at once, I'm yelling. I'm supposed to avoid stress, am I right? It was stress caused the fuckin' heart attack, so here I am yelling like a fuckin' Puerto Rican hooker, and when we get home I go in the television room to sleep, only I can't sleep because I'm thinking I better throw my gun in the river 'cause if she keeps at me this way, I'm gonna use it on her one day. Or hurt her very bad some other way. And I don't want to do that."

Detective Frank Connell of the Four-Seven looked across the desk at her.

"I don't know what to do," he said. "It's like I've got an enemy for a wife instead of a friend. A wife is supposed to be a friend, ain't she?

Ain't that why people get married? So there'll be somebody they can trust more than anybody else in the world? Instead, she makes me look like a fuckin' fool. I wouldn't do that to her in a million years, ridicule her in front of people she works with. She works in a law office, she's a legal secretary. I would *never* go in there and say she's this or that, she's no good at this or that, I would *never* hurt her that way. The way she hurts me when she says I'm a drunk."

"*Are* you a drunk?" Karin asked.

"No. I swear to God I am not."

"Do you want or need a drink when you get up in the morning?"

"Absolutely not. I go walk my fuckin' two miles, I eat my breakfast, and I go to work."

"Do you really have only two drinks when you get home at night?"

"Two. I swear."

"How big?"

"What do you mean? Like a regular drink. Some booze, some ice, some soda . . ."

"How *much* booze?"

"Two, three ounces."

"Which?"

"Three."

"That's six ounces."

"Which ain't a lot."

"Plus whatever wine you'll drink at . . ."

"Only when we go out. When we eat home, I usually have a Pepsi with dinner."

"Would you say you're a heavy drinker?"

"A moderate drinker. I know guys drink non-stop, day and night, I'm not one of . . ."

"Do you consider them drunks?"

"I consider them alcoholics. I rarely see them *drunk*, but I know they have drinking problems, I know they can't control their drinking."

"But you can."

"I do not consider two fucking drinks a day a *drinking* problem!"

"Now you're getting mad at me, huh?" Karin said, and smiled.

"I don't like being called a fuckin' drunk! It infuriates me! I'm not here because I have a *drinking* problem, I'm here 'cause I have a fucking *wife* problem. I love her to death, but . . ."

"But you've been talking about hurting her," Karin said.

"I know."

"Physically hurting her."

"Yes."

"Punching her out. Breaking her nose . . ."

Connell nodded.

"Breaking every bone in her body."

He nodded again.

"Even using your gun on her."

"This is what's tearing me apart," Connell said. "She's my wife, but when she starts on me I'd like to kill her."

"You said you love her to death," Karin said. "Do you?"

Connell thought about this for a moment.

"I guess so," he said, and fell silent.

Eileen Burke popped into her head again.

And do you love him?

Asking her about Bert Kling.

Eileen thinking it over.

And saying, "I guess so."

In which case, why had she stopped seeing him?

The offices of the David Pierce Advertising Agency were midtown on Jefferson Avenue, where most of the city's advertising agencies grew like poisonous toadstools. Carella and Meyer arrived there together at seven minutes past three that Friday afternoon. Peter Hodding was still out to lunch. This was the twentieth day of January. His daughter would be dead three weeks tomorrow. They were wondering if he'd killed her.

They were sitting on a chrome and leather sofa in the waiting room when he came in. He was wearing a raccoon fur coat. Cheeks ruddy from the cold outside, straight brown hair windblown, he looked the way Chastity Kerr had described him looking after his early morning walk on New Year's Eve. He seemed happy to see them. Asked them at once if there was any news. Led them to his private office in the agency's recesses.

Two walls painted yellow, a third painted a sort of lavender, the last banked with windows that looked out over a city hushed by snow. Photocopies of print ads tacked to the walls with pushpins. A storyboard for a television commercial. A desk with an old-fashioned electric typewriter on it. Sheet of paper in the roller. Hodding sat behind the desk. He offered the detectives chairs. They sat.

"Mr. Hodding," Carella said, "did you at any time on New Year's Eve leave the party at the apartment of Mr. and Mrs. Jeremy Kerr?"

Hodding blinked.

The blink told them they had him.

"Yes," he said.

"At what time?" Meyer asked.

Another blink.

"We left at a little after two."

"To go home. You and your wife."

"Yes."

"How about before then?"

Another blink.

"Well, yes," he said.

"You left the Kerr apartment before then?"

"Yes."

"At what time."

"Around one o'clock."

"Alone?"

"Yes."

"Where'd you go?" Carella asked.

"For a walk. I was drunk. I needed some air."

"Where'd you walk?"

"In the park."

"Which direction?"

"I don't know what you mean. Anyway, what's . . . ?"

"Uptown, downtown, crosstown? Which way did you walk?"

"Downtown. Excuse me, but what . . . ?"

"How far downtown did you walk?"

"To the statue and back."

"Which statue?"

"The Alan Clive statue. The statue there."

"At the circle?"

"Yes. Why?"

"Are you sure you didn't walk *uptown?*" Carella said.

Hodding blinked again.

"Are you sure you didn't walk uptown on Grover Avenue?" Meyer said.

"Four blocks uptown?" Carella said.

"To your apartment?"

"Getting there at ten after one, a quarter after one?"

"And staying there for a half-hour or so?"

There was a long painful silence.

"Okay," Hodding said.

"Mr. Hodding, did you commit those murders?" Carella asked.

"No, sir, I did not," Hodding said.

The affair with Annie Flynn . . .

He couldn't even properly call it an affair because their love wasn't fashioned in the classic adulterers' mold, it was more like . . .

He didn't know what to call it.

"How about cradle-snatching?" Carella suggested.

"How about seducing a girl half your age?" Meyer suggested.

They didn't particularly like this man.

To them, he was a cut above Fats Donner—who dug Mary Jane shoes and white cotton panties.

He wanted them to know that he'd never done anything like this before in his life. He'd been married to Gayle for the past five years now, he'd never once even *looked* at another woman until Annie began sitting for them. Annie was the only woman he'd ever . . .

"A *girl,*" Carella reminded him.

"A sixteen-year-old *girl,*" Meyer said.

Well, there were girls who became women at a very early age, listen she wasn't a virgin, this wasn't what you'd call seduction of the innocent or anything, this was—

"Yes, what was it?" Carella asked.

"Exactly what would you call it?" Meyer asked.

"I loved her," Hodding said.

Love.

One of the only two reasons for murder.

The other being money.

It had started one night early in October. She'd begun sitting for them in September, shortly after they'd adopted the baby, he remembered being utterly surprised by Annie's maturity. You expected a teenage girl to be somehow bursting with raucous energy, but Annie . . .

Those thoughtful green eyes.

The subtlety of her glances.

Secrets unspoken in those eyes.

The fiery red hair.

He'd wondered if she was red below.

"Look," Meyer said, "if you don't fucking mind . . ."

Meyer rarely used profanity.

"I didn't kill her," Hodding said. "I'm trying to explain . . ."

"Just tell us what . . . ."

"Let him do it his own way," Carella said gently.

"The son of a bitch was fucking a sixteen-year . . ."

"Come on," Carella said, and put his hand on Meyer's arm. "Come on, okay?"

"I loved her," Hodding said again.

In October, the beginning of October, she'd sat for them while he and his wife attended an awards dinner downtown at the Sherman. He remembered that it was a particularly mild night for October, the temperature somewhere in the seventies that day, more like late spring than early fall. Annie came to the apartment dressed in the colors of autumn, a rust-colored skirt, and a pale orange cotton shirt, a yellow ribbon in her hair, like the song. She had walked the seven blocks from her own apartment, schoolbooks cradled in her arms against abundant breasts, smiling, and bursting with energy and youth and . . .

Sexuality.

Yes.

"I'm sorry, Detective Meyer, but you have to understand . . ."

"Just get the fuck on with it," Meyer said.

. . . there was an enormous sexuality about Annie. A sensuousness. The smoldering green eyes, the somewhat petulant full-lipped mouth, the volcanic red hair, lava erupting, hot, overflowing. The short green skirt revealing long, lovely legs and slender ankles, French-heeled shoes, the short heels exaggerating the curve of the leg and the thrust of her buttocks and breasts, naked beneath the thin cotton shirt, nipples puckering though it was not cold outside.

They did not get home until almost three in the morning.

Late night. The dinner had been endless, they'd gone for drinks with friends after all the prizes were awarded—Hodding had taken one home for the inventive copywriting he'd done on his agency's campaign for a cookie company, he'd shown the plaque to Annie, she'd ooohed and ahhhed in girlish delight.

Three in the morning.

You sent a young girl out into the streets alone at three in the morning, you were asking for trouble. This city, maybe any city. Gayle suggested that her husband call down, ask Al the Doorman to get a taxi for Annie. Hodding said, No, I'll walk her home, I can use some air.

Such a glorious night.

A mild breeze blowing in off Grover Park, he suggested that perhaps they ought to take the park path home.

She said Oh, gee, Mr. Hodding, do you think that'll be safe?

Innuendo in her voice, in her eyes.

She knew it would not be safe.

She knew what he would do to her in that park.

She told him later that she'd been wanting him to do it to her from the minute she'd laid eyes on him.

But he didn't know that at the time.

Didn't know she wanted him as much as he wanted her.

It was only seven blocks from his apartment to where she lived with her parents. Well, seven and a half, because she lived in the middle of the block, off the avenue. He had seven and a half blocks to do whatever it was he planned to do . . .

He didn't have any plan.

. . . whatever it was he longed to do . . .

He yearned for her with every fiber in his being.

She began talking about her boyfriend. A kid named Scott Handler. Went to school up in Maine someplace. The asshole of creation, she said. She looked at him. Smiled. Green eyes flashing. Had she deliberately used this mild profanity? To tell him what? I'm a big girl now?

She said she'd been going with Handler since she was fifteen . . .

Rolling her eyes heavenward.

He guessed that at her age, dating someone for a year and more was an eternity.

. . . but that she was really beginning to feel tied down, you know? Scott all the way up there, and her down here, you know? They were supposed to be going *steady*, but what did that mean? How could you go *steady* with someone who was all the way up near the Canadian border? In fact, how could you *go* with him at *all*?

In the park now.

Leaves underfoot.

The rustle of leaves.

French-heeled shoes whispering through the leaves.

He was dying to slide his hands up her legs, under that rust-colored skirt. Open that cotton blouse, find those breasts with their erect nipples, teenage nipples.

You know, she said, a girl misses certain things.

His heart stopped.

He dared not ask her what things she missed.

Kissing, she said.

Scuffing through the leaves.

Touching, she said.

He held his breath.

Making love, she whispered.

And stopped on the path.

And turned to him.

And lifted her face to his.

That was the first time.

He had been with her a total of fourteen times since that October night, the fifteenth of October, the night he'd accepted the industry's coveted award, the night he'd been gifted, too, with this girl, this woman, this unbelievably passionate creature he'd coveted since September. Fourteen times. Including their hurried coupling on New Year's Eve.

His eyes brimmed with tears.

For Christmas he'd given her a small lapis pendant on a gold—

"You saw it," he said. "It was on the floor. Beside her. The chain must have broken when . . . when . . . do you remember it? A small teardrop-shaped piece of lapis with a gold loop holding it to the chain? I bought it in an antiques shop on Lamont. She loved it. She wore it all the time. I gave it to her for our first Christmas together. I loved her so much."

She had broken off with Handler by then.

Told him she no longer wished to see him. This was when he came down for the Thanksgiving holiday. Told him it was over and done with. Said she wanted nothing further to do with him. He accused her of having found a new boyfriend. Told her he'd kill them both.

Hodding was in bed with her when she reported this to him.

A room he'd rented in a hotel near the Stem.

Hookers running through the hallway outside.

They both laughed at Handler's boyish threat.

On New Year's Eve . . .

He covered his face with his hands.

Wept into his hands.

Meyer felt no sympathy.

Neither did Carella.

On New Year's Eve . . .

14

THE ASSISTANT DISTRICT ATTORNEY was a woman named Nellie Brand, thirty-two years old and smart as hell. Sand-colored hair cut in a breezy flying wedge, blue eyes intently alert. Wearing a brown tweed suit, a tan turtleneck sweater, and brown pumps with sensible high heels, she sat on the edge of the long table in the Interrogation Room, legs crossed, a pastrami sandwich in her right hand. A little cardboard dish of soggy French fries was on the table beside her, together with a cardboard container of Coca-Cola.

"Willing to risk a quickie, huh?" she said, and bit into the sandwich.

She was married, Carella noticed. Gold wedding band on the ring finger of her left hand. He was drinking coffee and eating a tuna and tomato on toast.

"According to what he told us," Meyer said, "he simply *had* to see her." He was still angry. Seething inside. Voice edged with sarcasm. Carella had never seen him this way. Nor was he eating anything. He was trying to lose seven pounds. This probably made him even angrier.

"Ah, *l'amour*," Nellie said and rolled her blue eyes.

In some countries, women wore the wedding band on the right hand. Carella had read that someplace. Austria? Maybe Germany. Or maybe both. Nellie Brand was a married woman who, Carella suspected, might not appreciate a married man her age playing around with a sixteen-year-old kid. He further suspected she might have preferred dining with her husband to eating deli with two weary detectives who'd spent most of the afternoon and evening with a man who may have killed his own baby daughter and the sixteen-year-old who'd been sitting with her. But here she was at eight o'clock on a cold and icy Friday night, trying to determine whether they had anything that would stick here should they decide to charge him. They would have to charge him soon or let him go. Those were the rules, Harold. Miranda-Escobedo. You played it by the rules or you didn't play at all.

"Got there at?" Nellie said.

"Quarter past one at the outside," Carella said.

"Doorman told you this?"

"Yes."

"Reliable?"

"Seems so."

"And left when?"

"Quarter to two."

"Half-hour even," Nellie said.

"*Had* to see her," Meyer said. Steaming. About to erupt. Thinking about his own daughter, Carella figured.

"How long did he say this'd been going on?"

"Since October."

"When?"

"The fifteenth," Carella said.

"Birth date of great men," Nellie said, but did not amplify. "Told you all this, huh?"

"Yeah. Which troubles *us,* too. The fact that he . . ."

"Sure, why would he?"

"Unless he's figuring . . ."

"Yeah, there's that."

"You know, the . . ."

"Sure, show 'em the death and they'll accept the fever," Nellie said.

"Exactly. If he thinks he's looking at murder, he'll settle for adultery."

"He gives us the old Boy-Meets-Girl . . ."

"Pulls a Jimmy Swaggart . . ."

"Tearfully begs forgiveness . . ."

"And walks off into the sunset."

Nellie washed down a fry with a swallow of Coke. "He knew what the autopsy report said, is that right?"

"About sperm in the . . . ?"

"Yeah."

"Yes, he was informed earlier."

"So he knew one of the possibilities was rape-murder."

"Yes."

"And now you've got him up here, and you're asking questions about New Year's Eve . . ."

"Oh, sure, he's no dummy. He had to figure we were thinking he was our man."

"Which you're *still* thinking," Nellie said.

"Otherwise we wouldn't have invited you here for dinner," Carella said, and smiled.

"Yes, thank you, it's delicious," Nellie said, and bit into the sandwich again. "So let me hear your case," she said. "You can skip means and opportunity, I know he had both. Let me hear motive."

"We'd have to wing it," Carella said.

"I've got all night," Nellie said.

Carella repeated essentially what Hodding had told them in this very room not an hour earlier.

If it had not been so cold on New Year's Eve, he would have planned to walk Annie home, the way he'd done that first time in October and several times since. Make love to her in the park. Annie standing under a tree with her skirt up around her hips and her panties down around her ankles, Hodding nailing her to the tree. His words. But it was so damn *cold* that night. He and his wife had virtually frozen to death just waiting for a taxi to take them over to the Kerr apartment, and Hodding knew that lovemaking in the park was out of the question, however strong his desire. He had it in his head that he and Annie had to usher in the new year by making love. An affirmation—

"Really gone over this kid, huh?" Nellie asked.

"Totally," Meyer said.

—an affirmation of their bond. To seal their relationship. Fuck her senseless at the start of the new year. His words again. And the more he drank—

"Was he really drunk? Or do you think that was an act? To get out of the place."

"I think he was really drunk," Carella said.

"Probably sobered up on the way over to the apartment," Meyer said.

"Doorman says he was sober."

"So you have him sober at the scene of the crime."

"Yes."

"Okay, go ahead."

The more he drank, the more the idea became an obsession with him. He had to get to his apartment, had to make love to Annie. When he talked to her on the phone at twelve-thirty, he whispered what he wanted to do . . .

"Did he tell you this?"

"Yes."

"That he whispered to her?"

"Yes."

"Said what?"

"Said, 'I want to fuck you.' "

"The son of a bitch," Meyer said.

"Uh-huh," Nellie said. "And she said?"

"She said, 'Good. Come on over.' "

"Precocious."

"Very."

"He told you all this?"

"We have it on tape."

"What was his response?"

"He said, 'In a little while.' "

"You've got all this on tape?"

"All of it. We've also got his hostess overhearing him. Chastity Kerr. We've got a statement from her."

"The exact words he gave you."

"Yes. Telling Annie, 'In a little while.' "

"Okay. Go ahead."

At one o'clock he leaves the Kerr party, ostensibly to clear his head. By the time he gets to his own building, four blocks uptown, he's cold sober. He goes upstairs, finds Annie waiting for him with nothing on under her skirt. They make passionate love on the living room couch, he goes in to kiss his baby daughter on her rosebud cheek, and then he leaves. The doorman clocks him coming out of the elevator at a quarter to two.

"Wham, bang, thank you, ma'am," Nellie said.

"That's how *his* story goes," Meyer said.

"And your version?"

"I think the strain of the relationship was beginning to tell on him," Meyer said. "The very fact that on New Year's *Eve,* he would risk running back to his apartment for a quick assignation . . ."

"Well, you yourself said he was totally gone on her."

"Exactly my point. And getting in deeper and deeper. On Christmas, for example, he . . ."

"No puns, please," Nellie said, and smiled.

Carella returned the smile. Meyer did not.

"On Christmas, he gave her a gift. Our first *Christmas* together," Meyer said, bitterly repeating Hodding's words. "And he caused her to break up with a decent . . ."

"What kind of a gift?" Nellie asked.

"Lapis pendant on a gold chain."

"Expensive?"

"I would guess moderately expensive."

"Well, there's cheap lapis, too," Nellie said.

"He bought this on Lamont."

"Okay, expensive," Nellie said.

"What I'm saying, this was a man out of control . . ."

"Uh-huh."

"Falling in love with a teenager to begin with . . ."

"Uh-huh."

"Getting in way over his head, buying her expensive gifts, making love to her in the *park,* for Christ's sake, meeting her in cheap hotels off the Stem, hookers parading the halls, taking risks no man in his right . . ."

"Detective Meyer, excuse me," Nellie said. "Why'd he kill her?"

"Because he couldn't see any other way out."

"Where'd you get that?"

"From everything he said."

"He told you he was in over his head?"

"No, but . . ."

"Told you he couldn't handle this?"

"Well . . ."

"Couldn't see any other way out?"

"Not in those exact words."

"What words then?"

"Mrs. Brand, excuse *me,*" Meyer said. "He was in that apartment making love to this girl between one-fifteen and a quarter to two. When he got home with his wife, forty-five minutes later, the girl is dead. Stabbed. Are we supposed to believe someone *else* got into that apartment during those forty-five minutes? Isn't it more reasonable to assume that Hodding either figured this was a good time to end his goddamn *problems* with this girl, or else he . . ."

"What problems? How did he indicate to you in any way that he considered this relationship a problem?"

"He said he *had* to see her, had to . . ."

"I don't see that as a problem. In fact, he was seeing her regularly. Seeing her was not a problem, Detective Meyer."

"Okay, then let's say they *argued* about something, okay? Let's say they made love and she told him she didn't want to see him anymore. She'd bounced her boyfriend in November, why couldn't she now do the same thing with Hodding? Over and done with, goodbye. Only he wasn't having any of it. Not after all the deception of the past few months. So he flies off the deep end, goes out to the kitchen for a knife—he knows where they are, he lives in this . . ."

"I've granted you means," Nellie said.

"And comes back and stabs her," Meyer said.

"Uh-huh," Nellie said.

"He was in that apartment for a half-hour," Meyer said.

"Okay, let's say all this happened," Nellie said. "They made love and she told him thanks, it was nice, but that's the last dance, goodbye and good luck, and he stormed out into the kitchen and grabbed the knife and did her in. Okay? Is that your scenario?"

"Yes," Meyer said.

"Let's say all of that—which you can't prove, by the way—is true. Then answer me one other question."

"Sure."

"Why'd he *then* kill his own daughter?"

And to that, there was no answer.

Henry Tsu did not enjoy being bad-mouthed.

As far as he was concerned, he was a trustworthy businessman and he did not like people spreading rumors about him. That his business happened to be illegal had nothing to do with whether or not he conducted it like a gentleman. True, Henry had been forced on occasion to break a few collarbones and heads, but even when force had been called for, the business community understood that such action had been an absolute necessity. Henry had a good reputation. He hated to see it going down the toilet because of a little spic cocksucker.

José Domingo Herrera, who years ago used to do some work for the Chang people when they had what was called the Yellow Paper Gang in Chinatown. Henry had heard that Herrera was very good at what he did. What he did was a secret between himself and Chang Tie Fei, otherwise known as Walter Chang here in this city. Then again, Henry's full and honorable name was Tsu Hong Chin. How he had got to be Henry was a mystery even to himself. Perhaps it was because he looked very much like Henry Fonda when he was young. With Chinese eyes.

Putting together the pieces, Henry figured that Herrera had served as a liaison between the Chang people and certain Colombian interests eager to establish a foothold here in the city. The Colombians were sick to death of having to deal with the wops in Miami, who thought they owned the whole fucking world. They didn't want to start dealing with them all over again up here so they went to the Chinese instead. The Chinese needed somebody who could understand these people who looked and sounded either like sombreroed and raggedy-assed bandidos in a Mexican movie or else pinky-ringed and pointy-lapeled gangsters in a movie about Prohibition days. So they landed on Herrera as a go-between.

Was what Henry figured.

Little José Domingo Herrera, building himself a rep with the Chinese and the Colombians as well.

How Herrera had got involved with a *Jamaican* posse was another thing.

Which was why Henry on this bleak Saturday morning, the twenty-first day of January, was talking to a man named Juan Kai Hsao, whose mother was Spanish—*really* Spanish, from Spain—and whose father was from Taiwan. The two men were speaking in English because Henry had no Spanish at all and Juan's Chinese was extremely half-assed, his father having come to this country at the age of two.

"Let me tell you what I suspect," Henry said.

"Yes," Juan said. "Please."

He had exquisite manners. Henry figured the manners were from his Chinese side.

"I believe Herrera is spreading this rumor in order to serve his own needs. Whatever they may be."

"This rumor that around Christmastime . . ."

"The twenty-seventh."

"Yes. That on the twenty-seventh, your people intercepted a shipment earmarked for the Hamilton . . ."

"Not the shipment. The money intended to *pay* for the shipment."

"Coming from where, this shipment?"

"How do I know?"

"You said . . ."

"I said that's the *rumor*. That I *knew* about this shipment. Knew where it would be delivered, and intercepted the money for it."

"Stole it."

"Yes, of *course,* stole it."

"From the Hamilton posse."

"Yes."

"Was this supposed to be a big shipment? In the rumor?"

"In the rumor, it was supposed to be three kilos."

"Of cocaine."

"Of cocaine, yes."

"But you don't know from where?"

"No. That's not important, from where. It could be Miami, it could be Canada, it could be the West—up through Mexico, you know—it could even be from Europe through the airport in a suitcase. Three kilos is a tiny amount. Why would I even *bother* with such a small amount? Three kilos isn't even seven fucking pounds. You can buy a Thanksgiving turkey that weighs more than that."

"But which doesn't cost as much," Juan said, and both men laughed.

"Fifty thousand," Henry said. "In the rumor."

"That you are supposed to have stolen."

"Not the cocaine."

"No, the money."

"Yes."

"From Herrera."

"Yes, this little . . ."

Henry almost said "spic," but then he remembered that his guest was half-Spanish.

"This little person Herrera, who by the way used to do work for the Chang people. When they had the Yellow Paper Gang. This was before your time."

"I've read a lot about Walter Chang," Juan said.

He was only twenty-four years old and still making a rep. He figured it didn't hurt to say he'd read a lot about every famous gangster this city had ever had. Make everyone think he had gone out of his way to learn such things. Actually, though, he did know about the Yellow Paper Gang because his father had once leaned on some people for them. Juan's father was six feet three inches tall and weighed two hundred and forty pounds, which was very large for a Chinese. Everybody joked that there must have been a eunuch in his ancestry someplace. Juan's father found this comical. That was because he had a keen reputation as a ladies' man.

"So as I understand this," Juan said, wanting to get the entire story straight before he went out of here on a wild pony, "you'd like to know what *really* went down on the night of December twenty-seventh."

"Yes. And why Herrera is saying we cold-cocked him."

"And stole the fifty."

"Yes. The story on the street is that Herrera went to take delivery of this lousy three keys . . ."

"Where? Do you know where?"

"Yes, in Riverhead. Where isn't important. Herrera is saying he *went* there with fifty dollars of Hamilton's money, to make the buy and take delivery, and as he was going in the building he was jumped by two Chinese men he later . . ."

"Your people? In the rumor?"

"Yes," Henry said. "I was about to say that he later identified them—this is all in the rumor that's going around—as two people who work for me."

"And none of this is true."

"None of it."

"And you think it's Herrera who's spreading the rumor?"

"Who else would be spreading it?"

"If it's someone else, you want to know that, too."

"Yes. And *why?* There has to be a reason for such bullshit."

"I'll find out," Juan promised.

But he wasn't sure he could.

It all sounded so fucking *Chinese*.

The way Hamilton had found out was through a person he'd done a favor for in Miami three years ago. The favor happened to have been killing the man's cousin. The man was a Cuban heavily involved in dealing dope. His name was Carlos Felipe Ortega. You kill a man's cousin for him, without charging him anything for it, the man might be grateful later on, if he could find an opportunity. Or so Hamilton thought at first.

The information was that the Tsu gang up here was going to take delivery on a million-dollar shipment of coke.

A hundred keys.

On the twenty-third of January.

The reason Ortega was calling—this was two weeks before Christmas—was that he'd found out the Miami people were insisting on a very low profile. They had gone along with Tsu's bullshit about testing and tasting five keys of the stuff in one place and taking delivery of the rest someplace else, but they didn't want a big fucking Sino-Colombian mob scene up there. In the first instance, they were insisting that one

guy from the Chinese side meet one guy from their side, fifty grand
here, five keys there. You test, you pay, you take the high road, we take
the low, it was nice seeing you. If the stuff tested pure, you sent two
other guys to pay for and pick up the rest of the shit. No *more* than two
guys. No crowds from the Forbidden City. Two guys who'd come and
go in the night, thank you very much, and so long. Tsu had agreed to
the terms. Which meant, Ortega said, that instead of a thousand guys
standing around with automatic weapons in their hands and threatening looks on their faces, you had a one-on-one in the first instance, and
only two people from each side when the later exchange took place.

"Which sounds very thin to me," Ortega had said.

"Very," Hamilton said.

"Unless, of course, there are no thieves in your city."

Both men chuckled.

"Do you want to know where all this is going to take place, Lewis?"
Ortega asked.

"That might be nice to know," Hamilton said.

"But no messing with the Miami people, please," Ortega said. "I live
here."

"I understand."

"Whatever you decide to do is between you and the Chinese."

"Yes, I understand."

"And if a little happens to fall my way . . ."

Ortega's voice shrugged.

"How much do you think should fall your way, Carlos?" Hamilton
asked, thinking You cheap bastard, I *killed* somebody for you. As a
fucking *gift*.

"I thought ten percent," Ortega said. "For the address of where the
big buy is going down."

"You have a deal," Hamilton said.

"Ten keys, correct?"

"No, that's more than ten percent."

"No, it's ten percent of a hundred keys."

"You told me five keys would be someplace else."

"I know. But ten keys is the price, Lewis."

"All right."

"Do we have a deal?"

"I said all right."

"You deliver."

"No. You pick up."

"Certainly," Ortega said.

"The address," Hamilton said.

Ortega gave it to him.

This was back in December.

Two weeks before Christmas. The tenth, the eleventh, somewhere in there.

Ortega had told him that the shipment would be arriving in Florida on the twenty-first of January. In Florida, there had to be at least eight zillion canals with private boats on them. A lot of those boats were Cigarette types—high-powered speedboats like an Excalibur or a Donzi or a Wellcraft Scarab that could outrun almost any Coast Guard vessel on the water. Zipped out to where the ship was waiting beyond the three-mile limit, zipped back in to their own little dock behind their own little house. Did it in broad daylight. Safer in the daytime than at night, when the Coast Guard might hail you and stop you. During the daytime, you were just some pleasure-seeking boaters out on the water to get some sun. Out there on the briny, you sometimes wouldn't see another vessel for miles and miles. Your ship'd be standing still out there, you lay to in her shadow, you could load seven *tons* of cocaine, there'd be nobody to see you or to challenge you. Coast Guard? Come suck my toe, man. What you needed to stop dope coming into Florida on *either* of its coasts was a fleet of ten thousand U.S. Navy destroyers and even *then* they might not be able to do the job.

The shipment would be coming up north by automobile.

No borders to cross, no Coast Guard vessels to worry about.

You drove straight up on interstate highways with the shit in the trunk of your car. You obeyed the speed limit. You drove with a woman beside you on the front seat. A pair of married tourists on vacation. *White* people, both of them, pure Wonder Bread. No blacks, no Hispanics. Nothing to raise even the slightest eyebrow of suspicion. You later met these people at a prearranged place in the city, usually one of the apartments you rented on a yearly lease for the specific purpose of using it as a drop, you paid them the money, you walked off with the shit.

This big shipment coming up was the reason Hamilton had hired Herrera.

What Herrera hadn't known, of course—

Well, maybe he *had* known, considering it in retrospect.

"I *still* don't know why you trusted that fucking spic with fifty dollars," Isaac said.

This was language the gangs had picked up from fiction.

It was funny the way life often imitated art.

None of the gangs in this city had ever read a book and they would never have heard of Richard Condon's *Prizzi's Honor* if there hadn't been a movie made from it. They liked that picture. It showed killers in a comical light. It also introduced real-life gangs to something Richard Condon had made up, the way his hoodlums talked about money in terms of singles instead of thousands. If Condon's crooks wanted to say five *thousand* dollars, they said *five* dollars. It was very comical. It was also an extension of real-life criminal parlance where, for example, a five-dollar bag of heroin became a nickel bag. That was when heroin was still the drug of choice, later conceding the title to cocaine and then crack, admittedly a cocaine derivative. A five-dollar vial was now a nickel vial. And when a thief said fifty dollars, he meant fifty *thousand* dollars. Which was the sum of money Lewis Randolph Hamilton had entrusted to José Domingo Herrera on the twenty-seventh day of December last year.

"Why?" Isaac asked now.

He knew he was risking trouble.

Hamilton was angry this morning.

Angry that Herrera had run off with fifty dollars belonging to him. Angry that Andrew Fields, who'd been sent out once *again* to dispatch the little spic, had been unable to find him anywhere in the city. Angry that he himself, Lewis Randolph Hamilton, had bungled the execution of the blond cop. Angry that the cop had taken a good look at him. All of these things were like a cluster of boils on Hamilton's ass. Isaac should have known better than to ask about Herrera at a time like this. But Isaac was still somewhat pissed himself over the way a week, ten days ago Hamilton had appropriated both of those German hookers for himself.

In many ways, Isaac and Hamilton were like man and wife. They each knew which buttons to push to get the proper response from the other. They each knew what the kill words were. Unlike most married couples, however, they did not fight fair. A marriage was doomed when either partner decided he or she would no longer fight fair. Hamilton had never fought fair in his life. Neither had Isaac. They weren't about to start now. But this was not threatening to their relationship. In fact, they each respected this about the other. They were killers. Killers did not fight fair.

"Not of the blood," Isaac said, shaking his head in exaggerated incredulity. "To have chosen someone not of the blood . . ."

"There's Spanish in you, too," Hamilton said.

"East Indian maybe, but not Spanish."

"A Spanish whore," Hamilton said.

"Chinese maybe," Isaac said, "but not Spanish."

"From the old days," Hamilton said. "From when Christopher Columbus was still there."

"That far back, huh, man?" Isaac said.

"Before the British took over."

"Oh my, a Spanish whore," Isaac said. He was letting all this roll off his back. This wasn't dirty fighting, it wasn't even fighting. Hamilton was just feinting, seeing could he get a rise without exerting too much effort. Isaac was the one with the power to punch below the belt today. Isaac was the one who insisted on knowing why Hamilton had handed fifty big ones to a spic.

"I thought you knew the Spanish were not to be trusted," Isaac said.

Of course, Hamilton might just tell him to fuck off.

"A race that writes on walls," Isaac said.

"You are not making sense, man," Hamilton said.

"It's a cultural thing," Isaac said. "Writing on walls. They also stare at women. It's all cultural. Go look it up."

"Come look up my asshole," Hamilton said.

"I might find a dozen roses up there," Isaac said.

Both men laughed.

"With a card," Isaac said.

Both men laughed again.

This was a homosexual joke. Neither of the men was homosexual, but they often made homosexual jokes, exchanged homosexual banter. This was common among heterosexual men, Harold. It happened all the time.

"To have trusted a *spic*," Isaac said, shaking his head again. "Whose credentials you never thought to . . ."

"He was checked," Hamilton said.

"Not by me."

"He was *checked*," Hamilton said again, hitting the word harder this time.

"If so, he was . . ."

"Thoroughly," Hamilton said.

And glared at Isaac.

Isaac didn't flinch.

"If *I* had checked the man . . ." he said.

"*You* were in Baltimore," Hamilton said.

"It could have waited till I got back."

"Visiting your *Mama,*" Hamilton said.

"There was no urgency . . ."

"Running home to Mama for Christmas."

He was getting to Isaac now. Isaac did not like to think of himself as a Mama's Boy. But he was always running down to see his mother in Baltimore.

"Running home to eat Mama's *plum* pudding," Hamilton said.

Somehow he made this sound obscenely malicious.

"While *you,*" Isaac said, "are having a spic checked by . . . who checked him, anyway?"

"James."

"James!" Isaac said.

"Yes, James. And he ran the check in a very pro . . ."

"You picked *James* to do this job? James who later used *baseball* bats on this very same . . ."

"I didn't know at the time that James would later fuck up," Hamilton said frostily. "*You* were in Baltimore. Someone had to do the job. I asked James to check on him. He came back with credentials that sounded okay."

"Like?"

"Like no current affiliations. A free-lancer. No police record. A courier once, long ago, for the Chang people. I figured . . ."

"Chinks are not to be trusted, either," Isaac said.

"*No* one is to be trusted," Hamilton said flatly. "You didn't know what the situation was, you were in *Baltimore.* I had to operate on my instincts."

"That's right, I didn't know what the situation was."

"That's right."

"And I *still* don't."

"That's right, too."

"All I know is Herrera stole the fifty."

"Yes, that's all you know."

"Do you want to tell me the rest?"

"No," Hamilton said.

The Ba twins had been Hamilton's idea, too.

They were named Ba Zheng Shen and Ba Zhai Kong, but people outside the Chinese community called them Zing and Zang. They were both twenty-seven years old, Zing being the oldest by five minutes. They were also extraordinarily and identically handsome. It was rumored that Zing had once lived with a gorgeous redheaded American girl for six months without her realizing that he and his brother were taking turns fucking her.

Zing and Zang knew that if the Chinese ever took over the world—which they did not doubt for a moment would happen one day—it would not be because Communism was a better form of government than democracy; it would be because the Chinese were such good businessmen. Zing and Zang were young and energetic and extremely ambitious. It was said in Chinatown that if the price was right, they would kill their own mother. And steal her gold fillings afterward. The very first time the Ba twins had killed anyone was in Hong Kong five years back when they were but mere twenty-two-year-olds. The price back then had been a thousand dollars American for each of them.

Nowadays, their fee was somewhat higher.

Back in December, for example, when Lewis Randolph Hamilton first contacted them regarding a courier named José Domingo Herrera, he'd offered them a flat three thousand dollars for messing up the little Puerto Rican and retrieving the fifty thousand dollars he would be carrying. Zing and Zang looked Hamilton straight in the eye—they were more inscrutable-looking than most Chinese, perhaps because they carried their extraordinary good looks with a defiant, almost challenging air—and said the price these days for moving someone around was four thousand for *each* of them, a total of eight thousand for the job, take it or leave it. Hamilton said he wasn't looking for God's sake, mon, to *dust* the little spic, he only wanted him *rearranged* a trifle. Eight thousand total, the Ba boys said, take it or leave it. Hamilton rolled his eyes and sighed heavily. But he took it.

Which made them wonder.

What they were wondering was the same thing Herrera had wondered when he'd been hired by Hamilton to carry the fifty K: Why is this man not using one of his own people to do this job? Why is he paying us eight thousand dollars for something his own goon squad can handle?

They also wondered how they could turn this peculiar situation to their own advantage.

The first way they figured they could pick up a little extra change was to contact the intended victim, this José Domingo Herrera character, and tell him they were supposed to move him around a little on the twenty-seventh of December, which was two days after Christmas.

"New Year you be on clutches," Zing said.

They both spoke English like Chinese cooks in a Gold Rush movie. This did not make them any less dangerous than they were. Pit vipers do not speak English very well, either.

Herrera, who was already wondering why Hamilton had hired him as a courier, now began wondering why these two fucking illiterate Chinks were telling him about the plan to cold-cock him. He figured they were looking for money *not* to beat him up. Play both ends against the middle. Which meant that the possibility existed he would lay some cash on them and they would beat him up, anyway. Life was so difficult in this city.

Herrera listened while they told him they wanted eight thousand dollars to forget their little rendezvous two weeks from now. Herrera figured this was what Hamilton was paying them to ambush him and take back his money. He'd been planning to steal the fifty he was delivering for Hamilton. Vanish in the night. Fuck the goddamn Jakie. But now these Chinks presented a problem. If they beat him up, they would take the fifty and return it to Hamilton. Leaving Herrera cold and broke in the gutter. On the other hand, if he paid them the eight . . .

"We have a deal," he said, and they all shook hands.

He trusted their handshakes as much as he trusted their slanty eyes.

But, oddly, Herrera started wondering in Spanish the same things the Ba brothers began wondering in Chinese.

Out loud and in English, Herrera said, "Why is he setting me up?"

Out loud, and in his own brand of English, Zang said, "Why use-ah two *Chinee?*"

They pondered this together.

It was obvious to all of them that Herrera was indeed being set up. At least to take a beating. And even though he had to admit that ten thousand dollars was a good price for getting roughed up—in this city, prizefighters had taken dives for less—he still wondered why. And why did the two men beating him up have to be Chinese?

Because . . .

Well . . .

They all looked at each other.

And then Herrera said, "Because something *Chinese* has to be coming down!"

"Ah, ah," Zing said.

Herrera was grateful he hadn't said, "Ah so."

"You want to go partners?" he asked.

The Ba brothers looked at him inscrutably. Fuckin' Chinks, he thought.

"You want to go in business together?"

"Ah, biz'liss, biz'liss," Zing said, grinning.

This they understood. Money. Fingers flying over the abacuses in their heads.

"Find out why he wants me hurt," Herrera said.

Everyone smiled.

Herrera figured the Ba brothers were smiling because maybe they'd stumbled on a way to become big players instead of handsome goons. Herrera was smiling because he was thinking he could maybe get out of this city not only alive but also rich.

Smiling, they shook hands all over again.

Eleven days later, the twins came back to him.

Frowning.

On Christmas Eve, no less.

No respect at all.

They were beginning to have misgivings about this new partnership. They had been to see Hamilton again, and he had paid them the agreed-upon fifty percent down payment for the job. But they were supposed to receive the remaining four thousand when they made delivery of the dope-cash Herrera would be carrying three nights from now.

"Now we no bling-ah cash, we no catchee monee!" Zang shouted.

"We lose-ah monee aw-relly!" Zing shouted.

"No, no," Herrera said patiently, "we can *make* money."

"Oh yeah how?" Zing asked.

The way he said it, it sounded like a Column B choice on a Chinese menu.

"If we can figure it out," Herrera said. "The deal."

The twins looked at him sourly and handsomely.

Fuckin' Chinks, Herrera thought.

"Did he say anything about *why?*" he asked patiently.

"He say we tell you Henny say hello."

A throw-away line.

"Henny?" Herrera asked.

"Henny Shoe."

Was what it sounded like.

He realized they were talking about Henry Tsu.

What they were saying was that when they beat him up on the twenty-seventh, they were supposed to give him Henry Tsu's regards, which would make it look as if two Chinks from Henry's big Chinatown gang had stolen Hamilton's money.

Ah so, he thought, and realized he was going native.

15

SUNDAY WAS NOT A DAY OF REST.

Not for the weary, anyway.

Jamie Bonnem of the Seattle P.D. was trying to sound patient and accommodating but he came over as merely irritated. He did not like getting called at home so early on a Sunday morning. Early for him, anyway. For Carella it was already ten o'clock. Besides, his case was still cold and Carella's call only reminded him of that bleak fact.

"Yes," he said brusquely, "we talked to the Gillette kid. We *also* talked to the other old boyfriend. Ain't that standard where you work?"

"It's standard here, yes," Carella said pleasantly. "How'd they check out?"

"We're still working Gillette."

"Meaning?"

"He's got no real alibi for where he was on the night of the murder."

"Where does he *say* he was?"

"Home reading. You know any twenty-year-old kid stays home *reading* at night? Eddie Gillette was home reading."

"Does he live alone?"

"With his parents."

"Where were they?"

"At the movies."

"Did you ask him where he was on New Year's Eve?"

"We asked *both* of them where they were on New Year's Eve. Because if this *is* tied to your kid kill . . ."

"It may be."

"The point ain't lost, Carella. We haven't been eliminating anyone just 'cause he was here in Seattle that night, but on the other hand, if somebody tells us he was roaming the Eastern seaboard . . ."

"What'd Gillette tell you?"

"He was right there on your turf."

"*Here?*" Carella said, and leaned in closer to the mouthpiece.

"Visiting his grandmother for the holidays."

"Did you follow up on that?"

"No, I went out to take a pee," Bonnem said. "You might want to check Grandma yourself, her name is Victoria Gillette, she lives in Bethtown, is there such a place as Bethtown?"

"There is such a place," Carella said.

"I talked to her on the phone, and she corroborated Gillette's story."

"Which was what?"

"That they went to the theater together on New Year's Eve."

"Gillette and Grandma?"

"Grandma is only sixty-two years old. And living with a dentist. The three of them went to see a revival of . . . what does this say? I can't even read my own notes."

Carella waited.

"Whatever," Bonnem said. "The dentist corroborates. The three of them went to see whatever the hell this is, Charlie's Something, and afterward they went out in the street with the crowd, and walked over to a hotel called the Elizabeth, is there such a hotel?"

"There is such a hotel," Carella said.

"To the Raleigh Room there, where Grandma and the dentist danced and Eddie tried to pick up a blonde in a red dress. All this according to Eddie and Grandma and the dentist, too, whose name is Arthur Rothstein. We do not have a name for the blonde in the red dress," Bonnem said drily, "because Gillette struck out."

"Where was he between one-forty-five and two-thirty?"

"Pitching the blonde."

"The dentist and Grandma . . ."

"Corroborate, correct."

"How about the other boyfriend?"

"Name's Harley Simpson, she dated him in her junior year, before she met Gillette. He has an alibi a mile long for the night she was killed. And he was here in Seattle on New Year's Eve."

"Mmm," Carella said.

"So that's it," Bonnem said.

"How's the old man taking this?"

"He doesn't even know she's dead. He's heavily sedated, on the way out himself."

"Is there anyone else in the family? Any other brothers or sisters?"

"No. Mrs. Chapman died twelve years ago. There were just the two sisters. And the husband, of course. Melissa's husband. You want my guess, they'll be out here settling a will before the week's out."

"He's that bad, huh?"

"Be a matter of days at most."

"How do you know there's a will?"

"Do you know any zillionaires who die intestate?"

"I don't know any zillionaires," Carella said.

"I know there's a will because I've been following an idea of mine out here. I'll tell you the truth, Carella, I don't think this is linked to your New Year's Eve case. I think what we have here are two separate and distinct cases. I guess you've been a cop long enough to know about coincidence . . ."

"Yes."

"Me, too. So while I ain't forgetting what happened there, I also have to treat this like a case in itself, you follow me? And I started thinking love or money, those are the only two reasons on God's green earth, and I started wondering if the old man has a will. Because you see, he was playing house with this younger woman before he got . . ."

"Oh?"

"Yeah, before he got sick. Her name's Sally Antoine, good-looking woman runs a beauty parlor downtown. Thirty-one years old to his seventy-eight. Makes you wonder, don't it?"

"It'd make *me* wonder," Carella said.

"About whether she's in the old man's will, right? If there *is* a will. So I started asking a few questions."

"What'd you find out?"

"Miss Antoine told me she has no idea whether she's in the old man's will. In fact, she said she saw no reason why she *should* be. But when I get an idea in my head, I ain't about to let go of it that easy. Because if the lady *is* in his will, and if the younger daughter found out about it somehow . . ."

"Uh-huh."

". . . then maybe she came out here to pressure the old man into *changing* the will while he could still sign his own name. Get the bimbo *out* of it. Though she isn't a bimbo, I can tell you that, Carella. She's a decent woman, divorced, two kids of her own, came up here from L.A., been working hard to make a go of it. I can hardly see her pumping two shots into Joyce Chapman."

"Did you take a look at the will?"

"You ought to become a cop," Bonnem said drily. "What I did, I couldn't ask the old *man* if there's a will because he's totally out of it. So I asked his attorney . . ."

"Who's that?"

"Young feller who took over when Melissa and her husband moved east. Hammond used to be the Chapman attorney, you know. Got the job shortly before Melissa married him, little bit of nepotism there, hmm? Met her when he got back from Vietnam, used to be in the army there, next thing you know he's the old man's lawyer."

"Did he draw the will for him?"

"Hammond? No. Neither did the *new* lawyer. Said he had no knowledge of it. Protecting his ass, I suppose. So I asked him who *might* have knowledge of it, and he suggested that I talk to this old geezer here in town, name's Geoffrey Lyons, used to be Chapman's attorney, retired just before the son-in-law took over. He told me he'd drawn a new will for Chapman twelve years ago, yes, right after Mrs. Chapman died, but a will's a privileged communication between attorney and client, and there was no way I could compel him to waive that privilege."

"Does he know you're investigating a murder?"

"Tough."

"Does Chapman have a copy of the will?"

"Yes."

"Where?"

"Where do you keep your will, Carella?"

"In a safe deposit box."

"Which is where Miss Ogilvy told me the old man keeps his. So I go for a court order to open the box, and the judge asks me if I know what's *in* this will, and I tell him 'No, that's why I want to open the box.' So he says 'Do the contents of this will provide probable cause for the crime of murder,' and I tell him that's what I'm trying to find out, and he says 'Petition denied.' "

"Who typed the will?" Carella asked.

"What do you mean? How the hell do I know who typed it?"

"You might try to find out."

"Why?"

"Legal typists have long memories."

The line went silent. Bonnem was thinking.

"Find the secretary or whoever," he said at last.

"Uh-huh," Carella said.

"Ask *her* does she remember what's in the will."

"It'd be a start."

"And if she says the will *does* name Sally Antoine . . ."

"Then you've got to go see Miss Antoine again."

"Won't that be fruit of the Poison Tree?"

"Once the old man dies, which you say is any day now . . ."

"Any day."

"Then the will goes to Probate and becomes a matter of public record. In the meantime, you're working a murder."

"Yeah. But you know, the Antoine woman was here in Seattle on New Year's Eve. So that would let out any connection with your case. Even if she *is* in the will."

"Let's see what the will says."

"The husband's back east, you know. Why don't you ask *him?*"

"Hammond? Ask him what?"

"What's in the will."

"How would he know?"

"Well, maybe he won't. But if *I'm* going to bust my ass looking for a person typed a will God knows how many years ago, the least you can do is pick up a telephone. Which, by the way, are you guys partners with AT&T?"

Carella smiled.

"Let me know how you make out," he said.

"I'll call collect," Bonnem said.

There had been times during the past month when Herrera wished his partners were Puerto Rican, but what could you do? The roll of the dice had tossed him two Chinks who, as agreed, had *not* given him either a beating *or* Henry Tsu's regards on the twenty-seventh day of December. Instead, on that day, Herrera had disappeared with the dope money, and Zing and Zang had gone back to Hamilton—seemingly shamefaced—to return his deposit. By the twenty-eighth of December, the year was running out through the narrow end of the funnel and Herrera was still sitting on the fifty K, hoping to turn it into a fortune overnight. He knew that the only way to do that was through dope. Any other way of turning money into more money was dumb. In America, there were no streets of gold anymore. Nowadays, the streets were heaped with cocaine. Coke was the new American dream. Herrera sometimes figured it was all a Communist plot. But who gave a shit?

On the twenty-eighth day of December, the Ba brothers came to report what they had learned.

At peril to their own lives, they said.

"Velly dange-ous," Zing said.

"Henny Shoe fine out, tssssst," Zang said, and ran his forefinger across his throat.

"You want to be wimps or winners?" Herrera asked.

The Ba brothers giggled.

Somehow, their laughter made them seem even more menacing.

Zing had done most of the talking. His English, such as it was, sounded a bit better than his younger brother's in that he never said ain't. Herrera listened intently. Partly because Zing was difficult to understand if you didn't listen intently and partly because the content of Zing's report was causing Herrera's hair to stand on end.

Zing was talking about a million-dollar dope deal.

"Millah dollah," he said.

A hundred kilos at ten thousand per. Discounted because Tsu was making a quantity buy.

"Hunnah kilo," Zing said.

The shipment was coming up from Miami by automobile.

On the twenty-third of January.

"Tessa-tay one play, pee up-ah ress not same," Zing said.

"What?" Herrera asked.

"Tessa-tay one play, pee up-ah ress not same," Zing repeated, exactly as he had said it the first time. He showed Herrera a slip of paper upon which several addresses were written in English in a spider-like hand. "Tessa-tay play," he said, indicating the first address.

"What?" Herrera asked.

"Tessa-tay."

"What the fuck does that mean?"

Through a series of pantomimes, Zing and his brother managed at last to transmit to Herrera the idea that the first address on the slip of paper was an apartment where the testing and tasting would take place . . .

"Fi' kilo," Zing said, and held up his right hand with the fingers and thumb spread.

"Five kilos," Herrera said.

"Yeh, yeh," Zing said, nodding.

"Will be tested and tasted at this place . . ."

"Yeh, tessa-tay play."

"And if it's okay, the rest'll be picked up at this second place."

"Yeh," Zing said, "pee up-ah ress not same," and grinned at his brother, letting him know the benefits of a second language.

"Where only *some* of the bags will be tested at random."

"Yeh, ony some."

"What if the first stuff tests bad?" Herrera asked.

Zing explained that the deal would be off and the Miami people and the Tsu people would go their separate ways with no hard feelings.

"No har feeyin," he said, and nodded.

"But if the girl is blue . . ."

"Yeh," Zing said, nodding.

"Then they hand over the five keys and Tsu's people hand over fifty thousand."

"Fiffee tousen, yeh."

"And then they go to this next address to do some random testing and pick up the rest of the shit."

"Yeh, ressa shit."

Herrera was thoughtful for several moments.

Then he said, "These Miami people? Are they Chinese?"

"No, no, Spanish," Ying said.

Which was what Herrera figured.

"I need to know how to get in touch with them," he said. "And I need to know any code words or passwords they've been using on the phone. Can you get that information for me?"

"Velly har," Zang said.

"Velly dange-ous," Zing said.

"You wanna make velly big money?" Herrera asked.

The Ba brothers giggled.

Herrera was thinking that if he could buy those five measly keys set aside for testing and tasting . . .

Buy those five shitty little keys with the money he'd stolen from Hamilton . . .

Why then he could turn the pure into fifty thousand bags of crack . . .

At twenty-five bucks a bag . . .

Jesus!

He was looking at a million and a quarter!

Which if he split with the Chinks as they'd agreed . . .

"Velly big money, you bet," Zing said, laughing.

"You bet," Herrera said and smiled at them like a crocodile.

Now—at twelve noon on the twenty-second day of January—Herrera made a long-distance call. Just dialing the 305 area code made him feel like a big shot. Spending all this money to make a telephone call. Then again, it was Hamilton's money he was spending.

The person who answered was a Colombian.

The two men spoke entirely in Spanish.

"Four-seven-one," Herrera said. The code numbers the resourceful Ba brothers had supplied. Chinese magicians.

"Eight-three-six," the man said.

The counter code.

Like spy shit.

"A change for tomorrow night," Herrera said.

"They're already on the way."

"But you can reach them."

"Yes."

"Then tell them."

"What change?"

"For the test. A new address."

"Why?"

"Heat."

"Give it to me."

"705 East Redmond. Apartment 34."

"Okay."

"Repeat it."

The man read it back.

"See you tomorrow," Herrera said.

The man said, "And?"

"And?" Herrera said, and realized in a flash that he'd almost forgotten the sign-off code. "Three-three-one," he said.

"*Bueno,*" the man said, and hung up.

The Cowboy's shop was closed on Sundays, and so he met Kling in a little tacos joint off Mason Avenue. At a quarter past one that afternoon, the place was packed with hookers who hadn't yet gone to sleep. Palacios and Kling were both good-looking men, but none of the women even glanced in their direction. Palacios was eager to get on with the business at hand. He did not like having his Sunday ruined with this kind of bullshit. Besides, he was not at all happy with what he'd come up with.

"There is no ship coming in tomorrow," he told Kling. "Not with dope on it, anyway. You said from Colombia?"

"That's my information."

"Scandinavian registry?"

"Yes."

"Nothing," Palacios said. "I talked to some people I know, the ports are dead right now. Not only for dope. I'm talking bananas, grapefruits, automobiles. There's people saying a strike's in the wind. Ships are holing up at home, afraid to make the trip, they get here there's nobody to unload."

"This one would be unloading outside."

"I know, you told me. A hundred keys. A million bucks' worth of coke. Aimed for a Jamaican posse."

"That's what I've got."

"Who gave you this? Herrera? Who, by the way, I know where he is."

"You do?" Kling said, surprised.

"He's shacked up with a chick named Consuelo Diego, she works for you guys."

"She's a cop?"

"No, she answers phones down 911. Civil service. She used to work in a massage parlor, so this is better. I guess. They moved into a place on Vandermeer a coupla days ago."

"Where on Vandermeer?"

"Here, I wrote down the address for you. After you memorize it, swallow the piece of paper."

Kling looked at him.

Palacios was grinning.

He handed Kling the slip of paper upon which he'd scrawled the address and apartment number. Kling looked at it and then slid it into the cover flap of his notebook.

"How reliable is this guy?" Palacios asked.

"I'm beginning to think not very."

"Because something stinks about this, you know?"

"Like what?"

"You say this is a Jamaican buy, huh?"

"That's what he told me."

"A hundred keys."

"Yes."

"So does that ring true to you?"

"What do you mean?"

"The Jamaicans aren't into such big buys. With them, it's small and steady. A kilo here, a kilo there, every other day. They step on that kilo, they've got ten thousand bags of crack at twenty-five bucks a bag. That's a quarter of a million bucks. You figure a key costs them on average fifteen thou, they're looking at a profit of two-ten per. Still want to be a cop when you grow up?"

Palacios was grinning again.

"So what I'm saying, you get a Jamaican posse making even a *five*-kilo buy, that's a lot for them. But a *hundred* keys? Coming straight up the water instead of from Miami? I'll tell you, that stinks on ice."

Which was why Kling liked hearing stuff that didn't come from police bulletins.

Henry Tsu was beginning to think that Juan Kai Hsao would go far in this business. Provided that what he was telling him was true. There was an ancient Chinese saying that translated into English as "Even good news is bad news if it's false." Juan had a lot of good news that Sunday afternoon—but was it reliable?

The first thing he reported was that the name of the Hamilton posse was Trinity.

"Trinity?" Henry said. This seemed like a very strange name for a gang, even a Jamaican gang. He knew there were posses called Dog, and Jungle, and even Okra Slime. But Trinity?

"Because from what I understand," Juan said, "it was started in a place called Trinity, just outside Kingston. In Jamaica, of course. This is my understanding."

"Trinity," Henry said again.

"Yes. And also it was three men who started it. So trinity means three. I think. Like in the Holy Trinity."

Henry didn't know anything about the Holy Trinity.

And didn't *care* to know.

"Was Hamilton one of these three?" he asked.

"No. Hamilton came later. He killed the original three. He runs the posse now, but he takes advice from a man named Isaac Walker. Who has also killed some people. In Houston. They are both supposed to be very vicious."

Henry shrugged. From personal experience, he knew that no one could be as vicious as the Chinese. He wondered if either Hamilton or Walker had ever dipped a bamboo shoot in human excrement and stuck it under the fingernail of a rival gang leader. Shooting a gun was not being vicious. Being vicious was taking pleasure in the pain and suffering of another human being.

"What about Herrera?" he asked. He was getting tired of all this bullshit about the Hamilton posse with its ridiculous religious name.

"This is why I'm telling you about Trinity," Juan said.

"Yes, why?"

"Because Herrera has nothing to do with it."

"With what? The posse?"

"I don't know about that."

"Say what you *do* know," Henry said impatiently.

"I do know that it's not Herrera who's spreading this rumor. It is definitely not him. He has nothing to do with it."

"Then who's responsible?" Henry asked, frowning.

"Trinity."

"The Hamilton posse?"

"Yes."

"Is saying we ambushed Herrera and stole fifty thousand dollars from him?"

"Yes."

"Why?"

"I don't know why," Juan said.

"Are you sure this is correct?"

"Absolutely. Because I talked to several people who were approached."

"What people?"

"Here in the Chinese community."

Henry knew he did not mean legitimate businessmen in the Chinese community. He was talking about Chinese like Henry himself. And he was saying that some of these people . . .

"Who approached them?" he asked.

"People in Trinity."

"And said we'd stolen . . . "

"Stolen fifty. From the posse. That a courier was carrying for them. Herrera."

"How many people did you talk to?"

"Half a dozen."

"And Hamilton's people had reached all of them?"

"All of them."

"Why?" Henry asked again.

"I don't know," Juan said.

"Find out," Henry said, and clapped him on the shoulder and led him to the door. At the door, he reached into his pocket, pulled out a money clip holding a sheaf of hundred-dollar bills, peeled off five of them, handed them to Juan and said, "Go buy some clothes."

Alone now, Henry went to a red-lacquer cabinet with brass hardware, lowered the drop-front door on it, took out a bottle of Tanqueray gin, and poured a good quantity of it over a single ice cube in a low glass. He sat in an easy chair upholstered in red to match the cabinet, turned on a floor lamp with a shade fringed in red silk, and sat sipping his drink. In China, red was a lucky color.

Why bad-mouth him?

Why say he'd stolen what he hadn't stolen?

Why?

The only thing he could think of was the shipment coming up from Miami tomorrow night.

A hundred kilos of cocaine.

For which he would be paying a million dollars.

In cash, it went without saying. In this business, you did not pay for dope with a personal check.

Did the Hamilton posse have its eye on that shipment? Trinity, what a ridiculous name! But assuming it did ... why bad-mouth Henry? Assuming the worst scenario, a Jamaican hijack of a shipment spoken for by a Chinese gang, why spread the word that Henry had stolen a paltry fifty thousand dollars?

And suddenly the operative words came to him.

Jamaican.

And Chinese.

If Hamilton had planned to knock over a shipment destined for another *Jamaican* gang, say the Banton Posse or the Dunkirk Boys, both far more powerful than his shitty little Trinity, he'd have done so without a by-your-leave. Go in blasting with his Uzis or his AK-47 assault rifles, Jamaican against Jamaican, head to head, winner take all.

But Henry was *Chinese*.

His gang was *Chinese*.

And if Hamilton's *Jamaican* people started stepping on *Chinese* toes, Buddha alone knew what reverberations this might cause in the city.

Unless.

All thieves understood retaliation.

In all cultures, in all languages.

If Henry had actually stolen fifty thousand dollars from the Hamilton posse, then Hamilton would be well within his rights to seek retaliation.

The fifty K plus interest.

A whole hell of a *lot* of interest when you considered that the stuff coming up from Miami was worth a million bucks, but honor among thieves was costly.

Hence the bullshit running around the city.

Hamilton setting up his excuse in advance: Tsu did *me* and now I am going to do *him*.

That's what *you* think, Henry thought, and reached for the telephone and dialed the same Miami number Herrera had called not five hours earlier.

It was already dark when they got to Angela Quist's apartment that Sunday evening. She had been rehearsing a play at the Y all day, she told them, and was exhausted. She really wished this could wait till morning because all she wanted to do right now was make herself some soup, watch some television, and go to sleep.

"This won't take long," Carella said. "We just wanted to check a lead the Seattle cops are following."

Angela sighed heavily.

"Really," Meyer said. "Just a few questions."

She sighed again. Her honey-colored hair looked frazzled. Her star sapphire eyes had gone pale. She was sitting on the couch under the Picasso prints. The detectives were standing. The apartment was just chilly enough to make overcoats seem appropriate.

"Did Joyce ever mention a woman named Sally Antoine?" Carella asked.

"No. I don't think so. Why?"

"Never mentioned that her father was seeing a woman? Any woman at all?" Carella asked.

"I don't recall her ever saying anything like that."

"Did she ever mention her father's will?"

"No."

"When she went out to Seattle, did she say *why* she was going?"

"Yes. Her father was very sick. She was afraid he might die before she saw him again." Angela looked at them, her eyes puzzled now. "Why don't you ask Joyce all this?" she said.

And they realized all at once that they hadn't told her.

She didn't know.

"Miss Quist," Carella said gently, "Joyce is dead. She was murdered last Monday night."

"Oh, shit," Angela said.

And bowed her head.

Sat there on the couch under the Picasso prints, head bent.

Nodding.

Saying nothing.

At last she sighed heavily and looked up.

"The same person?" she asked.

"We don't know."

"Boy."

She was silent again.

Then she said, "Does her sister know?"

"Yes.'"

"How's she taking it?"

"Okay, I guess."

"They were so close," Angela said.

Both detectives looked at her.

"Saw each other all the time."

They kept looking at her.

"*All* the time?" Meyer said.

"Oh, yes."

"Even *after* she got pregnant?"

"Well, sure. In fact, it was Melissa who did all the groundwork for her."

"*What* groundwork?" Carella asked.

"Finding an adoption agency," Angela said.

16

THEY DID NOT get to Richard and Melissa Hammond until eleven
o'clock on Monday morning because they'd had to make another stop
first. The Hammonds were packing when the detectives got there.
Melissa told them she'd received a call from Pearl Ogilvy in Seattle,
who had advised her that her father had passed away that morning at
seven minutes to eight Pacific time. The two were planning to catch an
early afternoon flight to the Coast.

Carella and Meyer expressed their condolences.

"There'll be a lot to take care of, won't there?" Carella said.

"Pearl will be a big help," Hammond said.

"I'm sure," Carella said, and smiled pleasantly. "I know this is a bad
time for you . . ."

"Well, it was expected," Hammond said.

"Yes. But I wonder if we can ask a few questions."

Hammond looked at him, surprised.

"Really," he said, "I don't think this is . . ."

"Yes, I know," Carella said. "And believe me, I wish three people
hadn't been murdered, but they were."

Something in his voice caused Hammond to look up from his open
valise.

"So, I'm sorry, really," Carella said, not sounding sorry at all, "but
we would appreciate a few more minutes of your time."

"Certainly," Hammond said.

On the other side of the bed, Melissa was neatly arranging clothing
in her open bag. The detectives stood just inside the door, uncomfortable in a room as intimate as the bedroom, further uncomfortable in
that no one had asked them to take off their coats.

"The last time we spoke to you," Carella said, "you mentioned that you hadn't seen Joyce since February sometime . . ."

"The twelfth of February," Meyer said, consulting his notebook.

"That's right," Melissa said.

Head still bent, packing.

"When she would've been four months pregnant," Carella said.

"Yes."

"But you didn't notice she was pregnant."

"No."

"Because all the Chapman women carry small, isn't that so, Mr. Hammond?"

"I'm sorry, what . . . ?"

"Isn't that what you said, Mr. Hammond? That all the Chapman women carry small."

"Yes."

"Which Chapman women did you have in mind?"

"I'm sorry, I really don't know what you're . . ."

"Your wife had only one sister. Joyce. You couldn't have meant Joyce because you'd never seen her pregnant. And the last time Melissa's *mother* was pregnant was twenty years ago. You didn't see *her* pregnant, did you?"

"No, I didn't."

"So which Chapman women did you mean?"

"Well, Melissa, of course . . ."

"Yes, of course. And who else?"

"What I *meant*," Hammond said, "was that everyone in the family always *said* the Chapman women carried small."

"Ah," Carella said. "Well, that explains that, doesn't it?"

"Mr. Carella, I'm not sure what you're going for here, but I know I don't like your tone. If you have anything you . . ."

"Mrs. Hammond," Carella said, "isn't it true that you suggested the Cooper-Anderson Agency to your sister?"

Melissa looked up from her suitcase.

"No," she said.

Flat out.

A flat-out lie.

"Before coming here this morning," Carella said, "we went to see a man named Lionel Cooper, one of the partners in the Cooper-Anderson . . ."

"What is this?" Hammond said.

"Mr. Cooper distinctly remembers having had several telephone conversations with you . . ."

"My wife never spoke to anyone named . . ."

". . . regarding your sister's pregnancy and the placement of her baby after it was born."

"Do you recall those conversations?" Meyer asked.

"No, I don't," Melissa said.

"But you do understand that if you *did* have those conversations, then we'd have reasonable cause to believe you *knew* your sister was pregnant."

"I did *not* know she was pregnant," Melissa said.

"So you told us. Because you weren't very close and you rarely saw her."

"That's right."

"Her roommate, a young woman named Angela Quist, seems to think you were *very* close and that you saw each other all the time. *Especially* after Joyce got pregnant."

"Miss Quist is mistaken," Hammond said flatly.

"Mr. Hammond, where were you on New Year's Eve, New Year's *Day,* actually, between one-forty-five and . . ."

"He was here with me," Melissa said.

"You were both here between . . ."

"That's it, gentlemen," Hammond said.

"Meaning what?" Carella said.

"Meaning I'm a lawyer, and this is the end of the conversation."

"I thought you might say something like that," Carella said.

"Well, you were right. Unless you have . . ."

"We do," Carella said.

Hammond blinked.

"We have a match."

Hammond blinked again.

"A report from the Federal Bureau of Investigation," Carella said, "stating that the fingerprints recovered from the handle of the knife used to murder Annie Flynn match the U.S. Army fingerprints on file for Richard Allen Hammond. That's you."

He was lying.

Not about the F.B.I. files. Bonnem in Seattle had told him that Hammond had served in the army during the Vietnam War, and so he knew his fingerprints would be on file as a matter of course. But the foreign prints on the handle of the murder weapon had been too smudged for any meaningful search. He was hoping Hammond hadn't been wearing gloves when he'd jimmied open the window to the Hodding apartment. He was hoping a lot of things. Meanwhile, he was taking his handcuffs from his belt.

So was Meyer.

Melissa seemed to realize all at once that one pair of cuffs was intended for her.

"My father just died," she said. "I have to go to Seattle."

Carella looked her dead in the eye.

She turned away from his icy gaze.

At ten minutes past eleven that Monday morning, Herrera came down the steps of the stoop outside 3311 Vandermeer and began walking eastward toward Soundview Boulevard.

Kling was right behind him.

He had got here at seven, not figuring Herrera for an early riser, but not wanting to take any chances, either. Herrera was walking along at a brisk clip now; well, sure, he hadn't been freezing his ass off on the street for the past four hours. Good arm swinging, head ducked into the wind, racing along like a man with a train to catch. Kling hoped he didn't plan to walk all over the goddamn city. His ears were cold, his hands were cold, his feet were cold, and his nose was cold. It bothered him that Herrera had most likely woken up in a warm bed an hour or so ago, made love to Consuelo Diego, and then eaten a hot breakfast while Kling was standing in a doorway across the street waiting for him to put in an appearance.

Herrera stopped to talk to someone.

Kling fell back, turned toward a store window, eyes glancing sidewards toward where Herrera was obviously asking directions.

The man he'd stopped was pointing up the street now.

Herrera thanked him, began moving again.

Cold as the frozen tundra out here.

Kling fell in behind him, staying a good fifty feet back. Herrera knew what he looked like. One glimpse and—

Stopping again.

This time to look up at the number over one of the shops.

In motion again.

Kling behind him.

Then, obviously having seen the storefront window ahead of him, recognizing it for what he'd been seeking, he turned immediately toward the door, opened it, and disappeared off the sidewalk.

The lettering on the window read:

GO, INC.

TRAVEL AGENCY

Kling was too cold to appreciate the pun.

He crossed the street, took up position in the doorway to a tenement building, pulled his head into his shoulders, and hunkered down to wait again.

An hour later, Herrera came flying out of Go, Inc. as though he were not only *going* but already *gone*. Big smile on his face, this was a man with tickets in his pocket, this was a man on his way to somewhere sunny and warm. Falling in behind him, Kling wished for a moment that he was going wherever Herrera was going. Get away from this city with the snow already turned soot black and the sidewalks slick with ice and the sky a gunmetal gray that seemed to threaten even more snow. Get away someplace. Anyplace.

So where are we going now? he wondered.

Where Herrera was going was right back to 3311 Vandermeer Avenue.

Climbed the front steps, walked directly inside, and poof.

Vanished.

Kling took up his position in the doorway across the street. The superintendent came out at a little after one to chase him away from the building. Kling went to the luncheonette several doors up, took a seat at a table near the front plate glass window, and sat eating a cheeseburger and a side of fries while he watched the building diagonally across the way. He was on his third cup of coffee when Herrera came out of the building, this time with a very pretty, dark-haired woman on his good arm. The woman was wearing a short fake fur over a micro miniskirt. Terrific legs. Smile all over her face. Consuelo, Kling figured. It was almost three P.M.

He followed them past the park on Soundview and then eastward to Lincoln and a movie theater complex named Gateway, where two different movies were playing in two different theaters, the Gateway I and the Gateway II. He could not get into line immediately behind Herrera because Herrera knew what he looked like. He waited until Herrera had bought two tickets to *something*, and then asked the girl behind the ticket-dispensing machine which movie the guy with his arm in a cast was seeing.

The girl said, "Huh?"

"The guy wearing the cast," Kling said. "Which theater did he go into?"

He did not want to flash the tin. Let the girl know he was a cop, everyone in the place would know it five minutes later. Herrera had eyes and ears.

"I don't remember," the girl said.

"Well, there are only two movies playing, which one did he buy tickets for?"

"I don't remember. You want a ticket or not?"

"Give me tickets to both movies," Kling said.

"*Both* movies?"

"Both."

"I never heard of such a thing," the girl said.

She was sixteen years old, Kling figured. One of the teenagers who nowadays were running the entire universe.

"How can you watch two movies at the same time?" she asked.

"I like to catch a little of each," Kling said.

"Well, it's your money," she said, her look clearly indicating that there were more nuts roaming this city than there were lunatics in the asylums. "That's fourteen dollars even," she said, punching out the tickets.

Kling took the tickets as they popped out of the machine. He gave her a ten and four singles. The girl counted the bills. "Ten and four make fourteen," she said, showing off.

Kling walked to where another teenager was standing beside a long vertical box, tearing tickets in half.

"Ticket, please," the boy said.

Kling handed him both tickets.

"Someone with you, sir?" the boy said.

"No, I'm alone."

"You have two tickets here, sir."

"I know."

"And they're for two different movies."

"I know."

The boy looked at him.

"It's okay," Kling said, and smiled.

The boy kept looking at him.

"Really," Kling said.

The boy shrugged, tore the tickets in half, and handed the stubs to Kling.

"Enjoy the show," he said. "Shows."

"Thank you," Kling said.

He tried Gateway I first. Waited at the back of the theater until his eyes adjusted to the darkness. Cautiously came down the aisle on the left, standing behind each row of seats so he wouldn't be made if Herrera was in here and happened to glance away from the screen. Checked each row. No Herrera. Went down the aisle on the opposite side of the theater, same routine. On the screen, somebody was saying he thought he was falling in love. His friend was saying something about him *always* falling in love, so what else was new? The two guys were teenagers. Who knew all about love, Kling guessed. One of the thousands of movies made for teenagers and starring teenagers. Kling tried to remember if there were any teenage stars when he was a teenager. He couldn't remember any teenage stars. He could only remember Marilyn Monroe's pleated white skirt blowing up over her white panties. Herrera was nowhere in the theater.

Kling came up the aisle, pushed open the door, turned immediately to the left, walked past the rest rooms and the concession and the video game machines, and then opened the door to Gateway II, and waited all over again while his eyes adjusted to the darkness. He spotted Herrera and Consuelo sitting in two aisle seats about midway down the theater on the right-hand side. He took a seat three rows behind them. The couple on the screen—both teenagers—were necking. The girl was struggling to keep her blouse buttoned. Kling remembered a time when unbuttoning a girl's blouse was tantamount to scaling Mount Everest. The boy on the screen unfastened an undoubtedly key button. The girl's breasts, contained in a white bra, popped out of her blouse and onto the screen. Kling figured she was supposed to be seventeen. She looked twenty-five. The boy looked twelve. Three rows ahead of him, Herrera was passionately kissing Consuelo. The position of his body seemed to indicate that he had his good hand up under Consuelo's skirt. Kling wondered why they didn't simply go back to the apartment. There was a new scene on the screen now. Two teenagers were fixing an automobile. The hood was up. They were talking about a girl named Mickey. Listening, Kling found Mickey somewhat less than fascinating. Herrera and Consuelo did not seem too interested in

Mickey, either. Herrera looked as if he now had his entire *arm* up under Consuelo's skirt.

Kling kept looking at his watch.

An average film was about two hours long; he did not want to get caught sitting here when the movie ended and the lights came up. He kept checking the action on the screen against his watch. The movie seemed to have sixteen endings. Each time he thought it was close to over, another teenage crisis sprang up, demanding immediate resolution. Kling wondered how teenagers managed to get through an entire day, all the serious problems they had to solve. The movie seemed to be peaking at about an hour and fifty minutes. He got up, walked to the back of the theater, and stood there until the movie did finally and truly end. As the credits began to roll, he stepped outside and walked over to one of the video game machines. Stood there with his back to the theater's doors, but with a good sideward shot at the exit doors to the street. Herrera and Consuelo walked through those doors some ten minutes later. Kling figured they'd both made rest-room stops. He tried to remember when he himself had last peed. It was now twelve minutes past five o'clock.

Already dark on the street outside. Streetlamps on. He followed Herrera and Consuelo back to the apartment on Vandermeer. Waited until they were inside and the lights came on in the third-floor front apartment. He ducked into the luncheonette then, used the rest room, and immediately came out onto the street again. The lights were still on in the third-floor apartment. Kling settled down to wait again.

At seven minutes past six, two Chinese men entered the building.

To most cops, all Chinese looked alike.

But *these* two could have passed for twins.

Hammond refused to say a word.

Advised his wife to remain silent as well.

But alone in the Interrogation Room with Nellie Brand and the detectives, Melissa finally burst into tears and told them everything they wanted to know. The time was a quarter past six. Until that moment, they'd been nervously watching the clock, aware of Miranda-Escobeda, knowing that time was running off down the drain. They figured Melissa's sudden outpouring was prompted by the presence of another woman, but they didn't give a damn about the why of it. All they wanted was a case that would stick; Nellie asked all the questions.

"Mrs. Hammond," she said, "do you now remember where your husband was between one-forty-five and two-thirty A.M. on the first day of January?"

"I don't know about the exact times," Melissa said. "But he left the apartment at . . ."

"By the apartment, do you mean . . . ?"

"*Our* apartment. In Calm's Point."

"Left it at what time?"

"Midnight. We toasted the New Year, and then he left."

"To go where?"

"To kill the baby."

The way she said those words sent a chill up the detectives' backs. Emotionless, unadorned, the naked words seemed to hover on the air. To kill the baby. They had drunk a midnight toast. He had left the apartment. To kill the baby.

"By the baby, do you mean Susan Hodding?" Nellie asked softly.

"Yes. My sister's baby."

"Susan Hodding."

"We didn't know what they'd named her."

"But you did know the adopting couple was named Hodding. Mr. and Mrs. Peter Hodding."

"Yes."

"How did you know that?"

"My husband found out."

"How?"

"Someone at the agency told him."

"By the agency . . ."

"Cooper-Anderson."

"The adoption agency."

"Yes."

"Someone at the agency revealed this information to him."

"Yes. He paid someone to get this information. Because, you see, the name of the people adopting the baby was only in two places. In the court records and in the agency records. The court records are sealed, you know, in an adoption, so Dick had to get the name through the agency."

"And, as I understand this, cash was given to . . ."

"Yes. Five thousand dollars."

"To someone in the agency."

"Yes."

"Who? Would you remember?"

Planning down the line. Getting her ducks in a row for when she had to prosecute this thing. Get the name of the agency person. Call him or her as a witness.

"You'll have to ask Dick," Melissa said.

"So once your husband had the name . . ."

"And address."

"Name and address of the Hoddings, he knew where to find the baby."

"Yes."

"And he went there on New Year's Eve . . ."

"Yes."

". . . to kill this infant."

"Yes."

"Specifically to kill this infant."

"Yes."

"How did he happen to kill Annie Flynn?"

"Well, I only know what he told me."

"What did he tell you, Mrs. Hammond?"

"He told me he was in the baby's room when . . . you see, what it was, he had the floor plans of the building. It's a new building, he went there pretending he was interested in buying an apartment. So he knew the layout of the apartment the Hoddings were in, do you see? There's a fire escape off the second bedroom, which he knew would be the baby's room, it's only a two-bedroom apartment. So he knew if he came down the fire escape from the roof, he could get right into the baby's room. And smother her. With her pillow. But the night he was there . . ."

"Why did he pick New Year's Eve?"

"He figured New Year's Eve would be a good time."

"Why? Did he say why?"

"No. He never told me why."

"Just figured it would be a good time."

"Well, yes. You'll have to ask him. Anyway, he was in there, and the girl . . ."

"Annie Flynn?"

"Yes, the sitter. You see, what he figured was that he'd just go in the baby's room, put the pillow over her face, and go right out again. I mean, this was a *baby*. There wouldn't be any resistance or anything, no noise, no yelling, he'd just go in and go out again. If the Hoddings were

home . . . well, this was New Year's Eve, they probably would've had a
few drinks, and anyway it was very late, they'd be sound asleep, he'd go
in very quietly, do what he had to do and get out without them hearing
a thing. This was a *baby,* you see. And if they were still out celebrating,
there'd probably be a sitter, and if *she* wasn't asleep . . ."

"There *was* a sitter, as it turned out, wasn't there?"

"Well, yes, but Dick knew where the living room was, and the baby's
room was all the way down the hall from it. So . . . what he figured, you
see, was that either way it would be . . . well, *easy.* This was a *baby.* He
wasn't expecting any problem at all."

"But there *was* a problem."

"Yes."

"What was the problem, Mrs. Hammond?"

"The mobile."

"The what?"

"The mobile. Over the crib. He was leaning in over the crib when he
hit the mobile. It was one of these . . . almost like wind chimes, do you
know? Except it didn't depend on wind. What it was, if you hit it, it
would make these chime sounds. It was hanging over where the baby's
hands would be, so the baby could reach up and hit it and make the
chime sounds. But Dick didn't know it was there, he'd never actually
been in the apartment, and when he leaned in over the crib, his head
hit the mobile, and it went off like an alarm."

"What happened then?"

"He yanked the mobile loose from the ceiling, but it had already
woken up the baby, the baby was screaming. And the sitter heard her
crying, and that's when all the trouble started. Otherwise it would've
gone smoothly. If it hadn't been for the mobile."

"So when Annie heard the baby crying . . ."

"Yes. Well, you have to understand we didn't know either of their
names. Not the baby's and not the sitter's. Until we heard them on
television."

"What happened when she heard the baby crying?"

"She yelled from the living room, wanted to know who was there,
and then she . . . she just *appeared* in the doorway to the room. With a
knife in her hand. A very *big* knife, in fact. And she came at Dick with
it. So he had to defend himself. It was self-defense, really. With the sitter, that's what it was. She was really coming at him with that knife. He
struggled with her for maybe three, four minutes before he finally got
it away from her."

"And stabbed her."

"Yes."

"Did he tell you that?"

"Yes."

"That he stabbed her?"

"Yes. That he had to kill her. In self-defense."

"Did he say how many times he'd stabbed her?"

"No."

"And the baby? When did he . . . ?"

"The baby was still crying. So he had to work fast."

"The baby was awake . . ."

"Crying, yes."

". . . when he smothered her?"

"Well, put the pillow over her face."

"Smothered her."

"Well, yes."

"Was there blood on his clothing when he got home?"

"Just a little. Some spatters."

"Do you still have that clothing?"

"Yes. But I soaked out the stains. With cold water."

Nellie was still planning her case. Seize the clothing as evidence. Send it to the lab. It was almost impossible to soak out all traces of blood. Compare the bloodstains with those recovered from the knife's wooden handle. Get herself a match that would prove Annie Flynn's blood was on the murder weapon and on the clothes Richard Hammond had worn on New Year's Eve.

"Tell me what happened on Monday night, the sixteenth of January," she said.

"I don't want to talk about that."

"That's the night your sister was murdered, isn't it?"

"I don't want to talk about it."

"Did your husband kill her?"

"I don't want to talk about it."

"Did he?"

"You know, there are some things . . ." Melissa said, almost to herself, and shook her head. "I mean, we'd be getting half when Daddy died, so why . . . ?" She shook her head again. "Half to me, half to Joyce," she said. "Plus the trust. Which is why the baby was so important. So . . . why get so greedy? Why go for it *all*?"

"Mrs. Hammond, did your husband kill Joyce Chapman?"

"You'll have to ask him. I don't want to talk about it."

"Was he going for all of the *inheritance*? Is that what you're saying?"

"I loved my sister," Melissa said. "I didn't care about the baby, I didn't even *know* the baby, but my sister . . ."

She shook her head.

"I mean, the baby meant *nothing* to me. And my husband was right, you know. Why *should* all that money go to a child that was . . . well, a bastard? I mean, Joyce didn't even know who the *father* was."

"All what money?" Nellie asked.

"I could understand that, it made sense. But my sister . . . I didn't know he was going to do that to her, I swear to God. If I'd known . . ."

"But you *did* know he was going to kill the baby."

"Yes. But not my sister. I'd have been happy with half, I swear to God. I mean, there are *millions,* why'd he have to get so damn *greedy* all at once? The other money, okay. Why *should* it go to a baby my sister never wanted? But then to . . ."

"What other money?" Nellie asked again.

"It's all in the will," Melissa said. "You'll have to look at the will."

"Has someone already contacted you about it?"

"About what?"

"The will. I understand your father died early this morning. Has his attorney . . . ?"

"No, no."

"Then . . ."

Nellie looked suddenly puzzled.

"Are you saying . . . ?"

"We knew what was in the will," Melissa said. "We found out almost a year ago."

"How did you find out?"

"Mr. Lyons told my husband."

"Mr. Lyons?"

"Geoffrey Lyons. Who used to be my father's attorney."

Nellie looked appalled.

"Told your husband the provisions of his client's *will?*" she said.

"Well, he was very fond of Dick," she said. "His own son was killed in Vietnam, they'd grown up together, gone to school together, I suppose he looked upon Dick as a sort of surrogate son. Anyway, there was nothing illegal about what he did. Or even unethical. My father was trying to make sure the family wouldn't just die out. He was trying to provide some incentive. Mr. Lyons gave Dick a friendly tip, that was all. Told him what was in the will. Said we'd better get going, you know?"

"Get going?"

"Well, you know."

"No, I don't know."

"Well, get on with it."

"I still don't know what you mean."

"Well, you'll have to look at the will, I guess," Melissa said, and turned away from Nellie.

And then, for some reason Carella would never understand, she looked directly into his eyes, and said, "I did love her, you know. Very much."

And buried her face in her hands and began weeping softly.

The apartment Herrera was using for the testing and tasting was only three blocks east of the one he had rented on Vandermeer. Both apartments were normally rented by the hour to prostitutes turning quickie tricks, and so the separate landladies had been happy to let Herrera have them at weekly rates that were lower but more reliable than the come-and-go, on-the-fly uncertain hooker trade.

Herrera had walked here with Zing and Zang. He was carrying fifty thousand dollars in hundred-dollar bills in a dispatch case that made him feel like an attorney. The five kilos of cocaine would go into that dispatch case once the deal was consummated. The three of them would then go back to the apartment on Vandermeer, where Zing and Zang expected to take possession of their half of the coke. Two and a half keys for them, two and a half for Herrera. Just as they'd all agreed. Gentlemen. Except that Herrera planned to kill them.

It was all a matter of having been born in this city, he figured.

You take two pigtailed Chinks from Hong Kong, they did not know that the minute the door to the apartment on Vandermeer closed behind them, he would shoot them in the back.

They did not understand this city.

You had to be born here.

They stopped now at the steps to 705 East Redmond.

"I have to go up alone," Herrera told them.

"Yeh," Zing said.

"Because that's the way Miami wants it."

"Yeh," Zang said.

"It may take a while. Make sure they ain't selling us powdered sugar."

"We be here," Zing said.

* * *

Kling saw Herrera go into the building.

The two Chinese men stayed outside, hands in the pockets of their overcoats. Both wearing long dark blue coats. No hats. Sleek black hair combed straight back from their foreheads. Neither of them had ever seen Kling before, he could move in closer for a better look.

Walked right past them on the same side of the street.

Brothers for sure.

Twins, in fact.

Didn't even seem to glance at them. But got enough on them in his quick fly-by to be able to spot them later, anytime, anywhere.

He continued on up the street. Walked two blocks to the west, crossed over, came back on the other side, this time wearing a blue woolen watch cap that covered his blond hair. The one thing you could count on in any slum neighborhood was a dark doorway. He found one three buildings up from the one Herrera had entered. Across the street, the Chinese twins were flanking the front stoop like statues outside a public library. Ten minutes later, a man with a mustache walked past the Chinese and into the building. Like Herrera, he, too, was carrying a dispatch case.

The man from Miami was a hulking brute with a Pancho Villa mustache. He said "Hello," in Spanish, and then "You got the money?"

"You got the shit?" Herrera asked.

No passwords, no code words, no number sequences. The time and the place had been prearranged. Neither of them would have known when and where without first having gone through all the security bullshit. So now they both wanted to get on with it and get it done fast. The sooner they got through with the routine of it, the safer the exchange would be.

There were people who said they could tell by a little sniff up the nose or a little speck on the tongue whether you were buying good coke or crap. Herrera preferred two simple tests. The first one was the old standby cobalt thiocyanate Brighter-the-Blue. Mix the chemical in with the dope, watch it dissolve. If the mix turned a very deep blue, you had yourself high-grade coke. The brighter the blue, the better the girl. Meaning if you got this intense blue reaction, you were buying cocaine that was purer than what you'd get with, say, a pastel blue reaction. What you had to watch out for was coke that'd been stepped on maybe two, three times before it got to you.

For the second test, Herrera used plain water from the tap.

The man from Miami watched in utter boredom as he scooped a spoonful of the white dust out of its plastic bag, and dropped a little bit of it into a few ounces of water. It dissolved at once. Pure cocaine hydrochloride. Herrera nodded. If the powder hadn't dissolved, he'd have known the coke had been cut with sugar.

"Okay?" the man from Miami said, in English.

"*Bueno,*" Herrera said, and nodded again.

"How much of this are you going to go through?" the man asked, in Spanish.

"Every bag," Herrera said.

From where he stood in the doorway across the street, Kling saw the man with the mustache coming out of the building, still carrying the dispatch case. He did not look at the two Chinese, and they did not look at him. He walked between them where they were still flanking the stoop, made a left turn and headed up the street. Kling watched him. He unlocked the door to a blue Ford station wagon, got in behind the wheel, started the car, and then drove past where Kling was standing in the doorway. Florida license plate. The numerals 866—that was all Kling caught. The street illumination was too dim and the car went by too fast.

He waited.

Five minutes later, Herrera came out of the building.

"No trubber?" Zing asked.

"None," Herrera said.

"You have it?" Zang asked.

"I've got it."

"Where?" Zing asked.

"Here in the bag," Herrera said. "Where the fuck you think?"

His eyes were sparkling. Just holding the dispatch case with all that good dope in it made him feel higher than he'd ever felt in his life. Five kilos of very *very* good stuff. All his. Take the Chinks back to the place on Vandermeer, kiss them off, leave them there for the cops to find when somebody complained about the stink in apartment 3A. Take his time disposing of the coke, so long as he got rid of it by the fifteenth of February. Catch the TWA plane to Spain on the fifteenth. The plane to Spain is mainly in the rain, he sang inside his head. Christ he was happy!

The twins were on either side of him now.
Like bodyguards.
Zing smiled at him.
"Henny Shoe say tell you hello," he said.

From where Kling stood across the street, he heard the shots first and only then saw the gun. In the hand of the Chinese guy standing on Herrera's right. There were three shots in rapid succession. Herrera was falling. The guy who'd shot him backed away a little, giving him room to drop. The other Chinese guy picked up the dispatch case from the sidewalk where it had fallen. They both began running. So did Kling.
"Police!" he shouted.
His gun was in his hand.
"Police!" he shouted again and watched them turn the corner.
He pounded hard along the sidewalk. Reached the corner. Went around it following his gun hand.
The street was empty.
His eyes flicked doorways. Hit doorways. Snapped away from them. Nothing. Where the hell had they . . . ?
There.
Partially open door up ahead.
He ran to it, kicked it fully open, fanned the dark entrance alcove with his gun. Open door beyond. Went to that. Through the doorway. Steps ahead. Not a sound anywhere in the hallway. An abandoned building. If he went up those steps he'd be walking into sudden death. Water dripped from somewhere overhead. A shot came down the stairwell. He fired back blindly. The sound of footfalls pounding up above. He came up the steps, gun out ahead of him. Another shot. Wood splinters erupted like shrapnel on the floor ahead of him. He kept climbing. The door to the roof was open. He came out into sudden cold and darkness. Flattened himself against the brick wall. Waited. Nothing. They were gone. Otherwise they'd still be firing. Waited, anyway, until his eyes adjusted to the darkness, and then covered the roof, paced it out, checking behind every turret and vent, his gun leading him. They were gone for sure. He holstered his gun and went down to the street again.
As he approached Herrera lying on his back on the sidewalk, he saw blood bubbling up out of his mouth. He knelt beside him.
"José?" he said. "Joey?"

Herrera looked up at him.

"Who were they?"

They won't let you live in this city, Herrera thought, but they won't let you out of it, either.

His eyes rolled back into his head.

Sitting in the automobile, Hamilton and Isaac watched the two Chinese men from the Tsu gang entering the building.

Hamilton smiled.

The thing about the Chinese, he thought, is that they know business but they have no *passion*. They are cool lemon yellow. And tonight, they were going to get *squeezed*.

The two men from Miami were waiting upstairs in apartment 5C.

This according to what Carlos Ortega had told him.

For ten percent, the ungrateful bastard.

The two men from the Tsu gang were now on their way upstairs to make payment and take delivery. The earlier testing and tasting, wherever the hell *that* had taken place, had apparently gone off without a hitch. Hamilton had no interest whatever in those shitty five keys that had vanished in the night. Upstairs in apartment 5C, there were ninety-five keys of cocaine and only four people to look after all that dope.

He nodded to Isaac.

Isaac nodded back and then flashed his headlights at the car up the street. He still didn't understand all the details of the deal. He only knew that tonight they were making a move that would catapult them into the big time where posses like Spangler and Shower roamed at ease. He was confident that Hamilton knew what he was doing. You either trusted someone completely or you didn't trust him at all.

Together, they got out of the automobile.

Up the street, the doors on the other car opened. Black men in overcoats got out. The doors closed silently on the night. The men assembled swiftly, breaths pluming on the frosty air, and then walked swiftly to the front steps of the building. Eight of them altogether. Hamilton, Isaac and six others. Hamilton knew the odds would be two to one in his favor.

Together they climbed to the fifth floor of the building.

Hamilton listened outside the door to apartment 5C.

Voices inside there.

Three separate and distinct voices.

There now.

A fourth voice.

He kept listening.

He smiled. Held up his right hand. Showed four fingers. Isaac nodded. Four of them inside there. As promised by Ortega. Isaac nodded to the man on his right.

A single burst from the man's AR-15 blew off the lock on the door.

The Jamaicans went in.

Hamilton was still smiling.

There were not four people in that apartment.

There were a dozen Colombians from Miami and a dozen Chinese from right here in the city.

Henry Tsu was one of those Chinese.

In the first ten seconds, Isaac—who still did not completely understand all the details of this deal—took seventeen slugs in his chest and his head. Hamilton turned to run. His way was blocked by the Jamaicans behind him. They, too, had realized all at once that they had walked into an ambush, and they were now scrambling in panic to get out of the trap. They were all too late. A second wave of fire cut them down before they reached the door. It was all over in thirty seconds. The only shot the Jamaicans had fired was the one that took off the lock.

Hamilton, still alive, started crawling over the bodies toward the doorway.

One of the Chinese said, "Henny Shoe say tell you hello."

Then he and another Chinese who looked remarkably like him fired twelve shots into Hamilton's back.

Hamilton stopped crawling.

Henry Tsu looked down at him.

He was thinking it was all a matter of which was the oldest culture.

17

CARELLA SIGNED for the Federal Express envelope at ten minutes past nine the following morning. It was from the Seattle Police Department and it contained a sheaf of photocopied pages and a handwritten memo. The memo read: *Thought you might like to see this.* It was signed: *Bonnem.* The pages had been copied from Paul Chapman's will. They read:

> My daughters are Melissa Chapman Hammond and Joyce Chapman.
>
> I give and bequeath to my trustee hereinafter named the sum of one million dollars ($1,000,000) to hold same in trust for the benefit of the first child born of my said daughters, and to manage, invest and reinvest the same and pay all costs, taxes . . .

"He was making sure the family line would continue after he was gone," Carella said.

"If his daughters were still childless at his death, he was giving them a good reason to change the situation," Meyer said.

"To get on with it."

"To get going."

"Melissa's words."

"Here's the motive," Carella said, tapping the page of the will that spelled out the firstborn provision.

"He was signing little Susan's death warrant," Meyer said.

"Because if she'd never been born . . ."

"Melissa's baby would be the firstborn child . . ."
"And that's where the million-dollar trust would go."
Both men continued reading in silence.

All the rest, residue and remainder of my estate, of whatsoever nature and wheresoever situated, which I may own or
to which I may in any way be entitled at the time of my
death, including any lapses or renounced legacies or devises,
is referred to in this, my will, as my residuary estate.

"Defining his terms," Carella said.
"The rest of his estate."
"Millions of dollars, isn't that what she said?"

I give, devise and bequeath any residuary estate in equal
shares to my daughters living at my death . . .

"Just what she told us."

. . . or if a said daughter shall predecease me . . .

"Here comes the motive for *Joyce's* murder . . ."

. . . then I give, devise and bequeath all of my residuary
estate to my then surviving daughter.

"Kill Joyce and Melissa gets it all," Carella said.
"Love or money," Meyer said and sighed. "It never changes."
There was more to the will.
But they already had all they needed.
And the phone was ringing again.

There were no windows in the room.
　　This was the first time Eileen noticed it.
　　Neither was there a clock.
　　Must be Las Vegas, she thought.
　　"Something?" Karin asked.
　　"No."
　　"You were smiling."
　　"Private joke," Eileen said.

"Share it with me."

"No, that's okay."

She was wearing a digital watch. Nothing ticked into the silence of the room. She wondered how many minutes were left. She wondered what the hell she was doing here.

"Let's play some word games," Karin said.

"Why?"

"Free association. Loosen you up."

"I'm loose."

"It's like snowballing. Cartoonists use it a lot."

"So do cops," Eileen said.

"Oh?"

"In a squadroom. You take an idea and run with it," she said, suspecting Karin already knew this. If so, why the expression of surprise? She wished she trusted her. But she didn't. Couldn't shake the feeling that to Karin Lefkowitz, she was nothing but a specimen on a slide.

"Want to try it?"

"We don't have much time left, do we?"

Hoping she was right. Not wanting to look at her watch.

"Twenty minutes, anyway," Karin said.

Christ, *that* long?

"I'll give you a word, and you give me the first word that pops into your head, okay?"

"You know," Eileen said, "I really don't enjoy playing games. I'm a grown woman."

"Yes, so am I."

"So why don't we just skip it, okay?"

"Sure. We can skip the whole damn thing, if you like."

Eileen looked at her.

"I think we're wasting each other's time," Karin said flatly. "You have nothing to say to me, and if you don't *say* anything, then I can't help you. So maybe we ought to . . ."

"The only help I need . . ."

"Yes, I know. Is quitting the force."

"Yes."

"Well, I don't think I can help you do that."

"Why not?"

"Because I don't think it's what you really want."

"Then why the hell am I here?"

"You tell me."

Eileen folded her arms across her chest.

"Here comes the body posture again," Karin said. "Look, I really don't think you're ready for this. I don't know why you came to me in the first place . . ."

"I told you. Sam Grossman sugg . . ."

"Yes, and you thought it was a good idea. So here you are, and you have nothing to tell me. So why don't we call it a day, huh?"

"You want to quit, huh?"

"Just for now, yes. If you change your mind later . . ."

"Too bad *I* can't quit just for *now*, huh?"

"What do you mean?"

"The force. Leaving police work is for*ever.*"

"Why do you say that?"

"Come on, willya?"

"I really don't know why you feel . . ."

"Don't you ever talk to cops? What do you do here? Talk to architects? Bankers? I mean, for Christ's sake, don't you know how cops *think?*"

"How do they think, Eileen? Tell me."

"If I quit now . . ."

She shook her head.

"Yes?"

"Never mind, fuck it."

"Okay," Karin said, and looked at her watch. "We've got fifteen minutes left. Have you seen any good movies lately?"

"I just don't like having to explain the simplest goddamn *things* to you!"

"Like what?"

"Like what everyone would think if I quit!"

"What would they think?"

"And why it would be impossible to . . ."

"What would they think, Eileen?"

"That I'm *scared*, goddamn it!"

"Are you?"

"I told you I was, didn't I? How would *you* like to get raped?"

"I wouldn't."

"But try to explain that to anyone."

"Who do you mean?"

"People I've worked with. I've worked with cops all over this city."

"Men?"

"Women, too."

"Well, surely the *women* would understand why you'd be afraid of getting raped again."

"Some of them might not. You get a certain kind of woman with a gun on her hip, she's sometimes worse than a man."

"But *most* women would understand, don't you think?"

"I guess so. Well, Annie would. Annie Rawles. She'd understand."

"Rape Squad, isn't that what you told me?"

"Annie, yeah. She's terrific."

"So who do you think might not understand? Men?"

"I've never heard of a man getting raped, have you? Except in prison? Most cops haven't been in prison."

"Then it's *cops* you're worried about. Men cops. You don't think they'd understand, is that it?"

"You should work with some of these guys," Eileen said.

"Well, if you quit, you wouldn't have to work with them anymore."

"And they'd run all over the city saying I couldn't cut it."

"Is that important to you?"

"I'm a good cop," Eileen said. "Was."

"Well, you haven't quit yet. So you're *still* a cop."

"But not a good one."

"Has anyone said that to you?"

"Not to my face."

"Do you think anyone has said that behind your back?"

"Who cares?"

"Well, you do, don't you?"

"Not if they think I'm scared."

"But you are scared. You told me you were scared."

"I know I am."

"So what's wrong with that?"

"I'm a cop."

"Do you think cops aren't scared?"

"Not the way I'm scared."

"How scared are you, Eileen? Can you tell me?"

She was silent for a long time.

Then she said, "I have nightmares. Every night."

"About the rape?"

"Yes. About giving him my gun. He has the knife to my throat, and I give him my gun. Both guns. The thirty-eight and the little backup pistol. The Browning. I give him both guns."

"Is that what happened in reality?"

"Yes. But he raped me, anyway. I thought . . ."

"Yes?"

"I don't know what I thought. I guess that . . . that if I . . . I cooperated, then he . . . he wouldn't cut me . . . wouldn't rape me. But he did."

"Cut you. And raped you."

"So fucking *helpless!*" Eileen said. "A *cop!*"

"What did he look like, do you remember?"

"It was dark."

"But you saw him, didn't you?"

"And raining. It was raining."

"But what did he look like?"

"I don't remember. He grabbed me from behind."

"But surely, when he . . ."

"I don't remember."

"Did you see him after that night?"

"Yes."

"When?"

"At the trial."

"What was his name?"

"Arthur Haines. Annie made the collar."

"Did you identify him at the trial?"

"Yes. But . . ."

"Well, what did he look like?"

"In the dream, he has no face."

"But while he was raping you, he had a face."

"Yes."

"And at the trial, he had a face."

"Yes."

"Which you identified."

"Yes."

"What did he look like, Eileen?"

"Tall. Six feet. A hundred and eighty pounds. Brown hair and blue eyes."

"How old?"

"Thirty-four."

"How old was the man you killed?"

"What?"

"How old was . . . ?"

"What's *he* got to do with this? I don't have nightmares about him."

"Do you remember how old he was?"

"Yes."

"Tell me."

"Early thirties."

"What'd he look like?"

"I already told you this. The second time I was here. We've been through all this."

"Tell me again."

"Blond," Eileen said, and sighed. "Six-two. Two hundred pounds. Eyeglasses. A heart-shaped tattoo with nothing in it."

"What color were his eyes?"

"Blue."

"Like the rapist."

"The eyes, yes."

"His size, too."

"Well, Bobby was heavier and taller."

"But they were both big men."

"Yes."

"You said you were alone with him in a room . . ."

"Bobby, yes."

"Because you'd lost your backups. By the way, do you always think of him as Bobby?"

"Well . . . I guess so. That's what he called himself. Bobby."

"Uh-huh."

"Is there anything wrong with that? Calling him Bobby?"

"No, no. Tell me how you lost your backups."

"I thought I already did."

"No, I don't think so. How many were there?"

"Two of them. Annie and a . . . Annie Rawles . . ."

"Yes."

". . . and a guy from the Seven-Two in Calm's Point. Mike Shanahan. Big Irishman. Good cop."

"How'd you lose them?"

"Well, Bert got it in his head that I needed help. So he drove out to the Zone . . ."

"Bert Kling."

"Yeah. Who I was still seeing at the time. I told him I didn't want him coming out there, but he came anyway. And . . . he's blond, you know. Did I mention he's blond? And there was a mix-up on the street, Shanahan saw Bert and thought he was the guy we were looking for, because Bobby was blond, too, you know, and about the same size. So by the time they straightened it out—it was the Feather in the Hat thing, you know, only nobody was wearing feathers—by the time Shanahan realized Bert was on the job, Bobby and I were gone."

"Gone?"

"Around the corner. On our way to the room."

"Did they ever catch up to you?"

"No."

"Then you really *did* lose them. I mean, permanently."

"Yes."

"Because Bert stepped into the play."

"Well, it wasn't his fault."

"Whose fault was it?"

"Shanahan's."

"Why?"

"Because he mistook Bert for the suspect."

"Didn't know Bert was a cop."

"That's right."

"But if Bert hadn't been there . . ."

"But he was."

"But if he *hadn't* been there . . ."

"There's no sense thinking that way. He *was* there."

"Eileen, if he hadn't been there, would there have been a mix-up on the street?"

"Well, no."

"Would you have lost your backups?"

"Probably not."

"Do you think they might have helped you in your situation with Bobby?"

"Who?"

"Your backups."

"I suppose so. If they'd got to me in time."

"Well, you said they're both good cops . . ."

"Oh, sure."

". . . who undoubtedly knew their jobs . . ."

"I'd have trusted my life with either of them. In fact, that's exactly what I *was* doing. Trusting them to get there on time if I needed them."

"But they weren't there when you needed them."

"Yes, but that wasn't *their* fault."

"Whose fault was it?"

"Nobody's. It was one of those dumb things that happen all the time."

"Eileen, if it *hadn't* happened—if there *hadn't* been the mix-up, if you *hadn't* lost Shanahan and Annie—do you think you'd have had to shoot Bobby?"

"I don't know."

"Well, think about it."

"How can I possibly . . . ?"

"Well, if they'd been following you . . ."

"Yes, but they weren't."

"*If* they'd been there behind you . . ."

"But you see . . ."

". . . *if* they'd seen where Bobby was taking you . . ."

"Look, there's no use crying over . . ."

". . . and *if* they'd got to you in time, would you have shot and killed Bobby Wilson?"

"I'd shoot him all over again," Eileen said.

"You didn't answer my question."

"Man with a knife? Coming at me with a knife? Of *course* I'd shoot the son of a bitch! I got cut *once*, thanks, and I don't plan to . . ."

Eileen stopped dead.

"Yes?" Karin said.

Eileen was silent for several moments.

Then she said, "I wasn't trying to get even, if that's what you think."

"What do you mean?"

"When I shot Bobby. I wasn't . . . I didn't shoot him because of . . . I mean, it had nothing to do with the rape."

"Okay."

"Nothing at all. In fact . . . well, I already told you."

"What was that?"

"I was beginning to like him. He was very charming."

"Bobby."

"Yes."

"But you killed him."

"I had to. That's the whole *point*, you know, the whole reason I'm here."

"Yes, tell me the reason."

"I already told you this, I don't know why I have to tell you every fucking thing a hundred times."

"What was it you told me?"

"That I want to quit because I'm afraid I'll . . ."

"Yes, I remember now. You're afraid . . ."

"I'm afraid I'll get so angry I'll kill somebody else."

"Angry?"

"Well, Jesus, if somebody's coming at you with a knife . . ."

"But I thought you were beginning to like him. Bobby."

"The man had already killed three other women! He was ready to kill me! If you think that doesn't start the adrenaline flow . . ."

"I'm sure it does. But you say it made you angry."

"Yes." She hesitated a moment, and then said, "I emptied the gun in him."

"Uh-huh."

"Six shots."

"Uh-huh."

"A big gun. A Smith & Wesson forty-four."

"Uh-huh."

"I'd do it again. In a minute."

"And that's what you're afraid of. That's why you want to quit the force. Because someday you might get angry all over again, and . . ."

"He had a knife!"

"Is that what made you angry? The knife?"

"I was all alone up there! I'd lost my . . . you know, I *told* Bert to stay out of it. I told him I could take care of it just fine, I had two backups who knew what they were doing, I didn't need any more help. But he came out there, anyway."

"And caused you to lose your backups."

"Well, that's what he did, didn't he? I mean, *I* didn't lose them! And Shanahan was only doing his job. It was Bert sticking his nose in that caused all the trouble. Because he thought I wasn't any good anymore. Thought I'd lost it, you see. Couldn't take care of myself. Couldn't do the job. When I found out later what'd happened out there on the street, I could've *killed* him!"

"So you were angry with him, too," Karin said.

"Well, later, yes."

"Yes. When you realized that if he hadn't interfered . . ."

"I wouldn't have been alone up there with Bobby. Yes."

The room went silent.

Karin looked at her watch.

Their time was up.

"But you told me you'd kill Bobby again," she said. "In a minute."

"I'd never killed anyone before, you know," Eileen said. "I used to . . . you know, my father and my uncle Matt both got killed on the job . . ."

"I didn't know that."

"Well, yeah. And . . . I used to think I'd . . . if I ever caught that guy with the red handkerchief over his face, I'd . . . blow him away without batting an eyelash. For what he did to . . . but . . . you know . . . when I . . . the third shot knocked him onto the bed, Bobby, he was lying flat on the bed, I'm sure he was already dead. But I . . . I fired the rest of the . . . three more bullets into . . . into his back . . . along the spine. And then I threw the gun across the room and began screaming."

Karin looked at her.

You're *still* screaming, she thought.

"Our time is up," she said.

Eileen nodded.

Karin rose from behind her desk. "We have a lot of work to do," she said.

Eileen was still sitting. Looking at her hands. Head bent, hands in her lap. Without looking up, she said, "I hate him, don't I?"

"Which one?" Karin asked, and smiled.

"Bert."

"We'll talk about it, okay?" Karin said. "Will I see you on Thursday?"

Eileen stood up.

She looked directly into Karin's eyes.

She did not say anything for several seconds.

Then she said, "Yes."

It was a beginning.

VESPERS

This is for Anne Edwards and Steve Citron

1

IT WAS HIS CUSTOM to reflect upon worldly problems during evening prayers, reciting the litany by rote, the prayers a mumbled counterpoint to his silent thoughts.

The Priest.

At such times, he thought of himself as The Priest. The T and the P capitalized. The Priest. As if by distancing himself in this way, by referring to himself in the third person as if he were someone not quite himself . . .

. . . a character in a novel or a movie, perhaps . . .

. . . someone outside his own body, someone exalted and remote, to be thought of with reverence as solely The Priest. By thinking of himself in this manner, by sorting out The Priest's problems as the problems of someone other than himself, Father Michael could . . .

Because, you see . . .

It was he, Father Michael, who could find comfort in the evening prayers, he who could whisper vespers for his solace as the shadows lengthened in the small, stone-paved garden behind the church rectory. But it was The *Priest* who had to cope with all the troubles that had befallen him since the middle of March, more than he quite knew how to handle, more than mere prayer could—but that was blasphemy.

Vespers was the sixth of the seven canonical hours.

At the seminary, he'd memorized the order of the prayers as a bit of rhyming doggerel:

> Matins is the morning prayer,
> At six comes Prime too soon.

Tierce comes three hours hence
And Sext is said at noon.

Nones is said at three P.M.
Nine hours past the sun.
Vespers is the evening prayer,
And when the day is done . . .
Complin's said.
And so to bed.

The Priest was thirty-two years old now.

Those soft, serene days at the seminary seemed a hundred years ago.

God, come to my assistance. Lord, make haste to help me. Glory to the Father.

The Liturgy of the Hours was as complex and as rigid as the Timetable for a space shot. Not only were there daily prayers for the seven different canonical hours, but there were special prayers as well for the Season of Advent and the Christmas Season, and for before and after Holy Week and before and after Ascension. And of course there were the Solemnities like Trinity Sunday and Corpus Christi and Sacred Heart and Christ the King, not to mention the Four-Week Psalter—just like a space shot. Deviate by a millisecond and you missed your window. The Priest wondered if such a simile was in itself blasphemy, but he heard his own voice whispering vespers into the evengloam, unperturbed.

His mind churned restlessly. He sought solutions where there seemed none. His voice said vespers by rote, but his thoughts flew helter-skelter . . . if only there were a way . . . a master plan . . . if only one could turn, for example, to the Proper of Saints, for example, to the twenty-first day of January, let's say, the Saint Day of St. Agnes, virgin and martyr, and find there the morning prayer . . . *My Lord Jesus Christ has espoused me with his ring; he has crowned me like a bride* . . . and then the directions to recite the psalms and canticle from Sunday, Week 1, on page 556, all so simple . . . *O God, you are my God, for you I long* . . . but, no, there was no such mortal scheme, you took your problems as they came, you tried to sort them out as you walked over stones laid a century and more ago in a part of the city now gone to ruin . . .

. . . the hateful threats in the rectory . . .

. . . this is blackmail, blackmail . . .

. . . the pounding at the central portal doors . . .

. . . the black boy running into the church, seeking sanctuary, Hey man, *hep* me, they goan *kill* me!

Blood running down his face

. . . gone to ruin, all to ruin.

Graffiti on the massive stones of the church, barbarians on ponies storming the gates. Almost six weeks since all of that—today was the twenty-fourth of May, the day of Ascension—all that time, almost six weeks, and he was still on his knees to . . .

I came forth from the Father and have come into the world; now I leave the world to return to the father, alleluia!

There was the sweet scent of roses on the evening air.

The roses were his pleasure and his vice, he tended them the way he tended the Lord's flock.

Something still and silent about tonight. Well, a Thursday. The name itself. Something dusky about the name, Thursday, as soft and silken as sunset. Thursday.

God is rich in mercy; because of his great love for us . . .

. . . I'll tell, I'll tell everything . . .

The boy's blood dripping on the marble floor before the altar.

The vengeful cries echoing inside the church.

Still on his knees.

. . . *by this favor are you saved. Both with and in Christ Jesus, he raised us up and gave us a place in the heavens.*

Beyond the high stone walls of the garden, The Priest could see the sooted upper stories of the buildings across the street, and yet above those, beyond those, the sunset-streaked springtime sky. The aroma of the roses was overpowering. As he moved past the big maple set exactly at the center of the garden, a stone bench circling it, he felt a sudden suffusion of love . . . for the roses, for the glorious sunset, for the power of the words that soared silently in his prayers, *God our Father, make us joyful in the ascension of your Son Jesus Christ, may we follow him into the new creation, for his ascension is our glory and our hope. We ask—*

—and noticed all at once that the gate in the wall was open.

Standing wide.

The setting sun striking it so that it cast a long arched shadow that reached almost to the maple itself.

He had thought . . .

Or surely, Martha would have . . .

He moved swiftly to the gate, painted a bilious green by a tasteless long-ago priest, and yet again recently with red graffiti on the side facing the street. The gate was wooden and some four inches thick, arched at its highest point a good foot above the stone walls on either side of it, an architectural touch that further displeased The Priest's meticulous eye. The narrow golden path of sun on the ground grew narrower yet as he swung the gate closed on its old wrought-iron hinges . . . narrower . . . narrower . . . and then was gone entirely.

Alleluia, come let us worship Christ the Lord as he ascends into heaven, alleluia!

The lock on the gate was thoroughly modern.

He turned the thumb bolt.

There was a solid, satisfying click.

Give glory to the King of kings, sing praise to God, alleluia!

His head bent, he turned and was walking back toward the rectory, past the shadow-shrouded maple, when the knife . . .

He felt only searing pain at first.

Did not realize until the second slashing blow . . .

Knew then that he'd been stabbed . . .

Turned . . .

Was *starting* to turn . . .

And felt the knife entering again, lower this time, in the small of the back . . .

Oh dear God . . .

And again, and again, and again in savage fury . . .

Oh Jesus, oh Jesus Christ . . .

As complete darkness claimed the garden.

Not a day went by without Willis expecting someone to find out about her. The open house tonight was on the twelfth floor of a renovated building about to go co-op. There were a great many strangers here, and strangers were dangerous. Strangers asked questions. What do you do, Mr. Willis? And you, Miss Hollis? Willis and Hollis, they sounded like a law firm. Or perhaps a dance team. And now, ladies and gentlemen, returning from their recently completed tour of the glittering capitals of Europe, we bring you . . . *Willis* . . . and *Hollis!*

The questions about himself were merely annoying; he wondered why everyone in America had to know immediately what everyone else in America *did*. He was sometimes tempted to say he sold crack to innocent schoolchildren. He wondered what sort of response *that* would get. Tell them you're a cop, they looked at you with raised eyebrows. Oh, really? Cut the crap and tell us what you *really* do. Really, I swear to God, I'm a cop, Detective/Third Grade Harold O. Willis, that's me, I swear. Looking you over. Thinking you're too short to be a cop, a detective, no less, and ugly besides with your curly black hair and wet brown eyes, let me see your badge. Show them the potsy. My, my, I never met a real live police detective before, do you work in one of those dreadful precincts we're always reading about, are you carrying a gun, have you ever killed anyone? The questions. Annoying, but not dangerous.

The questions they asked Marilyn were dangerous.

Because there was so much to hide.

Oh, not the fact that they were living together, this was already the Nineties, man, nobody even *thought* about such things anymore. You got married by choice, and if you chose not to, then you simply lived together. Had children together, if you could, did whatever you wanted, this was the Nineties. And perhaps . . . in such a climate of acceptance . . . you could even . . . well, perhaps . . . but it was extremely unlikely. Well, who the hell knew? Maybe they could, after all, come right out and say, *Look,* people, Marilyn used to be a hooker.

The raised eyebrows again.

Oh, really? Cut the crap and tell us what she *really* did.

No, really, that's what she really did, I swear to God, she used to be a hooker. She did it for a year or so in Houston, and ended up in a Mexican prison on a dope charge, and then picked up the trade again in Buenos Aires where she worked the streets for five years, more or less. Really. That's what she used to do.

But who would believe it?

Because, you know, you looked at Marilyn, you saw this woman who'd be only twenty-six in August, slender and tall, with long blonde hair and cornflower blue eyes and a complexion as flawlessly pale as a dipper of milk, and you thought No, not a hooker. You didn't survive being a hooker. You didn't come off six years of peddling tail—not to mention the time in that Mexican hellhole—and look like this. You just didn't. Unless you were Marilyn. Then you did. Marilyn was a survivor.

She was also a murderess.

That was the thing of it.

You opened the *hooker* can of peas, and everything else came spilling out.

The cocktail party was in a twelfth-floor corner apartment, what the real estate lady kept calling the penthouse apartment, although Willis didn't think it looked luxurious enough to warrant such a lofty title. He had been in court all day long and had come up here against his better judgment, at the invitation of Bob O'Brien who said there'd be good booze and plenty to eat and besides neither of them would run the risk of getting shot, a distinct possibility if ever you were partnered with a hard-luck cop like O'Brien.

He'd called Marilyn to tell her that O'Brien's girlfriend Maizie—who turned out to be as ditsy as her name—would be coming along, and maybe the four of them could go out to dinner later, and Marilyn had said, sure, why not? So here they were with the sun just gone, listening to a real estate lady pitching renovated apartments to supposedly interested prospects like O'Brien who, Willis discovered for the first time tonight, planned to marry Maizie in the not-too-distant future, lots of luck, pal.

It was Maizie who looked like a hooker.

She wasn't. She worked as a clerk in the D.A.'s office.

But she was wearing a fuzzy pink sweater slashed in a V over recklessly endangered breasts, and a tight shiny black skirt that looked like a thin coating of crude oil, and high-heeled, ankle-strapped black patent leather pumps, a hooker altogether, except that she had a tiny little girl's voice and she kept talking about having gone to high school at Mother Mary Magdalene or some such in Calm's Point.

The real estate lady was telling Willis that the penthouse apartment, the one they were standing in this very moment, was going for only three-fifty negotiable, at a fixed eight-and-a-quarter percent mortgage with no points and no closing fees. Willis wondered if he should tell her that he was presently living in a town house uptown that had cost Marilyn seven hundred and fifty thousand dollars. He wondered if there'd be any former hookers living in this fine renovated building.

In her high, piping voice, Maizie was telling someone that a nun named Sister Letitia used to hit her on her hands with a ruler.

O'Brien was looking as if he expected to get shot at any moment.

Marilyn wondered out loud how such a reasonable mortgage rate could be offered in this day and age.

The real estate lady told her that the sponsor was a bank in Minnesota, which meant nothing at all to Willis.

Then she said, "What do *you* do, Mrs. Willis?"

"It's Hollis," Marilyn said.

"I thought . . ." She turned to Willis. "Didn't you say your name was Willis?"

"Yes, but mine is Hollis," Marilyn said. "We're not married."

"Oh."

"The names *are* similar, though," Willis explained helpfully.

"And are you in police work, too, Miss Hollis?"

"No, I'm a student," Marilyn said.

Which was the truth.

"My education was interrupted," she said.

And did not amplify.

"What are you studying?"

All smiles, all solicitous interest; these were potential customers.

"Well, eventually, I want to be a social worker," Marilyn said. "But right now, I'm just going for my bachelor's."

All true.

"*I* wanted to be a doctor," the real estate lady said, and looked at Willis. "But I got married instead," she added, as if blaming him for her misfortune.

Willis smiled apologetically. Then he turned to O'Brien and said, "Bob, if you plan on staying a while longer, maybe me and Marilyn'll just run along, okay?"

O'Brien seemed to be enjoying the warm white wine and cold canapés.

"See you tomorrow," he said.

"Nice to meet you," Maizie said to Marilyn.

The church garden was crowded now with two ambulance attendants, three technicians from the Mobile Crime Unit, an assistant medical examiner, two detectives from Homicide, a woman from the Photo Unit, and a uniformed Deputy Inspector from Headquarters. The D.I. was here because the police department in this city was largely Irish-Catholic, and the victim was a priest.

Detective Stephen Louis Carella looked out at the assembled law enforcement officers, and tried to remember the last time he'd been inside a church. His sister's wedding, wasn't it? He was inside a church now. But not to pray. Well, not even *technically* inside a church, although the rectory was *connected* to the church via a wood-paneled corridor that led into the sacristy and then the old stone building itself.

He looked through the open rectory doorway and out into the garden where roses bloomed in medieval splendor. Such a night. On the paved garden floor, the priest lay as if dressed in mourning, wearing the black of his trade, festooned now with multiple stab and slash wounds that outrioted the roses banked against the old stone walls. A small frown creased Carella's forehead. To end this way, he thought. As rubble. On such a night. He kept looking out into the garden where the crowd of suits and blues fussed and fluttered about the corpse.

Carella gave the impression—even standing motionless with his hands in his pockets—of a trained athlete, someone whose tall, slender body could respond gracefully and effortlessly to whatever demands were placed upon it. His appearance was a lie. Everybody forgot that middle age was really thirtysomething. Ask a man in his mid-to-late thirties if he was middle-aged, and he'd say Don't be ridiculous. But then take your ten-year-old son out back to the garage and try to play one-on-one basketball with him. There was a look of pain on Carella's face now; perhaps because he had a splitting headache, or perhaps because he always reacted in something close to pain when he saw the stark results of brutal violence. The pain seemed to draw his dark, slanting eyes even further downward, giving them a squinched, exaggerated, Oriental look. Turn a group photograph upside down, and you could always pick out Carella by the slanting eyes—the exact opposite of almost anyone else in the picture.

"Steve?"

He turned from the open doorway.

Cotton Hawes was leading the housekeeper back in.

Her name was Martha Hennessy, and she'd become ill not five minutes ago. That is to say, she'd thrown up. Carella had asked one of the ambulance crew to take her outside, see what he could do for her. She was back now, the smell of her vomit still lingering in the rectory, battling for supremacy over the aroma of roses wafting in from outside. She seemed all right now. A bit pale, but Carella realized this was her natural coloration. Bright red hair, white skin, the kind of woman who would turn lobster red in the sun. Green eyes. County Roscommon all over her. Fifty-five years old or thereabouts, wearing a simple blue dress and sensible low-heeled shoes. She'd told them earlier that she'd found Father Michael in the garden as she'd come out to fetch him for dinner. That was at a little after seven tonight, fifteen minutes before she'd starting throwing up. It was now seven-forty; the police had been here for ten minutes.

"I sent one of the blues out for coffee," Hawes said. "Mrs. Hennessy said she might like some coffee."

"Actually," she said, "I asked Mr. Hawes if I could *make* some coffee. We've got a perfectly good stove . . ."

"Yes, but . . ."

"Yes," Carella said, almost simultaneously, "but the technicians will be working in there."

"That's what Mr. Hawes told me. But I don't see why I can't make my own coffee. I don't see why we have to send *out* for coffee."

Hawes looked at her.

He had explained to her, twice, that this entire *place* was a crime scene. That the killer might have been anywhere inside the church or the rectory before the murder. That the killer might even have been in the priest's small office, where one of the file cabinet drawers was open and papers presumably removed from that drawer were strewn all over the floor. Now the woman was questioning, for the *third* time, why she could not use the priest's kitchen—where, among other utensils, there were a great many knives. He knew he had adequately explained *why* she could not use the kitchen or anything *in* the kitchen. So how had he failed to communicate?

He stood in redheaded perplexity, a six-foot-two-inch, hundred-and-ninety-pound, solidly built man who dwarfed the Hennessy woman, searching for something to say that would clarify why they did not want her using the kitchen. There was an unruly white streak of hair over his left temple, a souvenir from a slashing years ago while he was investigating a burglary. It gave his haircut a somewhat fearsome Bride of Frankenstein look, which—when coupled with the consternation on his face—made it appear as if he might throttle the little housekeeper within the next several seconds, a premise entirely distant from the truth. Side by side, the two redheads stood, one huge and seemingly menacing, the other tiny and possibly confused, a blazing torch and a glowing ember.

Carella looked at both of them, not knowing Hawes had already explained the sanctity of the kitchen to her—twice—not knowing why Hawes was looking at her so peculiarly, and beginning to feel a bit stupid for not understanding what the hell was going on. Outside in the garden, the priest lay on blood-stained stones, his blood still seeping from the tattered wounds in his back. It was such a lovely night.

Getting away from the matter of the goddamn kitchen, Hawes said, "When did you last see Father Birney alive?"

"Father Michael," she said.

"Well, his name is Michael *Birney*, isn't it?" Hawes said.

"Yes," Mrs. Hennessy said, "but you can have a priest named . . . well, take Father O'Neill as used to be the pastor here. *His* name was Ralph O'Neill, but everybody called him Father O'Neill. Whereas Father Michael's name is Michael Birney, but everyone calls *him* Father *Michael*. That's the mystery of it."

"Yes, that's the great mystery of it," Hawes agreed.

"When *did* you last see him alive?" Carella asked gently. "Father Michael, that is."

Slow and easy, he told himself. If she's truly a stupid woman, getting angry isn't going to help either her *or* the situation. If she's just scared, then hold her hand. There's a dead man outside in the garden.

"When you last saw him alive," he prompted. "The time. What time was it?"

"A bit past seven," she said. "When I come to fetch him for dinner."

"Yes," Carella said, "but he was already dead by then, isn't that what you said?"

"Yes, God ha'mercy," she said, and hastily made the sign of the cross.

"When did you last see him *alive?* Before that."

"When Krissie was leaving," she said.

"Krissie?"

"Yes."

"Who's Krissie?"

"His secretary."

"And she left at what time?"

"Five. She leaves at five."

"And she left at five tonight?"

"Yes."

"And that's the last time you saw Father Michael alive?"

"Yes, when Krissie was leaving. He was saying good night to her."

"Where was this, Mrs. Hennessy?"

"In his study. I went in to clear the tea things . . . he takes tea in the afternoon, after he says his three o'clock prayers. Krissie was just going out the door, he was sayin' I'll see you in the morning."

"Krissie who?" Hawes asked.

"Krissie who's his secretary," Mrs. Hennessy said.

"Yes, but what's her full name?"

"Kristin."

"And her last name?"

"Lund. Kristin Lund."

"Does she work here full time?"

"No, only Tuesdays and Thursdays. Twice a week."

"And you? How often do . . . ?"

"Who gets the coffee?" a uniformed cop asked.

"Here's your coffee, Mrs. Hennessy," Hawes said, and took the cardboard container from him.

"Thank you," she said, and then, quite suddenly, "It was the Devil who done it."

The only problem was that Willis loved her to death.

It bothered him day and night that he loved a woman who'd killed someone. A pimp, yes—a fucking *miserable* pimp, as a matter of fact—but a human being, nonetheless, if any pimp could be considered human. He had never met a pimp he'd liked, but for that matter, he'd never met a hooker with a heart of gold, either. Marilyn was no longer a hooker when he'd met her, so she didn't count.

She *had* been a hooker, however, when she'd killed Alberto Hidalgo, a Buenos Aires pimp who by then had been living off the proceeds of prostitution for almost fifty years. In addition to Marilyn, there'd been six other whores in his stable. He was hated by each and every one of them, but by none so fiercely as Marilyn herself, whom he'd casually subjected first to an abortion and next to a hysterectomy performed by one and the same back-alley butcher.

So here was Willis—a police officer sworn to protect and enforce the laws of the city, state, and nation—in love with a former hooker, a confessed murderess, and an admitted thief, not necessarily in that order. Only two other people in this entire city knew that Marilyn Hollis had once been a prostitute; Lieutenant Peter Byrnes and Detective Steve Carella. Willis knew that the secret was safe with either of them. But neither of them knew that she was also a killer and thief. Willis alone had heard *that* little confession, he alone was the one to whom she'd . . .

"I did. I killed him."

"I don't want to hear it. Please. I don't want to hear it."

"I thought you wanted the truth!"

"I'm a cop! If you killed *a man . . ."*

"I didn't kill a man, *I killed a* monster! *He ripped out my insides, I can't have babies, do you understand that? He stole my . . ."*

"Please, please, please, Marilyn . . ."

"I'd kill him again. In a minute."

She'd used cyanide. Hardly the act of someone with a heart of gold. Cyanide. For rats.

And then . . .

"I went into his bedroom and searched for the combination to the safe because that was where my passport had to be. I found the combination. I opened the safe. My passport was in it. And close to two million dollars in Argentine money."

On the night she'd confessed all this to Willis, a night that now seemed so very long ago, she'd asked, "So what now? Do you turn me in?"

He had not known what to say.

He was a cop.

He loved her.

"Do they know you killed him?" he'd asked.

"Who? The Argentine cops? Why would they even *give* a damn about a dead pimp? But, yes, I'm the only one who split from the stable, yes, and the safe was open, and a lot of bread was gone, so yes, they probably figured I was the perpetrator, is that the word you use?"

"Is there a warrant out for your arrest?"

"I don't know."

And there had been a silence.

"So what are you going to do?" she'd asked. "Phone Argentina? Ask them if there's a warrant out on Mary Ann Hollis, a person I don't even *know* anymore? *What*, Hal? For Christ's sake, I love you, I want to live with you forever, I love you, Jesus, I *love* you, what are you going to *do?*"

"I don't know," he'd said.

He was still a cop.

And he still loved her.

But every time that telephone rang, he broke out in a cold sweat, hoping it would not be some police inspector in Buenos Aires, telling him they had traced a murder to the city here and were planning to extradite a woman named Marilyn Hollis.

It was easy to forget your fears on a night like tonight.

It was easy to forget that some problems might never go away.

At a little past ten o'clock, the city was ablaze with light. For all Willis knew, this could have been springtime in Paris: he'd never been there. But it felt like Paris, and it most certainly felt like spring, the balmiest spring he could ever remember. As he and Marilyn came out of the restaurant, a soft, fragrant breeze wafted in off Grover Park. Both of them smiled. He hailed a passing taxi and told the driver to take the park road uptown. They were still smiling. The windows were down. They held hands like teenagers.

Harborside Lane, where Marilyn owned the town house, was within the confines of the 87th Precinct, not quite as desirable as Silvermine Oval, but a very good neighborhood anyway—at least when one considered the *rest* of the precinct territory. Number 1211 was in a row of brownstones adorned with inaccessible spray-can scribblings. A wrought-iron gate to the right of the building guarded the entrance to a driveway that led to a garage set some fifty feet back from the pavement; the gate was padlocked. There were wrought-iron grilles on the ground-floor and first-floor windows, and razor wire on the roof overhanging the third floor. There were now two names in the directory set beside the bell button: M. Hollis and H. Willis.

Willis paid the driver and tipped him extravagantly; it was that kind of night. Marilyn was unlocking the front door as the taxi pulled away from the curb. It turned the corner and vanished from sight, the sound of its engine fading, fading, and then disappearing entirely. For an instant, the street, the small park across the way, were utterly still. Willis took a deep breath and looked up at the sky. Stars blinked overhead. A *Pinocchio* night. He expected Jiminy Cricket to come hopping up the sidewalk.

"Hal?"

He turned.

"Aren't you coming in?"

"It's so beautiful," he said.

He would later remember that these were the last words he'd said before the telephone rang. The last words before the terror started.

He went into the house and closed and locked the door behind him. The entry foyer and the living room beyond were paneled in mahogany. Old thick wooden beams crossed the ceiling. Marilyn began unbuttoning her blouse as she climbed the walnut-banistered staircase to the second story. Willis was crossing the living room, yanking down his tie and unbuttoning the top button of his shirt, when the telephone rang.

He looked automatically at his watch, walked to the phone on the dropleaf desk, and picked up the receiver.

"Hello?" he said.

There was a slight hesitation.

Then a man's voice said, "*Perdóneme, señor.*"

And then there was an empty click.

The altar was naked.

The altar was a twenty-seven-year-old woman who lay on her back on an elevated platform shaped as a trapezoid and covered with black velvet. Her head was at the narrow end of the trapezoid, her long blonde hair cushioned on a pillow covered with black silk. White against black, she lay with her legs widespread and dangling over the wide end of the platform, her arms at her sides, her eyes closed.

Lying between her naked breasts was a thick silver disc on a heavy silver chain, sculpted in relief with the Sacred Sign of Baphomet, the Black Goat, whose image hung on the wall behind her as well, its horns, ears, face and beard contained within the center and five points of an inverted pentagram:

Smoke from the torches illuminating this infernal symbol swirled upward toward the arched ceiling of the abandoned church. Smoke from the candles clutched in the hands of the woman who was the altar drifted up toward old wooden beams that long ago had crossed over an altar made not of flesh but of marble.

The mass had started at the stroke of midnight.

Now, at a little past one A.M., the priest stood between the spread legs of the altar, facing the celebrants, his back to the woman. He was wearing a black cotton robe embroidered in richer black silk with pine cones that formed a phallic pattern. The robe was slit to the waist on either side, revealing the priest's muscular legs and thighs.

The celebrants were here to mark the day of the Expulsion. Some twenty minutes earlier, during the Canon segment, they had each and separately partaken of the contents of a silver chalice offered by the priest. The chalice had tonight contained not the usual dark red wine symbolic of the blood of Christ, but something called Ecstasy, a hallucinogenic drug that was a potent mix of mescaline and speed. A capsule of Ecstasy sold for twenty dollars. There were at least two hundred people here tonight, most of them young, and each and every one of them had swallowed a cap of X immediately after the conclusion of the third segment of the mass.

Kissing the altar/woman full on her genitals, the priest had recited the timeless words, "Satan is Lord of the Temple, Lord of the World, he bringeth to me joyous youth, all praise Satan, all hail Satan!" and the celebrants had responded "All hail Satan!" and the girl acolyte had come to the altar and raised her garments to the priest, revealing herself naked beneath them. The boy acolyte had held a silver container to catch her urine, and the priest had dipped a phallus-shaped aspergill into the container and sprinkled the celebrants with the little girl's urine, *If thou hast thirst, then let thee come to the Lord Satan. If thou wouldst partake of the water of life, the Infernal Lord doth offer it.* And then he had passed among them with the chalice containing the Ecstasy capsules, and they had washed the caps down with thick red wine offered by the deacon and one of the subdeacons, sixty-one people times twenty bucks a pop came to twelve hundred and change.

The girl acolyte stood to the right of the altar now.

She was a darling little blonde girl, all of eight years old, whose mother was tonight serving as the altar. She was dressed entirely in black, as was her father who was sitting among the other stoned celebrants and feeling enormously proud of the separate important roles his wife and daughter were playing in tonight's ritual. The boy acolyte was only seven. He was standing to the left of the altar/woman, staring a bit wide-eyed at the tufted blonde patch above the joining of her legs. The priest was about to embark upon the fifth and final segment of the mass, called the Repudiation, especially significant tonight in that this twenty-fourth day of May was what the Christians had named Ascension, upon which day the body of Jesus Christ was supposed to have risen to Heaven, but which here within these walls was being celebrated as the *expulsion* of Jesus from Hell.

The priest had been supplied with a host consecrated at a church in another part of the city, stolen this morning at mass by a woman worshipper whose mouth had first been coated with alum to protect the wafer from her own saliva. He held the wafer between the thumb and forefinger of his left hand now, made a deep, mocking bow over it, and said, "I show you the body of Jesus Christ, the Forgotten One, pretender to the throne of Satan, monarch to slaves, confounder of minions stumbling to perdition."

He turned to face the altar/woman, his back to the celebrants now, his right hand raised in the sign of the horns, his left hand holding the wafer aloft to the goat symbol on the wall.

"All hail Satan!" he said.

"Hail, Satan!" the celebrants responded.

"All praise these splendid breasts that gave suck to the body of Jesus," he said mockingly, and touched the wafer first to the woman's right nipple and then to her left nipple. Kneeling between her legs, he rested the hand with the wafer on her mons veneris, and said, again mockingly, "Blessed be the generous womb that begat the body of Jesus," and passed the host over the lips of her vagina.

Now began the Repudiation in earnest.

Lifting the hems of his robe, fastening them into the black silken cord at his waist, he wet the fingers of his right hand and then touched them to the head of his now-erect penis. "Jesus Christ, messenger of doom, I offer you to worm and maggot . . ." he said, touching the wafer to the moistened head of his penis where it clung in desecration, moving closer to the widespread legs of the altar, the boy acolyte watching excited and amazed, "thrust you down with scorpion and snake . . ." approaching the altar where she waited open and spread for him, "show you storm and savage strife, curse you with famine and filth, burn you in eternal fire, cause you everlasting death to the end of time unending, and reward you with the enduring fury of our Lord, Satan!"

"Hail, Satan!" the celebrants chanted. "All hail Satan!"

Hurling himself onto the altar, thrusting himself into the woman, wafer and penis entering her, the priest said, "I descend anew, and ascend forever, saith the Infernal Lord. My flesh is your flesh . . ."

"My flesh is thy flesh," the woman murmured.

"My flesh is our flesh . . ."

"Thy flesh is our flesh," the celebrants intoned.

"In flesh, let us find the glory of Satan!"

"In flesh, find the glory of Satan!"

"In lust, let us know the goodness of Satan!"

"In lust, know the goodness of Satan!"

"In flesh and in lust, let us all praise Satan!"

"In flesh and in lust, we praise Satan's name!"

"Blessed be Satan!"

"Blessed be Satan!"

"All hail Satan!"

"Hail, Satan!"

This was four blocks away from where the police had chalked Father Michael's outline onto the blood-stained stones in the small church garden.

2

THE TWO MEN were speaking entirely in Spanish.

One of them was exceedingly handsome. Tall and slender, with black hair combed straight back from a pronounced widow's peak, he looked a lot like Rudolph Valentino. He did not know who Rudolph Valentino *was*, and so he wasn't flattered when people told him he looked like Rudolph Valentino. But he guessed that Rudolph Valentino had to be *some* handsome *hombre* because if there was one thing Ramon Castaneda knew for certain it was that he himself was handsome as sin.

The man sitting with him was named Carlos Ortega and he was exceptionally ugly. He had crooked teeth and a nose that had been broken often in street fights hither and yon, and a scar that ran through his right eyebrow and partially closed his right eye, and moreover he was bald and hulking and he resembled an escaped inmate from a hospital for the criminally insane, which he was not. But such was the vanity of men that he, too, thought he was handsome. In fact, many women had told him he was handsome. He believed them, even if all of them were hookers.

On this twenty-fifth day of May, another beautiful spring morning, the two men sat in a coffee shop close to their hotel, discussing why they were here in the city. It was still early in the morning, a little past seven; the place was full of people catching quick breakfasts before going to work. The two men were in no hurry. The handsome one, Ramon, had ordered steak and eggs for breakfast. Carlos, the ugly one who only thought he was handsome, had ordered pancakes and sausage. They sat sipping their coffee, waiting for the food to come, chatting idly.

ED McBAIN

Ramon said in Spanish that he thought it was a pity a man had answered the telephone last night. A man might complicate matters.

Carlos said in Spanish that he could break every fucking bone in the man's body, whoever he was, so what difference did it make if she was living with a man, a woman, or a chihuahua?

"*If* she's the right woman," Ramon said.

"Well, yes, we have to make sure she's the right woman," Carlos said.

"Which won't be easy without a photograph."

"But we have her description from the German whore."

The German whore was a buxom blonde who claimed she'd been openly abducted in Munich. Her name was Constantia. While they waited for their food, the two men discussed whether or not she was reliable. Ramon mentioned that she'd been a drug addict for many years. Carlos said he knew many people who were drug addicts who nonetheless made very reliable witnesses. They got sidetracked wondering if she was a good lay. When their food came, they fell silent for a while, Ramon eating with the exquisite table manners of a man who knew he was devastatingly handsome, Carlos eating like a brute who believed that handsome men like himself could eat any fucking way they *wanted* to.

"You think she could be so stupid?" Ramon asked.

"How do you mean?"

"To put her name in the book?"

"It says only M. Hollis," Carlos said. "Also, there are twenty-eight Hollises in the book."

"But only one M. Hollis."

"True. How's the steak?"

"Ours are better."

He was referring to Argentine beef; a bit of national pride there. But Carlos noticed that he was enjoying it. The pancakes he himself had ordered were only so-so. He wondered why he'd ordered pancakes, anyway; he didn't even *like* pancakes.

"So what we have to do," Ramon said, "is go up there and take a look."

"She could have changed what she looks like, you know," Carlos said.

"Yes, women can do that," Ramon said wearily, an observation a handsome man familiar with the strange and wonderful ways of women could make in utter boredom.

"She could be a redhead by now," Carlos said. "Or a brunette. Never mind the blonde. The blonde could be history by now."

"We can always look under her skirt," Ramon said, and smiled confidently.

"She could have changed it there, too. Or shaved it like a baby's. She could be an entirely different woman by now."

"The blue eyes, she can't change," Ramon said.

"She can wear contacts to make them green or brown or purple. A woman can change everything about herself. We could go up there, it could be the same woman, and we wouldn't recognize her."

"So what are you saying?" Ramon asked. "We *shouldn't* go up there?"

"We should go, we should go. But we shouldn't be disappointed if we look at her, and she doesn't fit the German whore's description. Who, by the way, may have been lying, anyway."

"Why would she have lied?"

"For the money. We gave her money."

"With the promise of more."

"*If* we locate the Hollis woman. If that's even her name."

"The German whore says that was her name. Mary Ann Hollis."

"So then why is there only an 'M' in the phone book?"

"Because if a woman puts an 'M.A.' in the phone book, a man immediately knows it's a woman," Ramon said.

"So if you put J. F. Kennedy in the phone book, it means it's a woman, correct?" Carlos said.

"Well, I don't *know* why she put only an 'M' in the phone book," Ramon admitted. "Maybe in this country it's cheaper than using two initials."

Carlos looked at him.

"Why do *you* think she put only an 'M'?" Ramon asked.

"Because, one, it could be the wrong woman . . ."

"Well, of course, but . . ."

"Or, two, it could be that the *man* who answered the phone is the one who's listed in the book, it's a *Mr.* M. Hollis . . ."

"No, it's only women who use initials," Ramon said.

"Or, three, she could have changed her name," Carlos said.

"That's true. But then why use an 'M'? Why not change it completely?"

"Even with an 'M,' it could be changed completely," Carlos said. "From Mary Ann, she could have changed it completely to Magdalena or Mercedes or Marta or . . ."

He was an Argentine, and so all these names were Spanish, naturally.

". . . Matilda or Maurita or Mirabella or Miranda or Modesta or . . ."

"I think I get the point," Ramon said.

"What I'm saying," Carlos said, "is we get uptown, we find a curly-haired redhead with big tits and a fat ass and brown eyes and her name is Margarita and we think we have the wrong number, but instead it's really Mary Ann Hollis who once upon a time was tall and thin and had blue eyes and straight blonde hair, is what I'm saying."

"So we have to be careful, is what you're saying."

"No, I'm saying we may have to beat the shit out of her," Carlos said.

"Well, of course," Ramon said, as if it went without saying that *all* women had to have the shit beat out of them every now and then.

"If she tells us she's not who we *think* she is," Carlos said.

"Yes," Ramon said.

"To find out who she *really* is, is what I'm saying," Carlos said.

"I agree with you entirely."

"So when do you want to go?"

"Let me finish my steak," Ramon said.

"You eat more slowly than any person I know."

"Because I was born rich," Ramon said. "Only the poor eat quickly. For fear someone will snatch the food away before they're finished."

"You were born rich, ha!" Carlos said.

"Yes, I was born rich, ha!" Ramon mimicked.

"What I want to do," Carlos said, "I want to be waiting when she comes out of the building. We take it slow and easy. Follow her, see where she goes, what she does. We make our move when we're *ready* to make it. And not near a house where a man answers the phone." He looked at the remaining bit of steak on Ramon's plate. "Now hurry up and finish, rich man," he said. "Because you'll be even richer once she gives us the money."

"*Sin duda,*" Ramon said.

Kristin Lund looked exactly like her name. Blonde hair and blue eyes, a full tempestuous mouth, and a figure that reminded Hawes of the gently sloping hills of Sweden, where he'd never been. Kristin Lund. Krissie sounded closer to home and just as beautiful. Krissie Lund. It rolled off the tongue like a balalaika riff. On this fine spring morning, she was wearing a pastel blue skirt, high-heeled pumps of the same subtle shade, and lemon-colored panty hose that matched her lemon-colored sweater. Krissie. She looked very much like spring. She smelled a lot like spring, too. If Hawes was not mistaken, she was wearing *Poison*.

She was not surprised to find two detectives on her doorstep so early in the morning; she had heard about Father Michael's murder late last night, on television. In fact, she had called 911 at once, to ask how she could get in touch with whoever would be investigating the case. The woman who'd answered the phone said, "What is the emergency, Miss?" When Krissie told her there *was* no emergency, the woman asked, "Do you wish to report a crime?" Krissie told her No, she didn't wish to report a crime, but she worked for the man whose murder she'd just heard reported on television and she wanted to know who'd be handling the case so she could contact them. The woman on the other end said, "One moment, please, I'll give you my supervisor." The supervisor came on and immediately said, "I understand you witnessed a murder," whereupon Krissie hung up, even if she was not a native of this city.

"But I *did* try to contact you," she said, and smiled so dazzlingly that Hawes almost swooned.

"When was this?" Carella asked.

"When?"

"When you tried to contact us."

"Oh. Right after the Eleven O'Clock News. I was going to call the church, but I called 911 instead. And then, after I spoke to that supervisor, I didn't know what to do. So I went to sleep. I figured you'd get to me sooner or later."

"Yes," Hawes said.

"So here you are," she said, and smiled again.

"Miss Lund," Carella said, "Father Michael's housekeeper . . ."

"Yes, Martha Hennessy."

"Yes, told us that the last time she saw him alive was when he was saying good night to you."

"That's the last time *I* saw him, too."

"At about five o'clock yesterday."

"Yes."

"Where did you go after that?"

"I came straight here."

They were in the kitchen of her small apartment on the fourth floor of a building downtown in The Quarter, far from the precinct territory. Coffee was brewing in a pot plugged into an outlet above a butcher block counter. Krissie leaned against the counter, her arms folded, waiting for the coffee to perk. She had set out three cups and saucers near the coffeepot. The detectives stood by the open window. A mild breeze fluttered the sheer white curtains on the window. Sunshine danced on the counter top, setting the bone white cups and saucers aglitter. Krissie lifted the pot and poured the three cups full. She carried them one at a time to a small round table near the window. The table was already set with teaspoons, paper napkins, a creamer, and a small bowl containing pink packets of a sugar substitute.

"Did you see anyone suspicious-looking outside the church?" Carella asked. "When you left last night?"

"Well, what do you mean by suspicious-looking? I mean . . . I guess you know that's a pretty rotten neighborhood. I mean, no offense, I know you guys do a good job. But to me, *everyone* up there looks suspicious."

"I was referring to anyone lurking about . . ."

Those words always made him feel foolish.

". . . anyone who seemed out of place . . ."

Those words, too.

". . . anyone who just didn't *belong* there," he said.

"Just the usual," Krissie said, and shrugged. Hawes loved the way she shrugged. "Milk?" she asked. "It's skim."

"By the usual . . . ?" Hawes asked.

"The usual," she said, and shrugged again. "I'm sure you know what's up there. The usual street mix. Crack dealers and buyers, hookers, hoodlums, the mix." She lifted her cup, sipped at the coffee.

"And last night, when you left . . . nothing but the mix."

"Just the mix."

"How about inside the church?" Carella asked. "See anything strange there? Anything out of the normal?"

"No."

"When you left the office . . . this was at five, you say?"

"Five, a little bit after."

"Were any of the file cabinets open?"

"They're never locked. We have keys, but . . ."

"No, I mean, were any of the drawers standing open?"

"No. Open? Why would they be?"

"Any papers on the floor?"

"No. Of course not."

"Everything neat and orderly."

"Yes."

"Miss Lund," Hawes said, "Father Michael's housekeeper mentioned that in recent weeks he'd been taking a strong church stand against . . ."

"Well, you don't think *that* had anything to do with his murder, do you?"

"What are you referring to?"

"The tithe."

"The tide?" Carella asked, puzzled.

"Tithe," she said, "tithe. The congregation is supposed to contribute ten percent of its earnings to the church. As a tithe. Aren't you familiar with that word? Tithe."

"Well, yes, it's just . . ."

He was thinking the word sounded medieval. He was thinking it did not sound like a word that should be lurking about in the here and now, a word that seemed out of place, a word that just didn't belong in this day and age. Tithe. Altogether archaic. Like a chastity belt. But he did not say this.

"What about this . . . tithe?" he asked.

"Well, she probably meant the sermons."

"What sermons?"

"Some pretty stiff sermons about shortchanging the church."

"Shortchanging?"

"Not dropping enough in the basket."

"I see. How many of these sermons were there?"

"Three. I know because I'm the one who typed them. All hellfire and brimstone. Unusual for Father Michael. He was normally . . ."

She hesitated.

"A very gentle man," she said at last.

"But not in these sermons," Hawes said.

"No. I suppose . . . well, the church really *is* in need of repair, hardly anything's been done to it in years. And, you know, the neighborhood *around* the church may be falling apart, but a lot of the parishioners come from five, six blocks away, where things are much better. Well, you know this city; you'll have a slum right next door to buildings with doormen. So he really *was* within his rights to ask for the proper tithe. Because, honestly, I think the neighborhood would be even *worse* by now if it wasn't for the work Father Michael does there. *Did* there," she said, correcting herself.

"What sort of work?" Carella asked.

"Well, trying to promote harmony," she said, "especially among the kids. The neighborhood up there is a mix of Italian, Irish, Hispanic and black—well, what am I telling you? Father Michael worked wonders with those kids. I'm sure you know what happened there on Easter Sunday . . ."

Carella shook his head.

So did Hawes.

"Well, it's *your* precinct," Krissie said, "I mean, don't you know what *happened* there? On Easter Sunday?"

"No, what happened there?" Carella asked, and tried to remember whether he'd had the duty on Easter Sunday.

"This was late in the afternoon," Krissie said, "this black kid came running into the church with his head all bloody. Half a dozen white kids were chasing him with stickball bats and garbage can covers, chased him right into the church, right up the center aisle to the altar. Father Michael stood his ground. Told them to get out of his church. Walked them right up the aisle to the door, escorted them out, told them not to come back until they knew how to behave in the house of God. I don't know who the kids were, neighborhood kids, I'm sure the incident is in your records, just look up Easter Sunday. Anyway, that's the kind of thing I mean. Father Michael was a meaningful force in that neighborhood. His congregation should have realized that. Instead of getting so offended. By the sermons, I mean."

"The money sermons," Carella said.

"The tithe sermons, yes," Krissie said.

"Some of his parishioners were offended by them?"

"Yes. By him calling the congregation . . . well, cheapskates, in effect."

"I see."

"From the pulpit."

"I see."

"One of the parishioners, I forget his name, distributed a letter that said Jesus had driven the money-changers from the temple and here they were back again . . . he was referring to Father Michael, you know. And the tithe sermons."

"They must have been pretty strong sermons," Hawes said.

"Well, no stronger than the *cult* sermons. I typed those, too."

"What cult sermons?" Carella asked.

"About the Church of the Bornless One."

"What's the Church of the Bornless One?"

"You mean you don't . . . come on, you're kidding me. It's right in the precinct. Only four blocks from St. Catherine's."

Hawes was wondering if Krissie Lund had ever thought of becoming a cop.

"I take it that the Church of the Bornless One is some kind of cult," he said.

"Devil worship," Krissie said.

"And you're saying that Father Michael wrote some sermons about . . ."

"About Satan being worshipped within a stone's throw of St. Catherine's, yes."

"Then that's what she was talking about," Hawes said, to Carella. "The housekeeper."

Carella nodded.

He reached into his jacket, took out his notebook, and removed a photograph from the front-cover flap.

"Ever see this before?" he asked, and handed the picture to Krissie.

The picture had been taken last night, by a police photographer using a Polaroid with a flash. Her exposure had been a bit off, and so the red wasn't as true as the actual red of the paint the graffiti artist had used, nor was the green of the gate quite as bilious. But it was a good picture nonetheless.

Krissie studied it carefully:

"What's it supposed to be?" she asked.

"Ever go around to the Tenth Street side of the church?"

"Yes?"

"Past the garden gate?"

"Yes?"

"This is what's painted on that gate."

"I'm sorry, I never noticed it," she said, and handed the photo back. "Does it mean something?"

Carella was thinking it meant that Satan was being worshipped within a stone's throw of St. Catherine's church, where a black kid had sought sanctuary from an angry white gang on Easter Sunday, and where an offended parishioner had circulated a letter about money-changers in the temple. He was thinking that in the world of the 87th Precinct, far uptown, any one of these things could be considered a reasonable cause for murder.

"Excuse me, Miss Lund," Hawes asked, "but is that *Poison?*"

"No," Krissie said, apparently knowing exactly what he was talking about. "It's *Opium.*"

She had trained herself never to respond to the name Mary Ann.

So when she heard the voice behind her now, speaking Spanish, using the name she'd discarded the moment she'd come to this city, she kept right on walking, paying no attention to it. She was *not* Mary Ann. She was certainly not Marianna to anyone speaking Spanish.

And then the voice said, "Ai, Mariucha," which was the Spanish diminutive for Mary. She had been called Mariucha in the Mexican prison. The nickname had followed her to Buenos Aires. And apparently here to this city as well. She kept walking. Her heart was pounding.

"Mariucha, *despacio,*" the voice said, and two men fell into step beside her, one on either side of her.

"Get away from me," she said at once, "or I'll yell for a cop."

"Oh dear," the handsome one said in Spanish.

"We don't want to hurt you," the ugly one said in Spanish.

Which meant he *did* want to hurt her, and *would* hurt her.

There was a switchblade knife in her handbag. She was prepared to use it if she had to.

They were coming up Concord, walking away from the cluster of buildings that in a city this size passed for a campus. The school was familiarly known as The Thousand Window Bakery, a reference too historically remote for Marilyn to understand, but accurate enough in that the university complex seemed to be fashioned entirely of glass. This was almost smack in the center of the island that was Isola, equidistant from the rivers bordering it north and south, only slightly closer to the old Seawall downtown than to the Riverhead bridges all the way uptown. The neighborhood was still a good one. Plenty of shops and restaurants, movie theaters, apartment buildings with door-men and—there ahead on the corner—a pair of uniformed cops basking in the spring sunshine.

"Don't do anything foolish," the handsome one said in Spanish.

She walked directly to the policemen.

"These men are bothering me," she said.

The cops looked at the two men.

The handsome one smiled.

The ugly one shrugged.

Neither of them said a word. They seemed to recognize that if they opened their mouths in this city and either Spanish or broken English came tumbling out, they'd be in serious trouble.

Marilyn kept waiting for the cops to do something.

The cops kept looking at the two men.

They were both well-dressed. Dark suits. White shirts. A red tie on one of them, a blue tie on the other. Both wearing pearl grey fedoras. Very neat. Very elegant-looking. Two legitimate businessmen enjoying a fine spring day.

"Guys," one of the cops said, "the lady doesn't wish to be bothered."

He said this in the fraternal tone that men adopt when they are suggesting to other men that this is a nice piece of ass here and we could all handily take our pleasure of her were we of a mind to, but out of the goodness and generosity of our masculine hearts, let's not bother the lady if she does not wish to be bothered, hmmhh? Marilyn almost expected him to wink at the handsome one and nudge the ugly one in the ribs.

The handsome one shrugged, as if to say We are all men of the world who understand the vagaries of women.

The ugly one sighed heavily, as if to say We are all occasionally burdened by these beautiful, unpredictable creatures, especially at certain times of the month. Then he took the handsome one's arm, and led him away quickly and silently.

"Okay?" the cop asked Marilyn.

She said nothing.

The ugly one was looking back at her.

There was a chilling promise in his eyes.

All of the windows in the station house were open. The barred windows on the ground-floor level, the grilled windows on the upper stories. It suddenly occurred to Carella that a police station looked like a prison. Even with the windows open, it looked like a prison. Grey, soot-covered granite blocks, a green-tiled roof stained with a century's worth of pigeon shit, green globes flanking the entrance steps and announcing in faded white numerals that here was the Eight-Seven, take it or leave it. Carella had been taking it for a good many years now.

The priest's papers were waiting on his desk.

Not eighteen hours after the discovery of Father Michael's body, his various papers—those strewn on his office floor, those still in his file cabinets or on his desk—had already been examined by the lab and sent back uptown again by messenger. This was very fast work. But the Commissioner himself—who happened to be black and who attended a Baptist church in the Diamondback section of the city where he'd been born and raised—had this morning made a television appearance on *The Today Show*, announcing by network to the nation at large that this city *could* not, and *would* not tolerate the wanton murder of a gentle man of God of whatever persuasion. Not too many day-watch cops caught the show because they were already out on the beat asking discreet questions in an attempt to aid and abet the investigating cops of the Eight-Seven while simultaneously mollifying the irate Commissioner himself. Up in the Eight-Seven, life went on as usual; priest or not, this was just another garden-variety murder, no pun intended, in a part of the city choked with weeds.

It was lunchtime in the squadroom.

The detectives sat around in shirt sleeves and pistols. Sandwiches and coffee, pizza and Cokes were spread on the desks before them. Only Meyer waved to Carella as he came in. The others were too busy listening to Parker.

"There is not going to be no mystery in these Dallas murders, I promise you," Parker said.

"There's *never* any mystery," Brown said.

"That I know. But what I'm saying, this is going to be even *less* of a mystery than there usually is. Especially since it's Texas."

"Love or money," Meyer said. "Those are the only two reasons for murder."

"That's why there are no mysteries, is what I'm saying," Brown said.

"Tell me all about it," Parker said. "But what *I'm* saying is the only mystery here is *who* the guy *is. What* he is, is a crazy."

"That's the third reason," Kling said. "Lunacy."

"There's nothing mysterious about any lunatic in the world," Parker said. "This thing in Dallas is gonna turn out to be just what the newspapers and the TV are saying it is, I'll bet you a hundred bucks. It's a crazy running around killing blondes. That's *all* it is. When they catch this guy, he'll be nuttier than a Hershey bar, you wait and see."

Carella wasn't particularly eager to tackle the priest's papers. Hawes had gone downtown directly after they'd left the Lund apartment, heading for Ballistics where he was trying to pry loose a report on a gun used in an armed robbery. This meant that Carella now had to wade through all this stuff by himself. The papers were in several large manila envelopes marked EVIDENCE. The papers themselves, however, were not *evidence* per se, in that the prints lifted from them had already been marked and filed downtown. Without the prints, the papers were merely *papers*, which might or might not contain information.

But the Police Department had a lot of manila envelopes of various sizes, all of them printed with the word EVIDENCE, and a cop was likely as not to grab one of these envelopes whenever he wanted to send or take something someplace, even if the something was a ham sandwich he planned to have for lunch. So whoever had examined these papers at the lab had later stuffed them into seven large EVIDENCE envelopes, and then had stamped the envelopes RUSH, and further stamped them BY MESSENGER because a priest had been killed in this city with an Irish-Catholic police department, and then had wrapped the little red strings around the little red buttons, and here they were on Carella's desk alongside another EVIDENCE envelope that did in fact contain a ham sandwich he planned to eat for lunch.

He hated paperwork.

This was a whole hell of a lot of paperwork on his desk.

The clock on the wall read ten minutes to one.

"What this is," Brown said, "is a guy whose mother was a blonde, she used to lock him in the closet every day 'cause he wet the bed. So now he's got a thing about blondes. He thinks all blondes are his mother. So he's got to kill every blonde in the world before one of them locks him in the closet again."

"Like I said," Parker said.

"My mother is blonde," Kling said.

"Did she lock you in the closet every day?"

"She chained me in the basement."

"Because you wet the bed?"

"I still wet the bed."

"He thinks he's kidding," Parker said.

"What this thing in Texas is," Kling said, "is a guy who has a blonde wife he hates. So first he kills the two blondes he already did, then the next one'll be his wife, and he'll kill two more blondes after that, and everybody'll think it's a crazy blonde-hater doing the murders. When instead it's just this little guy, he's an accountant or something, his wife is a big fat blonde he's been married to for forty years, he can't stand her, he has to get rid of her."

"No, I don't think this is no smoke screen," Parker said.

Carella figured he'd sooner or later have to dig into this mound of stuff here on his desk. It was just that it looked so *formidable.* All those envelopes full of papers. Stalling, he picked up the phone and dialed the lieutenant's extension.

"How do you feel?" Byrnes asked.

"What do you mean?"

"Your headache."

"All gone."

"The P.C. was on television this morning," Byrnes said.

"Yes, I know."

"A speech for every occasion, right? So what do you think? Any leads yet?"

"Not yet. I just got the priest's papers, there's a lot of stuff to look at here."

"What kind of papers?"

"Correspondence, sermons, bills, like that."

"Any diary?"

"Not according to the lab inventory."

"Too bad," Byrnes said, and then hesitated and said, "Steve . . ." and hesitated again and finally said, "I'd like to be able to tell the Commissioner something soon."

"I understand."

"So let me know the minute anything looks good."

"I will."

"It was probably some kind of bug," Byrnes said, "the headache."

And hung up.

Carella put his own phone back on the cradle, and looked at all those unopened evidence envelopes again. The pile hadn't diminished one damn bit. He decided to go to the Clerical Office for a cup of coffee. When he got back to his own desk, they were still talking about the murders in Dallas.

"You want to know what *I* think it is?" Genero said.

"What is it, Genero?"

"It's the full moon, is what it is."

"Yes, Genero, thank you," Parker said. "Go down the hall and take a pee, okay?"

"It's a known fact that when there's a full moon . . ."

"What has the full moon got to do with blondes?"

"Nothing. But . . ."

"Then what the fucka you talkin' about?"

"I'm saying in the same week there's two dead blondes is what I'm saying. And there happens to be a full moon this week."

"There is no such thing as a full moon that lasts a whole *week*," Parker said. "And also, what makes you think a full moon here in this city means there's also a full moon in Dallas, Texas, where this fuckin' *lunatic* is killin' these blondes?"

"It's a known fact," Genero said, "that there was a full moon on Monday when the first blonde turned up. And the moon was *still* pretty full *last* night when the *second* blonde turned up."

"Go take your pee, willya?"

Carella looked at all the evidence bags and wondered which one he should open first. He looked up at the clock. Almost a quarter past one. He could not think of a single other thing that might keep him from starting the paperwork. So he opened the bag with the ham sandwich in it.

Alternately chewing on his sandwich and sipping at his coffee, he began browsing—no sense jumping into icy-cold water all at once—through the papers in the first envelope. From the handwritten list on the outside of the envelope—written by someone at the lab whose initials were R.L.—and through his own corroboration of the list, the first envelope contained only bills, canceled checks, and check stubs. The checks were printed with the heading *St. Catherine's Roman Catholic Church Corporation*, and beneath that *Michael Birney, PSCCA*. All of the bills were for expenses Father Birney had incurred as parish priest. There were bills and consequent checks for electricity . . .

. . . and fuel oil . . .

. . . and snow plowing . . .

. . . and food . . .

. . . and postage . . .

. . . and salaries . . .

Martha Hennessy, for example, got a check every week for $224.98 after deductions of $21.02 for FICA and $34.00 for Federal Withholding Tax. Kristin Lund got a check every other week for $241.37 after deductions of \$21.63 for FICA and \$25.00 for Federal Withholding Tax . . .

"You want to know what this is?" Meyer said. "This is a guy who went out with this blonde, Mary, Marie, whatever her name was . . ."

"Matilda," Parker said. "The first one."

"Matilda, and it was a first date, and he tried to score but she turned him down. So he got so pissed off, he killed her. Then last night . . ."

"Where'd you get Mary or Marie?" Brown asked. "When the woman's name was Matilda?"

"What difference does it make what her name was? She's dead. The point is . . ."

"I'm just curious how you got Mary from Matilda?"

"I made it up, okay?"

"You musta."

. . . and telephone bills, and bills from a photocopying service and a local garage, and bills for the church's missalettes, and mortgage bills, and bills for maintenance of the church grounds, and medical insurance bills, and newspaper delivery bills, and bills for flowers for the altar, and dozens of other bills, all of which Father Michael paid like clockwork on the first and the fifteenth of every month. There were very few bills for personal clothing, and these for relatively small amounts. The biggest such item was for a new down parka at two hundred and twenty-seven dollars; it had been a severe winter.

"What I'm saying," Meyer said, "is that last night, this guy is *still* pissed off just *thinking* about it. So he goes out and finds himself another blonde to kill."

"How long's he gonna stay pissed off, this guy?"

"I'll bet you the one last night was the end of it."

"Until there's another full moon," Genero said.

"Will you fuck off with your full moon?" Parker said.

"One thing I'm glad of," Brown said.

"Tomorrow's your day off," Parker said.

"That, too. But I'm also glad this lunatic ain't doing it *here.*"

"Amen," Parker said.

The priest sent quarterly checks to the archdiocese—the last one had been written on the thirty-first of March—for something he listed as "cathedraticum" on the stub; Carella had no idea what this might be. Six checks had been written on the day of Father Michael's death:

A check to Bruce Macauley Tree Care, Inc. for "Spraying done on 5/19" in the amount of \$37.50.

A check to US Sprint for "Service thru 5/17" in the amount of $176.80.

A check to Isola Bank and Trust for "June mortgage" in the amount of $1480.75.

A check to Alfred Hart Insurance Company for "Honda Accord LX, Policy # HR 9872724" in the amount of $580.

A check to Orkin Exterminating Co. Inc. for "May services" in the amount of $36.50.

And a check to The Wanderers for "Band deposit" in the amount of $100.00.

That was it.

Each month, the balance in the St. Catherine's Roman Catholic Church Corporation checkbook leveled off at about a thousand dollars. There seemed to be nothing irregular about Father Michael's accounts.

The next evidence envelope contained his correspondence.

The first letter Carella took out of the package was written on blue stationery, addressed in a woman's hand to Father Michael Birney at St. Catherine's Church Rectory. He looked at the return address. Mrs. Irene Brogan. The postmark on the envelope was from San Diego, California, and it was dated May 19. He opened the envelope and took the letter from it:

My dearest brother,
*   I am now in receipt of yours of May 12th, and I cannot tell you with what a saddened heart I hasten to . . .*

"I'm back," Hawes said from the gate in the slatted rail divider. "Did you solve it yet?"

3

"WHAT'S THIS CASE you're working, anyway?" Parker said, turning to Carella.

Carella told him they had a D.O.A. priest, stab-and-slash, weapon unknown, housekeeper and secretary last ones to see him alive, wild prints all over the church and the rectory, random latents lifted from the papers here, but they were most likely the secretary's. He also told Parker that the housekeeper thought the Devil had dusted the priest and that in addition to the Devil the priest had also pissed off some local youngsters as well as his own congregation.

Parker thought this was very comical. He began laughing. So did Genero.

"This is his correspondence here," Carella told Hawes. "Just dig in."

"You're gonna have a lot of fun there," Parker said, "reading a priest's mail," and burst out laughing again. Genero started laughing again, too. Both men sat there giggling like teenagers. Hawes figured it was spring fever.

At his own desk, Carella went back to the letter from Father Michael's sister:

My dearest brother,
I am now in receipt of yours of May 12th, and I cannot tell you with what a saddened heart I hasten to respond. Michael, how have you managed to construct such a tower of doubt for yourself? And don't you feel you should relate your fears to the bishop of your diocese? I just don't know how to counsel or advise you.
I wish I could be closer to you during this difficult time. What makes matters worse is that Roger and I are leaving for Japan this

Saturday, and we won't be back till the tenth of June. I'll try to call
you before we leave, so we can have a good long telephone visit.
Perhaps, by then, the skies above will look a bit clearer.

Meanwhile, let me say only this: I know that you are a devout and
loyal servant of God and that however troubled you may now be,
you will find through prayer the way to enlightenment and salvation.

Your loving sister,
Irene

Carella turned over the envelope again.

He pulled the phone to him, lifted the receiver, asked the operator
for the San Diego area code, dialed 1-619-555-1212 for information,
and got a listing for a Roger Brogan at the address on the back of the
envelope. He dialed the number and let the phone ring twenty times
before hanging up.

"Here's something," Hawes said.

She did not think they were policemen. If they were policemen, they'd
have identified themselves at once to the street-corner cops she'd
approached. Flash the tin, reveal themselves as part of the great fraternal order of law enforcement officers. So no, they weren't cops.

They were Spanish-speaking. This frightened her. They had known
the name Mary Ann and had further known the nickname Mariucha.
This frightened her even more. They could have got the Mary Ann
from Houston, but not the Mariucha. This had to have come from
either *La Fortaleza* or Buenos Aires. So either they'd been asking questions at the prison, or else they'd been snooping around B.A. Either
way, they were here. Moreover, they had tracked her to the school.
Which meant they probably knew where she lived as well.

She knew she should tell Willis, but she was so afraid of losing him.
Afraid, too, that the trouble these men represented might somehow
rub off on him, cause problems for him on the job. She loved him too
dearly for that. So no, she couldn't tell him. She'd brought this trouble
upon herself, whatever it turned out to be, and she had to handle it
herself. Which was why she had to get a gun; the switchblade knife
seemed suddenly inadequate for defense, especially against the big,
ugly one. But how? And where?

The gun laws were tough in this state. You needed a permit before
you could walk into a shop and pick one off the shelf. And you needed a
damn good reason for *wanting* that permit. So how far would she have

to travel to buy a gun? Even in the immediately adjoining states, didn't shopowners have to file police applications well before letting you walk out with a gun? So where did the gun laws get easy? How far across the river and into the trees? How far north, east, south or west? Where in these surrounding United States could a person legally buy a gun to kill her husband or her mother, or, better yet, two Spanish-speaking goons who'd called her by her prison name, her Buenos Aires street name?

Where?

She was living with a cop and personally knew at least three dozen cops in this city, had gone out to dinner with them, been in their homes, but there wasn't a single one of them she could ask about getting a—well, maybe . . . yes, that was a possibility. Eileen Burke. Call her up, ask her out to lunch. Eileen was a cop, casually swing the conversation around to how and where a person might acquire a hot gun in this—no, she was too smart, she'd tip in a minute, know immediately that it was Marilyn herself who was looking for the gun. Besides, she wasn't sure Eileen even *liked* her. Wasn't sure, for that matter, that *any* of Willis's friends liked her. A hooker. A former hooker.

Hookers knew people who knew where to get guns.

In Houston, she'd have known where to get a gun.

In Buenos Aires, she'd have known where to get a gun.

But this was here and this was now, and she'd been out of the life too long.

Or had she?

"If you're looking for a motive, this could be a motive," Hawes said, and handed a sheet of paper across the desk. It was the sort of newsletter that years ago would have been typed first and then mimeographed. Today, it had started as a computer printout and had later been photocopied, several copier streaks across the page being the only clues to duplication. Carella wondered how many of them had been distributed. He also wondered how anyone had got along before Xeroxing was invented. Xeroxing? That was already the Stone Age. The Clerical Office's new fax machine was the *true* miracle.

My Fellow Parishioners:

For the past several weeks now, Father Michael Birney, the pastor assigned to guide the flock of St. Catherine's Church, has on more than one occasion seen fit to use the pulpit as a scolding board for our . . .

"What's a 'scolding board'?" Carella asked.

"Just keep reading," Hawes said, "it's self-explanatory."

... scolding board for our congregation. On these occasions, he has taken it upon himself to rail, nag, upbraid, revile, and berate ...

"See what I mean?" Hawes said.

"Mmm," Carella said.

... the good and decent people of this parish for failing to meet their financial obligations by way of the weekly tithe to the Lord Our God. He has pointed out that there are no less than forty-eight references to the tithe in scriptures. He has seen fit to quote many of these Old Testament passages, the most recent of which he included in last Sunday's sermon at a time of the year better suited to more spiritual matters. I quote it again now:

"From the days of your fathers you have turned aside from my statutes and have not kept them. Return to me, and I will return to you, says the Lord of hosts.

But you say, 'How shall we return?'

Will man rob God? Yet you are robbing me.

But you say, 'How are we robbing thee?'

In your tithes and offerings! You are cursed with a curse, for you are robbing me!

Bring the full tithes into the storehouse, that there may be food in my house!"

This from a spiritual leader, who has known nothing but kindness and generosity from the good people of this parish. My fellow parishioners, I would like to offer my own quote from the Holy Bible. This is from the Gospel According to John, Chapter 2, verses 14 to 16:

"In the temple he found those who were selling oxen and sheep and pigeons, and the money-changers at their business. And making a whip of cords, he drove them all, with the sheep and oxen, out of the temple; and he

poured out the coins of the money-changers and overturned their tables. And he told those who sold the
pigeons, 'Take these things away; you shall not make my
Father's house a house of trade!' "

Father Michael Birney is making our Father's house a
house of trade!

We are all well aware of our obligation to the Lord, we
know full well that five percent of our annual income is
expected by way of a weekly offering to the church. But we
refuse to be turned into a congregation of bookkeepers. Let
Father Michael count the offerings again and yet another
time, and then let him count his blessings as well. A noble
man of God might then do well to apologize from the pulpit
for accusing his parishioners of robbing from . . .

"Catch the last line," Hawes said.

. . . robbing from the Lord! Pride goeth before destruction,
and a haughty spirit before a fall.

Yours in Christ,
Arthur L. Farnes

"Well . . ." Carella said, and handed the letter back.
"I know. You dismiss a loony right off because you think nobody
mails such a letter to the whole congregation and then actually goes
out to *kill* somebody. But suppose . . ."
"Uh-huh."
". . . suppose this guy really *was* mad enough to go juke this priest? I
mean, he sounds pretty damn angry, doesn't he? I'm not a Catholic, so
I don't . . ."
"Me neither," Carella said. He considered himself a lapsed Catholic;
his mother said, "Shame on you."
"Okay, so I don't know how far you can go with yelling at the priest
assigned to your church, *if* in fact he *is* assigned, that's something I
don't know."
"Me neither."
"But let's *say* he's assigned and let's say you're unhappy with the
way he's bugging you about paying your dues . . ."
"Your tithe."

"Same thing, so you write a letter . . . for what purpose? To get him recalled? Do they do that in the Catholic Church? Recall a priest who isn't getting along with his congregation?"

"I really don't know."

"Neither do I."

"Or do you write to warn him that if he doesn't cut it out you're going to overturn his tables? I mean, really, Steve, a lot of the stuff in this letter sounds like a warning."

"Where does it sound like a warning?"

"You don't think this whole money-changer-in-the-*temple* stuff sounds like a warning?"

"No."

"You *don't?*"

"I really don't. Where else do you see a warning?"

"Where *else?* Okay, where else? How about here, for example? Dit-dah, dit-dah, di . . . *here.* 'Let him count his blessings.' Doesn't that sound like a warning?"

"No."

"Let the man count his *blessings?* That doesn't sound like a warning to you?"

"No, it doesn't."

"Let him count his blessings before it's too *late!*"

"Where does it say that?"

"Say what?"

" 'Before it's too late.' "

"It doesn't. I'm extrapolating."

"What does that mean, extrapolating?"

"It means to infer from what you already know."

"How do you know that?"

"I just happen to know it."

"I still don't think if you ask a man to count his blessings it's neces- sarily a warning."

"You don't."

"No, I don't."

"Okay, how about here? 'A noble man of God might then do well to apologize from the pulpit for accusing his parishioners of robbing from the Lord!' Or *else,* right?"

"Where does it say 'Or else'?"

"Right here. 'Pride goeth before destruction, and a haughty spirit before a fall.' "

"That doesn't say 'Or else.' "

"That's the *code* for 'Or else.' Look, you don't want to go talk to this guy, we won't go talk to him, forget it. I just thought . . ."

"He sounds like a very religious man, that's all," Carella said. "There are people like that in the world."

Like my father, Hawes thought, but didn't say. Who named me Cotton. After the Puritan Priest.

"You want to know something?" he said. "In this world, there are a lot of very religious people who are out of their minds, did you know that? And some of them have been known to stick knives in other people. Now I'm not saying this Arthur L. Farnes—which is the name of a lunatic to *begin* with—is the dude who done the priest, but I *am* saying you get a letter like this one, it could be a death threat is what I'm saying, and we'd be very dumb cops if we didn't go knocking on this guy's door right this minute, is what we should do."

"I agree with you," Carella said.

Schuyler Lutherson wanted to know who among his disciples had sprayed the inverted pentagram on St. Catherine's churchyard gate.

"Because, see," he said, "I don't want policemen coming here."

Schuyler Lutherson was not his real name. His real name was Samuel Leeds, a nice enough name except that the Samuel sounded like a prophet in the Old Testament (which was the last thing on earth he wanted to sound like) and the Leeds sounded like a manufacturing town in the north of England. Actually, his great-great-great-grandfather *had* been an ironmonger in Leeds before coming to America, but that was ancient history and Schuyler chose to trace his heritage more fancifully.

He had picked the given name Schuyler not because it meant a "scholar" or a "wise man" in Dutch (actually, he was quite unfamiliar with the Dutch language) but because it sounded like "sky," as in the skies above, or the heavens above, or the Kingdom of God above, from which an angel once had fallen. For was it not Satan himself who'd been unceremoniously expelled from Heaven, hurled from the upper stratosphere to the fiery lower depths? And was not Satan simultaneously known as Lucifer, whose name Samuel Leeds could not appropriate out of worshipful humility, but whose name he could at least echo alliteratively . . . Lucifer, Luther . . . and then rhyme slantingly . . . Lucifer, Lutherson . . . the surname achieving grandeur in retrospect, Lutherson, the son of Luther, the son of Lucifer, leader of the Church of the Bornless One, all hail Satan!

Not bad for a kid of nineteen, which was how old Schuyler had been when he originated his church in Los Angeles. He was now thirty-nine years old, that had been twenty years ago, away back in the days of the flower children, remember, Maude? When everyone was preaching love? Except Schuyler Lutherson on the pulpit of the Church of the Bornless One, where between the spread legs of a different voluntary "altar" each week, he preached the opposite of love, he preached hate, scorching pussy after pussy with the white-hot scorn of his seed. Everything in the worship of Satan was a study in opposites, an exercise in reversal or obversion. Through hate, love. Through denial, acceptance. Through darkness, light. Through evil, good.

Even Schuyler's carefully cultivated appearance supported the tenets of his creed. Not for him the sham look of a bearded devil with arched eyebrows, nor for him the silken crimson robes and peaked hood. Was he a true and sacred priest of a church dedicated to the Infernal One, or merely a Halloween caricature? Would the Devil on earth appear before man *as* the Devil, or would he in his infinite evil and guile assume the shape of some lesser form? And likewise, and even so, would the *son* of Satan—Lucifer's son, *Lutherson!*—lift the cuff of an earthly trouser to expose a furry ankle and a cloven hoof? Would he advertise his yellow eyes like beacons to unbelievers? Would he blow the foul breath of brimstone and piss from his nostrils, regurgitate purple vomit into the faces of fools, would this be the proper behavior and appearance of Lord Satan's son and servant?

Schuyler Lutherson was blond.

He had blue eyes.

He had begun lifting weights during a short stretch he'd served in a juvenile detention facility in California, back before he'd changed his name, and he still worked out at a gym near the church three times a week. As a result, he had the slim, lithe, sinewy body of a long-distance runner.

His nose would have been Grecian perfection, had it not once been broken at that selfsame detention facility, where the fair-haired, fuzzy-cheeked as-yet-unborn Schuyler Lutherson was forced to protect his ass from an older, huskier boy determined to have a taste of it at all costs. The "all costs" he'd had in mind did not include the ruptured spleen he'd suffered after he'd broken the nascent Schuyler's nose and declared his intention of making him his "private and personal pussy." The Schuyler-Lutherson-to-be used a two-by-four by way of discouragement, picking it up from a pile of lumber in the carpentry shop and wielding it like a baseball bat. The older boy never bothered him again. Neither did anyone else.

Schuyler had a wide androgynous mouth, with the full lower lip of a pouting screen siren, and the rather thin upper lip of a politician. He had even white teeth, the better to eat you with, my dear. That they were capped was a matter of small import or note. When he smiled, the gates to the infernal chambers opened wide and eternal midnight beckoned.

He was smiling now, wanting to know who—exactly—had painted the pentagram on the church gate.

He spoke deliberately and precisely.

"Who, exactly, painted the pentagram on the fucking gate?" he asked.

Through obscenity, purity.

The three looked at him.

Two women and a man. Each of the women had served as altars many time. Through Satan, Schuyler knew them intimately. The man knew them intimately as well, through the public rites of Satanic fornication that followed each ritual renunciation. One of the women was named Laramie. The other was named Coral. These were not their real names. The man was named Stanley. This *was* his real name; who on earth would want to change his name *to* Stanley unless he planned on becoming a dentist? Stanley was a salary-drawing church deacon. Laramie and Coral were disciples, and did not draw salaries per se, but money somehow stuck to their fingers. Laramie was black and Coral was white and Stanley was Hispanic; this was a regular United Nations here. Together they pondered who might have been foolish enough to decorate the church gate with a pentagram.

"Because now, see," Schuyler said, "the priest is dead."

Stanley shook his head, not in sorrow, but in dismay: the priest was now indeed dead, and someone had painted a pentagram on St. Catherine's gate. Stanley's head was massive and covered with long tawny, tangled hair that gave him the look of a middle-aged lion; when he shook his head, the gesture was monumental.

"We have nothing to hide here, that's true," Schuyler said.

Both women nodded, a symphony in black and white togetherness. Coral was wearing a paisley patterned skirt and a white peasant blouse, no bra. She had long blonde hair, eyes as blue as Schuyler's, and a button nose dusted with freckles. Laramie was wearing skin-tight jeans, boots, and a sweater. She was tall and strikingly good-looking, a Masai woman miraculously transported to the big bad city. By comparison, Coral looked like a prairie housewife—which incidentally she'd been before coming east to join Schuyler's church. The women were thinking hard. Who could have been dumb enough to paint a pentagram on the churchyard gate? This was the burning question of the day.

"But, see," Schuyler said, "suppose the police start raising some of the same questions that asshole priest raised? Suppose they come here and want to know this or that, see, as for example, are we popping X during the mass, which is a controlled substance, see? We can always tell the Man we are *not* doing Ecstasy nor anything *else* at our services, which by the way are private services, see, and not open to the public except by invitation, is what we could tell the Man. But then we'll have police shit, see, we'll have them coming around with search warrants and whatnot, looking for this or that, breaking our balls merely on principle, which is what cops know how to do very well. Because what they are going to figure, see, in their limited way, is that if somebody painted a pentagram on the fucking gate, then maybe that same person did the priest. And they're going to be all over us like locusts."

"Excuse me, Sky," Coral said.

"Yes, Coral."

Gently. His eyes caressing her. He would ask her to serve as altar again this Saturday night, May twenty-sixth, a night of no particular significance in the church calendar except that it followed immediately after the high holy solemnity of the Feast of the Expulsion. The two most important religious holidays, of course, were Walpurgisnacht and All Hallows' Eve. But these were nights of wild abandon, and the Feast of the Expulsion was traditionally more sedate. This was why the mass on Saturday following was generally anticipated as a time of greater release and realization. Coral would make a perfect altar. Lying on the draped trapezoid each time, her legs spread, her hands clutching those candelabra, she was a woman in constant motion, twitching in expectation. Even standing here before him now, she shifted from foot to foot, her right hand twisting her skirt like a little girl, twisting it.

"I feel we should open this to the entire congregation, Sky, put to them that someone in our midst—perhaps through overzealousness, or perhaps through just sheer stupidity—has placed the church in a precarious position, Sky. And we should ask whoever it was that painted the pentagram on the gate to come forward and admit it, and then perhaps go to the police voluntarily, himself or herself, and say

ED MCBAIN

what it was they done. So the investigation would end right there, with
whoever actually put that symbol on the gate. Is what I think, Sky."

Flat midwestern voice, little gap between her two upper front teeth.
Twisting her skirt like a little girl called on to recite. Like to do a mass
over her right this fucking minute, he thought.

"I think Coral's right," Stanley said, nodding his massive leonine
head. "Throw it open to the congregation . . ."

Throw it open *wide* to the congregation, Schuyler thought.

". . . this Saturday night, before the mass actually starts, before you
do the Introit. Explain to them we're in jeopardy here because of some
dumb thing somebody did in all innocence . . ."

"Un*less,*" Laramie said.

Woman of few words.

Said her piece, did her little Masai dance, and then got off the stage.

"Unless whoever painted the star *also* killed the priest."

Schuyler looked at her.

"Do you think that's really a possibility?" he asked.

"After what the priest said?"

She shrugged.

The shrug made it abundantly clear that whatever the priest had said
could, in the proper mind, have taken seed as a motive for murder.

"A total asshole," Schuyler said. "If he'd kept his mouth shut . . ."

"But he didn't."

This from Laramie again, who made an art of keeping her mouth
shut most of the time.

"No, that's true," Schuyler said, "he didn't. Which is why we now
find ourselves in a situation that is potentially, see, dangerous. I can tell
you I don't want policemen coming here. I don't want them looking
into this or that, discovering that little girls perform certain parts of the
ritual, discovering that on occasion we've used harmless though controlled substances in support of the mass, discovering that on occasion
we've even sacrificed small animals during the mass, though I can't
imagine *that's* against the fucking law, is it? The point is, see, the priest
made enough of a fuss from the pulpit, brought enough attention to us,
calling us—what was it, Stanley?—a neighborhood thorn in the side of
Christ, can you believe it? Which, of course, illustrates what a threat
our church actually *is*, illustrates clearly, see, how desperately the
Christ-lovers would love to drive us into non-existence, murder the
infant church in its cradle, see. But . . ."

"Sky."

From Coral. Softly.

"I think we ought to contact the police our ownselves," she said, "*before* the mass tomorrow night—right *away*, in fact—to tell them we're aware of what's painted on that gate and to let them know we're doing our own internal examination . . ."

The *words* she used.

". . . in an effort to determine who put the star on there, so he or she herself can come forward and reveal who they are, Sky. This way we're immediately letting the police know we're doing everything in our power to cooperate. So they won't think some kind of *cabal* connected with our church put the sacred sign on the priest's gate and then killed him."

"Un*less*," Laramie said.

They all turned to look at her.

"Unless that's exactly what *did* happen," she said.

Arthur Llewellyn Farnes was a tall, rangy white man with the speech of a born and bred city-dweller, and the look of a weather-hardened New England farmer. His men's clothing store was on The Stem between Carson and Coles, and he had just come back from lunch when the detectives walked in at two o'clock that afternoon. Most of his lunch seemed to have spilled onto his tie and his vest. Carella guessed he was the only man outside of Homicide Division who still wore a vest. He was willing to bet he also wore a fedora.

The detectives identified themselves and told him they were investigating the murder of Father Michael Birney. Farnes went into a long and apparently heartfelt eulogy on the priest he had only recently challenged in his open letter, now calling him a dedicated man of God, a true servant of the Lord, a kind and gentle shepherd to the church's flock, and a wonderful human being whose absence would be sorely felt.

All this with a straight face.

"Mr. Farnes," Hawes said, "we were looking through Father Michael's correspondence, and we came across this letter you sent to the congregation . . ."

"Yes," Farnes said, and smiled, and shook his head.

"You know the letter I mean, right?"

"Yes. The one I wrote in response to his sermons about the tithe."

"Yes," Hawes said.

"Yes," Farnes said.

He was still smiling. But now he was nodding. Yes, his head went. Yes, I sent that letter. Yes. In response to him chastening us about our church obligations. Yes, I'm the one who voiced resentment. Yes. Me. Nodding, nodding.

"What about that letter, Mr. Farnes?"

"What about it?" Farnes said.

"Well, I'd say it was a pretty angry letter, wouldn't you?"

"Only *pretty* angry? I'd say it was *monumentally* angry."

The detectives looked at him.

"In fact, Mr. Farnes," Hawes said, "you wrote some things in that letter . . ."

"Yes, I was furious."

"Uh-huh."

"Demanding money that way! As if we weren't *already* giving our fair share! All the man had to do was trust us! But, no! Runs his mouth off at the pulpit instead, week after week of fire-and-brimstone sermons better suited to Salem Village than to this parish! Never once trusting us! Excuse me," he said, and walked immediately to where a man was taking a pair of trousers from the rack. "May I help you, sir?" he asked.

"Just looking," the man said. "Are these all the forty-two longs you have?"

"Yes, from here to the end of the rack."

"Thank you," the man said.

"Let me know if I can be of any assistance," Farnes said, and walked back to the detectives. Lowering his voice, he said, "That man is a shoplifter. He walked out of here at Christmastime with an entire suit under the suit he was already wearing. I realized it after he was gone. Forgive me for watching him, but I'd like to catch the son of a bitch."

"So would we," Carella said.

"You were saying something about trust," Hawes said.

"Yes," Farnes said, his eyes following the man as he moved along the rack. "In many respects, the church is a business—and I mean no blasphemy. This is why a tithe is specified in the Bible, so there won't be any misunderstanding about the *business* the church is forced to conduct. In order to survive, do you understand? Ten percent, spelled out in black and white. Five in the basket every week, the other five as gifts to worthwhile charities. Do you follow me so far?"

"Yes, we follow you," Carella said.

"Okay. How do you know whether you're getting five percent in the basket? Instead of two percent or three and a half percent? The answer is you don't. You trust the congregation. By trusting them, you'll inspire their trust in turn, and you'll find that instead of getting a short count every week, you'll be generating even more revenue for the church. Any fool should . . ."

"Excuse me, but is this the dressing room?"

"Yes," Farnes said, "through the curtains there. Let me roll those trouser cuffs back for you, sir."

"That's all right, I can . . ."

"No problem at all, sir," Farnes said, and took the three pairs of trousers that were draped over the man's arm, and rolled back the cuffs, and said, "There you are, sir."

"Thank you," the man said.

"Let me know if you need any help," Farnes said, and came back to the detectives. Lowering his voice again, he said, "He's going in there with three pairs of pants. Let's see how many he walks out with."

"You were talking about trust," Hawes said.

"Yes," Farnes said. "I was saying that any fool should know you can't get anywhere in business—even if it's the business of saving souls for Jesus Christ—by not trusting the people you're doing business with. That's what I tried to explain to Father Michael, may God rest his soul, in my letter."

"It didn't sound as if your letter was about trust," Hawes said.

"It didn't? I thought it did."

"Well, for example, Mr. Farnes," Hawes said, having already gone over this with Carella and now considering himself an expert, "you don't think these words, do you, are about trust, here, this passage here," he said, unfolding the letter and finding what he was looking for, "here, Mr. Farnes, 'and he poured out the coins of the money-changers and overturned their tables.' Is that about trust, Mr. Farnes?"

"It's about not turning a place of worship into a place of commerce."

"Or how about this," Hawes said, gathering steam, "right here, Mr. Farnes, 'Let Father Birney count the offerings again and yet another time, and then let him count his blessings as well.' What did you mean by 'let him count his blessings as well'?"

"Let him realize that he is blessed with a good and generous congregation."

"And this? What does this mean? 'Pride goeth before destruction, and a haughty spirit before a fall.' Is that about trust?"

"It's about trusting the Lord to show the path that leads away from pride and haughtiness."

"Well, you certainly have an odd way of interpreting your own words," Hawes said. "Did you discuss any of this *personally* with Father Michael?"

"Yes. In fact, we had a good laugh over it."

"A good *what?*"

"A good laugh. Me and Father Michael."

"Had a laugh over this letter you wrote?"

"Oh, yes. Because I was so *incensed,* you see."

"And he found that funny, did he? That you were incensed enough . . ."

"Yes."

". . . by the sermons he'd given . . ."

"Yes."

". . . to have written a letter you yourself just described as 'monumentally angry.' He found that . . ."

"Yes, we both did."

". . . hilarious."

"Well . . ."

"Side-splittingly funny."

"No, but we *did* find it humorous. That I'd got so angry. That I'd written this righteous, indignant letter to the congregation when all I had to do, really, was go see Father Michael personally—as I finally did do—and have a pleasant chat with him, and straighten the whole thing out."

"So you straightened the whole thing out."

"Yes."

"When?"

"On Easter Sunday. I stopped by in the afternoon sometime, went back to the rectory with him. We had a good long talk."

"How'd you finally settle it?"

"Father Michael said he would ask each member of the congregation to confide in him the amount he or she could comfortably afford to contribute each Sunday, and then he would trust them to contribute that amount faithfully. It was all a matter of trust, you see. That's what I was able to explain to him when we talked. That he should just have a little trust." He glanced toward the curtains. The man who'd gone back with the three pairs of pants was just coming through into the store again. There were now only two pairs of pants slung over his arm.

"Just a minute, sir!" Farnes called.

"Ah, there you are," the man said. "I'll take the ones I'm wearing. Can I get them measured, please?"

"Why . . . why, yes, sir, certainly, sir," Farnes said, "please step right this way, the tailor's at the other end of the store."

"I left my own pants in the dressing room," the man said. "Will they be safe there?"

"Just have a little trust, sir," Hawes said.

Carella placed the call to the archdiocese at four-fifteen that afternoon. The man who answered the phone identified himself as Archbishop Quentin's secretary and told him that His Eminence was out at the moment but perhaps he could be of assistance. Carella told him this had to do with a murder he was investigating . . .

"Oh, dear."

"Yes, the murder of the priest up here . . ."

"Ah, yes."

"Father Michael Birney."

"Yes."

"And I'm calling because I'm trying to locate his sister, but there's no answer at the number I . . ."

"His Eminence has already taken care of that," the secretary said.

"Taken care of what?"

"Notifying Father Michael's sister."

"In Japan? How'd he . . . ?"

"Her husband's office number was in our files here. His Eminence was able to get the name of their hotel from Mr. Brogan's secretary, and he called Mrs. Brogan there. She'll be here Sunday in time for the funeral."

"Well, good," Carella said. "Would you happen to know if there are any other relatives? I'd like to . . ."

"I believe there was only the sister."

"And you say she'll be here Sunday?"

"She's already on the way, sir."

"Well, thank you very much."

"Not at all."

Carella put the phone back on the hook.

Already on her way, he thought.

Which meant that whatever had been troubling the good priest would have to wait till Sunday, after all.

The man sitting opposite Marilyn was a white man in his early fifties. His name was Shad Russell, and he knew why she was here, but he was making his pitch anyway because he figured it never hurt to take a chance. Shad used to be a gambler in Las Vegas before he came East and got himself settled in various other little enterprises. He had a pockmarked face from when he was a little kid, and he had a mustache that looked as if it could use some fertilizer, and he was as thin and as tall as Abraham Lincoln and he thought he had a devastating smile. Actually, he looked like a crocodile when he smiled. He was smiling now.

"So old Joe give you my number, huh?" he said.

"Yes," Marilyn said.

"Old Joe Seward," he said, and shook his head.

They were in his room on the second floor of the old Raleigh Hotel on St. Sebastian Avenue, near where the Warringer Theater used to be. Marilyn had come up here to Diamondback by taxi. She was wearing jeans and a leather jacket over a tan sweater. Her hair was pinned up under a woolen cap. It was one thing for a white woman to go alone into an exclusively black neighborhood to talk to someone a Texas pimp had recommended. It was another to go flashing long blonde hair.

"How is he?" Shad asked.

"I haven't seen him in years," she said.

"How come you know him?"

"He said you could help me find a gun."

"But that don't answer my question, does it?" Shad said, and smiled his crocodile smile. Marilyn had the sudden feeling that this was going to be harder than she'd thought.

"If you think I'm a cop or something . . ." she said.

"No, I . . ."

". . . you can call Joe on my credit card, and ask him to . . ."

"I already did."

The crocodile smile.

"Though not on your credit card."

The smile widening.

"On my own nickel. Right after you hung up. To ask him who this Mary Ann Hollis was that needed a gun so bad."

"And what'd he tell you?"

"He told me you used to work for him it musta been eight, nine years ago. When you were still in diapers. He said you used to have a piano-man pimp down there in Houston, but he got himself stabbed in a bar, which was when Joe come into your life. He also told me you got busted at the ripe old age of seventeen, and that he paid the five-bill fine and let you walk away from his stable 'cause you asked him nice and he happens to be a gent. So no, I'm not worried you're fuzz."

"Then why are you asking me things you already know?"

"I wanted to see if you'd lie."

"I would've."

"I figured. Why you need this piece?"

"Some people are bothering me."

"You going to shoot these people?"

"If I have to."

"And then what?"

"Then what what?"

"Who do you tell where you got the piece?"

"Not even my priest," Marilyn said.

"Yeah, I'll just bet you got a priest," Shad said, and smiled the crocodile smile again. "You still in the same line of work?"

"No."

"Too bad. 'Cause I could maybe find some major situations for somebody like you."

"Thanks, I'm not looking for any major . . ."

"Some *really* major . . ."

". . . or even *minor* ones. I need a gun. Can you sell me one? If not, *adiós.*"

"Think about the other for a minute."

"Not even for a second."

"Think about it," he said, and smiled. "Is there any harm thinking about it?"

"Yes, there is."

"Who you gonna shoot with this gun?"

"That's none of your business."

"If the gun comes back to me, then it *becomes* my business."

"It won't come back to you, don't worry."

"Are these people pimps? Does this involve prostitution?"

"No, I already told you, I'm not . . ."

" 'Cause I don't want some angry pimp comin' here yellin' one of his cunts tried to . . ."

"Goodbye, Mr. Russell," Marilyn said, and stood up, and slung her shoulder bag, and started for the door.

"What'd I do?" Shad asked. "Insult you? Too fuckin' bad. I got my own ass to protect here. I don't want no gun of mine involved in a family argument. You got a quarrel with your old man, go settle it with him quiet, you don't need no gun of mine."

"Thanks, I understand your position. It was nice meeting you."

"Look at her. All insulted on her fuckin' high horse. I hit it right on the head, didn't I? You want this gun to dust your pimp."

"Yep, right on the head. Goodbye, Mr. Russell. I'll be sure to tell Joe how helpful you were."

"Sit down, what's your fuckin' hurry? If this ain't a pimp, then what is it? Dope?"

"No."

"You say some people are bothering you, what are they bothering you for? Did you forget to pay them for their cocaine?"

"Do you have a gun for me, or don't you? I don't need this bullshit, I really don't."

"A gun will cost you," he said.

"How much?"

"It's a shame you ain't in the trade these days," he said, and smiled the crocodile smile. " 'Cause I have this very major Colombian merchant who'll be here in the city this weekend, I'm sure we could work out some kind of barter arrange—"

And suddenly he saw what was in Marilyn's eyes.

"All right, all right, all right," he said, "forget it, all right?"

And just as suddenly turned all business.

"What kind of gun did you have in mind?" he asked.

4

THE THREE who came into the squadroom on Saturday morning at the crack of dawn—well, at three minutes to eight, actually—looked either like a wandering band of twelfth-century minstrels or a gypsy troupe out of *Carmen,* depending on your perspective. The perspective from Cotton Hawes's desk was sunwashed and somewhat hazy, the light slanting in through open windows to create an almost prismatic effect of golden air afloat with dancing dust motes. Out of this refracting mass, there appeared the tentative trio, causing Hawes to blink as if he were witnessing either a mirage or a religious miracle.

There were two women and a man.

The man was between and slightly forward of the women, the point of a flying wedge, so to speak, for such it resembled as the three came through the gate in the slatted-rail divider and immediately homed in on the closest desk, which happened to be Hawes's. Perhaps his red hair had served as a beacon. Or perhaps he'd emanated a sense of authority that naturally attracted anyone seeking assistance. Or perhaps they gravitated toward him because he was the only person in the squadroom at this ungodly hour of the morning.

The man was wearing bright blue polyester trousers and a rugby shirt with a white collar and alternating red-and-blue stripes of different widths. He was a hairy giant of a man, with long tawny tresses and a solid, muscular build. One of the women flanking him was tall and black and the other was blonde and not quite as tall, and both women were dressed as if to complement the synthetic glitz of the hirsute giant.

The blonde was wearing a wide, flaring red skirt and a turtleneck shirt (no bra, Hawes noticed) that was the same color as the man's polyester trousers. She was also wearing sandals, although it wasn't yet summertime. The black woman was wearing an equally wide, flaring skirt (hers was green) and a turtleneck shirt (again, no bra, Hawes noticed) that was the color of the blonde's hair. She, too, was wearing sandals.

"There's a sign," Hawes said.

All three looked around.

Hawes pointed.

The hand-lettered sign just to the right of the gate in the railing read:

> STATE YOUR BUSINESS
> BEFORE ENTERING
> SQUADROOM

"Oh, sorry," the man said. "We didn't notice it."

Slight Hispanic accent.

"The desk sergeant said we should come up," the blonde said. Little tiny voice. Almost a whisper. But it compelled attention. Eyes as blue as the sky that stretched beyond the squadroom windows. Voice as flat as the plains of Kansas. Hawes visualized cornfields. "My name is Coral Anderson," she said.

Hawes nodded.

"I'm Stanley Garcia," the man said.

"Laramie Forbes," the black woman said.

"Is it all right to come in?" Coral asked.

"You're in already," Hawes said. "Please sit down."

Stanley took the chair alongside the desk. Quite the gent, Hawes thought. The women dragged chairs over for themselves. Sitting, they crossed their legs under voluminous skirts. The movement reminded Hawes of the days when hippies roamed the earth.

"How can I help you?" he said.

"I'm first deacon at the Church of the Bornless One," Stanley said.

The Church of the Bornless One. *Devil-worship,* Kristin Lund had said. Hawes wondered if Coral and Laramie were second and third deacons respectively. He also wondered what their real names were.

"We're disciples," Laramie said, indicating the blonde with a brief sideward nod.

She had a husky voice. Hawes wondered if she sang in the church choir. He wondered if there were choirs in churches that worshipped the Devil.

"We're here about the dead priest," Stanley said.

Hawes moved a pad into place.

"No, no," Stanley said at once. "Nothing like that."

"Nothing like what?" Hawes said. His pencil was poised above the pad like a guillotine about to drop.

"We had nothing to do with his murder," Stanley said.

"That's why we're here," Coral said.

"Let's get some square handles first," Hawes said.

They looked at him blankly.

"Your real names," he said.

"Coral *is* my real name," the blonde said, offended.

Hawes figured she was lying; *nobody's* real name was Coral.

Nor Laramie, either, for that matter.

"How about you?" he asked the other woman.

"I was born there," she said.

"Where's there?"

"Laramie, Texas," she said. Note of challenge in her husky voice. Dark eyes flashing.

"Does that make it your real name?" Hawes asked.

"How'd *you* like to be Henrietta all your life?"

Hawes thought Cotton was bad enough. The legacy of a religious father who'd believed that Cotton Mather was the greatest of the Puritan priests. He shrugged, wrote "Henrietta Forbes" on the pad, studied it briefly, nodded in agreement, and then immediately asked the blonde, "How do you spell Anderson?"

"With an 'O,' " she said.

"Where are you from originally, Coral?"

"Indiana."

"Lots of Corals out there, I'll bet."

She hesitated, seemed about to flare, and then smiled instead, showing a little gap between her two upper front teeth. "Well, it was Cora Lucille, I guess," she said, still smiling, looking very much like a Cora Lucille in that moment. Hawes imagined pigtails tied with polka-dot rags. He nodded, wrote "Cora Lucille Anderson" on the pad, and then said, "And you, Stanley?"

"Stanley," Stanley said. "But in Spanish."

"Which is?"

"Estaneslao."

"Thanks," Hawes said. "Now what about the priest?"

"We're here about the gate, actually," Coral said, uncrossing her legs and leaning forward earnestly, skirt tented, hands clasped, elbows resting on her thighs, the Sixties again. Hawes was swept with a sudden wave of nostalgia.

"What gate?" he said.

"The churchyard gate."

"What about it?"

"What's painted on the gate," Coral said. "The pentagram."

"The star," Stanley said.

"Inverted," Laramie said.

"Uh-huh," Hawes said.

Let them run with it, he thought.

"We know what you must be thinking," Stanley said. His accent sounded more pronounced now. Hawes wondered if he was getting nervous. He said nothing.

"Because of the star," Laramie said.

"And its association to Satanism," Coral said.

"Uh-huh," Hawes said.

"Which many people misunderstand, of course," Coral said, and smiled her gap-toothed smile again.

"In what way?" Hawes asked.

"Is the pentagram misunderstood?"

"Yes."

"In that it's upside down," Stanley said.

"Inverted," Laramie said.

"May I borrow your pencil?" Coral said.

"Sure," he said, and handed it to her.

"And I'll need a piece of paper."

He tore a page from the back of the pad and handed it to her.

"Thanks," she said.

He noticed that she was holding the pencil in her left hand. He wondered if left-handedness had anything to do with Devil worship. He wondered if they were *all* left-handed.

"This is what a star looks like," she said, and began drawing. "The star we see on the American flag, a sheriff's star, they all look like this."

Hawes watched as the star took shape.

"There," she said.

"Uh-huh," he said.

"And this is what a star looks like when you turn it upside down," she said.

"When you invert it," Laramie said.

"Yes," Coral said, her head bent over the sheet of paper, her left hand moving. "There," she said again, and showed the page to Hawes again. Side by side, the stars looked like a pair of acrobats turning cartwheels:

"Uh-huh," Hawes said.

"Do you see the difference?"

"Yes, of course."

"What's the difference?" Coral asked.

"The difference is that the one on the left . . ."

"Yes, the so-called *pure* pentagram . . ."

"Whatever, has only *one* point on top, whereas the other has *two*."

"Yes," Coral said. "And whereas the pure pentagram stands on *two* points, the symbol of Baphomet . . ."

"The *inverted* star . . ."

". . . stands on only one point."

"Indicating the direction to Hell," Laramie said.

"I see," Hawes said. Though he didn't really.

"If you look at the *pure* pentagram . . ." Coral said.

"The one on the left," Stanley said.

"Yes," Hawes said.

"You can imagine, can't you," Coral said, "a man standing with his legs widespread . . . those are the two lower points of the star . . . and his arms outstretched . . . those are the two middle points. His head would be the uppermost point."

"I see," Hawes said again, trying hard to visualize a man inside the upright star.

"In ancient times . . ." Coral said.

"Oh, centuries ago," Stanley said.

"The *white* magicians . . ."

"This has nothing to do with their *color,*" Laramie said.

"No, only with the kind of magic they performed," Coral said. "*White* magic."

"Yes," Hawes said.

"As opposed to *black* magic," Stanley said.

"Yes."

"These *white* magicians," Coral said, "used the pentagram to symbolize the goodness of man . . ."

". . . because it showed him standing upright," Laramie said.

"But in the church of the *opposite* . . ." Coral said.

"Where good is evil and evil is good . . ."

"In the church of the *contrary* . . ." Coral said.

"Where to lust is to aspire . . ."

"And to achieve is to satisfy all things carnal . . ."

"The pentagram has been turned upside down . . ." Coral said.

"Inverted," Laramie said.

"So that the horns of the goat . . ."

". . . the Satanic symbol of lust . . ."

". . . fit exactly into the two upper points . . ."

". . . which represent Good and Evil . . ."

". . . the universal duality in eternal conflict . . ."

"And the three *other* points," Coral said, "represent in their inverted form a *denial* of the trinity . . ."

". . . the Father, the Son and the Holy Ghost," Stanley said.

". . . doomed to burn eternally in the flames of Hell . . ." Laramie said.

". . . as indicated by the single point jutting directly downward," Stanley said.

"An upside-down star," Coral said.

"Inverted," Laramie said, and all three fell silent.

"What about it?" Hawes asked.

"Detective Hawes," Coral said, "we are aware . . ."

He wondered how she knew his name.

". . . that the star painted on St. Catherine's gate might link us in the minds of the police . . ."

Sergeant Murchison had probably given it to her downstairs.

". . . to the murder of the priest there."

"But," Laramie said.

"*But,*" Coral said, "we want you to know that we plan to question our congregation tonight and find out whether somebody if anybody painted that star on the churchyard gate."

"And if they did . . ." Stanley said.

". . . we'll make damn sure that person comes right over here to tell you about it his own self. So you can question them and see we had nothing to do with it. The murder. Even if someone, if anyone, *is* guilty of painting that gate."

"Guilt is innocence," Laramie said.

"We'll let you know," Stanley said, and all three rose in many-splendored radiance and disappeared into the sunlight and through the gate at which they had originally materialized.

Hawes wondered how Carella was doing out there on the street.

On a bright spring morning, it was difficult to think of the street as a slum. There seemed no visible evidence of poverty here. The people walking by at a leisurely pace were not dressed in tatters. There were flowerpots with blooms in them on fire escapes and windowsills. The window curtains flapping in the early morning breeze seemed clean and fresh as did the laundry hanging on backyard clotheslines. The sanitation trucks had been through early, and the garbage cans were lined up empty along wrought-iron railings that flanked recently swept front stoops. As Carella came up the street, a water truck was sprinkling the gutters, giving the black asphalt a sheen of rain-washed freshness. This could not be a slum.

But it was.

The endless crush of winter had departed, and in its place there was now the false hope of spring. But the people living in these tenements—true, the red brick did seem brighter in sunshine than it did beneath a grey and leaden sky—knew that hope was the thing with feathers, as elusive and as rare as happiness. This stretch of 87th Precinct territory was almost exclusively black. And here, despite the illusion of spring, there was indeed grinding poverty, and illiteracy, and drug addiction and malnutrition and desperation. The black man in America knew where it was at. And where it was at was not here, not in these mean streets. Where it was at was uptown someplace, so far uptown that the black man had never been there, could not even visualize it there, knew only that uptown was a shining city somewhere high on a hill, a promised land where everyone went to Choate and Yale and a thousand points of light glistened in every cereal bowl.

Read my lips, Carella thought.

Nathan Hooper lived in a tenement two blocks south of The Stem.

At eight-thirty that Saturday morning, Carella found him asleep in a back bedroom he shared with his older brother and his thirteen-year-old sister. Hooper was sixteen. The brother, dressed and out of the house already, was eighteen. The sister was wearing a white cotton slip. Hooper was wearing white Jockey undershorts and a white tank top undershirt. He was annoyed that his mother had let the police in while he was still asleep. He told his sister to cover up, couldn't she see there was somebody here? The sister shrugged into a robe and padded out to the kitchen, where Hooper's mother was having her morning coffee. She had already told Carella that she had to be at work at nine; on Saturdays and Sundays, she cleaned offices downtown. Rest of the week, she cleaned white people's houses uptown.

Hooper pulled on a pair of jeans and went out into the narrow hallway barefooted, Carella following. The bathroom was a six-by-eight rectangle containing a sink, an ancient yellowing claw-footed bathtub with a jerry-built shower over it, and an incessantly gurgling toilet bowl. A plastic curtain was drawn half-closed over the tub. The remainder of the curtain rod was hung with bikini panties. Hooper stepped in, and closed the door behind him. Standing in the hallway, Carella could hear him first urinating and then washing at the sink. When the door opened again, Hooper was drying his hands on a peach-colored towel.

Wordlessly, scowling, he went back into the bedroom again, Carella still following him. He opened the middle drawer of the only dresser in the room, took out a black T-shirt, and pulled it on over his head. He sat on the edge of the bed, pulled on a pair of white socks, and laced up a pair of black, high-topped sneakers. He was wearing his hair in what was called a High Top Fade, currently the rage among young black men in this city. The hairdo resembled a fez sitting on top of the head, with the lower part of the skull shaved almost clean, and it required very little maintenance other than an occasional bit of topiary. Hooper passed a pick comb through it, and walked out into the kitchen, still wordlessly, still scowling, Carella still patiently following. Hooper's sister was sitting at the table, a mug of coffee between her hands. She was staring through the open kitchen window at the clothes flapping on the backyard lines, watching them in fascination, as if they were brightly colored birds. Hooper's mother was just about to leave. She was a woman in her fifties, Carella guessed. Actually, he was high by about ten years.

"Offer the man some coffee," she said, and went out.

"You want some coffee?" Hooper asked grudgingly.

"I could use some," Carella said.

"You always come see people in the middle of the night?" the sister asked.

"Sorry I got here so early," Carella said, and smiled.

The girl did not smile back. Hooper was rummaging in the cupboard over the drainboard, searching for clean cups. He made a great show of exasperation, finally banged two cups down on the counter top, miraculously unscathed, and poured them three-quarters full. A container of milk was on the table. He poured from it into his own cup, and then shoved it across to where Carella had taken the chair alongside the girl's.

"Sugar?" the girl said, and offered Carella the bowl.

"Thanks," Carella said. "What's your name?"

"Why?" she said.

"Why not?" he said, and smiled.

"Seronia," she said.

"Nice to meet you."

"When you gonna lock up the shits beat up Nate?" she said.

"That's what I'd like to talk about," Carella said.

"Be the first one since it happened," Seronia said, and shrugged.

"That's not entirely true, is it?" Carella said. "The way *I* found out about it was from a report in our files. So *someone* had to . . ."

"Yeah, the blues," Hooper said. "But wasn't no detectives come around later is whut she means."

"Well, here's a detective now," Carella said.

"You don't look like no detective *I* ever seen," Seronia said. "Mama says you showed her a badge, but, man, you don't look like no detective to me."

"What do detectives look like?" he asked.

"Like pieces a shit," she said.

Carella wasn't looking for an argument here. Nor was he even certain the girl was trying to provoke one. He was here for information. A priest had been murdered. A priest who'd protected this boy on Easter Sunday.

"According to the report . . ."

"The report's full of shit," Hooper said. "The only thing they wanted to do was get out of that church *fast*, before they got lynched. They were scareder than I was. You never seen two cops writing so fast."

"They dinn even drive him to the hospital," Seronia said. "He's bleedin' like you shoulda seen him, man. Was the *priest* finely took him to the 'mergency room."

"Where was this?"

"Greer General."

"And you say Father Michael drove you there?"

"*Walked* me there, man," Hooper said. "You know like Christ walkin' with the fuckin' cross on his back and everybody jeerin' him, whatever? That was me, man. I'm bleedin' from the head from where one of them fucks hit me with a ball bat . . ."

"Start from the beginning," Carella said.

"What's the use?" Hooper said.

"What can you lose?" Seronia said, and shrugged again.

Easter this year had fallen on the fifteenth day of April, but even in its death throes winter tenaciously refused to loosen its grip and the day was howlingly windy, with what appeared to be a promise of snow on the air. A sullen roiling sky hung in angry motion over the city, giving it the look of an El Greco painting even in neighborhoods not entirely Hispanic. In this checkerboard precinct where black squares became white squares in the blink of an eye, Nathan Hooper lived in an area that was ninety-percent black, eight-percent Hispanic, and two-percent Asian. Not two blocks away was an entirely white neighborhood composed of Italians, Irish, and a sprinkling of Jews. The melting pot in this precinct has never really come to a boil. On this windy Easter Sunday, it is about to overboil.

Hooper rarely goes to church, but today he runs into a friend of his named Harold Jones, who the other guys all call Fat Harold. Fat Harold isn't truly fat; he is, in fact, rather thin and spindly-looking. He is also a crack addict who is on his way to church this Easter Sunday to pray that he can kick his habit and become a rich and famous black television star like Bill Cosby. Hooper decides to go along with him. Too fuckin' cold and windy to hang out, might as well join Fat Harold.

The church they go to is on the corner of Ainsley and Third, and it is called the First Baptist Abyssinian Church of Isola. Hooper is glad it's warm inside the church, because as far as he's concerned the rest of it is all bullshit. He's already dropped out of school because he doesn't do too good reading—none of his teachers ever once realized he was dyslexic—but one thing he did learn from all those history books he struggled through was that most of the wars that ever occurred on this planet was because one religion tried to tell another religion it was the only true way to God. So what the preacher is laying down in the church here this morning—all this stuff about Jesus getting crucified by the Romans or the Jews or whoever the fuck did it, Hooper doesn't know and doesn't give a damn—is all a lot of bullshit to him. These people want to believe fairy tales about virgins getting pregnant without nobody fucking them, that was their business. All Hooper was doing here was getting warm.

They're out of church by a little past noon. Fat Harold wants to go to this crack house he knows, buy himself a nickel vial, pass the time smoking some dope. But Hooper tells him what's the sense he just went to church and prayed his ass off for salvation if the next minute he's back on the pipe, does that make sense, man? He tells Fat Harold why don't he use the five bucks they go see a movie and buy some popcorn? Fat Harold thinks he rather go smoke some dope. So they part company on Ainsley—this is now maybe ten past twelve, a quarter past—and Fat Harold goes his way to the crack house where he's gonna find hope in a pipe, man, and Hooper walks crosstown and a little ways uptown on The Stem to where this movie theater is playing a new picture with Eddie Murphy in it.

Uptown.

Is where this movie theater is.

Uptown.

Where Eddie Murphy and Bill Cosby live.

Hooper knows he is walking into white turf, he wasn't born yesterday. But, man, this is Easter Sunday and all he's doing is going to a fuckin' movie where there's hundreds of white people standing on line outside, waitin' to see a black man up there on the screen. Handful of blacks on the line, too, here and there, guys all silked up, sportin' for they girls, this is Easter Sunday, it'll be cool, man, no sweat.

Hooper wishes he had a girl with him, too. But he broke up with this chick last month 'cause she was mad he dropped out of school, which was probably for the best if she didn't understand how he wasn't *getting* nowhere in that fuckin' school, what was the sense wastin' his *time* there? Learn more on a street corner in ten minutes than you did in school the whole fuckin' term. But on days like today, dudes all around him with they girls, he misses her. Always makes him feel like some kind of jerk, anyway, going to a movie alone.

Eddie Murphy takes care of that, though.

Eddie Murphy makes him feel good.

You see a handsome black man up there, smart as hell and not takin' any shit from Whitey, it makes you feel real good. Eddie Murphy probably lived in a big house on a hill overlooking the ocean. Probably had blonde girls coming in to suck his cock and wash his feet with they hair like the preacher was talking about Jesus's feet this morning. You was Eddie Murphy, you could buy anything in the world you wanted, have anything you wanted. Didn't matter you was black. You was Eddie *Murphy*, man! In the movie theater, sitting there in the dark with mostly white people, Hooper likes to wet his pants laughing every time Eddie Murphy does another one of his shrewd things. White people all around him are laughing, too. Not at any dumb *nigger* but at dumb *Charlie* who the nigger's fuckin' around. Hooper doesn't completely understand why all these white people are laughin' at they ownselves, but he knows it makes him feel *damn* good.

He is still feeling good when he comes out of the theater at two-thirty, around then. It isn't snowing yet, but it sure feels like it's gonna start any minute. Still windy as can be, great big gusts blowin' in off the River Harb and cuttin' clear to the marrow. He can walk home one of two ways. He can go down on The Stem to North Fifth, and then come crosstown the three blocks to his own building on Culver, where maybe some of the guys'll be hangin' out, or he can go directly crosstown on Eleventh where the theater is, and then walk downtown on Culver, six of one, half a dozen of the other—except that the Eleventh Street route will take him straight through an exclusively Italian neighborhood.

Hooper does not belong to any of the neighborhood street gangs. Neither does he do dope nor run dope for any of the myriad crack dealers who are what the newspapers call "a blight on the urban landscape." He is not a good student, but this does not make him a bad person. The color of his skin does not make him a bad person, either. He is black. He knows he is black. But he has never done a criminal thing in his life. Never. (He repeats the word fervently to Carella now: "*Never!*") This is no small achievement in a neighborhood where the word "bad" is often used with pride. I'm a *baaaad* nigger, man. If Hooper's gonna be *any* kind of nigger, it's gonna be a *good* one. Like Eddie Murphy. (He tells this to Carella, too, driving the point home by rapping a clenched fist on his T-shirted chest.)

The Italian-Americans on Eleventh Street are so far removed in time, space and attitude from their heritage in Naples or Palermo that they could, if they chose to, safely drop the hyphenated form. These are

Americans, period, born and bred on the turf they now inhabit with somewhat confused and confusing ethnic pride. These are kids whose great-*great*-grandparents came here as immigrants at the turn of the century. Kids whose *great*-grandparents were the first-generation Americans. Kids whose grandparents fought against Italy in World War II, whose parents were teenagers in the Sixties, and who themselves are now teenagers who do not speak Italian and who do not care to learn, thank you. They are Americans. And it is American to cherish home and family, American to protect one's neighborhood from evil infiltration, American to cherish God and country and to make sure no niggers fuck your sister.

Hooper is aware of them at once.

He has come perhaps a block and a half crosstown from The Stem when he sees them on the front stoop of the building. There are six of them. This is Easter Sunday and they are all silked out in their new Easter threads, hanging out and kidding around, laughing. He tells himself that's all they're doing is hanging out and kidding around, laughing, but warning hackles go up on the back of his neck, anyway. He should not be here. He should have gone down The Stem to Fifth Street instead, he was dumb to come across Eleventh where up ahead all of a sudden the horseplay stops and the laughter stops and there is a dead silence, they have spotted him.

He figures he should cross the street.

Would Eddie Murphy cross the street?

Sheee-it, man, *no!* Hooper's got as much right as these dudes to be wherever the fuck he *wants* to be, man—but his heart is pounding. He knows there is going to be trouble. He can smell it on the air, he can feel it coming his way on the wind, blowin' on the wind, man, touching his black skin like somebody usin' a cattle prod on him . . . trouble . . . danger . . . *run!*

But would Eddie Murphy run?

He does not run.

He does not cross the street.

He keeps walking toward where the six of them have now come off the stoop and are standing on the sidewalk in a casual phalanx, hands dangling loosely at their sides like gunslicks about to draw, narrow smiles on their faces, say somethin' smart, he thinks, say somethin' cool, be Eddie Murphy, man! But nothing smart comes. Nothing cool comes.

He smiles.

"Hey, man," he says to the closest one.

And the baseball bat comes swinging out of nowhere.

"Do you know which one used the bat?" Carella asked.

"No," Hooper said.

"They *all* had bats," Seronia said.

"That was later," Hooper said. "When they start chasin' me. All at once, they *all* got bats. Or garbage can lids. It was that first bat bust my head, though. 'Cause it took me by surprise. It musta been one of them standin' in the back had the bat hid, you know? So when I come up, I'm like a sittin' duck, you know? I give 'em my shit-eatin' grin, I say 'Hey, man' politely, and *wham* the bat comes from somewhere hid behind them, breaks my head open."

"What happened then?"

"I ran, man, whutchoo *think* happen? They six of them who all at once got ball bats, and they yellin' nigger and whatnot, man I know a lynch mob when I see one. I got the hell out of there fast as my feet could carry me. But that wasn't gonna be the end of it, far as they was concerned. They was right behind me, all six of 'em, cussin' and yellin' and chasin' me off they turf. I figured once I got to Culver I be okay, I could run downtown on Culver, get the hell off Eleventh Street . . ."

"You was crazy goin' in there in the first place," Seronia said.

"It was Easter," Hooper said in explanation, and shrugged.

"All right, they're chasing you," Carella said.

"Yeah, and I'm thinkin' I gotta get off the street, I stay here on the street, they goan kill me. I gotta be someplace where they witnesses, a restaurant, a bar, anythin' where they people can *see* what's happenin' if it goes that far. 'Cause it *sounds* like it's goan all the way, man, it sounds like they out to kill me."

"Then what?"

"All at once, I see this church up ahead. I never been inside it in my life, but there it is, and I figure there's got to be people inside a church, don't there, this is Easter Sunday. I like was losin' track of time by then, I didn't realize there wouldn't be no services two-thirty, three o'clock, whatever it was by then. But the front door was open . . ."

"Standing open?"

"No, no. Unlocked. I tried it and it was unlocked. They were right behind me, man, it's a good thing it *wasn't* locked, I'd be dead right there on the church steps. So I ran in with my head busted open and drippin' blood and them behind me yellin', and I hear *more* yellin' from someplace in the church, and the first thing I think is they got me surrounded, man, there's yellin' behind me and yellin' in front of me, I'm a dead man."

"What do you mean, yelling in front of you?"

"From like behind these columns. Two people yelling."

"Behind what columns?"

"Where they on the right side of the church, you know? They's like these columns and what I guess must be a little room back there 'cause . . ."

"Is that where the yelling was coming from? This little room behind the columns? On the right-hand side of the church?"

"I'm only *sayin'* it was a room, I was never in it. But this door opened, and a priest came out . . ."

"From the room?"

"From whatever was there behind the door. He heard all the yellin' in the church, you see. Heard them yellin' nigger and they was goan kill me, like that, and heard me yellin' Help, somebody help me! So he came out lookin' surprised and scared and first thing he sees is me spillin' blood from my head, and he goes, 'What's this, what's this?' like he can't believe it, you know, here's a nigger bleedin' on his floor and six white guys chasin' him. So I yell, 'Hey, man, *hep* me, they goan *kill* me!' and the priest sees what's happenin' now, gets it all in a flash, man, and steps between me and them and tells them get the fuck outa his church, tells them this is God's house, how dare they, all that shit. Meanwhile somebody'd called the cops, and by the time they showed up there was a big crowd outside, everybody yellin' and screamin' even if they didn't know what the fuck was happenin'. It was the priest walked me to the hospital. The cops were too scared. If you're gonna write up a report . . ."

"I am."

"You better mention them fucks was too scared to put me in the car and drive me the six blocks to Greer. I had to walk it with the priest."

"I'll mention it," Carella said.

A lot of good it'll do, he thought. The police protected their own. This was a simple, perhaps regrettable fact. But he would mention it.

"You say the priest was arguing with someone when you came into the . . ."

"Yeah."

"Who, do you know?"

"No. It was behind the door there."

"A man? A woman?"

"A man, I think. There were six fuckin' guys tryin'a *kill* me, you think I gave a shit who . . ."

"How do you know they were arguing?"

" 'Cause they were yellin' at each other."

"Did you hear anything they said?"

"Just these loud voices."

"Two voices? Or more than two?"

"I don't know."

"Well . . . after it was all over . . . did you *see* anyone?"

"What do you mean?"

"Coming out of that room."

"Oh. No. We went straight to the hospital. The cops opened up a path in the crowd out there, and me and the priest went through. I didn't see nobody else inside the church."

"You know Father Michael was killed on Thursday night, don't you?"

"Sure," Hooper said. "And I know who done it, too."

Carella looked at him.

"Them wops," Hooper said. "They made a blood vow they gonna get both me *and* the priest. For what happened on Easter. So now they got the priest, so that means I'm next. And for what? For walkin' on the street mindin' my own fuckin' business."

"For bein' *black,*" Seronia said.

Carella had no argument.

"It was very nice of you to come up here, Miss Lund," Hawes said. "I know it's Saturday, and I hate to intrude on your time."

"Not at all," she said. "Happy to help in any way I can."

The clock on the wall read twenty minutes past eleven. Krissie was wearing blue jeans, leather boots, a white T-shirt, and a fringed leather vest. No makeup except lipstick and eye liner. Long blonde hair pulled to the back of her head in a ponytail. She smelled of spring flowers.

"As I told you on the phone, the lab sent over this whole batch of let-ters and bills and whatnot, all Father Michael's stuff, you know, which I just finished going through. The point is, the lab found some very good latents on them, and we . . ."

"Latents?"

"Father Michael's, of course, but also some wild prints that may have been left by the killer. In case he'd been in the office looking through the files for something, which is still a possibility because of that open file drawer and the papers on the floor. Okay, so far?"

"Yes," Krissie said, and smiled.

"So what we're trying to do is track down the wild prints—the ones we know for sure weren't left by Father Michael—and eliminate whoever might have had a *legitimate* reason to be handling the papers. One of the logical . . ."

"Yes, his secretary," Krissie said, and smiled.

"Yes, would be a logical choice. Typing them, filing them and so on."

"Yes."

"You look very pretty this morning," he said.

The words startled her. They startled him, too. He hadn't expected to say them out loud. A second earlier, he'd only been *thinking* them.

"Well, thank you," Krissie said.

"Sorry," he said.

"No, no."

"But you do."

"Well, thanks."

There was an awkward silence. They stood side by side in a shaft of sunlight streaming through the window. The squadroom was unusually silent this morning. Somewhere down the hall, a telephone rang. Outside on the street, a horn honked.

"The thing is," he said, and cleared his throat, "if the killer *did* touch any of the papers—and chances are he at least had his hands on that stuff he threw all over the floor—then by eliminating as many of the latents as we can, we might have a shot at identification later on. If we come up with anybody. Which so far we haven't. But if we do."

"Yes."

"Which is why I asked you to stop by to have your prints taken, if it's no bother."

"No bother at all," she said.

"It'll take ten, fifteen minutes at the most."

"I've always wondered what it'd be like to have my fingerprints taken."

"Really? Well, here's your chance to find out."

"Yes," she said.

"Yes," he said, and cleared his throat again.

"Are you catching a cold?" she asked.

"No, I don't think so."

"Because you keep clearing your throat, you know . . ."

"No, that's . . ."

"So I thought maybe . . ."

"No, that's a nervous reaction," Hawes said.

"Oh," she said.

"Yes."

"Oh."

They looked at each other.

"Well, how do we do this?" she asked.

"Well . . . if you'll step over to this table . . ."

"Just like in the movies, huh?"

"Sort of."

"I've never had my fingerprints taken before," she said.

"Yes, I know."

"Did I tell you?"

"Yes."

"Oh. Then it must be true," she said.

"Yes. The first thing I have to do," he said, "is lock my pistol in the desk drawer there because what happened once—I don't know how long ago this was—a police officer somewhere in the city was finger-printing a felon and the guy grabbed the gun, and shot him dead."

"Oh my!" Krissie said.

"Yeah," Hawes said. "So now it's a rule that whenever we're finger-printing anyone, we have to take off the gun."

He walked over to his desk, dropped his pistol into one of the deep drawers on the right-hand side, locked the drawer, and then came back to the fingerprinting table. Krissie watched apprehensively as he began squirting black ink from a tube onto a pane of glass.

"This stuff washes right off with soap and water," he said.

"Thank God," she said.

"Oh sure, nothing to worry about."

"You must be an expert at this," she said.

"Well, it becomes second nature. Although we rarely do it anymore. This is all done at Central Booking now. Downtown. At Headquarters."

"Mugging and printing," she said. "Is that what you call it?"

"Yes."

"Mugging and printing," she said again.

"Yes."

He was rolling the ink onto the glass now, spreading it evenly. She watched him with great interest.

"You have to spread it, huh?" she said.

"Yes."

"Like blackberry jam," she said.

"I never thought of it that way," he said, and put down the roller. "There we go. Now I'll just take one of these cards . . ."

He took a fingerprint card from the rack at the back of the table.

"And if you'll let me have your right hand first . . ."

She extended her hand to him.

"I have to . . . uh . . . sort of . . . uh . . . if you'll just let your hand hang sort of . . . uh . . . loose . . . I have to roll them on the glass first, you see, each finger . . ."

"I hope this stuff really washes off," she said.

"Oh, yes, with soap and water, I promise. There, that's better."

She was sort of standing with her right hip sort of against him somewhat, his arms sort of cradling her arm, sort of holding her hand in both his hands as he rolled her fingers one at a time on the glass, and then rolled them in turn on the fingerprint card . . .

"Now the thumb," he said.

"Am I doing this right?" she asked.

"Just let me do it," he said, "just relax, that's the way . . ."

. . . sort of standing very close to each other in the silent sunwashed squadroom, he could smell the scent of her flowery perfume . . .

"Now the other hand," he said.

. . . sort of guiding each finger onto the glass, rolling it there, lifting it, rolling it onto the card, sort of moving together with a special rhythm now, her hand in his, her hip sort of molded in against him . . .

"This is sort of fun," she said.

"Yes," he said, "can you have dinner with me tonight?"

"I'd love to," she said.

She'd finally chosen the Walther PPK, a neat little .32 caliber automatic with an eight-shot capacity. Shad Russell had showed her some guns that had five, six-shot capacities, but she figured if push came to shove she might need those few extra cartridges. Seven in the magazine, he'd told her, another in the breech. He'd also showed her some .22 caliber pistols, but she insisted on the heavier firepower. Shad told her the caliber didn't mean a thing. You could sometimes do more damage with a .22 than with a .45. She didn't believe him. If you had to bring down a giant, you didn't go after him with a pea shooter.

She wasn't even sure *this* gun would do the job. But all of his bigger caliber guns seemed either too bulky or too heavy. The Walther had a short three-inch barrel, with an overall length of only five and a half inches, and the lightweight model she chose weighed only a bit more than twelve ounces. It fit snugly in her handbag, alongside of—and not very much bulkier than—her wallet. Shad had charged her six hundred dollars for the gun. She figured that his profit on this deal alone would pay for a vacation at Lake Como.

She had discovered that a person did not jaywalk when she was carrying an unlicensed pistol. She suspected that not many such guntoters exceeded the speed limit, either. Or spit on the sidewalk. Or even raised their voices in public places. She was breaking the law. And would break it further if she had to. Break it to the limit if she had to. Her bag felt heavier with the gun in it. The weight was reassuring.

She had spent this Saturday morning shopping in the midtown area, and had boarded an uptown-bound, graffiti-covered subway train at twenty past two. She was not in the habit of taking expensive taxi rides all over the city, and she did not plan on changing her habits now. Moreover, she sensed that there would be safety in crowded places; they had spooked yesterday when she'd led them directly to a cop.

The train rattled along in the underground dark.

Marilyn wondered if there were such things as passionate, poetic men who looked like lions and made their homes in subway caves. She wondered if there were alligators in the city's sewers. She wondered if there was such a thing as happily ever after.

The train pulled into a station stop.

The doors hissed open.

She watched the passengers coming on. She did not expect anyone even remotely resembling her two Hispanics to board. The doors hissed shut again. The train was in motion.

It was two-thirty-five when she got off the train uptown on The Stem and began walking northward toward the river. She was certain that they knew where she lived, had undoubtedly followed her from there to the school. As she approached Silvermine Oval now, her eyes swept both sides of the street ahead. Her handbag was slung on her left shoulder. Her right hand rested on its open top, hovering over the butt of the Walther.

Nothing.

She kept walking.

Entered the Oval, came around it. Nanny pushing a baby carriage in the bright sunshine. Such a lovely day. The weight of the gun in her bag. Around the Oval and onto Harborside. The small park across the street from her house. Potential danger there. A man approaching on the park side of the street. Short man wearing a tan sports jacket. Little mustache under his nose. Charlie Chaplin lookalike. Went on by, buried in his own thoughts. She scanned the park entrance.

Nothing.

1211 Harborside was just ahead, on her left. No one on either side of the street, not a sign of activity in the park. A pigeon fluttered overhead, glided over the park fence, settled on the walk inside the gate. She approached the building and fished into her bag for her keys, the back of her hand brushing up against the Walther. Found the keys, unlocked both locks on the door, came into the entryway, and secured the locks behind her. She was wearing a Chanel ripoff, blue skirt and blue jacket with a blue ruff. Unbuttoning the jacket, she went to the answering machine, saw that she'd had three messages, and pressed the playback button.

"Honey, it's me."

Willis's voice.

"Did you make dinner reservations for tonight? Because *I* didn't, and it's Saturday night, and we'll have a hell of a time this late. I kind of feel like Italian, don't you? Do you think you could try Mangia Bene? I'm at the lab, I should be home around four-thirty, see you then, love ya."

She looked at her watch.

Ten minutes to three.

"Hello, Miss Willis, this is Sylvia Bourne, I'm the real estate person you were talking to Thursday night, at the open house? Oliphant Realty? The co-op? I wonder if you and Mr. Hollis have had a chance to think about that penthouse apartment? I'm sure the sponsor would entertain a bid lower than the three-fifty, if you'd care to make an offer. Let me know what you think, won't you? It's negotiable. I know I gave you my card, but here's the number again."

As she reeled off the number—twice, no less—Marilyn wondered why no one could ever get their names straight. It would be worth getting married just so they'd have only *one* name to worry about.

"Hello, Marilyn?"

A woman's voice.

"It's Eileen."

Eileen?

"Burke. If you've got a minute, can you give me a call? At home, please. Few things I'd like to discuss with you. Here's the number."

Marilyn listened to the number, writing, thinking this had to be mental telepathy. Yesterday she'd thought of calling Eileen about a gun, and today Eileen was calling *her*. The difference was that today she already *had* a gun. And she *still* wasn't sure Eileen liked her very much. So why call me? And, conversely, do *I* like *her* enough to call her back?

First things first, she thought.

Mangia Bene.

She found the number in her personal directory, dialed it, said she was calling for Detective Willis—why *not* a little P.D. muscle on a Saturday night?—and asked if they could take two of them at eight o'clock. Unconsciously, she looked at her watch again. Three o'clock sharp. He'd be home in an hour and a half. She waited while the maître d' consulted his reservations book, clucking his tongue all the while. Finally, he said, "*Sì, Signora* Willis, two of you at eight, we look forward to seeing you then."

Willis again.

She cradled the phone, debated calling Eileen right that minute, get it over with, decided she'd rather bathe first. Slinging her shoulder bag, she went upstairs to the third floor of the house.

They were waiting for her in the bedroom.

5

SHE WENT FOR THE GUN.

She went for it at once, not a moment's hesitation, right hand crossing her body and dipping into the open mouth of the bag, fingers curling around the grip, gun coming up and out of the bag, forefinger inside the trigger guard, thumb snapping off the safety, gun leveling to—

He was on her in an instant.

The big one.

Moving swiftly across the Persian rug on the parqueted floor, past the canopied bed and the love seat upholstered in royal-blue crushed velvet. He was an experienced street fighter, he did not grab for the gun, the gun was where the danger was. He came up on her left side instead, ducking inside the gun hand and throwing his shoulder against her chest before she could pull off a shot. She stumbled backward. He hit her full in the face, his huge fist bunched. She felt immediate pain, and brought her left hand up at once, forgetting the gun, the pain shrieking, cupping her nose, pulling her hand away covered with blood. He took the gun out of her hand as if taking a toy from a naughty child. She knew he'd broken her nose. The pain was excruciating. Blood poured onto her hand, blood dripped through her fingers, blood stained her blouse and the front of her jacket, blood spattered onto the Persian rug, she wondered abruptly if the stains would come out, the pain, where was the gun?

He was grinning.

Big fucking gorilla standing there grinning while she held back the screams that bubbled into her throat, the small gun in his huge hand, King Kong standing on the Empire State Building swatting airplanes.

"No more of that," he said in Spanish, grinning.

The other one, the handsome one, was moving into the bathroom. She kept her eyes on the ugly one, the one who had hurt her. He did not know there was also a switchblade knife in her bag. She would slit his throat the moment she had a chance. The handsome one came out of the bathroom.

"Here," he said in Spanish and handed her one of her good bath towels. White. With the initials MH monogrammed on it in curlicued lettering fit for royalty. Gold on white. She did not want to stain her good towel. But she was bleeding all over the floor. She put the towel to her nose.

"Noses bleed a lot," the ugly one said in Spanish, as if making a comment on the weather.

The other one merely nodded.

"Do you have a license for this gun?" the ugly one said in Spanish, and laughed.

She said nothing.

Held the towel to her nose, trying to stop the flow of blood. Nothing to do for the pain. The pain shrieked and shrieked. She kept her teeth clenched to keep from screaming. She would not scream. She would not reveal her terror. She would wait for the proper moment, and then go for the knife. Cut him. Hurt him the way he had hurt her. And then go after the other one, the handsome one.

"Answer him," he said.

In Spanish. They were both speaking Spanish, assuming she understood, recognizing that if she was in fact Mary Ann Hollis, then she too would speak Spanish, she had learned Spanish in that fucking Mexican hellhole and had polished it on her knees in Buenos Aires. She pretended not to understand. Stupidity, she realized. The initials MH were on every towel in the bathroom.

"Did you hear me?" the handsome one said. "Answer him!"

"I don't understand you," she said in English.

"She doesn't understand us," he said in Spanish, "so knock out all her fucking teeth."

The big one moved toward her, turning the gun up in his hand, flipping it so that the butt was in striking position. He was grinning again.

"No," she said.

"No what?" the handsome one said.

In Spanish.

"No, don't hit me," she said.

In English.

"I don't understand you," he said in Spanish.

"*No me pegues, por favor,*" she said.

"*Muy bien,*" the handsome one said. "Now we will speak only Spanish, *comprendes?*"

"*Sí,*" she said, "*solo español.*"

Until I go for the knife, she thought.

"Do you know why we're here?" he asked.

"No."

"Do you know who we are?"

"No."

"My name is Ramon Castaneda. My colleague is Carlos Ortega." She nodded.

"Do you think it foolhardy of us? Telling you our names?" She said nothing.

"We trust you not to tell anyone after we're gone," Ramon said.

"Or we'll come back to kill you," Carlos said, and grinned.

The gun was no longer in his hand. Had he put it in his pocket? She should have been paying more attention, but she'd been too fucking intent on her Spanish lesson, too afraid the big one, Carlos, would really use the gun on her teeth. She had let them frighten her. They had won the first small battle, not even a battle, a tiny skirmish, frightening her into revealing that she spoke Spanish fluently. But they'd known this already. Just as they knew she was Marilyn Hollis. Or, more accurately, Mary Ann Hollis. On the street yesterday, they had called her first Marianna and then Mariucha. They knew her as Mary Ann Hollis. In which case she could claim . . .

"What do you . . . ?" she started in English, and immediately switched to Spanish. "What do you want here?"

"The money," Ramon said.

Straight to the point, she thought.

"What money?"

"The money you stole from Alberto Hidalgo," Carlos said.

Even more directly to the point.

"Four hundred million Argentine australes," Ramon said.

"Two million dollars American," Carlos said.

"We want it back."

A pair of international bankers discussing high finance in Spanish.

"I don't know what you're talking about," she said.

Still speaking Spanish. This was a cozy little meeting among highborn Spanish-speaking people. This was a tea party on the duchess's lawn. The duchess had invited the two bankers here to meet the daz-zling international traveler, Mary Ann Hollis, whose nose was still bleeding into a white towel.

"You must be mistaking me for someone else," she said in Spanish.

Everyone speaking Spanish. How nice to have a second language.

"No, there's no mistake," Ramon said.

"We know who you are, and we know you stole the money," Carlos said.

"And we'll kill you if you don't give it back to us," Ramon said sim-ply, a slight shrug of his narrow shoulders, this was merely one of the rules of international banking.

"*Marilyn* Hollis?" she said. "Are you looking for someone named *Marilyn* Hollis?"

"No, we're . . ."

"Because that's my name, you see, and . . ."

"Shut up," the ugly one said.

Very softly.

The word sounding not at all menacing in Spanish, *cállate,* the word rolling mellifluously off his tongue, *cállate,* shut up.

"Your name is Mary Ann Hollis," he said.

Still softly. Explaining something to a very young and possibly quite stupid child.

"Ah, *bien,*" she said, "there's the mis . . ."

"No," he said.

The word identical in English and in Spanish.

No.

Softly.

No, we've made no mistake. You are Mary Ann Hollis. And we are going to kill you if you don't give us the money you stole from Hidalgo.

All in that single word.

No.

The bag was still on her shoulder.

The knife was in the bag.

The clock on the mantel read 3:15.

I should be home around four-thirty, see you then, love ya.

No sense wishing for the cavalry. Do or die. Go for the knife, or . . .

The clock ticked into the room. Her nose had stopped bleeding. She tossed the towel aside, seeing her own reflection in the ornately framed mirror opposite the bed, her reverse image partially obscured by the backs of the two gentlemen from Buenos Aires.

"I have identification," she said. "My driver's license . . ."

The one to go for was the big one.

". . . my credit cards . . ."

Him first.

"We don't need identification," the handsome one said. Ramon. "We know exactly who you are."

"But that's just it, you see . . ."

Moving across the room toward where the big one stood with his hands dangling at his sides.

"If I can prove that I'm not who you *think* I am . . ."

Her hand dropping into the bag as she moved.

". . . then you'll realize your mistake, and you'll . . ."

"There *is* no mistake," Ramon said, shaking his head.

Fingers searching for the knife.

"But there is. Look, I'd be happy to pay you back . . ."

"Then pay us and shut up!" Ramon said.

Fingers closing on the handle of the knife.

". . . but I'm just not this person you think I am. I mean it. Truly."

"*Enough* of this shit!" Carlos said.

Verdad, she thought, and yanked the knife out of the bag.

Her mistake was going high.

She should have gone low instead, for the gut, plunge the blade in low, rip it across his belly, his hands would have had to cross in front of his body to block the thrust, a clumsy unnatural maneuver. But instead she went for the throat. Arm stiff and extended, right hand clutching the handle of the knife, blade going for his throat like a matador's sword, that was her mistake. Because his hands came up at once in a fighter's instinctive defensive stance, fists clenched for the tick of an instant, and then the hands opening when he recognized in another instant's beat exactly what was happening here, she was coming at him with a knife, this was a knife here!

His eyes said Oh, yeah?

Ah sí?

In which case I will break your fucking face.

She saw those eyes at once, read those eyes, had seen the message in those eyes many times before when she'd been repeatedly beaten and raped in that Mexican prison, and she thought No, mister, never again, and stopped the knife in mid-thrust because his hands were there and she did not want those massive fingers closing on her wrist.

She shifted her stance, stood wide-legged and fierce, the knife moving in tiny circles, waiting for his move. He was not going for the gun in his pocket or wherever the hell he'd put it. This meant that he respected the knife. You didn't grow up a fucking hoodlum in B.A. without having been cut at least once. You didn't spend time in a Mexican prison, either, without becoming an expert on reading eyes. The big one's eyes were saying that she was the one with the knife, and he did not want to get cut. *Her* eyes were saying If you make a move for for the gun, I'll go for your eyes. I'll blind you. Mexican standoff.

She'd forgotten the handsome one.

He moved in as gracefully and as swiftly as a flamenco dancer. She caught his motion almost a moment too late, spotted him from the tail of her eye, and turned immediately to her right as he lunged for her. She thought again, No, mister, and swung the knife out in a wide slashing arc, backhanded. He put out his hand as if trying to deflect the thrust, and then started to pull it back when he remembered this was cold hard steel—but he was too late. The knife caught him. It ripped through the meaty flesh on the edge of his hand, just below the pinky, slicing horizontally, opening a wide bloody gash. He yelled "Aiii," and caught the hand in his free hand, the left one, cradling it, trying to cradle it, pulling both hands in against his body, his face going pale, his eyes glazing over in fear, the blood covering both hands now—she went for him again.

And cut him again.

Slashed out viciously at both hands where he held them in tight against his belly, the blade ripping across the knuckles of the left hand, slashing through to the bone. He began whimpering. His nose was running. He stood there with terror in his eyes, his nose running, his hands bleeding, whimpering like a baby. She had them both in her line of vision now, the handsome one backing away toward the big one, whimpering, the gun still nowhere in sight, she wondered why the big one didn't pull the gun. And then she realized in a sudden exhilarating rush that they could not kill her; if they killed her, they would never get the money they'd come for. In the world they inhabited, you did not kill delinquent debtors except as an example to other debtors. If you wanted your money, you threatened and you maimed—yes, they could hurt her very badly—but you did not kill. Not if you wanted your money. They could not *kill* her!

She felt suddenly invincible.

"Come on," she said.

Knife swinging out ahead of her.

"Come on, you cocksuckers!"

In Spanish, so they'd know exactly what she was saying.

Knife testing the air.

"You want it? Come get it! Come *on!*"

The handsome one was still whimpering.

He kept his hands tucked in against his belly. His shirt was covered with blood.

The big one's eyes had naked murder in them.

She almost burst out laughing. He wanted to kill her but he couldn't. Anger twisted his features, frustration caused his lips to quiver. His fury was monumental, a towering rage that set him trembling like a volcano about to erupt. His face was livid, teeth clenched, mouth twitching, eyes blazing.

"Sure, come on," she said.

Hoping he *would* come.

Actually *wishing* he would come.

Blind you, she thought.

Put out your eyes.

He backed away from her instead, guiding the handsome one around her, his eyes never leaving the knife, edging cautiously back and away from her, around her toward the bedroom door, Marilyn turning so that the knife was always between them, prodding the air. The handsome one could not stop whimpering. At the door, the big one whispered, *"Volveremos."*

Which meant "We'll be back."

Nobody on Eleventh Street knew anything about what had happened on Easter Sunday. This meant that *everybody* in the neighborhood knew *exactly* what had happened. But around here, there was no need to talk to cops ever. If somebody was bothering you, you went to people who could do something about it. The only thing cops could do was write parking tickets and sit around with their thumbs up their asses.

Around here, they told a story about these four black guys went in the Capri Grot one night. This was a restaurant on Ainsley, it was actually named Il Grotto di Capri, but everybody called it the Capri Grot, even the guys who owned it. So these black guys walk in on a crowded Friday night, they're all strapped with huge guns like .45's or Magnums, it depended on who was telling the story. And they shove the guns in the cashier's face and they announce this is a stickup, man, and the headwaiter just stands there with his arms folded across his chest, shaking his head. Like he can't *believe* this is *happening,* man! Four dumb fucking niggers walking into a place has Mafia written up one side and down the other, they're here pulling a job. Amazing! So they clean out the cash register and go off in the night, and the headwaiter is still there shaking his head at the wonder of it all.

Next day one of the niggers comes back to the restaurant. His arm is in a sling, and his right eye is half-closed and there's a bandage wrapped around his head from where somebody busted it for him. He's carrying a briefcase. He asks to see the owner and then he tells him some friends of his made a terrible mistake last night, coming in here the way they done, and like, man, here's all the money back, let's let bygones be bygones, man, keep the briefcase, too, it's a Mark Cross.

People around here still laughed at that story.

Which is why nobody around here went to the cops when they had any kind of problem that needed solving. They went instead to the people who knew what to do about it. Which is why on any given Friday night, the customers at the Capri Grot could park their Benzes or their Jags outside and nobody would even *dream* of touching them. And if the cars happened to be double-parked in a clearly marked No Parking zone, that was okay, too, because some of the cops on the beat here were *also* in the pockets of the people you went to whenever you had a problem. Which is why you didn't tell cops a fucking *thing* around here, even if they asked you was your mother a virgin before she got married.

Nobody on the street knew who had busted that nigger's head on Easter Sunday.

Nobody on the street even knew there'd been any trouble at all that day.

Except Angelo Di Napoli.

Di Napoli was thirty-seven years old, a cop whose family name (which translated as "of Naples") promised short and dark with curly black hair but who was in fact an even six feet tall with blond hair and blue eyes. Di Napoli was a recent transfer to the Eight-Seven from the CPEP Unit at the Five-One in Riverhead. CPEP was an acronym for Community Police Enrichment Program, a law enforcement concept rudely imitative of the foot-patrol programs in several other large American cities. Here in this city, the centralized 911 emergency response system had gone into effect some thirty years ago, bringing with it the need for quick *motorized* response, and leaving in its wake a reduction in the number of foot patrols. Then, as so often happened when speed became confused with quality, many police officers began thinking that motorized patrol was in actuality a more diverse and interesting assignment, with the attendant result that those poor souls assigned to a foot beat approached the job with less than optimum enthusiasm. All by way of saying that the foot-patrol officer was almost entirely eliminated in the city's scheme of law enforcement and crime prevention.

CPEP—pronounced Cee-Pep by the police department—had been designed to correct what was now perceived as an error. Its sole intent was to reestablish the foot-patrol cop as an essential part of the process of essential contact between police and community. Di Napoli had been a part of the highly effective NarcPoc Drive, a combined blues-and-suits operation aimed at narcotic pockets in the Fifty-First precinct and resulting in a total of some ten thousand buy-and-bust arrests. It was a measure of the man that he considered it a challenge to be trans-ferred to the newly organized CPEP Unit at the Eight-Seven, under the command of a sergeant who'd initiated Operation Clean Sweep out of the notorious Hundred-and-First in Majesta. Di Napoli was a good cop and a dedicated cop. Like any good cop, he listened. And like any dedicated cop, he put what he heard to good use.

He would not have known that Carella was on the job if Carella hadn't introduced himself. Di Napoli couldn't recall seeing him around the station house, but then again he was new here. They exchanged the usual pleasantries . . .

"How's it going?"

"Little quiet."

"Well, give it time, it's Saturday."

"Yeah, I can't wait."

. . . and then Carella got straight to the point.

"I'm investigating the murder of that priest at St. Kate's," he said.

"Yeah, Thursday night," Di Napoli said.

"That's the one. I'm looking for whoever chased a black kid into the church on Easter Sunday."

"I wasn't here then," Di Napoli said. "I only got transferred the first of the month." He hesitated and then said, "I hear Edward-car pan-icked, huh?"

"Let's say they got out of there fast."

"The people around here laugh about it."

"I'll bet."

"Bad for the old image, huh?" Di Napoli said, and raised his eye-brows. "I bust my ass out here day and night and two jerks run when it gets hot."

"Have you heard anything about who it might have been?"

"That jumped the black kid?"

"Yeah."

"I'll tell you," Di Napoli said, "there's a thing happening around here where they're starting to be *proud* of it, you know what I mean? The neighborhood people. They *like* the idea these bums beat up the black kid and got away with it. That the cops cooled it, you know? For whatever reason, who the hell knows, maybe Edward-car was afraid they'd have a riot on their hands, who knows? The point is, a kid got beat up, and nobody paid for it. Nobody. So around here they're say-ing Yeah, it served him right, he shoulda stayed in his own neighbor-hood, why'd he come around here, and so on, this is a nice neighborhood, we don't need niggers coming in . . ."

Di Napoli shook his head.

"I'm Italian, you know," he said. "I guess you are, too, but I can't stand the way Italians feel about black people. It's a fuckin' *shame* the way they feel. Maybe they don't know how much prejudice there's still around about *us*, you know? Italians. Maybe they don't know you say somebody's Italian he's supposed to be a thief or a ditch-digger or a guy singing O Sole Mio in a restaurant with checked tablecloths and Chianti bottles dripping wax. I'm only a cop, I mean I know I'm not a fuckin' account executive or a bank president, but there're Italians who *are*, you realize that? So you get these dumb wops in this neighbor-hood—that's exactly what they are, excuse me, they're dumb fucking *wops*—they beat up this black kid and then they laugh about it later and *all* Italians suffer. All of us. I hate it. Man, I absolutely *hate* it."

"You sound like you know who did it," Carella said.

"Not completely. But I've been listening, believe me."

"And what've you heard?"

"I heard a guy in his forties, he's in the construction business, his name is Vinnie Corrente, I heard he's been bragging to people that his son Bobby was the one used the bat. I didn't hear him say this person-ally, otherwise his ass would be up the station house and I'd be reading him Miranda, the dumb fucking wop."

"On the other hand . . ."

"On the other hand, *you're* investigating a homicide . . ."

"Uh-huh."

"So maybe you got probable to pull him in."

"Let's say I'd like to talk to him."

"Let's say he's in apartment 41 at 304 North."

"Thanks," Carella said.

"Hey, come on," Di Napoli said, pleased.

304 North Eleventh was a five-story brick set in a row of identical buildings undoubtedly put up by the same contractor at the turn of the century, when the neighborhood was still considered desirable. At three-thirty that afternoon, several old women wearing the black mourning dresses and stockings you could see on widows all over Italy were sitting in late afternoon sunshine on the front stoop, chatting in Italian. Carella nodded good afternoon to them, and then walked through them and past them into the building foyer. He found a mailbox nameplate for V. Corrente in apartment 41, and began climbing the steps.

The building was scrupulously clean.

Mouth-watering cooking smells wafted in the hallways, suffused the stairwells. Oregano and thyme. Sweet sausage. Fresh basil. Delectable meats simmering in olive oil and garlic.

Carella kept climbing.

He found apartment 41 to the right of the staircase on the fourth-floor landing. He listened at the wood for a moment, heard nothing, and knocked on the door.

"Who is it?" a man's voice said.

"Police," Carella answered.

There was a brief silence.

"Just a minute," the man said.

Carella waited.

He heard several locks coming undone, and then the door opened some three inches or so, held by a night chain.

"Let's see your badge," the man said.

Gruff no-nonsense voice, somewhat gravelly. A smoker's voice. Or a drinker's.

Carella flipped open his leather case to show a blue-enameled, gold detective's shield and a laminated I.D. card. "Detective Carella," he said. "Eighty-seventh Squad."

"What's this about, Carella?" the man asked. He had still not taken the chain off the door. In the narrow wedge between door and jamb,

Carella could dimly perceive a heavyset man with a stubble on his cheeks, dark hooded eyes.

"Want to open the door?" he asked.

"Not till I know what this is about," the man said.

"Are you Vincent Corrente?"

"Yeah?"

Surprise in his voice.

"I'd like to ask you a few questions, Mr. Corrente, if that's okay with you," Carella said.

"Like I said, what about?"

"Easter Sunday."

"What about Easter Sunday?"

"Well, I won't really know until I can ask you some questions."

There was silence behind the door. In the wedge, Carella thought he detected the eyes narrowing.

"What do you say?" he asked.

"I say tell me more," the man said.

"Mr. Corrente, I want to ask you about an incident that occurred at St. Catherine's Church on Easter Sunday."

"I don't go to church," Corrente said.

"Neither do I," Carella said. "Mr. Corrente, I'm investigating a murder."

There was another silence. And then, suddenly and unsurprisingly—the word "murder" sometimes worked magic—the night chain came off with a rattle, and the door opened wide.

Corrente was wearing a pair of brown trousers and a tank top undershirt. He was a jowly, paunchy, unkempt man with a cigar in his mouth and a smile on his face, Hey, come in, how nice to see the Law here on my doorstep, come in, come in, don't mind the way the place looks, my wife's been sick, come in, Detective, please.

Carella went in.

A modest apartment, spotlessly clean despite Corrente's protestations and apologies. Little kitchen to the right, living room dead ahead, doors opening from either side of it, presumably to the bedrooms. From behind one of the closed doors, a television set was going.

"Come on in the kitchen," Corrente said, "so we won't bother my wife. She's got the flu, I hadda get the doctor in yesterday. You want a beer or anything?"

"Thanks, no," Carella said.

They went into the kitchen and sat opposite each other at a round, Formica-topped table. The air-shaft window was open. In the back-yard, four stories below, Carella could hear some kids playing Ring-a-Leevio. From the other room, he could hear the unintelligible drone of the television set. Corrente lifted an open can of beer that was sitting on the table, took a long swallow from it, and then said, "So what's this about St. Catherine's?"

"You tell me."

"All I know is I heard there was some fuss there on Easter."

"That's true."

"But I don't know what."

"A black boy was badly beaten by a gang of six white boys. We think the boys were from . . ."

"There are no gangs in this neighborhood," Corrente said.

"Anything more than two in number, *we* call a gang," Carella said. "Any idea who they might've been?"

"Why should that be important to you?" Corrente asked. His cigar had gone out. He took a matchbook from his trouser pocket, struck a match and held it to the tip of the cigar, puffing, filling the kitchen with billowing smoke. " 'Cause, you know," he said, "maybe this black kid had no right comin' to this neighborhood, you understand?"

"I understand that's the prevailing attitude, yes," Carella said.

"Which may not be the *wrong* attitude, hmmm?" Corrente said. "I know what you're thinking, you're thinking this is a bunch of preju-diced people here, they don't like the colored, is what you're thinking. But maybe the same thing woulda happened if this kid hadda been *white,* you follow me, Detective?"

"No," Carella said, "I'm afraid I don't."

He did not like this man. He did not like the beard stubble on his face, or the potbelly hanging over his belt, or the stench of his cigar, or his alleged barroom boasts that his son Bobby had wielded the bat that had broken Nathan Hooper's head. Even the way he said "Detective" rankled.

"This is a nice neighborhood," Corrente said. "A family neighbor-hood. Hardworking people, nice clean kids. We want to keep it that way."

"Mr. Corrente," Carella said, "on Easter Sunday, half a dozen nice clean kids from this neighborhood attacked a black kid with baseball bats and garbage can lids and chased him down the street to . . ."

"Yeah, the Hooper kid," Corrente said.

"Yes," Carella said. "The Hooper kid."

All of a sudden, Corrente seemed to know the name of the Easter Sunday victim. All of a sudden, he seemed to know all about the fuss that had happened at St. Catherine's, although not ten minutes ago he hadn't known nothing from nothing.

"You familiar with this kid?" Corrente asked.

"I've talked to him."

"What'd he tell you?"

"He told me what happened to him here on Eleventh Street."

"Did he tell you what he was *doing* here on Eleventh Street?"

"He was on his way home from the . . ."

"No, no, never mind the bullshit," Corrente said, taking his cigar from his mouth and waving it like a conductor's baton. "Did he tell you what he was *doing* here?"

"What was he doing here, Mr. Corrente?"

"Do you know what they call him down the schoolyard? On Ninth Street? The elementary school? You know what they call him there?"

"No," Carella said. "What do they call him there?"

"His nickname? Did he tell you his nickname?"

"No, he didn't."

"Go ask him what his nickname is down the schoolyard. Go ask him what he was doing here Easter Sunday, go ahead."

"Why don't you save me the trouble?" Carella said.

"Sure," Corrente said, and inhaled deeply on the cigar. Blowing out a cloud of smoke, he said, "Mr. Crack."

Carella looked at him.

"Is his nickname, right," Corrente said. "Mr. fucking nigger Crack."

There was a need that took him back here.

Something inexplicable that did, in fact, take him back to the scene of any murder he'd ever investigated, time and again, to stand alone in the center of a bedroom or a hallway or a kitchen or a roof or—as was the case now—a small cloistered garden suffused with the late afternoon scent of hundreds of roses in riotous bloom.

The Crime Scene signs had all been taken down, the police were through with the place so far as gathering evidence was concerned. But Carella stood alone in the center of the garden, under the spreading branches of the old maple, and tried to sense what had happened here this past Thursday evening at sunset. It was yet only a little before five, the priest had been slain some two hours later, but Carella was not here

now to weigh and to evaluate, to discern and to deduce, he was here to
feel this courtyard and this murder, to absorb the essence of it, breathe
it deeply into his lungs, have it seep into his bloodstream to become a
part of him as vital as his liver or his heart—for only then could he
hope to understand it.

Mystical, yes.

A detective searching for a muse of sorts.

He recognized the absurdity of what he was doing, but bowed to
it nonetheless, standing there in dappled shade, listening to the
sounds of the springtime city beyond the high stone walls, trying to
absorb through his very flesh whatever secrets the garden contained.
Had not something of the murderer's rage and the victim's terror
flown helter-skelter about this small, contained and silent space, to
be claimed by stone or rose or blade of grass, and held forever in
time like the image of a killer in a dead man's eye? And if so, if this
was in fact a possibility, then was it not also possible that the terror
and the rage of that final awful moment when knife entered flesh
could now be recovered from all that had borne silent witness here
in this garden?

He stood alone, scarcely daring to breathe.

He was not a religious man, but perhaps he was praying.

He stood there for what seemed a long time, some ten or fifteen minutes, head bent, waiting for . . .

He didn't know what.

And at last, he took a deep breath and nodded and went back into
the rectory and into the small office angled into a nook that—judging
from the replastering—had once served as something else, he could not
imagine what. There were secrets here, too; perhaps there were secrets
everywhere.

The report from the Fingerprint Section had informed him that any
latents recovered from the open drawer of the file cabinet had been too
smudged to be useful in any meaningful search. There had been latents
as well on the various papers scattered on the floor and separately
delivered in an evidence envelope marked CORRESPONDENCE:
FLOOR and then initialed by the lab's R.L., whoever he might be.
Some of the latents matched the prints lifted from the dead priest's fingers and thumbs. The rest of them were wild, with the possibility that
some had been left on the correspondence by Kristin Lund.

Carella knelt beside the filing cabinet.

The bottom drawer, the one that had been found open, was labeled:

CORRESPONDENCE
G–L

He opened the drawer, no danger in doing that since the Mobile Lab had been through here with everything from a vacuum cleaner to a pair of tweezers. He felt around inside, along the back of the front panel; sometimes people Scotch-taped things to the inside of a drawer, where no one but a cop or a thief would think of looking. Nothing. Correspondence, G–L. Presumably, whoever had thrown those papers all over the place was looking for something in this drawer, something beginning with the letters of the alphabet that fell between G and L. Six letters altogether. God only knew what piece of paper the vandal had been looking for or whether or not he'd found it. Or even whether the ransacking had had anything at all to do with the murder. Carella was getting to his feet again when a voice behind him said, "Excuse me, sir."

He turned from the filing cabinets.

Two young girls were standing just inside the entrance door to the office.

They could not have been older than thirteen, fourteen at the most.

A blonde and one with hair as black as pitch.

The blonde was a classic beauty with a pale oval face, high molded cheekbones, a generous mouth, and dark brown eyes that gave her a thoughtful almost scholarly look. The other girl could have been her twin: the same delicate face, the same sculpted look, except that her hair was black and her eyes were a startling almost electric blue. Both girls wore their hair in stylists' cuts that fell straight and clean to the shoulders. Both were wearing sweaters, skirts and—in a replay of the Fifties—bobby sox and loafers. They exuded a freshness that Americans arrogantly assumed only their own healthy young girls possessed, but which was actually an asset of most teenage girls anywhere in the world.

"Sir," the black-haired one said, "are you with the church?"

Same one who'd spoken not a moment before.

"No," Carella said, "I'm not."

"We thought they might have sent someone," the blonde said. "A new priest."

"No," Carella said, and showed his shield and I.D. card. "I'm Detective Carella, Eighty-seventh Squad."

"Oh," the black-haired one said.

Both girls huddled in the doorway.

"I'm investigating Father Michael's murder," Carella said.

"How terrible," the blonde said.

The black-haired one nodded.

"Did you know Father Michael?" Carella asked.

"Oh, yes," both girls said, almost in unison.

"He was a wonderful person," the black-haired one said. "Excuse me, I'm President of the C.Y.O. My name is Gloria Keely."

"I'm Alexis O'Donnell," the blonde said. "I'm nothing."

Carella smiled.

"Nice to meet both of you," he said.

"Nice to meet you, too," Alexis said. "C.Y.O. means Catholic Youth Organization."

Thoughtful brown eyes in her delicate, serious face. I'm nothing, she had said. Meaning she was not an officer of the club. But something indeed, in that she was easily the more beautiful of the two girls, with a shy and thoroughly appealing manner. He wondered how parents who had named their daughter Alexis could possibly have known she'd turn out to be such a beauty.

"Thank you," he said, and smiled.

"We were wondering about the funeral tomorrow," Gloria said. "About what time it'll be. So we can tell the other kids."

A grimace. A shrug. Still the little girl in the developing woman's body.

"I really don't know," Carella said. "Maybe you can call the archdiocese."

"Mm, yeah, good idea," she said. Electric blue eyes sparkling with intelligence, midnight hair cascading to her shoulders, head bobbing in agreement with a plan already forming. "You wouldn't happen to have the number, would you?"

"I'm sorry."

"Do you know what they'll be doing about mass tomorrow?" Alexis asked.

The same soft, shy voice.

"I really don't know."

"I hate to miss mass," she said.

"I guess we can go over to St. Jude's," Gloria said.

"I guess," Alexis said.

A heavy silence shouldered its way into the room, as if the priest's death had suddenly made itself irretrievably felt. Father Michael would not be here this Sunday to say mass. They guessed they could go to St. Jude's, but Father Michael would not be there, either. And then—he would never know which of the girls started it—both were suddenly in tears. And hugging each other. And holding each other close in clumsy embrace. And comforting each other with small keening female sounds.

He felt utterly excluded.

The twins were watching television in the family room at the other end of the house. Teddy Carella sat alone in the living room, waiting for her husband. He had called from the office to say he might be late, not to worry about dinner, he'd catch a hamburger or something. She wondered if he might be walking into danger again, there was so much danger out there.

There was a time when the shield meant something.

You said, "Police," and you showed the shield, and you *became* the shield, you were everything the shield represented, the force of law, the power of law, this was what the shield represented. The shield represented civilization. And civilization meant a body of law that human beings had created for themselves over centuries and centuries. To protect themselves against others, to protect themselves against themselves as well.

That's what the shield used to mean.

Law.

Civilization.

Nowadays, the shield meant nothing. Nowadays the law was overwritten with graffiti, scrawled in the blood of cops. She felt like calling the President on the telephone and telling him that the Russians weren't about to invade us tomorrow. Tell him the enemy was already here, and it wasn't the Russians. The enemy was here feeding dope to our kids and killing cops in the street.

"Hello, Mr. President?" she would say. "This is Teddy Carella. When are you going to *do* something?"

If only she could speak.

But, of course, she couldn't.

So she sat waiting for Carella to come home, and when at last she saw the knob turning on the front door, she leaped to her feet and was there when the door opened, relief thrusting her into his arms and almost knocking him off his feet.

They kissed.

Gently, lingeringly.

They had known each other such a long time.

She asked him if he'd like a drink . . .

Fingers flashing in the sign language he knew so well . . .

. . . and he said he'd love a martini, and then went down the hall to say hello to the kids.

When he came back into the living room, she handed him the drink she'd mixed, and they went to sit on the sofa framed in the three arched windows at the far end of the room. The house was the sort Stephen King might have admired, a big Victorian white elephant in a section of Riverhead that had once boasted many similar houses, each on its own three or four acres of land, all dead and gone now, all gone. The Carella house was a reminder of an era long past, a more gracious, graceful time in America, the gabled white building with the wrought-iron fence all around it, a large tree-shaded corner plot, no longer all those acres, of course, those days of land and luxury were a thing of the dim, distant past.

He sat drinking his gin martini.

She sat drinking an after-dinner cognac.

She asked him where he'd eaten—putting the snifter down for a moment so that she could have free use of her hands—and he watched her flying fingers and answered in a combination of voice and sign, said he'd gone to a little Chinese joint on Culver, and then he fell silent, sipping at his drink, his head bent. He looked so tired. She knew him so well. She loved him so much.

He told her then how troubled he was by the murder of the priest.

It wasn't that he was religious or anything . . .

"I mean, you know that, Teddy, I haven't been inside a church since my sister got married, I just don't *believe* in any of that stuff anymore . . ."

. . . but somehow, the murder of a man of God . . .

"I don't even believe in *that,* people devoting themselves to religion, devoting their lives to spreading religion, *any* religion, I just don't believe in any of that anymore, Teddy, I'm sorry. I know you're religious. I know you pray. Forgive me. I'm sorry."

She took his hands in her own.

"I wish I *could* pray," he said.

And was silent again.

And then said, "But I've seen too much."

She squeezed his hands.

"Teddy . . . this is really getting to me," he said.

She flashed the single word *Why?*

"Because . . . he was a priest."

She looked at him, puzzled.

"I know. That sounds contradictory. Why should the death of a *priest* bother me? I haven't even *spoken* to a priest since . . . when did she get married? Angela? When was her wedding?"

Teddy's fingers moved:

The day the twins were born.

"Almost eleven years ago," he said, and nodded. "That's the last time I had anything to do with a priest. Eleven years ago."

He looked at his wife. A great many things had happened in those eleven years. Sometimes time seemed elastic to him, a concept that could be bent at will, twisted to fit ever-changing needs. Who was to say the twins were not now *thirty* years old, rather than eleven? Who was to say that he and Teddy were not still the young marrieds they'd been back then? Time. A concept as confusing to Carella as was that of . . . well, God.

He shook his head.

"Leave God out of it," he said, almost as if he'd spoken his earlier thoughts aloud. "Forget that Father Michael was a man of God, whatever that means. Maybe there *are* no men of God anymore. Maybe the whole world . . ."

He shook his head again.

"Figure him only for someone who was . . . okay, not *pure*, nobody's pure, but at least *innocent*."

He saw the puzzlement on her face, and realized she had misread either his lips or his sloppy signing. He signed the word letter by letter, and she nodded and signed it back, and he said, "Yeah, think of him that way. Innocent. And, yes, pure, why *not*? Pure of *heart*, anyway. A man who'd never harmed another human being in his entire life. Would never have *dreamt* of harming anyone. And all at once, out of the night, out of the sunset, into his peaceful garden, there comes an assassin with a knife."

He drained his glass.

"That's what's getting to me, Teddy. On New Year's Eve, I caught a baby smothered in her crib, that was only five months ago, what's today, Teddy, the twenty-sixth of May, not *even* five full months. And now another innocent. If people like . . . like . . . if people like *that* are getting killed . . . if the . . . if even the . . . if nobody *gives* a damn any-

more . . . if you can kill a baby, kill a priest, kill a ninety-year-old grandmother, kill a pregnant woman . . .”

And suddenly he buried his face in his hands.

“There’s too much of it,” he said.

And she realized he was weeping.

“Too much,” he said.

She took him in her arms.

And she thought Dear God, get him out of this job before it kills him.

Seronia and her brother were eating pizza in a joint on The Stem. They
had ordered and devoured one large pizza with extra cheese and pepper-
oni, and were now working on the smaller pizza they’d ordered next.
Seronia was leaning forward over the table, a long string of mozzarella
cheese trailing from her lips to the folded wedge of pizza in her hand,
eating her way up the string toward the slice of pizza. Hooper watched
her as if she were walking a tightrope a hundred feet above the ground.

She bit off the cheese together with a piece of the pizza, chewed,
swallowed and washed it down with Diet Coke. She was very much
aware that the white guy throwing pizzas behind the counter was
watching her. She was wearing an exceptionally short mini made to
look like black leather. Red silk blouse with a scoop neck. Dangling red
earrings. Black patent pumps. Thirteen years old and being eyed up
and down by a white man shoveling pizza in an oven.

“You shoonta lied to him,” she told her brother. “He fine out *why*
you was on ’Leventh Street, he be back.”

“You the one say they was nothin’ to lose,” Hooper said.

“That dinn give you no cause to lie.”

“I tole him basely d’troof,” Hooper said.

“No, you lied about Fat Harol’.”

“So whut? Who gives a shit about that skinny li’l fuck?”

“Sayin’ as how he do crack. Sheee-it, man, he a momma’s boy doan
know crack fum his *own* crack.”

Hooper laughed.

“Sayin’ as how he wenn to a crack house, bought hisself a nickel vial.
An’ paintin’ yourself like a . . .”

“It was true we wenn t’church t’gether, though, me an’ Harol’,”
Hooper said.

“I doan do no dope,” Seronia said, imitating her brother talking to
Carella, “an’ I doan run dope for none a’these mis’able dealers comes
aroun’ here tryin’ a’spoil d’chirren.”

"This was the *Man* we talkin' to," Hooper said. "Whutchoo 'spec me to tell him?"

"I never done no crim'nal thing in my life," Seronia said, still doing a pretty fair imitation of her brother's deeper voice. "Never!" she said, and clenched her fist and rapped it against her small budding breast.

"Is 'zackly whut I tole the Man," Hooper said, and grinned.

"I like to wet my pants when I heerd that," Seronia said, and shook her head in admiration and pride. "I goan be *any* kine a'nigger, it's goan be a *good* one," she mimicked. "Like Eddie Murphy." And again shook her head and rolled her big brown eyes heavenward.

"Eddie Murphy, right," Hooper said.

"You goan wish you *was* Eddie Murphy when he comes roun' again," Seronia said. " 'Cause he look to me like the kine a'fuzz doan let go, bro. An' he goan *talk* to the people 'long 'Leventh Street, an' somebody gonna tell him sumpin' you *dinn* tell him. An' then he goan fine out whut happen 'tween you an' the pries', and then you goan be in deep shit, bro."

"Ain' nothin' happen 'tween me an' the pries'."

" 'Sep you hid yo' stash in the church," Seronia said, and bit into another slice of pizza.

6

WILLIS DID NOT GET BACK to the house on Harborside Lane until almost eight o'clock that Saturday night. He called her name the moment he stepped into the entry foyer.

There was no answer.

"Honey?" he called. "I'm home."

And again there was no answer.

He was a policeman, trained to expect the unexpected. He was, moreover, a policeman who had lived on the thin edge of anticipation from the moment he'd committed himself to Marilyn Hollis. The words he'd heard on the telephone this past Thursday night suddenly popped into his mind—*Perdóneme, señor*—and just as suddenly he was alarmed.

"Marilyn!" he shouted, and went tearing up the stairs two at a time, made a sharp right turn on the second-floor landing and was starting up the steps to the third floor when he heard her voice coming from somewhere down the corridor.

"In here, Hal."

She was in the kitchen. Sitting at the butcher block table, the stainless steel ovens, refrigerator and range forming a grey metallic curtain behind her. She was holding a dish towel to her nose. The towel bulged with angles. There was an empty ice cube tray on the table.

"I fell," she said.

Hand holding the dish towel to her nose, eyes wide above it and flanking it, flesh under the eyes already discolored.

"Down the stairs," she said. "I think I broke my nose."

"Well, Jesus, did you call the . . . ?"

"It just happened a few minutes ago," she said.

"I'll call him," he said, and went immediately to the phone.

"I don't think they can do anything for a broken nose," she said. "I think it has to heal by itself."

"They can set it," he said, and began searching through their personal directory on the counter under the wall phone. Rubenstein, the doctor's name was Rubenstein. Willis realized all at once that he was irrationally irritated; the way a parent might become irritated when a child did something that threatened its own well-being. He was relieved that Marilyn had not hurt herself more badly, but annoyed that she had hurt herself at all.

"How'd you manage to fall down the goddamn *stairs?*" he said, shaking his head.

"I tripped," she said.

"Isn't his number in this thing?" he asked impatiently.

"Try D," she said. "For doctor."

More annoyed now, he turned to the D section of the directory, and scanned through a dozen names and numbers in Marilyn's handwriting before he found a listing for Rubenstein, Marvin, Dr. He dialed the number. It rang four times and then a woman picked up. The doctor's answering service. She advised Willis that the doctor was out of town for several days and asked if she should notify his standby, a Dr. Gerald Peters. Somewhat curtly, Willis said, "Never mind," and hung the phone back on the wall cradle.

"Come on," he said, "we're going to the hospital."

"I really don't think . . ."

"Marilyn, *please,*" he said.

He hurried her out of the house and into the car. He debated hitting the hammer, decided against it. Use the siren on a personal matter, the Department would take a fit. The nearest hospital was Morehouse General on Culver and North Third, just inside the precinct's western boundary. He drove there as if he were responding to a 10-13, foot heavy on the accelerator, ignoring traffic signals unless a changing light posed a danger to another vehicle, and then made a sharp right turn on Third, and wheeled the car squealing up the driveway to the Emergency Room.

This was Saturday night.

Only eighteen minutes past eight, in fact, but the weekend had already begun in earnest, and the E.R. resembled an army field station. Two black cops with identifying 87 insignia on their uniform collars were struggling to keep apart a pair of lookalike white goons who had done a very good job of cutting each other to ribbons. Their T-shirts, once white, now clung in tatters to bloody streamers of flesh. One of the men had opened the other's face from his right temple down to his jaw. The other man had slashed through the first guy's bulging biceps and forearm all the way down to the wrist. The men were still scream-ing at each other, their hands cuffed behind their backs, shoulder-butting the cops trying to keep them separated.

A resident physician who looked Indian and undoubtedly was—in this city, there were more Indian interns than in the entire state of Rajasthan—kept saying over and over again, quite patiently, "Do you wish medical treatment, or do you wish to behave foolishly?" The two goons ignored this running commentary because they had *already* behaved foolishly, had probably been behaving foolishly all their lives, and weren't able to *stop* behaving foolishly now, just because a for-eigner was sounding reasonable. So they kept bleeding all over the E.R. while the two sweating black cops struggled with a pair of enraged men twice their size and tried to keep their uniforms clean, and a saintly nurse patiently stood by with cotton swabs, a bottle of antiseptic, and a roll of bandages and tried to keep *her* uniform clean, and an excitable orderly circled warily, trying to mop the goddamn floor as blood spat-tered everywhere in the air.

Elsewhere in the room sitting on the bench, or crowding the nurses' station, or standing about in various stages of distress and discomfort, Willis saw and registered with dismay:

A twelve-year-old Hispanic girl whose blouse was torn open to reveal a training bra and tiny budding breasts. Blood was streaming down the inside of her right leg. Willis figured she'd been raped.

A forty-year-old white man being supported by yet another police officer and yet another Indian resident, who were maneuvering him toward one of the cubicles so that the doctor could examine what looked to Willis like a gunshot wound through the left shoulder.

A black teenager sitting on the bench with one high-topped sneaker off and in his hands. His right foot was swollen to the size of a melon. Willis figured him for a non–crime victim, but in this precinct you never could tell.

There were also . . .

There was *Marilyn*, period.

"Excuse me, doctor," Willis said, and a redheaded resident standing at the nurses' station studying a chart glanced up as though wondering who had had the unspeakable audacity to raise his voice here in the temple. On his face, there was the haughtily scornful, one-eyebrow-raised look of a person who knew without question that his calling was godly. It was a look that managed to mingle distaste with dismissal, as though its wearer had already singled out and was now ready to punish whoever had dared fart in his immediate presence.

But Willis's woman had a broken nose.

Unintimidated, he flashed the tin, announced his own godly calling—"Detective Harold Willis"—and then slapped the leather case shut as though he were throwing down a glove. "I'm investigating a homicide, this woman needs immediate medical attention."

What a homicide had to do with this woman's broken nose—in a single glance, he was able to make this diagnosis—the redheaded resident couldn't possibly imagine. But the look on the detective's face said that the matter was extremely urgent, the matter was in fact positively critical, and there would be hell to pay if this woman's broken nose resulted in a bungled homicide investigation. So the resident ignored all the other people clamoring for attention in that Saturday night purgatory and immediately tended to the blonde woman's needs, determining (as he'd known at once, anyway) that the nose was in fact broken, and giving her an immediate shot for the pain, and then setting the nose, and dressing it with plaster (such a beautiful face, too) and writing a prescription for a pain-killer should she have difficulty getting through the night. Only then did he ask her how this had happened, and Marilyn told him unhesitatingly that she'd tripped and fallen down a flight of stairs.

This was when Willis fully realized something he had only partially known from the moment he'd found her in the kitchen with the ice pack to her nose.

Marilyn was lying.

"But why did you lie to them?" Sally Farnes asked.

This was eight-thirty P.M. The two of them were sitting on the little balcony outside their living room, looking out at the lights of the Saturday night city and the splendor of the sky overhead. Sunset had stained the western horizon an hour and a half ago. They had eaten an early dinner and then had carried their coffee out here onto the balcony, anticipating the brilliant show of color that had been their special treat these past several weeks. Tonight's spectacle had not been at all disappointing, a kaleidoscopic display of reds and oranges and purples and deeper blues culminating in a dazzle of stars wheeling across an intensely black sky.

"I didn't lie," he said.

"I would say that allowing them to think you and the priest had set-tled all your differences . . ."

"Which we did," Farnes said.

Sally rolled her eyes heavenward.

She was a big woman with brown hair, full-breasted and wide across the hips, a woman who had ironically chosen to remain childless while equipped with a body seemingly designed for childbearing. In a nation where being thin and staying young were the twin aspirations of every woman past the age of puberty, Sally Farnes at the age of forty-three thumbed her nose at all the models in *Vogue* and called herself volup-tuous, even though she was really twenty pounds overweight according to all the charts.

She had always been a trifle overweight, even when she was a teenager, but she'd never looked fat, she'd merely looked *zaftig*—a term she understood even then to mean voluptuous because a Jewish boy who later became class valedictorian told her so while he was feel-ing her up in the back seat of his father's Oldsmobile. Actually, the boy had been thinking of the word *wollüstig*, which indeed did mean voluptuous, whereas *zaftig* merely meant juicy. In any case, Sally had looked both voluptuous *and* juicy, and pleasantly plump besides, with a glint in her blue eyes that promised a sexiness wanton enough to arouse the desires of a great many pimply-faced young men.

She still looked supremely desirable. Even sitting alone here in the dark on her own balcony with her own husband, her legs were crossed in a provocative manner, and the three top buttons of her blouse were undone. There was a thin sheen of perspiration over her upper lip. She was wondering if her husband had killed Father Michael.

"You know you had a fight with him," she said.

"No, no," he said.

"Yes, yes. You went there on Easter Sunday . . ."

"Yes, and we shook hands and made up."

"Arthur, that is *not* what you told me. You told me . . ."

"Never mind what I told you," Farnes said. "We shook hands and made up is what I'm telling you now."

"Why are you lying?" she asked.

"Let me explain something to you," he said. "Those detectives . . ."

"You shouldn't have lied to them. You shouldn't be lying to me now."

"If you don't mind," he said, "you asked me a question."

"All right," she said.

"Do you want an answer, or do you want to keep interrupting?"

"I *said* all right."

"Those detectives came to see me because a priest was killed, do you understand that? A priest. Do you know who runs the police department in this city?"

"Who?"

"The Catholic Church. And if the church tells the cops to find whoever killed that priest, the cops are going to find him."

"That still doesn't . . ."

"That's right, interrupt again," Farnes said.

In the light spilling onto the balcony from the living room inside, his eyes met hers. There was something fierce and unyielding in those eyes. She could remember the last time she'd challenged him. She wondered again if he'd killed Father Michael.

"Catching the *real* killer isn't important to them," he said. "The only thing that matters is catching *a* killer, *any* killer. They came to the store trying to make a big deal out of my differences with Father Michael. Was I supposed to tell them we'd had an argument on Easter Sunday? No way. We shook hands and made up."

"But that's *not* what you did."

"That is what we did. Period."

From the street far below, the sounds of traffic filtered up. Distant, unreal somehow, the honking horns and ambulance sirens sounding like canned background sweetening for a daytime soap. They sat listening to the murmur of the city. The wingtip lights of an airplane blinked across the sky. She wondered if she should push this further. She did not want him to lose his temper. She knew what could happen if he lost his temper.

"You see," she said, as gently as she could, "I just think it was stupid to lie about something so insignificant."

"You must stop saying that, Sally. That I lied."

"Because certainly," she said, still gently, still calmly, "the police weren't about to think that a silly *argument* . . ."

"But that's exactly what they *were* thinking. That's exactly why they came to the store. Waving that damn letter I'd written! Finding something threatening in every paragraph! So what was I supposed to say? What did you want me to say, Sally? That the letter was only the beginning? That we had a violent argument shortly after I'd written it? Is that what you wanted me to say?"

"All I know is that policemen can tell when someone is lying."

"Nonsense."

"It's true. They have a sixth sense. And if they think you were lying about Father Michael . . ."

She let the sentence trail.

"Yes?" he said.

"Nothing."

"No, tell me. If they think I was lying about Father Michael, then what?"

"Then they may start looking for other things."

"What other things?"

"You know what things," she said.

Hawes was learning a few things about Krissie Lund.

He learned, to begin with, that she'd come to this city from a little town in Minnesota . . .

"I love it here," she said. "Do you love it here?"

"Sometimes."

"Have you ever been to Minnesota?"

"Never," he said.

"Cold," she said.

"I'll bet."

"Everybody runs inside during the winter. You can freeze to death out there in the snow and ice, you know. So they all run to the bunkers and lock up behind them and wait till springtime before they show their faces again. It's a sort of siege mentality."

It seemed odd to be talking about the dead of winter when everywhere around them springtime was very much in evidence. They had come out of the restaurant at a little after ten, and it was now almost ten-thirty and they were walking idly up Hall Avenue toward the Tower Building on Midway. On nights like tonight, it was impossible to believe that anyone ever got mugged in this city. Men and women strolled together hand in hand, glancing into brightly lighted store windows, buying pretzels or hot dogs or ice cream or yogurt or souvlaki or sausages from the bazaar of peddlers' carts on almost every corner, browsing the several bookstores that would be open till midnight, checking out the sidewalk wares of the nighttime street merchants, stopping to listen to a black tenor saxophonist playing a soulful rendition of *Birth of the Blues,* the fat mellow notes floating out of the bell of his golden horn and soaring upward on the balmy air. It was a night for lovers.

They were not yet lovers, Hawes and Krissie, and perhaps they'd never be. But they were learning each other. This was the difficult time. You met someone, and you liked what you saw, and then you hoped that what you learned about him or her would make sense, would mysteriously jibe with whatever person you happened to be at this particular stage of your life. The way Hawes figured it, everything depended on where you were and who you were at any given time. If he'd met Krissie a year ago, he'd have been too occupied with Annie Rawles to have initiated and pursued any other relationship. Five years ago, ten years ago, he found it difficult to remember which women had figured largely in his life at any given time. Once there had been another Krissie—well, Christine, actually, close but no cigar. Christine Maxwell. Who'd owned a bookshop. Hadn't she? May was the month for remembering. Or forgetting.

"How'd you happen to start working uptown?" he asked.

"There was an ad in the paper," she said. "I was looking for something part time and the job at the church sounded better than waitressing."

"Why part time?"

"Well, because I have classes, you know, and also I have to make rounds . . ."

Oh, Jesus, he thought, an actress.

"What kind of classes?" he asked hopefully.

"Acting, voice, dance . . ."

Of course, he thought.

"And I work out three times a week at the gym . . ."

Certainly, he thought.

"So the job at the church is just to keep me going, you know . . ."

"Uh-huh," he said out loud.

"Till I get a part in something . . ."

"Right, a part," he said.

Every actress he'd ever met in his life had been a totally egotistical, thoroughly self-centered airhead looking for a *part* in something.

"Which is why I *came* here, of course," she said. "I mean, we've got the Guthrie out there and all, but that's still regional theater, isn't it?"

"I guess you could call it that," Hawes said.

"Yes, well, it is, actually," Krissie said.

He had once dated an actress who was working in a little theater downtown in a musical revue called *Goofballs* written by a man who reviewed books while he was learning to become Stephen Sondheim. If he reviewed books as well as he wrote musical revues, the writers of the world were in serious trouble. The actress's name was Holly Tree, and she swore this was her real name even though her driver's license (which Hawes—big detective that he was—happened to peek at while she was still asleep naked in his apartment the morning after they'd met) read Marie Trenotte, which he later learned meant Three Nights, the Trenotte not the Marie. Three nights was the exact amount of time she spent with him before moving on to bigger and better things, like the reviewer who had composed the show.

He had known another actress who'd been living with a heroin dealer he'd arrested—this was before cocaine and then crack became the drugs of choice—and who told him she was up for the part of a lady cop on *Hill Street* and would he mind very much if she moved in with him while her man was away so she could do some firsthand research, who she didn't know was dealing drugs anyway. Her name was Alyce (with a y) Chambers and she was a beautiful redhead who mentioned that if they had any children their hair would be red since both their parents had red hair, did he ever notice that a lot of actresses and especially strippers had boyfriends who were cops? He had never noticed. She did not get the part on *Hill Street*. Nor any other part she ever tried out for, it was that son of a bitch in prison, she informed Hawes, pulling strings from all the way upstate. In all the while she lived with him, she never once talked about anything but herself. He began to feel like a mirror.

Then one day she met a man with a Santa Claus beard and twinkling blue eyes and a diamond pinky ring the size of Antigua and he told her he was producing a little show out in Los Angeles and if she cared to accompany him out there she could stay with him temporarily at a little house he owned on the beach at Malibu . . . not the *Colony*, but close to it . . . just south of it, in fact . . . closer to Santa Monica, in fact . . . if that's what she would like to do. She moved out the very next day. She still sent Hawes a card every Christmas, but somehow she seemed to think his name was *Corry* Hawes.

And he'd known another actress who washed out her panties in . . .

"Penny for your thoughts," Krissie said.

"I was just thinking how nice, an actress," Hawes said.

"Actually," she said, "it's not very nice at all."

He braced himself for an Actress Atrocity Story. Producer asking her to strip for a nude scene in a film that turns out to be a porn flick. Actor soul-kissing her while they're auditioning together for a theaterful of potential back . . .

"In fact," she said, and her voice caught, "I'm beginning to think I'm not so hot, you know what I mean?"

He looked at her, surprised.

"No," he said. "What do you mean?"

"Not such a good actress, you know?" she said, and smiled somewhat pallidly. "No talent, you know?"

He kept looking at her.

"But I don't want to spend the rest of the night talking about me," she said, and took his hand. "Tell me how you got into police work."

She had tried to get the blood stains out of the carpet, but Willis was a cop and he could spot a worked-over stain from a mile away. She had similarly tried to soak the blood out of the monogrammed hand towel from the master bedroom, a much more difficult job in that it was white whereas the carpet was a Persian with lots of red in it. She'd used Clorox on the towel and then had taken it downstairs to the washing machine off the kitchen on the second floor, thrown it in with a lot of other towels, but the stain was still just barely visible, blood was tough. He'd known murderers who'd worked for days trying to get blood stains out of a wooden knife handle or even the blade of a hatchet, witness Lizzie Borden, whom he had not known personally. Blood was blood. Blood told.

And now, so did Marilyn.

It was five minutes past eleven.

Saturday night was still with them.

Across town and downtown, Cotton Hawes was about to ask Krissie if she'd care to stop by his place for a nightcap.

Closer to home, at the Church of the Bornless One on Ninth and North End, Schuyler Lutherson was fastening a black silk cord about the waist of his black cotton robe, rehearsing aloud the words of the Introit which he would say at the beginning of the midnight mass.

She told Willis about the first approach the two men had made.

Ramon Castaneda and Carlos Ortega.

"They gave you their names?" he said.

"Not then," she said. "This afternoon."

She told him everything that had happened here in this bedroom this afternoon. Everything. He had found the window they'd jimmied on the third floor, and now he listened intently, his heart beating wildly, she could have been killed. But no, he agreed with her, they could not kill her if they expected to get money from her, you can't collect from someone who's dead.

"Give them what they want," he said at once. "Get rid of them."

"How?" she said.

"Sell the house, I don't *care* how. Get the money and give it to them, send them back to Argentina."

"In a minute, right? Put a house worth seven-fifty on the market, and hope to sell it in a minute."

"Then borrow against it. Mortgage it to the hilt. Liquidate whatever other assets you have, call your broker . . ."

"There isn't that much, Hal."

"You left Buenos Aires with two million dollars!"

"I put five hundred of that down on the house, and spent another three hundred furnishing it. I made some bad investments, a gold-mining operation in Papua New Guinea, an electronics firm in Dallas, some big loans to friends who never paid me back . . ."

"All right, how much *can* you raise?"

"If I sold off all the stock I have, let's say four, five hundred. Plus whatever I can get on a second mortgage. Unless somebody buys the house tomorrow. Even so . . ."

"Maybe they'll settle for that," Willis said.

"I don't think so."

"Because if not . . ."

She looked at him.

"I can't let anything happen to you," he said. "I love you too much."

The worshippers had been informed that the meeting before tonight's mass would begin at eleven-thirty, and so they had begun assembling in the old stone church at twenty past the hour. It was written in the sacred Black Book that all church business must perforce be concluded before the hour of midnight when it was further ordained that the Introit should be said and the mass begun. On most occasions, there was scant church business to discuss. Tonight there was the matter of who, if anyone, in the congregation had painted the sign of Baphomet on the murdered priest's gate.

The assemblage numbered some fifty-one people . . .

If divisible by two, impure . . .

. . . among whom were the nine who would preside over and partici-pate in the ritual of the mass . . .

If divisible by three, sublime.

The remaining forty-two were worshippers who had been told that the mass tonight would be more expressive of the *joys* of Satanism than had the more solemn Mass of the Expulsion earlier this week. But in contradiction to the announced purpose of the celebration tonight, the clothing they wore appeared conservative if not austere, the hues black or grey or dun for an overall appearance of unrelieved drabness, the cut angular and restrictive for an almost uniform look of severity.

It was only when one looked more closely . . .

A man standing at the rear of the church seemed to be wearing a long leather blacksmith's apron over black leather trousers. But when he turned in profile to greet a newcomer, it became evident that the trousers were in fact high boots and that between the tops of those boots and the hem of the apron there was naked flesh and nascent tumescence.

Through surmise, surprise.

A redheaded woman sat with her legs crossed on the aisle some three rows back from the altar, her auburn tresses caught and contained in a heavy black snood that added to them the seeming weight of mourning. She was wearing as well a black silk blouse, tailored grey slacks, and high-topped, laced, black leather shoes. But when she uncrossed her legs to lean forward and whisper something to a man on the row ahead of her, it became apparent that the slacks were crotchless and that beneath them she wore nothing. The revealed thatch of her fiery red pubic hair and lipstick-tinted nether lips were in direct contrast to the trapped hair on her head and the plainness of her unpainted mouth.

Throughout that vaulted holy place, then, there were unexpected . . .

Through ignorance, knowledge . . .

. . . glimpses of the flesh these celebrants were here tonight to honor. In Satan's name, they exposed discreetly and posed ingenuously. Speaking in whispers as befitted the sanctity of the Lord's meeting place, candid eyes met and held, glances neither roamed nor wavered, expressions never once indicated that a promised later offering to Satan was now being shown in fleeting preview:

A woman's severe black gown, cut high on the neck and low on the ankle with a cutout circle the size of a quarter exposing the nipple of her left breast painted a red as deep as blood . . .

A black man's grey homespun trousers, worn with a long-sleeved black shirt and a hangman's hood, his penis thrusting through an open-

ing in the trousers and held in an upright position by the silken white
ribbons wrapped around it and tied about his waist . . .

An exquisitely beautiful Chinese woman wearing a loosely crocheted
black dress, pale diamonds of flesh showing everywhere except where
tightly woven black covered her Venus mound and breasts . . .
Through concealment, revealment.

In many respects, this socializing before the mass began was not
too very different in tone or appearance from the little parties and
gatherings occurring all over the city tonight. Except that here in
this group, among these people openly worshipping the Devil, there
was in the reverse order of their beliefs an honesty of intent that
Schuyler Lutherson considered less hypocritical. Coming through
the black curtains at the rear of the church now, he reflected
solemnly upon the fervor of those who spoke most righteously for
any God they claimed to admire—be it Jesus, Muhammed, Buddha
or Zeus—and wondered if these people might not find a better home
here at the Church of the Bornless One. Because it seemed to him
that those who most vehemently denounced the sinful actions of
unbelievers were those who most vigorously and secretly *pursued*
those actions. And those who defended their religions against the
imagined onslaughts of infidels were those who, in the very name of
whichever god they professed to serve, most often vilified the sacred
teachings of that god.

Come to Satan, Schuyler thought, and made the sign of the goat in
greeting, and then went directly to the living altar and faced her, and
passed his tongue over the forefinger and middle finger of his left hand,
the Devil's hand, wetting his fingers, and then ran both fingers slick
and wet over the lips of Coral's vagina, from my lips to thy lips, and
said in Latin, "By your leave, most beloved Lord, I beseech thee,"
which was a plea upon Satan's own altar for the Unborn One to please
remain patient yet a moment longer while this tiresome church business was attended to.

The worshippers fell silent as Schuyler stepped forward. Immediately behind him was the living altar, Coral, with her legs spread and
bent at the knees, bare feet flat on the velvet-covered trapezoid, arms at
her sides, clutching in each hand a phallic-shaped candelabra in which
was an as-yet-unlighted black candle. The beginning of the mass would
be signaled by the lighting of these candles, followed by the recitation
of first the Introit and then the Invocation. For now, the deacon and
sub-deacons stood ranked behind the altar in readiness.

The four acolytes (four tonight rather than the customary two, in that this was a special mass following the high holy Feast of the Expulsion) stood seriously and solemnly in boy-girl pairs on either side of the altar. Two eight-year-old girls, one of whom was tall for her age, a boy who was also eight, and another who was nine, all of them barefooted and wearing silken black tunics beneath which they were naked. Coral's long blonde hair cascaded over the pointed end of the trapezoid, almost touching the cold stone floor.

Without preamble, Schuyler said, "The death of this priest is troublesome. It may bring unwanted, unneeded visitors to the church. It may lead to suspicion of our order, and possible harassment, see, from the police. Or perhaps even more serious measures from them, I don't know, I don't care. What I'm asking tonight is for anyone here among us, if he or she is responsible for painting an inverted pentagram on the gate of St. Catherine's church, to come up here and say you did it. If you did it, then you know who you are, and I want you to come forward and explain *why* you did it. So we can straighten this out."

There was silence out there in the congregation.

Hesitation.

And then a blond giant of a man rose and stepped out into the aisle. He was in his early twenties, weathered and suntanned and muscular and lean, wearing a pair of faded grey jeans and a T-shirt tie-dyed in varying swirls of black, black headband and black leather sandals. In further keeping with the tone and stated purpose of the mass tonight, a black leather thong was tied tightly around his left thigh some three inches below his crotch. No one so much as glanced at the thong, no one seemed to notice that it held fastened against the man's leg . . .

Through bondage, freedom . . .

. . . a penis enormous by any standards, hidden of course by the fabric of his jeans . . .

Through disguise, discovery . . .

. . . but clearly discernible in massive outline.

"I did it," he said. "I painted the priest's gate."

"Come on up," Schuyler said in a friendly manner, but he was scowling. Perhaps because he himself was blond and considerably handsome and so was the young man, and he may have felt this constituted a threat to his leadership. Or perhaps he sensed, even before the young man reached the front of the church, and even though he'd only heard him speak eight short words, that here in the Church of the Bornless One was yet another of Dorothy's friends, too damn *many* of whom had been attracted to the services here in recent weeks.

"Tell us your name," Schuyler said, still pleasantly. But something seemed coiled within him.

"Andrew Hobbs," the young man said. "I started coming here in March."

Something Southern in his speech. The lilt. The intonation. Something else as well. A more familiar lilt.

"Jeremy Sachs introduced me here."

Sachs. Jeremy Sachs. Schuyler searched his memory for an image to connect with the name. A face. A character trait. A verbal tic. Nothing came.

"Yes?" he said.

"Yes."

"And the gate?"

"I did it," he said.

Through confession, condemnation.

"Why?"

"Because of her."

"Who?"

Was it possible, then, that he was *not* one of Dorothy's friends? And yet the *look* of him, and the cleverness of the thong, the understatement of it. But he hadn't yet said "her" name. And among those who roamed Oz, the female pronoun was often substituted for the . . .

"Her," Hobbs said. "My mother."

Ah, then. Were we still on the yellow brick road?

"What about her?" Schuyler asked.

They often nursed long-term grievances against Mama.

"She went to him."

"Went to who?"

"The priest. And told him."

"Told him what?"

If only this wasn't so much like pulling *teeth*.

"That I've been coming here. That Jeremy took me here. That we've been doing . . . things here."

Jeremy. Sachs. And now the name took on visual dimensions, Jeremy Sachs, a squat, rather simian-looking young white homosexual—without doubt one of Dorothy's friends, a longtime traveler among the Munchkins—who'd declared fealty to the Devil by reversing his own

natural preferences and going down helter-skelter and willy-nilly on
every naked snatch offered to Satan within these sacrosanct walls.

Schuyler could not recall seeing his young blond friend at any of the
masses before tonight, but often there was wholesale confusion and
resultant obscurity. In any case, here he was now, the young friend of a
friend of Dorothy, perhaps homosexual himself, who had just now
confessed defiling the dead priest's gate because of his goddamn
mother. All mothers should be forced to suck a horse's cock, Schuyler
thought. Including my own.

"But why did you paint the gate?" he asked.

"As a statement," Hobbs said.

Schuyler nodded. So what this was, it was merely a case of someone
telling his Mama to keep out of his life. Completely understandable.
This was not someone with any hard feelings for the priest. No bad
intentions here at all. Just somebody making a personal family statement. But nonetheless . . .

"The statement you have to make *now,*" Schuyler said, "is to the
police. To let them know you didn't paint that pentagram as any kind
of warning or anything. This priest was killed, see, and we don't want
his murder connected to this church in any way. So what I suggest you
do is leave here right this minute, see, and go home and change your
clothes . . ."

"What's wrong with my clothes?" Hobbs asked.

"Nothing," Schuyler said. "In fact, what you're wearing is well-
suited . . ."

He didn't know he was making a pun.

". . . to the ceremony tonight. But it might be misunderstood by the
police, see, so go put on something that'll make 'em think you work in
a bank."

"I *do* work in a bank," Hobbs said.

There was laughter in the assemblage. Laughter of relief, perhaps.
This wasn't going to be as bad as it had appeared at first. Young homosexual here had argued with his mother, had gone off in a snit, and in
defiance had painted the sign of his religious belief on the enemy's gate.
He'd explain all this to the police and they'd understand, and send him
on his way, and everyone could go right on practicing his chosen religion in freedom again, this was a wonderful country, the U.S. of A.

It was four minutes to midnight.

Hobbs asked where the nearest police station was, and from where
he was standing behind the living altar, Stanley Garcia—who had been

there early yesterday morning—gave him directions to the 87th Precinct. Hobbs asked if he could come back here for the mass *after* he'd talked to the police, but Schuyler pointed out that the doors would be locked at the stroke of midnight, which in fact was now only three minutes away, so perhaps Hobbs had better get moving. Hobbs appeared to be sulking as he left the church. One of the worshippers closed and bolted the door behind him, and then dropped the heavy wooden crossbar into place, in effect double-locking the doors.

It was a minute to midnight.

The church was expectantly silent.

The redhead in the grey slacks sat with her knees pressed closely together, her head bent.

"It is the hour," Schuyler said, and signaled to his sub-deacons to come forward and light the candles. The sub-deacons tonight were two nineteen-year-old girls who looked like sisters but who weren't even cousins. Both brunettes with brown eyes, they were wearing the customary black robes of the church, naked beneath them, for it was a ritual that following consecration of the altar by the minister, his sub-deacons (traditionally female) would then in turn and in sequence be consecrated by the deacon.

Solemnly and silently, the girls—whose names were Heather and Patrice—went to the altar, knelt in reverence before her, and then parted, one going to the left, the other to the right, where Coral's hands clutched the thick phallic candelabra. Tapers sputtering, they lighted both candles, and then went behind the altar to where Stanley Garcia stood with an oxidized and blackened brass censer in each hand. The girls lighted the incense, and then accepted the thuribles from Stanley. Swinging them on the ends of their short black chains, they sweetened with incense first the altar and the surrounding apsidal chapters and then went up the center aisle to spread the cloying scent throughout the entire church. They returned then to stand flanking their deacon.

It was time for the Introit.

The word itself derived from the Middle English word for "entrance," from the Old French *introït* from the Latin *introitus*. It was pronounced not in the French manner but rather to rhyme with "Sin-Show-It," as many in the congregation were fond of explaining. In Christian churches, the introit was in fact an *entrance*, the beginning as such of the proper, and it consisted either of a psalm verse, an antiphon, or the Gloria Patri. In the true church of the Devil, however, the introit was a short and personal opening dialogue intended as a despoliation of innocence and an introduction to the Devil, who would be invoked more seriously later tonight. The ritual blasphemy that Schuyler and the four child acolytes were about to perform was, in essence, a rude dismissal of Jesus and an acknowledgment of Satan—*Daemon est Deus Inversus:* The Devil is the other side of God.

Schuyler nodded to his deacon.

Stanley rang the heavy bell nine times, three times facing south and the altar, and then kept turning counterclockwise to ring the bell twice at each remaining cardinal point of the compass.

The air now purified, Schuyler went to stand in the open angle formed by the naked legs of the altar. Facing the assemblage, he lifted both arms, and formed the sign of the goat with the fingers of both hands. At this signal the four acolytes came to face him, a boy and a girl on each side.

In Latin, Schuyler said, "*In nomine magni dei nostri Satanas . . .*"

In the name of our great god Satan . . .

". . . we stand before thy living altar."

And in their piping voices, the acolytes responded in unison and in Latin, "We beseech assistance, oh Lord, save us from the wicked."

"To our Lord who created the earth and the heavens, the night and the day, the darkness and the light," Schuyler intoned, "to our Infernal Lord who causes us to exult . . ."

"Oh Lord, deliver us from unjustness," the children chanted.

"Lord Satan, hearken to our voices," Schuyler said. "Demonstrate to us thy terrible power . . ."

"And give to us of thy immeasurable largess."

"*Dominus Infernus vobiscum,*" Schuyler said. "The Infernal Lord be with you."

And the children responded, "*Et tecum.* And also with you."

And the assemblage rose to its feet and shouted tumultuously and victoriously, "All hail Satan, all hail Satan!"

Detective Meyer Meyer was in the squadroom only by chance—trying to catch up on half a dozen reports that were already weeks late—when a blond young man wearing a dark pencil-stripe suit materialized on the other side of the wooden rail divider to the squadroom.

"Excuse me," he said.

"Yes?" Meyer said, looking up from his typewriter.

"I'm looking for whoever's investigating the priest murder. Sergeant downstairs told me there might be somebody in the squadroom."

"Not on the priest case," Meyer said, and thought, Never turn away a volunteer. "Come in, please," he said, "I'm Detective Meyer. Maybe I can help you."

Hobbs opened the gate and walked into the room. Judging from the way he looked it over, he'd never before been inside a police station. He shook hands with Meyer, accepted the chair he offered, introduced himself, and then said, "I'm the one who painted that garden gate."

Which, as it turned out, was the opening gun in a salvo aimed at Hobbs's mother, who—to hear him tell it—was the cause of all his miseries. Not only was she responsible for his homosexuality . . .

"I'm gay, you know," he said.

"Wouldn't have guessed," Meyer said.

"Yes," he said. "Which of course is *Abby's* fault, dressing me up in little girl's dresses and forcing me to wear my hair in a long blonde pageboy . . ."

At which point Meyer, while still wondering about the garden gate, was treated to the recitation of a childhood atrocity story no more horrifying than most atrocity stories he'd heard except that it had resulted in what Hobbs described as a human being "not moving left, not moving right"—a great many homosexuals knew Sondheim lyrics by heart.

Hobbs kept referring to his beloved mother as "Abby," sarcastically spitting out the word as though they were great good buddies whereas he hadn't seen her since she'd moved to Calm's Point six month ago, and neither knew nor cared to know her present address or telephone number. It was clear that he despised her and blamed her exclusively for his current life-style, which incidentally included worshipping the Devil. So, naturally, he had painted an inverted pentagram on St. Catherine's garden gate.

". . . to let her know I'd worship wherever I damn well please," he said. "It had nothing to do with the priest."

"Then why'd you pick *his* gate?" Meyer asked.

"To make a point," Hobbs said.

"What was the point?" Meyer asked. "I seem to be missing it."

"The point was she went to this priest and complained about me going to Bornless . . ."

"Bornless?"

"The Church of the Bornless One, when she had no right to do so. And incidentally, *he* had no right, either, preaching about our church to his congregation. No one was telling *his* congregation which church *they* should go to. Nobody at Bornless was running around saying Jesus is a menace, which by the way, he is, but we keep that to ourselves."

"But Father Michael wasn't keeping *his* beliefs to himself, is that what you're saying?"

"Only in passing, don't get me wrong. I had nothing at all against Father Michael. Though I must tell you, after *Abby* went *bleating* to him, he gave a few hot little sermons denouncing the Devil-worshippers up the block . . . well, *four* blocks away, actually, but close enough if you're wetting your pants worried that Satan's going to come burn down your shitty little church."

"So what you did," Meyer said, "was paint the Devil's sign . . ."

"Yes."

"On the priest's garden gate . . ."

"Yes."

"But not as a warning to the priest."

"No."

"Then why?"

"To let *Abby* know she should keep her big mouth shut."

"I see. And now you want us to understand you didn't paint that gate in malice."

"Correct. And I didn't kill that priest, either."

"Who said you did?"

"Nobody."

"Then why are you here?"

"Because Schuyler doesn't want you guys harassing us over this thing. He thought it'd be a good . . ."

"Schuyler?"

"Schuyler Lutherson, who runs Bornless."

"I see," Meyer said.

He was thinking he'd have to tell either Carella or Hawes about this pleasant early morning chat, because perhaps one or the other of them might wish to ask Schuyler Lutherson why he was so worried about police harassment.

"Thanks for stopping by," he said. "We appreciate your candor."

Hobbs wondered if he meant it.

Sitting on the third row of benches, the redhead in the grey tailored slacks watched the children as they rushed to escort Stanley to the altar, hurrying along on each side of him as he approached with a sword cushioned on a black velvet pillow. Schuyler grasped the sword by its silk-tasseled handle. The redhead's legs parted slightly. The children were back at the altar again. Schuyler raised the sword over his head, turned suddenly to point it at the hanging sign of Baphomet, and shouted in a voice hoarse with emotion, "Bornless One, I invoke thee!"

"Thou who didst create the universe," the assemblage chanted.

"Thou who didst create the earth and the heavens . . ."

"The darkness and the light . . ."

"Thou who didst create the seed and the fruit," Schuyler said, and on cue two of the acolytes—the tall eight-year-old girl and the shorter eight-year-old boy—stepped forward and faced each other. Holding the handle of the sword in one hand and the tip in the other, Schuyler lowered it horizontally over their heads. The redhead in the tailored grey slacks leaned forward expectantly.

In a high piping voice, the little boy said, "Behold! My staff is erect!" and lifted his tunic to show his limp little penis.

And the little girl responded, "Behold! My fruit drips nectar!" and raised her tunic to show her small hairless pudendum.

"My poison shall erupt and engulf!" the little boy said.

"My venom shall enclose and erode!" the little girl said.

"My lust is insatiable!" the little boy said.

"My thirst is unquenchable!" the little girl said.

"Behold the children of Satan," Schuyler said softly and reverentially.

Symbolically, he gently touched the tip of the sword first to the boy's genitals and then to the girl's. He returned the sword to the pillow. Stanley carried it back to where the two nineteen-year-old sub-deacons were waiting for him, the hems of their robes fastened above their waists, their hands resting on their naked flanks, palms turned outward toward the congregation.

The redhead on the third row placed her hands on her thighs and opened her legs a trifle wider.

Schuyler approached the altar.

"In thy name, oh Bornless One," he said, "I offer myself unto the altar of thy power and thy will."

He threw up his robe.

"Glory to God," he said, "may all hail Satan. Glory to Satan," he said, "whom we love and cherish. All hail Satan," he said, "we sing glory to thy name. All praise Satan," he said, "we sing honor to thy name. All bless Satan," he said, and positioned himself at the joining of the altar, "we adore thee, Great Lord, we thank thee, Infernal Lord, we cry unto thee, all hail Satan, all hail Satan, all hail Satan."

As he thrust himself onto and into the altar, the gong sounded three times and the assemblage chanted in unison and in Latin, *"Ave Satanas, ave Satanas, ave Satanas!"*

The redhead on the third row spread her legs wide.

The mass was beginning in earnest.

7

AT ELEVEN O'CLOCK that Sunday morning, the twenty-seventh day of May, they buried Father Michael Birney in the Cemetery of the Blessed Virgin Mary of Mt. Carmel, all the way uptown in Riverhead, where there was still a little ground left in which to put dead people. The priest who delivered the funeral oratory was a man named Father Frank Oriella, who had been appointed by the archdiocese of Isola East as temporary pastor of St. Catherine's Roman Catholic Church. Among the mourners was Detective Steve Carella of the 87th Precinct. Father Oriella chose to read his elegy from the first letter of the apostle Paul to the Corinthians.

"The first man was of earth," he read, "formed from dust. The second is from heaven. Earthly men are like the man of earth, heavenly men are like the man of heaven. Just as we resemble the man from earth . . ."

Carella studied the small group of assembled mourners.

Father Michael's sister, Irene Brogan—who had made the arduous trip from Japan via Los Angeles in order to be here for the funeral today—stood by the graveside now, listening intently to Father Oriella's carefully chosen text. Martha Hennessy, the priest's housekeeper, had introduced her to Carella when he'd arrived. A petite woman with travel-weary eyes, she told him she'd be happy to help with the investigation in any way possible. Carella said he was eager to talk to her, and asked if he could have a moment of her time after the service.

". . . to tell you a mystery. Not all of us shall fall asleep, but all of us are to be changed—in an instant, in the twinkling of an eye, at the sound of the last trumpet . . ."

The forecasters has promised continuing good weather for the entire Memorial Day weekend. A blazing sun shone down mercilessly on the shining black top of the coffin poised above the grave. A dozen or more young people stood beside the open grave, listening to Father Oriella. Carella recognized in the group of teenagers the two young girls he'd spoken to yesterday. They were dressed more sedately today, not in black—this was a largely alien color in a young person's wardrobe—but in dark shades of blue that seemed appropriate to the day's burden. They stood side by side, the one with the black hair (Gloria, was that her name?) and the blonde girl, Alexis. Both girls were crying. For that matter, so was the entire group of young people with them. He had been a well-loved man, this priest.

". . . then will the saying of Scripture be fulfilled: 'Death is swallowed up in victory. Oh, death, where is thy victory? Oh, death, where is thy sting?' The sting of death is sin, and sin gets its power from the law. But thanks be to God who has given us the victory through our Lord Jesus Christ . . ."

Poking about the fringes of the crowd like scavenger birds were half a dozen reporters and their photographers, but there were no television crews in evidence, and this surprised Carella. The priest story had received extensive coverage, especially on television, ever since it broke last Thursday. Carella was aware that this was already Sunday. The clock was ticking—and the older a case got, the wider became the murderer's edge.

"Lord, hear our prayers," Father Oriella said. "By raising your Son from the dead, you have given us faith. Strengthen our hope that Michael, our brother, will share in His resurrection."

Here in the sunshine, the assembled priests paid honor to one of their own, standing in solemn black at the edge of the grave, listening to Father Oriella's final words. High-ranking police officers were here, too, in blue and in braid, a show of color and support to let the citizens of this fair city know—via the newspaper people—that the police were still on the job, if only to weep huge crocodile tears at graveside.

"Lord God, you are the glory of believers and the life of the just. Your son redeemed us by dying and raising to life again. Our brother Michael was faithful and believed in our own resurrection. Give to him the joys and blessings of the life to come. We ask this, oh Lord, amen."

"Amen," the mourners murmured.

A hush fell over the grave site.

There must have been a signal, someone must have pressed a button because the coffin on its straps began lowering hydraulically, a photo opportunity that could not and would not be missed by the paparazzi, who moved forward as the coffin hung between heaven and earth, silhouetted blackly against the piercing blue sky. Another signal perhaps, because the lift stopped, and the coffin hung suspended now some several inches below the lip of the grave, and Father Oriella said another prayer, almost a private communication between him and his slain brother in Christ, whispering, his lips moving, and then he made the sign of the cross over the grave and knelt to scoop up a handful of moist spring earth and sprinkled it onto the coffin lid gleaming in sunshine.

The mourners came now with baby roses distributed by the funeral home, came in a last orchestrated effort to lend dignity to death, came in staged and solemn farewell, each passing this way for the last time, pausing at the grave with its shiny black coffin waiting to descend, tossing the roses onto the coffin, the priests from churches all over the city, the brass from Headquarters downtown, the priest's sister Irene Brogan, and some forty parishioners from St. Catherine's, and the dozen or more teenagers from the church's Catholic Youth Organization, all filing past to toss their roses in farewell, and now the pair from yesterday, Gloria, yes, and Alexis.

And then it was over.

As they moved past the grave and away from it, starkly illuminated in a clear sharp light the photographers must have loved, there was another unseen signal, and the hydraulic lift began humming again, and the coffin dropped slowly into the grave, deeper, deeper, until it was completely out of sight. Two gravediggers freed the canvas straps from beneath the coffin. They were beginning to shovel earth onto the coffin and into the grave when Carella walked over to where Irene Brogan was standing with Father Oriella, telling him what a beautiful service it had been.

He stood by awkwardly.

At last, she turned from the priest who had replaced her brother, and said, "I'm sorry to have kept you waiting. Please forgive me."

Tear-streaked face. Blue eyes shining with tears. Close up, in this harsh light, she looked to be in her early forties. A woman who just missed being pretty, her separate parts somehow not adding up to a completely satisfying whole. They walked together to where the funeral home limousines were waiting in line, shining in the sun. Standing beside the fender of the closest limousine, Carella watched the mourners moving past behind Irene, heading for their cars or the closest public transportation. Riverhead was a long way from home.

"Mrs. Brogan," he said, "I don't mean to intrude on your family privacy . . ."

She looked at him, puzzled.

"But in the course of the investigation . . . early on, as a matter of fact . . . I read a letter you wrote to your brother. Which was when I started calling you in San Diego."

"I think I know the letter you mean," she said.

"The one referring to *his* letter of the twelfth."

"Yes."

"In which he told you . . . I'm just putting all this together from what you wrote, Mrs. Brogan. But it seemed he was deeply troubled about something."

"He was."

"What would that have been?"

Irene sighed heavily.

"My brother was wholly devoted to God," she said.

"I've no doubt," Carella said.

And waited.

"But even Christ was sorely tempted in the wilderness," she said.

And still Carella waited.

"Let's . . . can we get in the car?" she asked.

He opened the back door of the limousine for her and then followed her into an interior as secluded as a confessional. The door closed behind him with a snug, solid click. And now, here in this dim and secret space with its tinted windows and its black leather seats, Irene Brogan seemed to find the privacy she needed to tell her brother's story. She described first the receipt of his letter . . .

"It was postmarked the twelfth, but I didn't get it on the Coast till the following Thursday, the seventeenth. My husband and I were leaving for Japan that Saturday. He sells heavy machinery, this was a business trip, he's still there, in fact. I . . . I called my brother that Friday. And when . . . when he told me what was *really* troubling him . . . the letter . . . you see, the letter had only hinted at it . . . but when I called him that Friday . . ."

At first, he is reluctant to speak about it, The Priest.

He tells her it's nothing, really, he shouldn't have written the letter at all, everything's fine now, she must be very excited about the trip to Japan, hm?

But Irene knows him too well. She was thirteen when he was born, which puts her at forty-five now, and she raised him almost as if he were her own child, her mother being a businesswoman who ran off to work every day and then complained of utter exhaustion all weekend long. She knows her brother all too well, and she knows he is hiding something now, excited about the trip to Japan indeed; she has accompanied her husband to Japan on every business trip he's made in the past six years! So she bides her time, and listens patiently to him telling her about someone in the congregation who took umbrage over his sermons about the tithe . . .

"He mentioned Arthur Farnes, did he?"

"I don't remember the man's name. But, yes, this was *one* of the things troubling him . . ."

. . . and someone's mother coming to seek solace and advice about her homosexual son's involvement with, of all things, *devil* worship . . . and something about . . .

"He was beginning to rattle on by then," Irene said, "do you know the way people sometimes do? When they're trying to avoid what's *really* troubling them? I'm not saying these things weren't actually bothering him . . . the tithe . . . and the drugs . . . and the . . ."

"The *what?*" Carella said.

"Well . . . drugs, yes. My brother seemed to think someone was using the church as a sort of storehouse. For drugs. He tore the whole place apart one weekend, looking for where they were hidden, but . . ."

"Are you saying illegal *drugs?* Controlled substances?"

"Well, yes, I'm sure that's what he meant."

"He found *drugs* inside the church?"

"Well, no, he didn't. But he certainly *looked* for them. At least, that's what he told me. As I said, he was starting to get a bit hysterical by then. Because he was coming to what the *real* problem was, and it didn't have a damn thing to do with any of the *little* things he was talking about. It had to do with . . ."

A woman.

Her brother is involved with a woman.

He does not tell Irene how this started or even how long it has been going on, but it is tormenting him that he has violated his vows of chastity and trapped himself in a situation from which there is no honorable escape. He loves Jesus Christ and he loves this woman and the two loves are incompatible and irreconcilable. He mentions that he has considered suicide . . .

"He told you this?"

"Yes. On the telephone."

"Had he considered a way of *doing* it?"

"What?"

"Did he tell you *how* he planned to kill himself?"

"Well, no. I mean, what difference would that make?"

"A lot," Carella said.

"It frightened me, I can tell you that," Irene said. "I almost canceled the trip. I thought I'd come east instead, be with my brother, see him through this . . ."

But he tells her that taking his own life would be an even greater sin than breaking his solemn vows. He swears to her and to the good Lord Jesus that he will not even *think* such thoughts again, swears this on the telephone. At Irene's urging, he swears as well that he will tell this woman he cannot go on with a relationship that is tearing him apart, cannot continue deceiving God in this way, destroying what is dearest to him. He will once again renounce the flesh, as he'd sworn to do so long ago, and pray for God's help in living forevermore a chaste and spiritual life.

He promises this to his sister.

"And then . . . when I got the call from Bishop Quentin . . . we'd just come upstairs from dinner . . . it was a lovely night there in Tokyo, the cherry blossoms still in bloom, the air so sweet . . . and he . . . he told me my brother was dead. And . . . and . . . the first thing I thought was that he'd killed himself. He'd done it. He'd broken his promise to me."

The limo went still.

"But this is worse, isn't it?" Irene asked. "Someone killing him that way."

Yes, Carella thought. This is worse.

Not to kill him, no. To *talk* to him. To ask him about her. Because you can't condemn a person without first hearing his side of the story, isn't that true? You can't just begin *hating* a person until you prove for sure that there's really a *reason* to hate him. Because this is a man of God, don't forget, this is not just someone like you or me, this is a man who's dedicated his life to God. And if he's going to break the rules that way, then he shouldn't be saying one thing and doing another thing. The rules should apply to everybody. That's the way rules work. Everybody knows you have to stop when a traffic light turns red. If you don't stop when it's red, then nobody is obeying the rules, and there'll be an accident, and someone might get killed. Of *all* people, he should be the one obeying rules, especially the promises he made to God. If you make a promise to God, you have to keep it or God will strike you dead. That's in the Bible, vengeance is mine, I will repay, says the Lord. Kissing her. But maybe there was some explanation. On the lips. Maybe he had some explanation for why he was doing that. Maybe there was something in church custom or church law that you had to kiss a woman on the lips in order to whatever. Bless her maybe. Greet one another with a holy kiss, that's in the Bible. It was all right to kiss in Scriptures, it was common practice. The one I shall kiss is the man and he came up to Jesus at once and said Hail, Master, and he kissed him. Or when he's sitting at table in the Pharisee's house and the sinner brings an alabaster flask of ointment and wets his feet with her tears and kisses his feet, this was Jesus getting his feet kissed. It was common in the Bible, look at Solomon, O that you would kiss me with the kisses of your mouth for your love is better than wine, your anointing oils are fragrant, your name is oil poured out, therefore the maidens love you. So maybe there was an explanation, and if you go to the person and ask him what the reason is, if there *is* a reason, then maybe he can tell you, explain that he was only greeting with a holy kiss, you shouldn't judge a book by its cover, ask and it shall be delivered unto you. Was the intention. To ask. To inquire. To discover. To hear from his own lips that this *kiss* was not what it appeared to be, was not a *man* kissing a *woman,* a beautiful woman, in fact, but was instead a *priest,* a holy priest, performing some kind of of of ceremony to do whatever it was he was doing. A holy kiss, it's in the Bible, there are holy kisses, what's in the Bible is true, every word of it. Not to kill him, no. To *talk* to him. To ask him about her. But how could he explain his hands under her skirt, her panties down around her ankles, this was not a holy kiss, this could not have been a holy kiss, not with her blouse open and her naked breasts showing, Oh, may your breasts be like clusters of the vine, and the scent of your breath like apples, and your kisses like the best wine that goes down smoothly, gliding over lips and teeth, goes down smoothly, goes down no this was not a holy kiss it was not that no.

The call came at twenty minutes to one that afternoon, not five minutes after Willis had gone out for the Sunday papers. The moment she heard the voice, Marilyn realized they'd been watching the house, waiting for him to leave before they placed the call.

In Spanish, the voice said, "Good afternoon."

Buenas tardes.

She recognized the voice at once. The handsome one. The one she had cut.

In Spanish, she answered, "I've been waiting for your call."

"Ah, did you know we would call?"

Politely. In Spanish. No sense playing games now. They knew who she was. If they were to do business, it would be simpler to do it in their native tongue. From now on, nothing but Spanish.

"Yes, in fact, I was *hoping* you'd call," she said. "We have business to discuss."

"Ah."

A note of sarcastic skepticism in that single word. The Spanish were wonderful at conveying shades of meaning by inflection of the voice alone.

"Yes. I want to pay you. But I'll need time."

"Time, yes."

"But I'm not sure I'll be able to raise the entire two million."

"Ah, what a pity."

"Because even if I sell everything I own . . ."

"Yes, that is surely what you must do."

". . . I'll still be short."

"Then perhaps you should sell yourself as well."

A smile in his voice. A nod to the former hooker. Sell yourself as well. We understand you were very good at selling yourself.

"Look," she said, "I think I can raise half a million, but that's all. More or less."

Más o menos.

There was a silence on the line. Then:

"You owe us a great deal more than half a million. More or less."

"To begin with, I don't owe you or your big friend *anything*. If that money belongs to *anyone*, it belongs to . . ."

"It belongs to whoever will kill you if you don't pay it."

"Let's talk straight here, please," she said. "You're not going to kill me."

"You're mistaken."

"No, I'm not mistaken. You kill me, you don't get *any* of the money. If I were you, I'd settle for the five hun . . ."

"If I were you," he said, slowly and silkenly, "I would recognize that there are worse things than being dead."

"Yes, I know that," she said.

"We thought you might know that."

"I do. But I've only got so many arms and legs . . ."

"*Y tu cara,*" he said.

And paused meaningfully.

"*Y tus pechos,*" he said.

And paused again.

"*Y así sucesivamente,*" he said.

Her face . . .

Her breasts . . .

And so on.

The last three words, though spoken softly and casually—*Y así suce-sivamente*—implied unspeakable acts.

She was suddenly very frightened again.

"Look, you're right," she said, "it's true, I don't want anything to happen to me. But . . ."

"Then you should learn not to cut people."

"If you're saying you're going to hurt me even if I *do* come up with the money . . ."

"I'm saying we'll *surely* hurt you if you *don't* come up with the money. Is what I'm saying."

"I understand that."

"I hope so."

"But what *I'm* saying is that it's impossible to come up with *all* of the money. Is what I'm saying."

"Then that's too bad."

"Look, wait a minute."

"I'm still here."

"How much time do I have here?"

"How much time do you need?"

"Even to raise the five hundred, I'd need a week, ten days."

"That is out of the question."

"Then how *much* time? Name a fucking amount of time!"

"Ah," he said.

Chastisingly. Scolding her for the language she'd used. Tsk, tsk, tsk.

She said nothing for several seconds. Regaining control. Calming herself. Then she said, "I need to talk to people who can turn assets into money. That takes time. I have to know exactly how much time I have."

"Wednesday," he said, and she had the feeling he'd picked a deadline out of the air.

"I don't think I can manage that," she said. "That's not enough time."

"It will have to be enough time."

"I don't think you understand."

"We understand completely."

"No. Look, can you listen to me a minute? Please? I want to pay you back, you have to understand that, I want this thing to be over and done with. But . . ."

"So do we."

"But you can't show up on someone's doorstep and expect them to raise two million dollars in . . ."

"You tell me," he said.

"How much time I'll need?"

"Yes. Tell me."

"You understand I can only raise half a million. It would be im-poss . . ."

"No, the full two million. How much time?"

"I . . ."

"Say."

"Can I get back to you?"

"We'll call you. Tell us when."

"This is Sunday . . ."

"Yes, a day of rest."

Sarcasm in his voice, the son of a bitch.

"I'll have to make some calls tomorrow, find out how long it'll take."

"Good. What time?"

"Can you call me at three-thirty? No later than that."

"Why? Will your boyfriend be coming home?"

"Three-thirty," she said. "Please. But, you know, I really think you should prepare yourself for . . ."

And hesitated.

Silence.

He was waiting.

The silence lengthened.

"Because you know . . . I really meant it when I said . . ."

And again she hesitated.

Because she knew what he would say if she told him again that it was impossible to raise much more than half a million. He would threaten her with punishment, raise fears of acid or steel, promise her mutilation. But the facts had to be stated.

"Listen," she said, "I'm being completely honest with you. I don't want to get hurt, but there's no way I can possibly raise more than half a million. Well, maybe a *little* more, I'm being honest with you, I hope you realize that, but two million is absolutely out of the question, I just can't do it, there's no way I can turn half a million into *two* million overnight."

There was another long silence.

And then he surprised her.

He did not threaten her again.

Instead, he offered a solution.

"There *is* a way," he said.

"No, there . . ."

"*Sí,*" he said. "*La cocaína.*"

And hung up.

Carella did not get back to the squadroom until almost two that Sunday afternoon, after extracting from Irene Brogan a promise that she would call her housekeeper in San Diego as soon as she returned to the hotel. He had previously asked her if she still had her brother's May twelfth letter. Irene said she thought it might be somewhere on her desk. The call to the housekeeper was to ask her to look for that letter. If she found it, she was to Fed Ex it to Carella at once. Irene seemed to understand why he wanted to read the letter himself: a fresh eye, an emotional uninvolvement, a mind trained to search for nuance of meaning. But she assured him once again that her brother—neither in his letter nor when she'd spoken to him on the telephone—had revealed the name of the woman with whom he was involved.

Meyer's note was waiting on Carella's desk.

It was typed on a D.D. form, but it was really a lengthy memo and not a report as such. Informal and chatty, it detailed Andrew Hobbs's visit to the squadroom late last night (early this morning, actually) to confess that he'd painted the pentagram on the church gate and to explain that "it was not the Devil who made him do it, but his mother Abby." Meyer's words. Touch of humor here at the old Eight-Seven. The report ended with the suggestion that either Carella or Hawes talk to Schuyler Lutherson at the Church of the Bornless One.

Carella carried the memo to the filing cabinet, found the file for the Birney case, and dropped it into the manila folder. He remembered again that this was Sunday. Even the hottest of cases got cold after a few days without a lead. This case had been cold from the beginning.

Nothing solid to pursue until this morning, when suddenly there was a woman in the priest's life. Solid enough, Carella suspected. But cause for murder? In this precinct, where looking cockeyed at another man's wife could result in a pair of broken legs, a *priest* fucking around could very well provoke murder, yes. Perhaps even those words—a priest fucking around—could incite riot.

He suspected that back in the good old days—when jolly friars were tossing up the skirts of giggling peasant girls and tickling their fancies on haystacks—religion wasn't taken quite as seriously as it was today. Perhaps something had been lost over the centuries. Maybe priests weren't supposed to be gods, maybe only God was supposed to be God. But didn't God ever smile? Wouldn't He perhaps find it comical that in a parish only four blocks from a congregation that openly worshipped the Devil, one of His faithful servants was—well, you find another way to describe it, Carella thought. To me, he was fucking around.

He suddenly realized that Father Michael's indiscretion—which was perhaps a better way of putting it—made him enormously angry.

Cherchez la femme, he thought. .

But first let's go find Bobby Corrente and ask him what *he* knows about the events that took place on Easter Sunday.

Bobby Corrente was an even six feet tall and he weighed at least a hundred and ninety pounds, every bit of it lean, hard muscle. He had sand-colored hair and hazel-colored eyes, and he bore no more resemblance to his father than a beanpole did to a fire hydrant. Carella figured his mother must have been a prom queen. All clean good looks and friendly charm, he rose from the stoop where he'd been sitting with two girls who appeared to be a year or so younger than he was, fifteen, sixteen, in there.

"Nice to meet you, Detective Carella," he said, and extended his hand.

They shook hands. The girls seemed more in awe of Bobby than they did of a visiting cop. Open-mouthed, wide-eyed, they looked up admiringly at this handsome young man who could talk so easily and naturally to a detective, even shake *hands* with him. When Bobby said, "Excuse us, won't you, girls?" signalling that he wanted the girls to depart as graciously as they could, Carella thought they would wet their pants in gratitude. Smiling, fumbling to their feet, bowing and scraping like handservants in a movie about ancient China, they managed to back away without tripping all over themselves, and then hurried off up the street, glancing back frequently at the radiant boy-emperor who had granted an audience with the local constabulary. Bobby gave a sort of embarrassed shrug coupled with a boyish grin that said, What're you gonna do when you're so handsome? Carella nodded in sympathetic understanding, even though he'd never had such a problem.

"I'm glad I found you," he said. "Few things I'd like to ask you about."

"Sure, anything," Bobby said.

"From what your father told me, Nathan Hooper was here trying to sell dope on Easter Sunday, is that right?"

"Mr. Crack," Bobby said, and nodded.

"That's his street name, huh?"

"That's what they call him at the school."

"Mr. Crack."

"Yeah, the kids at the elementary school. Which is why we didn't want him in the neighborhood. It's bad enough he's at the school, am I right? We warned him, we told him stay away from the school and stay away from where we live. But he came here, anyway."

"Why do you suppose he did that?" Carella asked.

"I still can't figure it," Bobby said, shaking his head. "I think he was just looking for trouble."

"Tell me what happened," Carella said.

What happened was it's two-thirty, three o'clock in the afternoon on Easter Sunday, and all the guys and girls are hanging around outside where Danny Peretti lives. This is 275 North Eleventh, near the Italian deli. It wasn't such a good day, Easter, do you remember? A lot of wind, very grey, in fact it looked like it might snow. We'd all gone to church that morning, well, the twelve o'clock mass, actually, this was Easter, we went to St. Kate's where Father Michael later chased us away. But you can't blame him, he didn't know what was happening. All he knew was a bunch of kids yelling and hollering inside his church.

So we were, I don't know, showing off for the girls, clowning around. I remember Allie was doing his imitation of what was supposed to be Tony Bennett singing I Lost My Heart in San Francisco, but he sounded more like Jerry Lewis, did you ever hear Jerry Lewis sing? Man. Anyway, we were making our own fun, you know what I mean? Because the weather was so terrible, and Easter's supposed to be spring, supposed to be sunshine—*Easter*, you know? So we were making the best of it.

And all at once, there he was.

I couldn't believe my eyes.

None of us could.

I mean, here's Mr. Crack in person, who we told at least a hundred times to keep his shit out of our neighborhood and out of the elementary school, and he comes strutting up the street like he owns it. Man. Allie stopped doing Tony Bennett, and all of us just sat there watching him come closer and closer. He wears his hair the way they're all wearing it now, shaved close all over and then what looks like an upside down flowerpot on top. He's all dressed up, it's Easter Sunday. He keeps coming. We're all watching him do his shuffle up the street. Sitting there dumbfounded. Trying to figure out is he crazy or what? He's got a big grin on his face. Big watermelon-eating grin. Here's Mr. Crack, boys and girls, here to dispense his goodies. Break out your five-dollar bills, here's the man's going to chase all your cares away.

Afternoon, ladies, he says, and nods to the girls.

As if he's Eddie Murphy, you know?

Instead of some nigger here to sell crack.

Boys, he says, how we doin'?

One of the guys, this is Jimmy Gottardi, he knew Hooper personally from when they were doing this Operation Clean-up on Fifth. What it was, the neighborhood people were cleaning out this lot that was full of garbage and junk and whatnot. Jimmy and some of the other guys on the block, but who weren't there that Sunday, volunteered to go over and lend a hand. So you see right off it isn't true what they say happened on Easter. I mean, these were *white* guys going over to a black neighborhood to help clean up an empty lot. They weren't getting paid for it, they were doing it as a community service. So whoever says this thing on Easter Sunday was racist is out of his mind.

Anyway, Jimmy knew Hooper from the Clean-up thing, so he says Hey, Nate—Hooper's first name is Nathan, he calls himself Nate when he ain't Mr. Crack—Hey, Nate, how you doing, and so on, like he's giving him the benefit of the doubt, he's giving him an opportunity to say he ain't here selling crack. And Hooper stands there grinning, telling Jimmy Oh so-so, man, ever'thin' cool, man—you know they go—and Jimmy says What brings you here to Eleventh Street, Nate, and Hooper slides his eyes up the street, checking it out, you know, and his eyes come back all serious and hard and there's no smile on his face anymore, and he says Anybody needin'?

What he means, of course, is does anybody need some crack. Because if we need it, he's here to sell it. He turns to one of the girls . . .

"This is only what you *figured*, right?" Carella said. "That he meant he was selling crack."

"Figured, what do you mean *figured*? He came right out and said it."

"I thought he only asked if . . ."

"No, no, that was at *first*. But then he turned to one of the girls, and he goes, 'Honey? You lookin' for some choice crack?' "

This is a fifteen-year-old girl he's talking to, Laurel Perucci, she lives in my building. Fifteen years old, I don't think she even knows what crack *is*, he's asking her is she looking for some choice crack. Man. But we still didn't do anything, I mean it. He was here, he was selling dope, but nobody got excited, nobody flew off the handle. In fact, Jimmy who worked with him on the Clean-up, looks at him and says Come on, Nate, this ain't that kind of neighborhood, something like that, letting him know this is where we live, we don't want no dope here, okay, cool it. And Hooper goes Oh, that right, man? This ain't that kind of neighborhood, that right? And he turns to Laurel again and he goes, Honey, how you like some of this sweet stuff, huh, baby? and he's holding the vial of crack like right where his cock is, you understand what I'm saying? There's like a double meaning. He's like spitting in our eye. He's saying not only is he gonna sell crack here, he's also gonna insult this innocent fifteen-year-old girl. So it happened.

"What happened?" Carella asked.

"A fight started, what do you *think* happened?"

"Someone hit him with a baseball bat, isn't that right?"

"No, what baseball bat? There was no baseball bat. It was a fist fight. This was Easter Sunday, who was playing baseball? Where was a baseball bat gonna come from?"

"Hooper says he got hit with a ball bat."

"Hooper's a lying bastard."

"He says he got chased up the street with baseball bats and garbage can lids."

"Sure. Because *he* was the one with the fucking *knife*."

"He had a knife?"

"A switchblade knife. He pulled it the minute the first punch was thrown."

"Who threw the first punch?"

"Me, I admit it," Bobby said, and grinned.

"And you say he pulled a knife?"

"First thing he did."

"Then what?"

"One of the guys hit him from behind, the back of the head. And he must've figured the knife wasn't going to help him here, he'd better get the hell out of here fast. So he began running. And we ran right after him."

"To the church."

"Yeah, he ran inside St. Kate's. We chased him inside, too. And then Father Michael started yelling we were hoodlums and all that, and get out of his church, and we tried to tell him this was a crack-dealer here, he was trying to sell dope in our neighborhood, he insulted one of our girls, he had a *knife,* for Christ's sake . . . I admit I said that in church, I admit I took the name of the Lord in vain. Father Michael had a fit. What? What did you say? How dare you? Get out of here, this is God's house, all that. So we left. Some things you walk away from, you know what I mean? Some things are a no-win situation."

"Then what?"

"Then *what* what? We went home. That was it."

"Did you see anyone else in the church? While you were there?"

"No. Just Father Michael."

"Hear anyone else?"

"No."

"You didn't hear two people arguing?"

"No. What two people?"

"Is it true that you made a blood vow to get both Hooper *and* Father Michael? For what happp . . ."

"What are you talking about? What blood vow?"

"For what happened on Easter Sunday."

"I don't even know what a blood vow is. What's a blood vow?"

"You didn't swear to get them, is that right?"

"For what? Did Hooper come back to the neighborhood since then? He didn't. Has he been hanging around the school peddling dope? He hasn't. So what's there to get him for? We got him good enough on Easter."

"And the priest? Father Michael?"

"He only did what he thought was right. He figured he was helping a poor innocent kid getting beat up by a gang of hoodlums. I'da done the same thing, believe me. If I thought somebody was in the right? The

very same thing. So why would we hold anything against him? In fact,
I've been to church every Sunday since. The other guys, too. Church is
like a meeting place for us. We go to ten o'clock mass every Sunday. We
go to the C.Y.O. dances on Friday nights. We had nothing against
Father Michael. In fact, he was like one of the guys until what happened on Easter. This was a terrible thing that happened to him. A terrible thing."

"When you say he was like one of the guys . . ."

"He was always kidding around with us, you know, telling jokes,
asking us about our problems, a real nice guy, I mean it, you sometimes
forgot he was a priest. I still think he did what he did on Easter because
he misunderstood the situation. He didn't know the kind of person
Hooper really is. In fact, I wouldn't be surprised . . ."

Bobby stopped, shook his head.

"Yes, what?" Carella asked.

"I wouldn't be surprised if it turned out Hooper had something to
do with his murder."

"Why do you say that?"

"A feeling, that's all."

"But what gives you that feeling?"

"I don't know. I just know that when a guy's selling dope, *anything*
can happen. Including killing somebody. That's all I know," Bobby
said, and nodded in utter certainty. "That's all I know."

Willis made the call from the squadroom at a little before three that
afternoon. With late afternoon sunlight streaming through the windows, he sat at his desk and direct-dialed first 0-1-1 and then 5-4-1,
and then the number listed in his international police directory. He
waited. The foreign ringing sounded somehow urgent. Across the
room, Andy Parker was typing up a report, pecking at the keys with the
forefingers of both hands. The squadroom was otherwise empty. The
phone kept ringing. He wondered what he could possibly say if the
lieutenant asked why he'd called Buenos . . .

"*Central de Policía,*" a woman's voice said.

"Hello," he said, "do you speak English?"

"*Perdóneme?*"

"I'm calling from the United States," he said, careful not to say
America, they were very touchy about that down there. "*Los Estados
Unidos,*" he said, "I'm a policeman, *un policía,*" trying his half-assed
Spanish, "*un detective,*" giving it what he thought to be the proper

Spanish pronunciation, day-tec-tee-vay, "is there anyone there who speaks English, please, *por favor?*"

"Juss a mom'enn, please," the woman said.

He waited.

One moment, two moments, three moments, a full *six* American moments which probably added up to one Argentinian moment, and then a man's voice came on the line.

"*Teniente* Vidoz, how can I be of assistance, please?"

"My name is Harold Willis," Willis said. "I'm a Detective/Third Grade with the 87th Squad here . . ."

"*Sí, señor?*"

"We're investigating a case you might be able to help us with."

"Oh?"

Warily.

There was not a cop in the world who wanted a foreign investigation added to his own already topheavy case load. Foreign meant anything outside the cop's own precinct. It could be the precinct right next door, this was still foreign. Bahía Blanca, some three hundred and more miles south of Buenos Aires, was very definitely foreign. Río Gallegos, all the way down near Chile, was practically *in* a foreign country. And the United States? All the way up *there?* Don't even ask.

But here was a person who'd identified himself as a third-grade detective, which Lieutenant Vidoz assumed was some sort of inferior in the police department, and he was investigating a case, and he needed help. Help. From the police in Buenos Aires. *Norteamericanos* were a nervy bunch.

"What kind of help?" Vidoz asked, hoping his voice conveyed the unmistakable impression that he desired not to help in any way, manner, or form. What he desired was to go to see his mistress before he went home. It was already a quarter to six in Argentina. This was what he desired.

"I have two names," Willis said. "I was hoping you'd be able to run them through for me."

"Run them through *what?*" Vidoz asked.

"Your computer. I think they may have criminal records. If so perhaps you can fax me the . . ."

"What sort of case *is* this?" Vidoz asked.

"Homicide," Willis said at once.

The secret password.

Homicide.

No cop in the world wanted to be burdened with a foreign case, but neither would any cop in the world turn his back on a homicide. Willis knew this. Vidoz knew it. Both cops sighed heavily. Willis in mock weariness after days and nights of working a murder he'd just invented, Vidoz because satisfying this request was a supreme pain in the ass but an obligation nonetheless.

"What are the names?" he said.

"Ramon Castaneda and Carlos Ortega," Willis said.

"Give me your fax number," Vidoz said.

Willis gave it to him.

The information from Buenos Aires came through on the fax at a little past seven that night, which made it a bit past eight down there in Argentina, where Lieutenant Francisco Ricardo Vidoz was feeding the photocopied records into the machine and cursing over having missed his evening *cita* with one Carla de Font-Alba. In the Clerical Office at the 87th Precinct, Sergeant Alfred Benjamin Miscolo pulled the pages as they inched their way out of the fax machine, remarked to his assistant Juan Luis Portoles that they were in Spanish, and then noticed that they were earmarked for "Det/3 Harlow Wallace," who he guessed was Hal Willis. Glancing at the pages—there were eight altogether—Portoles whistled and said, "These are *some* bad hombres, Sarge."

He probably referred to several words that had caught his eye, words such as . . .

Robo . . .

Asalto con Lesiones . . .

Violación . . .

. . . and especially *Homicidio.*

8

THE CALL FROM KRISTIN LUND came as something of a surprise that Monday morning. On her doorstep Saturday night, when she'd pointedly held out her hand for a good-night handshake, Hawes figured that was the end of that. But here she was now, bubbly and bright, asking if he'd had lunch yet.

"Well, no," he said.

"Because I'm cleaning out some things here at the church, and I thought since I'm in the neighborhood anyway . . ."

"I'd love to," he said. "Shall I pick you up there?"

"Why don't I come by the station house?" she said. "Maybe you can take my fingerprints again."

"Maybe," he said, and wondered why the handshake Saturday night. Actresses, he thought, and shook his head.

"Half an hour okay?"

"Fine," he said.

"I wasn't even sure you'd be working today," she said.

"How come?"

"Memorial Day."

"Oh. Yeah."

For cops, holidays came and went like any other day.

"But I'm glad you are," she said. "See you later."

And hung up.

He put up the receiver, and glanced at the clock. It was now a quarter past eleven. He sat for several seconds staring blankly at the sunshine streaming in through the grilled windows, still wondering.

A uniformed cop handed the Federal Express envelope to Carella some ten minutes after Hawes left the office. He explained that it had been buried under some other shit on the muster desk downstairs, and Sergeant Murchison had just now discovered it. When he apologized for any delay this may have caused, he sounded slightly sarcastic.

The red-and-blue package contained the letter Father Michael had written to his sister on the twelfth of May. It was written on church stationery, *St. Catherine's Roman Catholic Church* printed in raised black letters across the top of the page, the address just below that. Father Michael had written the letter by hand, but there was nothing in his handwriting to reveal the obvious emotional distress that had caused him to open his heart to his older sister. Instead, the hand was small and precise, the words marching evenly across the page as if to the steady cadence of a secret drummer:

My dear sister,

It's been a long time since you and I have talked meaningfully about anything, and I suppose much of this has to do with the disparate—and distant—lives we lead. Whatever the cause, I strongly miss the intensely personal and private talks we used to have when I was growing up, and the good advice you gave on more than one occasion. Not the least of which, by the way, was your advice to follow my heart about the call and to enter into the service of our Lord, Jesus Christ.

I write this letter in the hope that I may still reveal to you my deepest feelings.

Irene, I'm very troubled.

I have for the past little while now, since shortly before Easter as a matter of fact, been entertaining the most serious doubts about my ability to love God and to serve Him as devoutly as I've vowed to do. I now have reached the point where I feel incapable of facing a congregation on Sunday, of hearing confessions, of leading the young people in our youth organization, of counseling those in need of spiritual guidance—in short, of fulfilling the duties and obligations of the priesthood.

My self-loathing reached its highest peak on Easter Sunday, when I failed to extricate myself from a situation that had become all-consuming and debilitating. I realized then that I was caught in the Devil's own snare and had become a threat not only to myself and the lambs of my flock, but also to God.

I don't know what to do, Irene. Help me. Please.

Your loving brother,
Michael

Carella read the letter yet another time, and then he looked at the opening paragraph of Irene's return letter to him:

My dearest brother,

I am now in receipt of yours of May 12th, and I cannot tell you with what a saddened heart I hasten to respond. Michael, how have you managed to construct such a tower of doubt for yourself? And don't you feel you should relate your fears to the bishop of your diocese? I just don't know how to counsel or advise you.

This from a sister who, in the days of Michael Birney's youth, had given him "good advice on more than one occasion." To Carella, her letter read like a brush-off. Don't tell me your troubles, I'm on my way to Japan. I'll call you before I leave, we'll have a nice chat. By then, it'll be blue skies again, anyway. Besides, I know you'll be able to pray your way to enlightenment and salvation. Poor tormented son of a bitch is having an affair with someone, as it later turns out, but she can't be bothered. Eyes all full of tears at the funeral yesterday. Carella shook his head.

And then he went to the Clerical Office, and made a copy of Father Michael's letter, and used a yellow highlighter to mark those words or sentences that he thought might prove helpful to the case:

I have for the past little while now, since shortly before Easter as a matter of fact . . .

The affair, then, had started "shortly before Easter." "Shortly" being a relative term, it could have begun two *days* before Easter or two *weeks* or even two *months.* In any case, he hadn't said "For a long time now." His exact words were "For the past little while." Go pinpoint that.

My self-loathing reached its highest peak on Easter Sunday . . .

Here was Easter Sunday again. The day Nathan Hooper had sought sanctuary in the church. The day he'd heard Father Michael arguing with an unseen man. The day the priest had heatedly thrown out Bobby Corrente and his friends.

. . . when I failed to extricate myself from a situation that had become all-consuming and debilitating.

Was he referring here to the argument he'd had with this unseen, unknown man? Had they been arguing about the affair . . .

. . . that had become all-consuming and debilitating?

What had this man been telling him when Hooper burst into the church, dripping blood and chased by an angry mob?

I realized then that I was caught in the Devil's own snare . . .

The Devil's own snare, Carella thought, and wondered what the priest had meant.

"What were you cleaning out at the church?" Hawes asked.

"Oh, just some things in my desk. The priest who's replacing Father Michael is bringing his own secretary with him."

"Father Oriella? I thought he was only temporary."

"Well, apparently not," Krissie said, and tossed her hair the way actresses did. Hawes guessed there were acting classes where they taught you how to toss your hair. "I'll be looking for something else tomorrow. Unless a part comes along," she said, and shrugged.

On Saturday night, she had told him honestly and sincerely that sometimes she doubted a part would *ever* come along. But apparently hope sprang eternal. Here it was Monday, and she was singing the actress's same sad song again. A part will come along. And when it comes along, I'll be *up* for it. And if I lose it, it was because they were looking for someone who was taller. Or shorter. Or blonder. Or darker. Actresses, he thought, and wondered what the hell he was doing here.

They were eating in a new Italian restaurant on Culver. In this city restaurants sprang up like mushrooms (or, in some cases, toadstools) and most of the new ones were Italian, the American craze for pasta seemingly knowing no limits. Some of the restaurants survived. Most of them went under after struggling for two or three months. Krissie had ordered the veal piccata. Hawes had ordered the cannelloni. Judging from the taste of the sauce, he gave this joint two or three *weeks*.

"Would it bother you if I talked about the case?" he asked.

This morning, Carella had filled him in on what he'd learned at the cemetery yesterday. The priest having an affair. Hawes had listened silently. He guessed the news bothered him, but he didn't know quite why.

"Go right ahead," Krissie said.

"I was wondering . . . did Father Michael ever discuss personal matters with you?"

"Like what?"

"Well . . . personal matters."

"Like which dentist he should go to? Or whether or not he could afford a new car?"

"No, I was thinking more of . . . doubts . . . fears."

"No. Never."

"Did you ever open his mail? Or answer his telephone?"

"Yes, of course. All the time."

"Were there ever any letters or calls from . . . ?" He hesitated and then thought Go ahead, bite the bullet. "Were there ever any letters or calls from women?"

"Yes, of course," she said.

"Any woman in particular?"

"I don't know what you mean," she said.

"Any women who wrote or called more often than . . . well . . . might have seemed appropriate."

"I still don't know what you're saying."

"Well . . ." he said, and hesitated. "We have reason to believe that Father Michael may have been involved in something he didn't know how to handle. Something that was causing him distress. If you know of anything like that, you'd be helping us a lot by . . ."

"No, I don't know of anything that was troubling him," she said.

"Never mentioned any problems or . . ."

"Never."

"And these women who called or wrote . . ."

"Different women. Women in the parish mostly," she said.

"Would you remember their names?"

"Not offhand. But any letters would be in the file . . ."

"Yes, I saw them."

". . . and I kept a log of all telephone calls—unless the new secretary's already thrown it out."

"Where would it have been?"

"On my desk. To the right of the phone."

"A book, a pad . . . ?"

"One of those printed message pads. Pink. While You Were Out, and so on. And then a space for the message and the caller's name and number."

"These women who called . . . did any of them ever *visit* Father Michael?"

"Visit him?"

"Yes. Come to the church. To see him. To talk to him."

"There were women who came to the office, yes," Krissie said, and looked at him. "You know," she said, "I get the feeling you're . . . well . . . never mind, I'm sure I'm wrong."

"Maybe you're right," he said. "What are you thinking?"

"That . . . well . . . from the questions you're asking . . . well, you seem to be suggesting that Father Michael was . . . well . . ."

"Yes?"

"Well, was having an *affair* or something."

"Do you think that might have been the case?"

"No."

"You sound very positive."

"I think Father Michael was wholly devoted to God and to the Catholic Church. I doubt if he even *noticed* women as such. Or thought of them in that way."

"In what way?"

"A sexual way. He was very good-looking, you know . . . well, you saw him . . ."

Hawes had seen a corpse.

Someone repeatedly stabbed and slashed.

". . . all the little parish girls were crazy about him, those classic black-Irish looks, that Gene Kelly smile . . ."

The body on the stone floor of the garden had not been smiling.

They had caught a homicide, period.

The victim was a white male in his early thirties, dark hair, dark eyes.

Good-looking?

Hawes could not remember.

". . . is what I'm saying. He was sensitive and marvelously under-standing, and these are traits that women naturally find appealing. But he was a priest, don't you see? And as such, he couldn't dwell on . . . well . . . matters of the flesh. He couldn't think of himself as being attractive to women. And he certainly couldn't allow himself to be attracted to them."

"His sister thinks otherwise," Hawes said.

"Oh?" Krissie said.

"She seems positive her brother was having an affair with someone."

"Someone in the parish?"

"He didn't say, and she doesn't know."

"I'm surprised," Krissie said. "Really."

"You never saw any indication that he might have . . ."

"Not the slightest."

"Even though there were calls and letters . . ."

"Well, from *men*, too."

"And visits . . ."

"Yes, from both men *and* women. St. Catherine's is a busy parish and he was a responsive pastor. I remember how surprised I was when I first began working there, the number of people he found time to see. His energy was . . . well . . . amazing. I don't think the man ever slept, really."

"This was when?"

"When I started the job? The beginning of March, it was snowing I remember. I walked from the subway stop to the church . . ."

. . . and had trouble finding the entrance. You come in on the Culver Avenue side, you know, well, you've been there. The church is laid out like a cross, *all* churches are, with the central portal opposite the altar. The rectory at St. Catherine's is on the western side of the church, you come through this little arched door, and you go through the sacristy and then into a wood-paneled corridor and into the rectory. Father Michael's office is in a corner that once was part of the kitchen. In fact, there used to be a wood-burning stove where the filing cabinets now are, against the southern wall.

It's funny, but Krissie feels as if she's there auditioning for a part.

Maybe because there's another girl in the office when she arrives. You go to a theater to try out for something, there're always a hundred other girls there. In the theater, of course, you call anyone under the age of thirty a girl, but the girl in Father Michael's office on that blustery March morning really *is* a girl, thirteen years old if that, wearing jeans and a grey sweatshirt, and yellow rubber rain boots, her long dark hair spilling down over her face as she leans over the desk. He is saying, "You didn't put in the ticket price, Gloria," it turns out they're discussing a big church dance that won't take place till the beginning of June, and the beautiful little dark girl has designed the poster for it, and brought it here for Father Michael to look at. "What do you think of it?" he says to Krissie, lifting the poster off the desk and showing it to her.

She hasn't even told him who she is yet, hasn't even said she's here about the part-time secretarial job, but immediately he's getting her involved in church matters. She looks at the poster, which shows a lot of young girls and boys dancing, and features big fat black music notes floating on the air over their heads, and balloon-type lettering that announces The June Hop, to take place at St. Catherine's Hall on Friday night, the first of June. This is only the beginning of March, but Father Michael likes to get his young people involved long in advance of any planned event. "So?" he says, and grins at her . . .

"He really did have a Gene Kelly smile . . ."

. . . and waits for her answer as if the entire future of the Catholic Church depends upon it. The little girl—she's not truly *little,* she is in fact five feet six inches tall, but to Krissie she's only a little girl, twelve, thirteen, whatever—is also waiting for her decision, critics, critics everywhere. This is a first-night opening up here on North Eleventh Street, and they're waiting for the reviewer from Channel 4 to express an opinion. Gloria, he'd called her Gloria, is a beautiful little girl, with a pale oval face and high cheekbones, long black hair falling clean and straight to her shoulders, lips slightly parted, electric blue eyes opened wide in anticipation.

Krissie feels a sudden empathy for the girl, who obviously drew the poster and who is now yearning desperately for the priest's approval, which may or may not hinge upon what Krissie has to say about her effort. Krissie knows what it's like to be thirteen, however, and she also knows what a "sell" review can mean to a show, and so she expresses the opinion that the poster really makes a person want to come here and dance, at which point Gloria yells "Yippee!" or something equally adolescent and throws her arms around Krissie and gives her a great big hug.

Krissie is here for a job, remember. And she's beginning to think this isn't such a dignified first impression, a teenager jumping up and down in her arms and yelling when she hasn't even yet introduced herself. So she listens to Father Michael telling the girl that the poster is terrific except for the price she forgot to put in, and the girl is still so excited by Krissie's rave review and the priest's terrific Gene Kelly grin of approval and his gung-ho Let's Put On A Show contagion that she's almost wetting her pants there in the office. But finally she scoops up the poster and thanks Krissie again and leaves the office all adolescent happiness and smiles. The handsome young priest shakes his head when she's gone and says something about the wonderful kids in this parish, and *finally,* Krissie gets to introduce herself and to tell him she's here about the job. And do you know what he says?

"He says, 'Can you start today?' Just like that," Krissie said, and shook her head. "I guess he liked what happened there with Gloria, the way I handled myself with Gloria—who, by the way, is a terrific kid, president of the C.Y.O., bright as can be, and beautiful besides."

"I know," Hawes said, "Carella told me."

"The point is . . . well . . . he was a fine, decent man, and . . . look, I don't know his sister, I can't say whether she's telling the truth or not. But if she told you he was . . . involved with some woman . . . I mean, I find that hard to believe. That he was having an *affair* with some woman . . . I mean, I guess she said they were sexually involved, didn't she?"

"Yes, he told her he'd violated his vows of chastity."

"With some woman."

"Yes. A woman he said he loved."

Krissie shook her head sadly.

"What a pity," she said. "That he couldn't work it out. If it was true. That he loved this woman, and couldn't work it out."

"Yes," Hawes said.

Memorial Day.

Just what Marilyn needed.

A national holiday.

The banks closed, her stockbroker's office closed, and two hoods from Argentina expecting answers at three-thirty this afternoon. She looked at her watch. Five minutes past two. And ticking.

One of the men she'd known before she started seeing Willis was an attorney named Charles Ingersol Endicott, Jr., a man in his late fifties who carried as a holdover from his prep school days the nickname "Chip"—as if life did not have enough burdens. She dialed his number now and hoped he wasn't out on a boat for the weekend; sailing was Chip's passion. The phone rang four times, five, six. She was about to hang up when—

"Hello?"

"Chip?" she said. "It's me. Marilyn."

She had not spoken to him in months. She wondered suddenly, and with an odd sense of panic, whether he would even remember her. And then his voice boomed onto the line, deep and resonant and welcoming—"Marilyn, my God, how *are* you?"—and she visualized at once the good friend with whom she'd shared so many wonderful hours in a city where good friends and good men were scarce.

"I'm fine, Chip, how are you, I hope I'm not interrupting anything," remembering his kind handsome face and intelligent brown eyes, a man thirty-one years older than she was, the father she'd never known perhaps—

"Is something wrong?" he asked at once.

"No, no," she said, "I was just thinking about you and . . ."

She could not lie to him. He'd been too good a friend, and she hoped he was still a friend now. But either way, she could not lie to someone who'd once meant so much to her.

"I need advice," she said.

"Legal advice?"

"Not quite."

"Okay," he said, but now he sounded puzzled.

"Chip . . . what do you think I could get for a second mortgage on my house?"

"Why? What's the trouble?"

"No trouble. I need some money, is all."

"How much money?"

"A lot. I wouldn't be bothering you with this, but the banks are closed today, and this is somewhat urgent."

"You're alarming me, Marilyn."

"I don't mean to. I'm simply trying to get an estimate . . ."

"How much did the house cost?"

All business now.

"Seven-fifty."

"How much is the present mortgage?"

"Five hundred."

"You could expect something like a hundred and thirty-five thousand. That would be about eighty percent of the value."

"How long would it take to get it?" she asked.

"Usually a full month. How soon do you need it?"

"Yesterday," she said.

"Marilyn, I don't want to know what this is, truly. But if you need money, you don't have to go to a bank. I can lend you however much you want."

"Thank you, Chip, but . . ."

"I'm serious."

"Have you got two million bucks lying around?" she asked, and thought it amazing that she could still smile.

There was a silence on the line.

"What is it?" he said.

"An old debt came up."

"Gambling?"

"No."

"Then what?"

"A former time, a former life."

"Something you'd like to talk about?"

"No, Chip, I don't think so."

"I can go to five hundred thousand," he said. "Pay me back whenever you can."

"Chip . . ."

"No interest, no strings."

"I couldn't."

"You'll never know how much you meant to me," he said. "Come to my office tomorrow, I'll arrange a transfer of funds."

"I can't, Chip. But thank you, anyway."

"If you change your mind . . ."

"I don't think I will."

"We were such good friends," he said suddenly, his voice catching.

"Yes," she said.

"I miss you, Marilyn."

"I miss you, too," she said, and realized that she meant it.

"Marilyn, I'm serious," he said. "If you want the money, call me. It's here. And so am I. Call me, won't you? I'd like to talk to you every now and then. That's permitted, isn't it?"

"It is, Chip."

"Good," he said. "Stay well, darling," and hung up.

She lowered the receiver gently onto its cradle.

Her stockbroker was a man named Hadley Fields, but there was no sense calling him at the office today, and she did not have his home number. She went to the file cabinets in the study on the second floor of the house, and from the file marked STOCKS (she believed in generic labeling) she dug out the most recent statements. A glance at the last figure in the Market Value column showed that as of the last quarterly statement on March 31, the assets in her account totaled $496,394. Of this total, $443,036 was invested in equities, and the remainder was a cash equivalent of a bit more than $50,000 invested in what was called a short term income fund paying 8.6% interest. She began going down the list of stocks she owned:

500 Abbott Laboratories, bought in June two years ago at $45.125 per share for a total cost of $22,793. Now worth $54.75 per share or $27,435—up almost $5000 . . .

300 Walt Disney Co, bought at $57.00 a share in April two years ago, now worth $78.50 a share for a total increase of $6,270 . . .

500 Morton Thiokol Inc, bought in February of last year at $40.625 per share, now selling for $44.375 for a total gain of $1,657 . . .

There were losers, too:

1,000 Republic New York Corp purchased for $46,058 a year and a half ago, now worth $44,750, for a loss of $1,308 . . .

500 Sprague Technologies Inc. Purchased for $7872, now worth $5812 for a loss of a bit more than $2000 . . .

. . . but overall, the investments she'd made since coming to this city had increased in value by more than $60,000. Hadley Fields had been doing a good job for her; she would not be selling at a loss. Not that it made any difference. The proceeds would not be going to her. They would be going back to Argentina.

Tomorrow morning, she would call Hadley and advise him to sell everything she owned and to make a wire transfer of the proceeds to her bank account.

Meantime, she had to place another call to Shad Russell.

The man Willis spoke to at the Identification Section office that Memorial Day afternoon was fluent in Spanish, having been born of parents who'd made their way to the city from Puerto Rico back in the days when newcomers from that island were still called Marine Tigers. This was because the ship that had carried them to mainland America was called the *Marine Tiger*, Harold. Sergeant Miguel Florentino Morente was called Mike by the rest of the staff. He asked Willis to call him Mike now. This was nice of him in that sergeants in this city outranked even first-grade detectives. Willis was but a mere third.

Morente looked over the records that had been faxed by Vidoz, remarked as how the one named Carlos Ortega was perhaps the ugliest human being he'd ever seen in his life (but perhaps it was a bad fax) and then reeled off for Willis all the crimes Ortega and Castaneda had committed in tandem over the past twelve years. Willis, who'd already been filled in by Portoles, listened politely but impatiently. The list of crimes—Assault and Battery, Armed Robbery, Rape, Homicide and such—only raised his anxiety level. These were the people Marilyn was dealing with. These were the ones who wanted money from her.

"What I'm really interested in, Mike," he said politely, "is whether or not we've got anything on them *here.*"

"In this city, do you mean?"

"Or even in this *country,*" Willis said.

"These are common names," Morente said. "In Spanish. Very common. Castaneda? Ortega? Very common. If you'd of given me something like Hoyas de Carranza, or Palomar de las Heras, or . . ."

"Yes, but these are their names," Willis said.

"Oh, sure. I'm only saying. The computer's gonna have a ball with these names. You're gonna have four thousand Ortegas the first time around, you wait and see."

There were in fact only eighty-three listings for Ortega, Carlos, in the citywide Felony Offenders file, and forty-seven for Castaneda, Ramon. Armed with the records from Buenos Aires, however, Morente knew the birth dates of both men, and he also had information concerning height, weight, color of hair, color of eyes, scars, tattoos and so on, which he punched into the computer as well, and amazingly—the odds had to be *what*, ten million to one?—he came up with records for two men named Carlos Ortega who had been born on the very same day and who seemed to be just as ugly as the Carlos Ortega who'd presumably followed Marilyn up from Argentina. There were no Ramon Castanedas whose pedigrees matched the handsome one in the pair.

"You better call B.A., ask them to Fed Ex you a good set of prints," Morente said. " 'Cause I can tell you right off, we're not gonna get a match from this fax, no way."

"Any other way we can zero in?"

"Well, unless you're looking in prisons, you can count *this* one out," Morente said. "He's doing a five-and-dime at Castleview."

"How about the other one?"

"Carlos Ortega," Morente read out loud from the computer screen, and then turned to the faxed record and said, "Carlos Ortega," and then kept turning his head from screen to paper, like a spectator watching a tennis match, comparing records, speaking the facts out loud, "forty-two years old, born October fifteenth," and said in an aside to Willis "Birth date of great men" but did not amplify, "six feet three inches tall, two hundred and sixty-five pounds, brown eyes, bald with black sideburns, this is some kind of miracle, broken nose, knife scar over the right eye, they sound like twins except *your* guy was born in Argentina and *this* guy in El Salvador."

"How do their prison records match?"

"The only time *your* guy was out of jail, *this* guy was in."

"So they *could* be one and the same."

"If you conveniently forget El Salvador."

"That could be a clerical error."

"Sure, anything could be a clerical error."

"How long has your guy been in America?" Willis asked.

"Two years," Morente said, looking at the screen, and then turned. to study the faxed record. "Just about when *your* guy got out of jail."

"Why was *your* guy put away?"

"Dope."

"Where is he now?"

"Out. Naturally."

"Anything in *my* guy's record about dope?"

"Nothing. But here's his whole family history. His uncle was a pimp, a guy named Alberto Hidalgo, got him started picking pockets when he was still a little . . ."

"A guy named *what?*" Willis said, and reached for the fax.

"Don't *tear* the fuckin' thing," Morente said.

"Where does it say that?"

"Right here. That's what this means in Spanish, Living Off the Proceeds. And take a look at *this*. He's dead."

"Ortega?"

"No, the uncle."

Willis caught his breath.

"Hidalgo. Got himself killed a few years back. Cyanide."

"Do they . . . do they know who did it?" Willis asked.

"Doesn't say. This is *Ortega's* record, not his uncle's."

"His uncle," Willis said softly.

"Yeah. Is exactly what I said."

Willis was silent for several moments. Then he said, "When did *your* guy get out of jail?"

"October."

"Then it's at least possible."

"That they're one and the same person? Oh, sure," Morente said. "But I wouldn't wanna bet the farm on it."

"Have you got an address for him?" Willis asked.

It was the ugly one who called her at three-thirty sharp.

Like the handsome one, he spoke only in Spanish. There was in his voice a scarcely contained rage; he was forcing himself to be civilized. She knew that he would never forget the humiliation she had caused him to suffer. She knew that once she turned over the money they wanted, he would seek revenge, he would kill her. She did not yet know quite how she would deal with that. One step at a time, she told herself. But his voice was chilling.

"Do you have the money yet?" he asked.

"I forgot that today was a holiday," she said. "Everything's closed."

"When will you have it?" he asked.

"I'm sure I can get the five hundred tomorrow," she said. "Then I'll have to see what . . ."

"That is not two million," he said.

His voice was low. She felt he'd wanted to shout the words, but instead they came out softly, and were all the more terrifying: That is not two million. Almost a whisper. That is not two million.

"I realize that," she said. "But you know, you're the ones who suggested cocaine . . ."

"*Ustedes fueron los que sugerieron la cocaína . . .*"

"*Sí.*"

"So I was wondering . . . I'm sure you have contacts . . ."

"No."

"Because it would be so much simpler if I turned . . ."

"No."

". . . over the five hundred . . ."

"No, that is not satisfactory."

". . . and then *you* could handle the business of . . ."

"No. Five hundred is not two million."

"Of course not. But I'm sure you understand . . ."

Trying to appeal to his sense of fairness and justice . . .

". . . how difficult it is for a woman to handle such a trans . . ."

"You should have thought of that before you killed my uncle."

"What?" she said.

"*Nada,*" he said.

"No, what did you . . . ?"

"When will you have the two million?" he asked.

Had he said his *uncle?* Was that son of a bitch his uncle? Was *that* what this was all about? A little family vendetta here? We'd like the two mill, honey, sure, but there's also this matter of My Uncle the Famous Pimp Hidalgo.

"I'm still trying to make contact with someone," she said, "I told you, this is a *holiday.* But this is what I'm suggesting. Once I set the deal up, why don't you and your friend . . . ?"

"Are you dense?"

The word in Spanish was *pesada*. Meaning "thickheaded" or "obstinate." *Qué pesada eres.*

"We suggested cocaine as a way out of your problem. But the problem is *yours*, not ours. We don't want to become involved in anything illegal."

She almost burst out laughing.

"Do you understand what I'm telling you?" he said.

She understood perfectly. He didn't want to run any risks. She was the debtor, let *her* come up with the scratch.

"What if five hundred is all I can raise?" she said.

"You said you've already made contact with . . ."

"No, I said I'm *trying* to . . ."

"Then do what you have to do, and do it quickly!"

"I'm not in the habit of buying and selling dope, I'm . . ."

"Miss?"

Only the single word.

Señorita?

Loaded. About to explode.

"When will you have the money?"

Back to the point. No more bullshit. We're not interested in taking the five hundred and investing it in dope or in hogbellies. The only negotiable aspect of this deal is *time*. When will you have the money?

"I don't know yet. *If* I can buy the stuff . . . look, I simply don't know. I've been trying to reach this man . . ."

"When *will* you know?"

"That's just it. Until I . . ."

"When?"

"If you could let me have till the end of the week . . ."

"No."

"Please. I'm trying to work this out, I really am. If I could have till Friday . . ."

"Tomorrow."

"I can't promise anything by tomorr . . ."

"Then Wednesday."

"Can you make it Thursday?" she asked. "Please?" Groveling to the son of a bitch. "Thursday, okay?"

"No later," he said, and hung up.

Today, citizens all over America had lined the sidewalks of cities and towns, large and small, and watched the parades honoring their dead in foreign wars. Today, veterans of all ages had reminisced about their

infantry platoons or their bomber squadrons or their minesweepers or
their parachute drops. This was Memorial Day. A day set aside to pay
tribute to the dead. A day, also, that signaled the beginning of summer.
The swimming pools and outdoor tennis courts had been opened all
over America today, and all over America today the promise of summer
loomed large. For this was the twenty-eighth of May, and June was
only four days off and ready to bust out, summer was on the way, summer was in essence *here*—this was Memorial Day.

The town was full of tourists.

This was Memorial Day, this was the symbolic beginning of summer,
this was a time when most Americans dredged up memories not of
warfare and bloodshed, but of summers past . . . the summer of a first
kiss, the summer of a lost love, the summer all the lights went out, the
summer of distant music, the summer of girls in yellow dresses, summer after summer floating past in hot recall, this was Memorial Day.
The tourists came to the city not to remember either dead soldiers or
dead summers. They came to celebrate the *start* of a season of corn on
the cob and boiled lobsters, gin and tonic, beer frothing with foam.
Summertime. High cotton and good-looking women.

Carella had read over his own reports on the Hooper and Corrente
interviews, and there was no question but that the two men were in
absolute contradiction. It seemed to him that a *third* perspective might
be valuable, and he had gone to the Hooper apartment specifically to
talk to Seronia. Her mother told him where he could find her. Her
mother cleaned white people's houses and offices for a living. Got
down on her hands and knees to scrub floors. Her daughter got down
on her hands and knees to perform quite a different service. Carella
had not realized the girl was a hooker. That was the first shock.

"Arrest her," Mrs. Hooper told him. "On'y way she goan learn."

The second shock was actually seeing her.

He found her all the way downtown, standing under the marquee of
a movie theater playing a pair of triple-X-rated porn flicks. She was
wearing a purple satin mini and a lavender satin blouse. Amber beads
on her neck. Yellow flower in her hair. High-heeled purple leather
pumps to match the skirt and blouse. One hand on her hip, the other
clutching a small purple leather purse. Lips pursed to kiss the air as
strange men turned to look her over, whispered words. She looked
twenty-seven. She was thirteen.

"Want a date?" she asked Carella, and kissed the air as he
approached, and then recognized him, and started to turn away, and

realized it was too late to go anyplace, and stopped dead still, one hand on her hip. "Whut's this?" she said.

"Few questions," he said.

"You goan bust me?"

"Should I?"

"No crime to stan' outside a movie show," she said.

"I agree," he said. "Can I buy you a cup of coffee?"

"I'd p'fer some ice cream," she said.

They found an ice cream shop with tables in the back. At the counter, fresh-faced black girls in red-and-blue uniforms served up double-scoops on sugar cones and earned seven bucks an hour. At a table near the window, Carella watched Seronia Hooper eating a banana split with chocolate fudge sauce, whipped cream, and a maraschino cherry, and listened to her telling him that the girls behind the counter were assholes.

"They cud make two *hunn'id* an hour," she said, "they was to get lucky."

He figured she was talking fifty dollars a trick.

"I want to know what happened on Easter Sunday," he said.

"Nate tole you whut happen," Seronia said.

"I want to hear what he told *you.*"

"Same as he tole you."

"I don't think so."

"Look, man, whutchoo *want* fum me? Nate tole you the story, whyn't you go 'rest them cocksuckers busted his head?"

"Did your brother have a knife?"

"No. Who tole you he had a knife?"

"Did he go to Eleventh Street to sell crack?"

"Oh, man, doan make me laugh."

"Is his street name Mr. Crack?"

"Where you hear all this shit, man?"

"Somebody's lying, Seronia. Either your brother or a kid named Bobby Corrente, who . . ."

"Oh, *that* sum'bitch."

"You know him?"

"I know him, all right. Was him swung the fust bat, you ass me."

"Is that what your brother told you?"

"He tole me same as he tole you."

"He didn't tell me it was Bobby Corrente who swung the first bat. From the way he told it, the boys who attacked him were strangers."

"Then they was."

"But *you* know Corrente, huh?"

Silence.

"Seronia? How come you know Bobby Corrente?"

"I seen him aroun' is all."

"Where?"

"Aroun'."

"What are you hiding?"

"Nuthin'. You know Corren'ee, you go 'rest him. He the one broke Nate's head."

"How do you know that?"

"Jus' a guess is all."

"Is that what your brother told you? That Corrente swung the first bat?"

"You go ass Nate."

"I'm asking you."

"I got no more time to waste here," Seronia said, and wiped her mouth on the paper napkin and was preparing to get up from the table when Carella asked, "How'd you like to waste some time uptown?"

He felt no guilt whatever throwing muscle on a thirteen-year-old hooker.

"Waiting for the wagon to take you to Central Booking," he said, nailing the point home.

"On whut charge?" Seronia asked, supremely confident. "Anyway, my man get me out in half an hour."

"Good. Let's go then. I'm sure he'll love making bail."

"You think you bluffin' me?"

"Nope, I think I'm running you in on a Two-Thirty."

"Nobody offered you no sexual conduct, man."

"That's your word against mine," he said, and stood up. "Let's go."

"Sit down," she said, "you makin' a fuss here."

"Are we gonna talk about Easter Sunday or not?"

"They *both* lyin'," she said.

This is not *Rashomon,* not quite.

The movie *Rashomon,* as Carella remembers it, was not about people *lying.* It was about people sharing a single event but perceiving it separately and differently, so that each time the event was related, it had changed significantly. Listening to Seronia now, sitting with a thirteen-year-old hooker in an ice cream shop while she dug into her second banana split, aware that men thirty and forty years older than she is are eyeing her through the plate-glass window fronting the street, Carella begins wondering whether this version of the story, *Seronia's* version as related to her by Nate shortly after the incident occurred, is in fact the *true* version. Or is *she* lying as well?

In the game of Murder, only the murderer is allowed to lie; all the other players must tell the truth. But this is not the *game* of Murder, this is the death of a human being who also happened to be a priest, and it appears now as if *everyone* is lying, if only about what happened on Easter Sunday. And yet, there are areas where all three stories coincide, so that it becomes increasingly more difficult to tell who exactly was lying—or *is* lying—about which aspect of the Eleventh Street happening.

Seronia admits, for example, that her brother's street name is, in fact, Mr. Crack, and that he has been known to hang around the elementary school on Ninth Street enticing the little kiddies to try a bit of crack, a nickel a blow, this is not big money for kids who are ten, eleven years old. In this city, perhaps in every American city, kids are more and more often indulging in acts once exclusively reserved for adults. Seronia tells Carella—and presumably her line of work makes her an expert on the subject—that in the past three years, sex crimes committed by boys in the twelve-to-seventeen-year-old age bracket went up only twenty-eight percent, whereas sex crimes committed by boys *under* the age of twelve increased by two hundred percent. Moreover, since the rapist usually picks on someone *weaker* than he is, the female victims of these new-age sex criminals ranged in age from three years old to seven. In fact, Seronia feels she is doing a public service by engaging in sex with would-be rapists who might otherwise be chasing teeny little girls in the park.

But that is neither here nor there.

The point is that her brother, yes, is a dealer, yes. But this does not make him a bad person. This makes him a businessman filling a need in the community, much as she is a businesswoman—at thirteen, she thinks of herself as a woman, and why not, considering her occupation—filling a similar need in a different but possibly related community. All of this communicated to Carella in English that is not quite Black English, but neither is it the Queen's Own.

And on Easter Sunday, as happened on *every* Sunday, rain or shine, Christmas, Yom Kippur or Ramadān, Nathan Hooper goes uptown to Eleventh Street not to *sell* crack to the young wops gathered on their front stoops and freezing their asses off in their Easter finery, but instead to *buy* crack from his supplier, young Bobby Corrente . . .

"Are you making this up?" Carella asked.

"Do I *soun'* like I'm makin' it up, man?"

She did not sound like she was making it up.

"Bobby discounts it 'cause of the volume," she said. "Figure . . ."

. . . you can buy a vial of crack for five bucks, but you've got to go hustling customers and that takes time and energy. Bobby sells it to Nate for four bucks a vial, but he does a hundred vials in a single shot and goes home with four bills *without* having to run all over town. Nate makes a buck on each vial he sells, so on the initial investment of the four, he comes away with an *additional* hundred, which is a twenty-five percent return on the dollar, much better than you can do on Wall Street.

On this particular Sunday in question, which happens to be Easter Sunday, Nate goes uptown with three big ones in his pocket plus another hundred in twenties, intending to buy his usual hundred vials of crack from his usual dealer, Mr. Robert Victor Corrente, in case you didn't know his full name. But something happens that changes the entire complexion of the deal. What happens is that Nate hands over the money, and is reaching for the plastic bag with the vials of crack in it, same way they do business each and every time—

"An' by the way, this *wun't* on the front stoop in broad daylight, with all them silly wop girls sittin' an' watchin'. This is in the *hallway* . . ."

—where Nate is reaching for the plastic bag when Bobby tells him to disappear, vanish, get lost, nigger, words to that effect. Nate knows what it is at once, of course, but he pretends ignorance and so Bobby spells it out for him. What it is (Oh, man you got to be kiddin' me, Nate goes) is that *last* Sunday, when Nate made his usual buy, he paid for the dope with funny money (No man, you makin' a mistake, man, I mean it) and so *this* Sunday, Bobby is keeping the four bills, but he ain't giving Nate no dope for it, he's telling Nate instead to go shove his business up his ass, he doesn't like doing business with somebody who pays for merchandise with money printed in the cellar.

Hey, no, man, come on, man, Nate is going, but he knows Bobby's got him dead to rights, and he figures this is the end of this relationship here, he'll have to look for a supplier somewhere else. But you can't buy dope without cash, and Bobby has the four bills in his pocket already, and the only thing faintly resembling convertible cash around here is the plastic bag full of crack. A hundred vials of it. So, since the relationship is over and done with, anyway, and since Nate is a very fast runner with a good sense of rhythm . . .

"He grabs for the bag," Carella said.

"Is jus' whut he done," Seronia said.

. . . and starts running like hell, planning to get off Eleventh Street and stay off it till things cool down. Bobby Corrente wants to find him, let him come onto black turf, where *everybody* got rhythm, man, and where your life ain't worth a nickel if you start up with a brother. Which is just about when Bobby hits him on the back of the head with a baseball bat.

The blow sends Nate flying forward, he almost loses his grip on the bag of crack, but he keeps running, knowing he ain't gonna make it back home now, knowing he's bleeding too bad to make it back home, but not wanting to quit now, not with these hundred vials of crack in his hands. And all of a sudden he spots the church up ahead.

He tries the door, and it's unlocked. He runs into the church, and locks the door behind him, twists this big brass key that's sticking out of the heavy lock, and he hears the wops outside, charging up the steps, and he figures first thing he has to do is stash the dope because the dope is what this is all about, the reason he has a broken head is the dope. And now they're pounding on the door with their bats, and throwing themselves against the door, and maybe they've even got something they're using as a battering ram, Nate doesn't know. All he knows is that the door's going to give, and he's got to hide the dope. And then he hears somebody arguing someplace in the church, and he knows his time is running out, he's got to hide that dope before whoever's arguing comes out and finds him, or before that door smashes in, which it does about three seconds after he stashes the hundred vials.

"Where?" Carella said.

"I got no idea," Seronia said.

"But in the church someplace."

"In the church someplace," she said. "Doan y'think that's funny? Nate turnin' the church into a stash pad?"

"Yes, very funny," Carella said. "What's the rest of the story?"

"The rest is like he tole you. The pries' comes out yellin' an' hollerin' an' somebody calls the cops an' then ever'body goes home an' the pries' takes Nate to the hospital where they wrap his head in ban'ages. End of story."

Not quite, Carella thought.

"You mine if I go now?" Seronia said. "I got a livin' to make."

9

FATHER FRANK ORIELLA was a man in his early sixties, who'd been born into the Catholic Church when masses were still said in Latin, fish was eaten every Friday, and it was mandatory to go to confession before taking holy communion. Nowadays, he was often bewildered by the ecumenical changes that had taken place since he'd become a priest. He had only last week, for example, attended a funeral service in a church in Calm's Point, where—presumably to speed the deceased on his way to Heaven—the pastor had played a guitar and had sung what sounded like a pop song. This was in a Catholic church! This was not some little church down south with a tin roof. This was a big, substantial Catholic church! With a priest who played the guitar and sang! Father Oriella still shook his head in wonder at the memory.

That Tuesday afternoon, when Carella and Hawes arrived at the church, he was shaking his head and trying to put together a new office in the space that had once been occupied by Father Michael. This was a small church in a poor neighborhood. The rectory here at St. Catherine's was more a cottage than a true house. Fashioned of stone that echoed the floor of the adjoining garden, it consisted of two bedrooms, a small kitchen, and an even smaller office, the official church terminology for which was "chancellery." A long hall connected the rectory to the church, via the sacristy. Uptown, Father Oriella had enjoyed the use of a rather more opulent house.

His secretary of thirty years, a woman named Marcella Palumbo, to whom he spoke alternately in English and in Italian, was busily unpacking cardboard cartons of files which Father Oriella then transferred to the open drawers of green metal cabinets. Both Oriella and Marcella had white hair, and they were both wearing black. Looking very much like citified penguins, they bobbed busily about the small office, the priest complaining that it was inhuman to transfer a man from a parish he'd served for more than forty years, his secretary cluck- ing her tongue in sympathy while she unloaded box after box of files. It occurred to Carella that the files they were unloading pertained to Oriella's previous parish and would be of little worth here. But perhaps he'd carted them along for sentimental reasons.

"I can understand the bishop's thinking," he said, "but this does not make his decision any more bearable for me."

His accent was not *basso profundo buffone;* he did not sound like a recent immigrant. Rather, the intonations and cadences of his speech made it sound careful, studied, somewhat formal. In contrast, Marcella spoke with a thick Neapolitan accent that belied her presence on these shores for the past fifty-odd years.

"The bishop surmises," Oriella said, "that after a tragedy such as this one, it will take an older, more experienced priest to pull the parish together again. Not mine to question. But have they given any consider- ation to the shambles my *old* parish will become? There are people at St. John the Martyr who've been worshipping there since I first became a priest. That was forty-two years ago. Some of these people are eighty, ninety years old. How will *they* react to such a change? To a new priest?"

"Vergogna, vergogna," Marcella said, shaking her head and tackling yet another carton.

"It might have been wiser," Oriella said, "to send the newly appointed priest *here,* instead of to St. John's. This parish has *already* weathered a shock. Now there will be *two* shocks to overcome, one here and another one there."

"Sure, what do they know?" Marcella said.

It sounded like "Shoo, wottaday nose?"

"Marcella Bella here," he said, pleased when she waved away his playfully flattering nickname, "started working for me when the sub- ways were still clean and it wasn't worth your life to travel on them after ten o'clock. I had a difficult time convincing her to accompany me here. She lives in Riverhead, just a few blocks from St. John's. The commute is a difficult one for a woman getting on in years. And the neighborhood, with all due respect for what you people do, is not the best in the world, is it?"

"No, not the very best," Hawes admitted.

"But complaining about the pasture isn't going to mend the fences, is it?" he said. "These files are the accumulation of a lifetime, my sermons, letters from priests all over the world, articles on Jesus and the Catholic Church, reviews of inspirational books, anything pertaining to the spiritual life. To have left them behind at St. John's would have been like leaving my own children there."

"*Vergogna, vergogna,*" Marcella said again.

Hawes did not know what she was saying, but he gathered from the clucking of her tongue and the shaking of her head that she was not happy about Father Oriella's transfer here. Carella knew that she was saying, "Shame, shame," referring to the stupidity of the diocese in transferring the priest, the secretary, the files, the whole damn-a ting. She was not going to like this place. She knew that from the minute they'd walked into a rectory half the size of the one at St. John's. And what kind of housekeeper could an Irish be? Martha What*ever*, eh? This was a person to take care of an Italian priest? Or so Carella read it. *Vergogna, vergogna.*

"Actually, we'll have some more files for you in a little while," he said.

"Oh?" Oriella said.

"*Cosa?*" Marcella asked.

"More files," the priest said, and then, in Italian, "*Delle altre pratiche,*" and in English again, "What files?"

"Father Michael's. We're almost finished with them."

"They'll be useful to you," Hawes said. "For the receipts, records of payments . . ."

"Remind me to call the bishop," Oriella said, snapping his fingers, and turning to Marcella. "I have to ask him whether I should close out the St. John's account and start a new one here, or whether Father Daniel and I can simply use the old accounts." He turned back to the detectives and said, "They sent a young man straight out of the seminary, he's twenty-four years old, Daniel Robles, a Puerto Rican. He's going to be dealing with octogenarian Italians, young Daniel, he's going to be stepping into a lion's den."

Marcella burst out laughing.

"I should have left you there to help him out," Oriella said, teasing her.

"Hey, sure," Marcella said.

It sounded like "Ay, shoo."

"The reason we came by," Carella said, "is we'd like to do a search of the church, if that's all right with you."

"A search?"

"*Cosa?*" Marcella asked.

"*Una perquizione,*" Oriella said. "But a search for what?"

"Narcotics," Hawes said.

"Here?" Oriella said.

It was unthinkable that there would be narcotics here inside the church. This was like saying the Devil would be preaching next Sunday's mass. The single word "Here?" expressed not only surprise and disbelief but revulsion as well. Here? Narcotics? Dope? *Here?*

"If the story we have is reliable," Hawes said.

Marcella, who had apparently understood the word, was already shaking her head again.

"So we'd like to look around," Carella said, "see if we come up with anything. If there *is* dope here in the church, if dope *is* somehow involved in this . . . well . . . let's say that might change things."

"Of course," Oriella said, and shrugged as if to say This is entirely preposterous, dope inside a church, but if you wish to look for it, by all means go ahead, I am but a mere devoted servant of God transferred from my beloved parish uptown to an insufferable part of the city.

"We'll try not to get in your way," Hawes said.

"Is Mrs. Hennessy here?" Carella asked. "We thought she might show us around."

"She's in the kitchen," Marcella said.

It sounded like "She's inna kitch."

"I'll buzz her," Oriella said, and went to his desk. Pressing a button on the base of his phone, he waited, and then said, "Mrs. Hennessy, could you come in, please?" Marcella scowled. "Thank you," Oriella said, and put the phone back on the cradle. "She'll be right here," he said, and just then Alexis—the beautiful little blonde girl with the serious brown eyes and the solemn air—appeared in the doorway to the office, said, "Excuse me," and then recognized Carella.

"Hello, Mr. Carella," she said, "I'm Alexis O'Donnell, we met last Saturday."

"Yes, I remember," Carella said. "How are you?"

"Fine, thanks," she said, and hesitated, and then asked, "Have you learned anything yet?"

"Few things," he said.

Alexis nodded, her brown eyes thoughtful, her face bearing the same sorrowful expression that had preceded tears last Saturday. She was wearing a blue blazer with a gold embroidered school crest on the left breast pocket, pleated green plaid skirt, blue knee-high socks, brown walking shoes; Carella figured she had come here directly from school. She turned to Oriella and said, "I hope I'm not interrupting anything, Father . . ."

"Not at all," Oriella said.

"But we're not sure . . . the kids in the C.Y.O. . . . we're not sure what we should do about Friday night's dance." She turned to Carella and said, "This is the big dance we have every year at the beginning of June. We've been planning it for a long time," and then, to Father Oriella again, "We canceled last Friday's *regular* dance, but we don't know what we're supposed to do now. We don't want to do anything disrespectful to Father Michael's memory. But Gloria has the check Father Michael gave her, and she doesn't know whether to give it to Kenny or not. For the band Friday night."

"Kenny?" Father Oriella said.

"Kenny Walsh," she said. "He's leader of The Wanderers, the band that's supposed to play. He asked for a hundred-dollar deposit, and Father Michael gave Gloria the check, but now we don't know."

Oriella said, "Mmm," and thought about the problem for what seemed a long time. Then he asked, "Was Father Michael involved in the planning of this dance?"

"Oh, yes," Alexis said. "In fact, he was the one who *started* them. The First of June dances."

"For what purpose?" Oriella asked. "How are the proceeds used?"

Straight to the point, Carella thought, and wondered what Arthur L. Farnes—who'd taken a fit about the money-changers in the temple—would think of the new parish priest.

"We buy baskets for the poor," Alexis said.

"Baskets?"

"Food baskets, yes, Father. To take around on Christmas morning."

"Ah," Oriella said, and nodded in satisfaction to Marcella, who nodded in return.

"Last year, we made around two thousand dollars," Alexis said.

"And you say these dances on the first day of June were Father Michael's idea?"

"Oh, yes, Father. He started them three years ago."

"Then I think it would be a fitting memorial to hold the dance as scheduled. In honor of Father Michael's devotion to the needy of this parish. You may give Kenny his check," Oriella said. "And I will attend the dance myself, and give my blessing to everyone there."

"Thank you, Father," she said. "I'll tell Gloria."

She was starting out when Martha Hennessy appeared in the doorframe behind her. The tiny office was about to get crowded. Hawes
had been on too many small craft during his tour of duty in the Navy;
he was beginning to feel claustrophobic. "Mrs. Hennessy," he said,
"we'd like to look through the church, we were hoping you'd show us
around."

"I'd be happy to," she said, and then, to Alexis, "Hello, darlin', how
are you?"

"Fine, thanks, Mrs. Hennessy," Alexis said, "thanks, again, Father,
we'll look for you on Friday night," and stepped out into the small
entry that separated the chancellery from the remainder of the rectory.
As Hawes and Carella said their goodbyes to Father Oriella, she began
chatting with Mrs. Hennessy, and was still talking to her when they
came out a moment later. She turned to Carella at once, giving him the
impression that she'd been waiting for him.

"There's something I want to tell you," she said.

"Sure," he said.

"Could we talk privately?"

Something in her dark eyes signaled immediacy.

"I'll meet you in the church," he said to Hawes and then led Alexis
outside, to the garden where the priest had been slain. The roses were
still in bloom, their aroma overpowering. Where once there had been
the chalked outline of the priest on the uneven floor of the garden,
there was now only the grey and weathered stone itself. They walked
to the maple and sat on the low stone bench that circled it. There was
moss on the tree behind them. Ivy climbed the stone walls of the cottage. This could have been a courtyard in an English village.

"I don't want to get anyone in trouble," Alexis said.

He waited.

"But . . ."

The essential word.

Still, he waited.

"This was Easter Sunday," she said. "I was going crosstown to meet
my friend Gloria outside the movie theater on Eleventh and The
Stem. This must have been around two-thirty, a very windy day, I
remember . . ."

. . . skirts flapping about her legs, long blonde hair blowing in the
wind. She is supposed to meet Gloria outside the theater at three, an
Eddie Murphy picture is playing. Gloria and Alexis are both freshmen
at a private school on Seventh and Culver. The Graham School. One

of the few good schools in the precinct, it is only half a block away from a public school where an assistant principal recently was stabbed trying to break up a fistfight. She still has almost half an hour before she's supposed to meet her, though, she still has plenty of time. And although she's already been to mass early this morning, she is passing St. Catherine's again now, coming up the Tenth Street side where someone has painted a peculiar red star on the green gate leading to the garden and the rectory, planning to continue north to The Stem, where the theater is, but instead making a right on Culver, and impulsively going into the church through the big entrance doors, which are closed but unlocked . . .

"I thought I'd say a few extra prayers, this was, like, you know, Easter Sunday . . ."

. . . coming through the narthex, and walking up the center aisle under the nave, the church empty, her heels clicking on the polished wooden floors—this is Easter Sunday and she is wearing patent leather shoes with medium-high heels—clicking as she approaches the crossing, the transept on her left, the sacristy on her right, the brass chancel rail immediately ahead of her, and behind it the altar and the huge cross with Jesus hanging on it and bleeding from a dozen wounds in his side and his chest and . . .

". . . all at once there were voices, Father Michael's voice and someone else's . . ."

. . . coming from the paneled corridor that leads from the sacristy into the priest's small stone cottage, his rectory, the voices startling her because this is the first time she has ever heard Father Michael shouting in anger. She stops dead in the center of the crossing, here where the middle of Jesus's chest would be were this a true cross rather than the traditional stone-and-timber architectural representation of one, stands shocked and silent as the priest's voice comes down the corridor as if from the neck of a funnel into its open cup, rushing into the church, echoing into its vaulted ceiling, This is blackmail, he is shouting, *blackmail!*

She does not know quite what to do. She feels the sudden guilt of a child—she is wearing heels, but she is only thirteen—eavesdropping on an adult, fearful she will be discovered in the next instant and punished for her transgression, either by the priest or by the woman he is . . .

"A woman?" Carella said at once. "Not a man? He was with a *woman?*"

"Yes."

"And you heard him use the word blackmail?"

"Yes. And she said, 'I'm doing this for your own good.' "

"And then what?"

Alexis stands there at the middle of the stone-and-timber cross that is St. Catherine's Church, looking up at the huge plaster figure of Christ hanging on a genuine oaken cross behind the altar, the priest's voice coming again from her right, she is afraid to turn her head to locate the voice, she is afraid she will discover Father Michael lunging at her in a rage, shouting at her as he now shouts at the woman, Get out of my sight, how dare you, how dare you, and the woman is suddenly laughing, the laughter echoing, echoing, and there is the sound of a slap, flesh hitting flesh. Alexis turns and runs, terrified, they are *both* shouting behind her now, she runs for the entrance doors, heels strafing the wooden floor, slipping, almost losing her balance, grasping for the back of the nearest bench, righting herself, running again, running, running, she is not used to heels, throwing open the central portal doors and coming face to face with a black man, blood streaming down his . . .

"Nathan Hooper," Carella said.

"I screamed, I shoved myself past him, there were other men chasing him, I ran away from there as fast as I could."

She had called them men. And to her terrified eyes those husky young teenagers indeed must have appeared to be men. But hadn't she . . . ?

"Doesn't that name mean anything to you?" he asked. "Nathan Hooper?"

"Yes, of course, *now* it does, I saw his picture in the newspaper, I even saw him in person on television. But at the time, he was just this . . . this big black man with blood running down his face, and all I wanted to do was get out of there. I think in my mind I made some crazy kind of connection between Father Michael yelling and the woman yelling and all the yelling outside the church. I've never been so scared in my life. All that blood. All that anger."

"Did you *see* who the woman was?" Carella asked.

"I don't want to get anyone in trouble," Alexis said, and looked away.

He waited.

"But . . ." she said.

And still he waited.

"If she had anything to do with Father Michael's murder, then . . ."

Her eyes met his.

"Who was she?" he said. "Was she anyone you know?"

"I only saw her from the back," Alexis said.

"What'd she look like?"

"She was a tall woman with straight blonde hair," Alexis said. "Like mine."

And like Kristin Lund's, Carella thought.

"So what'd you do?" Shad Russell asked. "Rob a bank?"

"Not quite," Marilyn said.

"Then what? Saturday you're here haggling over the price of a gun—which, by the way, was a very good bargain—and Tuesday you're back with, *how* much did you say?"

"Five hundred thousand."

"You got that much change in your pocketbook there?"

"Sure," Marilyn said.

"I'll bet," Russell said knowingly. "So how'd you come into all this money?"

"Liquidation," she said.

"Of *who*? Who'd you dust, honey?"

"I understand that the normal return on a drug investment is eight to one," she said, straight for the jugular. "I need two million dollars. I'm assuming if I invest half a million . . ."

"Is *that* what we're talking here?" Russell said, surprised. "Dope?"

"I told you on the phone I was looking to make an investment."

"I thought you meant an investment of *time*. I thought you were all at once interested in one of my major situations."

"I am. The Colombian merchant."

"But not in the same way I *hoped* you'd be interested."

"No, not in that way," Marilyn said, and wondered if she'd have to go through the whole damn ex-hooker routine yet another time before they could settle down to the business at hand. They were in a little bar off St. Sebastian Avenue, three blocks from Russell's hotel. There were enough working girls in it, even at this early hour, to satisfy the needs of every major Colombian merchant in town. But they were all either black or Hispanic, and maybe Colombian gentlemen preferred blondes.

Smiling like a crocodile, Russell leaned over the table and said, "Maybe you could mix a little pleasure in with the business, what do you think?"

"I think no, and let's cut the crap, please. How many keys of cocaine can I get for the five hundred?"

"That kind of bread, that's peanuts nowadays," Russell said, immediately getting down to brass tacks. "There's no chance of a discount, you'd have to pay the going rate, which is very high these days because of all the pressure. Forty, fifty grand a key, depending on the quality. So what does that come to? Divide five hundred by fifty, what do you get?"

"Ten," she said, and wondered where he'd gone to school.

"Okay, that's if we're paying fifty, we get ten keys. If we're paying forty, what do we get?"

"Twelve and a half."

"So average it out, let's say you pay forty-five, let's say you get eleven keys for the five hundred, that'd be doing good these days."

"And how much would those eleven keys be worth on the street?"

"You're talking high, eight to one, that's high."

"Then what?"

"You step on a kilo even once, you come away with ten thousand bags of crack. Nowadays, a bag is selling for twenty-five bucks. That's a quarter of a mill you come away with, for the one key. That you paid forty-five for. That's around five and a half to one you'd be getting. So figure you can turn the five hundred into like two million seven, something in there. Exactly the amount you need," Russell said, and smiled his crocodile smile.

"No, all I need is two."

"Plus my commission," he said, still smiling.

"That seems very steep."

"Seven hundred thou is *steep?*" Russell said, looking offended. "You know somebody cheaper? In fact, you know anybody at *all?*"

"I can always call Houston again. I'm sure Sam can find me . . ."

"Sure, call him. Meanwhile, I got the feeling you were in some kinda hurry."

"Even so, that's steep," she said, shaking her head. "Seven hundred thousand? That's very steep."

Bargaining. When her fucking life was at stake.

Settle with the man, she thought.

"So is that it?" Russell said. "Are we finished talking here?"

"For that kind of money I'd expect you to handle the entire transaction," she said.

Still bargaining.

"Meaning what?"

"Setting it up, making the buy, turning the dope a . . ."

"I can tell you right now nobody's going to sell eleven keys to somebody invisible."

"Oh? Did you suddenly get invisible?"

"I'm talking about they smell I'm making the buy for somebody else, the Uzis come out. They like to know who they're doing business with."

"I can't get involved in this," she said.

Not bargaining this time. Merely thinking of Willis. Thinking that if something went wrong during the transaction, if the police came down, it might hurt Willis somehow. Thinking . . .

"Then don't get involved in moving dope," Russell said. "If you want to make a deal, I'll set up the buy for you. You show with the money, you make the buy yourself. Then I'll see about turning it around."

"I have to be *positive* you can turn it around."

"Tell you what. If I can't turn it around, you don't owe me a nickel. Is that fair?"

"Then what do I do with the eleven keys?"

"Snort it," Russell said, and smiled his crocodile smile. "When do you need this money?"

"How about tomorrow afternoon?"

"Impossible."

"Then when?"

"I can't set up the buy before Thursday night, soonest. Have you got your hands on this money already?"

"I have a cashier's check."

"Honey, please don't make me laugh. In this business? A check?"

"A cashier's check is as good as cash."

"Then cash it."

"All right."

"You know anything about high-grade coke?"

"A little."

"Enough to know whether they're selling you powdered sugar instead?"

"No."

"I'll teach you. They'll expect you to test the stuff. Everything's a fuckin' ritual with them. You test it, you taste it, you give them the cash, they give you the shit, and you go your separate ways. You deviate from the ritual, they think you're undercover and they blow you away. It ain't without its certain risks, this business," he said drily.

"When will you know for sure?"

"Tomorrow."

"I'll call you," she said.

"No, let me call you."

"No," she said.

"Why not?"

"Just no."

"Okay, you know where to reach me," Russell said, and shook his head as if to say there was no understanding the ways of beautiful broads who once earned a living on their backs. "Give me a call around this time tomorrow. If everything goes the way I figure, you better cash that check on Thursday and I'll let you know where they wanna meet you."

"No," she said. "Specify one-on-one. And I'll pick the place."

"They may not go for that."

"I'm paying top dollar. If they don't like the terms, tell them to go fuck themselves and we'll find somebody else."

"Tough lady," he said, and smiled. "You still got that gun I sold you?"

"No."

"You want my advice? Buy another one. From me or somebody else, it don't matter. A bigger one this time."

"What kind of gun did you have in mind?" she asked.

"We done this before, you know," Mrs. Hennessy said. "Father Michael and me. Went over the church top to bottom searching for the dope."

"Yes," Carella said. "His sister told me."

"Nice lady, ain't she? The sister."

"Yes," Carella said. "Very nice."

"I thought so first time I met her," Mrs. Hennessy said, smiling at the memory.

"When was that?"

"Shortly before Easter," she said. "Around St. Paddy's Day."

Which fell each year on the seventeenth of March. Which certainly would have qualified as "shortly before Easter" in that Easter this year had fallen on the fifteenth of April. Carella wondered if by then Father Michael had been involved with his mysterious lady. In which case, why hadn't he mentioned her to his sister while she was visiting here?

"... a search for dope?" Hawes was saying.

"Well, we got a phone call," Mrs. Hennessy said.

"What phone call?"

"Krissie took a phone call one afternoon, I was in the office when it . . ."

"When was this?"

"Last month sometime."

"When last month?"

"About a week after that black boy got beat up," Mrs. Hennessy said. "The call was for Father Michael. He took it, listened for a few minutes, said, 'I don't know what you're talking about,' and hung up."

"Who was it?"

"Who was who?"

"On the phone."

"Oh, I don't know. But Father Michael turned to Krissie and said, 'Kris, this guy says . . .' "

"Is that what he called her?" Hawes asked. "Kris?"

"Yes. Or sometimes Krissie."

Hawes nodded and said nothing. But Carella saw the look that crossed his face.

" 'Kris, this guy says there's dope hidden in the church here and he wants it back,' " Mrs. Hennessy said, and nodded.

"So it was a *man* on the phone," Hawes said.

"I guess so."

"Did Father Michael say who it was?" Carella asked.

"No, sir."

"He didn't say it was Nathan Hooper, did he?"

"No, sir."

"Did he say it sounded like a black person?"

"No, sir. He didn't say nothin' but what I just told you he said. 'This guy says there's dope hidden in the church here and he wants it back.' Is what Father Michael said. So we begun looking for it."

"Where'd you look?"

"Everywhere."

"Meaning?"

"Meaning *everywhere*. Places hadn't been cleaned or disturbed since the church was built, dust a hundred years thick. Nooks and crannies I didn't know existed. Secret passageways . . ."

"Secret *passage*ways?" Hawes said.

"This church used to be part of the underground railway," Mrs. Hennessy said. "Slaves escaping from the south used to come hide in the church here."

"What goes around comes around," Hawes said, and nodded.

Carella, deep in thought, missed Hawes's reference to history's little repetitions. He was remembering back to when Marilyn Hollis was a suspect in a poisoning, and Willis had fallen hopelessly in love with her. It had made things difficult—even though the ending turned out to be a happy one. Carella was all in favor of happy endings. But judging from the look that had crossed Hawes's face when he'd heard that the priest called his secretary either Kris or Krissie rather than Kristin or Miss Lund or Whatever the Hell, Carella suspected that his partner *this* time around had been similarly stricken, and he hoped with all his might that Krissie Lund turned out to be similarly clean.

Because *if* she was the woman who'd tried to blackmail Father Michael on Easter Sunday . . .

Or, worse, *if* she was the woman who'd been intimately involved with the priest . . .

Or, worse yet, *if* she was both adulteress *and* blackmailer at one and the same time . . .

"Show us the easy places first," Hawes told Mrs. Hennessy.

She always became apprehensive when he started drinking heavily before dinner. All the other times had happened when he'd come directly home from the store and started the evening by pouring himself a stiff drink. It was only a little past six now, and he'd already consumed two healthy gins-over-ice, and was pouring himself a third one at the counter near the kitchen sink. Ice-cube tray open on the counter. Tanqueray gin, he drank only the best. Tanqueray or Beefeater. Wouldn't allow a cheaper gin in the house. Asked her once if she knew that gin was made from juniper berries? And did she know that juniper berries were poisonous? She hadn't known whether he was kidding or not. He sometimes said things just to confuse her. He could be cruel that way.

She never knew whether one of his drunken . . . spells, she guessed you could call them . . . was triggered by something that had happened at the store that day, or whether they had something to do with the calendar, or the phases of the moon, or the tides—like a woman's period. She suspected there was something sexual about these spells of his, that what happened was some kind of substitute for sex, that he got off on first getting drunk and then . . .

"You disapprove, right?" he said.

"I'm making a nice dinner for us," she said.

"Which means you disapprove, right?"

Pouring the gin liberally over the ice cubes in the short fat tumbler. Fingers curled around the glass. Outside, there was thunder in the east. It had been days now since they'd had any rain. Rain would be welcome.

"I asked you a question, Sally."

She wondered if he was already drunk. Usually it took more than two of them, however heavily he'd poured them. She didn't want anything to start. And yet, whenever he got this way, no matter how carefully she tiptoed around him, there didn't seem to be anything she could do to prevent what came next. It was like a button inside him got pushed, and then all the gears started turning and meshing, and there was nothing you could do to stop the machine. Except maybe get out of here. Get *away* from the machine. Far away from it. She thought maybe she should get out of here right this minute, before the machine started again.

"Sally?"

"Yes, Art," she said, and realized this was a mistake the moment it left her mouth. His name was Arthur, he liked to be called by his full name. Arthur. Not Art, not Artie, but Arthur. Said Arthur sounded majestic, Arthur the King, whereas Art or Artie sounded like garage mechanics. "I'm sorry," she said at once.

"You still haven't answered my question," he said.

Good. He was ignoring the fact that she'd called him Art rather than Arthur. Maybe this wasn't going to be a bad one, after all, maybe tonight the machine would merely grind to a halt before it . . .

"Did you hear my question, Sally?"

"I'm sorry, Arthur . . ."

Making certain she called him Arthur this time.

". . . what was the question?"

"Do you disapprove of my drinking?"

"Not when you do it in moderation. Because I'm making us a nice dinner tonight, Arthur . . ."

"What nice dinner are you making us tonight?" he asked mockingly, and lifted the short fat tumbler to his lips, and drained it.

Outside, lightning flashed and thunder followed.

"Salmon steak," she said quickly. "With some lovely asparagus I got fresh at the Koreans'."

"I hate asparagus," he said.

"I thought you liked asparagus," she said. "I thought it was broccoli you hated."

"I hate asparagus *and* broccoli," he said, and went to the counter again and lifted two ice cubes from the tray and dropped them into the tumbler. She hoped he would not pour himself another drink.

He poured himself another drink.

"Asparagus and broccoli and cauliflower and all the *other* shitty vegetables you make that I *hate*," he said. "Brussels sprouts . . ."

"I thought you liked . . ."

". . . and cabbage and *all* of them," he said, and lifted the glass to his lips. "A man gets to be forty-nine years old, he's been married to the same woman for twenty-five years, you think she'd *know* what he likes to eat and what he *doesn't* like to eat. But oh no, not Fat Sally . . ."

The Fat Sally hurt.

He was going to hurt her tonight.

". . . Fat Sally goes her merry fat way, cooking whatever the fuck she *wishes* to cook, with never a thought as to what her husband might . . ."

"I give a lot of thought to . . ."

"Shut up!" he said.

I have to get out of here, she thought. The last time I waited too long, I waited until it got out of hand, and then there was no getting away. I don't care if the dinner burns to a crisp, she thought, I don't care if a *fire* starts in the stove, I have to get out of here. Now.

But she waited.

Giving him the benefit of the doubt.

Because after the last time, when she'd gone to Father Michael to tell him what had happened, things seemed to get a little better, this was what . . . almost two months ago, the beginning of April, shortly before Easter, right after he'd written that terrible letter. She'd asked him not to write the letter, she'd told him he'd be making a fool of himself before the entire congregation, but he'd insisted on typing it here in the apartment and then taking it to the bank to Xerox however many copies he'd needed, said he resented the way the priest was turning the church into a *financial* institution, his exact words. And, of course, the congregation *did* think he was a fool for writing that dumb letter, and the very next Sunday Father Michael made another sermon about money, this time mentioning the letter he'd received, the letter Arthur had sent . . . yes, that's right, this was exactly a week before Easter Sunday, this was the second Sunday in April. He'd got drunk that night. And the very next day, she'd gone to see Father Michael, her eyes puffy, her lip split . . .

"The very bad habit you have, Sally, is interrupting," he said.

"Oh, I *know,*" she said pleasantly, still giving him the benefit of the doubt, still hoping that her going to the priest had changed the situation here at home, that now that Arthur *realized* someone else knew what was going on here . . .

But the priest was dead.

Someone had killed the priest.

". . . even when I was a young girl," she said, her voice trailing, "I used to . . ."

And fell silent.

Interrupt, she thought.

All the time, she thought.

He was standing at the counter, putting more ice cubes into the glass. She had lost count of how many drinks he'd had already. Outside, there was more lightning, and then thunder, and then the rain came down in sheets, driven by a fierce wind. She kept staring at his back. He stood stock still at the counter, his hand wrapped around the lever that pried open the ice-cube tray. Little egg-crate compartments in the tray, the lever fastened to them. The tray empty now. The ice cubes all gone. The rain coming down in sheets outside.

"Miss Zaftig," he said. "Isn't that what your little Jew-boy used to call you?"

"Actually, he *did* refer to me as *zaftig,* yes," she said, "but he never called me *Miss* Zaftig as such."

Don't contradict him, she thought. Agree with everything he says!

"Little Miss Zaftig," he said, "running to the fucking priest!"

"Well, if you hadn't . . ."

"Washing our dirty laundry in public!"

"There wouldn't have *been* any dirty . . ."

"Taking our dirty laundry to church and washing it for the priest!"

"Next time, don't . . ."

His arm came lashing out at her in a backhanded swipe. His hand was still curled around the lever of the egg-crate divider, the metal outlining twelve empty squares now, the metal edges hitting her face but only barely scratching it because this was truly an ineffectual weapon, a silly weapon really, this aluminum tray divider dangling limply at the end of a lever, hardly a weapon at all.

The gin bottle was quite another thing.

The gin bottle was green and stout, and it had a little red seal on it that identified it as the genuine article, the Tanqueray, the good stuff. As quickly as he had swung the tray divider, he now dropped it clattering to the tiled kitchen floor, and immediately grasped the bottle by its neck and yanked it off the counter, and pulled it back as though preparing for a forehand tennis shot, the bottle coming around as if it were a racket level with a ball coming in about shoulder high, swinging it, eye on the ball, shoulder high was where her head was.

A red circle of blood splashed onto the bottle alongside the red seal. Gin sloshed from the open neck of the bottle onto his wrist, onto the floor, blood spurted now from the gash the bottle had opened alongside her left eye. The blood startled him. He seemed to realize all at once that he was attacking her with a lethal weapon, that this heavy bottle fashioned of thick green glass could very easily *kill* her if he were not terribly careful. He said, "Oh, *really?*" as if blaming her for his own stupidity in picking up the bottle, in using the bottle on her, "Oh, *really?*" and threw the bottle into the sink, deliberately smashing it, shards of green glass exploding up onto the air, caught for a moment against a dazzling backdrop of yellow-white light as lightning flashed again beyond the window.

Thunder rolled.

Oddly, he seemed more dangerous now.

Bereft of any weapons but his hands, miscalculating how powerful or how dangerous those hands could be (but she knew), he closed in on her where she stood cowering against the refrigerator door, blood gushing from the wound on her head, her bloody left hand clenched to her temple, her right hand held out like a traffic cop's, the fingers widespread. "Don't, Arthur," she said, "please, don't," but he just kept repeating over and over again, quite senselessly now, "Oh, *really?*" as if he were contradicting something she had just said, or perhaps asking for further explanation of what she'd said, "Oh, *really?*" while he slapped her over and again, methodically, his huge hands punishing her for whatever sin in his drunkenness he imagined she'd committed.

She reached for the knife on the drainboard.

And quite calmly stabbed him.

THE Q AND A took place in Lieutenant Byrnes's office at the 87th Precinct, not half an hour after Arthur Llewelyn Farnes was released from Greer General. He had been treated there for a knife wound in the left shoulder and had been charged immediately with Assault 1st Degree: "With intent to cause serious physical injury to another, causing such injury to such person or to a third person by means of a deadly weapon or a dangerous instrument," a Class-C Felony punishable by a minimum of three and a max of fifteen.

To sweeten the pudding, he had also been charged with Attempted Murder, a Class-B Felony punishable by a minimum of three and a max of twenty-five. His wife, Sally Louise Farnes, had been charged with the identical crimes, but opinion around the old station house was that she would easily beat both raps by pleading self-defense. The gathered detectives and an assistant district attorney named Nellie Brand were here this Wednesday morning at ten o'clock not so much to make certain their case against Farnes would stick—they knew they had real meat here—but to find out what he knew about the murder of Father Michael Birney.

Carella had called Nellie the moment he realized they had here a violent man whose wife had earlier gone to Father Michael to report previous abuses. This same man had written the priest a letter that in itself seemed to imply a threat, however veiled. And, by his own admission, he had gone to the church sometime during the afternoon of Easter Sunday, where at least one witness—Nathan Hooper—had reported hearing the priest in violent argument with a man.

Nellie was thirty-two years old, with alert blue eyes and sand-colored hair cut in a flying wedge that seemed appropriate to her breezy style. She was wearing this morning a dark blue skirt with a grey jacket, a pink man-tailored shirt with a narrow red-and-blue silk rep tie, and blue pumps with moderate heels. Carella liked her a lot; she reminded him somehow of his sister Angela, though she didn't resemble her in the slightest.

Sitting on the edge of the lieutenant's desk, she once again informed Farnes of his rights, and then asked him if he was certain he did not wish an attorney present. Like most amateurs who suddenly find themselves involved with the law, Farnes told her he didn't need a lawyer because he hadn't *done* anything, it was his *wife* who'd committed the goddamn crime here! Carella was thinking that every little cheap thief on the street asked for an attorney the moment he was clapped in cuffs.

Nellie dutifully informed Farnes that he could nonetheless stop the questioning at any time he chose to, or even request a lawyer whenever he felt he needed one, even though he'd declined one now, and asked him again if he understood all this, and Farnes rather testily said, "Of *course* I understand, do I look like an idiot? My wife tried to *kill* me!"

Miranda-Escobedo safely out of the way, Nellie switched on the tape recorder, nodded to the stenographer who was taking standby shorthand notes, said for the tape that this was 10:07 on the morning of May 30, identified the location and everyone in it, and then began the questioning:

Q: May I have your full name, please?
A: Arthur Llewellyn Farnes.
Q: And your address?
A: 157 Grover Park South.
Q: In what apartment, please?
A: 12C.
Q: Do you live in that apartment, at that address, with your wife, Sally Louise Farnes?
A: I do. Who tried to kill me last night.
Q: Mr. Farnes, were you treated at six-forty-five last night in the Emergency Room at Greer General for a knife wound in the left shoulder?
A: Damn *right* I was.
Q: And were you held for overnight observation at Greer General, and . . .
A: I was.

Q: . . . and released at nine-thirty-two this morning in custody of Detectives Hawes and Carella . . .

A: I was.

Q: . . . who transported you here to the 87th Precinct for questioning, is that correct?

A: That's correct.

Q: You've been informed, have you not, that you've been charged with First Degree Assault, a Class-C felony . . .

A: I have.

Q: And with Attempted Murder as well, which is a Class-B felony.

A: It was my *wife* who tried to kill *me!*

Q: But were you informed of these charges against you?

A: I was.

Q: And, of course, you were read your rights in accordance with the Supreme Court decisions in Miranda and Escobedo, and you said you understood those rights, did you not?

A: You read them to me, and I said I understood them.

Q: And declined your right to an attorney, is that also correct?

A: Yes.

Q: Very well, Mr. Farnes . . .

Leaning in closer to him now, conveying the impression that now that all the bullshit was out of the way, she was ready to take off the gloves.

Q: . . . can you tell me how you happened to get that knife wound in your shoulder?

A: She went crazy.

Q: Who do you mean, please?

A: Sally.

Q: Your wife, Sally Louise Farnes?

A: Yes.

Q: Went crazy, you say?

A: Yes.

Q: Can you tell me what you mean by that?

A: She went crazy, what do you *think* that means? We were sitting in the kitchen, and all at once she picked up the knife and stabbed me. Nuts! Totally nuts!

Q: Sitting where in the kitchen?

A: At the table.

Q: Doing what?

A: Talking.

Q: About what?

A: I don't remember.

Q: Try to remember.

A: How am I supposed to remember what we were talking about? She *stabbed* me, goddamn it!

Q: Do you remember telling your wife that she had a bad habit of interrupting you while you were . . . ?

A: No.

Q: The way you just interrupted me.

A: I'm sorry if I interrupted you. I thought you were finished with what you were saying.

Q: No, I wasn't.

A: Then I'm sorry.

Q: But isn't that what you told your wife? That she had a bad habit of interrupting?

A: I may have said that, I don't remember. It *is* a bad habit. You said so yourself.

Q: I don't believe I said that.

A: Well, you seemed to get upset when I interrupted you just now.

Q: Did you get upset when your wife interrupted you?

A: People shouldn't interrupt other people.

Q: Does that upset you? When your wife interrupts?

A: It would upset anyone. Getting interrupted. I suppose you realize, don't you, that she stabbed me, don't you? I mean, I really don't see the point of did she interrupt me, did I interrupt her, it was *me* who got stabbed, there are hospital records to prove I got stabbed, you said yourself there's a knife wound in my left shoulder, it didn't get there by *magic,* my wife *stabbed* me, goddamn it!

Q: Do you also remember telling your wife . . . ?

A: Did you hear what I just said?

Q: Yes, Mr. Farnes, I heard you.

A: I mean, did you hear a *word* of what I just said?

Q: I heard all of it, yes.

A: Then do you understand that my wife *stabbed* me?

Q: Yes, sir, I understand that. She has, in fact, admitted stabbing you.

A: Well, good, at least she had the decency to do *that!*

Q: Do you remember telling her that she also had a bad habit of washing your dirty linen in public?

A: No, I don't remember that.

Q: Of taking your dirty linen to the church and washing it for the priest?

A: No, why would I say anything like that?

Q: Washing it for Father Michael Birney.

A: No. No.

Q: Telling him about certain personal problems you were having.

A: We weren't having any personal problems.

Q: Mr. Farnes, did you strike your wife with the divider from an ice-cube tray?

A: No.

Q: Mr. Farnes, I show you this tray-divider which was recovered from apartment 12C at 157 Grover Park South and tagged as evidence by Detectives Carella and Hawes of the 87th Precinct. Do you recognize it?

A: I do not.

Q: Mr. Farnes, you are aware, are you not, that your fingerprints were taken when you arrived here at the station house?

A: I am.

Q: And you are aware, of course, that the Police Department's Fingerprint Section can recover latent prints from inanimate objects and compare those prints with, for example, your fingerprints taken here at the station house?

A: I am aware of that.

Q: Do you still say you do not recognize this tray-divider?

A: I never saw it in my life.

Q: Mr. Farnes, I show you the broken neck of a bottle recovered from the sink in apartment 12C at 157 Grover Park South and tagged as evidence by Detectives Carella and Hawes of the 87th Precinct. Keeping in mind what I just told you about fingerprints, I ask you now did you strike your wife with the bottle this neck was once a part of?

A: I did not.

Q: That is to say, a bottle containing what remained of a fifth of Tanqueray gin?

A: I did not.

Q: Mr. Farnes, where were you on Easter Sunday?

A: What?

Q: I asked you where you were on Easter Sunday.

A: Home, where do you think I was? Easter? Of *course* I was home.

Q: All day?

VESPERS   453

A: All day.
Q: Didn't you tell Detectives Hawes and Carella that you went to St.
   Catherine's Church sometime that afternoon?
A: Oh. Yes. I'd forgotten that.
Q: *Did* you go to the church that afternoon?
A: Yes.
Q: Why?
A: To talk to Father Michael.
Q: What about?
A: A letter I'd written to him. We'd had a misunderstanding about the
   letter. I wanted to clear it up with him.
Q: What time did you get to the church?
A: I don't remember.
Q: Would it have been between two-thirty and three?
A: I really don't know. There was a police car outside.

Oh, Jesus, Carella thought, there it goes, straight up the chimney!
Both Nathan Hooper and Alexis O'Donnell claimed to have heard the
priest arguing—with either a man *or* a woman, depending on whose
story you believed—sometime between two-thirty and three. But if
Edward-car was already there when Farnes came to the church, this
had to be sometime *after* the argument had taken place. So unless
Farnes was lying . . .

Q: Can you describe that car for me?

Trying to make certain the car had actually been there when he
arrived. She'd been briefed before the questioning began, she knew
that the half hour between two-thirty and three was critical. If Farnes
had come to the church *after* that time, then he could not have been
the person arguing with Father Michael.

A: It was a *police* car. What's there to describe about a police car?
Q: Do you remember the markings on it?
A: No. A blue-and-white car, like any other police car in this city.
Q: Mr. Farnes, where were you between seven and seven-thirty on the
   night of May twenty-fourth?

The night of the murder. She was going for the gold. Never mind
beating around the bush. Farnes could either account for his time while
the priest was being murdered—or he could not.

A: When was that? May twenty-fourth?

Q: Last Thursday. Do you remember where you were?

A: Last Thursday.

Q: Yes.

A: I'm trying to remember. I think I worked late last Thursday. I think I was at the store taking inventory.

Q: What do you mean by the store?

A: My store. I sell men's clothing.

Q: Where is this store, Mr. Farnes?

A: On The Stem. Between Carson and Coles. It's called C&C Men's Furnishings. Because of the cross streets. Carson and Coles. Up past Twentieth. Across the street from the new McDonald's.

Q: And you say you were there taking inventory on the night of May twenty-fourth.

A: Yes. I'm pretty certain that's where I was.

Q: Were you there at seven P.M.?

A: If I was there, then yes, I was there at seven P.M.

Q: And if you were there, were you also there at seven-thirty P.M.?

A: Yes, if I was there, I would have been there at that time, too.

Q: And at eight P.M.?

A: Yes.

Q: And at nine?

A: Yes. All night.

Q: *If* you were there.

A: Yes. But I'm fairly certain I was there.

Q: But you're not positive.

A: No, I'm not positive.

Q: Was anyone with you?

A: No.

Q: You were alone.

A: Yes.

Q: Do you normally take inventory alone?

A: Yes.

Q: So *if* you were at the store that night, you were there alone.

A: Yes.

Q: Which means we have only your word for your whereabouts on the night of May twenty-fourth.

A: Well, if I was there, there'd be a record.

Q: Oh? What kind of record, Mr. Farnes?

A: My inventory sheets would have a date on them. An inventory is worthless, you see, unless it's dated. The whole purpose of an inventory is to keep you up to date on what you have in stock. That's the whole purpose.

Q: Yes. And where would you have indicated this date?

A: In the inventory log. The date, and the quantity and size and color of any particular item. So I'll know when to reorder. That's the purpose of an inventory.

Q: Yes. Do you still have this inventory log?

A: I'm sure I do.

Q: Where is it?

A: At the store, most likely. I usually keep it at the store.

Q: And can you lay your hands on it at any time? To check the date? So that you can positively say you were in the store taking inventory all night long on May twenty-fourth?

A: Unless it's missing for one reason or another.

Q: Missing? Why would it be missing?

A: Well, you know this city. Things get stolen all the time.

Q: Are you saying that someone may have *stolen* your inventory log?

A: It's possible.

Q: Why would anyone want to steal an inventory log?

A: This city, who knows?

Q: So what you're saying, actually, Mr. Farnes, is that if the inventory log has been stolen, you have no way of verifying when this inventory-taking happened.

A: Or lost. The inventory log.

Q: Stolen or lost or misplaced, you would have no way of verifying where you were on the night of May twenty-fourth.

A: What has this got to do with my wife stabbing me?

Q: It has to do with someone stabbing a *priest*, Mr. Farnes.

A: Is that supposed to be a surprise?

Q: I beg your pardon?

A: I mean, you're oh-so-very *smart* here, aren't you, with your trick questions and beating all around the mulberry bush, do you think you're dealing with a fool here? I have a very successful business, I've been at the same location for fifteen years, I'm not a fool.

Q: No one said you were, Mr. Farnes.

A: Oh, no, you didn't come right out and *say* it, of course not. With the tape going? And this man taking notes? Of course not. But don't you think I realize what you're trying to do here? You're trying to make a mountain out of a molehill. You're trying to say that because I had an argument with Father Michael, that means . . .

Q: Did you have an argument with him?

A: I *told* you we had a misunderstanding.

Q: Yes, but you didn't say you'd had an argument.

A: A misunderstanding, I said, a misunder*stand*ing. Over a letter I sent to the entire . . .

Q: Yes, but just now you said you'd had an argument. When did you have this argument, Mr. Farnes?

A: A misunder*stand*ing. Listen, I want to make this clear . . . is that tape still going? I want it made perfectly clear on the tape that I *meant* to say misunderstanding, not argument. Misunderstanding. Your detectives came to *see* me about that damn letter. I *told* them the misunderstanding had been cleared up, Father Michael and I settled the whole thing on Easter Sunday. There was *no* damn *ar*gument, is that clear?

Q: On Easter Sunday, do you mean?

A: On Easter Sunday or any *other* time. We did not argue. Period.

Q: Ever?

A: Never.

Q: Mr. Farnes, I can ask for a search warrant to locate the inventory log you mentioned, but I feel certain you would want to help us find it. I wonder if you could accompany these detectives to your store . . .

A: No. I want a lawyer.

Nellie looked at Carella. Carella looked at Hawes. The stenographer looked up from his pad. Lieutenant Byrnes shrugged. The only sound in the room was the whirring of the tape recorder.

"Mr. Farnes," Nellie said at last, "am I to understand . . . ?"

"You've got it, sister."

"Am I to understand that you will *not* help us locate the log?"

"Not unless a lawyer tells me you can do this."

"What is it you think we're doing?"

"Taking me to the store against my will."

"Very well, Mr. Farnes, we'll request a search warrant. Any I to understand further that you wish the questioning to stop at this time?"

"You've got it, sister," Farnes said again.

Nellie snapped off the tape recorder.

"We're off the air," she said. "You ever call me sister again, I'll kick you in the balls, *got* it?"

"I'll mention that to my attorney," Farnes said.

"Please do," Nellie said, and walked out of the room.

* * *

It was not until one o'clock that afternoon that Carella and Hawes obtained both a search warrant from a Superior Court judge and a key to C&C Men's Furnishings from Sally Farnes. Sally said she hoped it turned out that her husband *had*, in fact, killed Father Michael, and she hoped further that he would be sent to prison for the rest of his natural life. She also mentioned that he usually kept his inventory log in the lower right-hand drawer of the desk in his office at the back of the store.

They found the office, they found the desk, and they found the log in the lower right-hand drawer.

The log indicated that Farnes had indeed taken inventory of his stock on the twenty-fourth of May.

"Nellie'll be disappointed," Carella said. "She was hoping we'd catch him in a lie."

"This could *still* be a lie," Hawes said. "Just 'cause he wrote the twenty-fourth doesn't mean he actually *did* it on that date. He could have done it a week earlier, three days earlier, whenever."

"Say he killed the priest," Carella said. "What do you see for his motive?"

"He's a nutcase," Hawes said. "He doesn't *need* a motive."

"Even a nutcase has what he *thinks* is a motive."

"Okay, he was annoyed that his wife ratted on him."

"Then why not kill *her*? Why the priest?"

"Because he had a *further* grievance with the priest."

"The whole business with the letter, huh?"

"Yeah, and being made to look foolish in the eyes of the congregation. Nutcases take themselves seriously, Steve."

"Yeah," Carella said.

Both men were silent for several moments.

Then Carella said, "Do *you* think he did it?"

"No," Hawes said.

"Neither do I," Carella said.

The way Martha Hennessy later described it, this was just another teenage wolf pack. You read about them all the time now, these gangs going totally crazy and doing unspeakable things. This was maybe a dozen strapping young men, all of them white—Mrs. Hennessy could have understood it if they'd been black or Hispanic, but *white*? Came storming into the church around three o'clock it must've been, she was in the rectory, heard a lot of noise in the church itself, ran through the paneled corridor leading to the sacristy where three of them were already there, knocking over things, tearing the place apart. Inside the church itself, Father Oriella was yelling in English and in Italian, and his secretary, this old Italian woman whose English was atrocious, was screaming for them to stop. Mrs. Hennessy ran back into the rectory and dialed 911 from the office telephone. A police car arrived in about three minutes flat.

The responding car was Edward-car, because the church was in the precinct's Edward Sector, and the two officers driving the car were the same man and woman who'd responded to the fracas here on Easter Sunday. The difference this afternoon, and the reason their response-time was so rapid, was that after the priest's murder, they'd been called downtown to Headquarters and asked a lot of questions about their behavior on Easter Sunday, which Inspector Brian McIntyre from Internal Affairs had found somewhat less than exemplary in a community rife with white-black tensions. Mindful of the inspector's diatribe and reprimand, the moment Officers Joseph Esposito and Anna Maria Lopez caught the 10-39—a Crime In Progress, specified by the dispatcher as a "rampage at St. Catherine's Church"—they hit the hammer and screeched over to the church, where if this wasn't a rampage it sure as hell looked like one. Officer Lopez got on her walkie-talkie and called in an Assist Police Officer, and within another three minutes, cars from the adjoining David and Frank sectors and half a dozen foot-patrol officers assigned to CPEP were responding to the 10-13 and swarming all over the church and the church garden and the rectory, rounding up what eventually turned out to be six teenagers, all of them white, all of them with Italian names, least of whom was Robert Victor Corrente.

Bobby and his pals all seemed to be rather high on an unidentified substance of a controlled nature. He seemed not to care that he was now in handcuffs, in a police squadroom, being charged with an assortment of crimes, among which was an assault upon Father Frank Oriella with a brass candlestick Bobby had seized from the main altar while his friends were knocking over the altar, and ripping the altar clothes from it, and otherwise ransacking the church. Bobby was screaming that he wanted a lawyer. His assorted friends, some handcuffed to desk legs in various parts of the squadroom, some already in the detention cage in the corner of the room, parroted every word he said. Bobby wanted a lawyer, *they* wanted a lawyer. He yelled for his father, they yelled for *their* fathers. It was an opera here in the squadroom, with everyone in fine voice. Carella wished he had ear plugs.

When Vincent Corrente arrived at the squadroom at four P.M. that afternoon, he looked much as he had the day Carella talked to him, except that he was not wearing a tank top undershirt. Or, if he was, it was not visible under the Hawaiian print, short-sleeved sports shirt he wore hanging outside his tan slacks. Otherwise, he was still jowly and paunchy and unkempt and he was still smoking an El Ropo cigar that lent a distinctive olfactory dimension to the auditory squadroom medley of yelling teenagers, clacking typewriters, ringing telephones, and cops telling everyone to shut the fuck up. Corrente was furious. It was difficult to tell, however, whether he was angrier with his son or with the people who'd arrested him.

"You dumb bastard," he told Bobby, "wha'd you do to the church, hah?" and belted him upside the head. To Carella, he shouted, "You! Take these cuffs offa my son or you're in deep shit!"

Carella looked at him calmly.

"You hear me? I know people!" Corrente shouted.

"Mr. Corrente," Carella said, "your son has been charged with . . ."

"I don't care *what* he's been charged with, he's a juvenile!"

"He's been charged as an adult."

"He's only seventeen!"

"That's an adult, Mr. Corrente. And he's been charged with . . ."

"I want a lawyer!" Bobby shouted.

"Shut up, you dumb bastard!" Corrente said. To Carella, he said, "He don't say anything till my lawyer gets here."

"Fine," Carella said calmly.

He was wondering when Bobby would come down off his high.

The lawyer Corrente called was a man named Dominick Abruzzi.

This was getting to be a regular reunion of WOPS, the World Order for the Prevention of Subterfuge, a watchdog society dedicated to the proposition that any American born with an Italian name must keep that name forever, neither changing it completely, nor even Anglicizing it, lest he be mercilessly and eternally hounded to his grave with reminders that he is merely an ignorant peasant with hoity-toity pretensions. Abruzzi looked as Italian as Richard Nixon. Carella guessed his teeth were capped.

Thirty-five, thirty-six years old, wearing a tailored suit, a button-down shirt, and a somber tie, he breezed into the squadroom as if he'd been in it (or one similar to it) a thousand times before. He said hello to Corrente, waved to Bobby who seemed to be sinking lower and lower into a depressive mire, and then asked, pleasantly enough, "What seems to be the trouble here?"

Carella told him what the trouble seemed to be. The trouble seemed to be First-Degree Assault, Second-Degree Burglary, First-Degree Criminal Mischief, and Reckless Endangerment of Property.

"That's what the trouble seems to be," he said.

"Well, that's *your* contention, Detective," Abruzzi said.

Carella was aware of the sense in which Abruzzi was using the word "Detective." His intonation made it sound like "Pig."

"No, that's not *my* contention, Counselor," he said, "that's what Robert Corrente's been charged with."

He did not like attorneys who defended criminals. He especially did not like Italian-American Attorneys who defended criminals, especially when they looked like Richard Nixon and smelled of snake oil, and especially when the criminal was himself an Italian-American.

Abruzzi was aware of the sense in which Carella was using the word "Counselor." His intonation made it sound like "Shyster." Abruzzi hated high and mighty Italian-American Law Enforcement Officers who thought their calling was as pure and exalted as a priest's. In a democracy, everyone was entitled to counsel and everyone was innocent until he was proved guilty, and Abruzzi was here to make certain that no American citizen would ever be deprived of his rights, God bless America.

"If you don't mind, Detective," he said, "I'd like to talk to my client and his father privately."

"Sure," Carella said. "Go right ahead. Counselor."

A uniformed cop escorted Abruzzi and the Correntes down the hall to the Interrogation Room. Carella went to the cage, threw back the slip bolt, opened the door, and said, "One at a time, you first, son. Want to step outside, please?" The kid was eighteen and looked fifteen. Dark hair, wide brown eyes, a pretty mouth. Like Bobby, he had come down from the high induced by whatever the hell they'd ingested and now looked as if he'd been run over by a railroad locomotive. Carella took him over to his desk. Hawes was coming from the Clerical Office with a cup of tea; he liked his afternoon tea.

"What's your name, son?" Carella asked the kid.

"Rudy Perucci," the kid said.

"Rudy, you're in trouble," Carella said, and read him his rights. Rudy listened gravely. Carella asked him if he'd understood everything he'd heard. Rudy said he had. Carella asked him if he wanted an attorney.

"Do I need one?" Rudy asked.

"I'm not permitted to advise you on that," Carella said. "You can have one or not, it's entirely up to you. Either way, it won't reflect upon your guilt or innocence."

"It wasn't me who hit the priest," Rudy said.

"Rudy, before you say anything else, I have to know whether you want an attorney. If you want one, you can have one. Either your own, or we're required by law to get one for you if you don't have one. So please tell me now if you want an attorney."

"What else do they say I done?" Rudy asked.

Carella read off the list of charges.

"That's serious, huh?" Rudy said.

Carella started to tell him exactly how serious it was. The assault charge was punishable by a max of fifteen. The burglary charge . . .

"We didn't steal anything," Rudy said.

"Rudy, please don't say anything else, okay?" Carella said. "Let me tell you what these charges mean, and then you can decide about a lawyer. You can get up to fifteen years for the assault, fifteen for the burglary, twenty-five for the reckless endangerment, and seven for the criminal mischief."

"I only went along," Rudy said. "I didn't do anything."

"Do you want a lawyer, Rudy?"

"If I didn't do anything, why do I need a lawyer?"

"Yes or no, Rudy?"

"No, I don't need a lawyer."

"Are you willing to answer questions without a lawyer present?"

"Yes. I don't need a lawyer, I didn't do anything."

"Can you tell me what happened?"

"I only went along," Rudy said.

"How did it start?"

"We were trying some stuff Bobby got hold of."

"What stuff? What'd you take, Rudy?"

"I don't even know the name of it. We just said yes."

He grinned. He had just made a joke about Nancy Reagan's famous and foolish slogan. Anybody who'd ever smoked only so much as a joint knew exactly how stupid the Just Say No campaign had been. Rudy was testing Carella now. To see if *he* knew how dumb it had been. Carella smiled back. Two old buddies familiar with the ways of drug abuse. But only one of them had gone berserk inside a church.

"It was real good, man," Rudy said, still grinning.

Carella was willing to bet it had been real good.

"So what happened?" he asked pleasantly.

"Bobby wanted to go get his stuff back."

"What stuff?"

"The stuff the nigger ripped off."

"Ripped off?"

"Yeah, you know."

"No, I don't know. Tell me."

This is the fifth episode of *Rashomon*. After this, there will be no more installments. This is the final chapter. At least Carella *hopes* it is the final chapter. They are back to Easter Sunday again, the same windy, shitty day, everyone seems to agree on the weather. And it is still two-thirty, three o'clock in the afternoon, everyone agrees on the time as well. And the star player, or at least *one* of the star players in this tedious and interminable little melodrama, is once again coming up Eleventh Street, doing what Rudy calls his Nigger Shuffle, and grinning into the wind like he owns the world. Alexis has not said anything about *this* part of the saga because she was not witness to it, but so far Hooper's, Bobby's, and Seronia's versions are all in agreement. But they are coming to the dope part again, which dope Hooper was first there to *sell*, and next there to *buy*, and next ran off with after Bobby accused him of using funny money the last time they traded. And, sure enough, they are going into the hallway again, and another dope transaction is about to go down, these two—Bobby and Hooper—are in the *habit* of exchanging money for dope, you see, and vice versa, Mrs. Reagan, which is why little girls in red hoods should not go wandering off into the woods where evil and corruption lurk, hmmm?

So there in the hallway, out comes the crack. A hundred vials, identical to the tiny glass tubes perfume samples come in, except that *these* vials don't contain *Eau du Printemps*. These vials contain little crystals that look like exaggerated grains of salt but which are actually cocaine base, which is made by heating a mixture of baking soda, cocaine hydrochloride and water, and then letting it cool. *These* little vials are deadly.

Out comes the crack . . .

"And out comes the piece," Rudy said.

"The what?"

"The piece."

"A gun?"

"A gun."

"Bobby pulled a gun?"

"No, no. The *nigger* pulled the gun."

... because what he has in mind, you see, is taking these hundred vials worth four hundred bucks and not giving Bobby a red cent for them. That is what the piece is for. Which upon closer examination looks like a .38 caliber Smith & Wesson Regulation Police Model 33, capable of putting very large holes in anyone's head who is stupid enough to try grabbing that plastic bag of crack away from Hooper. Unless the someone is standing a little to the side of and slightly behind the nigger, and unless there's a baseball bat (and also a softball and a mitt, but it is only the bat that is of importance) in the corner of the hallway, where one of the kids left it when his mother called him upstairs to Easter dinner. The bat is propped against the wall, and the mitt and the softball are on the floor, the ball in the pocket of the mitt (although this is an insignificant detail) and the kid standing slightly behind and to the left of Hooper is not Bobby Corrente but his kid brother Frankie Corrente, who is rapidly learning the ways of the street, and especially how to seize the opportunity.

Not to mention the handle of a ball bat.

Which he does, in fact, seize.

And swings the bat with practiced ease at the target that is Nathan Hooper's head. From the corner of his eye, Hooper sees the bat coming, and he kind of raises his left shoulder, sort of hunkering down into it, turning at the same time, trying to deflect the blow, which he partially succeeds in doing in that the bat hits his shoulder first and only then bounces off to graze his head. This is not enough to prevent a serious wound, but it is enough to prevent concussion and possible coma. It is also enough to cause his grip on the gun to loosen before he can fire a shot. And as the gun clatters to the floor and young Frankie pulls back the bat for yet another swing at the fences, Hooper recognizes it is time to get the hell out of here, but not without the dope for which he has now paid with a broken head. So off he goes with the bag of dope in his left hand and the pack in full cry behind him, and the rest of the story ends in church—not once, but twice.

"The second time is today," Rudy said. "When we went back to look for the stuff."

Because, yes, Virginia, it *is* true that Hooper stashed the dope someplace inside the church. Bobby and his pals know this is so. Not because when he came out with the priest on the way to the hospital, they couldn't see the bag of crack nowhere in sight; he could've had it in his pocket, right? But because pretty soon after the incident on Easter, Hooper began bragging around Fifth Street that as soon as it was safe to go back to St. Kate's he was gonna be one rich nigger. And also, this must've been three, four days before the priest got killed, they were fooling around with a pussy kid named Fat Harold, kidding around with him, you know, giving him knucks and the burn, this was near the school, and he told them he was with Hooper when he called the church and warned the priest he wanted his dope back.

So the dope is there inside the church, right?

Someplace inside the church.

Four hundred *dollars* worth of crack.

And there hasn't been a single black guy snooping around looking for it because first of all there aren't any blacks go to St. Catherine's, and second of all, they know what happened to Hooper on Easter, and they don't want a taste of the same medicine.

This doesn't mean Bobby and the guys haven't been in there tiptoeing around half a dozen times looking for it, but they can't *find* the fucking stuff, the nigger hid it too good. So it's beginning to look like four hundred bucks is going straight down the toilet.

Until today.

Today, Bobby gets sore.

And he tells them they're going to that church and they're gonna turn it upside down till they find that fuckin' dope.

Which is what they done.

"But not me," Rudy said. "I just went along. I didn't hit the priest, I didn't knock over any of the things, the candlesticks, the altars, the thing with the incense, I didn't do any of those things. And, also, how is it burglary if nobody stole nothing?"

Carella explained that it was burglary if someone knowingly entered or remained unlawfully in a building with intent to commit a crime.

"But we *didn't* go there to commit a crime," Rudy said. "We went there looking for dope rightfully belongs to Bobby."

Carella explained that criminal mischief was a crime. And so was assault. And so was reckless endangerment.

Rudy shook his head over the inequity of the law.

"Good thing I didn't do none of those things," he said.

"Who *did?*" Carella asked.

The entire reason for this little exercise. Get one of them talking, get him to nail one of the others. Then get another one talking to save his own skin, and have him nail yet another one. The Domino Theory of law enforcement and criminal investigation.

"I just went along," Rudy said.

"Too bad you've been charged," Carella said sympathetically. "But you get a thing like this, a bunch of guys acting in concert . . ." He shook his own head over the inequity of the law.

"I don't see why I should take the rap for something I didn't do," Rudy said, beginning to sound a bit indignant.

"Yeah, it's too bad," Carella said. "But if you didn't see who knocked over the altar, for example, or who hit the priest . . ."

"Bobby hit the priest."

"Bobby Corrente?"

"Yeah. I saw him grab the candlestick and hit him with it. And Jimmy Fava knocked over the altar, the big one. And . . ."

And that was the beginning.

When Dominick Abruzzi came back into the squadroom after having talked to his client, he said, "May I have a word with you, Detective Carella?"

No more sneering of the word "Detective."

"Sure," Carella said.

"My client went into the church because he was having an allergy attack," Abruzzi said.

Carella looked at him.

"Lots of pollen in the air this time of year. The church is relatively pollen free. It was a haven for him."

"I'm sure," Carella said. "Dust free, too, probably."

Abruzzi looked at him.

"The wagon gets here at six," Carella said. "After that, you can talk to your client downtown. Good night, Mr. Abruzzi," he said, and went to the lieutenant's door and knocked on it.

"Come!" Byrnes shouted.

11

HERE IN THIS CHURCH, here in this hallowed place, *Our father who art in Heaven, hallowed be Thy name,* searching now behind a life-sized plaster statue of the Virgin Mary holding the crucified Christ in her arms, here in this place, on his hands and knees but not praying, lifting altar cloths instead and looking under them, groping along stone walls inch by inch, inspecting niches in which there were statues of saints he did not recognize or could not remember, Carella was transported back to a time when a young boy who looked somewhat like the man he'd grown into, sat in a church not too far away from this one—the family had not yet moved uptown to Riverhead—sat Sunday after Sunday listening to the drone of ritual, barely able to keep his eyes open.

Sunday after Sunday.

He was inside a church again today, seeking not salvation but dope. Because Lieutenant Byrnes had told him to find that dope. Because if there was dope inside the church, then the black girl was telling the truth about her brother stashing it there and Mrs. Hennessy was telling the truth about somebody calling up and wanting it back, and the possibility existed that Corrente or somebody else had come back for it sometime *before* this afternoon. And if that was the case, then maybe the somebody'd who'd come looking for it had run into the priest instead. And such a chance encounter called up a great many possibilities, least of which was violence. Where there was dope, the possibility of murder always existed. So find the goddamn dope and at least maybe you had your goddamn motive!

Sunday after Sunday.

Sundays with sunshine blazing through the long high windows on either side of the church, illuminating stained glass that had been fashioned by a local artisan here in this Italian section of the city (which was no Firenze, that was certain), dust motes climbing to the ceiling while from the organ loft soft fat notes floated out onto the scintillated air, and a boy with slanting eyes and unruly hair listened to the priest and wondered what it was all about.

On the day of his first holy communion when he was ten or eleven, somewhere in there—a spiritual life was so alien to him now that he could no longer remember the exact dates of the most important events in a young Catholic's life—his mother slicked down the cowlick at the back of his head, and he walked to the church with her and his father and his Uncle Lou, all so long ago.

Carella—he was called Stevie back then, a name he'd always sort of liked until a girl a few years later dubbed him Stevie-Weevie in an attempt to make him feel childish; he was twelve and she was fourteen, a vast difference at that age, he'd gone home in tears. But on the day of his first holy communion Stevie Carella accepted the wafer on his tongue, allowed it to melt there, careful not to bite it because this was the flesh and the blood of Jesus Christ, and the wafer would bleed in his mouth, Christ's blood would flow in his mouth, or so he'd been given to understand by one of the nuns who'd taught him his catechism every Monday and Wednesday afternoons after school.

He'd felt a deep and reverent attachment to God that day. He did not know exactly what it was he believed, it was all mumbo-jumbo of a sort to him, but he knew that he felt an inner glow when that wafer dissolved in his mouth, and he knelt there at the altar railing with his head bent and his cowlick plastered down, and he felt somehow enriched by what had happened this day, so very long ago. Enriched. And somehow joyous. He'd gone to his first confession the day before, nothing to confess at that age, he truly was without sin, an innocent . . . well . . . I lied, Father, and I ate meat on Friday, and I talked back to my mother. Sins. A boy's sins. Forgiven, absolved with a handful of Hail Marys, a couple of Our Fathers, and an Act of Contrition, pure again, the lamb again, joyous in the presence of God on the following day, the Sunday of his first holy communion.

A year or so later, two years, so difficult to remember now, he was confirmed in that very same church, wearing the same blue suit, which he was beginning to outgrow, red arm ribbon on his sleeve, his Uncle Lou looking tall and handsome in a blue suit that matched his own, neatly trimmed little mustache, his father gave him a gold signet ring with his new initial on it, L for Louis, in honor of his godfather, SLC for Stephen Louis Carella, today I am a man. Sunday after Sunday in that church and then in the smaller church in Riverhead, three blocks from the house his parents were renting, Carella had his own bedroom, he was a man now, he no longer shared a bedroom with his sister Angela. No one called him Stevie anymore. He was Steve now. Sunday after Sunday.

Rainy Sundays in the new church, rainsnakes slithering down the windows, plain glass here in Riverhead, he missed the stained glass they'd had in Isola, the priest's sonorous voice floating out over the heads of the worshippers, the scent of incense wafting from thuribles, a lightning flash, the boom of thunder, the scent of something else now, imagined or real, the perfume of young girls, its scent much headier than the incense, he was beginning to notice, his mind wandered, he thought of panties when he should have been thinking of God.

Years later, on the Saturday before Easter—he must have been fifteen or sixteen, he could hardly remember anymore—he was infused with the same sort of spiritual fervor he'd felt on that day of his first communion, and he'd got on his bicycle, a black and white Schwinn with a battery-powered horn, and he'd pedaled over to the church, and locked the bike to the wrought-iron fence outside . . .

His father used to tell stories about the days when you didn't even have to lock your front door, but that was when there were chariots in the streets . . .

. . . and he took off his hat . . .

He used to wear this shabby blue baseball cap that had seen better days, but it was the good luck hat he'd worn when he pitched a no-hitter . . .

. . . and he went into the church and dipped his hand into the font of holy water and made the sign of the cross, and then sat down and waited his turn to enter the confession box. And he knelt on the padded kneeling bar, and the little door slid open and he could vaguely see the priest's face behind the screen partition, and he crossed himself and said, "Bless me, Father, for I have sinned, this is six months since my last confession."

There was a silence behind the screen.

Carella waited.

And then the priest said, "And you pick the busiest time of the year to come?"

Carella confessed his sins. He had done a lot of bad things that had kept him away from the church for six months because he'd been afraid of telling all those things to a priest, evil things like feeling up an Irish girl named Marge Gannon, and masturbating a little . . . well, a lot . . . and saying Fuck you, and You dirty bastard. The priest told him what he had to say as penance, and Carella said, "Thank you, Father," and left the confession box, and was starting down the center aisle toward the altar, fully intending to say the penance so that tomorrow he could receive communion and feel the same glow he'd felt that first time, when all at once he stopped dead in the middle of the aisle, and he thought What do you *mean,* the busiest time of the year? Does God have busiest times of the year? I was feeling *good* when I came in here, I wanted to be near *God!* So what the hell do you mean—he actually thought those words, what the hell, here in the church, standing in the middle of the aisle halfway to the altar—what the hell do you *mean,* the busiest time of the year?

And he turned his back to the altar, and walked up the aisle, and out of the church, and he slammed his lucky baseball cap down on his head, and he unchained his bike, and rode away from the church without looking back at it. He had not been inside a church again until his sister's wedding eleven years ago.

He was in one today.

Looking for dope.

Father Michael had searched the church thoroughly, and undoubtedly he'd known its nooks and crannies more completely than any outsider could have. And Carella had searched it again with Hawes, and Bobby Corrente and his friends had done another more reckless search, and no one had come up with the hundred vials of crack. So maybe the crack wasn't here, after all, maybe *all* the versions of *Rashomon* were false. And even if the crack *was* here, what were we talking about? Five hundred dollars? That was the street value of the crack Nathan Hooper allegedly had stashed inside St. Catherine's. A lousy five hundred dollars. Was that enough to kill someone for? In this city, yes. In this city five hundred *pistachio* nuts was enough to kill someone for. And if someone had come to this church to retrieve that dope . . .

And had been intercepted by Father Michael . . .

Perhaps challenged by him . . .

Yes, it was possible. The lieutenant was right. Where there was dope, there was often murder.

Sighing heavily, he started the search one more time.

From the top.

Playing his own *Rashomon* tune.

Imagining himself as Nathan Hooper entering this church on Easter Sunday with the pack in full cry behind him.

Through the massive center doors. Urn of holy water on the left. Stainless steel, sitting on a black wrought-iron stand. Little upright brass cross fastened to the top of its lid. Little brass spigot on the container below. He pressed the button on the spigot. A drop of water fell onto the fingers of his right hand. He could remember back to a time when all the fonts of holy water in a church were filled to the brim every day of the week. Now, they were empty except on Sundays. The urn was simpler. It held . . . what, three gallons of water? You didn't have to run all around the church filling all those little basins all the time.

To the right of the entrance doors was a rack containing religious reading matter. Newspapers titled *National Catholic Register* and *Our Sunday Visitor* and *Catholic Twin Circles*. Pamphlets with titles like *Serving God's People with a Bequest in Your Will* and *Students Pursue the Infinite Wisdom of God* and *Proclamation: Aids for Interpreting the Lessons of the Church Year,* this particular issue subtitled *Lent.* The rack was fashioned of wood, with troughlike partitions holding the printed matter. He had felt inside those troughs, searching behind the newspapers, when he'd gone through the church with Hawes. He did it again now. Nothing.

The offerings box stood alongside the newspaper rack; one was expected to make donations for the reading material. There were twenty-two of these boxes scattered throughout the church; he had counted them on his earlier search. Each box resembled nothing so much as a black iron chest with a black iron tower growing out of it. The box was a foot square, with a heavy padlock fastened to its front, where the box opened. The tower sprang from the center of the box, rising to about Carella's belt buckle. It was a three-inch-square chute with a slit in the top of it. The slit was perhaps three inches long and half an inch wide. Big enough to accept even a wadded bill.

Or a vial of crack.

But wouldn't Father Michael have emptied all the boxes in the church since Easter Sunday? And even if Hooper had dropped a dozen vials here and there in offerings boxes around the church . . .

But this would have taken time.

He was being chased by an angry mob.

But, hold it. *Rashomon,* okay?

He comes running into the church, carrying his plastic bag with his precious hundred vials in it. The vials are identical to the ones perfume samples come in. In fact, most crack dealers get their vials from wholesale specialty houses. The sale of these tiny containers has skyrocketed since crack came into vogue. If you checked the books of these houses, you'd think half the population of this city had suddenly gone into the perfume business. Little perfume tubes containing the crack crystals, most of them white, some of them with a yellowish tint, little clear crystals looking as if they've been chipped from a larger rock, it is sometimes *called* rock because of its appearance. White or yellow, when you smoke the shit, when you melt it and inhale the vapors, it produces an immediate high that knocks the top of your head off. So he's carrying his hundred vials of crack in a small plastic bag . . .

They'd have fit in a small bag.

They're what, those vials? An inch long? Quarter of an inch in diameter? Little plastic cap sealing the top of the vial, well, just like the perfume sample vials, those are what these deadly little containers *are*. So yes, they were small enough to fit inside the smallest of the commercial plastic bags, one of those sandwich-sized things and yes, practically the first thing he'd have seen when he came running into the church would have been the offerings box with its black conning tower. It wouldn't have taken him more than a few minutes to dump those vials into the slot on top of the tower, turn over the bag maybe, sort of funnel them in, using the edge of his free hand as a shovel, it was possible. Two, three minutes at most. If he *had* two, three minutes. With all of them roaring up behind him?

But suppose he'd been too frightened to pause there in the entrance narthex, suppose he'd run into the church instead . . .

Carella stepped through the doors into the nave . . .

. . . and was suddenly confronted with a veritable *feast* of offerings boxes. There were shrines to his right and to his left . . . *Dedicated to the very Reverend* . . . there were more statues of saints, there were marble altars with goldleaf screens above them, there were standing racks holding votive candles and there were racks fastened to the wall and holding yet more votive candles, and everywhere the candles flickered, there was an offerings box. Nathan Hooper had to have seen what Carella was seeing now. Candles everywhere. Candles and flowers. The stations of the cross starting on the north wall of the church, to the right of the altar . . . *Jesus is condemned to death . . . Jesus is made to bear His cross . . . Jesus is nailed to the cross . . .*

Carella walking up the side aisle now . . .

. . . a stained glass window with an air-conditioner under it.

He passed his fingers over the evaporating fins. About an inch of space between each fin. Had Hooper dropped his vials into one of the air-conditioners set under windows everywhere around the church? But he was being *chased!* He didn't have time to look, to find, to . . .

More candles against the wall.

And another offerings box.

Maybe Farnes had been right about the good priest's obsession with the tithe.

Jesus falls the first time under His cross . . .

And more candles.

And an offerings box.

And a shrine with a statue of Jesus with his open heart revealed in his chest, radiating gold-leaf rays, fresh flowers under the statue. And votive candles. And an offerings box.

Jesus meets His afflicted Mother . . .

A candle rack fastened to the stone wall had a metal lip at its topmost edge, forming a troughlike angle with the wall. He felt behind the lip. Nothing.

Double rows of candles flickering.

Where? he thought.

There were niches all over the church, rounded little insets in the stone, all of them containing statues.

He felt behind each statue for the third time, fingers widespread, searching. Nothing.

Niches everywhere.

He passed a font designed for bearing holy water, little steel basin sitting in a stone cavity. He lifted the empty basin. It fit the cavity exactly, there was not a millimeter of an inch to spare. No place to hide crack here, and besides it would have contained water on Easter Sunday, Hooper was being *chased,* he wouldn't have had time to . . .

Hey.

Hey, *wait* a minute.

Wait a holy goddamn minute!

He came running up the right-hand side of the church, passing the stations of the cross in reverse order . . .

Jesus is placed in the sepulchre . . .

. . . running past the arched doorway that led to the sacristy and the rectory beyond . . .

Jesus is taken down from the cross . . .

. . . passed another little shrine with a statue of yet another saint, flowers at his feet . . .

Jesus dies on the cross . . .

. . . opened the center inner doors, and stepped into the entrance lobby, and turned instantly to his right.

Because if the offerings box with its black tower was one of the first things Hooper had seen immediately upon entering the church, then the *next* thing he'd have seen, *had* to have seen, was the urn of holy water.

Stainless steel, sitting on a black wrought-iron stand. Little upright brass cross fastened to the top of its lid. Little brass spigot on the container below. He did not know how often this urn was refilled. But it looked too heavy to be carried to a water tap, and he was willing to bet it was regularly filled right here on the spot. Which, if true, meant that someone would simply lift the lid and pour water into the urn. He took off his jacket, unbuttoned the right-hand sleeve of his shirt, shoved the sleeve up to his elbow, and with his left hand, reached out for the brass cross fastened to the urn's lid. Virtually holding his breath, he lifted the lid and reached into the water with his free hand. Felt around. And . . .

There.

He lifted the plastic bag dripping out of the water.

It was sealed with one of those little yellow plastic ties.

He loosened it.

Kneeling, he shook the contents of the bag onto the stone floor. The bag wasn't waterproof, and so the first thing that spilled out onto the floor was a small amount of water. The vials came spilling out next. He could tell at once that water had seeped into some of them as well, partially dissolving many of the crystals, melting others entirely. But what remained looked a hell of a lot like crack.

It occurred to him that if the urn had been refilled since Easter Sunday . . .

And if Father Michael had blessed the water between then and the time of his death . . .

Then the *crack* was holy, too.

Which, in a way, in America today, it probably was.

It began raining again later that evening, just as Willis was heading crosstown to a shop called *El Castillo de Palacios*. He was going there because nobody at 1147 Hillsdale knew anyone named Carlos Ortega.

This was the address Ortega had given his Parole Board when he was released from prison in October of last year. If there was now a new address, the Department of Corrections was unaware of it. Trying to find a Carlos Ortega in a city that had locked up eighty-three of them in the last little while was akin to finding a pork roast in the state of Israel.

El Castillo de Palacios would have been ungrammatical in Spanish if the *Palacios* hadn't been a person's name, which in this case it happened to be. *Palacio* meant "palace" in Spanish, and *palacios* meant "palaces" and when you had a plural noun, the article and noun were supposed to correspond, unlike English where everything was so sloppily put together. *El Castillo de los Palacios* would have been the proper Spanish for "The Castle of the Palaces," but since Francisco Palacios was a person, *El Castillo de Palacios* was, in fact, correct even though it translated as "Palacios's Castle," a play on words however you sliced it, English *or* Spanish.

Francisco Palacios was a good-looking man with clean-living habits (now that he'd served three upstate on a burglary rap) who owned and operated this pleasant little store that sold medicinal herbs, dream books, religious statues, numbers books, tarot cards, and the like. His silent partners were named Gaucho Palacios and Cowboy Palacios, and they ran a store *behind* the other store, and *this* one offered for sale such medically approved "marital aids" as dildos, French ticklers, open crotch panties (*bragas sin entrepierna*), plastic vibrators (eight-inch and ten-inch in the white, twelve-inch in the black), leather executioner's masks, chastity belts, whips with leather thongs, leather anklets studded with chrome, penis extenders, aphrodisiacs, inflatable life-sized female dolls, condoms in every color of the rainbow including puce, books on how to hypnotize and otherwise overcome reluctant women, ben-wa balls in both plastic and gold plate, and a highly popular mechanical device guaranteed to bring satisfaction and imaginatively called Suc-u-lator.

Selling these things in this city was not illegal; the Gaucho and the Cowboy were breaking no laws. This was not why they ran their store *behind* the store owned and operated by Francisco. Rather, they did so out of a sense of responsibility to the Puerto Rican community of which they were a part. They did not, for example, want a little old lady in a black shawl to wander into their backstore shop and faint dead away at the sight of playing cards featuring men, women, police dogs and midgets in fifty-two marital-aid positions, fifty-*four* if you counted the jokers. Both the Gaucho and the Cowboy had community pride to match that of Francisco himself. Francisco, the Gaucho, and the Cowboy were, in fact, all one and the same person, and they were collectively a police informer.

Naturally, the police had something on Palacios in any one of his incarnations; nobody—well, hardly anybody—becomes a snitch merely because he believes he will be performing a community service while simultaneously enjoying a life of romantic adventure. What they had on Palacios was a small tax-fraud violation that would have sent him to a federal prison for a good many years had they chosen to exercise their option to arrest him. Palacios cheerfully accepted the grip the police held over him, and tried to lead an exemplary life. If every now and then he did a little something illegal—like moving hot CD players along with his dildos and doodads—he figured there wasn't much more he could lose. With a federal rap hanging over his head, all else seemed minor.

Willis went to him not because he was a better informer than Fats Donner—actually Donner had a slight edge when it came to providing quality information—but only because over the years Donner's penchant for young girls had become more and more unbearable; being in the same room with him was like inhaling a mix of baby powder and spermicidal gel. The Cowboy was actually pleasant to be with. Moreover, Carlos Ortega was of Hispanic origin, and so was the Cowboy, whose shop was in a section of the Eight-Seven known as *El Infierno*, which until the recent influx of Jamaicans, Koreans and Vietnamese had been almost exclusively Puerto Rican.

He was combing his hair when Willis, soaking wet after a two-block run from the bus stop, came into the back of the shop. High pompadour, the way kids used to wear it back in the Fifties. Dark brown eyes. Matinee idol teeth. It was rumored in The Inferno that Palacios had three wives, which was also against the law, but they already had him on the tax fraud. One of the wives was supposed to have been a movie star in Cuba before Castro took over. That had to put her in her fifties or sixties, Willis guessed. He got straight to the point.

"Carlos Ortega," he said.

"Gimme a break," Palacios said. "You guys come in here with Spanish names that all sound alike."

"Forty-two years old, ugly as homemade sin."

"What'd he do?"

"Nothing that we know of right now, except he's not where he's supposed to be."

"Where's that?"

"1147 Hillsdale."

"Tough neighborhood," Palacios said, which was sort of comical in that he lived in a neighborhood that had racked up three dozen corpses since the beginning of the year.

"He was busted on a drug charge," Willis said. "Did good time, got paroled in October. He's really *very* ugly, Cowboy, that might be where you start."

"If I had a nickel for everybody's ugly in this city . . ."

"Big bald guy, knife scar over his right eye, partially closing . . ."

"Popeye Ortega," Palacios said.

Which is the way it went sometimes.

The one thing Palacios forgot to tell him was that this was a crack house.

"Here's where you'll find him," he said, and gave him an address and an apartment number. If Willis had known where he was going, he might have realized that the twelve-year-old kid standing outside the building was a lookout. As it was, he walked past him as innocent as the day is long, which is maybe why the kid didn't challenge him. Or maybe it was because he didn't look at all like a cop. Five-eight, slender and slight, wearing a sports shirt open at the throat, sleeves rolled up to his elbows, blue slacks, and scuffed loafers, he could have been anyone who lived here in a housing development where blacks, whites, Hispanics and Asians lived side by side in a volatile mix. The twelve-year-old scarcely gave him a passing glance.

Still all unaware, Willis went into the lobby and took the elevator up to the third floor. Apartment 37, Palacios had told him. Ask for Popeye. A kid of about sixteen or seventeen was lounging against the wall opposite the elevator doors. The moment Willis stepped out into the third floor corridor, he said, "You looking for something?" Big husky white kid wearing a T-shirt and jeans. The shirt had the call letters of a rock radio station on it. You looking for something? And all at once, the twelve-year-old downstairs registered and Willis realized that the Cowboy had sent him to a crack house.

"I'm supposed to meet Popeye Ortega," he said.

The kid nodded.

"You know the apartment number?"

"Yes," Willis said. "Thirty-seven."

"End of the hall," the kid said, and stepped out of his way.

He did not want to go in here as a cop. If he flashed the tin, the roof would come down around his ears. But passing the scrutiny of a twelve-year-old outside and a sixteen-year-old here in the hallway was not quite the same thing as slipping undetected through enemy lines. He thought at once that he should split, put the joint under surveillance, come back another time with a hit team. But he wanted Popeye Ortega.

He went to the door of apartment 37, knocked on it.

A peephole opened.

"I'm supposed to meet Popeye Ortega," he said.

If it worked once, he figured it might work again. It did. The door opened. The man standing just inside was a big, good-looking black man who could've got a job playing the sidekick cop on a police show. The first thing he said was, "Have I seen you here before?"

"No," Willis said.

"I didn't think so."

"Popeye told me to meet him here."

"He's upstairs. What can I get you?"

"Nothing right now," Willis said.

The man looked at him.

"I'll just go talk to him," Willis said, and walked past him into the apartment. Kitchen on the left. Dead ahead, in what would have been the living room, three young men sat at a table. One black, one white, one Hispanic. Crack pipes on the table. Butane torch. Butane fuel. Crack vials. Three cream-colored rocks in a vial, cost you five bucks here and in L.A., fifteen in D.C., the nation's capital. Three rocks. Good for an instant high that lasted about thirty minutes. Then you were back in the toilet again till your next hit.

On the Coast, they called it rock. In D.C., they called it Piece of the Mountain. In this city, there were a dozen different names for it. You made the stuff in your own kitchen. You mixed cocaine powder in a pot with baking soda and you stirred it till you had a thick paste. Then you cooked the paste on your stove and you let it dry out until it resembled a round bar of soap. You broke it into chips. Another name for it. Chip. If you were a roller, you packaged it and sold it under your own brand name. If you used crack made from coke powder that had already been cut with some deadly shit like ephedrine or amphetamine, you could end up in the morgue. Users liked to know what they were smoking. They looked for brand names they could count on. Lucky Eleven. Or Mister J. Or Royal Flush. Or Paradise. Or Tease Me.

Actually, you didn't *smoke* the stuff, you *inhaled* it.

Although you *could* crunch up the rocks, and sprinkle them inside a marijuana cigarette. You called this "whoolie," the pot laced with crack, and it was one way you *could* actually smoke the product.

But you didn't normally burn it the way you burned tobacco or pot. Normally, you *melted* it.

The three young men at the table were ready to go.

They were each holding a glass pipe. This did not resemble a *real* pipe the way a glass slipper resembled a *real* slipper. This "pipe" was fashioned of a clear glass bowl with two glass tubes protruding from it on opposite sides at right angles to each other, one vertical, one horizontal. It looked more like a laboratory instrument than a smoking apparatus. You expected to see it over a Bunsen burner, with some mad scientist's evil brew boiling in it. The bowl was about the size of a tennis ball, and it had a hole in it through which water could be poured. Each glass tube was about five inches long, with a diameter of half an inch or so. You wedged your rocks—each rock weighed about a hundred milligrams—into the top of the vertical glass tube, which after very few uses became blackened, and you put the horizontal glass tube in your mouth, and you picked up the butane torch . . .

"Beam me up, Scotty," one of the young men said.

Intent on what they were doing now. Sucking flame into the tube. The rocks beginning to melt. Sucking the vapors through the water in the bowl of the pipe. Up through the other glass tube, lips tight around it, inhale the vapors, a five-second journey from the lungs to the brain, and *whammo!*

The equivalent of an orgasm, most addicts said.

Rapture.

Euphoria.

In laboratory tests, rats ignored electric shocks to get at their cocaine doses, chose cocaine over food, chose it over sex, allowed it to dictate the very course of their lives. By the end of a month, nine out of ten of them were dead.

Willis watched the young men sucking up death.

The crack house was in actuality three separate apartments on the second, third and fourth floors of the building. The floor and ceiling of the third-floor apartment had been broken through and ladders set up to allow access to the second floor below and the fourth floor above. There were entrance doors on each floor, of course, but anyone wanting to come in and smoke away the time had to come in on the third floor, where he paid his money for his vial and his pipe. The three-level arrangement also served a more practical purpose. In the event of a raid, the second and fourth floors could be emptied in a flash while the cops milled about on the entrance floor of the dope sandwich.

He found Popeye Ortega on the fourth floor.

He was sitting at a table in the far corner of the second bedroom, looking through a rain-lashed window, at least a dozen empty vials of crack spread on the table top before him. Willis did not know how long he'd been here. He looked as if he had not changed his clothes or shaved in days, and he smelled of the stench of his own urine. He kept staring through the window at the rain outside, as if viewing somewhere in the streaked greyness colors and images mere mortals could not see.

"Ortega?" Willis said.

"Scotty got dee chip, man," he said.

He was, in truth, as ugly as Marilyn had described him, as ugly as his picture and/or his description in the Buenos Aires documents and the I.S. printouts. But there was something missing here.

Willis stepped out of the room, opened a window in the hallway, and allowed the cool, clean scent of fresh rain to sweep into the apartment. He would wait until Ortega came down from his high, and then he would question him. But he already knew for certain that the man sitting in there, staring out the window and stinking of his own piss, could not be the same man who was threatening Marilyn's life. What was missing in this man was the vitality Marilyn had described. The huge ugly man in there had long ago lost all sense of direction, ambition or drive. Crack had stolen his life force. He was, in effect, already dead.

Willis took a cigarette from the package in his pocket, lighted it, and stood by the window puffing on it, looking out at the rain, wondering how long it would be before Ortega surfaced. He could hear voices from downstairs welling up in the hole that had been cut in the ceiling. The good-looking black man greeting a customer. Willis figured that while he was here, and just so it shouldn't be a total loss, he might as well ruffle a few feathers. He went down the ladder again to the third floor. He walked past the three young men sitting at the table. They had been joined by a fourth man, who was at the very moment firing up. This has to be China in the 1800's, Willis thought. This has to be a nation of drug addicts. This has to be the disgrace of the planet. This has to be an America that makes you ashamed.

The good-looking black man was sitting at a table in the kitchen.
Willis walked in with his gun in one hand and his shield in the other.

"What's this?" the black man said.

"What do you think it is?" Willis asked.

"Hey, come on, man."

"Meaning what?"

"Meaning you know."

"No, I *don't* know. Tell me."

"Come on, man."

Meaning, of course, that the fix was in. As simple as that. Hey, come
on, man, this has been taken care of, huh? Go talk to your people, man,
they tell you let it slide, huh, man? With the numbers involved in the
drug trade, there would always be somebody letting it slide, somebody
looking the other way.

"What's your name?" Willis asked.

"Come on, man."

"What's your fucking *name?*"

"Warren Jackson."

"Mind if I use your phone, Warren?"

"You steppin' in deep shit, man."

"Wait'll you see what *you're* steppin' in," Willis said, and yanked the
phone from the wall hook, and dialed the precinct number. Charlie-car
showed up in five minutes. The driver looked surprised. So did the man
riding shotgun. Both of them knew Willis.

"Gee, Hal," one of them said, "when did *this* joint spring up?"

"Surprises every day of the week," Willis said.

Warren Jackson was scowling at both of the Charlie-car cops. Willis
figured they were both in on the deal. Partners. Helping Young America smoke its fucking brains out.

"More detectives on the way," he said conversationally.

"Good," the shotgun cop said.

"You know Detective Meyer? He's on the way."

"Oh, sure," the driver said. "Meyer Meyer. The bald guy, right?"

"Right. He's got young kids."

Both cops looked at him.

"He has a thing about crack," Willis said, smiling pleasantly.

So far Warren Jackson wasn't saying anything. He was possibly
waiting for somebody to tell Willis to fuck off. But nobody was doing
it. Not yet. The young crack addicts sitting around the table knew
something was going on, but they were so far out of it, so high up on

the third moon of the planet Belix in the galaxy Romitar that they figured maybe those guys in blue uniforms were the palace guard, standing there with the big black eunuch and the short curly-haired jester, all of them guarding the Emperor Pleth's harem, this was a good movie.

"Where's your sergeant?" Warren said at last.

This was Charlie Sector, the Patrol Sergeant's name was Mickey Harrigan, a big redheaded red-faced hairbag who'd been on the force since Hector was a pup. It was entirely possible that Harrigan was in on it, too. Maybe every cop in the *sector* was in on it, including the CPEP cops on the beat.

"Call your fuckin' sergeant," Warren said, "tell him we got a misunderstandin' here."

The Charlie-car cops looked at each other. They were trying to figure what the protocol was here. They knew their Patrol Sergeant outranked Willis, but if it came to a matter for Internal Affairs, rank didn't mean a goddamn thing. Unless Willis himself was in on the deal. In which case . . .

"Sure, call him," Willis said.

They figured he wasn't in on the deal.

"Go ahead," Willis said.

The shotgun cop's name was Larry Fitzhenry. He raised Harrigan on the walkie-talkie and asked him could he please, Sarge, stop by this apartment here on Ainsley and Fifth, apartment 37, Sarge, where there seems to be some sort of misunderstanding here? Harrigan said he'd be right over. His voice sounded noncommittal. Over the years, Willis had learned that you should never trust anyone named Mickey unless his last name was Mouse.

Meyer got there before Harrigan did.

He did not like what he saw. Willis took him aside and told him he thought the proprietor was ready to blow the whistle. He figured some uniforms were about to hit the fan, at least one of them decorated with a gold shield. Meyer looked even more annoyed. The Charlie-car cops looked extremely nervous. Warren Jackson was getting angrier and angrier over the untrustworthiness of the police department.

When Harrigan showed up, he said, "What is this? What is this?"

Warren Jackson told him to get his men in line, this wasn't what three grand a week was supposed to buy.

Harrigan told the detectives he didn't know what the fuck Jackson was talking about.

Meyer said, "You're full of shit, Mickey."

Willis went upstairs to talk to Ortega.

Shad Russell refused to discuss it on the telephone.

When they met later that night, at a delicatessen on The Stem, he told her why.

"It occurs to me that perhaps you're setting me up," he said.

This was already nine o'clock. The dinner-hour rush had peaked, but neighborhood people were still straggling in and taking seats at tables near the window, where they could watch the springtime rain drilling the sidewalk outside. There were still things in this city that were nice.

"You still think I'm a cop, huh?" she said.

"Or *working* for the cops, yes," he said.

"Setting you up for *what?*"

"First for dealing guns and next for dealing dope."

"Don't be ridiculous," she said.

"Maybe I am being ridiculous," he said, and shrugged. "But maybe I'm not."

"I thought you called Houston."

"I did."

"I thought you talked to Sam Seward, how could I be a cop?"

"Maybe *he's* in their pocket, too, the Houston cops. And maybe they got you sewed up here, the cops here. All I know is first you come around looking to buy a gun, and next thing I know you've got five hundred K, and you wanna buy dope. To me, that sounds like a setup."

"Well, it isn't."

"For all I know you're wired. For all I know, you got a mike hung between your knockers. I set up a drug buy for you, I end up in a holding cell."

"I'm not wired."

"Prove it."

"How?"

"Strip," he said.

She looked at him.

She sighed heavily.

"So we're back to that again, huh?" she said.

"No, we're *not* back to *that* again," he said, mimicking her, "get your fuckin' mind out of the gutter. I call up this lady friend of mine, we go to her place, you strip for *her*, not me. She tells me you're clean, we talk."

"Did you find a deal for me?"

"No strippee, no talkee," he said.

"I cashed that check today," she said.

Shad looked at her and said nothing.

"I've got five hundred thousand in hundred-dollar bills."

Still he said nothing.

"Come on, don't be a jackass," she said.

"Lady," he said, and stood up, "it was nice meeting you."

"Sit down," she said.

"My friend lives on Darrow," he said. "Near the old Franklin Trust building. Yes or no?"

Marilyn was shaking her head in amazement.

"Yes or no?" Shad said.

Russell's lady friend was a hooker, for sure, but her apartment was tidy and well-furnished, and Marilyn guessed she worked solo. Her name—or at least the name by which she introduced herself—was Joanne. This was a common hooker name. Like Kim or Tracy or Julie or Deborah. She looked to be in her mid-thirties, but Marilyn guessed she was at least a decade younger. She told Marilyn she could undress in the bathroom.

The bathroom was spotlessly clean. Through force of habit, Marilyn checked out the medicine cabinet and found several bottles of mouthwash, three boxes of condoms, and a bottle of Johnson's Baby Oil. She took off her clothes and folded them neatly on the small wooden table opposite the sink. There were two robes hanging on the back of the door. Marilyn put on one of them. Silk. The aroma of perfume clinging to it. Something she recognized but could not for the life of her name. Not a cheap scent. She fastened the sash at her waist and came out into the bedroom wearing only the robe and her own high-heeled pumps.

Joanne looked at the robe and said, "Make yourself at home, why don't you?"

"Sorry, I thought . . ."

"You mind taking it off, please?"

Shad was sitting on the edge of the bed.

Marilyn looked at him.

"This is a *search*," Joanne said, "take off the fuckin' robe."

Shad got up, and went into the other room. Marilyn took off the robe. Joanne looked her up and down.

"Nice," she said.

"Thanks."

"Your own?"

"Yes."

"Nice," she said again. "Turn around."

Marilyn turned.

"Nice," Joanne said again. "You gay?"

"No."

"Bi?"

"No."

"That's a shame. Take off the shoes, okay?"

Marilyn slipped out of the pumps. Joanne picked them up, felt inside each of them, tested each heel to see if she could slide it away from the body of the shoe, and then handed the shoes back.

"I'll check your clothes," she said, and went into the bathroom.

Marilyn put the robe on again, and sat on the edge of the bed, her legs crossed. She desperately wanted a cigarette. In the bathroom, Joanne picked up each article of clothing—the skirt, the blouse, the bra, the slip, the pantyhose—and patted them down. She opened Marilyn's handbag, then, and whistled when she found the .38.

"Shad sold that to me," Marilyn said.

"I don't want to know," Joanne said, and continued rummaging through the bag. At last, she snapped the bag shut, said, "I'll tell him you're clean, you can dress now," and went out into the living room. Marilyn went into the bathroom, looked for her package of cigarettes, immediately lighted one, and then closed and locked the door. In the living room, she could hear their muffled voices. Alternately puffing on the cigarette and resting it on the edge of the sink, she dressed silently, and then flushed the cigarette down the toilet. When she walked out into the living room, Joanne was gone.

"She said we can talk here," Shad said.

"Fine."

"Sit down."

"Thanks."

He was sitting on a sofa covered with a pale blue fabric. Behind him was a Van Gogh poster, all yellows and oranges and bolder blues. She took a chair opposite his, crossed her legs. At the far end of the room, rain lashed the window.

"What'd you think of her?" he asked.

"Nice lady," she said.

"She told me she'd like to go down on you."

"Sorry, I'm not interested."

"You're a difficult person," he said, and sighed.

"Shad, can we talk business? Please?"

"That *is* her business," he said, and smiled the crocodile smile. "I'm glad you were clean. It really bothered me to think that maybe you were fuzz."

"Good, now let's get on with it. Have you found . . . ?"

"Did you really cash that check?"

"Yes."

"Half a mill in hundreds, huh?"

"Yes."

"What'd they say?"

"What do you mean?"

"What'd you *tell* them? Why you wanted the C-notes."

"They didn't ask."

"But didn't you feel funny? Getting all that bread in hundred-dollar bills?"

"I told them I was buying an antique vase, and the man wouldn't accept anything but cash."

"An antique vase, huh?"

"Yes. Ming Dynasty."

"Ming Dynasty, huh?"

"Museum quality."

"And they bought that, huh?"

"I'm a regular customer at the bank, they never asked me why I wanted . . ."

"But you told them, anyway, huh?"

"Yes."

"Because you felt funny, right?"

"No, because it was an unusual transaction."

"And because you used to be a hooker, right?"

Marilyn looked at him.

The rain beat a steady tattoo on the window.

"I can understand why you walked easy," he said.

"I wasn't walking *easy*," she said. "The bank *knows* me. But I felt my request *was* a bit . . ."

"But they don't know you used to be a hooker, I'll bet."

Big smile on his face. Little man with a big smile and a big secret. She wished he'd get off this tack, but he kept coming back to it, the blonde used to be a hooker, what do you know?

"So did you find a deal for me?" she asked.

"Yes," he said, "I found a deal for you."

"Good. Who?"

"A man up from Colombia, I done deals with him before."

"When will it be?"

"He'll have the eleven keys by tomorrow night."

"Good. Did you tell him I wanted to pick the place?"

"I told him. He didn't like it *but* . . ."

Shad shrugged and smiled again.

"Did you tell him one-on-one?"

"I told him. He agreed to it."

"Where'd you leave it?"

"He'll call me tomorrow night, when he's got the stuff together. I call you, you tell me where you want him to come, he'll be there in ten minutes, provided it ain't in Siam."

"What's his name?"

"Why do you need to know that?"

"I guess I don't."

"You guess right, you don't. All you need is the money."

"After I've got the stuff . . ."

"Yeah, well, first you gotta get it."

"Yes. But *after* I have it, how long do you think it'll take to turn it around?"

"Depends on who I can find. Two days maybe. Somebody to step on it—it'll cost, you know . . ."

"Yes."

"And then somebody else'll take it off your hands. All in time. Two, three days."

"Because the thing is, I haven't *got* much time, you see."

"I figured."

"I'm getting a lot of pressure, you see."

"Mmm."

"So the sooner we can turn it around, the happier I'll be."

"Oh, sure," he said. "But first you gotta make the buy, don't you?"

"Yes. But that's tomorrow night."

"Provided," Shad said.

"What do you mean *provided*? You *said* tomorrow night, didn't you?"

"Yeah, to meet him."

"Yes."

"Test the stuff, taste it . . ."

"Yes."

"Which you don't know how to do, right?"

"Well . . . that shouldn't be a problem. You said you'd . . ."

"Yeah, I said I'd teach you."

"Yes."

"To taste it," he said, and smiled.

She looked at him.

A fresh wind swept torrents of rain against the window.

"You really want me to put you in touch with this guy, don't you?" he said.

Smiling.

She kept looking at him.

"Well, don't you?" he said.

"You know I do."

"Because this deal is very important to you, right?"

"Yes," she said.

"Very important," he said.

"Yes."

"Sure."

Smiling.

"Well, don't worry about it," he said. "Everything'll be all right."

"I hope so," she said.

"Oh, sure," he said. "Provided."

His eyes met hers.

The rain and the wind rattled the window.

"Come here, baby," he said, and began unzipping his fly.

She went immediately to the door.

It was locked.

A dead bolt.

The key gone.

In prison that first time, the door had been locked from the outside. The warden—*El Alcaide,* a squat little man wearing jodhpurs and high, brown-leather boots, a riding crop in his hand—had asked her to raise her gown for him. She'd run to the door, but it was locked. She'd twisted the unresponsive doorknob again and again, shouting "Help!" in English and then *"Socorro!"* in Spanish, the warden coming up behind her, the riding crop raised . . .

Never again, she thought.

She took the .38 from her handbag.

"Unlock the door," she said.

He looked at the gun in her fist.

"Now," she said.

"You're a hooker," he said. "What's another blowjob more or . . . ?"

She almost shot him dead on the spot that very minute. Her finger almost tightened that last millimeter on the trigger, she almost spattered his brains on the wall. Instead, she turned to the door and leveled the gun at it, and fired repeatedly at the wood, splintering the area around the lock. Shad sat bolt upright on the sofa, his words cut off by the explosions, his eyes saucer wide, his fly open. Marilyn twisted the knob, and pulled open the door, tearing the latch assembly from the tattered wood, its bolt still engaged in the doorframe's striker plate.

"Now there'll be cops," he said, almost petulantly.

"Good," she said. "*You* explain it to them."

Doors were opening all up and down the hallway. Curious tenants who knew that a hooker lived in 6C, and who were expecting trouble sooner or later, and here it was on a rainy spring night. She walked swiftly past them, and went down the steps and out into the street. People who had heard the shots were gathering near the front stoop. She could hear a police siren in the distance. She walked away swiftly, through the rain.

She was thinking that now she'd have to kill the two men from Argentina.

12

THE TWO DETECTIVES stood before Lieutenant Byrnes's desk like a pair of apprehensive schoolboys about to be birched by the headmaster. The fact that it was still raining that Thursday did little to help the pervasive feeling of impending doom. This was the last day of May. It was now two in the afternoon. In just five hours, the priest would have been dead for a full week.

Silvery rainsnakes slithered down each of the lieutenant's corner windows, the grey beyond much duller than the grey of his hair, which was still short-cropped but growing increasingly whiter over the years. Frowning, he sat behind his desk, hands folded in front of him. The knuckles were oversized, a legacy from his youthful days as a street fighter. His shaggy white brows were lowered over flinty blue eyes. The rain oozed on either side of him.

"Let me hear it," he said.

"I went to see Bobby Corrente late last night," Carella said. "He's already out on bail . . ."

"Naturally."

". . . I found him at home with his parents. I figured since we've already got him for tearing a church apart and assaulting a priest . . ."

"Yes, yes," Byrnes said impatiently.

"But he's got an alibi for the night of the murder."

"A reliable witness?"

"His father."

"Worthless," Byrnes said.

"Hooper's got an alibi, too," Hawes said. "I talked to him this morning."

"Who's *his* witness?"

"His sister."

"Also worthless," Byrnes said.

"But they both knew there was crack hidden inside . . ."

"Where was it, by the way?"

"In the holy water urn."

"Jesus," Byrnes said, and shook his head. "How about the weapon? Have you found that yet?"

"Not anywhere in the church. And we've searched it a hundred times already. The point is, if either Hooper *or* Corrente went back for that dope . . ."

"Except you're just telling me they've both got alibis."

"Which *you're* telling me are worthless," Carella said.

"Which they are," Byrnes said. "What about this Farnes character, is that his name?"

"Farnes, yes."

"What's *his* alibi?"

"His inventory log," Carella said.

"Which he himself dated," Hawes said.

"So far you're giving me nothing but alibis that aren't alibis at all," Byrnes said. "What else have you got?"

"Only *more* alibis that aren't alibis," Carella said. "This gay guy who painted the star . . ."

"His name again?"

"Hobbs. Andrew Hobbs. He claims he was in bed with a man named Jeremy Sachs on the night of the murder."

"Terrific."

"We haven't been able to locate his mother . . ."

"Her name?"

"Abigail. I guess. He calls her Abby, I guess it's Abigail."

"Okay, Abigail Hobbs, what about her?"

"She went to Father Michael for help. We want to ask her just how angry this made him."

"The son?"

"Yeah. Meyer says he was *still* pissed about it. The priest was stabbed seventeen times, Pete. That's anger."

"Agreed. So find her."

"We're trying."

"What about the secretary?" Byrnes asked.

"What about her?" Hawes said.

Defensively, it seemed to Carella.

"Could she have been the one the priest was diddling?"

"I don't think so," Hawes said.

"On what do you base that?"

"Well . . . she just doesn't seem like the sort of person who'd get involved in something like that."

Byrnes looked at him.

"She just doesn't," Hawes said, and shrugged.

"The Class Valedictorian, right?" Byrnes said.

"What?" Hawes said.

"Brightest kid in the class, handsome as can be, witty, ambitious, kills his mother, his father, both his sisters and his pet goldfish. But he didn't *seem* like that sort of person. Right?"

"Well . . ."

"Don't give me *seems*," Byrnes said. "And don't tell me there aren't any secretaries who fool around with their bosses. Find out where she was and what she was doing on the night of the murder."

"Yes, sir," Hawes said.

"And locate this gay guy's mother, Hobbs, find out what the hell *that's* all about."

"Yes, sir," Carella said.

"So do it," Byrnes said.

A good time to visit a church devoted to worshipping the Devil was on a rainy day, Carella guessed. As he came up the street, he saw through the falling rain the old soot-stained stones of what had first and very long ago been a Catholic church, and then a storehouse for grain during the Civil War, and briefly a Baptist church, and then a warehouse for sewing machines, and then a convenient location for antiques shows and crafts shows until the neighborhood began crumbling everywhere around it. Now it was The Church of the Bornless One, though nothing advised the casual observer of this fact.

He saw only wet, sootened stones against a gunmetal sky, the outline of a building that seemed to squat on its haunches ready to pounce, tethered to the earth by flying buttresses. He climbed the low flat steps to the entrance and tried the knobs on both doors. Both were locked. He went around the side to what he guessed was the rectory door. A bell button was set into the stone. A tarnished brass escutcheon over it read *Ring for Service*. He rang for service. And waited in the rain.

The woman who answered the door had long blonde hair, a button nose dusted with freckles, and eyes the color of cobalt. She was wearing blue jeans and a white T-shirt with a tiny red devil's head as a discreet logo over the left breast. Carella figured he'd come to the right place.

"Yes?" she said.

"I'm looking for Mr. Lutherson," he said, and showed her his shield and his I.D. card.

"You're not the one we spoke to," she said.

"No, I'm not," Carella admitted. "May I come in, please? It's a little wet out here."

"Oh, *yes,*" she said, *"excuse* me, come in, come in, please."

She stepped back and away from him. She was barefoot, he noticed. They were standing in what was a small oval entrance foyer fashioned of stone and lined with niches similar to the ones at St. Catherine's, except that these were devoid of statues.

"Didn't Andrew Hobbs come talk to you?" she asked at once.

"Not to me personally," Carella said. "But, yes, he did speak to us."

"Then you know he's the one who . . ."

"Yes, painted the star."

"The pentagram, yes."

"Yes."

"Let me tell Sky you're here," she said. "What was your name again?"

"Carella. Detective Carella."

"I'll tell him," she said, and turned and went padding off into the gloom.

He waited in the foyer. Outside a water spout splashed noisily. He wondered what they did here. He wondered if they were breaking any laws here. You read stories about all these sensational ritual murders, people killing people for the Devil, you began to think the whole *world* was worshipping Satan. Slitting the throats of little babes, dripping their blood into sacrificial basins. Most of these cults sacrificed chickens or goats, hardly any of them were foolish enough or reckless enough to dabble in human sacrifice. In this city, there were no laws as such against sacrificing animals. Who was to say that tossing a lobster into a pot of boiling water wasn't sacrifice of a sort? There were, however, laws against inhumane methods of slaughtering, and if you were in a mood to bust a cult that practiced animal sacrifice, you could always nail them on a bullshit violation. He was not here to bust a cult. He was here to learn a bit more about . . .

"Mr. Carella?"

He turned.

A tall blond man had materialized in the foyer, stepping from the darkness beyond one of the arched portals. Like the woman who'd answered the door, he too was wearing jeans and the white T-shirt with the devil's-head logo. He, too, was barefoot. The body of a weight lifter, lean and clean, Carella was willing to bet next month's salary that this cat had done time. A bend in the otherwise perfect nose, where it had once been broken. A Mick Jagger mouth. Pearly white teeth. Eyes as blue as the woman's had been, were they brother and sister?

"I'm Schuyler Lutherson," he said, smiling, "welcome to The Church of the Bornless One."

He extended his hand. Carella took it, and they shook hands briefly. Lutherson's grip was firm and dry. Carella had read someplace that a firm, dry grip was a sign of character. As opposed to a limp, wet one, he guessed. He was willing to bet another month's salary that a great many murderers in this world had firm, dry grips.

"Come on inside," Lutherson said, and led him through an arched portal opposite the one through which he'd entered, and down a stone corridor, more empty niches in the walls, and then opened a heavy oaken door that led into a wood-paneled room that had once been a library, but which was now lined only with empty shelves. A thriftshop desk was in the center of the room. There was a chair behind it and two chairs in front of it. A standing floor lamp with a cream-colored shade was in one corner of the room. Lutherson sat behind the desk. Carella sat opposite him.

"So," Lutherson said. "I hope you're making progress with your case."

Hands tented, fingers and thumbs gently touching. Looking at Carella over his hands. Smiling pleasantly.

"Not very much," Carella said.

"I'm sorry to hear that. I thought when we offered our cooperation, this would at least, see, clear up any doubts along *those* lines. That anyone here at Bornless might be involved, see. In the murder of the priest."

"Uh-huh," Carella said.

"Which is why we asked him to go to the police. Hobbs. The minute we found out he was the one who'd defaced that gate."

"As a matter of fact, he's the reason I'm here today."

"Oh?"

Blue eyes opening wide.

"Yes. We've been trying to locate his mother, but we can't find a telephone listing for her, and we . . ."

"Why don't you ask Hobbs?"

"We did. He doesn't know."

"He doesn't know his own mother's *telephone* number?"

"They don't get along. She moved six months ago, and neither of them has made any attempt to contact each other since."

"Well, I wish I could help you, but . . ."

"Did Hobbs ever mention her to you?"

"No. In fact, the first time I ever *spoke* to Hobbs was last Saturday night."

"I thought he was a regular member of your congregation. According to Jeremy Sachs . . ."

"Yes, I know Jer . . ."

". . . he introduced Hobbs to your church in March sometime."

"I do know Jeremy, and that may be true. But people come and go, see, it's a transient group. A lot of people are attracted by the novelty of it, and then they realize that this is a serious *religion* here, see, we're serious *worshippers* here, and they drop out."

"But you'd never talked to Hobbs before last Saturday."

"Correct."

"You'd seen him here, though, hadn't you?"

"Not that I can recall. But I'm sure if Jeremy says he's been coming here since March, then I have no reason to doubt his word. It's just that I wasn't familiar with him personally."

"And so you wouldn't have any information about his mother."

"No."

"Abigail Hobbs."

"No. I'm sorry."

"You wouldn't have met her . . ."

"How would I have met her?"

"Well, she could have come here in an attempt to . . ."

"No, I've never met anyone named Abigail Hobbs."

"I guess you'd remember if she came here."

"Yes, I'm sure I'd remember."

"Before going to see Father Michael. To ask you to talk to her son, convince him to leave the church, whatever. You don't remember anything like that, is that right?"

"Nothing like that, no. I can say very definitely that I don't know anyone named Abigail Hobbs."

"Well, thank you, Mr. Lutherson," Carella said, and sighed. "I appreciate your time."

"Not at all. Feel free to stop in whenever you like," Lutherson said, and rose from behind the desk and extended his hand again.

The men shook hands. Firm and dry, the grip of the Devil's disciple.

"I'll show you out," Lutherson said, which Carella thought happened only in movies.

She'd told him she was going to a cattle-call audition that afternoon and that he could meet her outside the Alice Weiss Theater downtown at about five o'clock, by which time she hoped she'd be through. Hawes waited under the theater marquee now, watching the falling rain, watching the pedestrians rushing past on their way to the subways and home. He wanted to be going home, too. Instead, he stood here waiting for Krissie Lund.

Right after their meeting in the lieutenant's office, Carella had told him that Alexis O'Donnell had seen a blonde woman with Father Michael on Easter Sunday. Whether or not the blonde had been Krissie was yet another matter; there were a great many blondes in this world, including Alexis herself. But it bothered Hawes that she might have been. Because *whoever* the blonde was, Father Michael had accused her of blackmail. And blackmail, otherwise known as extortion, was defined in Section 850 of the state's Penal Law as "the obtaining of property from another induced by a wrongful use of force or fear." And listed under the threats that constituted extortion was: *To expose any secret affecting him.*

If, for example, the blonde arguing with Father Michael on Easter Sunday had threatened to expose his love affair unless he paid her a substantial sum of money or gave her property *worth* money—a house in the country, a diamond bracelet, an Arabian show horse—this would have been blackmail.

This is blackmail, the priest had shouted.

According to Alexis O'Donnell.

Who had seen a blonde.

Blackmail, or extortion, was punishable by a max of fifteen years.

A long stretch up the river if you threatened to tattle unless someone paid you off. Which potential stay in the country often provided a good reason for murder. Most often, of course, it was the intended victim who murdered his blackmailer. Better murder than exposure. But what if the victim threw all caution to the winds and threatened to *report* the blackmail attempt? Oh, yeah? Take this, you dirty rotten rat!

Not so funny when it happened in real life.

If Alexis O'Donnell had heard and seen correctly, a blonde had been with Father Michael on Easter Sunday, and she had threatened him with what he'd considered blackmail. If that blonde was Krissie Lund . . .

"Hi, have you been waiting long?" she said, and took his arm.

Carella was waiting outside the First Fidelity Savings and Trust when Andrew Hobbs came out of the bank at a quarter past five that afternoon. Hatless and without an umbrella, he pulled up the collar of his raincoat, ducked his head, and plunged bravely into the teeming rain.

"Mr. Hobbs?" Carella said, and fell into step beside him. "I'm sorry to bother you again . . ."

"Yes, well, you *are*," Hobbs said.

"But we've been unable to reach your mother . . ."

"I don't want to hear another word about that bitch."

The rain was relentless. Both men virtually galloped through it, Hobbs obviously intent on reaching the subway kiosk on the corner, Carella merely trying to keep up. When at last they'd reached the sanctuary of the underground station, Carella grabbed Hobbs's arm, turned him around, and somewhat angrily said, "Hold *up* a minute, will you?"

Hobbs was reaching into his trouser pocket for a subway token. His blond hair was plastered to his forehead, his raincoat, trouser legs, and shoes were thoroughly soaked. He shook off Carella's hand impatiently, found his token, glanced toward the platform to see if a train was coming in, and then impatiently said, "What is it you want from me?"

"Your mother's phone number."

Sodden, homeward-bound commuters rushed past on their way to the token booth and the turnstiles. Standing against the graffiti-sprayed tile wall some four or five yards away were two young men, one of them playing acoustic guitar very badly, the other sitting against the wall with a cardboard sign hanging around his neck. The sign read: WE ARE HOMELESS, THANK YOU FOR YOUR HELP. Hobbs glanced again toward the platform, and then turned back to Carella and said in the same impatient voice, "I don't *have* her number, I already *told* you that. Why don't you look it up in the damn phone book?"

"We have, she's not listed."

"Don't be ridiculous. Abby not listed? Abby taking the risk of missing a phone call from a *man*? Really."

"Mr. Hobbs," Carella said, "your mother was one of the people who'd had contact with Father Michael in the several weeks before his death. We'd like to talk to her."

"You don't think *she* killed him, do you?"

"We don't know *who* killed him, Mr. Hobbs. We're merely exploring every possibility."

"Wouldn't *that* be a hoot! Abby killing the asshole who was supposed to save me from the Devil!"

"The point is . . ."

And here Carella launched into a somewhat creative improvisation, in that the *real* reason he wanted to talk to Abigail Hobbs was to explore further her son's anger and his potential for violence . . .

". . . whatever Father Michael may have said to her, however unimportant it might have seemed at the time, could possibly be of enormous value to us now, in retrospect, if it sheds light on events in the past that could conceivably relate to the murder, though at the time it may have appeared insignificant."

Hobbs tried to digest this.

Then he said, "You're not suggesting he might have *confided* in Abby, are you? Because quite frankly, Mr. Carella, that would be tantamount to confiding in a boa constrictor."

"We won't know until we talk to her, will we?" Carella said.

"Don't you people have ways of getting unlisted numbers?"

"We do. And we tried them. The phone company doesn't have a listing anywhere in the city for anyone named Abigail Hobbs."

"Small wonder," Hobbs said, and smiled.

Carella looked at him.

"Her name isn't Abigail Hobbs."

"Your mother's name . . ."

"She divorced my father ten years ago," Hobbs said. "She's been using her maiden name ever since."

The hotel had a French name but its staff was strictly American and when the maître d' in what was called the *Café du Bois* said, "Bonn swarr, mess-yoor, will there be two for drinks?" Hawes didn't feel particularly transported to Gay Paree. The maître showed him through a glade of real birch trees under a glass canopy, usually nourished by sunshine but not today when the rain was beating steadily overhead. At the far end of the lounge a man was playing French-sounding songs on the piano. Krissie slung her shoulder bag over the back of the chair, sat, tossed her hair, and said, "I have to call my agent when I get a minute. She'll want to know how it went."

On the way here in the rain, she'd told Hawes that they'd asked her to read *two* scenes rather than the one scene they'd asked all the other actresses to read. She considered this a good sign. Hawes said he hoped she'd get the part. He ordered drinks for both of them now—the gin and tonic Krissie requested, and a Diet Pepsi for himself since he was still on duty—and then he said, "There are some questions I have to ask you, Krissie, I hope you don't mind."

"Don't look so serious," she said.

"I want you to tell me, first of all, where you were between six-thirty and seven-thirty on the night of May twenty-fourth."

"Oh, my," she said, and rolled her eyes. "This *is* serious, isn't it?"

"Yes."

"That's when Father Michael was killed, isn't it?"

"Yes."

"And you want to know where I . . ."

"Where you were while he was being killed, yes."

"My, my."

"Yes," he said.

"What are you going to ask next? Was I having an affair with him?"

"Were you?"

"As for where I was that night," she said, "I can tell you in a minute."

"Please do," he said.

"Because I write down everything in my appointment calendar," she said, and swung the shoulder bag around so that she could reach into it, and pulled out a binder book with black plastic covers. "Although I can't say I appreciate your inviting me for a drink under false pretenses."

"Krissie," he said wearily, "I'm investigating a murder."

"Then you should have told me on the phone that this was a *business* meeting."

"I told you I . . ."

"You said you wanted to see me," she said, angrily flipping pages, "not that you wanted to see me to *question* me. Here," she said, "May," she said, "let's see what I was doing on the twenty-fourth, okay?"

The waiter came back to the table.

"The gin and tonic?" he asked.

"The lady," Hawes said.

It occurred to him that she had not yet said whether or not she was having an affair with Father Michael.

The waiter put down her drink, and then turned to Hawes and said, "And a Diet Pepsi," giving him a look that indicated *real* men drank *booze.* "Enjoy your drinks, folks," he said, and smiled pleasantly, and walked off. At the other end of the room, the piano player was playing a song about going away. Krissie took a sip of her drink and turned immediately to her calendar again.

"May twenty-fourth," she said.

Hawes waited.

"To begin with, the twenty-fourth was a Thursday, so I was *working* that day, I worked at the church on Tuesdays and Thursdays, remember?"

"Yes."

"Which meant I was there from nine to five, so my first appointment was at five-thirty, do you see it here?" she said, "with Ellie, here's her name," turning the book so Hawes could see it. "That's my agent, Ellie Weinberger Associates, I met her at The Red Balloon at five-thirty."

"Okay," Hawes said. He was already reading ahead in the calendar space for Thursday, the twenty-fourth of May. On that day, Krissie's next appointment was . . .

"At eight o'clock, I met this man for dinner, he was putting together an off-Broadway revue of famous vaudeville skits, and he wanted to talk to me about directing one of them. I've never directed before, this would have been a wonderful opportunity for me. His name is Harry Grundle, I met him at a restaurant called . . . do you see it here? Eight P.M., Harry Grundle, Turner's? That's where I was."

"What time did you leave your agent?"

"Around six-thirty."

"Where's The Red Balloon?"

"On the Circle."

"Where'd you go when you left her?"

"Home to bathe and change for my dinner date."

"And where's Turner's?"

"In the Quarter. Near my apartment, actually."

"Do you drive a car?"

"No."

"How'd you get from one place to the other?"

"By subway from the church to The Red Balloon. I took a taxi home, and walked from my apartment to Turner's."

"Do you remember what you were wearing?"

"I wore a cotton dress to work and to meet Ellie. Then I changed into something dressier."

"Like what?"

"A blue suit, I think. Also cotton. It was a very hot day."

"What color was the dress you wore to work?"

"Blue."

"Both blue, is that it?"

"It's my favorite color," she said, and closed the book.

He was thinking that it would not have taken more than twenty minutes by subway from the church to Grover Park Circle. If she'd left her agent at six-thirty, as she said she had, she could have been back uptown again by ten minutes to seven. The priest was killed sometime after seven. And she'd still have had time to taxi downtown to meet Grundle.

He was also thinking that he would have to check with Mrs. Hennessy to get a description of the dress Krissie had been wearing to work that day, and he would have to look up Harry Grundle to ask him what she'd been wearing that night. Because if she *hadn't* gone home to bathe and change her clothes . . .

"How about Easter Sunday?" he said. "Does your calendar have anything for Easter Sunday?"

"I don't like you when you're this way," she said.

"What way?"

"Like every shitty cop I've ever met in my life."

"Sorry," he said, "but I *am* a cop."

"You don't have to be a shitty one."

"Where were you on Easter Sunday between two-thirty and three P.M.?"

"You know, it occurs to me that maybe I ought to have a lawyer here."

"Shall I read you your rights?" he asked, and tried a smile. But there was something that truly bothered him here. Not that she had no real alibi for the hour and a half between six-thirty and eight on the twenty-fourth of May, but because her attitude had become so very defensive the moment he began asking questions. Maybe his technique was rotten, maybe that was it. Or maybe . . .

"I really don't think you need a lawyer," he said. "Do you *know* where you were on Easter Sunday?"

"Yes, of *course* I know where I was," she said, and flipped the book open again, and said, "When the hell was Easter Sunday?"

"The fifteenth, I think. Of April."

"I'm pretty sure I was in the country. My friends have a house in the country, I'm pretty sure I spent Easter with them."

She kept flipping pages until she came to April.

"The fifteenth," she said, almost to herself.

"Yes," he said.

"I have nothing for that day," she said, and looked up. "That's odd. Because I could swear I went to the country. I can't imagine being alone on Easter Sunday. Unless I was in rehearsal for something. In which case . . ." She looked at the book again. "Well, sure, here it is. I did a showcase on the twenty-first, a Saturday night. I was probably learning lines the Sunday before because—here, do you see it?—rehearsals began the next day, Monday the sixteenth, here."

She was tapping the calendar box with her forefinger.

Rehearsal, the entry read.

YMCA.

7:00 P.M.

"Was anyone with you?" he asked.

"Oh, yes. We were rehearsing a scene from a new play, there were at least . . ."

"On Easter. While you were learning your lines."

"I believe I was alone."

"No one to cue you?"

"No, I believe I was alone."

"You didn't go up to St. Catherine's that day, did you?"

"Why would I do that?"

"I have no idea. Did you?"

"No."

"What was your relationship with Father Michael?"

"I *wasn't* having an affair with him, if we're back to that."

"Was there ever anything between you that went beyond a strictly business relationship?"

"Yes," she said, surprising him.

"In what way?" he asked.

"I found him extremely attractive. And I suppose . . . if I'm to be perfectly honest with myself . . . I suppose I flirted with him on occasion."

"Flirted how?"

"Well, the walk . . . you know."

"What walk?"

"Well, you know how women walk when they want to attract attention."

"Uh-huh."

"And eye contact, I guess. And an occasional show of leg, like that. Well, you know how women flirt."

"Are you Catholic?" he asked.

"No."

"So you found it perfectly okay, I guess, to flirt with a priest."

"You sound angry," she said, and smiled at him.

"No, I'm not angry, I'm simply trying to . . ."

"But you sound angry."

"It was okay to flirt with a priest, is that right? The walk, the eye contact, the occasional show of leg, isn't that what you called it, all that? That was all perfectly okay."

"Oh, come on, we've all had that fantasy, haven't we? Nuns? Priests? What do you think *The Thorn Birds* was all about, if not wanting to go to bed with a priest? Didn't you read *The Thorn Birds?*"

"No," he said.

"Or see the mini-series?"

"No."

"Only everybody in the entire *world* saw the mini-series."

"But not me. Was that *your* fantasy? Wanting to go to bed with Father Michael?"

"I thought about it, yes."

"And apparently acted on it."

"Acting's a pretty good word for it, actually. Because in many ways it was almost like playing Meggie in *The Thorn Birds*. Or Sada Thompson in *Rain,* do you know *Rain?* I did it in class last year. You have to try *all* sorts of parts, you know, if you want to stretch your natural talent. These women involved with priests are very interesting. Or the Bette Davis character in *Of Human Bondage,* do you know that one? He's not a priest, of course, he's a cripple, but that's sort of the same thing, isn't it? Not that I'm suggesting a priest is a cripple, but only that he's a person handicapped by his vows, who can't give vent to his natural instincts or desires, his urges really, because he's bound by these vows he's made, he's handicapped in *that* way . . . well, he *is* sort of crippled, actually. So it was . . . well, very interesting. To be playing this sort of part, and to . . . well . . . observe his reactions. It made the job more interesting. I mean, the job was *very* boring, you know. This made it interesting."

"Sure," Hawes said.

Actresses, he thought.

"But it never went beyond that," he said.

"Never."

"You never . . ."

"Well," she said, and hesitated.

He waited.

"I could see he was interested, you know."

"Uh-huh."

"I mean . . . he was *aware* of me, let's put it that way."

"Uh-huh."

"Watching me, you know."

"Uh-huh."

"Aware of me."

She sipped at her drink, and then looked thoughtfully into her glass, as if searching for truth under the lime and ice cubes.

"I have to admit," she said, and again hesitated. "If he'd made the slightest move . . . if he'd taken it that single step beyond . . . you know . . . *looking* . . . I might have gone all the way. Because, I'll tell you the truth, I'm being perfectly honest with you, I'm scared to death of sex these days. Because of AIDS. I haven't been to bed with anyone in the past year, I'm telling you the absolute truth. And I thought . . . and maybe this is why I started it, the flirting, you know . . . I thought at least *this* would be safe. Sex with a priest would be completely safe."

She looked up into his face.

Her eyes met his.

"I don't know," she said, "do you think I'm terrible?"

"Yes," he said.

But that didn't mean she'd killed him.

"I'll just get the check," he said.

Abigail Finch was a beautiful blonde woman wearing yellow tights, a black leotard top, and high-heeled black leather pumps that added a good three inches to her already substantial height. When she let Carella into her Calm's Point apartment at seven o'clock that evening, she explained that she'd just come in from exercise class when he called, and hadn't had time to change. Except for your shoes, he thought, but did not say.

Miss Finch . . .

"Please call me Abby," she said at once . . .

. . . had to have been at least forty (her son was, after all, in his twenties) but she looked no older than thirty-two or -three. Proud of her carefully honed appearance, she walked ahead of him into the living room, offered him a seat, asked if he'd like something to drink, and then turned to face him on the sofa, her knees touching his briefly before she repositioned herself, folding her long legs under her, placing her hands demurely in her lap. There was incense burning somewhere in the room, and Miss Finch herself—*Abby*—was wearing a perfume thick with insinuation. Carella felt as if he'd inadvertently dropped into a whorehouse in Singapore. He decided he'd better get to the point fast and get the hell out of here. That was exactly how threatened he felt.

"It was good of you to see me, Miss Finch," he said. "I'll try not to . . ."

"Abby," she said. "Please."

"I'll try not to take up too much of your time," he said. "It's our understanding . . ."

"Are you sure you wouldn't like a drink?"

Leaning toward him, placing one hand lightly on his arm.

A toucher, he thought.

"Thank you, no," he said, "I'm still officially on duty."

"Would you mind if I had one?"

"Not at all," he said.

She swiveled off the sofa, moved like a dancer to a bar with a dropleaf front, opened it, looked back over her shoulder like Betty Grable in the famous World War II poster, smiled, and said, "Something soft?"

"Nothing, thank you," he said.

She poured something dark into a short glass, dropped several ice cubes into it, and came back to the sofa.

"To the good life," she said, and smiled mysteriously, as if she'd made a joke he could never hope to understand.

"Miss Finch," he said, "it's our . . ."

"Abby," she said, and raised her eyebrows in reprimand.

"Abby, yes," he said. "It's our understanding that you went to see Father Michael to ask for his assistance in . . ."

"Yes, in March sometime. Toward the end of March. Because I'd learned that my son was fooling around with witchcraft . . ."

"Well, not witchcraft, certainly . . ."

"The same thing, isn't it? Devil worship? Worse, in fact."

And smiled again, mysteriously.

"And you wanted his help, you wanted him to talk to your son . . ."

"Well, yes, would you want *your* son involved in such stuff? I went to see Father Michael because Bornless was so *close* to St. Catherine's. And I thought if Andrew got a call from a priest . . . he was raised as a Catholic, you know . . . it might carry some weight."

"How'd you find out your son was attending services . . . if that's what they're called . . ."

"Masses," she said. "I guess. I forget who told me. It was someone I ran into, she said did I know my son was involved in Satanism? A woman who knew both me *and* Andrew."

"But why did you care?"

"I'm sorry?"

"You and your son are estranged, why'd you care *what* he was doing?"

"My son worshipping the *Devil?*" she said, looking astonished. "How would you like to have *that* going around town? That your faggot son is also involved in *Satanism?*"

"You mean . . . well, I'm not sure what you mean. Were you afraid this would reflect upon you in some way?"

"Of course it would. God knows I'm not a good Catholic anymore, but a person can't just forget her upbringing *entirely,* can she?"

And smiled mysteriously again, as if mocking her own words.

"So you went to see Father Michael . . ." Carella said.

"Yes. That was the church I used to attend. Before my fall from grace," she said, and lowered her eyes like a nun, and again he had the feeling that she was mocking him, but he could not for the life of him imagine why.

"I see," he said. "And you told him . . ."

"I told him my son was worshipping the Devil. Three, four blocks from his own church! And I asked him to get in touch with Andrew . . ."

"Which he did."

"Yes."

"Which made your son very angry."

"Well, I really don't care how *angry* it made him. I just wanted him to stop going to that damn church."

"And this was toward the end of March? When you went to see him."

"Yes, the first time."

"Oh? Were there other times?"

"Well, I . . ."

Her blondeness suddenly registered on him.

That and her blatant sexuality.

"How often *did* you see him?" he asked.

"Once or twice."

"Including your initial visit toward the end of March?"

"Yes."

"Then it was only twice."

"Well, yes. Well, maybe three times."

"Which?"

"Three times. I guess."

"Starting sometime toward the end of March."

"Yes."

"*When* in March?"

"Would you mind telling me . . . ?"

"Do you remember when?"

"Why is this important to you?"

"Because he was killed," Carella said flatly.

Her look, accompanied by an almost indiscernible shrug, said *What's that got to do with* me?

"When in March?" he asked again.

"It was a Friday," she said. "I don't remember exactly when."

Carella took out his notebook, and turned to the calendar page at the back of the book. "The last Friday in March was the thirtieth. Was that it?"

"No. Before then."

"The twenty-third?"

"Possibly."

"And the next time?"

"In April sometime."

"Can you remember the date?"

"I'm sorry, no. Look, I know the man was killed, but . . ."

"Were you with him on Easter Sunday?" Carella asked.

Sometimes, when you zeroed in that way, they figured you were already in possession of the facts. You had them. They didn't know how, but they knew you already knew, and there was no sense lying.

"As a matter of fact, I was," she said.

Rashomon never ends.

Carella has already heard five tellings, count 'em, *five,* of the Easter Sunday Saga, as it is now known to the entire literate world, but there is yet another version to come and this one will be Abigail Finch's, Her Story, and she is going to tell it full out, no holds barred, a premise—

and a promise—that is evident in her first eight words: "I went there to make love to him."

By that time . . .

This is now the fifteenth day of April, and a blustery day at that, perfect for making love in the cozy stone corners of a rectory . . .

By that time, they've been doing *exactly* that—here and there, on and off, so to speak—for a good two weeks, ever since the first of April, when she went to see the priest for the *second* time. As she reports it now, it was there in the rectory on that April Fool's Day that she was mischievously prompted, in the spirit of the occasion, to seduce the good father. Attracted at their first meeting to his Gene Kelly smile and his breezy unpriestlike manner, she had begun wondering what he *wore* under that silly cassock of his, and she was now determined to find out. She was astonished to learn, however . . .

For whereas she *knows* she's an enormously desirable woman who takes very good care of herself, after all, not only the exercise classes, but also bicycling in the park, and milk baths for her skin, she's been told by people who should know that she possibly ranks among the city's great beauties, of which there are many, well, she doesn't wish to sound immodest . . .

. . . but she was nonetheless enormously surprised, on that first day of April, by his extreme state of *readiness*. It was almost as if some designing woman had been *preparing* him for her—working him over, softening the ground, so to speak—because as it turned out, the good father was an absolute pushover, Little Mr. Roundheels himself, head over cassock, a flash of eye, a show of leg, and he was on her in a minute, fumbling for the buttons of her blouse and confessing that once upon a time, before he joined the ministry, he'd done it on a rooftop for the first and last time with a fourteen-year-old girl named Felicia Randall.

Abby admits to Carella now that there was something deliciously sinful about doing it with a priest, something that kept her coming . . .

"You should pardon the expression . . ." she said.

. . . back to the church again and again, three, four times a week, morning, noon and night . . .

"I lied about only having seen him a few times . . ."

. . . something that took her back there on Easter Sunday as well. Which, after all, is a time for celebration, isn't it, Easter? The Resurrection of Christ, and all that? So why not celebrate? Which she is there to do on this Holy Day of the Sixth Telling of Rashomon,

Easter Sunday, the fifteenth day of April in the Year of Our Lord, Amen.

She is wearing for the occasion of the priest's twelfth despoiling—she has counted the number of times they've done it since April Fool's Day—a simple woolen suit appropriate to the chill of the season, beneath which are a garter belt and silk tap pants she bought at Victoria's Secret, and seamed silk stockings and nothing else, the priest having told her on more than one occasion that he loves watching her naked breasts spill free each time he unbuttons her blouse, perhaps recalling his similar experience with the young but bountiful Felicia on the rooftop. But all to her surprise, he tells Abby that he wants to end it, that their relationship is filling him with guilt and remorse, that he feels a traitor to his church, his God, and his sacred vows, and that he has even contemplated suicide . . .

"A lot of men have told me that," she said.

. . . so please, Ab, we must end it, this is driving me crazy, Ab . . .

"He used to call me Ab, it was a pet name . . ."

. . . please, have mercy on me, let me end it, please, my dearest.

"He also called me his dearest . . ."

. . . which Ab, his dearest, has no intention of doing. Ending it, that is. She is enjoying this too much, this sinful expedition into the darkest heart of religiosity, this corruption of a priest, this sticking it to God, so to speak, in his own house, oh no, she is not about to end it now. Not now when her pleasure is so fulfilling, not now when she is at the peak of her ardor and he is at the peak of his delirium. So she tells him . . .

"I told him if he ended it now, I'd let the whole world know about it."

She smiled at Carella, mysteriously.

"Which is when he started . . ."

"Which is when he started yelling blackmail," Carella said.

"Oh?" Abby said.

"You were heard and you were seen," Carella said, lying only a little bit, in that Alexis hadn't seen her face.

"Well, yes, that's exactly what he started yelling. Blackmail. This is blackmail, this is blackmail, how dare you . . . how *silly,* really! I told him it was for his own good. Because, really, I *was* incredibly good for him."

"What happened then?" Carella asked.

"*Everything,*" Abby said. "A black kid came running into the church, bleeding, and there was pounding on the doors, and the doors caved in, and a bunch of white kids came running in after him, and mister, I have to tell you, I was out the back door as fast as my feet would carry me."

"When did you see him again?"

"Who?"

"Father Michael."

"Never. I figured if he wanted out, fuck him."

She looked up at Carella and smiled.

"Would *you* have wanted out?" she asked.

He ignored the question.

"Where were you on May twenty-fourth between six-thirty and seven-thirty?" he asked.

"I wasn't out killing a priest, that's for sure."

"Okay, now we know where you weren't," he said. "Can you tell me where you *were?*"

"Not without getting personal," she said, and smiled that same infuriating, mysterious smile.

"Miss Finch . . ." he said.

"I was right here," she said. "All night long. With a man named Dwight Colby. Check it," she said, "he's in the phone book."

"Thank you," he said. "I will."

"He's black," she said.

The ugly one again.

"*Qué tal?*"

His first words. Signaling that they would speak only in Spanish, *his* language. She went along with it. Tomorrow it would be over and done with. Forever.

In Spanish, she said, "*Yo tengo el dinero.*"

I have the money.

"Oh?" he said, surprised. "That was very fast."

"I met with my contact last night. The deal is too complicated to explain, but . . ."

"No. Explain it."

"Not on the telephone. You can understand that. Let me say only that it turned out to be simpler than I thought it would."

"Well, that's very nice, isn't it?"

Forced joviality in his voice.

Pero, eso está muy bien, no?

"Yes," she said. "Can you come here tomorrow afternoon?"

"I'm not sure we *want* to come there," he said. "You live in a dangerous place. A person can get hurt in that place."

Reminding her that there was still an *additional* debt she owed.

For the cutting of the handsome one. The two million would pay for the killing of Alberto Hidalgo . . . maybe. But she knew the ugly one would not be content until the cutting was paid for as well. *Machismo* was invented by Spanish-speaking people. So was *venganza*.

"Well, I'm sorry," she said, "but I'm not about to go out on the street carrying two million dollars in cash."

Show them the green.

"You have the full amount, eh?"

"All of it."

"In what denominations?"

"Hundreds."

"How many hundreds?"

He almost trapped her. She surely would have counted that much money, she surely would have known how many hundred-dollar bills there were in two million dollars. Her mind clicked like a calculator. Drop two zeros, you come up with . . .

"Twenty thousand," she said at once, and then embroidered the lie. "Two hundred banded stacks, a hundred bills in each stack."

"Good," he said.

"Can you be here at three tomorrow?"

Willis would be working the day watch again. He'd leave here at a quarter past eight, and he wouldn't be home till four-fifteen, four-thirty. By that time it would be finished.

"Three-thirty," he said.

"No, that's too . . ."

"Three-thirty," he repeated.

"All right," she said, sighing. "You'll have fifteen minutes to count the money and get out."

"I hope there won't be any tricks this time," he said.

The word *trucos* meant only that in Spanish. Tricks. It did not have the secondary or tertiary meanings it had in English, where a trick was either a prostitute's client or the service she performed for him. He was not making veiled reference to either her own or his uncle's former occupations. Too much the gentleman for that. No Shad Russell here, this man's mind wasn't in the gutter. He was simply warning her not to come up with any surprises.

"No guns," he said, "no knives, eh?"

Reminder of the debt again.

The cutting of the handsome one.

"No tricks," she said. "I just want this over and done with."

"Yes, so do we."

The something in his voice again. The promise. Running deep and dark and icy cold beneath the surface of his words.

"I'll see you at three-thirty tomorrow," she said, and hung up.

And realized all at once that she was trembling.

13

HE WENT BACK to the church again at noon that Friday, the first day of June. He had called ahead to ask if he could look through the dead priest's files again, and Father Oriella had told him it would be no bother at all, he himself had a meeting at the archdiocese downtown, and would be out of the office most of the day. "If you need any assistance," he'd added, "just ask Marcella Bella."

Marcella Palumbo, as it happened, was out to lunch when Carella got there. It was Mrs. Hennessy who let him into the rectory and then took him back to the small office. Where there had been papers scattered all over the floor on the night of the murder, and cartons stacked everywhere when the new priest was moving in, there was now order and a sure sense of control.

"What is it you're looking for?" Mrs. Hennessy asked.

"I'm not sure," Carella said.

"Then how will you know where to look?"

Good question.

He was here, he guessed, to do paperwork again. To some people, Hell was eternal flames, and to others it was getting caught in midtown traffic, but to Carella it was paperwork. He was being punished now for having walked out of church without having said his penance all those years ago. A vengeful God was heaping more paperwork on him.

He asked Mrs. Hennessy if she knew where Father Oriella had put the calendar, checkbooks, and canceled checks that had been returned to him by the police. She said she thought Mrs. Palumbo had filed them in the M–Z file drawer, though she had no idea why the woman had put them there since checks and calendars both started with a C, so why hadn't she put them in the A–C drawer? Carella had no idea, either. But sure enough, there they were, at the front of the M–Z drawer. He thanked Mrs. Hennessy, declined her offer of a cup of coffee, sat down at the desk and began going through the material yet another time.

As earlier, the priest's appointment calendar told him nothing of importance. On the day of his murder, he had celebrated masses at eight A.M. and twelve noon, and then had done the Miraculous Medal Novena following the noon mass. He had met with the Altar Society Auxiliary at two, and the Rosary Society at four. He was scheduled to meet with the Parish Council at eight that night, presumably after dinner, an appointment he never kept. That was it for the twenty-fourth day of May. Carella skimmed back through the pages for the preceding week. Again, there was nothing that seemed significant.

He put the appointment calendar aside, took the St. Catherine's Roman Catholic Church Corporation checkbook from the drawer, and began looking through the stubs for checks the priest had written during the month of May. Here again were the checks for photocopying and garage, mortgage and maintenance, medical insurance, flowers, missalettes, and so on. Carella turned to the check stubs for May 24.

The first stub on the page was numbered 5699. In a hand that was not Father Michael's, and which Carella assumed to be Kristin Lund's, the stub recorded that a check had been written to Bruce Macauley Tree Care, Inc. for spraying done on 5/19 in the amount of $37.50. As he'd done last Friday in the squadroom, Carella now went down the stubs one after the other, all of them dated May 24, each numbered sequentially:

	5700
To:	US Sprint
For:	Service thru 5/17
	$176.80

	5701
To:	Isola Bank and Trust
For:	June mortgage
	$1480.75

```
           5702
To:        Alfred Hart Insurance Co.
For:       Honda Accord LX, Policy
           # HR 9872724
                        $580.00
```

```
           5703
To:        Orkin Exterminating Co. Inc.
For:       May services
                        $36.50
```

```
           5704
To:        The Wanderers
For:       Band deposit
                        $100.00
```

That was the last check Father Michael had written on the day of his murder.

Carella closed the checkbook.

Nothing.

Paperwork, he thought. That's why he was here. Punishment. The ransacked G-L file. The eighth circle of Hell would be going through that file yet another time, and trying to discern what was *missing* from it. Because no one zeros in on a single file, pulls that file drawer out, searches through that file in haste, tosses papers recklessly into the room and onto the floor, unless that someone is *looking* for something. And if the something had in fact been found and taken from the priest's office, then the something may have been the *reason* for the priest's murder. So perhaps if he studied the papers in order, as they'd been filed, he might discover a break in the continuity, a lapse, a gap, a hole in the records. And then, by studying the *surrounding* papers, and by using his admittedly weak powers of deductive reasoning, he hoped he might be able to figure out what the purloined something had been. In short, he planned to study the doughnut in order to define the hole.

It occurred to him that Father Oriella might have replaced the dead priest's G-L file with a G-L file of his own. But no, the fastidious Marcella had refiled the dead priest's papers exactly where they'd been on the night of the murder, there to be consulted whenever or if ever his successor had need to look up something concerning the church. Carella opened the drawer—the bottom one on the left—took out the first hanging folder in line, made himself comfortable at the desk again, and began going through the folders one by one.

He thought, at one point, that he'd found a meaningful absence in a file labeled GUTTERS. Last autumn, Father Michael had been in correspondence with a man named Henry Norton, Jr., at a firm called Norton Brothers Seamless Gutter Company, regarding the repair and possible replacement of the church's leaders and gutters. He had written a letter on September 28, making an appointment with Mr. Norton to visit the site and give an estimate, and then he'd written another letter on October 11, stating that he would like to see a *written* estimate in addition to the verbal estimate Mr. Norton had given him after his visit, and then a further letter on October 16, stating that he was now in receipt of the written estimate and that this would serve as agreement to the terms. It closed saying he would be looking forward to word as to when the actual work would commence. The missing document was the written estimate Father Michael said he'd received. It turned out, however, that the estimate had been misfiled. Carella ran across it later, in a folder labeled HOLY NAME SOCIETY. There it was. On a Norton Brothers Seamless Gutter Company letterhead. An estimate of $1,036 to repair the leaders and gutters at St. Catherine's Church. Filed between the minutes of the Holy Name Society meetings for January and February of this year.

The last folder in the file was a hefty one labeled LENT.

Carella read every last document in that folder.

There was nothing else in the G-L drawer.

Sighing heavily, he replaced the folder in the bottom file drawer, and pushed the drawer back into the cabinet. It did not close all the way. He pulled it open again. Eased it shut. It still would not close completely. An inch or more of the drawer jutted out from the cabinet frame. He opened the drawer again and checked the slide mechanism. The drawer was seated firmly on its rollers, nothing seemed to be snagging. So what the hell . . . ?

He tried closing it again. It slid back into the cabinet and then abruptly stopped. Something at the back of the drawer, or perhaps behind the drawer, was preventing it from sliding all the way into the cabinet. He opened the drawer again, got down on his hands and knees, leaned in over the drawer, and reached in behind it. Something was stuck down there. He couldn't see what it was, but . . .

He yanked back his hand in sudden searing pain.

A thin line of blood ran across his fingertips.

The something back there was a knife.

He had found the murder weapon.

The defense attorney, a man named Oscar Loring, leaned in closer to Willis and said, "And what time was this, exactly, Detective?"

He had a bristly mustache and the breath of a lion who'd just eaten a warthog. It was now a quarter to three. Willis had been on the stand for an hour and a half this morning, and had been on again since two o'clock, when court had reconvened. Trying to explain, first, why he'd requested a no-knock warrant, and next why he'd shot a man who'd tried to kill him with an AR-15. This had been in October of last year, during a raid on a stash pad. The case had just come to trial. Loring was attempting to show that Willis had lied on his affidavit making application for the search warrant, that he'd had no reasonable cause to believe there'd be either weapons *or* contraband material in the suspect apartment, and that in fact he'd *planted* both the weapons and the contraband after he'd kicked in the door!

He now wanted to know *exactly* what time it was that Willis—*and* Bob O'Brien *and* four uniformed cops from CPEP—had kicked in the door to the apartment.

"It was nine o'clock in the morning," Willis said.

"*Exactly* nine o'clock?" Loring asked.

"I don't know if it was *exactly*. We had the raid scheduled for nine o'clock, it's my belief we were assembled by nine and went in at nine."

"But you don't know if it was *exactly* . . ."

"Excuse me," the judge said, "but where are you going with this?"

His name was Morris Weinberg, and he had a bald head fringed with sparse white sideburns, and he was fond of telling people that he'd lost all his hair the moment he'd been appointed to the bench.

"Your Honor," Loring said, "it's essential to my client's case that we know at *exactly* what time illegal entry was . . ."

"Objection!"

The prosecuting attorney. Bright young guy from the D.A.'s office, hadn't let Loring get away with so much as an inch of bullshit.

"Sustained. What difference will it make, Mr. Loring, if the police went in at a minute before nine or a minute after nine? What possible . . . ?"

"If Your Honor will permit me . . ."

"No, I'm not sure I will. You've kept this officer on the stand for almost two and a half hours now, picking at every detail of a raid he and other policemen made under protection of a no-knock warrant duly signed by a justice of the Superior Court. You've questioned his integrity, his motives, his methods, and everything but the legitimacy of his birth, which I'm sure you'll get around to before the . . ."

"Your Honor, there *is* a jury pres . . ."

"Yes, I'm aware of the jury. I'm also aware of the fact that we're wasting a great deal of time here, and that unless you can tell me *why* it's so important to pinpoint the time of entry, then I will have to ask you to leave off this line of questioning."

"Your Honor," Loring said, "my client was awake and eating his breakfast at nine o'clock."

"So?"

"Your Honor, this witness claims they kicked in the door at nine o'clock and found my client in bed. Asleep, Your Honor."

"So?"

"I'm merely suggesting, Your Honor, that if the detective is willing to perjure himself on . . ."

"Objection!"

"Sustained. Now cut that out, Mr. Loring. You know better than that."

"If the detective is *mistaken* about what actually happened on the morning of the raid, then perhaps he made a similar mistake regarding cause."

"Are you referring to probable cause for the search warrant?"

"Yes, Your Honor."

"Detective Willis," Weinberg said, "why did you believe there were weapons and contraband materials in that apartment?"

"An undercover police officer had made several buys there, Your Honor, in advance of the raid. Of a controlled substance, namely cocaine. And he reported seeing weapons there. Of a type, I might add, that was fired at us the moment we entered the apartment."

"What's his name? This undercover officer?"

"Officer Charles Seaver, Your Honor."

"His precinct?"

"Same as mine, Your Honor. The Eight-Seven."

"Does that satisfy you as to probable cause, Mr. Loring?"

"I'm just hearing of this, Your Honor. This was not stated on Detective Willis's petition for a . . ."

"I said information based on my personal knowledge and be . . ."

"You didn't mention a police officer . . ."

"What difference does it make? The warrant was *granted,* wasn't it? I went into that damn apartment with a . . ."

"Just a minute now, just a minute," Weinberg said.

"Sorry, Your Honor," Willis said.

"Can we get Officer Seaver here this afternoon?" Weinberg asked.

"I'd need time to prepare, Your Honor," Loring said.

"Tomorrow morning, then. Be ready to call him at nine A.M."

"Your Honor . . ."

"This court is adjourned until nine A.M. tomorrow morning," Weinberg said, and banged his gavel, and abruptly stood up.

"All rise!" the Clerk of the Court shouted, and everyone in the courtroom stood up as Weinberg swept out like a bald Batman, trailing his black robes behind him.

The clock on the wall read 2:55 P.M.

They were due at three-thirty.

When they announced themselves over the speaker at the front door, she would tell them the door was open. When they stepped into the entrance foyer, she would call, "I'm in here." And as they walked into the living room . . .

The entire house was already in disarray.

She had spent the past hour yanking out dresser drawers and strewing their contents onto the floor, unplugging television sets and stereo equipment, gathering up silverware, jewelry and fur coats, carrying all of this down to the living room where it would appear they had assembled it after ransacking the house. Her story to the police would be that she had walked in on two armed men . . .

She hoped they'd be armed. If not, she would change her story . . .

. . . two armed men whom she'd shot dead in self-defense. Two armed intruders shot to death while burglarizing a house they thought was empty. Criminal records a mile long on both of them, Willis had shown her copies. Open and shut, don't cry for me, Argentina.

She did not have a permit for the gun she'd bought from Shad Russell, but she was willing to look that charge in the eye when the time came, even if it meant going to prison again. The important thing was to make certain none of this rubbed off on Willis. She did not see how it could. The day watch was relieved at a quarter to four. He would not be home until four-fifteen, four-thirty. It would be over by then. All of it.

She looked at the mantel clock now.

Seven minutes to three.

She picked up the gun Russell had sold her.

A .38 caliber Colt Detective Special. Six-shot capacity. Three for each of them. She had better shoot fast and she had better shoot straight.

She rolled out the cylinder, checked that the gun was fully loaded, and then snapped it back into the barrel.

The clock read five minutes to three.

The two girls came down the front steps of the Graham School on Seventh and Culver, both wearing pleated green skirts, white blouses, blue knee-high socks, brown walking shoes, and blue blazers with the school crest over the left breast pocket. They were both giggling at something another girl had said. Books held against their budding bosoms, girlish laughter spilling onto the springtime air, sparkling and clear now that the rain had stopped. One of them was a killer.

"Hello, girls," Carella said.

"Hi, Mr. Carella," Gloria said. Blue eyes still twinkling with laughter, long black hair dancing in sunshine as she came down the steps.

"Hi," Alexis said. She wore the solemn look even in the aftermath of laughter, her brown eyes thoughtful, her face serious. I'm nothing, she had told him. Blonde hair falling to her shoulders, bobbing as she came down the steps. They could have been twins, these two, except for their coloring. But one of them was a killer.

"See you guys," the other girl said, and waved as she went off.

They stood in the sunlight, the detective and the two schoolgirls. It was three o'clock sharp. Students kept spilling out of the school. There was the sound of young voices everywhere around them. Neither of the girls seemed particularly apprehensive. But one of them was a killer.

"Alexis," he said, "I'd like to talk to you, please."

She looked first at him, and then at Gloria. The serious brown eyes looked suddenly troubled.

"Okay," she said.

He took her aside. They chatted quietly, Alexis's eyes intent on his face, concentrating on everything he said, nodding, listening, occasionally murmuring a few words. A girl wearing the Graham School's uniform and a senior hat that looked like a Greek fisherman's cap, except that it was in the orange-and-blue colors of the school, came skipping down the front steps, said, "Hi, Lex," and then walked off toward the subway kiosk on the corner.

Some little distance away, Gloria watched them in conversation, her books pressed against her narrow chest, her eyes squinted against the sun.

Carella walked back to her.

"Few questions," he said.

"Sure," Gloria said. "Is something wrong?"

Books still clutched to her chest.

Behind them and off to the left, Alexis sat on the school steps and tucked her skirt under her, watching them, puzzled.

"I spoke to Kristin Lund before coming here," Carella said. "I asked her if she'd seen you at the church on the day of the murder. She said she hadn't. Is that correct?"

"I'm sorry, but I don't understand the question."

"Did you go to the church at any time before five o'clock on the day of the murder?"

"No, I didn't."

"I also spoke to Mrs. Hennessy. She told me *she* hadn't seen you, either."

"That's because I wasn't there, Mr. Carella."

Blue eyes wide and innocent. But clicking with intelligence.

"Gloria," he said.

Those eyes intent on his face now.

"When I talked to Alexis last week—and I just now verified this with her, to make sure I wasn't mistaken—she told me you had the check for the band deposit and wanted to know whether the dance was still on. This was on Tuesday afternoon, the twenty-ninth of May. Is that right? Were you in possession of the deposit check at that time?"

"Yes?"

Wariness in those eyes now.

"When did Father Michael give you that check?"

"I don't remember."

"Try to remember, Gloria."

"It must have been on Wednesday. Yes, I think I stopped by after school and he gave me the check then."

"Are you talking about Wednesday, the twenty-third of May?"

"Yes."

"The day before the murder?"

"Yes."

"What time on Wednesday, would you remember?"

"After school. Three, four o'clock, something like that."

"And that was when Father Michael gave you the deposit check made out to The Wanderers, is that correct? For a hundred dollars."

"Yes."

"Gloria, when I spoke to Kristin Lund, I asked her if she was the person who'd written that check. She told me she was. She wrote that check and then asked Father Michael to sign it."

Eyes steady on his face.

"She wrote it on the twenty-fourth of May, Gloria."

Watching him, knowing where he was going now.

"You couldn't have picked it up on the twenty-third," he said.

"That's right," she said at once. "It was the twenty-fourth, I remember now."

"*When* on the twenty-fourth?"

"After school. I told you. I went to the church right after school."

"No, you told me you didn't go to the church at *all* on the day of the murder."

"That was when I couldn't remember."

"Are you telling me now that you *were* at the church?"

"Yes."

"Before five o'clock?"

"I'm not sure."

"Kristin left at five. She says you . . ."

"Then it must have been *after* five."

"What time, Gloria?"

"I don't remember exactly, but it was long before seven."

He looked at her.

They had not released to the media the estimated time of the priest's death. Only the killer knew that. He saw realization in her eyes. So blue, so intelligent, darting now, on the edge of panic. He did not want to do this to a thirteen-year-old, but he went straight for the jugular.

"We have the knife," he said.

The blue eyes hardened.

"I don't know what you're talking about," she said.

Which words he had heard many times before, from murderers much older and wiser than young Gloria here.

"I'd like you to come with me," he said.

And in deference to her youth, he added, "Please."

Maybe she's scared them off, he thought.

They hadn't heard from the two Argentinians since the day she'd cut the handsome one. That was on Saturday afternoon. A week tomorrow. And no word from them. Every night this past week, when he'd come home from work, his eyes had met hers expectantly. And every night she'd shaken her head, no. No word. So maybe they'd given her up as a lost cause. Maybe they'd bandaged the handsome one's hands and packed up and gone home, no sense trying to ride a tigress.

Maybe.

He came down the steps from the street outside the Criminal Courts Building, into the tiled subway passageway, and was walking toward the turnstiles when he saw the roses. Lavender roses. A man selling long-stemmed lavender roses, just to the left of the token booth. A dollar a rose. In the Mexican prison, there'd been a woman from Veracruz who'd wistfully told Marilyn that all the days were golden there, all the nights were purple. Lovely in Spanish. Lovely the way Marilyn repeated it. *En Veracruz, todos los días eran dorados, y todas las noches violetas.*

The roses weren't quite purple, but lavender would do.

Maybe it *was* time to celebrate, who the hell knew?

Maybe they were really gone for good.

"I'll take a dozen," he told the vendor.

The clock on the wall of the token booth read ten minutes past three.

In this city, the Afghani cab drivers had a private radio network. You got into the taxi, you told them where you wanted to go, they threw the flag, and that was the last you heard from them. For the rest of the trip, they ignored the passenger entirely and talked incessantly into their radios, babbling in a language incomprehensible to the vast majority of the city's population. Maybe they were all spies. Maybe they were plotting the overthrow of the United States government. This did not seem likely. More reasonable was the assumption that they were homesick and needed the sound of other Afghani voices to get them through the grinding day.

Carlos Ortega didn't *care* what the needs of the Afghani people might be. He knew only that someone with an impossible name printed on the Hack Bureau license affixed to the dashboard of his taxi was shrieking into the radio at the top of his lungs in an unintelligible language that was abrasive and intrusive.

"You!" he said in English.

The cabbie kept babbling.

"You!" he shouted.

The cabbie turned to him.

"Shut up!" Carlos said.

"What?" the cabbie said.

"Shut your mouth," Carlos said in heavily accented English. "You're making too much noise."

"What?" the cabbie said. "What?"

His ethnic group back home in the Wākhān Corridor was Kirghiz, although a moment ago he'd been speaking not the language of that area, but Farsi instead—which was the *lingua franca* of the city's Afghani drivers. His ancestors, nonetheless, had come from Turkey, and he tried now to muster some good old Turkish indignity, which disappeared in a flash the moment he looked at the ugly giant sitting in the back seat. He turned away at once, muttered something soft and Farsic into his radio, and then fell into an immediate and sullen silence.

Carlos merely nodded.

He was used to people shutting up when he told them to shut up.

In Spanish, now that the chattering din had subsided, he said, "I don't trust her, do you?"

"Beautiful women are never to be trusted," Ramon said.

He was still angry over the fact that she'd cut him. His hands were still bandaged and medicated and for the most part his wounds had healed. But there were some wounds that never healed. You did not cut the hands of a person as handsome as Ramon Castaneda. You did not even *touch* Ramon Castaneda unless he gave you permission to do so. For her indiscretion, the blonde whore would pay. As soon as she gave them the money.

"Why her house?" Carlos asked.

"Because she's stupid," Ramon said.

"No, she's very smart, give her that at least."

"I'll give her *this*," Ramon said, and grabbed his genitals.

"Yes," Carlos said, and smiled. "After she gives us the money."

"And then *this*," Ramon said, and took from his pocket a small bottle with a glass stopper in its top. The bottle was full of a pale yellowish liquid. The liquid was nitric acid. Ramon hoped that Marilyn Hollis would live to have many children and grandchildren, so that she could tell all of them how her face had come to be scarred in such a hideous manner. You did not cut someone who looked like Ramon Castaneda, no.

"Put that away," Carlos said.

Ramon put the bottle away.

"Why her house?" Carlos asked again. "Will the police be there? Has she notified the police?"

"She murdered your uncle," Ramon reminded him.

"Still."

"If you had murdered someone, would you call the police?"

"The police in Argentina aren't looking for her."

"True. But she doesn't know that. Believe me, Carlos, she hasn't called the police."

"Then why her house?"

"I told you. She's stupid," Ramon said again. "*All* beautiful women are stupid."

"Can she be planning a trap?"

"Stupid people don't know how to plan traps."

"I think we should be careful."

"Why? We'll roll over her like a tank. Take the money, fuck her, throw the acid in her face," Ramon said, and nodded at the utter simplicity of it all.

But Carlos was still concerned.

"Why do you think she chose the house?" he asked again. "Why not a public place?"

"She *told* you why. She's afraid of carrying all that money on the street."

"A public place would be safer for her."

"Women think their own houses are the safest places in the world. They think their houses are nests."

"She'll be armed in her nest," Carlos said.

"Certainly. She was armed last time."

Both men fell silent.

Carlos looked at his watch.

The time was a quarter past three.

Suddenly, he grinned. He looked particularly ugly when he grinned. "Do you remember how we got in last time?" he asked.

Ramon grinned, too.

She heard the key in the front door at exactly twenty-eight minutes past three. There were only two people who had keys to this house. The person opening the front door had to be . . .

"Marilyn?"

Willis's voice. Calling from the entry hall. Calling to her where she sat in the red leather armchair facing the open-arch entrance to the living room, the .38 Colt Detective Special in her fist.

Exactly what she hadn't wanted. Willis home and the other two not here yet. Willis stepping into the middle of it. The one person she wanted to keep *out* of it, *clear* of it . . .

"Hi, honey," he said, and came into the room with a bouquet of flowers wrapped in white paper, and saw the gun in her hand. The flowers made her want to weep, the incongruity of flowers when she was expecting . . .

His eyes suddenly shifted to the left, toward the stairs, and she knew even before his hand snapped up to his shoulder holster that they were already in the house. Somehow, they had got into the house again.

The spring-release on Willis's holster snapped his pistol up and out into his hand.

She came up out of the chair just as he fired.

He must have hit one of them—she heard someone yelling in pain just as she turned toward the stairway—and then there was shooting from the steps, and she stuck the .38 out in front of her the way she had seen lady cops do on television shows, holding it in both hands, leveling it. The big one was hit and was lurching toward Willis, firing as he stumbled into the living room. The handsome one was on the left, coming toward her, a gun in his hand. She fired at once. The bullet went low, she'd been aiming for his chest. But she was sure she'd hit him because she saw a dark stain appear where his jacket pocket was and at first she thought it was blood, but it wasn't dark enough for blood, and suddenly he began screaming. His screaming startled her, but there was no time to wonder what was causing it, there was time only to fire again because the hit hadn't stopped him, he was still coming at her, screaming, his handsome face distorted in anger and pain. The big one was still headed straight for Willis. Both of them still coming. The bad and the beautiful in one spectacular fireworks package.

Willis had his pistol stuck out straight in front of him, holding it in both hands the way she'd seen detectives do it on television, except that he happened to be a *real* detective and not Don Johnson. He was aiming very carefully at the ugly one's chest, taking his time, because this one was for the money. He fired in the same instant that the ugly one did. She fired, too. And saw the handsome one throw back his arms, the way extras did in movies, and then fly over backward as if he'd been hit by a football linebacker. Except that the stain on his pocket seemed to be spreading and his chest was suddenly spurting blood.

So was hers.

She didn't realize at first that she'd been hit.

And then she saw the blood, saw her white blouse turning red with blood, saw the blood spurting up out of the hole in her blouse, the hole in her chest, spreading into the fabric, turning the entire blouse red, and knew that she'd truly been hit badly, and felt the pain all at once, came down all at once off the excitement of all the shooting, felt the pain like an elephant stepping on her chest and thought, oh Jesus, he's really done me, and thought oddly and belatedly that she had not yet returned Eileen Burke's call of almost a week ago. And then she fell to the floor with her mouth open and her chest still spurting blood.

Willis stood over the big one, the gun still in both hands, the gun leveled at his fucking head, ready to blow his head off if he so much as blinked an eyelash, but nobody was blinking, they were both down, he turned immediately to Marilyn.

And saw her on the Persian carpet, all covered with blood.

Saw blood spurting up from her chest.

Her heart pumping out blood.

And thought Oh Jesus no.

And ran to her.

And fell on his knees beside her.

And said, "Marilyn?"

A whisper.

"Marilyn?"

And realized all at once that he was still holding the bouquet of lavender roses in his left hand.

In the city and state for which these men and women worked, Section 30 of the Criminal Law Statutes was titled INFANCY, and Subdivision 1 of this statute read: A person less than 16 years old is not criminally responsible for conduct.

Gloria Keely had turned thirteen in February.

Her parents insisted on an attorney. The attorney said he would apply at once for removal of the action to the Children's Court. They reminded him that the crime was murder. He reminded them that she was scarcely thirteen years old, and that children (he punched home the word *children*) of thirteen, fourteen and fifteen years of age were juvenile offenders under the laws of this state. They, in turn, reminded him that the moment she hit her thirteenth birthday, she lost infancy under the laws of this state if the crime was Murder, Subdivision One or Two. Ergo, she could no longer be considered a juvenile offender, and they were charging her as an adult.

Gloria's attorney told them that the laws of this city and this state specifically forbade the questioning of a juvenile offender in a police station. They reminded him again that the crime was murder, and that she was no longer a juvenile offender. They also mentioned that the intent of that particular restriction was to keep juveniles separate and apart from hardened criminals, and besides she was no longer a juvenile—for the *third* time. The attorney said the questioning was academic, anyway, since he would not allow his young client to answer any questions put to her by the police.

They were all walking on eggs here.

The girl was only thirteen years old.

They were saying she'd killed a priest by stabbing or slashing him seventeen times.

The police were in possession of what they were certain was the murder weapon, a knife with its handle and blade caked with dried blood almost certainly the priest's. Presumably, there were also fingerprints on that knife. And presumably, the fingerprints would match Gloria's. But her attorney argued that taking her fingerprints here in a police station would be tantamount to questioning her here, which would be in violation of not only her basic rights under Miranda-Escobedo, but also in violation of the statute specifically forbidding the questioning of a person under the age of fifteen in a police station.

They told him yet another time that she had lost infancy when she'd turned thirteen, and that under Miranda-Escobedo they would *not* be taking incriminating testimony without permission if they fingerprinted or photographed Gloria, or asked her to submit to a blood or breathalyzer test, or examined her body, or put her in a lineup, because the difference between these actions and a statement in response to interrogation was simply the difference between *non-testimonial* and *testimonial* responses on the part of the prisoner. There was no question that Gloria was a prisoner. She was in custody. They were going to charge her with the crime of Murder, Subdivision One: With intent to cause the death of another, causing the death of such person.

But this was a tough one.

Nellie Brand, who'd been called in because of her familiarity with the case, couldn't do a Q and A because Gloria's attorney said he would not permit her to answer any questions. The attorney was now saying they'd had no cause to bring her in here in the *first* place, were they perchance familiar with the expression "false arrest"? Carella had already briefed Nellie on his reason for bringing in Gloria, and whereas she considered his deduction sound enough, she also recognized that absent a fingerprint match, they were treading shaky ground. Carella was using the girl's possession of the last check written by Father Michael as proof that she'd been to the church on the day of his murder. If her fingerprints were on that knife, all well and good. If not . . .

A fingerprint match was essential to their case.

And even though Nellie felt positive that they were permitted to take Gloria's fingerprints (and the Police Department's Legal Bureau concurred on this point) she didn't want to risk what appeared to be a good case by giving anybody reason to complain about a rights violation later on; these were trigger-happy times. Anyway, once they charged the girl and booked her—and they would do that downtown at Central Booking, as soon as they quit tap-dancing here—fingerprints and photographs would be taken as a matter of course, juvenile or not. So why push Miranda-Escobedo now?

The attorney would not let go of it. So they argued it back and forth, Mr. and Mrs. Keely putting in their two cents every now and then with strident comments about what a good girl and excellent student their daughter was, espousing Lieutenant Byrnes's "Class Valedictorian" line of reasoning, the lawyers and detectives quoting chapter and verse of the various applicable laws, and in the midst of all this, as the shouting and gesticulating reached a heated climax, Gloria suddenly said, "I killed him."

Her attorney immediately said, "Gloria, I must advise you . . ." but she rolled over him like a steamroller flattening a fly. And since neither the police nor the district attorney were required by Miranda-Escobedo or any other law in the land to warn a person of her rights if she was *volunteering* a statement, they stood by silently and let her run with it.

I didn't mean to do it, she said.

I only went there to pick up the check. This was around six o'clock or so, I went in through the garden, the gate was open, I left it open because I figured maybe they wanted it that way, whoever'd left it open. The rectory door was open, too, the wooden one, not the screen door, that was closed. I opened the screen door and went right in. I'd promised Kenny the check, Kenny Walsh, he's leader of The Wanderers, he plays lead guitar and writes most of the songs, he said he needed the deposit check right away if we expected him to play the job. So I only went there to get the check.

I went into the rectory, and . . .

There's like this little bend before you come to the office, this sort of little turn after you come out of the entry, and I heard the . . . the voices . . . before . . . before I made the turn . . . the moaning . . . the woman moaning . . . and Father Michael saying, Oh God oh God oh God, and the woman saying Give it to me, *give* it to me, Michael!

And . . .

I'm not a child, you know. I know about such things. A lot of the girls at Graham *do* these things, they *talk* about these things, I'm not a child, I knew what they were doing even before I . . .

I should have turned back, I guess.

I should have left the minute I heard them.

But I . . .

I went around the . . . the turn there . . . the little bend there where the . . . the bench is . . . that you sit on when you're waiting to see the priest, and I . . .

I looked.

And he was . . . they were . . . her back was to me, her skirt was up, she was holding her skirt up, she was naked under the skirt, her panties down around her ankles, her legs apart, his hands were up under her skirt, they were kissing, oh dear God, and she kept moaning and moving against him, they were, you know, they were, they were making love there in his office, her long blonde hair trailing down her back, twisting her head, moaning, and him saying I love you Ab, oh God how I love you, a priest! And then he he sort of of of *slid* down her, his hands moving down the backs of her legs, and he he got on his knees in front of her as if he was praying, and I realized all at once what he was doing to her, and I covered my face with my hands and ran through the sacristy into the church and prayed to God for guidance.

I waited till she was gone. She came out through the church, I guess she didn't want anyone to see her leaving on the rectory side. I was still sitting in a pew near the altar. Praying. This was about half an hour after I'd seen them, maybe forty minutes, I don't know, she came clicking out of the sacristy on her high heels, tall and beautiful and clicking by in a hurry, a smile on her face, she was smiling. I watched her, I could see the line of her panties under the yellow skirt, I turned to look up at Jesus hanging on the cross and I looked at his sad eyes, do you know his sad eyes, I cry when I look at those eyes, and it seemed to me he was saying I should *discuss* this with Father Michael, ask him about it, find out what he what he why he he was *doing* this, why he had *done* this.

I didn't mean to kill him.

I only wanted to ask him why he was betraying not only God but also *me*, too, yes, because I'd trusted him, I'd thought we were friends, I thought we could tell each other things we couldn't tell anyone else, hadn't I said things in the confession box, hadn't I told him things I'd never told another human being on earth, not even Alexis? So that's what I planned to do. Just ask him how he could *do* such a thing. He was supposed to be a *priest* but instead he was behaving like a like a, I just wanted to *tell* him.

He was sitting in the rectory alone, behind his desk, this had to have been, I don't know, seven, a little before seven, ten to seven, something like that? He looked up when I came in, and he smiled, and said You're here for the check, am I right? Something like that. And I said Yes, Father Michael, and he gave me the check and I put it in my purse and I I I was waiting there because I didn't know how to start this, and he said Is there something, Gloria? And I said, Father Michael, I saw you and that woman. And he said, What woman, Gloria? And I said A blonde woman, Father Michael, the one who was here earlier. And he looked me in the eye and he said I don't know what you're talking about, Gloria. I said Father Michael, why are you doing this, it's a *sin!* And he looked me in the eye again and he said You must be mistaken, Gloria, please go now.

I went out of the office.

I don't know why I took the knife from the kitchen.

Mrs. Hennessy wasn't in there, I don't know where she was.

There were things cooking on the stove.

It smelled good in the kitchen.

I took the knife and . . .

And went back to the rectory to look for him, but he wasn't there. This made me . . .

I don't know why, but it made me angry. I mean, I wasn't going to *hurt* him, so why was he *hiding* from me? And then I . . . I heard him out in the garden . . . walking out there in the garden, and I went to the rectory door, the sun was beginning to set, the sky was red like blood, and I realized he was praying and all at once the *hypocrisy* of it, his praying to God, the *lie* of it . . .

I guess I stabbed him.

I don't know how many times.

God forgive me.

Afterwards, I . . . I went . . . I had to get rid of the knife, you see. There wasn't any blood on my clothes or on my hands . . . isn't there supposed to be a lot of blood? The blood was all over his his back, all

over the knife, but none of it was on me. I couldn't go out on the street
with with . . .

I ran into the rectory again . . .

Mrs. Hennessy didn't see me, she was in the kitchen . . .

Everything was happening so fast . . .

I ducked into the office . . .

I pulled open the bottom file drawer, and threw the knife into the
space at the back of the drawer, and then kept yanking things out of
the drawer to make it look as if somebody had come there to rob the
church and had killed . . .

Oh dear God.

Had killed the priest.

Oh dear God.

Had killed dear Father Michael.

Carella listened now to the numb recitation of how she'd made her
way home through streets already dark, how her parents had found her
in the living room reading a book when they'd got home from work,
how she'd told her mother the roast was already in the oven.

Thirteen, he was thinking, she's only thirteen.

And he recognized with a heavy sadness that nighttime in this city he
loved seemed to come too swiftly nowadays. And he wondered if it
wasn't already too late to say vespers.

Nellie Brand was watching him. As if reading his mind and thinking
exactly the same thing. Their eyes met. In the distance, there was the
sound of an ambulance siren.

Marilyn Hollis was being taken to Morehouse General, where they
would declare her dead on arrival.

Night had come.

The sky was black with rolling clouds. They were sitting in the little
garden behind the church. They could hear the sound of an ambulance
siren fading in the distance. Faraway lightning flashes crazed the sky.

"I haven't seen you in a long time," he said.

He was wearing a black cotton robe embroidered in richer black silk
with pine cones that formed a phallic pattern, slit to the waist on either
side to reveal his muscular legs and thighs.

"Well, there were problems," she said.

She was wearing a red leather skirt slit to the thigh. Black silk blouse
carved low over her breasts. Red high-heeled shoes. Bloodred lipstick.
Dangling red earrings.

"Tell me," he said.

She told him the story.

He listened thoughtfully.

Sipped at his drink and listened.

"There was a simpler way," he said at last.

"I didn't think so."

"I'd have kicked him out, see. Plain and simple."

"I didn't want you to know I had a twenty-two-year-old son."

"So you went to a Catholic priest instead."

"Yes."

"To ask him to intervene."

"Yes. Because how could I continue coming here if *Andrew* was here with his goddamn faggot boyfriend?"

"Andrew Hobbs."

"Yes."

"I never once suspected."

"That was my married name. Hobbs."

"A twenty-two-year-old son," he said.

"Yes."

"Abigail Finch has a twenty-two-year-old son," he said, and shook his head in wonder.

"Yes. So now you know I'm a hag," she said, and smiled.

"Oh yes, some hag," he said, and returned the smile.

"The point is," she said, "it backfired. And I'm truly penitent about that."

"Backfired how?"

"I didn't expect him to get on his pulpit about *Bornless*. I only wanted him to give Andrew a little heart-to-heart. Quit seeing the Devil, son, it's bad for your soul. That sort of thing."

"Yes."

"Sure. Instead, he made a federal case out of it."

"Yes."

He was silent for a moment, sipping thoughtfully at his drink. He looked up then, and said, "Maybe you should be punished, Ab. The church can punish you, you know."

"I know that, and that's entirely up to you and the deacons, Sky. I *am* penitent, though, I really am. And you know . . ."

"Yes?"

"I *did* get him to stop, I really did. When I realized what was happening, his sermons and all, I went to him and told him I'd tell all

about us if he didn't quit harassing Bornless. He said it was blackmail. I
told him it was for his own good. I was being sarcastic, you know. For
his own good. Walking with Satan would be for his own good."

Schuyler began laughing.

"Yeah," she said, and laughed with him. "But that was what really
ticked him off, my saying that, and then laughing in his face. He
slapped me, the bastard, can you believe it? Five minutes earlier he was
worshipping at the mound, and all at once he slapped me. Because I'd
offended his beloved *Jesus,* you know, who he'd only been betraying
since the first of April, fucking me six ways from Sunday. A priest, can
you believe it! Some priest. I made him pay for that slap later. But he
stopped the sermons, Sky. There weren't any more sermons after
Easter, did you notice?"

"To tell the truth, Ab, I didn't notice the ones *before* Easter, either."

Both of them laughed.

And sipped at their drinks.

And looked up at the threatening black sky.

There was another flash of lightning.

"Rain coming," he said.

"There's another thing, too," she said. "If you're thinking of
leniency."

"And what's that?"

"I really think I *accomplished* something for the church, Sky."

"How do you figure that?"

"I seduced a Catholic priest. I seduced a servant of Jesus Christ. I
think that's something, Sky."

"You do, huh?"

"Something worth considering, yes. If you're thinking of forgiving
me."

"I'll see."

There was more lightning, closer now. A faint roll of thunder.

"He told me he loved me," she said, and turned to look at him, a
small pleased smile on her face.

"I can't blame him."

"Through love, lust. Right?"

"Vice versa, actually."

"I had him lusting for me, Sky. He'd have done anything for me. A
Catholic priest, Sky. I had him panting for me. On his knees to me. Not
to Jesus, Sky. To *me.*"

She looked directly into his eyes.

Lightning flashed closer. There was a loud boom of thunder.

"We're going to win," she said earnestly. "Eventually, we're going to win, Sky."

"I think we've *already* won," he said softly.

It was going to rain any moment now.

He took her hand. They rose together and started back into the church just as the first huge drops began pelting the path.

"Would you care to serve as altar tomorrow night?" he asked.

"I'd be honored," she said.

WIDOWS

This is for Jane Powell and Dick Moore

1

SHE'D BEEN BRUTALLY stabbed and slashed more times than Carella chose to imagine. The knife seemed to have been a weapon of convenience, a small paring knife that evidently had been taken from the bartop where a bottle opener with a matching wooden handle sat beside a half-full pitcher of martinis, an ice bucket, and a whole lemon from which a narrow sliver of skin was missing.

Someone had been drinking a martini. With a twist. Presumably the paring knife had been used to peel back the skin of the lemon before the knife was used on its victim. The martini was still on the coffee table alongside which she was lying. The lemon twist lay curled on the bottom of the glass. The paring knife was on the floor beside her. The blade was covered with blood. She was bleeding from what appeared to be a hundred cuts and gashes.

"Natural blonde," Monoghan said.

She was wearing a black silk kimono patterned with oversized red poppies. The kimono was belted at the waist, but it had been torn open to reveal her long, slender legs and the blonde pubic patch upon which Monoghan had based his clever deduction. Her blue eyes were open. Her throat had been slit. Her face had been repeatedly slashed, but you could still see she'd been a beauty. Nineteen, twenty years old, long blonde hair and startling blue eyes, wide open, staring at the ceiling of the penthouse apartment. Young beautiful body under the slashed black kimono with poppies the color of blood.

The men in suits and jackets stood around her, looking down at her, plastic-encased ID cards clipped to their coat collars. Monoghan and Monroe from Homicide North; Detective/Second Grade Steve Carella from the Eight-Seven; Detective/Third Grade Arthur Brown, same precinct. Nice little gathering here at a little past eight o'clock on a hot, muggy night late in July. Monoghan and Monroe kept staring down at the body as if pondering the mystery of it all. There were slash and stab marks on her breast and her belly. Her wounds shrieked silently to the night. The insides of her thighs had been slashed. There was blood everywhere you looked. Torn white flesh and bright red blood. Shrieking. The men were waiting for the medical examiner to arrive. This weather, cars and people all over the streets, it took time to get anywhere. There was a pained look on Carella's face. Brown looked angry, the way he normally did, even when he was deliriously happy.

"Girls like this, they can get in trouble, this city," Monroe said.

Carella wondered, Girls like *what*?

"You get a young, pretty girl like this one," Monoghan said, "they don't know what this city is like."

"What this city can do to you," Monroe said.

"This city can do terrible things to young girls," Monoghan said.

They stood there with their hands in the pockets of their suit jackets, thumbs showing, identical navy-blue suits and white shirts and blue ties, looking down at the dead woman. Girl, they had called her. Nineteen, twenty years old at most. Carella wondered if she'd thought of herself as a woman. On all the subsequent reports, she would be labeled merely FEMALE. Generic labeling. No fine distinction for feminists to pursue, no quarrel over whether it should be girl or woman, no such bullshit once you became a victim. The minute you were dead, you became *female,* period.

The pained look was still in his eyes.

Dark brown eyes, slanting downward to give his face a somewhat Oriental look. Brown hair. Tall and slender. His nose was running, a summer cold. He took out his handkerchief, blew his nose, and looked toward the front door. Where the hell was the M.E.? The apartment felt sticky and damp, was there a window open someplace, diluting the airconditioning? No window units here, everything hidden and enclosed, this was an expensive apartment. High-rise, high-rent condo here on what passed for the precinct's Gold Coast, such as it was, overlooking the River Harb and the next state. Two blocks south you had your tenements and your hot-bed hotels. Here, on the floor of the building's only penthouse apartment, a young woman in an expensive silk kimono lay torn and bleeding on a thick pile carpet, a martini in a stemmed glass on the coffee table behind her. Liquid silver in the glass. Yellow twist of lemon curling. Lipstick stain on the glass's rim. Enough still left in the pitcher on the bar to pour half a dozen more glasses like this one. Had she been expecting company? Had she voluntarily admitted her own murderer to the apartment? Or *was* there a window open?

"They say it's gonna be even hotter tomorrow than it was today," Monoghan said idly, and turned away from the victim as though bored with her lifeless pose.

"Who's *they?*" Monroe asked.

"The weather guys."

"Then why didn't you say so? Why do people always say *they* this, *they* that, instead of who the hell *they* is supposed to be?"

"What's the matter with you tonight?" Monoghan asked, surprised.

"I just don't like people saying *they* this, *they* that all the time."

"I'm not people," Monoghan said, looking offended and hurt. "I'm your partner."

"So stop saying *they* this, *they* that all the time."

"I certainly will," Monoghan said, and walked over to where a second black leather sofa rested under the windows on the far side of the room. He glanced angrily at the sofa, and then heavily plunked himself down onto it.

Brown couldn't believe that the M&Ms were arguing. Monoghan and Monroe? Joined at the hip since birth? Exchanging heated words? Impossible. But there was Monoghan, sitting on the sofa in a sulk, and here was Monroe, unwilling to let go of it. Brown kept his distance.

"People are always doing that," Monroe said. "It drives me crazy. Don't it drive you crazy?" he asked Brown.

"I don't pay much attention to it," Brown said, trying to stay neutral.

"It's the *heat's* driving you crazy," Monoghan said from across the room.

"It ain't the goddamn heat," Monroe said, "it's people always saying *they* this, *they* that."

Brown tried to look aloof.

At six feet four inches tall and weighing two hundred and twenty pounds, he was bigger and in better condition than either of the two Homicide dicks. But he sensed that the argument between them was something that could easily turn against him if he wasn't careful. Nowadays in this city, a black man had to be careful, except with people he trusted completely. He trusted Carella that way, but he knew nothing at all about the religion or politics of the M&Ms, so he figured it was best not to get himself involved in what was essentially a family dispute. One thing he didn't want was a hassle on a hot summer night.

Brown's skin was the color of rich Colombian coffee, and he had brown eyes and kinky black hair, and wide nostrils and thick lips, and this made him as black as anyone could get. Over the years, he had got used to thinking of himself as black—though that wasn't his actual color—but he was damned if he would now start calling himself African-American, which he felt was a phony label invented by insecure people who kept inventing labels in order to reinvent themselves. Inventing labels wasn't the way you found out who you were. The way you did that was you looked in the mirror every morning, the way Brown did, and you saw the same handsome black dude looking back at you. That was what made you grin, man.

"You get people saying things like 'They say there's gonna be another tax hike,' " Monroe said, gathering steam, "and when you ask them who they mean by *they*, they'll tell you the investment brokers or the financial insti . . ."

"You just done it yourself," Monoghan said.

"What'd I do?"

"You said you ask them who they mean by *they*, they'll tell you the investment . . ."

"I don't know what you're talking about," Monroe said.

"I'm talking about you complaining about people saying *they* this and *they* that, and you just said *they* this yourself."

"I said nothing of the sort," Monroe said. "Did I say that?" he asked Brown, trying to drag him into it again.

"Hello, hello, hello," the M.E. said cheerily from the door to the apartment, sparing Brown an answer. Putting down his satchel, wiping his brow with an already damp handkerchief, he said, "It's the Sahara out there, I'm sorry I'm late." He picked up the satchel again, walked over to where the victim lay on the carpet, said, "Oh my," and knelt immediately beside her. Monoghan got off the sofa and came over to where the other men stood.

They all watched silently as the M.E. began his examination.

In this city, you did not touch the body until someone from the Medical Examiner's Office pronounced the victim dead. By extension, investigating detectives usually interpreted this regulation to mean you didn't touch *anything* until the M.E. had delivered his verdict. You could come into an apartment and find a naked old lady who'd been dead for months and had turned to jelly in her bathtub, you waited till the M.E. said she was dead. They waited now. He examined the dead woman as if she was still alive and paying her annual visit to his office, putting his stethoscope to her chest, feeling for a pulse, counting the number of slash and stab wounds—there were thirty-two in all, including those in the small of her back—keeping the detectives in suspense as to whether or not she was truly deceased.

"Tough one to call, huh, Doc?" Monoghan asked, and winked at Monroe, surprising Brown.

"Cause of death, he means," Monroe said, and winked back.

Brown guessed they'd already forgotten their little tiff.

The M.E. glanced up at them sourly, and then returned to his task.

At last he rose and said, "She's all yours."

The detectives went to work.

The clock on the wall of the office read eight-thirty P.M. There was nothing else on any of the walls. Not even a window. There was a plain wooden desk probably salvaged from one of the older precincts when the new metal furniture started coming in. There was a wooden chair with arms in front of the desk, and a straight-backed wooden chair behind it. Michael Goodman sat behind the desk. *Dr.* Michael Goodman. Who rated only a cubby hole office here in the Headquarters Building downtown. Eileen Burke was singularly unimpressed.

"That's Detective/Second, is it?" he asked.

"Yes," she said.

"How long have you been a detective?"

She almost said Too long.

"It's all there in the record," she said.

She was beginning to think this was a terrible mistake. Coming to see a shrink recommended by another shrink. But she trusted Karin. She guessed.

Goodman looked at the papers on his desk. He was a tall man with curly black hair and blue eyes. Nose a bit too long for his face, mustache under it, perhaps to cradle it, soften its length. Thick spectacles with rims the color of his hair. He studied the papers.

"Put in a lot of time with Special Forces, I see," he said.

"Yes."

"Decoy work."

"Yes."

"Mostly Rape Squad," he said.

"Yes," she said.

He'd get to the rape next. He'd get to the part that said she'd been raped in the line of duty. It's all there in the record, she thought.

"So," he said, and looked up, and smiled. "What makes you think you'd like to work with the hostage team?"

"I'm not sure I would. But Karin . . . Dr. Karin Lefkowitz . . ."

"Yes."

"I've been seeing her for a little while now . . ."

"Yes."

"At Pizzaz. Upstairs."

Psychological Services Assistance Section. P.S.A.S. Pizzaz for short. Cop talk that took the curse off psychological help, made it sound jazzier, Pizzaz. Right upstairs on the fifth floor of the building. Annie Rawles's Rape Squad office was on the sixth floor. You start with a Rape Squad assignment on the sixth floor and you end up in Pizzaz on the fifth, Eileen thought. What goes up must come down.

"She suggested that I might find hostage work interesting."

Less *threatening* was what she'd actually said.

"How did she mean? Interesting?"

Zeroing right in. Smarter than she thought.

"I've been under a considerable amount of strain lately," Eileen said.

"Because of the shooting?" Goodman asked.

Here it comes, she thought.

"The shooting, yes, and complications arising from . . ."

"You killed this man when?"

Flat out. You killed this man. Which, of course, was what she'd done. Killed this man. Killed this man who'd murdered three prostitutes and was coming at her with a knife. Blew him to perdition. Her first bullet took him in the chest, knocking him backward toward the bed. She fired again almost at once, hitting him in the shoulder this time, spinning him around, and then she fired a third time, shooting him in the back, knocking him over onto the bed. At the time, she couldn't understand why she kept shooting into his lifeless body, watching the eruptions of blood along his spine, saying over and over again, "I gave you a chance, I gave you a chance," until the gun was empty. Karin Lefkowitz was helping her to understand why.

"I killed him a year ago October," she said.

"Not this past October . . ."

"No the one before it. Halloween night," she said.

Trick or treat, she thought.

I gave you a chance.

But had she?

"Why are you seeing Dr. Lefkowitz?"

She wondered if he knew her. Did every shrink in this city know every other shrink? If so, had he talked to her about what they'd been discussing these past several months?

"I'm seeing her because I'm gun-shy," she said.

"Uh-huh," he said.

"I don't want to have to kill anyone else," she said.

"Okay," he said.

"And I don't want to do any more decoy work. Which is a bad failing for a Special Forces cop."

"I can imagine."

"By the way," she said, "I don't particularly like psychiatrists."

"Lucky I'm only a psychologist," he said, and smiled.

"Those, too."

"But you *do* like Karin."

"Yes," she said, and paused. "She's been helpful."

Big admission to make.

"In what way?"

"I have other problems besides the job."

"First tell me what your problems with the job are."

"I just told you. I don't want to be placed in another situation where I may have to shoot someone."

"Kill someone."

"Shoot, kill, yes."

"You don't see any difference?"

"When someone's coming at you and you've got three seconds to make a decision, there's no difference, right."

"Must have been pretty frightening."

"It was."

"Are you still frightened?"

"Yes."

"Just how frightened are you, Miss Burke?"

"Very frightened."

She could admit this now. Karin had freed her to do this.

"Because you killed this man?"

"No. Because I was raped. I don't want to get raped again, I'd *kill* anyone who tried to rape me again. So I don't want to be . . . to be constantly put in situations where someone may *try* to rape me, which frightens the hell out of me, and where I'll . . . I'll have to kill him, which . . . which also frightens me, I guess. Having to kill someone again."

"Sort of a vicious circle, isn't it?"

"If I stay with Special Forces, yes."

"So you're thinking of the hostage team."

"Well, Karin thought I should come up here and talk to you about it. See what it was all about."

"It's not about killing people, that's for sure," Goodman said, and smiled again. "Tell me about these other problems. The ones that *aren't* related to the job."

"Well, they're personal."

"Yes, well, hostage work is personal, too."

"I understand that. But I don't see what *my* personal problems have to do with . . ."

"I just interviewed a detective who's been with Narcotics for the past ten years," Goodman said. "I've been interviewing people all day long. There's a high burnout rate on the team, lots of stress. If the inspector and I can keep a good negotiator for eight months, that's a long time. Anyway, this detective hates drug dealers, would like to see all of them dead. I asked him what he'd do if we were negotiating with a hostage-taker who was a known drug dealer. He said he'd try to save the lives of the hostages. I asked him who he thought was more important, the hostages or the drug dealer. He said he thought the hostages were more important. I asked him if he'd kill the drug dealer to save the hostages. He said yes, he would. I told him I didn't think he'd be right for the team."

Eileen looked at him.

"So what about these personal problems you're working on?" he asked.

She hesitated.

"If you'd rather . . ."

"The night I shot Bobby . . . that was his name," she said, "Bobby Wilson. The night I shot him, I had two backups following me. But my boyfriend . . ."

"Is he the personal problem? Your boyfriend?"

"Yes."

"What about him?"

"He figured he'd lend a hand on the job, and as a result . . ."

"Lend a hand?"

"He's a cop, I'm sorry, I should have mentioned that. He's a detective at the Eight-Seven."

"What's his name?"

"Why do you need to know that?"

"I don't."

"Anyway, he walked into what was going down, and there was a mix-up, and I lost both my backups. Which is how I ended up alone with Bobby. And his knife."

"So you killed him."

"Yes. He was coming at me."

"Do you blame your boyfriend for that?"

"That's what we're working on."

"You and Dr. Lefkowitz."

"Yes."

"How about you and your boyfriend? Are you working on it, too?"

"I haven't seen him since I started therapy."

"How does he feel about that?"

"I don't give a damn *how* he feels."

"I see."

"I'm the one who's drowning," Eileen said.

"I see."

They sat in silence for several moments.

"End of interview, right?" she asked.

They found the letters in a jewelry box on the dead woman's dresser.

They had ascertained by then—from the driver's license in her handbag on a table just inside the entrance door—that her name was Susan Brauer and that her age was twenty-two. The picture on the license showed a fresh-faced blonde grinning at the camera. The blue cloth backing behind her told the detectives that the license was limited to driving with corrective lenses. Before the M.E. left, they asked him if the dead woman was wearing contacts. He said she was not.

The box containing the letters was one of those tooled red-leather things that attract burglars the way jam pots attract bees. A burglar would have been disappointed with this one, though, because the only thing in it was a stack of letters still in their envelopes and bound together with a pale blue satin ribbon. There were twenty-two letters in all, organized in chronological order, the first of them dated the eleventh of June this year, the last dated the twelfth of July. All of the letters were handwritten, all of them began with the salutation *My darling Susan.* None of them was signed. All of them were erotic.

The writer was obviously a man.

In letter after letter—they calculated that he'd averaged a letter every other day or so—the writer described in explicit language all the things he intended to do to Susan . . .

. . . standing behind you in a crowded elevator, your skirt raised in the back and tucked up under your belt, you naked under the skirt, my hands freely roaming your . . .

. . . and all the things he expected Susan to do to him . . .

. . . with you straddling me and facing the mirror. Then I want you to ease yourself down on my . . .

As the detectives read the letters in order, it seemed possible that Susan had been writing to him in return, and that her letters were of the same nature, his references to her requests . . .

. . . when you say you want to tie me to the bed and have me beg you to touch me, do you mean . . .

. . . indicating an erotic imagination as lively as his own. Moreover, it became clear that these were no mere unfulfilled fantasies. The couple were actually *doing* the things they promised they'd do, and doing it with startling frequency.

. . . on Wednesday when you opened your kimono and stood there in the black lingerie I'd bought you, your legs slightly parted, the garters tight on your . . .

. . . but then last Friday, as you bent over to accept me, I wondered whether you really enjoyed . . .

. . . quite often myself. And when you told me that on Monday you thought of me while you were doing it, the bubble bath foaming around you, your hand busy under the suds, finding that sweet tight . . .

. . . known you only since New Year's Day, and yet I think of you all the time. I saw you yesterday, I'll see you again tomorrow, but I walk around eternally embarrassed because I'm sure everyone can see the bulge of my . . .

The letters went on and on.

Twenty-two of them in all.

The last one was perhaps the most revealing of the lot. In part, before it sailed off into the usual erotic stratosphere, it dealt with business of a sort:

My darling Susan,

I know you're becoming impatient with what seems an inter-minable delay in getting you into the new apartment. I myself feel uneasy searching for a taxi when I leave there late at night, know-ing the streets to the south of the Oval are neither well-lighted nor well-patrolled. I'll be so much happier when you're settled down-town, closer to my office, in a safer neighborhood, in the luxurious surroundings I promised you.

*But please don't take the delay as a sign of indifference or chang-
ing attitude on my part. And please don't become impatient or for-
getful. I would hate to lose this apartment before the other one
comes free—which I've been assured will be any day now. I'll
make sure you have the cash to cover any checks you write, but
please pay all of the apartment bills promptly. You can't risk losing
the lease on default.*

*I've been going to my post office box every day, but nothing from
Susan. Is little Susan afraid to write? Is little Susan losing interest? I
would hate to think so. Or does sweet Susan need reminding that
she's mine? I think you may have to be punished the next time I see
you. I think I'll have to turn you over my knee, and pull down your
panties, and spank you till your cheeks turn pink, watch your ass
writhing under my hand, hear you moaning . . .*

This letter, too, was unsigned.

It was a shame.

It made their job more difficult.

The clock on the squadroom wall read twelve minutes to midnight.
The Graveyard Shift had just relieved, and Hawes was arguing with
Bob O'Brien, who didn't want to be the one who broke the news to
Carella. He told Hawes he should stick around, do it himself, even
though he'd been officially relieved.

"You're the one the sister talked to," O'Brien said. "You're the one
should tell Steve."

Hawes said he had an urgent engagement, what did O'Brien want
him to do, leave a note on Carella's desk? The urgent engagement was
with a Detective/First Grade named Annie Rawles who had bought
him the red socks he was wearing. The socks matched Hawes's hair
and the tie he was wearing. He was also wearing a white shirt that
echoed the white streak of hair over his left temple. Hawes was dressed
for the summer heat. Lightweight blue blazer over gray tropical slacks,
red silk tie and the red socks Annie had given him.

This was the seventeenth day of July, a Tuesday night, and the temperature outside the squadroom was eighty-six degrees Fahrenheit. By
Hawes's reckoning that came to thirty degrees Celsius, which was
damn hot in any language. He hated the summer. He particularly
hated *this* summer, because it seemed to have started in May and it was
still here, day after day of torrid temperatures and heavy humidity that
combined to turn a person to mush.

"Can't you just do me this one simple favor?" he said.

"It's not such a simple favor," O'Brien said. "This is the most traumatic thing that can happen in a man's life, don't you know that?"

"No, I didn't know that," Hawes said.

"Also," O'Brien said, "I have a reputation around here as a hard-luck cop . . ."

"Where'd you get *that* idea?" Hawes said.

"I got that idea because I have a habit of getting into shoot-outs, and I know nobody likes being partnered with me."

"That's ridiculous," Hawes said, lying.

"Now you're asking me to tell Steve this terrible thing, he'll confuse the messenger with the message and he'll think Here's this hard-luck cop bringing hard luck to *me.*"

"Steve won't think that at all," Hawes said.

"I won't think what?" Carella said from the gate in the slatted-rail divider, taking off his jacket as he came into the room. Brown was right behind him. Both men looked wilted.

"What won't I think?" Carella asked again.

O'Brien and Hawes looked at him.

"What is it?" Carella said.

Neither of them said anything.

"Cotton?" he said. "Bob? What is it?"

"Steve . . ."

"What?"

"I hate to have to tell you this, but . . ."

"*What,* Bob?"

"Your sister called a little while ago," O'Brien said.

"Your father is dead," Hawes said.

Carella looked at them blankly.

Then he nodded.

Then he said, "Where is she?"

"Your mother's house."

He went directly to the phone and dialed the number from memory. His sister picked up on the third ring.

"Angela," he said, "it's Steve."

She'd been crying, her voice revealed that.

"We just got back from the hospital," she said.

"What happened?" he asked. "Was it his heart again?"

"No, Steve. Not his heart."

"Then what?"

"We went there to make positive identification."

For a moment he didn't quite understand. Or didn't choose to understand.

"What do you mean?" he said.

"We had to identify the body."

"Why? Angela, what happened?"

"He was killed."

"Killed? What . . . ?"

"In the bakery shop."

"No."

"Steve . . ."

"Jesus, what . . . ?"

"Two men came in. Papa was alone. They cleaned out the cash register . . ."

"Angela, don't tell me this, please."

"I'm sorry," she said.

And suddenly he was crying.

"Who's . . . who's . . . is it the . . . the . . . it's the Four-Five, isn't it? Up there? Who's working the . . . do you know who's working the . . . the . . . Angela," he said, "honey? Did they . . . did they hurt him? I mean, did they . . . they didn't *hurt* him, did they? Oh God, Angela," he said, "oh God oh God oh God . . ."

He pulled the phone from his mouth and clutched it to his chest, tears streaming down his face, great racking sobs choking him. "Steve?" his sister said. "Are you all right?" Her voice muffled against his shirt where the receiver was pressed fiercely to his chest. "Steve? Are you all right? Steve?" Over and over again. Until at last he moved the phone to his mouth again, and still crying, said, "Honey?"

"Yes, Steve."

"Tell Mama I'll be there as soon as I can."

"Drive carefully."

"Did you call Teddy?"

"She's on the way."

"Is Tommy there with you?"

"No, we're alone here. Mama and me."

"What do you . . . ? Where's Tommy?"

"I don't know," she said. "Please hurry."

And hung up.

2

THE TWO DETECTIVES from the 45th Squad in Riverhead felt uncomfortable talking to the detective whose father had been killed. Neither of the men knew Carella; the Eight-Seven was a long way from home. Moreover, both detectives were black, and from all accounts the two men who'd robbed Tony Carella's bakery shop and then killed the old man were black themselves.

Neither of the detectives knew how Carella felt about blacks in general. But the murderers were blacks in particular, and the way the black/white thing was shaping up in this city, the two Riverhead cops felt they might be treading dangerous ground here. Carella was a professional, though, and they knew they could safely cut through a lot of the bullshit. He *knew* what they'd be doing to apprehend the men who'd killed his father. They didn't have to spell out routine step by step, the way you had to do with civilians.

The bigger of the two cops was named Charlie Bent, a Detective/Second. He was wearing a sports jacket over blue jeans and an open-collared shirt. Carella could see the bulge of his shoulder holster on the right-hand side of his body. Left-handed, he figured. Bent spoke very quietly, either because he was naturally soft-spoken or else because he was in a funeral home.

The other cop was a Detective/Third, just got his promotion last month, he mentioned to Carella in passing. He was big, too, but not as wide across the shoulders and chest as Bent was. His name was Randy Wade, the Randy being short for Randall, not Randolph. His face was badly pockmarked, and there was an old knife scar over his left eye. He looked as mean as Saturday night, but this was ten o'clock on Wednesday morning, and they were inside the Loretti

Brothers Funeral Home on Vandermeer Hill, and so he was speaking softly, too.

Everyone was speaking softly, tiptoeing around Carella, who for all they knew might be as bigoted as most white men in this city, but whose father had certainly been killed by two black men like themselves, bigot or not. The three detectives were standing in the large entrance foyer that separated the east and west wings. Carella's father was in a coffin in Chapel A in the east wing.

There was a hush in the funeral home.

Carella could remember when he was a kid and his father's sister got run over by an automobile. His Aunt Katie. Killed instantly. Carella had loved her to death. They'd laid her out in this very same funeral home, in one of the chapels over in the west wing.

Back when Aunt Katie died, the family still had older people in it who'd come from the Other Side, as they'd called Europe in general. Some of them could barely speak English. Carella's mother, and sometimes his father—but not too often because his own English showed traces of having been raised in an immigrant home— laughed at the fractured English some of their older relatives spoke. Nobody was laughing when Aunt Katie was here in this place. Aunt Katie was twenty-seven years old when the car knocked her down and killed her.

Carella could still remember the women keening.

The women keening were more frightening than the fact that his dear Aunt Katie lay young and dead in a coffin in the west wing.

Today, there was no keening. The old ways had become American, and Americans did not keen. Today, there was only the hush of death in this silent place where two black cops tiptoed around a white cop because his father had been killed by two black men like themselves.

"The witness seems reliable," Bent said softly. "We've been showing him . . ."

"When did he see these two men?" Carella asked.

"Coming out," Wade said.

"He was in the liquor store next door. He thought he heard shots, and when he turned around to look, he saw these guys . . ."

"What time was this?"

"Around nine-thirty. Your sister told us your father sometimes worked late."

"Yes," Carella said.

"Alone," Bent said.

"Yes," Carella said. "Baking."

"Anyway," Wade said, "he saw them plain as day under the street lamp . . ."

"Getting into a car, or what?"

"No, they were on foot."

"They'd been cruising, we figure, looking for a mark."

"They had to pick my father, huh?"

"Yeah, well," Bent said sympathetically, and shook his head. "We've got the witness looking through mug shots, and we've got an artist working up a drawing, so maybe we'll come up with some kind of positive ID. We're also checking the M.O. file, but there's nothing special about the style of this one, we figure it was maybe two crack addicts cruising for an easy score."

Nothing special about it, Carella thought.

Except that it was his father.

"They're both black," Bent said. "I guess your sister told you that."

"She told me," Carella said.

"We want you to know that our being black . . ."

"You don't have to say it," Carella said.

Both men looked at him.

"No need," he said.

"We'll be doing our best," Wade said.

"I know that."

"We'll keep you informed every step of the way," Bent said.

"I'd appreciate that."

"Meanwhile, anything we can do to help your family, look in on your mother, whatever you need, just let us know."

"Thanks," Carella said. "Whenever you have anything . . ."

"We'll let you know."

"Even if it seems unimportant . . ."

"The minute we get anything."

"Thanks," Carella said.

"My father was killed in a mugging," Wade said out of the blue.

"I'm sorry," Carella said.

"Reason I became a cop," Wade said, and looked suddenly embarrassed.

"This city . . ." Bent started, and let the sentence trail.

Brown had been in the apartment for an hour before Kling arrived to lend a hand. Kling apologized for getting there so late but he didn't get the call from the lieutenant till half an hour ago, while he was still in bed. This was supposed to be his day off, but with Carella's father getting shot and all—

"Are they any good up there?" he asked Brown. "The Four-Five?"

"I don't know anything about them," Brown said.

"That's like the boonies up there, isn't it?"

"Well, I think they have crime up there," Brown said dryly.

"Sure, but what *kind* of crime? Do they ever have murders up there?"

"I think they have murders up there," Brown said.

Kling had taken off his jacket and was looking for a place to hang it. He knew the techs were finished in here and it was okay to touch anything he liked. But he would feel funny putting his jacket in a closet with the dead woman's clothes. He settled for tossing it over the back of the living-room sofa.

He was wearing brown tropical-weight slacks and a tan sports shirt that complemented his hazel eyes and blond hair. Loafers, too, Brown noticed. Mr. College Boy. They made a good pair, these two. Most thieves figured Kling for an innocent young rookie who'd just got the gold shield last week. With all that blond hair and that shit-kicking, apple-cheeked style, it was hard to guess he was a seasoned cop who'd seen more than his share of it. Your average thief mistook him for somebody he could jerk around, play on his sympathies, get him to talk Big Bad Leroy here into looking the other way. Kling and Brown played the Good Cop/Bad Cop routine for all it was worth, Kling restraining Brown from committing murder with his bare hands, Brown acting like an animal just let out of his cage. It worked each and every time.

Well, once it hadn't.

"How's Steve taking it?" Kling asked.

"I haven't seen him this morning," Brown said. "He was pretty shook up last night."

"Yeah, I can imagine," Kling said. "Is your father alive?"

"Yes. Is yours?"

"No."

"So I guess you know."

"Yeah."

"Did the lieutenant say how long you'd be on this?"

"Just till Steve's done with the funeral and everything. He pulled me off a stakeout me and Genero are working on Culver. These grocery-store holdups."

"Yeah," Brown said.

"What are we looking for?" Kling asked.

"Anything that'll give us a line on the guy who wrote these letters," Brown said, and tossed the packet to Kling. Kling sat on the sofa and undid the blue ribbon around the envelopes. He unfolded the first letter and began reading it.

"Don't get too involved there," Brown said.

"Pretty steamy stuff here, Artie."

"I think you may be too young for that kind of stuff."

"Yeah, I agree," Kling said, and fell silent, reading. "*Very* good stuff here," he said.

"It gets better."

"You go on and do whatever you have to do, I'll see you next week sometime."

"Just read the last letter."

"I thought I might read all of them."

"Last one's got everything you need to know."

Kling read the last letter.

"Paying for the apartment here, huh?" he said.

"Looks that way."

"He sounds old, don't you think?"

"What's old to you?"

"In his fifties, maybe. Doesn't he sound that way to you?"

"Maybe."

"Just the words he uses. And the tone. How old was this girl?"

"Twenty-two."

"That sounds very young for this guy."

"You might want to look through some of that stuff in her desk, see if you find anything about anyone named Arthur. I think his name night be Arthur."

"That's *your* name," Kling said.

"No kidding?"

"You sure *you* didn't write these letters? Listen to this," Kling said, and began quoting. "*And afterward, I'll pour oil onto your flaming cheeks, and should any of this oil accidentally flow into your . . .*"

"Yeah," Brown said.

"Some imagination, this guy."

"Check out the desk, will you?"

Kling folded the letter, put it back into its envelope, retied the bundle, and tossed it onto the coffee table. The desk was on the wall opposite the sofa. The drawer over the kneehole was unlocked. He reached into it for a checkbook in a green plastic cover.

"What makes you think his name is Arthur?" he asked.

"I've been going through her appointment calendar. Lots of stuff about Arthur in it. Arthur this, Arthur that. Arthur here at nine, Arthur at Sookie's, call Arthur . . ."

"That's a restaurant on The Stem," Kling said. "Sookie's. He probably figured the turf up here was safe."

"What do you mean *safe?*"

"I don't know," Kling said, and shrugged. "He says his office is downtown, so I figure he knows people down there. So up here would be safe. He may even *live* downtown, for all we know. So up here would be safe from his wife, too. I figure he's married, don't you?"

"Where do you see anything about that?"

"I don't. But if he's single and he lives *downtown* . . ."

"There's nothing there that says he lives downtown."

"How about him taking a cab when he leaves late at night?"

"That doesn't mean he's going downtown."

"All right, forget downtown. But if he isn't married, then why's he keeping a girl *any*place? Why don't they just live together?"

"Well . . . that's a point, yeah."

"So he's this old married guy keeping this young girl in a fancy apartment till he can get her an even *fancier* one."

"Is 'Phil' another restaurant?"

"Phil? I don't know any restaurant named Phil."

"It says here 'Arthur at Phil, eight P.M.'"

"When was that?"

"Last Wednesday night."

"Maybe he's a friend of theirs. Phil."

"Maybe."

"You know how much the rent on this joint comes to each month?" Kling said, looking up from the checkbook.

"How much?"

"Twenty-four hundred bucks."

"Come on, Bert."

"I'm serious. Here are the stubs. The checks are made out to somebody named Phyllis Brackett, for twenty-four hundred a shot, and they're marked Rental. Rental March, Rental April, Rental May, and so on. Twenty-four hundred smackers, Artie."

"And he's trying to find her a *better* place, huh?"

"Must be a *rich* old geezer."

"Here he is again," Brown said, tapping the calendar with his finger. " 'Arthur here, nine P.M.' "

"When?"

"Monday."

"Day before she caught it."

"I wonder if he spent the night."

"No, what he does is take a taxi home to his beloved wife."

"We don't know for sure that he's married," Brown said.

"Got to be," Kling said. "*And* rich. I'm clocking five-thousand-dollar deposits every month on the first of the month. Here, take a look," he said, and handed Brown the checkbook. Brown began leafing through it. Sure enough, there were deposits listed for the first of every month, each for an even five thousand dollars.

"Probably won't help us," Brown said. "His letter . . ."

"Cash, I know," Kling said.

"Even if those deposits were checks, we'd need a court order to get copies of them."

"Might be worth it."

"I'll ask the loot. What was that woman's name again?"

"Brackett. Phyllis Brackett. With a double *T* on the end."

"Take a look at this," Brown said, and handed Kling the calendar. In the square for Monday, the ninth of July, Susan had scrawled the name *Tommy!!!!*

"Four exclamation points," Kling said. "Must've been urgent."

"Let's see what we've got," Brown said, and picked up a spiral book bound in mottled black plastic, Susan Brauer's personal directory.

The only possible listing they found for anyone named Tommy was one under the letter *M: Thomas Mott Antiques.* Brown copied down the address and phone number and then leafed back to the pages following the letter *B.* There was a listing for a Phyllis Brackett at 274 Sounder Avenue. A telephone number was written in below the address. He copied both down, and then they read through the calendar and the directory and the checkbook yet another time, making notes, jotting down names, dates, and possible places Susan Brauer might have visited with the elusive Arthur Somebody during the weeks and days before her murder.

They went through every drawer in the desk and then they turned over the trash basket under the desk and sorted through all the scraps of paper and assorted debris that tumbled out onto the carpet. They spread newspapers on the kitchen floor and went through all the garbage in the pail under the sink. They could find nothing that gave them a last name for the man who was paying the rent on this apartment.

In Susan's bedroom closet, they found a full-length mink coat and a fox jacket . . .

"He's getting richer and richer by the minute," Kling said.

. . . three dozen pairs of shoes . . .

"Imelda Marcos here," Brown said.

. . . eighteen dresses with labels like Adolfo, Chanel, Calvin Klein, Christian Dior . . .

"I wonder what his *wife* wears," Kling said.

. . . three Louis Vuitton suitcases . . .

"Planning a trip?" Brown said.

. . . and a steel lockbox.

Brown picked the lock in thirty seconds flat.

Inside the box, there was twelve thousand dollars in hundred-dollar bills.

The doorman was a dust-colored man with a thin mustache under his nose. He was wearing a gray uniform with red trim and a peaked gray hat with red piping, and he spoke with an almost indecipherable accent they guessed was Middle Eastern. It took them ten minutes to learn that he had been on duty from four P.M. to midnight last night. Now what they wanted to know was whether or not he'd sent anyone up to Miss Brauer's apartment.

"Dunn remembah," he said.

"The penthouse apartment," Kling said. "There's only one pent-house apartment, did you send anybody up there last night?"

"Dunn remembah," he said again.

"Anybody at all go up there?" Brown asked. "A whiskey delivery, anything like that?"

He was thinking about the martinis.

The doorman shook his head.

"Peckage all the time," he said.

"*Package,* is that what you're saying?"

"Peckage, yes."

"People delivering packages?"

"Yes, all the time."

"But this didn't have to be a delivery," Kling said. "It could've been *anyone* going up there to the penthouse. Do you remember *anyone* going up there? Did you buzz Miss Brauer to tell her anyone wanted to come up?"

"Dunn remembah," he said. "Peckage all the time."

Brown wanted to smack him in the mouth.

"Look," he said, "a girl was killed upstairs, and you were on duty during the *time* she was killed. So did you let anyone in? Did you send anyone upstairs?"

"Dunn remembah."

"Did you see anyone suspicious hanging around the building?"

The doorman looked puzzled.

"Suspicious," Kling said.

"Someone who didn't look as if he belonged here," Brown explained.

"Nobody," the doorman said.

When finally they quit, it felt as if they'd been talking to him for a day and a half. But it was only a little after three o'clock.

274 Sounder was a brownstone on a street bordered by trees in full summer leaf. It had taken them close to an hour in heavy traffic to drive from the penthouse apartment on Silvermine Oval all the way down here to the lower end of Isola, and they did not ring Phyllis Brackett's doorbell until almost four o'clock that afternoon.

Mrs. Brackett was a woman in her early fifties, they guessed, allowing her hair to go gray, wearing no makeup, and looking tall and slender and attractive in a wide blue skirt, thong sandals, a sleeveless white blouse, and a string of bright red beads. They had called before coming, and not only was she expecting them, she had also made a pitcher of cold lemonade in anticipation of their arrival. Brown and Kling almost kissed her sandaled feet; both men were hot and sticky and utterly exhausted.

They sat in a kitchen shaded by a backyard maple. Two children were playing in a rubber wading pool under the tree. Mrs. Brackett explained that they were her grandchildren. Her daughter and her son-in-law were on vacation, and she was baby-sitting the two little blonde girls who were splashing merrily away outside the picture window.

Brown told her why they were there.

"Yes," she said at once.

"You were renting the apartment to Susan Brauer."

"Yes, that's right," Mrs. Brackett said.

"Then the apartment is yours . . ."

"Yes. I used to live in it until recently," she said.

They looked at her.

"I was recently divorced," she said. "I'm what is known as a grass widow."

Kling had never heard that expression before. Neither had Brown. They both gathered it meant a divorced woman. Live and learn.

"I didn't want alimony," she said. "I got the apartment and a very large cash settlement. I bought this brownstone with the settlement money, and I get twenty-four hundred a month renting the apartment. I think that's a pretty good deal," she said, and smiled.

They agreed it was a pretty good deal.

"Was anyone handling this for you?" Brown asked. "Renting the apartment uptown? A real estate agent, a rental agent?"

"No. I put an ad in the paper."

"Was Susan Brauer the one who answered the newspaper ad?"

"Yes."

"I mean *personally*," Brown said. "Was she the one who wrote . . . or called . . . ?"

"She called me, yes."

"She herself? Not anyone calling for her? It wasn't a man who called, was it?"

"No, it was Miss Brauer."

"What happened then?" Brown asked.

"We arranged to meet at the apartment. I showed it to her, and she liked it, and we agreed on the rent, and that was it."

"Did she sign a lease?"

"Yes."

"For how long?"

"A year."

"And when was this?" Kling asked.

"In February."

Fast worker, Kling thought. He meets her on New Year's Day, and he's got her set up in an apartment a month later. Brown was thinking the same thing.

"I don't know what to do now that she . . . well, it's just a terrible tragedy, isn't it?" Mrs. Brackett said. "I suppose I'll have to contact my lawyer. The man who drew the lease. I guess that's the thing to do."

"Yes," Kling said.

"Yes," Brown said. "Mrs. Brackett, I want to make sure we've got this absolutely right. You were renting the apartment *directly* to Miss Brauer, is that right?"

"Yes. She sent me a check each month. To this address."

"No middleman," Brown said.

"No middleman. That's the best way, isn't it?" she said, and smiled again.

"Do you know anyone named Arthur?" Kling asked.

"No, I'm sorry, I don't."

"Did Miss Brauer ever introduce you to anyone named Arthur?"

"No. I only saw her once, in fact, the day we met at the apartment. Everything since then has been through the mail. Well, several times we spoke on the telephone, when she . . ."

"Oh? Why was that?"

"She needed to know how to work the disposal . . . there's a switch on the wall . . . and she wanted the combination to the wall safe, but I wouldn't give her that."

"Did she say why she wanted the combination?"

"No. I assume to put something *in* the safe, wouldn't you guess?"

I would guess, Kling thought.

Like twelve grand, Brown thought.

"Thank you very much for your time," Kling said. "We appreciate it."

"Some more lemonade?" she asked.

Outside, the little girls kept splashing in the pool.

Thomas Mott was a man in his late forties, early fifties, with stark white hair, deep brown eyes, and a face that seemed carved from alabaster. Brown guessed his height at five-eight, his weight at a hundred and forty. Slender and slight, wearing skintight black jeans, a red cotton sweater, and black loafers without socks, he flitted among the treasures in his Drittel Avenue shop like a dancer in a Russian ballet. Brown wondered if he was gay. There was something almost too delicate about the way he moved. But he was wearing a narrow gold wedding band.

Kling could not have named or dated any of the antiques here if he were being stretched on a rack or roasted on a spit, but he knew he was in the presence of objects of extreme beauty. Burnished brass and wood rubbed to a gleaming patina, tiny clocks that ticked like chickadees, stately clocks that tocked in counterpoint, beautiful bottles in ruby reds and emerald greens, silver-filigreed boxes and bronze lamps with stained-glass shades that glowed with vibrant color. There was a hush in the place. He felt as if he were in an ancient cathedral.

"Yes, of course I know her," Mott said. "A terrible shame, what happened to her. A lovely person."

"Why'd she come in here on the ninth?" Brown asked.

"Well, she was a customer, she stopped by every now and then, you know."

"But was there something special about the ninth?" Kling asked. He was thinking of those exclamation points.

"No, not that I can remember."

"Because her appointment calendar made it look like something important," Kling said.

"Well, let me see," Mott said.

"How well did you know her?" Brown asked, biting the bullet.

"As well as I knew any of my customers."

"And how well was that?"

"As I said, she came in every now and . . ."

"Well enough to call you Tommy?"

"All my customers call me Tommy."

"When was the last time she came in?"

"Last week sometime, I suppose."

"Would it have been last Monday?"

"Well, I . . ."

"The ninth?"

"I suppose it could have been."

"Mr. Mott," Kling said, "we've got this idea that Miss Brauer felt it was important for her to come in here last Monday. Would you happen to know why?"

"Oh," he said.

Comes the dawn, Brown thought.

"Yes, now I remember," Mott said. "The table."

"What table?"

"I'd told her I was expecting a butler's table from England . . ."

"When did you tell her that, Mr. Mott?"

"Well . . . last month sometime. She came in sometime last month. As I told you, she stopped by every . . ."

"Every now and then, right," Brown said. "So when she was in last month, you mentioned a butler's table to her . . ."

"Yes, that was coming from England on or about the ninth, was what I told her."

"What kind of table is that?" Kling asked. "A butler's table?"

"Well, it's a . . . I'd show it to you, but I'm afraid it's already gone. This was solid cherry, quite a good buy at seventeen hundred dollars. I thought she might be able to find a place for it in her apartment. She jotted down the date I was expecting it, and said she'd give me a call."

"But instead she came to the shop."

"Yes."

"On Monday the ninth," Kling said.

"Yes."

"So that's what was so urgent," Brown said. "A cherrywood butler's table."

"A quite beautiful piece," Mott said. "She couldn't use it . . . from what I was able to gather, she was renting a furnished apartment . . . but it went in a minute. Well, only seventeen hundred dollars," he said, and raised his eyebrows and moved his hands in an accompanying extravagant gesture.

"What time did she come in here?" Kling asked. "Last Monday."

"It was toward noon. Shortly before noon. Sometime between eleven-thirty and twelve o'clock."

"You remember, huh?" Brown said.

"Yes. It was about that time." As if on cue, somewhere in the shop a clock began chiming the hour. "A Joseph Knibb," Mott said, almost idly. "Quite rare, quite valuable, such lovely chimes."

The clock chimed six times.

Mott looked at his watch.

"Well, I guess that's it," Brown said. "Thanks a lot, Mr. Mott."

"Thanks," Kling said.

The moment they were out on the street again, Brown said, "You think he's gay?"

"He was wearing a wedding band."

"I caught it. That doesn't mean anything."

"What's a butler's table?" Kling asked.

"I don't know," Brown said, and looked up at the sky. "I hope Carella gets good weather tomorrow," he said.

Deputy Inspector William Cullen Brady was telling the trainees that he took no credit for organizing the hostage negotiating team. Listening to him, Eileen felt uncomfortable because she thought she was over-dressed.

This was the first meeting of the training class.

Thursday morning, the nineteenth day of July. Nine o'clock.

For work she'd normally have worn either slacks or a wide skirt, comfortable shoes, big tote bag—unless they were dolling her up for the street. But she hadn't decked herself out as a decoy since the night she'd killed Robert Wilson. Bobby. She supposed that was known as shirking the work. Not precisely doing the job for which she was getting paid. Which was why she was here today, she guessed. So she could go back to doing an honest job someplace in the department.

She was wearing a simple suit, brown to complement her red hair and green eyes, tan blouse with a stock tie, sand-colored pantyhose, low-heeled pumps, fake alligator-skin bag. Service revolver in the bag, alongside the lipstick. Overdressed for sure. The only other woman in the room, a tiny brunette with a hard, mean look, was wearing jeans and a white cotton T-shirt. Most of the men were dressed casually, too. Slacks, sports shirts, jeans, only one of them wearing a jacket.

There were five trainees altogether. Three men, two women. Brady was telling them that the unit had been organized by former chief of patrol Ralph McCleary when he was still a captain some twenty years back. ". . . never would have *been* a team," he was saying. "We'd still be breaking down doors and going in with shotguns. His ideas worked then, and they still work. I take credit for only one new concept. I put women on the team. We've already got two women in the field, and I hope to have another two out there . . ."

A nod and a smile to Eileen and the brunette.

". . . by the time we finish this training program."

Brady was in his early fifties, Eileen supposed, a tall, trim man with bright blue eyes and a fringe of white hair circling his otherwise bald head. Nose a bit too prominent for his otherwise small features. Gave his face a cleaving look. He was the only man in the room wearing a tie. Even Dr. Goodman, who sat beside him at the desk in front of the classroom, was casually dressed in a plaid sports shirt and dark blue slacks.

"Before we get started," Brady said, "I'd like to take a minute to introduce all of you. I'll begin here on the left . . . *my* left, that is . . . with Detective/First Grade Anthony . . . am I pronouncing this correctly . . . Anthony Pellegrino?"

"Yes, sir, that's it, Pellegrino, like the mineral water."

Short and wiry, with dark curly hair and brown eyes. Badly pock-marked face. Olive complexion. Eileen wondered why Brady had questioned the pronunciation of a simple name like Pellegrino. Especially when it *was* the brand name of a widely known mineral water. Hadn't Brady ever been to an Italian restaurant? But there were people in this city who got thrown by any name ending in an *o*, an *a*, or an *i*. Maybe Brady was one of them. She hoped not.

"Detective/First Grade Martha Halsted . . ."

The petite brunette with the Go-to-Hell look. Cupcake breasts, the narrow hips of a boy.

"Martha's with the Robbery Squad," Brady said.

Figures, Eileen thought.

"I forgot to mention, by the way, that Tony's with Safe, Loft and Truck."

He kept going down the line, Detective/Third Grade Daniel Riley of the Nine-Four, Detective/Second Grade Henry Materasso—had no trouble pronouncing *that* one—of the Two-Seven, and last but not least Detective/Second Grade Eileen Burke . . .

"Eileen is with Special Forces."

Martha Halsted looked her over.

"I'm not sure whether Dr. Goodman . . ."

"Mike'll do," Goodman said, and smiled.

"I'm not sure whether *Mike*"—a smile, a nod—"explained during the interviews that while you're attached to the hostage unit, you'll continue in your regular police duties . . ."

Oh, terrific, Eileen thought.

". . . but you'll be on call here twenty-four hours a day. As I'm sure you know, hostage situations come up when we least expect them. Our first task is to get there fast before anyone gets hurt. And once we're on the scene, our job is to make sure that nobody *gets* hurt. That means *nobody*. Not the hostages and not the hostage-takers, either."

"How about *us*, Inspector?"

This from Henry Materasso of the Two-Seven. Big guy with wide shoulders, a barrel chest, and fiery red hair. Not red like Eileen's, which had a burnished-bronze look, but red as in carrot top. The butt of a high-caliber service revolver was showing in a shoulder holster under his sports jacket. Eileen always felt a shoulder holster spelled macho. She was willing to bet Materasso had been called "Red" from the day he first went outside to play with the other kids. Red Materasso. The Red Mattress. *And* the class clown.

Everyone laughed.

Including Brady, who said, "It goes without saying that *we* don't want to get hurt, either."

The laughter subsided. Materasso looked pleased. Martha Halsted looked as if *nothing* pleased her. Poker up her ass, no doubt. Eileen wondered how many armed cowboys she'd blown away in her career at Robbery. She wondered, too, what Detective/First Grade Martha Halsted was doing here, where the job was to make sure nobody got hurt. And she also wondered what she *herself* was doing here. If this wasn't going to be a full-time job, if they could still put her on the street to be stalked and—

"How often do these hostage situations come up, Inspector?"

Halsted. Reading her mind. How often do these situations come up? How often will we be pulled off our regular jobs? Which in Eileen's case was strutting the streets waiting for a rapist or a murderer to attack her. Wonderful job, even if the pay wasn't so hot. So how often, Inspector? Will this be like delivering groceries part time for the local supermarket? Or do I get to work more regularly at something that doesn't involve rape or murder as a consequence of the line of duty?

I don't want to kill anyone else, she thought.

I don't want anybody to get hurt ever again.

Especially me.

So how often do I get a reprieve, Inspector?

"We're not talking now about *headline* hostage situations," Brady said, "where a group of terrorists takes over an embassy or an airplane or a ship or whatever. We're lucky we haven't had any of those in the United States—at least not *yet*. I'm talking about a situation that can occur once a week or once a month or once every six months, it's hard to give you an average. We seem to get more of them in the summer months, but all crime statistics go up during the summertime . . ."

"*And* when there's a full moon," Riley said.

A wiry Irishman from the Nine-Four, as straight and as narrow and as hard-looking as a creosoted telephone pole. Thin-lipped mouth, straight black hair, deep blue eyes. Matching blue shirt. Tight blue jeans. Holster clipped to his belt on the left hand side for a quick cross-body draw. Plant him and the dame from Robbery in the same dark alley and no thief in the world would dare venture into it. Eileen wondered how the people in this room had been chosen. Was compassion one of the deciding factors? If so, why Halsted and Riley—who looked mean enough to pass for the Bonnie and Clyde of law enforcement?

"That's statistically true, you know," Goodman said. "There *are* more crimes committed when the moon is full."

"Tell us about it," Materasso said, grinning, and looked around for approval.

Everyone laughed again.

It occurred to Eileen that the only person in the room who hadn't said a word so far was Detective/Second Grade Eileen Burke. Of Special Forces.

Well, Pellegrino hadn't said much, either.

"This might be a good time to turn things over to Mike," Brady said.

Goodman rose from where he was sitting, nodded, said, "Thanks, Inspector," and walked to the blackboard.

Actually, it was a greenboard. Made of some kind of plastic material that definitely wasn't slate. Eileen wondered if the movie she'd seen on late-night television last week would have made it as *Greenboard Jungle*. She also wondered why everyone in the room was on a first-name basis except Deputy Inspector William Cullen Brady, who so far wasn't either William or Cullen or Bill or Cully but was simply and respectfully Inspector, which *all* deputy inspectors in the police department were called informally.

Goodman picked up a piece of chalk.

"I'd like to start with the various types of hostage-takers we can expect to encounter," he said.

His eyes met Eileen's.

"Inspector Brady has already mentioned . . ."

Or was she mistaken?

". . . terrorists, the political zealots who are the most commonly known of all takers," Goodman said, and chalked the word onto the board:

TERRORIST

"But there are two other types of takers we'll . . . let's get used to that shorthand, shall we?" he said, and chalked another word onto the board:

TAKER

"The takers we'll most frequently encounter . . ."

No, she wasn't mistaken.

". . . can be separated into three categories. First, as we've seen, we have the terrorist. Next, we have the criminal caught in the . . ."

*   *   *

He rode in the limo with the three women dressed in black. Sat between his mother and his wife, his sister on the jump seat in front of them, everyone silent as the big car nosed its way through the Thursday morning heat and humidity, moving slowly in convoy toward the cemetery where Aunt Katie was buried. His father was in the hearse ahead. He had talked to his father on the telephone only last week. It occurred to him that he would never talk to his father again.

Teddy took his hand.

He nodded.

Beside him, his mother was weeping into a small handkerchief edged with lace. His sister, Angela, stared woodenly through the window, gazing blankly at the sunlit landscape moving past outside the car.

It was too hot to be wearing black.

They stood in the hot sun while the priest said the words of farewell to a man who had taught Carella the precepts of truth and honor he had followed all his life. The coffin was shiny and black, it reflected the sun, threw back the sun in dazzling bursts of light.

It was over too soon.

They were lowering the coffin into the ground. He almost reached out to touch it. And then his father was gone. Gone from sight. Into the ground. And they moved away from the grave. His arm around his mother. A widow now. Louise Carella. A widow. Behind them, the gravediggers were already shoveling earth onto the coffin. He could hear the earth thudding onto the hot, shiny metal. He hoped his mother would not hear the earth hitting the coffin, covering his father.

He left his mother for a moment, and walked up the grassy knoll to where the priest was standing with Angela and Teddy. Angela was telling the priest how beautiful the eulogy had been. Teddy was watching her lips, reading them, eyes intent. They stood side by side in black in the sun, both of them dark-haired and dark-eyed—he wondered suddenly if that was why he'd chosen Teddy Franklin as his wife all those years ago.

Angela was in her early thirties now, enormously pregnant and imminently parturient with her second child. She still wore her brown hair long, cascading straight down on either side of eyes surprisingly Oriental in a high-cheekboned face. The face was a refinement of Carella's, pretty with an exotic tint that spoke of Arabian visits to the island of Sicily in the far-distant past.

Teddy was a far more beautiful woman, taller than her sister-in-law, her midnight-black hair worn in a wedge, intelligence flashing in her dark eyes as she turned now to study the priest's mouth, translating the articulation of his lips into words that filled the silence of her world: Teddy Carella was deaf; nor had she ever spoken a word in her life.

Carella joined them, thanked the priest for a lovely service, although secretly—and he would never tell this to a soul, not even Teddy—he'd felt that the priest's words could have applied to *anyone*, and not to the unique and wonderful man who'd been Antonio Giovanni Carella, so-named by an immigrant grandfather who'd never once realized that such names would never be in fashion in the good old U.S. of A. Nevertheless, Carella invited the priest to join the family at the house, where there'd be something to eat and drink—

"Well, thank you, no, Mr. Carella," the priest said, "I must get back to the church, thank you anyway. And, once again, be cheered by the knowledge that your father is now at peace in God's hands," he said, which caused Carella to wonder whether the priest had even the faintest inkling of how *much* at peace his father had been while he was still alive. To make this point clear, the priest took Carella's hand between both his own and pressed it, from God's hands to Father Gianelli's hands, so to speak, in direct lineage. Carella remained unimpressed.

Teddy had noticed that her mother-in-law was now standing alone some ten yards or so down the knoll. She touched Carella on the arm, signed to him that she was going to join his mother, and left him there with the priest still sandwiching Carella's hand between his own, Angela looking on helplessly. Standing in black, her hands resting on her big belly, her back hurting like hell, she knew damn well that the priest's eulogy had been boilerplate. Fill in the blanks and the dead man could have been anyone. Except that it had been her father.

"I must be on my way," the priest said, sounding like a vicar in an English novel. He made the sign of the cross on the air, blessing God only knew whom or what, picked up his black skirts, and went off toward where his sexton was standing beside the parish car.

"He didn't know Papa at all," Angela said.

Carella nodded.

"You okay?" he asked.

"Yes, fine," she said.

The sexton gunned the priest's car into life. Down the knoll, Teddy was gently hugging Carella's mother, who was still crying into her handkerchief. The car moved off. On the lawn below, the two figures in black were etched in silhouette against the brilliant sky. On the knoll above, Carella stood with his sister.

"I loved him a lot," she said.

"Yes."

He felt inadequate.

"We'd better get to the house," she said. "There'll be people."

"Have you heard from Tommy?" he asked.

"No," she said, and turned suddenly away.

He realized all at once that she was crying. Mistaking her tears as grief for his father, he started to say, "Honey, please, he wouldn't have wanted . . ." and then saw that she was shaking her head, telling him wordlessly that he did not understand the tears, did not know why she was crying, stood there in black in pregnancy in utter misery, shaking her head helplessly in the unrelenting sunlight.

"What is it?" he asked.

"Nothing."

"You told me you thought he was still in California . . ."

Shaking her head.

"You said he was trying to get back in time for the funeral . . ."

Still shaking her head, tears streaming down her face.

"Angela, what is it?"

"Nothing."

"*Is* Tommy in California?"

"I don't know."

"What do you mean, you don't know? He's your husband, where is he?"

"Steve, please . . . I don't know."

"Angela . . ."

"He's gone."

"Gone? Gone where?"

"Gone. He left me, Steve. He walked out."

"What are you saying?"

"I'm saying my husband walked out on me."

"No."

"For Christ's sake, do you think I'm making this *up?*" she said fiercely, and burst into fresh tears.

He took her in his arms. He held her close, his pregnant sister in black, who too many years ago had been afraid to come out of her bedroom to join her future husband at the altar. She'd been wearing white that day, and he'd told her she was going to be the prettiest bride the neighborhood had ever seen. And then he'd said . . .

Oh, Jesus, as if it were yesterday.

He'd said . . .

Angela, you have nothing to worry about. He loves you so much he's trembling. He loves you, honey. He's a good man. You chose well.

His sister was trembling in his arms now.

"Why?" he asked her.

"I think he has someone else," she said.

Carella held her at arm's length and looked into her face. She nodded. And nodded again. Her tears were gone now. She stood in bloated silhouette against the sky, her brother's hands clasping her shoulders.

"How do you know?" he asked.

"I just know."

"Angela . . ."

"We have to get back to the house," she said. "Please, it'll be a sin."

He had not heard that expression since he was a boy.

"I'll talk to him," he said.

"No, don't. Please."

"You're my sister," he said.

"Steve . . ."

"You're my sister," he said again. "And I love you."

Their eyes met. Chinese eyes meeting Chinese eyes, dark brown and slanting downward, the Carella heritage clearly evident, brother and sister reaffirming blood ties as powerful as life itself. Angela nodded.

"I'll talk to him," he whispered, and walked her pregnant down the grassy knoll to where Teddy and his mother stood waiting in black in the sunshine.

3

THE GUN had been a gift from him.

Everyone in this city should have a gun, he'd said, should know how to use a gun if and when the need arose. Said the police were worthless when it came to protecting the lives of ordinary citizens. The police were too busy tracking down prostitutes and drug addicts.

Where he'd bought the gun was anybody's guess.

He traveled a lot by car, he could have picked it up in any of the states that thought America was still the Wild West with hostile Indians massing to attack, better get those wagons in a circle and unholster the Mac 10s. *Bought you something,* he'd said. *I'll teach you to use it.*

That was the irony of it.

The gun was a .22-caliber Colt Cobra.

He'd explained that it was a part-aluminum version of the higher-caliber Detective Special, but people shouldn't let the caliber of a gun fool them, a .22 could do as much damage—even more damage some-times—as a higher-caliber gun. The reason for this was that the lower-caliber slug would bounce around inside the body without the power to exit, and it could wreak havoc with all the organs in there. Wreak havoc. Those had been his exact words. Wreak havoc. Which was exactly what was planned for tonight. The wreaking of a little more havoc.

The gun was a revolver with a six-shot capacity. It weighed only fif-teen ounces, and he had chosen the one with the two-inch barrel, which made it nice in that it wouldn't snag on your clothing. A nice gun. It had been easy learning how to use it, too, he'd kept his promise. That was the irony.

This time, it would be deliberate.

Malice aforethought, wasn't that what they called it?

Tuesday afternoon had been different.

Tonight would be simpler.

Tonight there was the gun.

The building was tree-shaded, and so the sidewalks had not been baking under a merciless sun for hours on end; the street at nine o'clock was refreshingly cool. Cool here in the shadows across the street from the building. Cool waiting here under a big old tree with thick leaves, right hand wrapped around the butt of the Cobra, index finger inside the trigger guard. He would walk his dog at nine o'clock sharp. A creature of habit. Walk a dog at nine, fuck a mistress any chance he got. In ten minutes, he would be dead.

Waiting.

Dressed entirely in black, a black cotton jumpsuit, black socks and jogging shoes, black woolen ski hat pulled down over the ears, sweltering in the woolen hat, but it covered the hair, concealed the color of the hair, no stray pedestrian or motorist would later be able to come up with a good description.

He came out of the building at two minutes to nine, eight fifty-eight on the digital watch, said something to the doorman who was out taking the air, and then started toward the corner, leading his dog. Eight fifty-nine now, and a dark empty street. No cars, no people. Even the doorman had gone back inside again. *Go!*

Cross the street diagonally . . .

Gun out and ready . . .

Step onto the sidewalk and into his path and level the gun at him . . .

"Are you crazy?" he said.

"Yes."

Calmly.

And shot him four times in the head.

And shot the whimpering dog, too, for good measure.

The neighborhood was still largely Italian, the bakery shop wedged between a grocery store and a sausage shop that had an Italian sign in the window, SALUMERIA. Two- or three-story buildings along the street here, clapboard and frame, stores on the ground-floor level, owners usually occupying the upper floor or floors. There were still trees along this street. No graffiti on the buildings. Still something Old World about it.

Carella could remember growing up in this neighborhood when many of the cadences were still Italian, when Italian-language radio stations still played songs like *"La Tarantella"* and *"O Sole Mio"* and *"Funiculì-Funiculà,"* the music floating out on the summertime air through open windows all up and down the street. He could remember helping his father in the bakery shop on weekends, when the crowds were thickest, kneading the dough for the bread while his father handled the more delicate art of pastry-making. Carella's hands would be covered with flour. Kneading the dough. When he turned fourteen, fifteen—who could remember now, he'd been a late bloomer—he began to think the dough felt exactly like a girl's breasts. Kneading the dough. Well, exactly like Margie Gannon's breasts, in fact, because this was after he'd experienced his first heavy petting session with her. Or with anyone, for that matter.

Margie Gannon.

Freckled all over, including her breasts, which he'd released from her blouse and her bra one Saturday afternoon while the rain and her breasts came tumbling down, he and she feverish and intent in the living room of the two-story brick house two houses down from his own, her parents out doing the marketing or the shopping or wherever they were, the only thing that mattered was that they'd be gone all afternoon—*They won't be back till four or five,* she'd told him, *come in out of the rain, Steve.*

He had gone there to read comic books with her. Margie had the best comic-book collection in the neighborhood. Kids used to come from blocks away, boys and girls, all of them barely pubescent, to read Margie Gannon's comic books. Her parents encouraged it as a nice clean way of socializing. But they should not have left their lovely young daughter (heh-heh) in the clutches of the mad beast named Stephen the Horny, certainly not on a sultry afternoon in August, with lightning flashing and thunder booming outside, and with all his adolescent juices coming to a boil, not to mention hers.

Alone with Margie Gannon in the ground-floor living room of her house. Parents gone. Rain pelting the windows. Their heads bent over the comic book. Heads almost touching. His arm on the couch behind her. She was holding one side of the comic book in her right hand, he was holding the other side in his left. Heads together. There was the sudden feel of her hair against his cheek. Long reddish-blonde hair. Silken hair against his cheek. Green-eyed, freckle-faced, Irish Margie Gannon sitting beside him with her hair touching his cheek. He was suddenly erect in his pants.

He could not remember now which comic they were reading. Something to do with cops and archcriminals? He could not remember. He remembered what she was wearing, though, still remembered *that*. A short, faded blue-denim skirt and a white, short-sleeved blouse buttoned up the front. Freckled pretty Irish face, freckled slender arms, freckled everything, he was soon to discover, but for now there was only the tingling thrill of her silken hair touching his cheek. She reached up with her left hand, brushed the hair back from her face. Their cheeks touched.

It was as if an intensely sharp light suddenly spilled onto the open comic book. Not daring to look at her, he concentrated his vision on the brilliantly illuminated pages, alive now with pulsating primary colors, red and blue and yellow outlined in the blackest black, focused his white-hot gaze on the action-frozen figures and the shouted oversized words, POW and BAM and BANG and YIIIIKES leaping from the pages, repeating in print the triphammer of his heart, POW, BAM, BANG, echoing the fierce erection in his pants, YIIIIKES!

He turned his face toward hers, she turned her face toward his.

Their noses banged.

Their lips collided.

And oh, dear God, he kissed sweet Margie Gannon, and she moved into his suddenly encircling arms, the comic book POW-ing and BAM-ing and BANG-ing and sliding off her knees and falling to the floor with a whispered YIIIIKES as lightning flashed and thunder boomed and rain relentlessly drilled the sidewalk outside the street-level living room. They kissed for he could not remember how long. He would never again in his life kiss anyone this long or this hard, pressing her close, lips fusing, adolescent yearnings merging, steamy young passions crazing the sky with blue-white flashes, rending the sky with blue-black explosions.

His hand eventually discovered the buttons on her blouse. He fumbled awkwardly with the buttons, this was his goddamn *left* hand and he was *right*-handed, fumbling, fearful she would change her mind, terrified she would stop him before he managed to get even the *top* button open. They were both breathing audibly and hard now, their hearts pounding as he tried desperately to get the blouse open. She helped him with the top button, her own trembling hand guiding his, and then the next button seemed to pop open magically or possibly miraculously, and the one after that and oh my God her bra suddenly appeared in the wide V of the open blouse, a white bra, she was wearing a white bra.

Lightning flashed, thunder boomed.

He thought Thank you, God, and touched the bra, the cones of the bra, white, her breasts filling the white bra, his hand still trembling as he touched the bra awkwardly and tentatively, fumbling and unsure because whereas he'd *dreamt* of doing this with girls in general and Margie Gannon in particular, he never thought he would ever really *get* to do it.

But here he was, actually *doing* it—thank you God, oh Jesus *thank you*—or at least *trying* to do it, wondering whether he should slide his hand down inside the bra, or lower the straps off her shoulders, or get the damn thing *off* somehow, they fastened in the back, didn't they? Trying to dope all this out in what seemed like an hour and a half but was only less than a minute until Margie moved out of his arms, a faint flushed smile on her face, and reached behind her, arms bent, he could see the freckles on the sloping tops of her pretty breasts straining in the bra as she reached behind her to unclasp it, and all at once her breasts came tumbling free, the rain kept tumbling down in torrents, and oh dear God, her breasts were in his hands, he was touching Margie Gannon's sweet naked breasts.

He wondered what had ever become of her.

He could never walk the streets of this neighborhood without thinking of Margie Gannon on that rainy August afternoon.

Carella did not know what had led him back here tonight. Perhaps he wanted only to be near the place where his father had spent most of his waking hours. Be there to feel again the essence of the man he had been. Until it faded entirely. There was a light on in the back of his father's bakery shop. Nine-thirty on a Friday night, a light burning. Just as if his father were still alive, baking his pastries and bread for the big weekend rush. The guys from the Four-Five must have forgotten to—

A shadow suddenly appeared on the shade covering the upper glass panel of the rear door to the shop.

Carella tensed, threw back the flap of his jacket, unholstered his gun.

The shadow moved.

He walked stealthily to the side of the building.

A good policeman never entered a room or a house without first listening at the door, ear pressed to the wood, trying to ascertain whether anyone was inside there. He knew someone was inside his father's shop, but he didn't know how many were in there or who it was. There was a window on the side of the shop, better than a door in that he could *see* who was in there without having to guess at sounds or voices filtered through a door. He skirted the window, approached it from the side, and ducked below the sill. Cautiously, he raised his head.

It was his mother inside there.

He sat alone in the living room, crying. The room was dark except for the soft glow of the imitation Tiffany lamp behind him. He sat in the big easy chair under the lamp, his shoulders quaking, tears streaming down his face.

Teddy could not hear his sobs.

She went to him, sat on the arm of the chair, gently pulled his head to her shoulder. He had never been a man who'd thought of crying as shameful or embarrassing. He cried because he was pained, and whereas the emotion was painful, the act itself was not; this was a distinction someone more macho might not have appreciated. He cried now. His head cradled on his wife's shoulder, he cried until there were no more tears left in him. And then he raised his head and dried his face with a handkerchief already soggy and looked at her and nodded, and sighed heavily and forlornly.

She signed *Tell me.*

He told her with his mouth and with his hands, words forming on his lips and his fingers, spilling into the silence of the living room where only the imitation Tiffany glowed. The grandfather clock standing against the far wall struck the hour, eleven o'clock, but Teddy could not hear the bonging, could not hear her husband's words except as she watched them on his lips and on his fingers.

He told her he'd watched his mother through the window at the side of the shop. Watched her touching things. Moving around the shop touching things his father had used. The rolling pins and baking pans, the spatulas and spoons, the pastry sheets—even the handles on the big oven doors. He'd watched her for a long time. Moving about the shop silently, touching each item lovingly.

He'd gone around back at last to where the Crime Scene signs were tacked to the back door of the shop, the police padlock gone, but the signs still there. The shade was drawn, his mother's shadow flitted on the shade as she moved silently about the shop. He rapped gently on the glass panel.

She said, "Who is it?"

"It's me," he said. "Steve."

"Ah," she said, and came to the door and unlocked it.

He went in and took her in his arms. She was a good head shorter than he was, wearing the mourning black she would wear for a long time to come, following the tradition of the old country even though she'd been born here in the United States. He held her gently and patted her back. Tiny little pats. I'm here, Mama, it's all right. I'm here.

She spoke against his shoulder.

She said, "I came here to see if I could find him, Steve."

Patting her. Comforting her.

"But he's gone," she said.

Carella looked up at his wife now, looked directly into her eyes intent on his face, and said, "I've been crying for her, Teddy. Not Papa, but her. Because she's the one who's alone now. She's the widow."

The doorman at 1137 Selby Place was telling the detectives that he'd talked to the victim not three minutes before he heard the shots.

"We exchanged a few words about the weather," he said. "That's all everybody talks about these days is the weather. 'Cause it's been so hot."

It had cooled off a bit, the forecasters said there'd be rain tonight.

The detectives were standing on the sidewalk where the technicians still worked within the rectangle defined by the yellow crime-scene tapes stretching from trees and police stanchions to the wall of the apartment building. Monoghan and Monroe had left half an hour ago. So had the medical examiner and the ambulance taking the body of the dead man to the morgue. Hawes and Willis had caught the squeal and they were the only ones left with the technicians, who were busily searching the sidewalk and gutter for whatever they could find.

The doorman was shorter than Hawes but taller than Willis—well, almost everybody was taller than Willis, who'd barely cleared the department's five-foot-eight-inch height requirement when he joined the force all those years ago. Things had changed since then. Now you had women cops who were a lot shorter than that, though Hawes still hadn't seen any midgets in uniform. He didn't like being partnered with Willis. The man was too damn sad these days. He could understand grieving for a loved one, but that didn't mean you had to inflict the pain on everyone around you.

Hawes had scarcely known the woman Willis was living with. Marilyn Hollis. Victim of a felony murder, pair of burglars broke in, put her away, something like that, Hawes never had got it straight. There'd been a lot of tiptoeing around this one, something about Willis being at the scene and blowing the two perps away, Carella and Byrnes both advising Hawes not to ask too many questions. This was two, three months ago, time moved like molasses in this precinct, especially in the summertime.

Willis was handling the questioning now.

Asking about the dead man in a dead man's voice.

"His name?"

"Arthur Schumacher."

"Apartment number?"

"Sixty-two."

Sad brown eyes intent on his pad. Curly black hair, the slight slender build of a matador. Detective Hal Willis. The sadness seeping out of him like sweat.

"Married, single, would you know?"

A dead toneless voice.

"Married," the doorman said.

"Any children?"

"Not living here. He's got grown daughters from a previous marriage. One of them comes to see him every now and then. *Came* to see him."

"Would you know his wife's name?" Hawes asked.

"Marjorie, I think. She's away just now, if you planned on talking to her."

"Away where?"

"They have a summer place out on the Iodines."

"How do you know she's there?"

"Saw her when she left."

"Which was when?"

"Wednesday morning."

"You saw her leaving?"

"Yes, said good morning to her and all."

"Do you know when she's coming back?"

"No, I don't. They usually split their time between here and there in the summer months."

The doorman seemed to be enjoying all this. Except for the killer, he was the last person to have seen the victim alive, and he was clearly relishing his role as star witness, looking ahead to when they caught the killer and the case came to trial. He would take the stand and tell the district attorney just what he was telling the detectives now, though it was hard to believe the tiny little guy here was actually a detective. The big one, yes, no question. But the little one? In the doorman's experience, most detectives in this city were big, that was a fact of life in this city. You hardly ever saw a small detective.

"What time would you say Mr. Schumacher came downstairs with the dog?" the little one asked.

"Little before nine." Practicing for what he'd tell the district attorney. "Same as every night. Unless him and his wife were going out someplace together, in which case he'd walk the dog earlier. But weeknights, it was usually nine o'clock when he took down the dog."

Hawes guessed the doorman considered Friday night a weeknight. Hawes himself considered it the start of the weekend. He would be spending this weekend with Annie Rawles. Lately, he had been spending *most* of his weekends with Annie Rawles. He wondered if this could be considered serious. To tell the truth, it was a little frightening.

"What happened then?" Willis asked.

"He started walking up the street," the doorman said. "With the dog."

"Where were you?"

"I went back inside."

"Did you see anyone before you went back in?"

"Nobody."

"Across the street? Or up the block?"

"Nobody."

"When did you hear the shots?"

"Almost the minute I went back in the building. Well, maybe a few seconds later, no more than that."

"You knew they were shots, huh?"

"I know shots when I hear them. I was in Nam."

"How many shots?"

"Sounded like a full clip to me. The dog got shot, too, you know. Nice gentle dog. Why would anyone want to kill a dog?"

Why would anyone want to kill a *human?* Willis wondered.

"You'll want these," one of the technicians said, walking over. He was wearing jeans, white sneakers, and a white T-shirt. He handed Willis a small manila envelope printed with the word EVIDENCE. "Four bullets," he said. "Must've went on through."

Overhead, there was a sudden flash of lightning.

"Gonna rain," the doorman observed.

"Thanks," Willis said to the technician, and took the envelope, and sealed it, and put it in the right-hand pocket of his jacket. Hawes looked at his watch. It was a quarter past eleven. He wondered how they could reach Mrs. Schumacher. He didn't want to hang around here all night.

"You have a number for them out on the Iodines?" he asked.

"No, I'm sorry, I don't. Maybe the super has. But he won't be in till tomorrow morning."

"What time tomorrow?"

"He's usually here by eight."

"Would you know which island?"

"I'm sorry, I don't know that, either."

"Was the dog barking or anything?" Willis asked.

"I didn't hear the dog barking."

"Did you hear Mr. Schumacher say anything?"

"Nothing. All I heard was the shots."

"What then?"

"I came running outside."

"And?"

"I looked up and down the street to see where the shots had come from . . ."

"Uh-huh."

". . . and saw Mr. Schumacher laying on the sidewalk there." He glanced toward where the technicians had chalked the outline of Schumacher's body on the pavement. "With the dog laying beside him," he said. The technicians had not chalked the dog's outline on the sidewalk. "Both of them laying there. So I ran over, and I knew right away they were both dead. Mr. Schumacher and the dog."

"What was the dog's name?" Willis asked.

Hawes looked at him.

"Amos," the doorman said.

Willis nodded. Hawes was wondering why he'd wanted to know the dog's name. He was also wondering where they'd taken the dog. They didn't take murdered dogs to the morgue for autopsy, did they?

"Did you see anyone at that time?" Willis asked.

"No one. The street was empty."

"Uh-huh."

The technicians were still working the scene. Hawes wondered how long they'd be here. Another lightning flash crazed the sky. There was a crash of thunder. When it rained, the blood would be washed away.

"Was she carrying a suitcase when she left?" he asked. "Mrs. Schumacher?"

"Yes, sir, a small suitcase."

"So you're pretty sure she went out to the Iodines, huh?"

"Well, I can't swear to it, but that's my guess, yes, sir."

Hawes sighed.

"What do you want to do?" he asked Willis.

"Finish up here, then start the canvass. If we can't get a phone listing for her, we'll just have to talk to the super in the morning."

"Tomorrow's my day off," Hawes said.

"Mine, too," Willis said.

Something in his voice made it sound as if he was wondering what he would do on his day off.

Hawes looked at him again.

"Well," Willis said to the doorman, "thanks a lot, we'll get in touch with you if we have any more questions."

"Okay, fine," the doorman said, and looked again at the chalked outline on the pavement.

Suddenly, it was raining.

On Saturday morning, the twenty-first day of July, Steve Carella went back to work. The first thing he found on his desk was a copy of a Detective Division report signed by Detective/Third Grade Harold O. Willis and written by him before he'd left the squadroom at one o'clock this morning. At that time, he had not yet been able to contact Arthur Schumacher's widow. There *was* a phone listed to an Arthur Schumacher in Elsinore County, but the number was an unpublished one and the late-night telephone-company supervisor refused to let Willis have it until someone from Police Assistance okayed it in the morning.

Lieutenant Byrnes's memo, paper-clipped to Willis's report, suggested that someone—he did not recommend who—should contact the telephone company again in the morning and get to Mrs. Schumacher as soon as possible. Neither Willis nor Hawes, who'd caught the squeal, would be back in the squadroom till Monday morning, and someone—again, Byrnes did not say who—should set the 24-24 in motion. Because the report had been left on his desk, Carella shrewdly detected that the someone the lieutenant had in mind was he himself.

Elsinore County consisted of some eight communities on the Eastern Seaboard, all of them buffered from erosion and occasional hurricane force winds by Sands Spit, which—and with all due understanding of the city's chauvinist attitudes—*did* possess some of the most beautiful beaches in the world. Sands Spit ran pristinely north and south. The Iodines were the smaller islands that clustered around it like pilot fish around a shark.

There were six Iodine islands in all, two of them privately owned, a third set aside as a state park open to the public, the remaining three rather larger than their sisters and scattered with small private houses and, more recently, high-rise condominiums and hotels, their fearless occupants apparently willing to brave the hurricanes that infrequently—but often enough—ravaged Sands Spit, the clustering Iodines, and sometimes the city itself.

The Schumachers had shared a house on Salt Spray, the Iodine closest to the mainland. It was there that Carella reached the dead man's widow at nine-fifteen that morning, after having finally pried the phone number loose from a telephone-company liaison officer in the Police Assistance section. It was his sorry task to tell her that her husband had been murdered.

They arrived at the Schumacher apartment on Selby Place at two o'clock that Saturday afternoon. Margaret Schumacher (and not *Marjorie,* as last night's doorman had surmised) had started into the city from Sands Spit shortly after talking to Carella, and was waiting to greet them now. She was in her late thirties, Carella guessed, an attractive woman with blue eyes and blonde hair rather too long for her narrow face. She was wearing a brown skirt cut some two inches above her knees, a tangerine-colored blouse, and low-heeled pumps. She told them that she'd just got home an hour or so ago. Her eyes, puffy and red, indicated that she'd been crying all morning. Carella knew exactly how she felt.

"This is a second marriage for both of us," Margaret said. "I was hoping it would last forever. Now this."

She told them she'd been divorced for almost three years when she met Arthur. He was married at the time . . .

"He's a good deal older than I am," she said, without seeming to realize she was still using the present tense. Her husband had been shot dead the night before, four gunshot wounds in his head according to the autopsy report, but she was still talking about him as if he were alive. They did this. It caught up with them all at once sometimes, or sometimes it never did. "I'm thirty-nine, he's sixty-two, that's a big age difference. He was married when I met him, with two daughters as old as I was—one of them, anyway. It was a difficult time for both of us, but it worked out eventually. We've been married for almost two years now. It'll be two years this September." Still the present tense.

"Could you tell us his former wife's name, please?" Carella asked.

He was thinking that divorced people sometimes did more terrible things to each other than any strangers could. He was thinking there were four bullet holes in the man's head. One would have done the job.

"Gloria Sanders," Margaret said. "She went back to using her maiden name."

Which perhaps indicated a bitter divorce.

"And his daughters?"

"One of them is still single, her name is Betsy Schumacher. The other one is married, her name is Lois Stein. Mrs. Marc Stein. That's with a *c*, the Marc."

"Do you have addresses and phone numbers for them? It would save us time if . . ."

"I'm sure Arthur has them someplace."

Something there, Brown thought. The way she'd said those words.

"Did you get along with his daughters?" he asked.

"No," Margaret said.

Flat out.

No.

"How about your husband? How was his relationship with them?"

"He loved Lois to death. He didn't get along with the other one."

"Betsy, is that it?" Carella asked, glancing at his notes.

"Betsy, yes. He called her an aging hippie. Which is what she is."

"How old would that be?"

"My age exactly. Thirty-nine."

"And the other daughter. Lois?"

"Thirty-seven."

"How'd he get along with his former wife?" Brown asked.

Circling around again to what he'd heard in her voice when she'd said her husband probably had the phone numbers someplace, whatever it was she'd said exactly. The peculiarly bitter note in her voice.

"I have no idea."

"Ever see her, talk to her, anything like . . . ?"

"Him or me?"

"Well, either one."

"There's no reason to talk to her. The daughters are grown. They were grown when we met, in fact."

The daughters.

Generic.

"Any alimony going out to his former wife?" Brown asked.

"Yes."

The same bitter note.

"How much?"

"Three thousand a month."

"Mrs. Schumacher," Carella said, "can you think of anyone who might have done this thing?"

You asked this question of a surviving spouse not because you expected any brilliant insights. Actually, it was a trick question. Most murders, even in this day and age of anonymous violence, were incestuous affairs. Husband killing wife or vice versa. Wife killing lover. Boyfriend killing girlfriend. Boyfriend killing boyfriend. And so on down the line. A surviving husband or wife was always a prime suspect until you learned otherwise, and a good way of fishing for a motive was to ask if anyone *else* might have wanted him or her dead. But you had to be careful.

Margaret Schumacher didn't give the question a moment's thought.

"Everyone loved him," she said.

And began crying.

The detectives stood there feeling awkward.

She dried her tears with a Kleenex. Blew her nose. Kept crying. They waited. It seemed she would never stop crying. She stood there in the center of the living room of the sixth-floor apartment, sealed and silent except for the humming of the air conditioner and the wrenching sound of her sobs, a tall, good-looking woman with golden hair and a golden summer tan, seemingly or genuinely racked by grief. Everyone loved him, she had said. But in their experience, when *everyone* loved someone, then *no* one truly loved him. Nor had she said that *she* loved him. Which may have been an oversight.

"This is a terrible thing that's happened," Brown said at last, "we know how you must . . ."

"Yes," she said. "I loved him very much."

Perhaps correcting the oversight. And using the past tense now.

"And you can't think of any reason anyone might have . . ."

"No."

Still crying into the disintegrating Kleenex.

"No threatening letters or phone . . ."

"No."

". . . calls, no one who owed him money . . ."

"No."

". . . or who *he* may have borrowed from?"

"No."

"Any problems with his employer . . . ?"

"It's his own business."

Present tense again. Swinging back and forth between past and present, adjusting to the reality of sudden death.

"What sort of business would that be?" Carella asked.

"He's a lawyer."

"Could we have the name of his firm, please?"

"Schumacher, Benson, and Loeb. He's a senior partner."

"Where is that located, ma'am?"

"Downtown on Jasper Street. Near the Old Seawall."

"Was he having trouble with any of his partners?"

"Not that I know of."

"Or with anyone working for the firm?"

"I don't know."

"Had he fired anyone recently?"

"I don't know."

"Mrs. Schumacher," Brown said, "we have to ask this. Was your husband involved with another woman?"

"No."

Flat out.

"We have to ask this," Carella said. "*You're* not involved with anyone, are you?"

"No."

Chin up, eyes defiant behind the tears.

"Then this was a happy marriage."

"Yes."

"We have to ask," Brown said.

"I understand."

But she didn't. Or maybe she did. Either way, the questions had rankled. Carella suddenly imagined the cops of the Four-Five asking his mother if *her* marriage had been a happy one. But this was different. Or was it? Were they so locked into police routine that they'd forgotten a *person* had been killed here? Forgotten, too, that this was the person's wife, a person in her own right? Had catching the bad guy become so important that you trampled over all the good guys in the process? Or, worse, did you no longer believe there *were* any good guys?

"I'm sorry," he said.

"Mrs. Schumacher," Brown said, "would it be all right if we looked through your husband's personal effects? His address book, his appointment calendar, his diary if he kept . . ."

"He didn't keep a diary."

"Anything he may have written on while he was making or receiving telephone calls, a notepad, a . . ."

"I'll show you where his desk is."

"We'd also like to look through his clothes, if you don't . . ."

"Why?"

"Sometimes we'll find a scrap of paper in a jacket pocket, or a matchbook from a restaurant, or . . ."

"Arthur didn't smoke."

Past tense exclusively now.

"We'll be careful, we promise you," Carella said.

Although he had not until now been too overly careful.

"Yes, fine," she said.

But he knew they'd been clumsy, he knew they had alienated her forever. He suddenly wanted to comfort her the way he'd comforted his mother, but the moment was too far gone, the cop had taken over from the man, and the man had lost.

"If we may," he said.

Margaret showed them where her husband's clothes were hanging in the master bedroom closet. They patted down jackets and trousers and found nothing. A smaller room across the hall was furnished as a study, with a desk and an easy chair and a lamp and rows of book-shelves bearing mostly legal volumes. They found the dead man's address book and appointment calendar at once, asked Margaret if they might take them for reference, and signed a receipt to make it all legal. In the desk drawer above the kneehole, in a narrow little box some three inches long and seven inches wide, they found a stack of blank wallet-sized refill checks and a small red snap-envelope containing the key to a safe-deposit box.

Which was how, on Monday morning, they located another bundle of erotic letters.

4

Hi!

I'm putting on my new sexy lingerie, a red demi-bra (so-called because it pushes up my breasts and leaves my nipples uncovered), a garterbelt with red silk stockings, and the tiniest red panties you ever saw in smooth soft silk. On top of that I'll wear the new suit I got yesterday. It cost an arm and a leg but it was irresistible, a prim-looking blue thing with a short, double-breasted jacket and— the pièce de résistance—a skirt with an interesting arrangement in front: a big split artistically draped with intricate folds so that it looks very decent when I stand up but when I sit down and spread my legs a little I'm practically inviting the man sitting next to me to put his hand through that split and touch me between the legs.

Is this the sort of letter you want me to write? I think I may enjoy this.

In my fantasy, we'll check into a hotel and then go down to the restaurant together and find a booth in an out-of-the-way corner somewhere and you would be that man sitting next to me and you would put your hand through that split in the skirt and you would touch my cunt, which would be very hot, very wet, and very very hungry for your attention. In no time at all, you would bring me to climax, and then it would be my turn. I would unzip your fly and find your cock, which I'm sure would already be stone hard. It would spring out into my hand, and I would play with it under the table until it got harder and harder, and then when nobody was looking, I would pretend to pick up a napkin from the floor, and I would lower my mouth onto your cock, and suck you till you begged me to let you come but I wouldn't let you no matter how hard you begged, I'd just keep sucking your big cock until you were almost weeping, and then I'd say, "Come on, let's go up to the room."

We would compose ourselves, leave the restaurant, and take the elevator back upstairs. And inside the room, I'd take off the blue suit, and you'd tear off that wisp of red panty, and you'd say something about me driving you crazy, and I'd unzip you once again, and sink to my knees, and put your big cock in my mouth again. You'd take off the rest of your clothes, and slowly slip out of my mouth, and then you'd lift me to you and start licking my breasts. I would come again, you always make me come so fast, even just sucking my nipples, but I would know you weren't finished with me yet, I would know you wanted more from me, you always want more and more from me. You would pick me up and carry me to the bed, and you would kneel over me with my legs wide open and your cock in your hand, and you would begin fucking me slow and steady, and then harder and harder and harder, give it to me, baby, fuck me now.

See you later.

Bye!

"Gives me a hard-on, this woman," Brown said, and shook his head, and said, "Whooosh," and slid the letter back under the rubber band that held the stack of letters together. He was sitting beside Carella in one of the squad's unmarked cars, a three-year-old Plymouth sedan with the air conditioner on the fritz, both men sweltering as they drove uptown again to the Schumacher apartment. It had taken them an hour and a half this morning to get a court order to open Schumacher's safe-deposit box, and another half hour to get to the bank, not far from his office on Jasper Street. The box had contained only the letters and a pair of first-class airline tickets to Milan, one in Schumacher's name, the other in Susan Brauer's.

There were seventeen letters in all, five fewer than Schumacher had written. The first one—the one Brown had been reading—was dated three days after Schumacher's first letter, and seemed to be in direct response to it. Like his letters, none of these were signed. Each of the letters was neatly typed. Each started with the same salutation and ended with the same complementary close. *Hi!* and *Bye!* Like a vivacious little girl writing to someone she'd met in camp. *Some* little girl, Brown thought.

"You think he was losing interest?" he asked.

"I'm sorry, what?" Carella said.

His mind had been drifting again. He could not shake the image of his mother in the bakery shop, wandering the shop, touching all the things that had belonged to his father.

"I mean, he meets her on New Year's Day, and this is only June when he gets her to write him these hot letters. Sounds as if he was maybe losing interest."

"Then why would he be taking her to Europe?"

"Maybe the letters got things going again," he said, and was silent for a moment. "You ever write any kind of letters like these?"

"No, did you?"

"No. Wish I knew how."

They were approaching the Selby Place apartment. Carella searched for a parking spot, found one in a No Parking zone, parked there anyway, and threw down the visor to display a placard with the Police Department logo on it. It seemed cooler outside the car than it had inside. Little breeze blowing here on the tree-shaded street. They walked up the street, announced themselves to the doorman, and then took the elevator up to the sixth floor.

What they had already concluded was that Arthur Schumacher and Susan Brauer had been exchanging intimate letters and that they'd been planning to fly to Italy together at the end of the month. What they did *not* know was whether Margaret Schumacher had known all this. They were here to question her further. Because if she *had* known . . .

"Come in," she said, "have you learned anything?"

Seemingly all concerned and anxious and looking drawn and weary; her husband had been buried yesterday morning. They had to play this very carefully. They didn't want to tell her everything they knew, but at the same time it was virtually impossible to conduct a fishing expedition without dangling a little bait in the water.

Carella told her they were now investigating the possibility that her husband's death may have been connected to a previous homicide they'd been investigating . . .

"Oh? What previous homicide?"

. . . and that whereas when they were here on Saturday they'd merely been doing a courtesy follow-up for the two detectives who'd initiated the investigation into her husband's death . . .

"A *courtesy* follow-up?" she said, annoyed by Carella's unfortunate choice of a word.

"Yes, ma'am," he said, "in order to keep the investigation ongoing . . ."

. . . but under the so-called First Man Up rule, the previous homicide demanded that *both* cases be investigated by the detectives who'd caught the first one. This meant that her husband's case was now *officially* theirs, and they'd be the ones . . .

"What previous homicide?" she asked again.

"The murder of a woman named Susan Brauer," Carella said, and watched her eyes.

Nothing showed in those eyes.

"Do you know anyone by that name?" Brown asked.

Watching her eyes.

"No, I don't."

Nothing there. Not a flicker of recognition.

"You didn't read anything about her murder in the papers . . ."

"No."

". . . or see anything about it on television?"

"No."

"Because it's had a lot of coverage."

"I'm sorry," she said, and looked at them, seemingly or genuinely puzzled. "When you say my husband's death may have been connected . . ."

"Yes, ma'am."

". . . to this previous homicide . . ."

"Yes, ma'am, that's a possibility we're now considering."

Lying, of course. It was no longer a mere possibility but a definite probability. Well, yes, there *did* exist the remotest chance that Arthur Schumacher's death was totally unrelated to Susan Brauer's, but there wasn't a cop alive who'd have accepted a million-to-one odds on such a premise.

"Connected how?"

The detectives looked at each other.

"Connected how?" she said again.

"Mrs. Schumacher," Carella said, "when we were here on Saturday, when we found that key in your husband's desk, you said the only safe-deposit box you had was up here at First Federal Trust on Culver Avenue, that's what you told us on Saturday."

"That's right."

"You said you didn't know of any box at Union Savings, which was the name of the bank printed on that little red envelope. You said . . ."

"I *still* don't."

"Mrs. Schumacher, there *is* a box at that bank, and it's in your husband's name."

They were still watching her eyes. If she'd known what was in that box, if she now realized that *they,* too, knew what was in it, then something would have shown in her eyes, on her face, something would have flickered there. But nothing did.

"I'm surprised," she said.

"You didn't know that box existed."

"No. Why would Arthur have kept a box all the way downtown? We . . ."

"Union Savings on Wellington Street," Brown said. "Three blocks from his office."

"Yes, but we have the box up here, you see. So why would he have needed another one?"

"Have you got any ideas about that?" Carella asked.

"None at all. Arthur never kept anything from me, why wouldn't he have mentioned a safe-deposit box down there near his office? I mean . . . what was *in* the box, do you know?"

"Mrs. Schumacher," Brown said, "did you know your husband was planning a trip to Europe at the end of the month?"

"Yes, I did."

"Italy and France, wasn't it?"

"Yes, on business."

Coming up on it from the blind side, trying to find out if she'd known about those tickets in the safe-deposit box, if she had somehow *seen* those tickets . . .

"Leaving on the twenty-ninth for Milan . . ."

. . . or had learned in some other way, *any* other way, about the affair her husband was having with a beautiful, twenty-two . . .

"Yes."

". . . and returning from Lyons on the twelfth of August."

"Yes."

"Had you planned on going with him?"

"No, I just told you, it was a business trip."

"Did he often go on business trips alone?"

"Yes. Why? Do you think the trip had something to do with his murder?"

"Do *you* think it might have?" he asked.

"I don't see how. Are you saying someone . . . I mean, I just don't understand how the trip could have had anything to do with it."

"Are you sure he was going alone?" Carella asked.

"Yes, I think so," she said. "Or with one of his partners."

"Did he *say* he was going with one of his partners?"

"He didn't say either way. I don't understand. What are you . . . ?" and suddenly her eyes narrowed, and she looked sharply and suspiciously at Carella and then snapped the same look at Brown. "What is this?" she asked.

"Mrs. Schumacher," Carella said, "did you have any reason to believe your husband . . ."

"No, what is this?"

". . . might *not* be traveling alone?"

"What the hell is this?"

So there they were, at the crossroads.

And as Yogi Berra once remarked, "When you come to a crossroads, take it."

Carella glanced at Brown. Brown nodded imperceptibly, telling him to go ahead and bite the bullet. Carella's eyes flicked acceptance.

"Mrs. Schumacher," he said, "when we were here last Saturday, you told us your husband had *not* been involved with another woman. You seemed very definite about that."

"That's right, he wasn't. Would you mind . . . ?"

"We now have evidence that he *was,* in fact, involved with someone."

"What? What do you mean?"

"Evidence that links him to Susan Brauer."

Both of them alert now for whatever effect the revelation might have on her. Watching her intently. The eyes, the face, the entire body. They had just laid it on the line. If she'd known about the affair . . .

"*Links* him to her?" she said. "What does that mean, *links* him to her?"

"Intimately," Carella said.

What seemed like genuine surprise flashed in her eyes.

"Evidence?" she said.

"Yes, ma'am."

"What evidence?"

The surprise giving way to a look of almost scoffing disbelief.

"Letters she wrote to him," Carella said. "Letters we found in his safe-deposit . . ."

"Well, what does . . . ? Letters? Are you saying this woman wrote some *letters* to my husband?"

"Yes, ma'am."

"Even so, that doesn't mean . . ."

"We have *his* letters, too. The letters he wrote to her."

"*Arthur* wrote . . . ?"

"Yes, ma'am."

"Don't be ridiculous."

"We found the letters in her apartment."

"Letters *Arthur* wrote to her?"

"They weren't signed, but we feel certain . . ."

"Then how do you . . . ? Where *are* these letters? I want to see these letters."

"Mrs. Schumacher . . ."

"I have a right to see these letters. If you're saying my husband was involved with another woman . . ."

"Yes, ma'am, he was."

"Then I want to see proof. You're trying to . . . to . . . make it seem he was having an *affair* with . . . this . . . this *woman,* whatever her name was . . ."

"Susan Brauer."

"I don't *care* what it was! I don't believe a word of what you're saying. Arthur was *never* unfaithful to me in his life! Don't you think I'd have *known* if he was unfaithful? Are you deliberately trying to hurt me?" she shouted. "Is that it?" Eyes flashing now, entire body trembling. "I don't have to answer any more of your questions," she said, and went immediately to the phone. "My husband was a partner in one of the biggest law firms in this city, you can just go *fuck* yourself," she said, and began dialing.

"Mrs. Schumacher . . ."

"There's the door," she said, and then, into the phone, "Mr. Loeb, please."

Carella looked at Brown.

"Please *leave!*" Margaret shouted. Into the phone, in a quieter but still agitated voice, she said, "Lou, I have two detectives here who just violated my rights. What do I . . ."

They left.

In the hallway outside, while they waited for the elevator, Carella said, "What do you think?"

"Tough one to call," Brown said.

"This isn't new, you know."

"You're talking about last week, right?"

"Yeah, Saturday. I mean, she got angry from minute one, today isn't something new."

"Maybe we've got shitty bedside manners."

"I'm sure," Carella said.

The elevator doors slid open. They got into the car and hit the button for the lobby. They were both silent as the elevator hummed down the shaft, each of them separately thinking that Margaret Schumacher had just treated them to a fine display of surprise, shock, disbelief, indignation, anger, and hurt over the news of her husband's infidelity, but there was no way of knowing if any of it had been genuine.

As they stepped out of the building, the heat hit them like a closed fist.

"You think her lawyer's gonna call us?" Brown asked.

"Nope," Carella said.

He was wrong.

A detective named Mary Beth Mulhaney was working the door.

She normally worked out of the Three-One; Eileen had met her up there, oh, it must've been four years ago, when they'd called Special Forces for a decoy. Guy was beating up women on the street, running off into the night with their handbags. Eileen had run the job for a week straight without getting a single nibble. The hairbag lieutenant up there told her it was because she looked too much like a cop, S.F. should've sent him somebody else. Eileen suggested that maybe *he'd* like to go out there in basic black and pearls, see if *he* couldn't tempt the mugger to hit on him. The lieutenant told her not to get smart, young lady.

There was a lot of brass down here outside the lingerie shop. Emergency Service had contained the owner of the shop and the woman she was keeping hostage, barricading the front of the place and cordoning off the street. Mary Beth was working the back door, far from the Monday morning crowd that had gathered on the street side. The brass included Chief of Patrol Dylan Curran, whose picture Eileen had seen in police stations all over town, and Chief of Detectives Andrew Brogan, who all those years ago had reprimanded Eileen for talking back to the hairbag lieutenant at the Three-One, and Deputy Inspector John Di Santis who was in command of the Emergency Service and whom Eileen had seen on television only the other night at the Calm's Point Bridge where a guy who thought he was Superman was threatening to fly off into the River Dix. But Brady was the star.

A sergeant from Emergency Service was softly explaining to Eileen and the other trainees that the lady in there had a .357 Magnum in her fist and that she'd threatened to kill the only customer still in her shop if the police didn't back off. The reason the police were here to begin with was that the lady in there had already chased another customer out of her shop when she complained that the elastic waistband on a pair of panties she'd bought there had disintegrated in the wash.

The lady—whose name was Hildy Banks—had yanked the Magnum she kept under the counter for protection against armed robbers and such, and had fired two shots at the complaining customer, who'd run in terror out of the shop. Hildy had then turned the gun on the other terrified woman and told her to stop screaming or she'd kill her. The woman had not stopped screaming. Hildy had fired two more shots into the air, putting a hole in the ceiling and knocking a carton of half-slips off the topmost shelf in the store. The police were there by then. One of the responding blues yelled "Holy shit!" when Hildy slammed another shot through the front door. That was when Emergency Service was called. After which they'd beeped—

"Can we keep it down back there?"

Inspector Brady. Standing beside Mary Beth, who was talking calmly to the lady behind the door. Turning his head momentarily to scold the Emergency Service sergeant, and then giving Mary Beth his full attention again. Eileen wondered how long Mary Beth had been working with the unit. Brady seemed to be treating her like a rookie, whispering instructions to her, refusing to let her run with it. Mary Beth shot him an impatient look. He seemed not to catch it. He seemed to want to handle this one all by himself. Eileen guessed the only reason Mary Beth was outside the door was because the taker inside was a woman.

"Hildy?"

Mary Beth outside the door, cops everywhere you looked in that backyard. The rear door of the shop opened onto a small fenced-in courtyard. It was on the street-level floor of an apartment building, and clotheslines ran from the windows above to telephone poles spaced at irregular intervals all up and down the block. Trousers and shirts hung limply on the humid air, arms and legs dangling. Just in case Hildy in there decided to blow her head off, Mary Beth was crouched to one side of the door, well beyond the sight-lines of the single window on the brick wall. She was a round-faced woman with eyes as frosty blue as glare ice, wearing a blue shirt hanging open over a yellow T-shirt and gray slacks. No lipstick. No eye shadow. Cheeks rosy red from the heat.

Perspiration dripping down her face. Eyes intent on that door. She was hoping nothing would come flying through it. Or the window, either.

"Hildy?" she said again.

"Go away! Get out of here! I'll kill her."

Voice on the edge of desperation. Eileen realized the woman in there was as terrified as her hostage. The cops outside here had to look like an army to her. Chief of Patrol Curran pacing back and forth, hands behind his back, a general wondering whether his troops would take this one or blow it. Chief of Detectives Brogan standing apart with two other beefy men in plainclothes, whispering softly, observing Mary Beth at the door. Uniformed policemen with rifles and handguns—out of sight, to be sure.

You promise them no guns, no shooting, Eileen thought. And you meant it. Unless or until. All these cops were here and ready to storm the joint the moment anyone got hurt. Kill the hostage in there, harm the hostage in there, you took the door. Hurt a cop outside here, same thing. You played the game until the rules changed. And then you went cop.

"Hildy, I'm getting that coffee you asked for," Mary Beth said.

"Taking long enough," Hildy said.

"We had to send someone down the street for it."

"That was an hour ago."

"No, only ten minutes, Hildy."

"Don't argue with her," Brady whispered.

"Should be here any second now," Mary Beth said.

"Who's that with you?" Hildy asked.

Voice touched with suspicion.

Mary Beth looked at Brady. Eyes questioning. What do I tell her, Boss?

Brady shook his head. Touched his index finger to his lips. Shook his head again.

"Nobody," Mary Beth said. "I'm all alone here."

"I thought I heard somebody talking to you."

Brady shook his head again.

"No, it's just me here," Mary Beth said.

Why is he asking her to *lie?* Eileen wondered.

"But there are cops out there, I know there are."

"Yes, there are."

"But not near the door, is that what you're saying?"

"That's it, Hildy. I'm all alone here at the door."

Brady nodded, pleased.

"Why don't you open the door just a little?" Mary Beth said.

This surprised Brady. His eyes popped open. As blue and as crisp as Mary Beth's, but clearly puzzled now. What was she doing? He shook his head.

"Then you can see I'm alone here," Mary Beth said, and waved Brady away with the back of her hand.

Brady was shaking his head more vigorously now. Standing just to Mary Beth's left, bald head gleaming in the sunshine, hawk nose cleaving the stiflingly hot air, head shaking No, no, no, what the hell are you *doing?*

Mary Beth shooed him away again.

"Open the door, Hildy. You'll see . . ."

Brady shook his head angrily.

". . . I'm alone here."

She lifted her head to Brady, shot him an angry glance. Their eyes locked. Blue on blue, flashing, clashing. Brady stomped off. Michael Goodman was standing with the trainees. Brady went directly to him.

"I want her off that door," he said.

"Inspector . . ."

"She'll open the door when the coffee comes, Mulhaney's moving too fast."

"Maybe she senses something you don't," Goodman said. "She's the one talking, Inspector. Maybe she . . ."

"I was standing right there all along," Brady said. "I heard everything they said to each other. I'm telling you she's trying to get that door open too damn soon. The woman in there'll open it and start shooting, that's what'll happen."

He doesn't trust her, Eileen thought.

"Let's give her another few minutes," Goodman said.

"I think we should ease in another talker. Wait till the coffee comes, and then . . ."

"Look," Eileen said.

They turned to follow her gaze.

The door was opening. Just a crack, but it was opening.

"See?" Mary Beth said. "I'm all alone here."

They could not hear Hildy's reply. But whatever she'd said, it seemed to encourage Mary Beth.

"Why don't you leave it open?" she said. "I like to see who I'm talking to, don't you?"

Again, they could not hear her reply. But she did not close the door.

"Be careful with that gun now," Mary Beth said, and smiled. "I don't want to get hurt out here."

This time they heard Hildy's voice:

"Where's *your* gun?"

"I don't have one," Mary Beth said.

"You're a cop, aren't you?"

"Yes, I am. I told you that. I'm a Police Department negotiator. But I haven't got a gun. You can see for yourself, now that the door is open," Mary Beth said, and spread her hands wide. "No gun. Nothing. See?"

"How do I know you haven't got one under your shirt?"

"Well, here, I'll open the shirt, you can see for yourself."

Mary Beth opened the blue shirt wide, like a flasher, showing Hildy the yellow T-shirt under it.

"See?" she said.

"How about your pockets?"

"Would you like to put your hand in my pockets? Make sure I haven't got a gun?"

"No. You'll try something funny."

"Why would I do that? You think I want to get hurt?"

"No, but . . ."

"I don't want to hurt you, and I don't want to get hurt, either. I have a three-year-old son, Hildy. I don't think he'd want me getting shot out here."

"Do you really?"

"I really do, his name is Dennis," she said.

"Dennis the Menace, huh?"

"You said it," Mary Beth said, and laughed.

From inside the shop, they could hear the woman laughing, too.

"You got any children?" Mary Beth asked.

"I think she'll be all right," Goodman said.

"So the sexist bastard fires her," Eileen said. "Not from the *police* department, even *that* dictatorial son of a bitch couldn't swing that. But he kicked her off the team, sent her back full time to the Three-One. And you know why?"

"Why?" Karin asked.

They were in her office on the fifth floor of the building. Dr. Karin Lefkowitz. Five o'clock that afternoon, her last appointment of the day. A big-city Jewish girl who looked like Barbra Streisand, people told her, only much prettier. Brown hair cut in a flying wedge. Sharp intelligence in her blue eyes, something like anger in them, too, as she listened to Eileen's atrocity story about Inspector William Cullen Brady, commander of the hostage negotiating team. Good legs, crossed now, wearing her signature dark blue business suit and Reeboks, leaning forward intently, wanting to know why the son-of-a-bitch sexist bastard had fired Mary Beth Mulhaney.

"Because she wasn't doing it *exactly* his way," Eileen said. "You do it exactly his way, or so long, sister, it was nice knowing you. But Mary Beth's way was *working,* it *did* work, she got the hostage *and* the taker out of there without anyone getting hurt. You know what this is?"

"What is it?" Karin asked.

"It's the old-guard mentality of the police department," Eileen said. "They can say what they want about the gun on the hip making us all equal, but when push comes to shove, the old-timers still think of us as *girls.* And us *girls* need a lot of help, don't we? Otherwise we might *endanger* all those hairy-chested *men* out there who are doing their best to maintain law and order. I say *fuck* law and order and fuck all thick-headed Irishmen like Brady who think sweet little Irish girls like me and Mary Beth should be in *church* saying novenas for all the brave *men* out there in the streets!"

"Wow," Karin said.

"Damn right," Eileen said.

"I've never seen you so angry."

"Yeah."

"Tell me why."

"Why do you think? If Brady can do that to Mary *Beth,* who was with the team for six months and who was doing an absolutely *great* job, then what's he going to do to *me* the first time *I* screw up?"

"Are you worried about screwing up?"

"I've never even worked the door yet, I'm just saying . . ."

"Do you want to work the door?"

"Well, that's the whole idea, isn't it? I mean, I'm in training as a hostage negotiator, that's what negotiators do. We work the door, we try to get the taker and the hostages . . ."

"Yes, but do you *want* to work the door? Are you looking forward to working the door?"

"I think I've learned enough now to give it a shot."

"You feel you're prepared now to . . ."

"Yes. We've simulated it dozens of times already, different kinds of takers, different kinds of situations. So, yes, I feel I'm prepared."

"Are you looking forward to your first time?"

"Yes."

"Your first *real* situation?"

"Yes. I'm a little nervous about it, of course, but there'll be supervision. Even if I was alone at the door, there'd be other people nearby."

"Nervous how?"

"Well, this isn't a game, you know. There are lives at stake."

"Of course."

"So I'd want to do it right."

"Are you afraid you might do it wrong?"

"I just wouldn't want anyone to get hurt."

"Of course not."

"I mean, the reason I hate *decoy* work . . ."

"I know."

". . . is because there's . . . there's always the possibility you'll have to . . ."

"Yes?"

"Put someone away."

"Yes. Kill someone."

"Kill someone. Yes."

"And you feel that would be a danger? When you're working the door?"

"Whenever there's a gun on the scene, there's a danger of that happening, yes."

"But in this situation, you wouldn't be the one with the gun, isn't that right."

"Well, yes, that's right."

"The taker would have the gun."

"The taker would have the gun, that's absolutely right."

"So there's no possibility that *you* would have to shoot anyone. Kill anyone."

"Well, you know, *I* don't want to get hurt, either, you know? The person in there has a *gun*, you know . . ."

"Yes, I know."

"And if I screw up . . ."

"What makes you think you'll screw up?"

"I *don't* think I'll screw up. I'm only saying *if* I should screw up . . ."

"Yes, what would happen?"

"Well, the person in there might use the gun."

"And then what?"

"We'd have to come down."

"You'd have to take the door by force."

"Yes. If the taker started shooting."

"And if the door was taken by force . . ."

"Well . . . yes."

"Yes *what*, Eileen?"

"The taker might get hurt."

"Might get killed."

"Yes. Might get killed."

"Which you wouldn't want to happen."

"I wouldn't want that to happen, no. That's why I want to get out of *decoy* work. Because . . ."

"Because you once had to kill a man."

"Bobby."

"Bobby Wilson, yes."

"I killed him, yes."

The women looked at each other. They had gone over this ground again and again and again. If Eileen heard herself telling this same story one more time, she would vomit all over her shoes. She looked at her watch. She knew Karin hated it when she did that. It was twenty minutes past five. Monday afternoon. Hot as hell outside and not much cooler here in this windowless room with faulty municipal-government air-conditioning.

"Why does Brady make you so angry?" Karin asked.

"Because he fired Mary Beth."

"But you're not Mary Beth."

"I'm a *woman*."

"He hasn't fired *you*, though."

"He might."

"Why?"

"Because he doesn't think women can do the job."

"Does he remind you of anyone you know?"

"No."

"Are you sure?"

"Positive."

"You can't think of a single other man who . . ."

"I'm not going to say Bert, if that's what you want me to say."

"I don't want you to say anything you don't want to say."

"It wasn't that Bert didn't think I could do the job."

"Then what was it?"

"He was trying to protect me."

"But he screwed up."

"That wasn't his fault."

"Whose was it?"

"He was trying to help me."

"You mean you no longer think . . . ?"

"I don't know *what* I think. *You* were the one who suggested I talk to Goodman about joining the team, *you* were the one who thought . . ."

"Yes, but we're talking about Bert Kling now."

"I don't want to talk about Bert."

"Why not? Last week you seemed to think he was responsible . . ."

"He *was*. If I hadn't lost my backups . . ."

"Yes, you wouldn't have had to shoot Bobby Wilson."

"*Fuck* Bobby Wilson! If I hear his name one more time . . ."

"Do you *still* think Bert was responsible for . . ."

"He was the one who made me lose my backups, yes."

"But was he responsible for your shooting Bobby Wilson? For your killing Bobby Wilson?"

Eileen was silent for a long time.

Then she said, "No."

Karin nodded.

"Maybe it's time we talked to Bert," she said.

Carella had spent his early adolescence and his young manhood in Riverhead. He had moved back to Riverhead after he married Teddy, and it was in Riverhead that his father had been killed. Tonight, he drove to a section of Riverhead some three miles from his own house, to talk to his brother-in-law, Tommy. He would rather have done almost anything else in the world.

Tommy had moved back to the house that used to be his parents' while he was away in the army. Nowadays, you did not have to say which war or police action or invasion a man had been in. If you were an American of any given age, you had been in at least one war. The irony was that Tommy had come through *his* particular war alive while his parents back home were getting killed in an automobile accident. He still owned the house, still rented it out. But there was a room over the garage, and he was living in that now.

Angela had told Carella that he'd moved out at the beginning of the month, after they'd had a terrible fight that caused their three-year-old daughter to run out of the room crying. Actually, Angela had *kicked* him out. Screamed at him to get the hell out of the house and not to come back till he got rid of his bimbo. That was the word she'd used. Bimbo. Tommy had packed some clothes and left. Two weeks ago, he'd called to tell her he had to go to California on business. Last night, he'd called to say he was back. Tonight, Carella was here to see him.

He had called first, he knew he was expected. He did not want to ring this doorbell. He did not want to be here asking Tommy questions, he did not want to be playing *cop* with his own brother-in-law. He climbed the steep flight of wooden steps that ran up the right hand side of the garage. He rang the bell. It sounded within.

"Steve?"

"Yeah."

"Just a sec."

He waited.

The door opened.

"Hey." Arms opening wide. "Steve." They embraced. "I didn't know about your father," Tommy said at once. "I would've come home in a minute, but Angela didn't call me. I didn't find out till last night. Steve, I'm sorry."

"Thank you."

"I really loved him."

"I know."

"Come in, come in. You ever think you'd see me living alone like this? Jesus," Tommy said, and stood aside to let him by. He had lost a little weight since Carella had last seen him. You get a little older, your face gets a look of weariness about the eyes. Just living did that to you, even if you weren't having troubles with your marriage.

The single room was furnished with a sofa that undoubtedly opened into a bed, a pair of overstuffed easy chairs with flowered slipcovers on them, a standing floor lamp, a television set on a rolling cart, a dresser with another lamp and a fan on top of it, and a coffee table between the sofa and the two easy chairs. On the wall over the sofa, there was a picture of Jesus Christ with an open heart in his chest radiating blinding rays of light, his hand held up in blessing. Carella had seen that same picture in Catholic homes all over the city. There was a partially open door to the left of the sofa, revealing a bathroom beyond.

"Something to drink?" Tommy asked.

"What've you got?" Carella asked.

"Scotch or gin, take your choice. I went down for fresh limes after you called, in case you feel like a gin and tonic. I've also got club soda, if you . . ."

"Gin and tonic sounds fine."

Tommy walked to where a sink, a row of cabinets, a Formica countertop, a range, and a refrigerator occupied one entire wall of the room. He cracked open an ice-cube tray, took down a fresh bottle of Gordon's gin from one of the cabinets, sliced a lime in half, squeezed and dropped the separate halves into two tall glasses decorated with cartoon characters Carella didn't recognize, and mixed two hefty drinks that he then carried back to where Carella was already sitting on the sofa.

They clinked glasses.

"Cheers," Tommy said.

"Cheers," Carella said.

The fan on top of the dresser wafted warm air across the room. The windows—one over the sink, the other on the wall right-angled to the sofa—were wide open, but there wasn't a breeze stirring. Both men were wearing jeans and short-sleeved shirts. It was insufferably hot.

"So?" Carella said.

"What'd she tell you?"

"About the fight. About kicking you out."

"Yeah," Tommy said, and shook his head. "Did she say why?"

"She said you had someone else."

"But I don't."

"She thinks you do."

"But she's got no *reason* to believe that. I love her to death, what's the *matter* with her?"

Carella could remember organ music swelling to drown out the sound of joyful weeping in the church, his father's arm supporting Angela's hand as he led her down the center aisle to the altar where Tommy stood waiting . . .

"I told her there's nobody else but her, she's the only woman I ever . . ."

. . . the priest saying a prayer and blessing the couple with holy water, Tommy sweating profusely, Angela's lips trembling behind her veil. It was the twenty-second day of June, Carella would never forget that day. Not only because it was the day his sister got married, but because it was also the day his twins were born. He remembered thinking he was the luckiest man alive. Twins!

". . . but she keeps saying she *knows* there's somebody else."

Teddy sitting beside him, watching the altar, the church expectantly still. He remembered thinking his little sister was getting married. He remembered thinking we all grow up. For everything there is a season . . .

*Do you, Thomas Giordano, take this woman as your lawfully wed-
ded wife to live together in the state of holy matrimony? Will you love,
honor, and keep her as a faithful . . .*

. . . a time to plant, and a time to pluck up what is planted . . .

"I've never cheated on her in my life," Tommy said. "Even when we
were just going together . . . well, you know that, Steve. The minute I
met her, I couldn't even *look* at another girl. So now she . . ."

*. . . and forsaking all others keep you alone unto her 'til death do you
part?*

Yes. I do.

*And do you, Angela Louise Carella, take this man as your lawfully
wedded husband to live together in the state of holy matrimony? Will
you love, honor, and cherish him as a faithful woman is bound to do, in
health, sickness, prosperity, and adversity . . .*

Tommy lifting his bride's veil and kissing her fleetingly and with
much embarrassment. The organ music swelling again. Smiling, the
veil pulled back onto the white crown nestled in her hair, eyes
sparkling, Angela . . .

"Why does she think you're cheating, Tommy?"

"Steve, she's pregnant, she's expecting any day now, you know what
I mean? I think it's because we aren't having sex just now is why she
thinks I've got somebody else . . ."

. . . a time to embrace, and a time to refrain from embracing . . .

"I'm being completely honest with you. That's all I think it is."

"No other reason?"

"None."

"Nothing she could have got in her head . . . ?"

"Nothing."

"Something you did . . . ?"

"No."

"Something you said?"

"No."

"Tommy, look at me."

Their eyes met.

"Are you telling me the truth?"

"I swear to God," Tommy said.

5

LIEUTENANT BYRNES had advised him—*everyone* had advised him—to let the Four-Five run with it, stay out of it, he was too emotionally involved to do anything effective on the case. But this was now a week since his father had been shot and killed, and despite all the promises from the two detectives investigating the case, Carella hadn't heard a word from them. At nine o'clock that Tuesday morning, he called Riverhead.

The detective who answered the phone in the squadroom up there said his name was Haley. Carella told him who he was, and asked for either Detective Bent or Detective Wade.

"I think they're in the field already," Haley said.

"Can you beep them and ask them to give me a call?"

"What's this in reference to?"

"A case they're working."

"Sure, I'll beep them," Haley said.

But the way he said it made Carella think he had no intention of beeping anybody.

"Is your lieutenant in?" he asked.

"Yeah?"

"Would you put me through to him?"

"He's got somebody in with him just now."

"Just buzz him and tell him Detective Carella's on the line."

"I just told you . . ."

"Pal," Carella said, and the single word was ominous with weight. "Buzz your lieutenant."

There was a long silence.

Then Haley said, "Sure."

A different voice came on the line a moment later.

"Lieutenant Nelson. How are you, Carella?"

"Fine, thank you, Lieutenant. I was wond . . ."

"I got a call from Lieutenant Byrnes a few days ago, asking me to give this case special attention, which I would have done anyway. Bent and Wade are out on it right this minute."

"I was wondering how they made out with that witness."

"Well, he turned out not to be as good as we thought. All of a sudden he couldn't remember this, couldn't remember that, you know what I mean? We figure he thought it over and chickened out. Which happens lots of times."

"Yeah," Carella said.

"But they're out right this minute, like I told you, chasing down something they came up with yesterday. So don't worry, we're on this, we won't . . ."

"What was it they came up with?"

"Let me see, I had their report here a minute ago, what the hell did I do with it? Just a second, okay?"

Carella could hear him muttering as he shuffled papers. He visualized a mountain of papers. At last, Nelson came back on the line. "Yeah," he said, "they been looking for this kid who told his girlfriend he saw the punks who shot your father running out of the shop. They got his name and address . . ."

"Could I have those, sir? The name and . . ."

"Carella?"

"Yes, sir?"

"You want my advice?"

Carella said nothing.

"Let Bent and Wade handle it, okay? They're good cops. They'll get these guys, believe me. We won't disappoint you, believe me."

"Yes, sir."

"You hear me?"

"Yes, sir."

"Better this way."

"Yes, sir."

"I know how you feel."

"Thank you, sir."

"But it's better this way, believe me. They're out on it right this minute. They'll find those punks, believe me. Trust us, okay? We'll get 'em."

"I appreciate that."

"We'll stay in touch," Nelson said, and hung up.

Carella wondered why the hell they hadn't stayed in touch till now.

The kid began running the moment he saw them.

He was standing on the corner, talking to two other guys, when Wade and Bent pulled up in the unmarked car. It was as if the car had neon all over it, blaring POLICE in orange and green. Wade opened the door on the passenger side and was stepping out onto the curb when the kid spotted him and started running. Bent, who'd been driving the car and who was also out of it by this time, yelled, "He's going, Randy!" and both men shouted, almost simultaneously, "Police! Stop!"

Nobody was stopping.

Neither were any guns coming out.

In this city, police rules and regs strictly limited the circumstances in which a weapon could be unholstered or fired. There was no felony in progress here, nor did the detectives have a warrant authorizing the arrest of a person known to be armed. The kid pounding the pavement up ahead hadn't *done* anything, nor was he threatening them in any way that would have warranted using a firearm as a defensive weapon. The guns stayed holstered.

The kid was fast, but so were Wade and Bent. A lot of detectives in this city, they tended to run to flab. You rode around in a car all day long, you ate hamburgers and fries in greasy-spoon diners, you put on the pounds and you had a hell of a time taking them off again. But Wade and Bent worked out at the Headquarters gym twice a week, and chasing the kid hardly even made them breathe hard.

Bent was six-two and he weighed a hundred and ninety pounds, all of it sinew and muscle. Wade was five-eleven and he weighed a solid hundred and seventy, but the knife scar over his left eye made him look meaner and tougher than Bent, even though he was smaller and lighter. The kid up ahead was seventeen, eighteen years old, lean and swift, and white in the bargain. Just to make sure he hadn't mistaken them for a pair of bad black dudes looking to mug him, they yelled "Police!" again, "Stop!" again, and then one more time for good measure, "Police! Stop!," but the kid wasn't stopping for anybody.

Over the hills and dales they went, the kid leaping backyard fences where clothes hung listlessly on the sullen air, Wade and Bent right behind him, the kid leading the way and maintaining his lead because he *knew* where he was going whereas they were only following, and the guy paving the way usually had a slight edge over whoever was chasing him. But they were stronger than he was, and more determined besides—he had possibly seen the two people who'd killed the father of a cop. The operative word was *cop*.

"There he goes!" Wade yelled.

He was ducking into what had once been a somewhat elegant mid-rise apartment building bordering Riverhead Park but which had been abandoned for some ten to twelve years now. The windows had been boarded up and decorated with plastic stick-on panels made to resemble half-drawn window shades or open shutters or little potted plants sitting on windowsills, the *trompe-l'oeil* of a city in decline. There was no front door on the building. A bloated ceiling in the entryway dripped collected rainwater. It was dark in here. No thousand points of light in here. Just darkness and the sound of rats scurrying as the detectives came in.

"Hey!" Wade yelled. "What are you running for?"

No answer.

The sound of the water dripping.

His voice echoing in the hollow shell of the building with the fake window shades and shutters and potted plants.

"We just want to talk to you!" Bent yelled.

Still no answer.

They looked at each other.

Silence.

And then a faint sound coming from upstairs. Not a rat this time, the rats had done all their scurrying, the rats were back inside the walls. Bent nodded. Together, they started up the stairs.

The kid broke into a run again when they reached the first floor. Wade took off after him and caught him as he was rounding the steps leading up to the second floor. Pulled him over and backward and flat on his back and then rolled him over and flashed his police shield in the kid's face and yelled as loud as he could, "Police, police, police! Got it?"

"I didn't do nothin'," the kid said.

"On your feet," Wade said, and in case he hadn't understood it, he yanked him to his feet and slammed him up against the wall and began tossing him as Bent walked over.

"Clean," Wade said.

"I didn't do nothin'," the kid said again.

"What's your name?" Bent asked.

"Dominick Assanti, I didn't do nothin'."

"Who said you did?"

"Nobody."

"Then why'd you run?"

"I figured you were cops," Assanti said, and shrugged.

He was five-ten or -eleven, they guessed, weighing about a hundred and sixty, a good-looking kid with wavy black hair and brown eyes, wearing blue jeans, sneakers, and a T-shirt with a picture of Bart Simpson on it.

"Let's talk," Bent said.

"I didn't do nothin'," Assanti said again.

"Broken record," Wade said.

"Where were you last Tuesday night around nine-thirty?" Bent asked.

"Who remembers?"

"Your girlfriend does."

"Huh?"

"She told us you were near the A & L Bakery Shop on Harrison. Is that right?"

"How does she know where I was?"

"Because you told her."

"I didn't tell her nothin'."

"Were you there or weren't you?"

"I don't remember."

"Try remembering."

"I don't know *where* I was last Tuesday night."

"You went to a movie with your girlfriend . . ."

"You walked her home . . ."

"And you were heading back to your house when you passed the bakery shop."

"I don't know where you got all that."

"We got it from your girlfriend."

"I don't even have no girlfriend."

"She seems to think you're going steady."

"I don't know where you got all this, I swear."

"Dominick . . . pay attention," Wade said.

"Your girlfriend's name is Frankie," Bent said. "For Doris Franceschi."

"Got it?" Wade said.

"And you told her you were outside that bakery shop last Tuesday night at around nine-thirty. Now were you?"

"I don't want no trouble," Assanti said.

"What'd you see, Dominick?"

"I'm scared if I tell you . . ."

"No, no, we're gonna put these guys away," Bent said, "don't worry."

"What'd you see?" Wade asked. "Can you tell us what you saw?"

"I was walking home . . ."

He is walking home, he lives only six blocks from Frankie's house, his head is full of Frankie, he is dizzy with thoughts of Frankie. Wiping lipstick from his mouth, his handkerchief coming away with Frankie's lipstick, he can remember her tongue in his mouth, his hands on her breasts, he thinks they're backfires at first. The shots. But there are no cars on the street.

So he realizes these are shots he just heard, and he thinks Uh-oh, I better get out of here, and he's starting to turn, thinking he'll go back to Frankie's house, ring the doorbell, tell her somebody's shooting outside, can he come up for a minute, when all at once he sees this guy coming out of the liquor store with a brown paper bag in his hands, and he thinks maybe there's a holdup going on in the liquor store, the guy is walking in his direction, he thinks again I better get out of here.

Then . . .

Then there were . . .

"I . . . I can't tell you," Assanti said. "I'm scared."

"Tell us," Wade said.

"I'm scared."

"Please," Wade said.

"There were . . . two other guys. Coming out of the bakery next door."

"What'd they look like?"

Assanti hesitated.

"You can tell us if they were black," Bent said.

"They were black," Assanti said.

"Were they armed?"

"Only one of them."

"One of them had a gun?"

"Yes."

"What'd they look like?"

"They were both wearing jeans and black T-shirts."

"How tall?"

"Both very big."

"What kind of hair? Afro? Dreadlocks? Hi-top fade? Ramp? Tom?"

"I don't know what any of those things are," Assanti said.

"All right, what happened when they came out of the bakery?"

"They almost ran into the guy coming out of the liquor store. Under the streetlight there. Came face to face with him. Looked him dead in the eye. Told him to get the hell outta their way."

Bent looked at Wade knowingly. Their star witness, the guy coming out of the liquor store. Chickenhearted bastard.

"Then what?"

"They came running in my direction."

"Did you get a good look at them?"

"Yeah, but . . ."

"You don't have to worry, we're gonna send them away for a long time."

"What about all their *friends*? You gonna send *them* away, too?"

"We want you to look at some pictures, Dominick."

"I don't want to look at no pictures."

"Why not?"

"I'm scared."

"No, no."

"Don't tell me no, no. You didn't see this Sonny guy. He looked like a gorilla."

"What are you saying?"

"You saying a name?"

"You saying Sonny?"

"I don't want to look at no pictures," Assanti said.

"Are you saying Sonny?"

"Was that his name? Sonny?"

"You know these guys?"

"Was one of them named Sonny?"

"Nobody's gonna hurt you, Dominick."

"Was his name Sonny?"

"Sonny what?"

"We won't let anybody hurt you, Dominick."

"Sonny what?"

He looked at them for a long time. He was clearly frightened, and they thought for sure they were going to lose him just the way they'd lost the guy coming out of the liquor store. He did, in fact, shake his head as if to say he wasn't going to tell them anything else, but he was only shaking it in denial of something inside him that was telling him he'd be crazy to identify anyone who had killed a man.

"The one with the gun," he said softly.

"What about him, Dominick?"

"His name was Sonny."

"You know him?"

"No. I heard the other guy calling him Sonny. When they were running by. Come on, Sonny, *move* it. Something like that."

"Did you get a good look at them, Dominick?"

"I got a good look."

"Can we show you some pictures?"

He hesitated again. And again he shook his head, telling himself he was crazy to be doing this. But he sighed at last and said, "Yeah, okay."

"Thank you," Wade said.

The only white man he could trust with this was Carella. There were things you just knew.

"My goddamn skin," Brown said, as if Carella would understand immediately, which of course he didn't.

"All that *crap* I got to use," Brown said.

Carella turned to look at him, bewildered.

They were in the unmarked car, on their way downtown, Brown driving, Carella riding shotgun. So far, it had been an awful morning. First the disappointing promises-promises conversation with Lieutenant Nelson at the Four-Five and then Lieutenant Byrnes of their very own Eight-Seven asking them into his office and telling them he'd had a call from a lawyer named Louis Loeb, who'd wanted to know why a grieving widow named Margaret Schumacher had been harassed in her apartment yesterday morning by two detectives respectively named Carella and Brown.

"I realize you didn't harass her," Byrnes said at once. "The problem is this guy says he's personally going to the chief of detectives if he doesn't get written apologies from both of you."

"Boy," Carella said.

"You don't feel like writing apologies, I'll tell him to go to hell," Byrnes said.

"Yeah, do that," Brown said.

"Do it," Carella said, and nodded.

"How does the wife look, anyway?" Byrnes asked.

"Good as anybody else right now," Brown said.

But, of course, they hadn't yet talked to anyone else. They were on their way now to see Lois Stein, Schumacher's married daughter, Mrs. Marc with-a-c Stein. And Brown was telling Carella what a pain in the ass it was to be black. Not because being black made you immediately suspect, especially if you were *big* and black, because no white man ever figured you for a big, black *cop*, you always got figured for a big black *criminal*, with tattoos all over your body and muscles you got lifting weights in the prison gym.

The way Brown figured it—and this had nothing to do with why being black was such a very *real* pain in the ass—drugs were calling the tune in this America of ours, and the prime targets for the dealers were black ghetto kids who, rightly or wrongly (and Brown figured they were right) had reason to believe they were being cheated out of the American dream and the only dream available to them was the sure one they could find in a crack pipe. But a drug habit was an expensive one even if you were a big account executive downtown, especially expensive *uptown* where if you were black and uneducated the best you could hope for was to serve hamburgers at McDonald's for four-and-a-quarter an hour, which wasn't even enough to support a heavy *cigarette* habit. To support a *crack* habit, you had to steal. And the people you stole from were mostly white people, because they were the ones had all the bread. So whenever you saw Arthur Brown coming down the street, you didn't think here comes a protector of the innocent sworn to uphold the laws of the city, state, and nation, what you thought was here comes a big black dope-addict criminal in this fine country of ours where the vicious circle was drugs-to-crime-to-racism-to-despair-to-drugs and once again around the mulberry bush. But none of this was why it was a supreme pain in the ass to be black.

"You know what happens when a black man's skin gets dry?" Brown asked.

"No, what?" Carella said.

He was still thinking about Brown's vicious circle.

"Aside from it being damn uncomfortable?"

"Uh-huh," Carella said.

"We turn gray is what happens."

"Uh-huh."

"Which is why we use a lot of oils and greases on our skin. Not only women, I'm talking about men, too."

"Uh-huh."

"To lubricate the skin, get rid of the scale. What was that address again?"

"314 South Dreyden."

"Cocoa butter, cold cream, Vaseline, all this crap. We have to use it to keep from turning gray like a ghost."

"You don't look gray to me," Carella said.

" 'Cause I use all this crap on my skin. But I got a tendency to acne, you know?"

"Uh-huh."

"From when I was a teenager. So if I use all this crap to keep my skin from turning gray, I bust out in pimples instead. It's another vicious circle. I'm thinking of growing a beard, I swear to God."

Carella didn't know what *that* meant, either.

"Up ahead," he said.

"I see it."

Brown turned the car into the curb, maneuvered it into a parking space in front of 322 South Dreyden, and then got out of the car, locked it, and walked around it to join Carella on the sidewalk.

"Ingrown hairs," he said.

"Uh-huh," Carella said. "You see a boutique? It's supposed to be a boutique."

The shop was named Vanessa's, which Lois Stein explained had nothing to do with her own name, but which sounded very British and slightly snobbish and which, in fact, attracted the upscale sort of women to whom her shop catered. She herself looked upscale and elegantly groomed, the sort of honey blonde one usually saw in perfume commercials, staring moodily out to sea, tresses blowing in the wind, diaphanous skirts flattened against outrageously long legs. Margaret Schumacher had told them her stepdaughter was thirty-seven years old, but they never would have guessed it. She looked to be in her late twenties, her complexion flawless, her grayish-blue eyes adding a look of mysterious serenity to her face.

In a voice as soft as her appearance—soft, gentle, these were the words Carella would have used to describe her—she explained at once how close she had been to her father, a relationship that had survived a bitter divorce and her father's remarriage. She could not now imagine how something like this could have happened to him. Her father the victim of a shooting? Even in this city, where law and order—

"Forgive me," she said, "I didn't mean to imply . . ."

A delicate, slender hand came up to her mouth, touched her lips as if to scold them. She wore no lipstick, Carella noticed. The faintest blue eye shadow tinted the lids above her blue-gray eyes. Her hair looked like spun gold. Here among the expensive baubles and threads she sold, she looked like an Alice who had inadvertently stumbled into the queen's closet.

"That's what we'd like to talk to you about," Carella said, "how something like this could've happened." He was lying only slightly in that on his block, at this particular time in space, anyone and everyone was still a suspect in this damn thing. But at the same time . . .

"When did you see him last?" he asked.

This because a victim—especially if something or someone had been troubling him—sometimes revealed to friends or relatives information that may have seemed unimportant at the time but that, in the light of traumatic death, could be relevant . . . good work, Carella, go to the head of the class. He waited. She seemed trying to remember when she'd last seen her own father. Who'd been killed last Friday night. Mysterious blue-gray eyes pensive. Thinking, thinking, when did I last see dear Daddy with whom I'd been so close, and with whom I'd survived a bitter divorce and subsequent remarriage? Brown waited, too. He was wondering if the Fragile Little Girl stuff was an act. He wasn't too familiar with very many white women, but he knew plenty of black women—some of them as blonde as this one—who could do the wispy, willowy bit to perfection.

"I had a drink with him last Thursday," she said.

The day before he'd caught it. Four in the face. And by the way, here's a couple for your mutt.

"What time would that have been?" Carella asked.

"Five-thirty. After I closed the shop. I met him down near his office. A place called Bits."

"Any special reason for the meeting?" Brown asked.

"No, we just hadn't seen each other in a while."

"Did you normally . . ."

"Yes."

". . . meet for drinks?"

"Yes."

"Rather than dinner or lunch?"

"Yes. Margaret . . ."

She stopped.

Carella waited. So did Brown.

"She didn't approve of Daddy seeing us. Margaret. The woman he married when he divorced Mother."

The woman he married. Unwilling to dignify the relationship by calling her his *wife*. Merely the woman he married.

"How'd you feel about that?"

Lois shrugged.

"She's a difficult woman," she said at last.

Which, of course, didn't answer the question.

"Difficult how?"

"Extremely possessive. Jealous to the point of insanity."

Strong word, Brown thought. Insanity.

"But how'd you feel about these restrictions she laid down?" Carella asked.

"I would have preferred seeing Daddy more often . . . I love him, I loved him," Lois said. "But if it meant causing problems for him, then I was willing to see him however and whenever it was possible."

"How'd *he* feel about that?"

"I have no idea."

"You never discussed it with him?"

"Never."

"Just went along with her wishes," Carella said.

"Yes. He was married to her," Lois said, and shrugged again.

"How'd your sister feel about all this?"

"He never saw Betsy at all."

"How come?"

"My sister took the divorce personally."

Doesn't everyone? Brown wondered.

"The whole sordid business beforehand . . ."

"What business was that?" Carella asked at once.

"Well, he was having an affair with her, you know. He left Mother *because* of her. This wasn't a matter of getting a divorce and then meeting someone *after* the divorce, this was getting a divorce because he wanted to marry Margaret. He already *had* Margaret, you see. There's a difference."

"Yes," Carella said.

"So . . . my sister wouldn't accept it. She stopped seeing him . . . oh, it must've been eight, nine months after he remarried. In effect, I became his only daughter. All he had, really."

All he had? Brown thought.

"What'd you talk about last Thursday?" Carella asked.

"Oh, this and that."

"Did he say anything was bothering him?"

"No."

"Didn't mention any kind of . . ."

"No."

". . . trouble or . . ."

"No."

". . . argument . . ."

"No."

". . . or personal matter that . . ."

"Nothing like that."

"Well, did he *seem* troubled by anything?"

"No."

"Or worried about anything?"

"No."

"Did he seem to be *avoiding* anything?"

"Avoiding?"

"Reluctant to *talk* about anything? *Hiding* anything?"

"No, he seemed like his usual self."

"Can you give us some idea of what you talked about?" Brown asked.

"It was just father-daughter talk," Lois said.

"About what?"

"I think we talked about his trip to Europe . . . he was going to Europe on business at the end of the month."

"Yes, what did he say about that?" Carella asked.

"Only that he was looking forward to it. He had a new client in Milan—a designer who's bringing his line of clothes here to the city—and then he had some business in France . . . Lyons, I think he said . . ."

"Yes, he was flying back from Lyons."

"Then you know."

"Did he say he was going alone?"

"I don't think Margaret was going with him."

"Did he mention who *might* be going with him?"

"No."

"What else did you talk about?"

"You know, really, this was just *talk.* I mean, we didn't discuss anything *special,* it was just . . . a nice friendly conversation between a father and his daughter."

"Yes, but about *what?*" Brown insisted.

Lois looked at him impatiently, squelching what appeared to be a formative sigh. She was silent for several seconds, thinking, and then she said, "I guess I told him I was going on a diet, and he said I was being ridiculous, I certainly didn't need to lose any weight . . . oh, and he told me he was thinking of taking piano lessons again, when he was young he used to play piano in a swing band . . ."

Blue-gray eyes looking skyward now, trying to pluck memory out of the air, corner of her lower lip caught between her teeth like a teenage girl doing homework . . .

". . . and I guess I said something about Marc's birthday . . . my husband, Marc, his birthday is next week, I *still* haven't bought him anything. You know, this is *really* very difficult, trying to remember every word we . . ."

"You're doing fine," Carella said.

Lois nodded skeptically.

"Your husband's birthday," Brown prompted.

"Yes. I think we talked about what would be a good gift, he's so hard to please . . . and Daddy suggested getting him one of those little computerized memo things that fit in your pocket, Marc loves hi-tech stuff, he's a dentist."

Carella remembered a dentist he had recently known. The man was now doing time at Castleview upstate. Lots of time. For playing around with poison on the side. He wondered what kind of dentist Marc Stein was. It occurred to him that he had never met a dentist he had liked.

". . . which Marc never even wore. That was last year. Daddy said you had to be careful with gifts like that. I told him I'd thought of getting Marc a dog, but he said dogs were a lot of trouble once you got past the cute puppy stage, and I ought to give that a little thought."

Two bullets in the dog, Brown thought. Who the hell would want to kill a man's *dog*?

"Did your father's dog ever bite anyone?" he asked.

"*Bite* anyone?"

"Or even *scare* anyone, *threaten* anyone?"

"Well . . . I really don't know. He never mentioned anything like that, but . . . I just don't know. You don't think . . . ?"

"Just curious," Brown said.

He was thinking there were all kinds in this city.

"Betsy hated that dog," Lois said.

Both detectives looked at her.

"She hates *all* dogs in general, but she had a particular animosity for Amos."

Amos, Brown thought.

"What kind of dog was he?" he asked.

"A black Lab," Lois said.

Figures, he thought.

"Why'd your sister hate him?" Carella asked.

"I think he symbolized the marriage. The dog was a gift from Margaret, she gave it to Daddy on their first Christmas together. This was when Betsy was still seeing him, before the rift. She hated the dog on sight. He was such a sweet dog, too, well, you know Labs. But Betsy's a very mixed-up girl. Hate Margaret, therefore you hate the dog Margaret bought. Simple."

"Is your sister still living on Rodman?" Carella asked, and showed her the page in his notebook where he'd jotted down Betsy Schumacher's address.

"Yes, that's her address," Lois said.

"When did you see her last?" Brown asked.

"Sunday. At the funeral."

"She went to the funeral?" Carella asked, surprised.

"Yes," Lois said. And then, wistfully, "Because she loved him, I guess."

"Nice view," the girl said.

"Yeah," Kling said.

They were standing at the single window in the room. In the near distance, the Calm's Point Bridge hurled its lights across the River Dix. Aside from the spectacular view of the bridge and the buildings on the opposite bank, there wasn't much else upon which to comment. Kling was renting what was euphemistically called a "studio" apartment. This made it sound as if an artist might live quite comfortably here, splashing paint on canvases or hurling clay at wire frames. Actually, the studio was a single small room with a kitchen the size of a closet and a bathroom tacked on as a seeming afterthought. There was a bed in the room, and a dresser, and an easy chair, and a television set and a lamp.

The girl's name was Melinda.

He had picked her up in a singles bar.

Almost the first thing she'd said to him was that she'd checked out negative for the AIDS virus. He felt this was promising. He told her that he did not have AIDS, either. Or herpes. Or any other sexually transmitted disease. She'd asked him whether he had any *non*sexually transmitted diseases, and they'd both laughed. Now they were in his studio apartment admiring the view, neither of them laughing.

"Can I fix you a drink?" he asked.

"That might be very nice," she said. "What do you have?"

At the bar, she'd been drinking something called a Devil's Fling. She told him there were four different kinds of rum in it, and that it was crème de menthe that gave the drink its greenish tint and its faint whiff of brimstone. She said this with a grin. This was when he began thinking she might be interesting to take home. Sort of a sharp big-city girl edge to her. Whiff of brimstone. He liked that. But he didn't have either crème de menthe or four different kinds of rum here in his magnificent studio apartment with its glorious view. All he had was scotch. Which, alone here on too many nights, he drank in the dark. He was not alone tonight. And somehow scotch seemed inadequate.

"Scotch?" he said tentatively.

"Uh-huh?"

"That's it," he said, and shrugged. "Scotch. But I can phone down for anything you like. There's a liquor store right around the . . ."

"Scotch will be fine," she said. "On the rocks, please. With just a splash of soda."

"I don't think I have any soda."

"Water will be fine then. Just a splash, please."

He poured scotch for both of them, and dropped ice cubes into both glasses, and then let just a dribble of water from the tap splash into her glass. They clinked the glasses together in a silent toast, and then drank.

"Nice," she said, and smiled.

She had brown hair and brown eyes. Twenty-six or -seven years old, Kling guessed, around five-six or thereabouts, with a pert little figure and a secret little smile that made you think she knew things she wasn't sharing with you. He wondered what those things might be. He had not had another woman in this room since Eileen left him.

"Bet it looks even better in the dark," she said.

He looked at her.

"The view," she said.

Secret little smile on her mouth.

He went to the lamp, turned it off.

"There," she said.

Beyond the window, the bridge's span sparkled white against the night, dotted with red taillight flashes from the steady stream of traffic crossing to Calm's Point. He went to stand with her at the window, put his arms around her from behind. She lifted her head. He kissed her neck. She turned into his arms. Their lips met. His hands found her breasts. She caught her breath. And looked up at him. And smiled her secret smile.

"I'll only be a minute," she whispered, and moved out of his arms and toward the bathroom door, smiling again, over her shoulder this time. The door closed behind her. He heard water running in the sink. The only light in the room came from the bridge. He went to the bed and sat on the edge of it, looking through the window where the air conditioner hummed.

When the telephone rang, it startled him.

He picked up the receiver at once.

"Hello?" he said.

"Bert?" she said. "This is Eileen."

She could remember a telephone call a long time ago, when they were both strangers to each other. It had been diffcult to make that call because she'd inadvertently offended him and she was calling to apologize, but it was more difficult to make this call tonight. She was not calling to apologize tonight, or perhaps she was, but either way she would have given anything in the world not to have to be making this call.

"Eileen?" he said.

Totally and completely surprised. It had been months and months.

"How are you?" she said.

She felt stupid. Absolutely stupid. Dumb and awkward and thoroughly idiotic.

"Eileen?" he said again.

"Is this a bad time for you?" she asked hopefully.

Looking for a reprieve. Call him back later or maybe not at all, once she'd had a chance to think this over. *Damn* Karin and her brilliant ideas.

"No, no," he said, "how are you?"

"Fine," she said. "Bert, the reason I'm calling . . ."

"Bert?" she heard someone say.

He must have covered the mouthpiece. Sudden silence on the other end of the line. There was someone with him. A woman? It had sounded like a woman.

* * *

Melinda was wearing only bikini panties and high-heeled pumps. She stood in partial silhouette just inside the bathroom door, her naked breasts larger than they'd seemed when she was fully dressed, the smile on her face again.

"Do you have a toothbrush I can use?" she asked.

"Uh . . . yes," he said, his left hand covering the mouthpiece, "there should be . . . I think there's an unopened one . . . uh . . . in the cabinet over the sink . . . there should be a new one in there."

She glanced at the phone in his hand. Arched an eyebrow. Smiled again, secretly. Turned to show her pert little behind in the skimpy panties, posed there for a moment like Betty Grable in the famous World War II poster, and then closed the bathroom door again, blocking the wondrous sight of her from view. "Eileen?" he said.

"Yes, hi," she said, "is there someone with you?"

"No," he said.

"I thought I heard someone."

"The television set is on," he said.

"I thought I heard someone say your name."

"No, I'm alone here."

"Anyway, I'll make this short," she said. "Karin . . ."

"You don't have to make it short," he said.

"Karin thinks it might be a good idea if the three of us . . ."

"Karin?"

"Lefkowitz. My shrink."

"Oh. Right. How is she?"

"Fine. She thinks the three of us should get together sometime soon to talk things over, try to . . ."

"Okay. Whenever."

"Well, good, I was hoping you'd . . . I usually see her on Mondays and Wednesdays, how about . . . ?"

"Whenever."

"How about tomorrow then?"

"What time?"

"I've got a five o'clock . . ."

"Fine."

". . . appointment, would that be all right with you?"

"Yes, that'd be fine."

"You know where her office is, don't you?"

"Yes, I do."

"Headquarters Building, fifth floor."

"Yes."

"So I'll see you there at five tomorrow."

"I'll see you there," he said, and hesitated. "Been a long time."

"Yes, it has. Well, goodnight, Bert, I'll . . ."

"Maybe she can tell me what I did wrong," he said.

Eileen said nothing.

"Because I keep wondering what I did wrong," he said.

Her beeper went off. For a moment, she couldn't remember where she'd put it, and then she located it on the coffee table across the room, zeroed in on the sound as if she were a bat or something flitting around in the dark, reached for the bedside lamp and snapped it on—they used to talk to each other on the phone in the dark in their separate beds—the beeper still signaling urgently.

"Do *you* know what I did wrong?" he asked.

"Bert, I have to go," she said. "It's my beeper."

"Because if *someone* can tell me what I . . ."

"Bert, really, goodbye," she said, and hung up.

6

THERE WERE CHILDREN in swimsuits.

The fire hydrant down the block was still open, its spray nozzle fanning a cascade of water into the street, and whereas not a moment earlier the kids had been splashing and running through the artificial waterfall, they had now drifted up the street to where the real action was. Outside the building where the blue-and-white Emergency Service truck and motor-patrol cars were angled into the curb, there were also men in tank tops and women in halters, most of them wearing shorts, milling around behind the barricades the police had set up. It was a hot summer night at the end of one of the hottest days this summer; the temperature at ten P.M. was still hovering in the mid-nineties. There would have been people in the streets even if there hadn't been the promise of vast and unexpected entertainment.

In this city, during the first six months of the year, a bit more than twelve hundred murders had been committed. Tonight, in a cluttered neighborhood that had once been almost exclusively Hispanic but that was now a volatile mix of Hispanic, Vietnamese, Korean, Afghani, and Iranian, an eighty-four-year-old man from Guayama, Puerto Rico, sat with his eight-year-old American-born granddaughter on his knee, threatening to add yet another murder to the soaring total; a shotgun was in his right hand and the barrel of the gun rested on the little girl's shoulder, angled toward her ear.

Inspector William Cullen Brady had put a Spanish-speaking member of his team on the door, but so far the old man had said only five words and those in English: "Go away, I'll kill her." Accented English, to be sure, but plain and understandable nonetheless. If they did not get away from the door on the fifth-floor apartment where he lived with

his son, his daughter-in-law, and their three children, he would blow
the youngest of the three clear back to the Caribbean.

It was suffocatingly hot in the hallway where the negotiating team
had "contained" the old man and his granddaughter. Eileen and the
other trainees had been taught that the first objective in any hostage situation was to contain the taker in the smallest possible area, but she
wondered now exactly *who* was doing the containing and who was
being contained. It seemed to her that the old man had chosen his own
turf and his own level of confrontation, and was now calling all the
shots—no pun intended, God forbid! The narrow fifth-floor hallway
with its admixture of exotic cooking smells now *contained* at least
three dozen police officers, not counting those who had spilled over
onto the fire stairs or those who were massed in the apartment down
the hall, which the police had requisitioned as a command post, thank
you, ma'am, we'll send you a receipt. There were cops all over the
rooftops, too, and cops and firemen spreading safety nets below, just in
case the old man decided to throw his granddaughter out the window,
nothing ever surprised anybody in this city.

The cop working the door was an experienced member of the negotiating team who normally worked out of Burglary. His name was
Emilio Garcia, and he spoke Spanish fluently, but the old man wasn't
having any of it. The old man insisted on speaking English, a rather
limited English at that, litanizing the same five words over and over
again: "Go away, I'll kill her." This was a touchy situation here. The
apartment was in a housing project where only last week the Tactical
Narcotics Team had blown away four people in a raid, three of them
known drug dealers, but the fourth—unfortunately—a fifteen-year-old
boy who'd been in the apartment delivering a case of beer from the
local supermarket.

The kid had been black.

This meant that one of the city's foremost agitators, a media hound
who liked nothing better than to see his own beautiful face on television, had rounded up all the usual yellers and screamers and had pick-
eted both the project and the local precinct, shouting police brutality
and racism and no justice, no peace, and all the usual slogans designed
to create more friction than already existed in a festering city on the
edge of open warfare. The Preacher—as he was familiarly called—was
here tonight, too, wearing a red fez and a purple shirt purchased in
Nairobi and open to the waist, revealing a bold gold chain with a cruci-
fix dangling from it; the man was a minister of God, after all, even if he

preached only the doctrines of hate. He didn't *have* to be here tonight, though, shouting himself hoarse, nobody needed any help in the hate department tonight.

The guy inside the apartment was a Puerto Rican, which made him a member of the city's second-largest minority group, and if anything happened to him or that little girl sitting on his lap, if any of these policemen out here exercised the same bad judgment as had their colleagues from TNT, there would be bloody hell to pay. So anyone even remotely connected with the police department—including the Traffic Department people in their brown uniforms—was tiptoeing around outside that building and inside it, especially Emilio Garcia, who was afraid he might say something that would cause the little girl's head to explode into the hallway in a shower of gristle and blood.

"*Oigame*," Garcia said. "*Solo quiero ayudarle.*"

"Go away," the old man said. "I'll kill her."

Down the hall, Michael Goodman was talking to the man's daughter-in-law, an attractive woman in her mid-forties, wearing sandals, a blue mini, and a red tube-top blouse, and speaking rapid accent-free English. She had been born in this country, and she resented the old man's presence here, which she felt reflected upon her own Americanism and strengthened the stereotyped image of herself as just another spic. Her husband was the youngest of his sons—the old man had four sons and three daughters—but even though all of them were living here in America, he was the one who'd had to take the old man in when he'd finally decided to come up from the island. She had insisted that the old man speak English now that he was here in America and living in her home. Eileen wondered if this was why he refused to speak Spanish with their talker at the door.

She was standing with the other trainees in a rough circle around the woman and Goodman, just outside the open door to the command post apartment, where Inspector Brady was in heavy discussion with Deputy Inspector Di Santis of the Emergency Service. Nobody wanted this one to flare out of control. They were debating whether they should pull Garcia off the door. They had thought that a Spanish-speaking negotiator would be their best bet, but now—

"Any reason why he's doing this?" Goodman asked the woman.

"Because he's crazy," the woman said.

Her name was Gerry Valdez, she had already told Goodman that her husband's name was Joey and the old man's name was Armando.

Valdez, of course. All of them Valdez, including the little girl on the old man's lap, Pamela Valdez. And, by the way, when were they going to go in there and *get* her?

"We're trying to talk to your father-in-law right this minute," Goodman assured her.

"Never mind *talking* to him, why don't you just *shoot* him?"

"Well, Mrs. Valdez . . ."

"Before he hurts my daughter."

"That's what we're trying to make sure of," Goodman said. "That nobody gets hurt."

He was translating the jargon they'd had drummed into them for twelve hours a day for the past six days, Sunday included, time-and-a-half for sure. Never mind containment, never mind establishing lines of communication, or giving assurances of nonviolence, just cut to the chase for the great unwashed, dish it out clean and fast, we're trying to talk to him, we're trying to make sure nobody gets hurt here.

"Not him, not *anybody*," Goodman said, just in case the woman didn't yet understand that nobody was going in there with guns blazing like Rambo.

Martha Halsted, the tight-assed little brunette with the Go-to-Hell look, seemed eager for a chance to work the door. She kept glancing down the hall to where Garcia kept pleading in Spanish with the old man, her brown eyes alive with anticipation, if you relieve Garcia, then choose me, pick me, I can do the job. Eileen guessed maybe she could.

She had asked Annie Rawles what she knew about her. Annie remembered her from when she was still working Robbery. She described her as a "specialist." This did not mean what Eileen at first thought it meant. A specialist in robbery or related crimes, right? Wasn't that what Annie meant? Annie explained that, well, no, the term as it was commonly used—hadn't Eileen ever heard the expression? Eileen said No, she hadn't, all eyes, all ears. Annie explained that a specialist was a woman who . . . well . . . a woman adept at oral sex, come on you're putting me on, you *know* what a specialist is. My, my, Eileen thought. Martha Halsted, a specialist. For all her hard, mean bearing and her distant manner, Martha Halsted was all heart, all mouth. Live and learn, Eileen thought, and never judge a book by its cover.

She figured Martha had as much chance of working the door on *this* one as she had of playing the flute with the Philharmonic. Unless she'd been blowing sweet music in the inspector's ear, so to speak, or perhaps even the good doctor's, who knew what evil lurked? Even so, neither of them would risk putting a trainee on the door a week after those Narcotics jerks had blown away a teenager. However much they taught that everything was theory until it was put into practice, and nothing was as valuable as actual experience in the field, nobody in his right mind was going to trust anyone but a skilled professional in a situation like this one. So eat your heart out, Martha. Tonight is a night for specialists of quite another sort.

From down the hall, Garcia was signaling.

Hand kept low at his side so that the old man in the apartment wouldn't see it, wouldn't spook and pull the shotgun trigger. But signaling distinctly and urgently, somebody get *over* here, *will* you please? Martha was the first one to spot the hand signal, busy as she was with watching the door and waiting for her golden opportunity. She told Goodman the guy at the door wanted something. Goodman went in to tally to Brady, and the inspector himself went down the hall to see what it was Garcia wanted. He had already decided to pull Garcia off the door. Now he had to decide who would replace him. A knowledge of Spanish was no longer a priority; the old man obviously spoke English and would speak nothing *but* English. In a situation as volatile as this one, Brady was thinking that he himself might be the right man for the job. Anyway, he went down the hall to see what the hell was happening.

Gerry Valdez was telling Goodman and the assembled trainees that her father-in-law was a sex maniac. She'd caught him several times fondling her daughters, or at least trying to fondle them. That was what had started it all today. She had caught him at it again, and she had threatened to ship him back to the goddamn island if he didn't quit bothering her daughters, and the old man had got the shotgun out of where Joey kept it in the closet, and had grabbed Pamela, the youngest one, the eight-year-old, and had yelled he was going to kill her unless everybody left them alone in the apartment.

Goodman was thinking they had a serious problem here.

Brady was coming back up the hall with Garcia. There was no one at the door now. Just a lot of uniformed cops milling around down the hall, waiting for God only knew what.

"Mike?" Brady said. "Talk to you a minute?"

The three of them went inside the command-post apartment. Brady closed the door behind them.

Gerry Valdez began telling the trainees that she didn't *really* think the old man was a *sex* maniac, it was just that he was getting senile, you know? He was eighty-four years old, he sometimes forgot himself, forgot he wasn't still a little boy chasing little girls along the beach, you know? It was really a pity and a shame, but at the same time she didn't want him fooling around with her kids, that was child abuse, wasn't it?

Eileen guessed it was.

She wondered what they were talking about inside that apartment.

Were it not for the shotgun, it would have been comical.

The old man wanted a girl.

"What do you mean, a girl?" Goodman said.

"He told me he'd trade his granddaughter for a girl," Garcia said.

"A girl?"

"He said if we send in a girl, he'd give us his granddaughter."

"A girl?" Goodman said again.

This was unheard of. In all his years of hostage negotiation, Goodman had never had anyone request a girl. He'd had takers who'd asked for cigarettes or beer or a jet plane to Miami or in one instance spaghetti with red clam sauce, but he had never had anyone ask for a girl. This was something new in the annals of hostage negotiation. An eighty-four-year-old man asking them for a girl.

"You mean he wants a *girl?*" he said, shaking his head, still unwilling to believe it.

"A girl," Garcia said.

"Did he tell you this in Spanish or in English?" Brady asked.

"In Spanish."

"Then there was no mistake."

"No mistake. He wants a girl. *Una chiquita,* he said. I'm sure he meant a hooker."

"He wants a hooker."

"Yes."

"The old goat wants a hooker," Brady said.

"Yes."

"Mike?" Brady said. "What do you think?"

Goodman looked amused. But it wasn't funny.

"Can we send out for a hooker?" Brady said.

"And a dozen red roses," Goodman said, still looking amused.

"Mike," Brady said warningly.

"It's just I never heard of such a request," Goodman said.

"Can we get him a goddamn hooker or not?" Brady said. "Swap him a hooker for the little girl?"

"Absolutely not," Goodman said. "We never give them *another* hostage, that's a hard-and-fast rule. If we sent a hooker in there and she got blown away, you know what the media would do with *that*, don't you? Last week a fifteen-year-old kid, this week a hooker?"

"Yeah," Brady said glumly.

Garcia had been the talker on the door so far, and he didn't want anything to go wrong here, didn't want the old man to blow away either his granddaughter or anybody they might send in there. Garcia was only a Detective/Second, he didn't want any shit coming down on him. Do the job and do it right, but protect your ass at all times; he'd been a cop too long not to know this simple adage. So he waited for whatever Brady might come up with. Brady was the boss. Goodman was a civilian shrink who didn't matter, but Brady was rank. So Garcia waited for whatever he might decree.

"We've got two girls right outside," Brady said.

He was referring to the two women police officers in his training program.

Apparently, the old man did not know that Martha Halsted was a specialist. He took one look at her and told Garcia, in Spanish, that if they didn't get a better-looking girl he would kill his granddaughter on the spot. He gave them ten minutes to get him a better-looking girl. Martha, supremely egotistical, felt his rejection of her had to do with the fact that she was wearing white sneakers, jeans, and a T-shirt; the old man had been expecting someone who looked more like a hooker. She suggested that Eileen—who was dressed almost identically, except for the sneakers—looked more like a hooker.

"So what do you say, Burke?" Brady asked.

"Sir?"

"You want to go in there or not?"

Decoy work all over again, Eileen thought. Either they put you on the street in hooker's threads or you go sit on an old man's lap in blue jeans and a T-shirt, and you try to talk him out of a shotgun. Or maybe you shoot him. She was not in this program because she wanted to shoot people.

"If the shotgun comes out, I go in," she said.

"That's not the deal we made with him," Brady said.

"What was the deal?"

"He sends out his granddaughter, we send in a girl."

"Then what?"

"Then the kid is safe," Brady said.

"How about me? Am I safe?"

Brady looked at her.

"We can't send in a real hooker," he said.

"I realize that. I'm asking if you're swapping my life for the kid's, sir. That's what I'm asking."

"It's up to you to calm him down, get that shotgun away from him."

"How do I calm him down?" Eileen asked.

"We've had run-throughs on situations like this one," Brady said.

"Not exactly, sir, no, sir. We didn't do any run-throughs on a man expecting a hooker and getting a talker instead."

"This is only a variation of a classic hostage situation," Brady said.

"I don't think so, sir. I think he may get very upset when he finds out I'm really a cop. I think he may decide to use that gun when he . . ."

"There's no reason for him to know you're a cop," Brady said.

"Oh? Do I lie to him, sir? I thought once we established communication, we told the truth all the way down the line."

"In this instance, we can bend the truth a little."

Goodman looked at him.

"Inspector," he said, "I think we may be confusing Detective Bur . . ."

"I'm certainly not trying to confuse her," Brady said. "But I've got an eight-year-old girl in there with a crazy old man who wants a hooker or he's going to blow her away. Now do I give him a hooker or don't I? That's the only pertinent question at this moment in time."

"I'm not a hooker, sir," Eileen said.

"I realize that. But you're a police officer who's impersonated hookers in the past."

"Yes, sir, I have. The point is . . ."

"Are you willing to do so now?" Brady asked reasonably. "That's the point, Detective Burke. Are you willing to impersonate a prostitute in order to save that little girl's life?"

How about *my* life? Eileen thought.

"Sir," she said, "how do you suggest I get that shotgun away from him? Once I'm inside that apartment, and he realizes I'm a police negotiator and not a hooker, how do I get him to give up that shotgun?"

"Detective Halsted was willing to go into that apartment within the parameters we've set up," Brady said, hurling down the gauntlet: Are you as good a man as Halsted? Do you have *cojones*, Detective Burke? "She was willing to accept the challenge of negotiating with him from a position of extreme vulnerability. Now I understand the risks involved here, don't you think I understand the risks? I've been in this game a long time now . . ."

Game, Eileen thought.

". . . and when I say I don't want *anyone* hurt, I mean *anyone*, not the taker, not his hostage, and certainly not any member of my team. I'm not asking you to do anything I wouldn't do myself . . ."

Then go *do* it yourself, Eileen thought.

". . . believe me, I'm as concerned for your safety as I would be for my own . . ."

Go in there in drag . . .

"But the situation has reached this point in time where we've got to make a decision. We've either got to satisfy the old man's desire or risk his killing that little girl. He's given us ten minutes, and eight of those minutes are already gone. So what would you like us to do, Detective?"

"Sir, you're asking me to go in there unarmed . . ."

"That's what we promised, that's what we always promise. No guns, no one gets hurt."

"But he *does* have a gun, sir."

He happens to have a goddamn *gun,* sir.

"They always have guns," Brady said. "Or knives. They always have weapons of some sort, yes."

"A double-barreled shotgun, sir."

"Yes, that's the situation here," Brady said.

"I'd have to be crazy, right?" Eileen said.

"Well, that's for you to decide, that's the nature of the work." Brady looked at his watch. "What do you say, Burke, we're almost out of time here. Yes or no? Believe me, there are plenty of female police officers in this city who'd be happy to work with this team."

Female police officers, she thought.

Can you cut it or not, Detective Burke?

Are you a man or a mouse?

Bullshit, she thought.

"We negotiate *before* I go in," she said.

Brady looked at her.

"I work the door. The old man can believe what he wants, but nobody's going inside that apartment until he hands over the little girl *and* the shotgun. Take it or leave it."

He kept looking at her.

She figured whichever way this went, she'd be off the team tomorrow morning. Same as Mary Beth Mulhaney.

"Take it or *leave* it?" Brady said.

Or maybe off the team right this minute.

"Yes, sir," she said. "Take it or leave it."

Both you *and* the old man, she thought.

"If anything happens to that little girl . . ." Brady said, and let the sentence trail.

The old man thought the redhead was a vast improvement over the skinny one with the look of a mongrel. It was a pity she couldn't speak Spanish, but at his age he couldn't expect perfection. Enough that she had eyes as green as the sea and breasts as softly rolling as the hills of his native land. Freckles sprinkled like gold dust on her cheeks and across the bridge of her nose. A beauty. He was a very lucky man.

"We have to talk," she said. "My name is Eileen."

The door to apartment 5L was open just a crack, the night chain holding it. He could see her face and her body in the narrow opening. He knew she could see the shotgun against his granddaughter's ear. His finger was inside the trigger guard. There were two shells in the shotgun. His son always kept the shotgun loaded in the closet. This was a bad neighborhood now that all the strangers had begun moving in.

"What is there to talk about?" he asked.

"About my coming in there," she said.

She had been taught not to lie to them. She would try not to lie to him now. She would not say she was a hooker. But neither would she say she wasn't. It was an omission she could live with. Unless someone got hurt. Then she would never be able to live with it again.

"I can't come in there as long as you have that gun in your hands," she said.

In the crack between the door and the doorjamb, she could see him smiling wisely. A wrinkled old man with gray-white beard stubble, a terrified little dark-haired, dark-eyed girl on his lap, the double barrel of a shotgun against her head. If anything happened to that little girl . . .

"I'm afraid to come in there while you have that gun in your hands," Eileen said.

"Yes," the old man said.

What the hell does *that* mean? she wondered.

"But that is precisely why they've sent you to me, *verdad?*" he asked. "*Because* I have this gun in my hands."

Heavily accented English, but clearly understandable. And perfectly logical, too. The only reason they were submitting to the old man's wishes was that he had a gun. Give up the gun, he gave up his power to negotiate.

"Your granddaughter must be frightened, too," she said.

"I love my granddaughter," he said.

"Yes, but I'm sure she's terrified of that gun."

"No, she's all right. You're all right, aren't you, *querida?*" he said to the girl, and chucked her under the chin with his free hand. "Besides, I will let her go when you come in here," he said. "That is our understanding, eh? You come in, I let her go. Everybody's happy."

"Except me," she said, and smiled.

She knew she had a good smile.

"Well, I certainly don't want to make you unhappy," the old man said flirtatiously. "I will certainly do my best to make you happy."

"Not if you have a gun in your hands. I'm afraid of guns."

"Once you're in here," he said, "I'll let the little girl go. Then we can lock the door, and I'll put down the gun."

Oh, sure, she thought, Fat Chance Department.

"I'll make you very happy," he said.

Oh yes, she thought, I'm sure.

"Listen to me," she said. Her voice lowering conspiratorially. "Why don't you send out the little girl?"

Hostage first, weapon later.

All according to the book.

"When you come in, she goes out," he said. "That was the deal."

"Yes, but when they made the deal, they didn't know I'd be so afraid of guns."

"A pretty girl like you?" he said, flirtatiously again. "Afraid of a little gun like this one?"

Gently, he nudged his granddaughter's temple with the barrel of the shotgun. The girl winced.

Don't let it go off, Eileen thought. Please, God.

"I really am afraid," she said. "That's why, if you send her out, we can talk about the gun. Privately. Just the two of us."

"Tell me what else we will do privately."

"First send out the little girl," Eileen said.

"No. You come in here and then you can tell me what we'll do privately."

"Why don't you take the chain off the door?" she said.

"Why should I?"

"So I can see you better."

"Why do you want to see me?"

"It's just difficult to talk this way."

"I find it very easy to talk this way," he said.

You stubborn old bastard, she thought.

"Don't you want to see *me* better?" she asked.

"Yes, that would be nice."

"So take off the chain," she said. "Open the door a little wider."

"Are you a policeman?" he asked.

Flat out.

So what now?

"No, I'm not a policeman," she said.

The absolute truth. A police *woman*, yes. A police *person*, yes. But not a police *man*. She guessed she could live with that.

"Because if you're a policeman," he said, "I'll kill the little girl."

Which she could *not* live with.

"No," she said again, "I'm not a policeman. You said you wanted a woman . . ."

"Yes."

"Well, I'm a woman."

In the wedge between the door and the jamb, she saw him smile again.

"Come in here and show me what kind of woman you are," he said.

"For me to come in, you have to take the chain off the door."

"Will you come in then?"

"I'll come in if you take the chain off the door . . ."

She hesitated.

"And let the little girl come out . . ."

She hesitated again.

"And put down the gun."

Silence.

"Then I'll come in," she said.

Another silence.

"You want a lot," he said.

"Yes."

"I'll give you a lot," he said, and winked.

"I hope so," she said, and winked back.

Double meanings flying like spears on the sultry night air.

"Open your blouse," he said.

"No."

"Open your blouse for me."

"No."

"Let me see your breasts."

"No," she said. "Take off the chain."

Silence.

"All right," he said.

She waited. He leaned forward. Did not get out of the chair. The little girl still on his lap. The shotgun still to her head. His finger still inside the trigger guard. Leaned forward, reached out with his left hand, and slid the chain along its track until it fell free. She wondered if she should shove the door inward, try knocking him off the chair. He was so old, so frail. But the shotgun was young, the shotgun was a leveler of age.

Gently, with the toe of her foot, she eased the door open just a trifle wider. She could see the old man more completely now, a blue wall behind him deep inside the apartment, blue wall and blue eyes and gray hair and grizzled gray beard. He was looking directly into her eyes, an anticipatory smile on his face.

"Hello," she said.

"You're even prettier than I thought," he said.

"Thank you. Do you remember our deal?"

"Yes, you're coming in here."

"Only after you let the little girl go and put down the gun."

"Yes, I know."

"So do you want to let her go now?"

"How do I know . . . ?"

"You have my word."

"How do I know you'll come in here to me?"

"I said I would. I gave you my word."

"And are you a woman of your word?"

"I try to be."

Which meant she would break her word if he made the slightest move to harm either her or the little girl. She was unarmed . . .

That's what we promise. No guns, no one gets hurt . . .

. . . but there were backup cops to her right, and all she had to do was signal for them to storm the door. She hoped the old man would not do anything foolish.

"So let her come out now, okay?" she said.

"Pamela?" he said. And then in Spanish, "Do you want to go outside now, *querida*? Do you want to leave Grandpa here with the nice lady?"

Pamela nodded gravely. Too terrified to cry or to show relief. She knew this was her grandfather, but she also knew this was a gun. It was difficult for her to reconcile the two. She nodded. Yes, I want to go outside. Please let me go outside, Grandpa.

"Go on then," he said in English, and looked to Eileen for approval. Eileen nodded.

"Come on, sweetheart," she said, and extended her arms to the little girl. "Come on out here before your grandfather changes his mind."

Pamela scrambled off his lap and out into the hall. Eileen clasped her into her arms, swung her around, and planted her securely in the arms of an Emergency Service cop, who swooped her up and hurried off down the hall with her.

Now there was only the old man and his gun.

No bargaining power anymore. If they wanted to blow him away, they could do so without any fear that a hostage was at risk. But that wasn't the name of the game. And she had given him her word.

"Now put down the gun," she said.

He had swung the shotgun toward the opening in the door. It sat in his lap, his finger still inside the trigger guard, the barrels angled up toward Eileen's head. From where he was sitting, he could not see the policemen in the hallway to her right. But he knew someone had taken the girl, he knew she had passed the girl on to someone, he knew she was not alone.

"Who's out there with you?" he asked.

"Policemen," she said. "Do you want to put down the gun, Mr. Valdez?"

"Do they have guns, these policemen?"

"Yes."

The truth. Tell him the truth.

"If I put down the gun, how do I know they won't shoot me?"

"I promise you we won't hurt you."

A slip.

We.

Identifying herself as a cop.

But he hadn't caught it.

Or had he?

"I promise you none of the policemen out here will hurt you."

Correcting it. Or compounding it. Which? How smart was he? Blue eyes studying her now, searching her face. Could he trust her?

"How do I know they won't shoot me? I made . . ."

"Because I . . ."

". . . a lot of trouble for everybody," he said.

"Yes, you did. But I promise they won't shoot you. No one will hurt you if you put down the gun. I promise you. I give you my word."

"Will they forget the trouble I made for everybody?"

She could not promise him this. There'd be the weapons charge, that wasn't a toy gun in there. And God knew what other charges there'd be on top of that. He wouldn't walk away from this clean, that wasn't the way it worked, the promises didn't extend that far. He was only a senile old man, true, who thought he was six years old and playing doctor under the coconut palms—but he'd broken the law, broken several laws, in fact, and these were policemen here, sworn to uphold those laws.

"They'll help you," she said. "They'll try to help you."

Which was true. Psychiatric observation, therapy, the works, whatever seemed indicated.

But the shotgun was still in his lap, angled up at her.

"Come on," she said, "let's put down the gun, okay?"

"Tell them I want to see them. The policemen in the hall."

"I don't have any authority to tell policemen what to do."

"Ask them," he said. "Do you have authority to ask them?"

The smile on his face again.

Was he toying with her?

"He wants to see who's out here," she shouted down the hall to Brady, who was standing behind four Emergency Service cops with riot guns in their hands and sidearms strapped to their waists. The E.S. cops were all wearing ceramic vests. So what do you say, Inspector? she thought. Want to come in the water?

That's what we promise. No guns, no one gets hurt.

Except that now it was show time.

"Let him see you," Brady said to the E.S. men.

They lumbered down the hall in their heavy vests, toting their heavy guns, lining up against the wall behind Eileen, where the old man could see them.

"Are there any others?" he asked.

"Yes, but not right here," she said. "All the way down the hall."

"Tell them to put down their guns."

"I can't give them orders," Eileen said.

"Tell the other one. The one you were talking to."

Eileen nodded, turned away from the door, and shouted, "Inspector Brady!"

"Yes?"

"He wants them to put down their guns."

Silence.

"Or I'll shoot you," the old man said.

"Or he'll shoot me," she called to Brady, and then smiled and said to the old man, "You wouldn't do that, would you?"

"Yes, I would," he said, returning the smile.

"He means it," she shouted down the hall.

Behind her, the E.S. cops were beginning to fidget. Any one of them had a clear shot at the old bastard sitting there in full view with the shotgun in his lap. If they put down their guns, as he was now asking them to do, there was no guarantee that he wouldn't start blasting away. A ceramic vest was a very handy tool in a situation like this one, but you couldn't pull a ceramic vest over your head. If he cut loose at this range, nobody outside the door was safe. The E.S. cops were hoping this dizzy redhead and her boss knew what the hell they were doing.

"Put down your guns, men," Brady called.

"Now just a second, Bill!" another voice shouted.

Deputy Inspector John Di Santis, in command of the Emergency Service, and coming from behind Brady now to stand beside him in the hallway. Eileen could hear them arguing. She hoped the old man's ears weren't as good as hers. Di Santis was saying he was willing to go along with all this negotiating shit up to a point, but that point did not include standing four of his men against the wall for a firing squad. Brady answered him in a voice Eileen could not hear. Made aware, Di Santis lowered his voice, too. Eileen could not hear what either of them was saying now. Their whispers cascaded down the hallway. White-water whispers. Inside the apartment, the old man was watching her. She suddenly knew that he would in fact shoot her if the men behind her didn't put down their guns.

"What do you say, Inspector?" she called. "The man here's getting itchy."

Valdez smiled.

He knew what itchy meant.

She smiled back.

Little joke they were sharing here. The man's getting itchy, he's going to blow off my goddamn head, aren't you darling? Smiling.

"Inspector?"

The whispers stopped. Eileen waited. Somebody—either her or the old man or one or more of the cops standing behind her—was going to get hurt in the next few seconds, unless . . .

"All right, men, do what Inspector Brady says."

Di Santis.

Behind her, one of the E.S. cops muttered something Eileen couldn't understand, a word in Spanish that made the old man's smile widen. She heard the heavy weapons being placed on the floor . . .

"The other guns, too," the old man said.

"He wants the sidearms, too!" she yelled down the hall.

"All your weapons, men!" Di Santis shouted.

More muttering behind her, in English this time, soft grumbles of protest. They had been dealt a completely new hand, but the old man was still holding all the cards.

"Now you," Eileen told him.

"No," he said. "Come inside here."

"You promised me," she said.

"No," he said, smiling. "You're the one who made all the promises."

Which was true.

I promise they won't shoot you.

No one will hurt you . . .

"If you put down the gun," she reminded him.

"No."

Shaking his head.

"I promised that no one would hurt you if you put down the gun," she said.

"No one can hurt me, anyway," he said, smiling. "No one has a gun now but me."

Which was also true.

"Well, I thought I could trust you," she said, "but I see I can't."

"You can trust me," he said. "Open your blouse."

"No," she said.

"Open your goddamn *blouse*," one of the E.S. cops whispered urgently.

She ignored him. "I'm going to leave now," she told the old man. "You broke your word, so I'm leaving. I can't promise what these men will do when I'm gone."

"They'll do nothing," he said. "I have the gun."

"There are others down the hall," she said. "I can't promise you anything anymore. I'm going now."

"No!" he said.

She hesitated.

"Please," he said.

Their eyes met.

"You promised," he said.

She knew what she'd promised. She'd promised that no one would be hurt. She'd promised she would go in to him if he put down the gun. She had given him her word. She was a woman of her word.

"Put down the gun," she said.

"I'll kill you if you don't come in here," he said.

"Put down the gun."

"I'll kill you."

"Then how will I be able to come in?" she asked, and the old man burst out laughing because the logic of the situation had suddenly become absurdly clear to him. If he killed her, she could not go in to him; it was as simple as that. She burst out laughing, too. Surprised, some of the E.S. cops behind her began laughing, tentatively at first, and then a bit more boldly. Down the hall, Eileen heard someone whisper, "They're laughing." Someone else whispered, *"What?"* This seemed funny, too. The cops in their ceramic vests began laughing harder, like armored knights who'd been told their powerful king was in fact impotent. Defenseless, their weapons and holsters and cartridge belts on the floor at their feet, contained here in this stifling hot hallway, they quaked with laughter, thinking how silly it would be if the old man actually *did* kill the redhead, thereby making it impossible for her to go in to him. The old man was thinking the same thing, how silly all of this had suddenly become, thinking too that maybe he should just put down the gun and get it over with, all the trouble he'd caused here, his blue eyes squinched up, tears of laughter running down his wrinkled face into his grizzled gray beard. Down the hall there were puzzled whispers again.

"Oh, dear," Eileen said, laughing.

"¡Dios mío!" the old man said, laughing.

Any one of the E.S. cops could have shot him in that moment. He had lowered the shotgun, it sat across his lap like a walking stick. No one was in danger from that gun. Eileen took a tentative step into the room, reaching for it.

"No!" the old man snapped, and the gun came up again, pointing at her head.

"Aw, come on," she said, and grimaced in disappointment like a little girl.

He looked at her. The tears were still streaming down his face, he could still remember how funny this had seemed a moment ago.

"Mr. Valdez?" she said.

He kept looking at her.

"Please let me have the gun."

Still looking at her. Weeping now. For all the laughter that was gone. For all those days on the beach long ago.

"Please?" she said.

For all the pretty little girls, gone now.

He nodded.

She held out her hands to him, palms up.

He put the gun into her hands.

Their eyes locked.

She went into the apartment, the gun hanging loose at her side, the barrels pointing toward the floor, and she leaned into the old man where he sat frail and weeping in the hardbacked chair, and she kissed his grizzled cheek and whispered, "Thank you," and wondered if she'd kept her promise to him after all.

7

GLORIA SANDERS was covered with blood.

This was ten o'clock on the morning of July twenty-fifth in the nurses' lounge at Farley General Hospital, downtown on Meriden Street. Her white uniform was covered with blood, and there were also flecks of blood in her blonde hair and on her face. They'd had a severe bleeder in the Emergency Room not ten minutes earlier, and Gloria had been part of the team of nurses who, working with the resident, had tried to stanch the flow of blood. There'd been blood all over the table, bed, blood on the walls, blood everywhere, she had never seen anyone spurting so much blood in her life.

"A stabbing victim," she told Carella and Brown. "He came in with a patch over the wound. The minute we peeled it off, he began gushing."

She was dying for a cigarette now, she told them, but smoking was against hospital rules, even though the people who'd *made* the rule had never worked in an emergency room or seen a gusher like the one they'd had this morning. Or the kid yesterday, who'd fallen under a subway car and had both his legs severed just above the knee. A miracle either of them was still alive. And they wouldn't let her smoke a goddamn cigarette.

Arthur Schumacher's taste for blue-eyed blondes seemed to go back a long way. His former wife's eyes were the color of cobalt, her hair an extravagant yellow that blatantly advertised its origins in a bottle. Slender and some five feet six or seven inches tall, Gloria strongly resembled the one daughter they'd already met, but there was a harder edge to her. She'd been around a while, her face said, her body said, her entire stance said. Life had done worse things to her than being bled on by a stabbing victim, her eyes said.

"So what can I do for you?" she asked, and the words sounded confrontational and openly challenging. I've seen it all and done it all, so watch out, boys. I'd as soon kick you in the groin as look at you. Blue eyes studying them warily. Blonde hair bright as brass, clipped short and neat around her head, giving her a stern, forbidding look. This was not the honey-blonde hair her daughter Lois had; if this woman were approaching you at night, you'd see her a block away. She reminded Carella of burned-out prison matrons he had known. So what can I do for you?

"Mrs. Sanders," he said, "we went . . ."

"*Ms.* Sanders," she corrected.

"Sorry," Carella said.

"Mm," she said.

It sounded like a grunt of disapproval.

"We went to your daughter's apartment on Rodman this morning . . ."

Eyes watching them.

"The address we have for her on Rodman," Brown said.

". . . and the super told us he hadn't seen her for the past several days."

"Betsy," she said, and nodded curtly.

"Yes."

"I'm not surprised. Betsy comes and goes like the wind."

"We're eager to talk to her," Carella said.

"Why?"

Leaning forward in the leather chair. The walls of the lounge painted white. She hadn't had a chance to wash before coming to talk to them; there were tiny flecks of blood in her yellow hair. Blood on the front of the white uniform. Blood on the white shoes, too, Brown noticed. He tried to visualize the bleeder. Most bleeders he'd seen were already dead.

"We understand she didn't get along with your former husband," Carella said.

"So what?" Gloria said. "Neither did I."

The challenge again. Is that why you're here? Because I didn't get along with my husband who's now dead from four bullets in the head?

"That *is* true, isn't it?" Carella said. "That your daughter . . ."

"She didn't kill him," Gloria said flatly.

"No one said she did," Carella said.

"Oh no?" she said, and pulled a face. "There are cops all over the E.R. every day of the week," she said, "uniformed cops, plainclothes cops, all kinds of cops. There isn't a cop in the world who doesn't first look to the family when there's any kind of trouble. I hear the questions they ask, they always want to know who got along with whom. Man's got a bullet in his belly, they're asking him did he get along with his wife. So don't lie to me about this, okay? Don't tell me we're not suspects. You know we are."

"Who do you mean, Ms. Sanders?"

"I mean Betsy, and me, and maybe even Lois, for all I know."

"Why would you think that?"

"I *don't* think that. *You're* the ones who think it."

"Why would *we* think it?"

"Let's not play games here, Officer. You told me a minute ago that you understood Betsy didn't get along with her father. So what does that mean? What are you, a social worker looking for a reconciliation? You're a cop, am I right? A detective investigating a murder. Arthur was killed, and his daughter didn't get along with him. So let's find her and ask her where she was last Friday night, Saturday night, whenever the hell it was, I don't know and I don't care. No games. Please. I'm too tired for games."

"Okay, no games," Carella said. He was beginning to like her. "Where's your daughter? She was at her father's funeral on Sunday, and now she's gone. Where is she?"

"I don't know. I told you. She comes and goes."

"Where does she go *to* or come *from?*" Brown asked. *He* didn't like her at all. He'd had a teacher like her in the fourth grade. She used to hit him on the hands with a ruler.

"This is the summertime. In the summer, hippies migrate. They cover the earth like locusts. Betsy is a thirty-nine-year-old hippie, and this is July. She could be anywhere."

"Like *where* anywhere?" Brown insisted.

"How the hell should I know? You're the cop, you find her."

"Ms. Sanders," Carella said, "no games, okay? Please. I'm too tired for games. Your daughter hated him, and she hated his dog, and now both of them are . . ."

"Who says so?"

"What do you mean?"

"That she hated the dog."

"Lois. Your daughter Lois. Why? *Didn't* Betsy hate the dog?"

"Betsy seemed to hate the dog, yes."

"Then why'd you question it?"

"I simply wanted to know who'd told you. I thought it might have been *her.*" Almost snarling the word.

"Who do you mean?" Brown asked.

"Haven't you talked to her yet? His precious peroxide blonde?"

Pot calling the kettle, Carella thought.

"Do you mean Mrs. Schumacher?" Carella asked.

"*Mrs.* Schumacher, yes," she said, the word curling her upper lip into a sneer. She flushed red for a moment, as if containing anger, and then she said, "I thought she might have been the one who told you Betsy hated that dumb dog."

"How'd *you* feel about that dumb dog?" Carella asked.

"Never had the pleasure," Gloria said. "And I thought we weren't going to play games."

"We won't."

"Good. Look, let me make it easier for you, okay? I hated Arthur for what he did to me, but I didn't kill him. Betsy hated him for much the same reasons, but I'm sure she didn't kill him, either. I know you'll find out about the will, so I might as well tell you right now that I wouldn't grant a divorce until I made sure both my daughters were in his will for fifty percent of his estate. That's twenty-five percent each, which in Arthur's case comes to a hell of a lot of money."

"How much money?"

"I don't know the exact amount. A lot. But I know that neither of my daughters killed him for his money. Or for *any* reason at *all*, for that matter."

Both detectives were thinking that the only two reasons for murder were love or money. And hate was the other side of the love coin.

"How about you?" Brown asked. "Are *you* in that will?"

"No."

"Would you know if the present Mrs. Schumacher . . . ?"

"I have no idea. Why don't you ask *her?* Or better yet, ask Arthur's beloved partner, Lou Loeb. I'm sure he'll know all there is to know about it."

"Getting back to your daughter," Brown said. "Betsy. Did you talk to her after the funeral on Sunday?"

"No."

"When *did* you talk to her last?"

"I guess the day after he got killed."

"That would've been Saturday," Carella said.

"I suppose. It was on television, it was in all the papers. Betsy called and asked me what I thought about it."

"What'd you tell her?"

"I told her good riddance to bad rubbish."

"How'd *she* feel about it?"

"Ambivalent. She wanted to know whether she should go to the funeral. I told her she should do what she felt like doing."

"Apparently she decided to go."

"Apparently. But when we talked, she wasn't certain."

"Did she mention where she'd been the night before?" Carella asked.

"No games," Gloria reminded him.

He smiled.

"How about Lois?" he asked. "Did she call you, too?"

"Yes. Well, this was a shocking thing, a man gunned down right outside his apartment. Although in this city, it's starting to be the norm, isn't it?"

"*Any* city," Brown said, suddenly defensive.

"Not like here," Gloria said.

"Yes, like here," he said.

"When did Lois call you?" Carella asked.

"Saturday morning."

"To talk about her father?"

"Of course."

"How'd you feel about her continuing relationship with him?"

"I didn't like it. That doesn't mean I killed him."

"How'd she seem? When she called?"

"Seem?"

"Was she in tears, did she seem in . . ."

"No, she . . ."

". . . control of herself?"

"Yes."

"What'd she say?"

"She said she'd just read about it in the paper. She was surprised that her *stepmother*"—giving the word an angry spin—"hadn't called her about it, she was sure she must have known before then."

"You don't like Mrs. Schumacher very much, do you?"

"I loathe her. She stole my husband from me. She ruined my marriage and my life."

Carella nodded.

"But I didn't kill him," she said.

"Then you won't mind telling us where you were Friday night," he said, and smiled.

"Games again," she said, and did not return the smile. "I was home. Watching television."

"Anyone with you?"

"No, I was alone," she said. "I'm a sixty-year-old grass widow, a bitter, unpleasant woman who doesn't get invited out very often. Arthur did that to me. I never forgave him for it, and I'm glad he's dead. But I didn't kill him."

"What were you watching?" Brown asked.

"A baseball game."

"Who was playing?"

"The Yankees and the Minnesota Twins."

"Where?"

"In Minnesota."

"Who won?"

"The Twins. Two to one. I watched the news afterward. And then I went to bed."

"You still have no idea where we can find Betsy, huh?" Carella said.

"None."

"You'd tell us if you knew, right?"

"Absolutely."

"Then I guess that's it," he said. "Thank you very much, Ms. Sanders, we appreciate your time."

"I'll walk you out," she said, and rose ponderously and wearily. "Catch a cigarette in the alley," she added in a lower voice. And winked.

The trouble with a name like Sonny was that too many criminals seemed to favor it. This was a phenomenon neither Bent nor Wade quite understood. As kids growing up in the inner city, they had known their share of blacks named Sonny, but they hadn't realized till now just how popular the nickname was. Nor had they realized that its popularity crossed ethnic and racial barriers to create among criminals a widespread preference that was akin to an epidemic.

Bent and Wade were looking for a *black* Sonny.

This made their job a bit more difficult.

For whereas the computer spewed out a great many Sonnys who'd originally been Seymours or Stanislaws or Sandors, it appeared that blacks and people of Italian heritage led the pack in preferring the nickname Sonny to given names like Seward or Simmons or Salvatore or Silvano.

The detectives were further looking for a black Sonny who may or may not have had an armed-robbery arrest record. This made their job even more difficult in that the computer printed out a list of thirty-seven black Sonnys who within the past three years had done holdups in this city alone. As a sidelight, only six of those Sonnys were listed as wearing tattoos, a percentage much lower than that for the general armed-robber population, white, black, or indifferent. They did not bother with a nationwide search, which might have kept them sitting at the computer all day long.

Eight of the thirty-seven black armed robbers named Sonny were men who'd been born during the two years that Sonny Liston was the world's heavyweight boxing champion and considered a worthy role model. They were now all in their late twenties, and Wade and Bent were looking for a black Sonny who'd been described as being in his twenties. They knew that to most white men all black men looked alike. That was the difficulty in getting a white man to identify a black man from a photograph—especially a police photograph, which did not exactly qualify as a studio portrait. Dominick Assanti was no different from any other white man they'd ever known. To Dominick, only two black men were instantly recognizable: Eddie Murphy and Bill Cosby. All other black men, including Morgan Freeman and Danny Glover, looked alike. To Assanti, Bent and Wade probably looked alike, too.

First they showed him each of the eight mug shots one by one.

"Recognize any of them?" they asked.

Assanti did not recognize any of the men in the mug shots.

He commented once that he would not like to meet *this* guy in a dark alley.

Wade and Bent agreed.

Then they placed the mug shots on the table side by side, all eight of them, and asked him to pick out the three Sonnys who *most* resembled the Sonny who'd run past them with a gun in his fist on the night of the Carella murder.

Assanti said none of them looked like the man he'd seen.

"Are you sure?" Bent asked.

"I'm positive," Assanti said. "The one I seen had a scar on his face."

"Ah," Bent said.

So it was back to the computer again, this time with new information. Recognizing the difficulty of judging a man's age when he's rushing by you at night with a gun in his hand, the gun taking on more immediacy than the year of his birth, they dropped the age qualification. Recognizing, too, that the bakery shop holdup did not necessarily indicate a *history* of armed robbery, they dropped this qualification as well and ran a citywide search for any black man convicted of a felony within the past five years, provided he was named Sonny and had a scar on his face. They turned up sixty-four of them. This was not surprising.

It was almost impossible to grow up black in the inner city without one day acquiring a scar of one sort or another. And because keloids—scars that extended and spread beyond the original wound—were more prevalent in black skin than in white, these scars were usually highly visible. The knife scar over Wade's left eye was a keloid. He'd been told it could be treated with radiation therapy combined with surgery and injection of steroids into the lesion. He'd opted to wear the scar for the rest of his life. Actually, it didn't hurt in his line of work.

They now had sixty-four new mug shots to show Assanti. He pondered the photos long and hard. He was really trying to be cooperative, but he was severely limited in that he was white. In the long run, he simply gave up.

Bent and Wade hit the streets again.

Eileen was already there when Kling got to the office at five-ten that Wednesday afternoon. He apologized for being late and then took the chair Karin Lefkowitz offered him. He found it difficult to keep his eyes off Eileen. She was dressed casually—well, almost sloppily, in a faded denim skirt and a cotton sweater that matched her eyes—but she looked fresh and beautiful and radiantly happy. Karin explained that they'd just been talking about Eileen's first success with the hostage negotiating team. Last night, she'd . . .

"Well, it wasn't a major *triumph* or anything like that," Eileen said quickly.

"A baptism of fire, more or less," Karin said, and smiled.

"Bad word to use," Eileen said. "Fire."

Both of them were smiling now. Kling felt suddenly like an outsider. He didn't know how Eileen was using the word, and he felt somewhat like a foreigner here in his own country. Fire meant combustion. Fire meant to terminate someone's employment. Fire also meant to shoot.

But Karin seemed to know exactly which meaning or meanings Eileen had intended, and this sense of shared intimacy was somehow unsettling to him.

"So," Karin said, "I'm glad you could make it."

But what had happened last night? Weren't they going to tell him?

"Happy to be here," he said, and smiled.

"I'll tell you where we are," Karin said. "Then maybe you can help us."

"Happy to," he said, and realized he'd repeated himself, or almost, and suddenly felt foolish. "If I can," he said lamely. Help them with what? he wondered.

Karin told him where they were.

Recounted the whole confusing tale of the Halloween night that had only been last year but that seemed centuries ago, when he'd stuck his nose into what was admittedly none of his business, causing Eileen to lose her two backups and placing her in an extremely dangerous and vulnerable position with a serial killer.

"Since that time," Karin explained, "Eileen has been blaming you for . . ."

"Well, you know," Kling started, "I was only trying to . . ."

"I know that," Eileen said.

"I mean, the *last* thing I wanted was to come between you and your backups. I know Annie Rawles," he said, turning back to Karin, "she's a good cop. And whereas this other guy . . ."

"Shanahan," Eileen said.

"Shanahan," he said, nodding to her in acknowledgment, "was a stranger to me . . ."

"Mike Shanahan."

"Which, by the way, is how the mixup came about. I didn't know him, he didn't know me . . ."

"I know," Eileen said.

"What I'm saying is I'd rather have cut off my right arm than put you in any kind of situation where you'd have to face down a killer."

The room went silent.

"I think Eileen knows that," Karin said.

"I hope so," Kling said.

"She also knows . . . don't you, Eileen? . . . that whereas you *were* to blame for losing her backups . . ."

"Well, as I told you . . ."

". . . you were *not* to blame for her having to kill Bobby Wilson."

"Well . . . who said I was?"

"Eileen thought you were."

"You didn't think that, did you?" he asked, turning to her.

"Yes, I did."

"That I was . . . how could you think that? I mean, the guy was coming at you . . ."

"I know."

". . . with a knife . . ."

"I know."

"So how could I have had anything to do with that? I mean, *anybody* . . . any police officer . . ."

"Yes, Bert, I know that now."

"Jesus, I really didn't think you were blaming me for that, Eileen."

"It's complicated," she said.

"Well, I know that. But you can't blame . . ."

"It's involved with the rape, too."

"Well, yeah, that," he said.

Eileen looked at him.

"Bert . . ." she said. "Don't just dismiss it."

"I'm not dismissing it, Eileen, you know that."

"Just don't fucking *dismiss* it, okay?"

He felt as if he'd been slapped in the face. He looked at her, stunned.

"It wasn't well, yeah, *that*," she said. "It was *rape!*"

"Eileen, I didn't mean it that way. I meant . . ."

He stopped dead, shaking his head.

"Yes, what did you mean, Mr. Kling?" Karin asked.

"Never mind, forget it."

"No, I think it may help us here."

"Help *who* here?" he asked. "Are you trying to help *me*, too, or are you trying to blame me for everything that happened since the rape? Or maybe even for the rape itself, who the hell knows, you're blaming me for everything else, why not the rape, too?"

"No one's blaming you for the rape," Eileen said.

"Thanks a lot."

"But, yes, I think you did have a lot to do . . ."

"Oh, listen . . ."

". . . with what happened *since* the rape, yes."

"Okay, I lost your backups, I admit it. I shouldn't have been there, I should have let them handle it. But that's not the crime of the cent . . ."

"You're *still* doing it," Eileen said.

"Doing *what*, for Christ's sake?"

"He doesn't even realize it," she said to Karin.

"What is it I don't realize? What do you want me to say? That *I'm* the one who really killed that cocks . . . ?"

He cut himself short.

"Yes?" Karin said.

"I didn't kill Bobby Wilson," he said. "But if it makes you happier to think I was responsible for it, I'll take the rap, okay?"

"What were you about to call him?"

Kling hesitated.

"Go ahead," Karin said.

"A cocksucker," he said.

"Why'd you stop?"

"Because I don't know you well enough to use such language in your presence."

Eileen started laughing.

"What's funny?" he said.

"You never used that word in *my* presence, either," she said.

"Well, I guess that's a sin, too," he said, "watching my language when there's a lady around."

"If only you could hear yourself," Eileen said, still laughing.

"I don't know what's so funny here," he said, beginning to get angry again. "Do you know what's so funny?" he asked Karin.

"Why'd you go to the Canal Zone that night?" Karin asked.

"I told you."

"No, you didn't," Eileen said.

"I went there because I didn't think Annie and Shanahan could handle it."

"No," Eileen said.

"Then why'd I . . . ?"

"You thought *I* couldn't handle it."

He looked at her.

"Yes," she said.

"No. I didn't want to trust your safety to two people . . ."

"You didn't want to trust my safety to *me*."

"Eileen, *no* cop trusts himself alone in a situation . . ."

"I know that."

"That's why there are backups . . ."

"Yes, yes . . ."

"The *more* backups the better."

"But you didn't trust *me*, Bert. Ever since the rape . . ."

"Oh, Jesus, here's the *rape* again! Ever since the rape, ever since the *rape* . . ."

"*Yes*, goddamn it!"

"*No*, goddamn it! You're talking about *trust?* Well, who didn't trust *who?* I don't like being blamed for something I . . ."

"I blame you for losing faith in me!"

"No. You blame me for wanting to protect you!"

"I didn't *need* your protection! I needed your understanding!"

"Oh, come on, Eileen. If I'd been any more understanding, I'd have qualified for the priesthood."

"What does that mean?"

"Well, you figure it out, okay?"

"No, what does it mean?"

"It means who wouldn't let me touch her after the rape?"

"Oh, is *that* what it gets down to?"

"I guess it gets down to I'm not the one who raped you, Eileen. I didn't rape you, and I didn't come at you with a knife, either, and if you've got me mixed up in your head with *either* of those two . . . *cocksuckers*, okay? . . . then there's nothing I can do to help you."

"Who asked for your help?"

"I thought I was here to . . ."

"Nobody asked for your help."

"She said maybe I could . . ."

"Nobody needs your goddamn help."

"Well, okay, I guess I misunderstood."

"And let's get one thing straight, okay?" Eileen said. "I didn't *ask* to be a victim."

"Neither did I," he said.

She looked at him.

"The only difference is I haven't made a career of it," he said.

"I'm sorry," Karin said, "our time is up."

The house Tommy was now living in was not quite a mile from the church Carella used to attend when they moved up here to Riverhead. Our Lady of Sorrows, it was called. He'd stopped going to mass when he was fifteen, sixteen, he could hardly remember now, because of something stupid one of the priests had said to him, but that hadn't kept him from attending the Friday night dances in the church basement. Thinking back on it now, it seemed to him that most of his early sex life was defined by those dances in the church basement. Had God known what was happening on that dance floor? All that steamy adolescent activity, had God known what was going on? If so, why hadn't He sent down a lightning bolt or something?

And if God Himself wasn't noticing, if He was busy someplace else, visiting plagues or something, then couldn't the *priest* see all that feverishly covert grinding, all that surreptitious clutching of buttock and breast, all that secret dry-humping there in the semi-dark? Standing there beaming at his flock while they slow-danced their way to virtual orgasm, didn't the priest at least *suspect* that no one was silently saying five Hail Marys? Father Giacomello, his name was. The younger priest. Always smiling. The older one was the one who'd scolded Carella for coming to confession at the busiest time of the year.

Not a smile from where he stood tonight, watching the garage from the shadow of the trees across the street, waiting for Tommy to come out, *if* he was coming out. Angela had told Carella that her husband had a bimbo. Well, okay, if there was a bimbo, this was as good a time as any to be seeing her. He'd been kicked out of the nest, this was as good a time as any to seek comfort and solace. *If* there was a bimbo.

He waited in the dark.

Playing cop with his own brother-in-law.

He shook his head.

There were roses in bloom, he could smell the roses on the still night air. They used to walk home from those Friday night dances, roses blooming in the soft summer night, he and his sister when she got old enough, walking home together, talking about things, talking about everything. At the time, he was closer to her than to any other human being on earth, he guessed, but he hated it nonetheless when she came to the dances because he felt she was intruding on his sexual freedom. How could a person dry-hump Margie Gannon when a person's own sister was dancing with some guy not four feet away? And, also, how could you keep an eye on your sister to make sure some sex fiend wasn't dry-humping *her* while you were busy trying to dry-hump Margie Gannon? It got complicated sometimes. Adolescence was complicated.

He remembered talking things over with his father.

So many things.

He remembered telling his father one time—the two of them alone in the shop late at night, the aroma of good things baking in the oven, breads and cakes and pastries and muffins and rolls, he would never forget those smells as long as he lived—he remembered telling him that the longest walk he ever had to make in his life was across a dance floor to ask some girl to dance, any girl, a pretty one, an ugly one, just taking that walk across the floor to where she was sitting, that was the longest walk in the world.

"It's like torture," he said. "I feel like I'm walking a mile across the desert, you know?"

"I know."

"Over hot sand, you know?"

"Yes, of course."

"To where she's sitting, Pop. And I hold out my hand, and I say Would you like to dance, or How about the next dance, or whatever, standing there, everybody watching me, everybody knowing that in the next ten seconds she's gonna say Get lost, jerk . . ."

"No, no," his father said.

"Sometimes, Pop, yeah, I mean it. Well, not those exact words, but you know they'll say like I'm sorry or I'm tired just now or I already promised this one, whatever, but all it means is Get lost, jerk. And then, Pop, you have to walk *back* to where you came from, only now everybody *knows* she turned you down . . ."

"Terrible," his father said, shaking his head.

". . . and the walk *back* is even longer than the walk when you were coming over, the desert is now a hundred miles long, and the sun is scorching hot, and you're gonna drop dead before you reach the shade, and everybody's laughing at you . . ."

"Terrible, terrible," his father said, and began laughing himself.

"Don't they *know?*" Carella said. "Pop, don't they *realize?*"

"They don't know," his father said, shaking his head. "But they're so beautiful, even the ugly ones."

There was activity across the street. The door to the room over the garage opening, a rectangle of light spilling onto the platform just outside the door. Tommy. Reaching inside to snap off the interior lights. Only the spot over the steps shining now. He locked the door and then came down the steps. He was wearing jeans and a striped polo shirt. Head bent, watching the steps as he came down. Carella ducked deeper into the shadows.

Was there a bimbo?

He gave him a decent lead, and then fell in behind him. Not too close to be spotted, not too distant to lose him. Tailing his own brother-in-law, he thought, and shook his head again.

He'd once talked to his father about faithfulness. Or rather *listened*
to his father talking about it, listened carefully to every word because
by then Carella was old enough to realize that his father had come
through many of these same things himself and was able to discourse
on them without sounding like the wise old man of the world. Without
sounding like—a father. Sounding like just another man you happened
to like a lot. A friend. Possibly the best friend Carella had or ever would
have.

This was just before he married Teddy. A week before the wedding.
He and his father were in the bakery shop—all of their important conversations seemed to take place near the ovens, the aroma of baking
bread wafting on the air—and Carella was experiencing what he
guessed could be defined as prenuptial jitters, wondering out loud
whether or not he was about to enter a contract that might be, well,
too limiting. Too restrictive, you know what I mean, Pop?

He guessed he felt the way he had when Angela started coming to
those Friday night dances with him, that his *turf* was being invaded, his
space threatened. He'd never told his father that he used to dry-hump
Margie Gannon on the dance floor, or that his sister's presence had
cramped his style somewhat. Neither had he ever mentioned that he'd
later moved onward and upward to the blissful actuality of *truly* hump-
ing Margie in the backseat of the family Dodge, but he suspected his
father knew all this, understood that his only son had been leading a
fairly active sex life with a wide variety of women before he'd met
Teddy Franklin, the woman he was now about to marry, the woman to
whom he was about to commit the rest of his life.

He was troubled, and his father realized it.

He'd never signed any kind of contract in his entire life, not for a
car, not for an apartment, not for anything, and here he was about to
sign a contract that would be binding forever. He'd never sworn to
anything in public except to uphold the laws of the city, state, and
country when he took his oath as a policeman, but now he was about
to swear before his relatives and friends and her relatives and friends
that he would love her and keep her and all that jazz so long as they
both should live. It was scary. In fact, it was terrifying.

"Do you love her?" his father asked.

"Yes, I love her, Pop," he said. "I love her very much."

"Then there's nothing to be scared of. I'll tell you something, Steve.
The only time a man considers taking another woman is when he no
longer loves the woman he already has. Do you think that's going to

happen? Are you afraid the time will come when you won't love Teddy anymore?"

"How can I know that, Pop?"

"You can know it. You can feel it in your bones and in your blood. You can know you'll love this woman till the day you die, and you'll never want another woman but her. And if you don't know this *now* . . . don't marry her."

"Now isn't tomorrow," he said.

"Yes, now is tomorrow. Now is forever," his father said.

The shop fell silent.

"Listen to me," his father said.

"Yes, Pop."

His father put his hands on Carella's shoulders. Big hands covered with flour. He looked into Carella's eyes.

"How do you feel about anyone else touching her?" he asked.

"I would kill him," Carella said.

"Yes," his father said, and nodded. "You have nothing to worry about. Marry her. Love her. Stay with her and no one else. Or I'll break your head," he said, and grinned.

And now, all these years later, Carella was following his sister's husband because the possibility existed that a time had come when he didn't love her anymore. He supposed that time could come to anyone. He did not think it would ever come to him. But he wondered now if that was because he truly loved Teddy to death or only because his father had threatened to break his head. In the darkness, quickening his pace as Tommy rounded a corner ahead, he smiled to himself.

He must have been trailing Tommy for at least half a mile, ten blocks or so, the area changing from strictly residential to commercial, elevated train tracks overhead now, stores still open on this gaudy summer night, July still flaunting her passion, men and women in the streets— was he planning to take a train? Was he heading for the platform on the next . . . ?

No, he walked right past the stairway leading up to the platform and the tracks, staying on the avenue, his stride deliberate, his step that of a man who knew where he was going, a man with a destination. A little past nine o'clock now, the earlier lingering dusk now snuffed, the moonless sky black, the only illumination coming from store lights and sidewalk lamps and the red and green traffic lights on the tracks above and the streets below. Tommy was moving at a pretty fast clip, looking at his watch every now and then, continuing on up the avenue until he reached Brandon, and then turning left, off the avenue, down to Willow where the brick library Carella used as a kid stood on the southern side of the street, mantled in darkness now.

A car was parked up the street, some short distance from the library. Tommy walked directly to the car.

He opened the door on the passenger side, triggering the interior light, the light going out again the instant he slammed the door behind him. The headlights came on. Carella ducked away from their sudden glare. The driver gunned the engine into life and set the car in motion. Carella moved deeper into the shadows as it approached the corner. A red Honda Accord sped by.

A woman was at the wheel.

8

"HE WANTED TO FIRE YOU," Goodman said. "I talked him into a thirty-day probation period."

"*Fire* me?" Eileen said. "But why?"

They were having lunch together in a seafood joint down near the Headquarters Building. Special Forces was on the tenth door, Goodman's office was on the fourth. It was convenient. But she'd believed, until this moment, that he'd asked her to lunch to offer congratulations.

"You have to understand him," Goodman said.

"Oh, I understand him, all right."

"Well, yes, that," he said.

She loved the way men brushed off matters of enormous concern to women. Bert yesterday with his *Well, yeah, that* in reference to what had merely been the most traumatic experience in her life, and now Goodman with his *Well, yes, that,* when he knew she'd been referring to Brady's blatantly sexist attitude.

"He just *adores* the class clown," she said, "and he . . ."

"Well, you have to admit Materasso's a pretty funny guy."

"How about Pellegrino? Or Riley? They're not too comical, and Brady treats them like long-lost brothers. He's got two women on the team only because . . ."

"Give credit where it's due, Eileen. He's the one who *put* women on the team in the first place."

"I wonder why."

"Certainly not because he's sexist."

"Then what was the 'Well, yes, that' all about?"

"I thought you knew."

"No, Mike, I'm sorry, I don't."

Using the name for the first time, realizing she hadn't called him *anything* until now, not Dr. Goodman, not Michael, and certainly not Mike. But there it was. Mike.

"I'm willing to bet he's never trusted a woman in his life."

"You'd lose."

"Would I?"

"I'm starved," he said, suddenly peering at her from behind his eyeglasses, raising his eyebrows and looking very much like a hungry little boy. "Aren't you?"

"I can eat," she said.

"Good, let's order."

They both ordered the steamed lobster. Eileen ordered a baked potato, he ordered fries. Eileen asked for Roquefort on her salad, he asked for creamy Italian. The salads came first. He ate ravenously. It was almost comical watching him. No manners at all. Just dug in. She wondered if he'd come from a large family.

"So tell me," she said.

"He lost one," Goodman said.

"What does that mean?"

"A negotiator. A woman."

"What are you saying?"

"Early on. The first woman he put on the team."

"You're kidding me."

"No, no. This was a long time ago, you probably weren't even on the job at the time. Woman named Julie Gunnison, worked out of Auto Theft, good cop, a Detective/Second. It was summertime, same as now. First time she worked the door. Woman in an apartment with her three kids, suddenly went bananas, threw one kid out the window before the police got there, was threatening to do the same with the other two if they didn't pull back. He put Julie on the door because it was a woman in there. There was a theory at the time that women confided more freely in other women, we now know it doesn't always work that way. But that was the thinking back then. Hostage negotiation was a new thing. You got a woman taker, you gave her a woman talker."

"What happened?" Eileen asked.

"Who gets the baked?" the waitress asked.

"I do."

The waitress put down their plates.

"Anything to drink?" she asked.

"Eileen, some wine? Beer?"

"I'm working," she said.

"Right. Coke? Pepsi?"

"Coke."

"I'll have a Heineken beer," Goodman said.

"One Coke, one Heineken," the waitress said, and rushed off looking harried.

"I'm listening," Eileen said.

"Julie was on that door for six hours straight, performing a high-wire act that defied all the laws of gravity. Every five minutes, the lady inside there grabbed one of her kids and rushed to the window and hung the kid outside it, upside down, holding him by the ankles, swinging him, yelling she was going to let go if the cops didn't back off. Cops and firemen all over the street, trying to figure out where to run with the net, which way she was going to swing that kid before she dropped him. Julie at the door, talking her out of it each time, telling them all they wanted to do was help her, help the kids, help each other, come on out of there and we'll talk it over. Woman had a meat cleaver in her hands. Her husband was a butcher. The kid she dropped out the window before they got there, she'd cut off his hands at the wrist."

"Wow," Eileen said.

"Heineken and a Coke," the waitress said, and put down the drinks, and rushed off again.

"Anyway," Goodman said, "Julie started to think she was making some progress. For the past hour—this was now eight o'clock at night, she'd been on the door since two in the afternoon, they'd already sent out for pizza and sodas. The woman had asked for beer, but you know we never let them have anything alcoholic . . ."

Eileen nodded.

". . . and she'd already fed herself and the kids and was beginning to feel chatty and at least for the past hour she hadn't tried to throw anyone out the window. So Julie starts telling her about her own kids, the way Mary Beth did with that woman in the lingerie shop last week, and they're getting along fine, and Julie's got her convinced she isn't armed, takes off her jacket, pats herself down . . . no guns, see? Nobody gets hurt, right? And then she takes a chance, she asks the lady to send out one of the kids, nobody's going to hurt her, the kids must be sleepy, they've got a cot set up down the hall, why doesn't she send out one of the kids? And the lady says Let me see again that you don't have a gun, and Julie shows her she doesn't have a gun, which is the truth, and the lady says Okay, I'll let you have one of the kids, and she opens the door and splits Julie's head in two with the cleaver."

"Jesus!" Eileen said.

"Yeah. So the E.S. cops stormed the door and killed the lady and that was the end of the story. Except that Brady got called on the carpet downtown, the Commish wanting to know what had happened there, a kid dead, a woman dead, a police officer dead, what the hell had gone wrong? If there was already a person dead when the hostage team *got* there, why didn't they just storm the door to begin with? Brady explained that we didn't work that way, whatever had happened *before* we got there didn't matter, it was a clean slate, our job was to make sure nobody got hurt *after* we were on the scene. Which the Commish must have thought was ridiculous because people *had* got hurt, there were three people dead and television was having a field day.

"The TV people were angry because Brady wouldn't let any of them near where the lady was contained—well, that's still a rule, no television cameras. So they began questioning the entire validity of the program. Almost wrecked it, in fact. All the hard work Chief McCleary had done getting it started, all the advances Brady had made when he took over, all of it almost went down the drain. The newspapers went after him, too. They'd all endorsed the incumbent mayor, who'd lost the election, and the new mayor had appointed a new commissioner and now the Commish was being blamed for what Brady had done, and naturally the buck stopped at Brady, it was his program, he was in command of the team. It was a hell of a mess, believe me."

Goodman was working on his lobster as he said all this. Delicately taking it apart with nutcracker, fingers, and fork, dipping the succulent meat into the butter sauce, chewing, popping a fry into his mouth, back to the lobster, working on the claws now, a gulp of beer, another fry, eating, talking.

"Brady blamed himself, of course, he's that kind of man. Got it into his head that he hadn't adequately trained Julie . . . which wasn't true, we've since learned there's only so much you can teach in a classroom. And, anyway, she was really a top-notch negotiator with a great deal of experience. Played it just the way she should have, in fact. Her bad luck was to come up against a lady who'd've snapped under any circumstances."

Goodman fell silent. Eileen watched him demolishing the rest of the lobster. Huge gulp of beer now. Another fry.

"Big family?" she asked.

"Just the three kids," he said.

"I meant you."

"No, I'm . . . huh?"

"The way you're eating."

"Oh. No, I've always eaten this way," he said, and shrugged. "I get hungry."

"I see that."

"Yeah," he said, and shrugged again, and drained what was left of his beer. "Took him a long time to get over it," he said. "For a while there, he wouldn't have any women on the team at all. Then he hired Georgia . . . I don't think you've met her . . . and Mary Beth. I don't know why he fired her, I thought she was doing a good job. Maybe he began feeling helpless again. A woman working the door, another woman contained, the entire situation a volatile one. Maybe he fired Mary Beth because he was afraid something would happen to her."

"Mike . . ."

Using the name again, getting used to the name.

". . . however you slice it, that's a sexist attitude. Has he fired any *men?*"

"One. But the guy had a drinking problem."

"Well, there you are."

"I'm not sure it's that simple."

"Do you think he'll fire me?"

"I don't know."

"Well . . . did he feel I was in danger yesterday?"

"You *were* in danger. He shouldn't have put you on the door. I argued against it, in fact. Sending in either you or Martha."

"Why?"

"Too early. Not enough observation yet, not enough training."

"But it worked out."

"Luckily. I don't think Martha would have been successful, by the way. It's a good thing the old man turned her down."

"Why do you say that?"

"Too eager, too aggressive. I'm not sure she'll *ever* make a good negotiator, for that matter."

"Have you told that to Brady?"

"I have."

"How about me? Do you think I'll make a good one?"

"You're already a pretty good one. You handled some things clumsily, but it was an enormously difficult situation. I like to call a spade a spade, Eileen. A police negotiator is a police negotiator and we should *never* lie about that, *whatever* the taker may want. Pretending to be a hooker . . ." He shook his head. "I told Brady I didn't like the idea. When he insisted we go ahead with it, I told him we should call Georgia, get her to come in. If we were going to lie to the taker, then we needed an experienced negotiator to pull it off. Georgia's done undercover work, by the way, decoy work, too. I'm surprised you don't know her."

"What's her last name?"

"Mobry. M-O-B-R-Y. Georgia Mobry."

"Doesn't ring a bell."

"She works mostly with Narcotics."

"No."

"Anyway, she could've handled it nicely yesterday. Trouble is she's on vacation. But . . . as you said . . . it worked out."

"Luckily. As *you* said."

"Well . . . however."

"I *was* lucky, wasn't I?"

"I think it could have gone either way. We shouldn't have lied to him. If he'd found out . . ."

"I tried to keep it ambiguous. If that's the word."

"That's the word. But the fact is we were passing you off as a hooker. And if he once discovered we were deceiving him . . ." Goodman nodded knowingly. "There was a little girl in that apartment. And a shotgun."

"Why'd Brady take the chance?"

"On you? Or the whole deception?"

"Both."

"You because the old man turned down Martha. Brady preferred her, she was his first choice. The deception? I don't know. He probably thought it would work. And if it might save that little girl's life . . ."

"It *did* save her life."

"As it turned out."

"So why'd he want to fire me?"

"I'm not sure how his mind works. I've been with him for ten years now . . ."

"That long?"

"Yes. Why?"

"You look younger."

"I'm thirty-eight."

"You still look younger. Why'd he want to fire me?"

"I don't know. It came as a total surprise to me. First he picks Martha over you, and then he agrees to your terms for working the door. So you get the old man *and* the kid out without anybody getting hurt, and he decides to fire you. *Meshugge*, do you understand Yiddish?"

"I know what *meshugge* means. And I think I know why he wanted to fire me, too."

"Why?"

"Because I didn't do it *his* way."

"He knew you weren't going to do it his way when you told him nobody went in till the old man let go of the kid *and* the gun. That wasn't Brady's way, that was *your* way. His way was the kid comes out and you go in, an even trade."

"That's exactly what I'm . . ."

"You're missing my point. If he wanted to fire you because you didn't do it his way, then why didn't he fire you on the spot? When you *refused* to do it his way?"

"I don't know. Why didn't he?"

"Maybe he realized you were right. But then, after it was all over, he *had* to fire you to show he's still the boss."

"But he *didn't* fire me."

"Only because I talked him out of it."

"How'd you do that?"

"I told him you were fearless and honest and sympathetic and smart and that you'd probably turn out to be the best negotiator the team ever had, male *or* female."

"Fearless, huh? You should only know."

"Fearless," he said. "And all those other things, too."

"And that's why he gave me the thirty-day probation."

"Well, I also told him you were beautiful."

"You didn't," she said.

"I did," he said. "Want to go to a movie tonight?"

She looked at him.

"What do you say?"

"What's playing?" she asked.

Louis Loeb told Carella on the telephone that his partner's will had already been filed and was a matter of record and he had neither the time nor the inclination to discuss it in detail with the detectives investigating his murder, certainly not after they had violated the civil rights of Mr. Schumacher's widow, an offense for which he—Mr. Loeb and not Mr. Schumacher—was still awaiting an apology. Carella said, "Thank you, Mr. Loeb," and hung up.

At two o'clock that afternoon—after having spent an hour and a half poring over the will in what was called Surrogate's Court in this city but which in many other cities was called Probate Court—he and Brown drove uptown onto Jefferson Avenue and parked the car in a neighborhood sprinkled with antiques shops, boutiques, beauty salons, and art galleries. Nestled between two of these galleries was a shop called Bide-A-Wee Pets. The woman who owned the shop was named Pauline Weed. She had sold a black Labrador retriever puppy to Margaret Schumacher for her to give to her husband on the occasion of their first Christmas together—and now she'd been named in Arthur Schumacher's will as the legatee of ten thousand dollars.

The woman was astonished.

Blonde and beautiful, in her early thirties, Carella guessed, slender and tall in black dancer's tights, black pumps, and a blue smock that matched her eyes, she accepted the news with disbelief at first, asking them if they were playing a joke on her, and then taking a closer look at the gold, blue-enameled shields they showed yet another time, and then bringing her hand up to her mouth and giggling behind it and shaking her head, all in what appeared to be a genuine display of surprise and delight.

"I can't believe this," she said, "it's so impossible."

"You had no idea, huh?" Brown said.

"None at all," she said, "this is a total and unimaginable surprise! Ten thousand dollars, that's a *fortune!* For *what?* I hardly *knew* the man. Are you sure this isn't a mistake?"

They assured her it was not a mistake.

They showed her the paragraph they had copied from the will:

In appreciation of the excellent medical services provided to my beloved Labrador retriever, Amos, by the NBB Veterinary Hospital at 731 Derwood Street, Isola, I give to Dr. Martin Robert Osgood the sum of Ten Thousand Dollars ($10,000.00) to further his work with animals. In similar appreciation of the excellent consultation and advice she gave to me regarding the care of the aforesaid Amos, I leave to Pauline Byerly Weed, owner of Bide-A-Wee Pets at 602 Jefferson Avenue, Isola, the sum of Ten Thousand Dollars ($10,000.00). Inasmuch as I have made prior arrangements with the Hollybrook Pet Cemetery and Crematory at 4712 Liberty Road in Pinesdale for the burial and perpetual grave-side care of the aforementioned Amos, I request that my wife Margaret, should she survive me, or my daughter Lois Stein, should she survive my said wife, determine that Hollybrook Pet Cemetery and Crematory honors its contractual obligations.

Of the rest, residue and remainder of my estate . . .

"This is amazing," she said, "truly. I don't know what to say. I haven't seen him in . . . God, it must be six, seven months since he last came in. This is incredible. Excuse me, but I can't get over it."

"What sort of 'consultation and advice' did you give him?" Carella asked. "About the dog?"

"Well, the first time he called . . . gee, this had to've been at *least* a year ago. Listen, are you *positive* this isn't a gag? I mean, all I did was sell his wife a *dog.*"

"You do remember the dog?"

"Amos? Oh, sure, an adorable puppy. Well, you know Labs, they're the gentlest dogs on earth. I've got some back here now, come take a look."

She led them through the shop, past cages of puppies and kittens, past hanging cages of brightly colored birds and tanks of tropical fish, yet more cages with hamsters in them, endlessly paddling their wheels. There was the aroma of feathers and fur and an almost indiscernible aroma of what might have been cat piss disguised by litter. The Labrador retriever pups were in a cage at the back of the shop, two of them, looking up expectantly and . . . well, yes, *cheerfully* at Pauline as she approached them.

"Hello, babies," she said, "here're two people who brought me some very good news today."

She poked her forefinger between the strands of the cage and waggled it at the dogs, scratching first one puppy's head and then the other's, and then allowing them to nip and lick at her finger. The puppies were still frisking around the cage as she led the detectives back to the front of the shop again, explaining that she didn't like to stray too far from the cash register when she was alone in the shop . . . well, she guessed they knew what this city was like.

"So this first time he called . . ." Carella prompted.

"It was about a flea collar, actually. He wanted to know how old the dog should be before he put a flea collar on him. He'd named the dog by then, on the phone he kept calling him Amos, a cute name actually . . ."

Brown frowned.

". . . Amos this and Amos that, and I told him if he planned to take the dog out to the beach—they had a house at the beach, Mr. and Mrs. Schumacher—or any place where there'd be plant life and ergo fleas or ticks—then he ought to put a collar on him right away, the dog was already three months old. So he came in sometime that week, and I sold him a collar specifically designed for puppies, there are different strengths, you know, this was a Zodiac puppy collar. I still can't get over this, forgive me," she said, shaking her head. "Just *telling* you about it—I mean, I hardly *knew* the man."

"And you say he came in every so often . . ."

"Yes, oh, once a month, once every six weeks, something like that. He'd be passing by . . . there are wonderful shops in the neighborhood, you know . . . and he'd stop in and buy a little something for Amos, a rawhide bone, or some kind of toy, we're always getting new shipments of toys, and we'd talk about the dog, he'd tell me stories about the dog, how Amos did this, how Amos did that . . ."

"In his will, he says you gave him consultation and advice . . ."

"Well, hardly *consultation*. But advice, yes, I guess so. I mean, well, yeah, I'd give him little tips I'd picked up, things to make a dog happy, well, *any* animal. Animals are like people, you know. They're all individuals, you have to treat them all differently. He'd bring Amos in every now and then, I'd look him over, tell him what a good dog he was, like that. I remember once . . . well, I really shouldn't take any credit for this because I'm sure the vet would've discovered it anyway the next time Mr. Schumacher took him in. But I was patting Amos on the head, and he had his tongue hanging out, panting, you know, and looking up at me, and I don't know what made me look in his mouth, I guess I wanted to see how his teeth looked, you can tell a lot about a dog's health by looking at his teeth and his gums. And I saw—I didn't know *what* it was at first—this sort of *ridge* across the roof of his mouth, like a narrow ridge on his palette. And I reached in there and it was . . . you won't believe this . . . he'd bitten down on a twig, and it had got wedged in there across his mouth, running from one side of his mouth to the other, where his teeth had bitten it off, wedged up there on the roof of his mouth with his teeth holding it in place on either side. And I yanked that out of there. . . . *Jesus!* He didn't even bleed. The thing just came free in my hand and that dog looked as if he was going to get up on his hind legs and kiss me! Can you imagine the pain that must've been causing him? Wedged up there like that? Like a toothache day and night, can you imagine? That poor dog. But, you know . . . that wasn't worth ten thousand dollars. I mean, *nothing* I did was worth ten thousand dollars."

"Apparently Mr. Schumacher thought so," Carella said.

"But you didn't know you were in the will, is that right?" Brown asked.

"Oh my God, *no!* Wait'll I tell my mother! She'll die."

"He never mentioned it to you."

"Never."

"Not any of the times he stopped by . . ."

"Never."

"When did you say the last time was?" Brown asked.

"That he came in? January? February? At *least* that long ago. I really can't believe this!"

"How about his wife? Did she ever come into the shop?"

"Not after she bought the dog, no."

"You never talked to her after that?"

"Never."

"Or saw her?"

"Never. Look at me, I'm shaking. I am positively shocked!"

Brown was wondering how come *he* didn't know any people who might want to leave *him* ten thousand smackers.

Arthur Schumacher had really loved that dog.

He could not have known they would die together in the same angry fusillade, but nonetheless he had made provision in his will for "the burial and perpetual graveside care of the aforementioned Amos," in addition to the ten grand each he'd left to Dr. Martin Osgood and Miss Pauline Weed for remembered little courtesies and services.

Of the rest, residue, and remainder of his estate, of whatsoever nature and wheresoever situated, he had given, devised, and bequeathed fifty percent to his wife, Margaret Schumacher, twenty-five percent to his daughter Lois Stein, and twenty-five percent to his daughter Betsy Schumacher. The detectives still didn't know the total worth of the estate, but according to Gloria Sanders, his embittered grass widow, it came to a considerable sum of money.

There was no mention of Susan Brauer in the will.

But in addition to the safe-deposit box Schumacher had kept at Union Savings downtown near his office, there was also a checking account in his name. A perusal of his statements—after obtaining a court order granting the privilege—revealed that he had, in fact, been taking five thousand dollars in cash from this account at the beginning of every month, and there now seemed little doubt that this money found its way into Susan's personal checking account. Unaccounted for, however, was the twelve thousand dollars they'd found in her closet cash box. Had Schumacher been giving her additional money? If so, where had it come from?

Maybe he was stealing it, Teddy signed.

Carella looked at her, wondering how such a generous and lovely person could come up with thoughts that attributed such devious machinations to human beings.

From his firm, she signed. *Or from his wife's account, if she had one.*

"I don't think he was stealing," Carella said, talking and signing at the same time.

But where *had* the money come from?

"Maybe he had some other bank accounts," he said. "He was keeping *this* one from his wife, so why not some others? I mean, the guy wasn't exactly what you'd call trustworthy, was he? Divorced Gloria to marry *one* blonde and then started carrying on with yet another one. So maybe he kept secret bank accounts as a life-style. In preparation, you know?"

Teddy watched his hands as if she were watching a television miniseries, his words conjuring banks all over town, tall granite pillars and brass tellers' cages, long black limousines and beautiful blonde women, champagne chilling in silver buckets, clandestine passion on red silk sheets.

But he was kind to his dog, she signed, her hands somehow managing to convey the dryness of her words.

"Oh *yes,*" Carella said. *"And* the vet who took care of the dog, *and* the woman who'd sold Margaret the dog. Ten thousand each, can you imagine? Margaret," he said, seeing her puzzlement, and signing the name letter by letter. "The *first* blonde. Susan was the *second* one. Susan. S-U-S-A-N."

Maybe I should open a pet shop, Teddy signed. *Or become a vet.*

"Good idea, we can use the money. She was pretty foresighted, wasn't she? Gloria, I mean, the first wife. The bleached blonde, Gloria.

G-L-O-R-I-A. Getting it put in their settlement agreement, I mean. That he'd leave the daughters fifty percent of the estate? Lots of guys remarry, they forget they ever *had* kids. Speaking of which . . . Mark!" he yelled. "April! Five minutes."

"Aw, shit!" Mark yelled from down the hall.

"We still can't find the hippie daughter," Carella said. "Remember I was telling you . . . ?"

Teddy nodded.

"She disappeared," Carella said. "Let me go tuck them in, I'll be right back. There's something else I have to tell you."

She looked up at him.

"When they're asleep."

She frowned, puzzled.

He mouthed the word *Tommy*.

Teddy sighed.

The twins were in the bathroom brushing their teeth. Eleven years old already, my how the time flew by.

"Mark said shit," April said.

"I heard him."

"You're supposed to fine him."

"I will. That's ten cents, Mark."

"Did Mom hear it?"

"No."

"Then it's only a nickel."

"Who says?"

"If only one of you hears it, it's half the price."

"He's making that up, Dad."

"I know he is. Ten cents, Mark."

"Shit," Mark said, and spat into the sink.

"That's twenty," Carella said. "Go kiss your mother, then bedtime."

"Why don't *you* ever curse?" Mark asked his sister as they went out of the bathroom.

"I do," she said. "I know even dirtier words than you."

"So how come I never hear you saying them?"

"I say them in the dark."

"That's ridiculous," Mark said.

"Maybe, but it doesn't cost me any money."

He could hear them in the living room, saying goodnight to Teddy. He waited in the hallway, very tired all at once, remembering his father all at once. When he and Angela were small, his father used to read them to sleep every night. He sometimes thought his father got a bigger kick out of the bedtime stories than either of the kids did. Now there was only television.

"See you in the morning!" April called. A ritual with her. Saying it would make it true. She would see them in the morning if only she said it each night. He took them to their rooms, separate rooms now, they were getting older, separate prayers. He tucked Mark in first.

"I like swearing," Mark said.

"Okay, so pay for it."

"It isn't fair."

"Nothing is."

"Grandpa said to always be fair."

"He was right. You should."

"Do you miss him?"

"Yes. Very much."

"I do, too."

Carella kissed him on the forehead.

"Goodnight, son," he said.

"G'night, Dad."

"I love you."

"Love you too."

He went into the room next door and listened to April's prayers and at last said, "Goodnight, angel, sleep well."

"See you in the morning," she said.

"See you in the morning."

"I don't really, you know," she said. "Curse in the dark."

"Much better to light a single candle," Carella said, and smiled.

"Huh?" she said.

"I love you," he said, and kissed her on the forehead.

"I love you, too. See you in the morning," she said.

"See you in the morning," he said.

Teddy was waiting in the living room. Sitting under the Tiffany-style lamp, reading. She put down the book the moment he came in. Her hands signed *Tell me.*

He told her about following Tommy the night before. Told her he'd seen Tommy getting into a red Honda Accord driven by a woman.

"I don't know what to tell Angela," he said.

Just be sure, Teddy signed.

Their informant told them he'd seen these two dudes from Washington, D.C., one of them named Sonny and the other named Dick, in an abandoned building off Ritter. There was a girl with them, but he didn't know the name of the girl at all; she wasn't from Washington, she was from right here in this city. All three of them were crackheads.

This was the information Wade and Bent had.

They had got it at a little after nine o'clock that night from a man who himself was a crackhead and who had volunteered the information because they had him on a week-old pharmacy break-in. He said word was out they was looking for a dude named Sonny and that's who he'd seen earlier tonight, Sonny and this other dude and a girl couldn't be older than sixteen, he was being cooperative, wasn't he? They told him he was being real cooperative, and then they clapped him in a holding cell downstairs to wait for the ten o'clock van pickup.

The building was around the corner from Ritter Avenue, on a street that had once been lined with elegant apartment buildings, most of them occupied by Jews who'd moved up here a generation after their parents made the long journey from Poland and Russia to settle in the side streets of Lower Isola. The Jews had long since left this section of Riverhead. The area became Puerto Rican until they, too, left because landlords found it cheaper to abandon rent-controlled buildings than to maintain them. Ritter Avenue and its surrounding side streets now looked the way London or Tokyo or Berlin had looked after World War II—but America had never suffered any bombing raids. What had once been a thriving commercial and residential community was now as barren as a moonscape. Here there was only an unsteady mix of rubble and buildings about to fall into rubble. Here there was no pretense of rescue, no fancy plastic flowerpot decals promising later reconstruction; the jungle had already reclaimed what had once been a rich and vibrant community.

Sonny and Dick and the sixteen-year-old girl were presumably holed up at 3341 Sloane, the only building still standing in a field of jagged brick and concrete, strewn mattresses and rubbish, roaming dogs and skittering rats. Clouds scudded across a thin-mooned sky as the detectives got out of their car and looked up at the building. Something flickered in one of the gutted windows.

Third floor up.

Wade gestured.

Bent nodded.

They both figured it was a candle flickering up there. Too hot for a fire unless they were cooking food. Probably just sitting around a candle, smoking dope. Sonny and Dick and the sixteen-year-old girl. Sonny who had been carrying a gun on the night Anthony Carella got killed. Sonny who was maybe still carrying that same gun unless he'd sold it to buy more crack.

Neither Wade nor Bent said a word. Both of them drew their guns and entered the building. The shots came as they rounded the second-floor landing. Four shots in a row, cracking on the night air, sundering the silence, sending the cops flying off in either direction, one to the right, one to the left of the staircase, throwing themselves out of the line of fire. Someone was standing at the top of the stairs. A cloud passed, uncovering a remnant moon, revealing a man in silhouette on the roofless floor above, huge against the sky, gun in hand, but only for an instant. The figure ducked away. There was noise up there, some frantic scrambling around, a girl's nervous giggle, a hushed whisper, and then rapid footfalls on the night—but no one coming down this way. Wade stepped out. Bent covered him, firing three shots in rapid succession up the stairwell. Both men pounded up the steps, guns fanning the air ahead of them. The apartment to the right of the stairwell was vacant save for a handful of empty crack vials and a guttering votive candle in a red glass holder. It took the detectives only a moment to realize where everyone had gone; there was a fire escape at the rear of the building.

But there were spent cartridge cases at the top of the staircase, and they now had something they could compare with what they'd found on the floor of the A & L Bakery on the night Anthony Carella was killed.

9

FRIDAY COULD NOT make up its mind. It had been threatening rain since early morning, the sky a dishwater gray that changed occasionally to a pale mustard yellow that promised sunshine and then dissipated again into the drabs. At six that evening, the heat and humidity were still with the suffering populace, but nothing else was constant. There was not the slightest breeze to indicate an oncoming storm, and yet the sky seemed roiling with the promise of rain.

Outside the old gray stone Headquarters Building downtown on High Street, Kling waited on the sidewalk in front of the low flat steps, watching the homeward-bound troops coming out of the building; invariably, they looked up at the sky the moment they came through the big bronze doors at the top of the steps. Karin Lefkowitz emerged at twenty minutes past the hour. She did not look up at the sky. She was carrying one of those small folding umbrellas and probably didn't give a damn *what* the weather did. She was also carrying a shoulder bag in which she'd undoubtedly placed her Reeboks; in their place, she was wearing high-heeled blue leather pumps to match her blue linen suit. He fell into step beside her.

"Hi," he said.

She turned to him in surprise, hand tightening on the umbrella as if she were getting ready to swing it.

"Oh, hi," she said, recognizing him. "You startled me."

"Sorry. Have you got time for a cup of coffee?"

She looked at him.

"Mr. Kling . . ." she said.

"Bert," he said, and smiled.

"Does this have to do with the meeting we had on Wednesday?"

"Yes, it does."

"Then I'd prefer two things. One, whatever this is, I'd like to discuss it in my office . . ."

"Okay, wherever you . . ."

". . . and I'd like Eileen to be present."

"Well, I came down here alone because I didn't *want* Eileen to be present."

"Discussing anything that concerns Eileen . . ."

"Yes, it does concern . . ."

". . . would be inappropriate."

"Is it inappropriate for you and Eileen to discuss *me?*"

"You're not my client, Mr. Kling."

"I just want to tell *my* side of it."

She looked at him again.

"A cup of coffee, okay?" he said. "Ten minutes of your time."

"Well . . ."

"Please," he said.

"Ten minutes," she said, and looked at her watch.

Carella had been waiting outside the bank since three o'clock, wondering if and when it would rain, and it was now six-thirty but it still hadn't rained. He hadn't expected Tommy to come out at three, because Tommy was an executive who went to meetings that sometimes lasted well into the night. Tommy's job was trying to rescue loans the bank had made. If the bank made a three-million-dollar loan to someone who ran a ball-bearing company in Pittsburgh, and the guy started to miss his payments, Tommy got sent out to see how they could help the guy make good on the loan. The bank didn't want to own a ball-bearing company; the bank was in the money business. So if they could work something out with the guy, everybody would be happy. That was Tommy's job, and it took him all over the country, sometimes even to Europe. Carella could see how such a job might allow for the opportunity to fool around, if a man was so inclined to begin with.

Tommy came out of the bank at twenty minutes to seven. There was a woman with him, an attractive brunette who appeared to be in her late twenties, smartly dressed in a tailored suit and high-heeled pumps, and carrying a briefcase. From across the street, Carella could not tell whether she was the same woman who'd been in the car last night. He gave them a lead, and then began following them, staying on the opposite side of the street, walking parallel and almost abreast of them.

They seemed to have nothing to hide. Carella guessed she was a business associate. They walked past the subway kiosk up the street; neither of them was planning to take a train anyplace. They continued on up the street toward a parking garage, and then walked past that as well, and continued walking some several blocks until they came to a second garage. The woman turned in off the sidewalk, Tommy at her side. She opened her handbag and handed him a yellow ticket. Carella immediately hailed a taxi.

He got in and showed the driver his shield.

"Just sit here," he said.

The driver sighed heavily. Cops, he was thinking.

Tommy was at the cashier's booth, paying to retrieve the parked car. He came back to where the woman was standing, and the two fell into conversation again. From the backseat of the taxi across the street, Carella watched.

Some two minutes later a red Honda Accord came up the ramp.

It was the same car Tommy had got into last night.

In this area of courthouses and state and municipal buildings, there were not many eating establishments that stayed open beyond five, six o'clock, when the streets down here became as deserted as those in any ghost town. But there was a delicatessen on the cusp of the area, closer to a genuine neighborhood, and it had a sign in its window that announced it was open till 9:00 P.M.

Kling urged Karin to have something to eat.

The smells coming from the kitchen were hugely tempting.

She admitted that she was starving and said it would take her an hour or more to get home; she lived across the river, in the next state.

Kling suggested the hot pastrami.

She told him she *loved* hot pastrami. She said that when she was a kid her mother used to take her for walks around the neighborhood . . .

"I'm Jewish, you know."

"Gee, really?"

". . . past all these wonderful delis. But she wouldn't let me eat anything they served, I was only allowed to stand outside and *smell* the food. 'Take a sniff,' she would say, 'take a good sniff, Karin.' "

She smiled with the memory now, though to Kling it seemed like extraordinarily cruel and unusual punishment.

"So what'll it be?" he asked.

She ordered the hot pastrami on rye. He ordered it on a seeded roll. They both ordered draft beer. There was a big bowl of sour pickles on the table. They sat eating their sandwiches. Reaching for pickles. Sipping beer. There was only a handful of other diners in the place, men in short-sleeved shirts, women wearing summer dresses. The air was hushed with the expectation of rain.

"So why'd you want to see me?" Karin asked.

"I don't like what happened on Wednesday," he said.

"What didn't you like?"

"You and Eileen ganging up on me."

"Neither of us . . ."

"Because it just isn't true, you see. That whatever happened to Eileen is all my fault."

"No one says it was, Mr. Kling . . ."

"And I wish to hell you'd call me Bert."

"I don't think that would be appropriate."

"What do you call Eileen?"

"Eileen."

"Then why isn't it appropriate to call me Bert?"

"I told you. Eileen is my client. You're not. And whereas it may not be true that you were responsible for . . ."

"Never mind the buts. It *isn't* true."

"I'm not suggesting it was. I'm saying that Eileen *perceived* it as the truth. Which, by the way, she no longer does."

"Well, I hope not. If she wants to think of herself as some kind of damsel in dis . . ."

"I'm sure she doesn't. In fact, she never did."

"I think she did, where it concerns that night, where it concerns her having to put that guy away. Damsel in distress, woman in jeopardy, whatever you want to call it. When the plain truth of the matter is she was a *cop* in a showdown with a serial killer. It was her *job* to put him away. She was only doing her goddamn job."

"It would be nice if it were that simple," Karin said, and bit into her sandwich again. "But it isn't. Eileen was raped. And unfortunately, the rapist resembled you. So when you later step into a situation that . . ."

"I didn't know that."

"He had blond hair. The rapist. Like yours."

"I really didn't know."

"Yes. And he was armed with a knife . . ."

"Yes."

". . . was threatening her with a knife. Cut her, in fact. Thoroughly terrified her."

"Yes, I know."

"So now there's a *second* man with a knife, coming at her again, and she's alone with him because *you* caused her to lose her backups."

"I didn't deliberately . . ."

"But you *did*. This isn't merely her perception, it's reality. If you had stayed home that night, Eileen would have had two capable and experienced detectives following her, and chances are she wouldn't have found herself in a confrontational situation with a serial killer. But there she was. Because of you."

"Okay. I'm sorry it happened. But . . ."

"And you're wrong when you say she *had* to put him away. She didn't have to. Her perception—and, again, the reality as well—was that this man was going to cut her if she didn't stop him, she was going to get cut again if she didn't stop this man. But she didn't have to *kill* him in order to stop him. The man was armed only with a knife, and she had her service revolver—a .44-caliber Smith & Wesson—*plus* a .25-caliber Astra Firecat in a holster strapped to her ankle, *and* a switchblade knife in her handbag. She certainly did not have to kill him. She could have shot him in the shoulder or the leg, wherever, anything of the sort would have effectively stopped him. The point is she *wanted* to kill him."

Kling was shaking his head.

"Yes," Karin said. "She wanted to kill him. Even though he wasn't the man she *really* wanted to kill. The man she *really* wanted to kill was the man who'd raped her and cut her, and who—I say 'unfortunately' again—looked somewhat like you. If it weren't for the blond rapist, she wouldn't have to kill this man. If it weren't for *you* . . ."

Shaking his head, no, no, no.

"Yes, this is what her *mind* was telling her. If it weren't for *you*, she wouldn't have to kill this man. I gave you a chance, she told him, meanwhile pumping bullets into his back, I gave you a chance. Meaning she gave *you* a chance. To prove yourself, to show you still believed in her . . ."

"I *did* believe in her, I *do* believe in her."

"But you didn't. You followed her to the Canal Zone . . ."

"Yes, but only . . ."

"Because you didn't trust her, Bert, you didn't think she could take care of herself. It was your failure of confidence that caused the mixup, caused the confrontation, and eventually caused the murder."

"It wasn't murder, it was self . . ."

"It was murder."

"Justified then."

"Perhaps."

There was the soft sound of rain pattering the sidewalk outside. They both looked up.

"Rain," he said.

"Yes," she said.

"Heading uptown," the cabdriver said.

"Stay with them," Carella said.

Windshield wipers snicked at the lightly falling rain. Tires hissed against the pavement. Up ahead, the red Honda Accord moved steadily through the gray curtain of drizzle and dusk. Carella leaned over the back of the front seat, peering through the windshield.

"Pulling in," the driver said.

"Go past them to the corner."

He turned his head away as they passed the other car and then he looked back through the rear window to keep the car in sight. The woman was maneuvering it into the curb now, across the street from a playground where children stood under the trees looking out at the rain.

Carella paid and tipped the driver, got out of the cab, and ducked into a doorway just as Tommy climbed out of the Accord on the passenger side. A moment later, the woman joined him on the sidewalk. Together, they ran through the rain to a brownstone some twenty feet up from where she'd parked the car. Carella watched them entering the building. He walked up the street.

He was copying down the address on the brownstone when his beeper went off.

Brown was waiting for him in the rain.

The woman lay on the sidewalk under the trees. Blood seeping from her, mingling with the rain, diluted by the rain, running in rivulets into the gutter. Long blonde hair fanned out around her head. Raindrops striking her wide-open blue eyes. When Carella's father was taken to the hospital with his heart attack three years ago, it was raining. One of the nurses walking alongside the stretcher as he came out of the ambulance said, "He doesn't like it." The other nurse said, "It's raining on his face," and tented a newspaper over it. His father had always recounted that story with amusement. The idea that he was suffering a massive heart attack and the nurses were discussing rain in his face. Big Chief Rain in the Face, he'd called himself.

Lying on her back with her blonde hair spread on the slick gray pavement and her blood-drenched face shattered by the impact of the bullets that had entered it, Margaret Schumacher wasn't concerned about the rain in her face.

"When?" Carella asked.

"Boy One called it in an hour ago."

"Who found her?"

"Kid over there under the awning."

Carella looked up the street to where a white sixteen-year-old boy was standing with the doorman.

"He saw the whole thing," Brown said, "yelled at the perp, got shot at himself. He ran inside the building, got the doorman to call nine-one-one. Boy One responded."

"Homicide here yet?"

"No, thank God," Brown said, and rolled his eyes.

"Let's talk to him some more," Carella said.

They walked through the rain to where the doorman was counseling the kid on how to handle interviews with cops. This was the same doorman who'd been on duty the night Arthur Schumacher and his dog were killed. Now Schumacher's wife was lying dead on the sidewalk in almost the identical spot; it was getting to be a regular epidemic. Carella introduced himself and then said, "We'd like to ask a few more questions, if that's all right with you."

He wasn't talking to the doorman, but the doorman immediately said, "I called nine-eleven the minute he ran in here."

"Thanks, we appreciate it," Carella said, and then to the kid, "What's your name, son?"

"Penn Halligan," the kid said.

"Can you tell us what happened?"

The kid was handsome enough to appear delicate, almost feminine, large brown eyes fringed with long black lashes, a high-cheekboned porcelain face with a cupid's bow mouth, long black hair hanging lank with rain on his forehead. Tall and slender, he stood under the awning with the doorman and the detectives, hands in the pockets of a blue nylon windbreaker. He was visibly trembling; he'd had a close call.

"I was coming home from class," he said. "I take acting lessons."

Carella nodded. He was thinking Halligan was handsome enough to be a movie star. Though nowadays that certainly wasn't a prerequisite.

"On The Stem," he said, gesturing with his head. "Upstairs from the RKO Orpheum. I go every Monday, Wednesday, and Friday afternoons. Five o'clock to seven o'clock. I was on my way home when . . ." He shook his head. The memory caused him to shiver again.

"Where do you live?" Brown asked.

"Just up the block. 1149 Selby."

"Okay, what happened?"

"I was coming around the corner when I saw this guy running across the street from under the trees there," he said, turning to point. "There was this blonde lady walking toward me on *this* side of the street, and the guy just crossed sort of diagonally, running from under the trees to where the blonde was walking, like on a collision course with her. I was just coming around the corner, I saw it all."

"Tell us everything you saw," Carella said. "Don't leave anything out."

"I was walking fast because of the rain . . ."

Head ducked against the rain, a gentle rain but you can still get pretty wet if you're coming from eight blocks away on Stemmler. He has walked all the way down to Butterworth and is continuing on down the four blocks to Selby, and is turning the corner onto his own street when he sees this blonde lady walking toward him. Tall good-looking blonde wearing a short, tight mini and rushing through the rain even though she's got this bright orange-and-white umbrella over her head, one of these huge things that looks like it should be covering a hot-dog stand. High heels clicking on the sidewalk, rain pattering everywhere around her, he's thinking here comes a sexy young mother, which he's been told is the most passionate woman you can find, a young mother . . .

Carella suddenly wonders if the kid's delicate good looks have ever raised questions about his masculinity. Else why the gratuitous comment about a woman lying dead on the sidewalk not twenty feet away?

. . . coming at him in the rain, long legs flying through the rain, when all of a sudden he sees this movement from the corner of his eye, on his left, just a blur at first, almost a shadow, a black shadow moving from the deeper black shadow of the trees across the street, flitting across the wet black pavement merging with the blackness of the asphalt and the grayness of the rain, there is a gun in the man's hand.

The man is dressed entirely in black, wearing like black mechanic's overalls, you know? Like what you see mechanics wearing all covered with grease, except it's entirely black, and he's wearing black socks and shoes, running shoes, and a black woolen hat pulled down over his forehead, almost down onto his eyes, he's got the gun sticking out ahead of him, did you ever see *Psycho?* Do you remember when Tony Perkins comes out of that doorway upstairs with the big bread knife raised high over his head, just rushes out in the hallway to stab Marty Balsam? He's in drag, do you remember, we're supposed to think it's his crazy mother running out, but it's the knife held high over his head in that stiff-armed way that scares you half to death. Well, this guy all in black . . .

And Carella suddenly knows it's a *woman* this kid saw.

. . . is rushing across the street with the gun already pointing at the blonde, the arm straight out and stiff, the gun like following the blonde's progress, like tracking her on radar, like a compass needle or something, rushing across the street in the rain, with the gun zeroing in on her. She doesn't see the guy, he's moving very fast, like a dancer, no, like a bullfighter, I guess, more like a bullfighter . . .

And Carella is positive now that this is a *woman* the kid is talking about . . .

. . . coming at her, she's under the orange-and-white umbrella, she doesn't even *see* him. I'm the only one who sees them both, the blonde coming toward me where I'm already around the corner, the guy rushing across the street with this gun in his hand, I'm the only one who knows what's about to happen, I'm like the camera, you know, I'm like *seeing* this through the wide-angle viewfinder on a camera. My first reaction is to yell . . .

"Hey!" he yells. "Hey!"

The guy keeps coming. The blonde looks up because she hears the yell, she thinks at first Halligan is the one to worry about, Halligan is the one yelling, Halligan is the crazy lunatic in this city full of crazy lunatics, Halligan is coming at her from the corner, yelling at her, Hey, hey, hey! She hasn't yet seen the guy in black, she doesn't yet know that a gun is pointed at her head, she doesn't yet realize that the threat is angling in on her from diagonally across the street, ten feet away from her now, eight feet . . .

"Hey!" he yells again. "Stop!"

. . . six feet away, four feet . . .

And the gun goes off. Bam, bam on the wet night air, bam again, and again, four shots shattering the steady patter of the rain. "Hey!" he yells, and the man turns to face him squarely, the blonde tumbling in slow motion to the sidewalk behind him, the man turning in slow motion, everything suddenly in slow motion, the blonde falling, crumbling in

slow motion, the rain coming down in slow motion, each silvery streak
sharp and clear against the blackness of the night, the gun swinging
around in slow motion, a yellow flash at its muzzle as it goes off, the
explosion following it in seeming slow motion, reverberating on the
rain-laden air, he thinks Jesus *Christ!* and the gun goes off again.

He is already hurling himself to the sidewalk and rolling away, he
has seen a lot of movies, not for nothing is he a drama student. He rolls
away toward the opposite side of the gun hand, the gunman is right-
handed, the pistol is in his right hand, he does not roll *into* the gun, he
rolls away from it, you have to watch movies carefully. He expects
another shot, he has not been counting, when you are about to wet
your pants you don't count shots exploding on the night. He knows he
will be dead in the next ten seconds, suspects that the blonde lying in a
bleeding crumpled heap on the sidewalk is already dead, hears the
man's footfalls in the rain, pattering through the pattering rain . . .

A woman, Carella thinks.

. . . to where he is lying against the brick wall of the building now,
waiting for the fatal shot, it's a miracle he hasn't been shot yet, it's a
miracle he isn't already dead.

He hears a *click* and another *click* and the word *Shit!* whispered on
the night, hissing on the night, and the man turns and runs, he does not
see the man running, he only hears the footfalls on the night, in the
rain, rushing away, fading, fading, and finally gone. He lies against the
wall trembling, and then at last he gets to his feet and realizes that he
has in fact either wet his pants or else he was lying in a puddle against
the wall. He looks into the darkness, into the rain. The man is gone.

"Could it have been a woman?" Carella asked.

"No, it was very definitely a man," Halligan said.

"Are you sure he was right-handed?" Brown asked.

"Positive."

"The gun was in his right hand?"

"Yes."

"What'd you do then?" Brown asked. "After he was gone."

"I came over here and told the doorman what I'd just seen."

"I called nine-eleven right away," the doorman said.

"You're sure this wasn't a woman, huh?" Carella asked.

"Positive."

"Okay," Carella said, and thought maybe it was only the reference
to Tony Perkins in drag.

"I called nine-eleven right away," the doorman said again.

* * *

They found Betsy Schumacher the very next day.

Or rather, she found them.

It was still raining.

Brown and Carella were just about to leave for the day. The shift had been relieved at a quarter to four, and it was a quarter past when she came into the squadroom, dripping wet in a yellow rain slicker and a yellow rain hat, straight blonde hair cascading down on either side of her face.

"I'm Betsy Schumacher," she said. "I understand you've been looking for me."

Betsy Schumacher. Arthur Schumacher's alienated daughter. Whom they'd been trying to locate ever since her father's murder, because— for one reason—she'd been named in his will as the legatee of twenty-five percent of his estate.

So here she was.

As blue-eyed as the blue out of which she'd appeared.

"I read about Margaret in the newspaper," she said.

So had everyone else in this city. The newspapers were clearly having a ball with this one. First a beautiful blonde bimbo in a love nest, then her elderly lover, and then the elderly lover's equally beautiful and equally blonde wife. Such was the stuff of which American headlines were made. But when you're in love, the whole world's blonde, Carella figured, because here was yet another beauty wearing neither lipstick nor eye shadow, the slicker and hat a brighter yellow than her honey-colored hair, cornflower eyes wide in a face the shape of her sister's and—come to think of it—her mother's as well. Betsy Schumacher, how do you do?

"I figured I'd better come up here," she said, and shrugged elaborately. "Before you started getting ideas."

The shrug seemed all the more girlish in that she was thirty-nine years old. This was no teenager standing here, despite the dewy complexion and the freshness of her looks. Her own father had called her an aging hippie, and her mother had corroborated the description: *Betsy is a thirty-nine-year-old hippie, and this is July. She could be anywhere.*

"Where've you been, Miss Schumacher?" Carella asked.

"Vermont," she said.

"When did you go up there?"

"Last Sunday. Right after the funeral. I had some heavy thinking to do."

He wondered if she'd been thinking about how she would spend her money.

"How'd you learn we were looking for you?"

"Mom told me."

"Did she call you, or what?" Brown asked.

A trick question. Gloria Sanders had told them she didn't know where her daughter was.

"I called *her*," Betsy said. "When I read about Margaret."

"When was that?"

"Yesterday."

"How'd your mother feel about it?"

"Gleeful," Betsy said, and grinned mischievously. "So did I, in fact."

"And she told you we wanted to see you?"

"Yeah. So I figured I'd better come on down. Okay to take off my coat?"

"Sure," Carella said.

She unclipped the fasteners on the front of the slicker and slipped it off her shoulders and arms. She was wearing a faded denim mini, somewhat tattered sandals, and a thin, white cotton T-shirt with the words SAVE THE WHALES printed across its front. She wasn't wearing a bra. Her nipples puckered the words SAVE on her right breast and WHALES on her left breast, the word THE falling someplace on her neutral sternum. She did not take off the hat. It sat floppily on her head, like a wilted wet sunflower, its petals framing her face. She looked around for a place to hang the slicker, spotted a coatrack near the water cooler in the corner, carried the slicker to it, hung it on one of the pegs, had herself a drink of water while she was at it—bending over the fountain, denim skirt tightening over her buttocks—and then came back to where the detectives were waiting for her. There was a faint secret smile on her face, as if she knew they'd been admiring her ass, which in fact they had been doing, married men though they both were.

"So what would you like to know?" she asked, sitting in the chair beside Carella's desk and crossing her legs, the skirt riding up recklessly. "I didn't kill the bimbo, and I didn't kill *Mrs.* Schumacher, either . . ."

Same malicious twist to the dead woman's true and courteous title . . .

"And I *certainly* didn't kill the fucking mutt."

Poor Amos, Brown thought.

"So who else is left?" she asked, and grinned in what Carella could only interpret as a wise-ass hippie challenge of the sort she'd extended all too often when the world was young and nobody wore a bra and everybody had long blonde hair and all cops were pigs.

"Nobody, I guess," he said, and turned to Brown. "Can you think of anybody else, Artie?"

"Gee, no," Brown said. "Unless maybe her father."

"Oh, right, right," Carella said. "*He* was killed, too, wasn't he? Your father."

Betsy scowled at him.

"But let's start with the first one," Carella said. "The bimbo. Susan Brauer. That would've been Tuesday night, the seventeenth. Can you tell us . . . ?"

"Am I going to need a lawyer here?" she asked.

"Not unless you want one," Carella said. "But that's entirely up to you."

"Because if you're going to ask me where I was and all that shit . . ."

"Yes, we're going to ask you where you were," Brown said.

And all that shit, he thought.

"Then maybe I need one," she said.

"Why? Were you someplace you shouldn't have been?"

"I don't remember where I was. I don't even know *when* that was."

"Today's Saturday, the twenty-eighth," Carella said. "This would've been eleven days ago."

"A Tuesday night," Brown said.

"The seventeenth," Carella said.

"Then I was in Vermont."

"I thought you went up to Vermont after your father's funeral."

"I went *back* up. I've been there since the beginning of July."

"Did your mother know this?"

"I don't tell my mother everything I do."

"Where do you go up there?" Brown asked.

"I have a little place my father gave me after the divorce. I think he was trying to win me over. He gave me this little house up there."

"Where?"

"Vermont. I told you."

"*Where* in Vermont?"

"Green River. It's a little house in the woods, I think one of his clients gave it to him years ago, instead of a fee. This was even before he married Mom. So it was just sitting there in the woods, practically falling apart, and he asked me if I wanted it. I said sure. Never look a gift horse, right?"

Carella was thinking she wouldn't even give her father the time of day, but she accepted a little house from him.

"Anyway, I go up there a lot," she said. "Get away from the rat race."

"And your mother doesn't know this, huh?" Brown said. "That you go up to Vermont a lot to get away from the rat race."

"I'm sure my mother knows I go up to Vermont."

"But she didn't know you went up there on the first day of July . . ."

"The *beginning* of July. The *fifth,* actually. And I don't remember whether I told her or not."

"But you were up there when Susan Brauer was killed, is that right?"

"If she was killed on the seventeenth, then I was up there, yes."

"Anybody with you?"

"No, I go up there alone."

"How do you get there?" Carella asked.

"By car."

"Your own car? Or do you rent one?"

"I have my own car."

"So you drive up there to Vermont in your own car."

"Yes."

"All alone?"

"Yes."

"How long does it take you to get there?"

"Three, three-and-a-half hours, depending on traffic."

"And it takes the same amount of time to get back, I suppose."

"Yes."

"When did you come back down again?"

"What do you mean?"

"You said you went up on the fifth . . ."

"Oh. Yes. I came down again right after my sister called me."

"When was that?"

"The day after my father got killed. She called to give me the news."

"That he'd been murdered."

"Yes."

"Then your sister also knew you were in Vermont."

"Yes."

"Both your mother *and* your sister have the number up there."

"Yes, they both have the number."

"So the day after your father got killed . . ."

"Yes."

"Your sister called you."

"Yes."

"That would've been Saturday, the twenty-first."

"Whenever."

"What time would that have been?"

"She called early in the morning."

"And you say you came back to the city right after she called?"

"Well, I called my mother first. After I spoke to my sister."

Which checked with what Gloria Sanders had told them.

"What'd you talk about?"

"About whether or not I should go to the funeral."

Which also checked.

"And what'd you decide?"

"That I'd go."

"So what time would you say you left Vermont?"

"I had breakfast, and I dressed and packed some things . . . it must've been eleven o'clock or so before I got out of there."

"Drove straight back to the city, did you?"

"Yes."

"Took you three, three-and-a-half hours, right?" Brown said.

"About that, yes."

They were both thinking that Vermont wasn't the end of the world. You could get up there in three hours. You could be here in the city killing somebody the night before and you could be back in Vermont taking a telephone call the next morning. People could see you coming and going in Vermont, into a grocery store, into a bakery, into a bookshop, into a bar, and no one would know whether you were in residence in your little house in the woods or commuting back and forth to the city to do murder.

"Did you know that under the provisions of your father's will, you would inherit twenty-five percent of his estate?" Carella asked.

"Yes, I knew that."

"How'd you happen to know?"

"Mom constantly told us."

"What do you mean by constantly?"

"Well, all the time. *Certainly* while they were negotiating the settlement . . . we weren't children, you know, this was only two years ago. Mom told us she wouldn't give him a divorce unless he agreed to put both of us in the will. Me and Lois. For half the estate. Together, that is. Sharing half the estate. So we knew about it at the time, and since then she's repeated the story again and again, with a great deal of pleasure and pride. Because she felt she'd done something very good for us. Which she had."

"Where were you on Friday night, Miss Schumacher?" Brown asked.

"Vermont. I told you."

The hippie grin again. Her mother's daughter for sure. No tricks, please. Just the facts, ma'am.

"You weren't down here in the city?"

"No. I was in Vermont."

"Anyone with you?"

"I told you. I go up there alone."

"I didn't ask if you went up there with anyone," Brown said pleasantly. "I asked if anyone was with you on the night Margaret Schumacher was killed."

"No. I was home alone. Reading."

"Reading what?" Carella asked.

"I don't remember. I read a lot."

"What kind of books?"

"Fiction mostly."

"Do you read murder mysteries?"

"No. I *hate* murder mysteries."

"You said you read about Margaret Schumacher's murder in the newspaper . . ."

"Yes."

"Local Vermont paper?"

"No. I picked up one of our papers at the . . ."

"*Our* papers?"

"Yes. From here in the city. We *do* get them up there, you know."

"And that's when you saw the headline . . ."

"It wasn't a headline. Not in the paper I bought. It was on page four of the metropolitan section."

"A story about Mrs. Schumacher's murder."

"Yes. *Mrs.* Schumacher's murder."

Repeating the title scornfully, so that it sounded dirty somehow.

"And you say you felt gleeful . . ."

"Well, perhaps that was too strong a word to use."

"What word would you use now?"

"Happy. The story made me happy."

"Reading about a woman's brutal murder . . ."

"Yes."

". . . made you happy."

"Yes."

"She'd been shot repeatedly in the head and chest . . ."

"Right."

"And reading about this made you happy."

"Yes," Betsy said. "I'm glad someone killed her."

Both detectives looked at her.

"She was a rotten bitch who wrecked our lives. I used to pray she'd fall out a window or get run over by a bus, but it never happened. Well, now someone got her. Someone gave it to her good. And yes, that makes me happy. In fact, it makes me *gleeful,* yes, that *is* the right word, I'm overflowing with *glee* because she's dead. I only wish she'd been shot a *dozen* times instead of just four."

There was a satisfied smile on her face.

You couldn't argue with a smile like that.

You could only wonder whether the newspapers had mentioned that Margaret Schumacher had been shot four times.

It was getting late.

They'd been talking in the living room of the house Angela had shared with Tommy until just recently, three-year-old Tess asleep in the back room, Angela telling her brother she was dying for a cigarette but her doctor had forbidden her to smoke while she was pregnant. Carella thought suddenly of Gloria Sanders, who'd been dying for a smoke when they'd talked to her at the hospital. He could not shake the persistent feeling that Penn Halligan had been describing a *woman* running through the rain. Or had the image been created by the foreknowledge that three women had survived Arthur Schumacher: two daughters, and an ex-wife who hated him.

"But it won't be long now," Angela said.

"You should *stay* off them," Carella said.

"Tough habit to kick," she said, and shrugged.

His father hadn't known that Angela smoked. Or at least had *pretended* not to know. Carella could remember one Sunday afternoon when all the family was gathered together . . . this was when he himself still smoked. A long time ago. Shortly after Angela and Tommy got married. An Easter Sunday, was it? A Christmas? The entire family gathered. They'd just finished the big afternoon meal—with Italian families, every meal was a feast—and he patted down his pockets, and realized he was out of cigarettes, and he went across the room to where Angela was sitting at the old upright piano, playing all the songs she'd learned as a little girl, a grown woman now with a husband, and he'd said, "Sis? Have you got a cigarette?" And Tony Carella, sitting in an easy chair listening to his daughter playing, suddenly shook his head and put his finger to his lips, shushing Carella, letting Carella know that his father wasn't supposed to know his darling daughter smoked, the sly old hypocrite.

Carella smiled with the memory.

"They say it's easier to kick heroin than nicotine," Angela said.

"But you've *already* kicked it," Carella said. "Eight, nine months now, that's kicking it."

"I *still* want a cigarette."

"So do I."

"And I'm gonna *have* one. As soon as the baby's born . . ."

"I wish you wouldn't," he said.

"Why the hell *not?*" she asked.

And suddenly she was crying.

"Hey," he said.

She shook her head.

"Hey, come on."

Raised her hand in mild protest, still shaking her head, no, please leave me alone. He went to her, anyway. Put his arm around her. Handed her his handkerchief.

"Here," he said. "Dry your eyes."

"Thanks," she said.

She dried her eyes.

"Okay to blow in it?" she asked.

"Since when do you ask?"

She blew her nose. She sniffed some more. She dried her eyes again.

"Thanks," she said again, and handed the handkerchief back to him.

"Cigarettes mean that much to you, huh?"

"Not cigarettes," she said, and shook her head.

"Tell me," he said.

"I just figured what the hell's the use? Smoke my brains out, die of cancer, who cares?"

"Me, for one."

"Yeah, you," she said. She seemed on the edge of tears again.

"Why do you think Tommy's having an affair?" he asked.

"Because I know he is."

"*How* do you know?"

"Just by the way he's been acting lately. I haven't found any hand-kerchiefs with lipstick on them, and he doesn't stink of perfume when he comes home, but . . ."

"Yes, but what?"

"I just *know*, Steve. He *behaves* differently. His mind is someplace else, he's got another woman, I just know it."

"How is he behaving differently?"

"He's just *different*. He tosses and turns all night long . . . as if he's thinking of someone else, can't get her out of his mind, can't fall asleep . . ."

"What else?"

"I'll be talking to him and his mind starts wandering. And I look at him and I just know he can't concentrate on what I'm saying because he's thinking of *her*."

Carella nodded.

"And he . . . well, I don't want to talk about it."

"Talk about it," Carella said.

"No, really, I don't want to, Steve."

"Angela . . ."

"All right, he doesn't want to make love anymore, all right?" she said. "Oh!" she said and suddenly grabbed for her belly. "Oh!" she said again.

"Sis?" he said.

"Oh!"

"What is it?"

"I think . . . oh!"

"Is it the baby?"

"Yes, I . . . oh!" she said, and clutched for her middle again.

"Which hospital?" he said at once.

From the squadroom, he'd have used the TDD on his desk, "talking" to Teddy directly, tapping out the letters of his message on the machine's keyboard, hitting the GA key for Go Ahead, reading her message in return. But he was calling home from the hospital waiting room, and public telephones hadn't yet caught up with state-of-the-art technology. Fanny Knowles answered the phone.

"Carella household," she said.

He visualized her standing at the kitchen counter, fiftyish and feisty, hair tinted a fiery red, wearing a pince-nez and standing with one hand on her hip as if challenging whoever was calling to say this was police business that would intrude on the sanctity of the home.

"Fanny, it's me," he said.

"Yes, Steve," she said.

E D M C B A I N

"I'm at Twin Oaks, Teddy knows the hospital, it's where the twins
were born."

"Yes, Steve."

"Can you tell her to catch a cab and come on over? Angela's
already in the delivery room."

"Do you want me to call your mother?"

"No, I'll do that now. Twin Oaks, the maternity wing."

"I've got it."

"Thank you, Fanny. Everything all right?"

"Yes, fine. I'll tell her right now."

"Thanks," he said, and hung up, and fished in his pocket for
another quarter, and then dialed his mother's number.

"Hello?" she said.

Her voice the same dull monotone he'd heard ever since his
father's death.

"Mama, it's me," he said. "Steve."

"Yes, honey."

"I'm here with Angela at the hospital . . ."

"Oh my God!" she said.

"Everything's all right, she's in the delivery room now, do you want
to . . . ?"

"I'll be right there," she said.

"Twin Oaks Hospital, the maternity wing," he said. "Call a taxi."

"Right away," she said, and hung up.

He put the receiver back on the hook and went to sit next to a
balding man who looked extremely worried.

"Your first one?" the man asked.

"It's my sister," Carella said.

"Oh," the man said. "It's my first one."

"It'll be all right, don't worry," Carella said. "This is a good hospital."

"Yeah," the man said.

"My twins were born here," Carella said.

"Yeah," the man said.

All those years ago, Carella thought. Meyer and Hawes pacing the
floor with him, Meyer consoling him, telling him he'd been through
it three times already, not to worry. Teddy up there in the delivery
room for almost an hour. Twins. Nowadays . . .

"We're having a boy," the balding man said.

"That's nice," Carella said.

"*She* wanted a girl."

"Well, boys are nice, too," Carella said.

"What do you have?"

"One of each," Carella said.

"We're going to call him Stanley," the man said. "After my father."

"That's nice," Carella said.

"*She* wanted to call him Evan."

"Stanley is a very nice name," Carella said.

"I think so," the man said.

Carella looked up at the clock.

Up there for twenty minutes already. He suddenly remembered Tommy. Tommy should be here. Whatever problems they were having, Tommy should be here. He went to the phone again, took out his notebook, found the number for the room over the garage, and dialed it. He let it ring a dozen times. No answer. He hung up and went to sit with the worried balding man again.

"What's she having? Your sister."

"I don't know."

"Didn't she have all the tests?"

"I guess so. But she didn't tell me what . . ."

"She should have had the tests. The tests tell you everything."

"I'm sure she must have had them."

"Is she married?"

"Yes."

"Where's her husband?"

"I just tried to reach him," Carella said.

"Oh," the man said, and looked at him suspiciously.

Teddy got there some ten minutes later. The man watched them as they exchanged information in sign language, fingers moving swiftly. Signing always attracted a crowd. You could get a crocodile coming out of a sewer in downtown Isola, it wouldn't attract as big a crowd as signing did. The man watched, fascinated.

She was asking him if he'd called his mother.

He told her he had.

I could have picked her up on the way, she signed.

"Easier this way," he said, signing at the same time.

The man watched goggle-eyed. All those flying fingers had taken his mind off his worries about his imminent son Stanley.

Carella's mother came into the waiting room a few minutes later. She looked concerned. She had come to this same hospital eleven days earlier, to identify her husband in the morgue. Now her daughter was here in the delivery room—and sometimes things went wrong in the delivery room.

"How is she?" she asked. "Hello, sweetie," she said to Teddy, and kissed her on the cheek.

"She went up about forty minutes ago," Carella said, looking at the wall clock.

"Where's Tommy?" his mother said.

"I've been trying to reach him," Carella said.

A look passed between him and Teddy, but his mother missed it.

Teddy signed *Forty minutes isn't very long.*

"She says forty minutes isn't very long," he repeated for his mother.

"I know," his mother said, and patted Teddy on the arm.

"Did Angela tell you what it would be?" Carella asked.

"No. Did she tell you?"

"No."

"Secrets," his mother said, and rolled her eyes. "With her, everything's always a secret. From when she was a little girl, remember?"

"I remember," he said.

"Secrets," she said, repeating the word for Teddy, turning to face her so she could read her lips. "My daughter. Always secrets."

Teddy nodded.

"Mr. Gordon?"

They all turned.

A doctor was standing there in a bloodstained surgical gown.

The worried balding man jumped to his feet.

"Yes?" he said.

"Everything's fine," the doctor said.

"Yes?"

"Your wife's fine . . ."

"Yes?"

"You have a fine, healthy boy."

"Thank you," the man said, beaming.

"You'll be able to see them both in ten minutes or so, I'll send a nurse down for you."

"Thank you," the man said.

Angela's doctor came down half an hour later. He looked very tired.

"Everything's fine," he said.

They always started with those words . . .

"Angela's fine," he said.

Always assured you about the mother first . . .

"And the twins are fine, too."

"Twins?" Carella said.

"Two fine healthy little girls," the doctor said.

"Secrets," his mother said knowingly. And then, to Carella, "Where's Tommy?"

"I'll try to find him," Carella said.

He drove first to the house Tommy had inherited when his parents died. No lights were showing in the room over the garage. He climbed the steps, anyway, and knocked on the door. It was only a quarter past eleven, but perhaps Tommy was already in bed. There was no answer. Carella went back down to the car, thought for a moment before he started the engine, and then started the long drive downtown.

He hoped Tommy would not be with his girlfriend on the night his twin daughters were born.

The playground across the street from the brownstone was deserted. Raindrops plinked on the metal swings and slides. This was an alternate-side-of-the-street parking zone. Water ran in sheets off the streamlined surfaces of the cars lining the curb that bordered the fenced-in playground. Carella found a spot dangerously close to a fire hydrant, threw down the visor with its police department logo, locked the car, and began running up the street in the rain.

He'd been a cop too long a time not to have noticed and recognized at once the two men sitting in a sedan parked across the street from the brownstone. He went over to the car, knocked on the passenger-side window. The window rolled down.

"Yeah?" the man sitting there said.

"Carella, the Eight-Seven," he said, showing his shield, shoulders hunched against the rain. "What's happening?"

"Get in," the man said.

Carella opened the rear door and climbed in out of the rain. Rain beat on the roof of the car. Rainsnakes trailed down the windows.

"Peters, the Two-One," the man behind the wheel said.

"Macmillen," his partner said.

Both men were unshaven. It was a look detectives cultivated when they were on a plant. Made them look overworked and underpaid. Which they were, anyway, even without the beard stubbles.

"We got cameras rolling in the van up ahead," Peters said, nodding with his head toward the windshield. Through the falling rain, Carella could make out a green van parked just ahead of the car. The words HI-HAT DRY CLEANING were lettered across the back panel, just below the painted-over rear window.

"Been sitting the building for a week now," Macmillen said.

"Which one?"

"The brownstone," Peters said.

"Why? What's going on over there?" Carella asked.

"Cocaine's going on over there," Macmillen said.

10

IT WAS MONDAY MORNING, and all the Monday-morning quarterbacks were out. Or at least one of them. His name was Lieutenant Peter Byrnes, and he was telling his assembled detectives what he hoped they should have known by now.

"When you're stuck," he said, "you go back to the beginning. *You* start where *it* started."

He was sitting behind his desk in the corner office he warranted as commander of the 87th Squad, a compact man with silvering hair and no-nonsense flinty-blue eyes. There were six detectives in the office with him. Four of them had already given him rundowns on the various cases they were investigating. The *big* case had waited patiently in the wings till now. The big case was multiple murder, the tap-dancing, singing, piano-playing star of this here little follies. Like a network television executive lecturing six veteran screenwriters on basics like motivation and such, the lieutenant was telling his men how to conduct their business.

"This case started with the dead girl," he said.

Susan Brauer. The dead girl. Twenty-two years old, a girl for sure, though Arthur Schumacher had considered her a woman for sure.

"And that's where *you* gotta start all over again," Byrnes said. "With the dead girl."

"You want my opinion," Andy Parker said, "you already *got* your perp."

Carella was thinking the same thing.

"Your perp's the hippie daughter," Parker said.

Exactly, Carella thought.

Looking at Parker in his rumpled suit, wrinkled shirt, and stained tie, his cheeks and jowls unshaven, Carella remembered for the hundredth time the two cops planted outside that brownstone downtown. He still hadn't talked to his brother-in-law because he hadn't yet figured out how the hell to handle this. Nor had he yet told Angela that her husband's sudden behavioral changes had nothing whatever to do with sex with a perfect stranger, but were instead attributable to what most cocaine addicts considered far more satisfying than even the *best* sex. He was hoping neither Peters nor Macmillen had pictures of Tommy marching in and out of a house under surveillance for drugs; how could he have been so goddamn dumb?

". . . the will for a quarter of the estate to begin with," Parker was saying. "Reason enough to kill the old . . ."

"That isn't starting with the dead girl," Byrnes reminded him.

"The dead girl was a smoke screen, pure and simple," Parker said breezily and confidently.

"Was *she* in the will?" Kling asked. "The dead girl?"

His mind was on Eileen Burke. On Monday mornings, it was sometimes difficult to get back to the business at hand, especially when the business happened to be crime every day of the year.

"No," Brown said. "Only people in the will are the two daughters, the present wife . . ."

"Now dead *herself*," Parker said knowingly.

". . . the vet, and the pet-shop lady," Brown concluded.

"For *how* much?" Hawes asked. "Those two?"

"Ten grand each," Carella said.

Hawes nodded in dismissal.

"The point is," Parker said, "between them, the two kids are up for fifty percent of the estate. If *that* ain't a good-enough motive . . ."

"*How* much did you say?" Hawes asked again. "The estate?"

"What the hell are *you* this morning?" Parker asked. "An accountant?"

"I want to know what the estate was, okay?" Hawes said.

"Supposed to be a lot of money," Carella said. "We don't have an exact figure."

"*Whatever* it is," Parker said, and again nodded knowingly, "it's enough to get the hippie daughter salivating."

This was a big word for him, *salivating*. He looked around as if expecting approval for having used it.

"What's this about she knew four bullets did the wife?" Willis asked.

"Yeah," Carella said.

"Was that in the papers?"

"No, but it was on one of the television shows."

"Who gave it out?" Byrnes asked.

"We're trying to find out now," Brown said. "It might've been the M&Ms. Or *anybody* from Homicide, for that matter."

"Homicide," Byrnes said, and shook his head sourly.

"That don't mean *she* didn't put those four slugs in the wife herself," Parker said. "Get rid of her, too, make it a clean sweep. She kills the old man to get her quarter of the pot . . ."

"Assuming she knew that," Byrnes said.

"She knew it, Pete."

"From when she was on her mother's knee," Parker said.

"Well, both daughters were grown at the time of the divorce, this was only two years ago. But they knew they were in the will for a quarter."

"Who gets the wife's share of the estate?" Kling asked. "Now that she's dead."

"Her will leaves it to a brother in London."

"Sole heir?"

"Yeah. But we called him and that's where he is, London. Hasn't visited the States in four years."

"Forget him," Parker said, "London's a million miles away. The hippie daughter was after the money, case closed."

"Then why'd she kill the other two?" Kling asked.

"Hatred, pure and simple," Parker said.

"You should hear the way she says, 'Mrs. Schumacher,' " Carella said.

"The *first* wife, too," Brown said. "She says it the same way. *Mrs.* Schumacher. She hated both of them. The old man, the new wife . . ."

"So'd the hippie daughter," Parker said, defending his case.

"No, wait a minute, don't let go of that so fast," Willis said. "The old lady hates Schumacher . . ."

"Right," Kling said, nodding.

"So she not only wipes out *him*, but also all the women in his life."

"Kills two birds with one stone," Kling said. "Gets the mistress *and* the present wife . . ."

"*Three* birds," Hawes corrected. "When you count Schumacher himself."

"Well, yeah, but I'm not talking body count. What I mean is she knocks over the women, and at the same time she puts her daughters in line for the cash."

"Yeah, but she has to kill Schumacher to do that."

"Well, sure."

"Is all I'm saying," Hawes said.

"Sure."

"How about the three of them did it in *concert*," Willis suggested. "Maybe we're looking at *three* killers instead of just one. Like the Orient Express."

"What the fuck's the Orient Express?" Parker asked.

"You know, Agatha Christie."

"Who the fuck's that, Agatha Christie?" Parker asked.

"Forget it," Willis said.

"Anyway, that was more than three people," Hawes said.

"And the younger daughter loved him," Carella said. "I don't think she'd have . . ."

"*Claims* she loved him," Willis said.

"Well, that's true, but . . ."

"Butter wouldn't melt," Brown said.

"Those are sometimes the worst kind," Willis said. "And I *know* it was more than three people, Cotton. I was just using it as an example."

"What is this, the public library?" Byrnes asked.

"Huh?" Parker said, looking bewildered.

"What about this pet-shop lady?" Kling asked.

"What about her?"

"Did *she* know she was in the will?"

"Claims she knew nothing about it," Carella said.

"Seemed genuinely surprised," Brown said.

"Anyway," Hawes said, "who'd kill somebody for a lousy ten grand?"

"*Me,*" Parker said, and everyone laughed.

"Besides, she hardly knew the guy," Brown said.

"Just gave him occasional advice on the pooch," Carella said.

"Also she knew the dog from when he was a pup," Hawes said. "Whoever blew away that mutt was somebody who hated him."

"Right, the hippie daughter," Parker said, nodding. "I was you, I'd pick her up, work her over with a rubber hose."

Everybody laughed again. Except Byrnes.

"Where'd that twelve grand come from?" he asked.

"What twelve grand?" Hawes said.

"The twelve grand in the cash box in her closet," Byrnes said. "And how'd the killer get in the apartment?"

"Well, we don't actually . . ."

"Anybody talk to the doorman who was on?"

"Yes, sir," Kling said. "Me and Artie."

"So what'd he say?"

"He didn't see anybody suspicious."

"Did he or did he not let anyone in that apartment?"

"He said there's deliveries all the time, he couldn't remember whether anyone went upstairs or not."

"He couldn't remember," Byrnes repeated flatly.

"Yes, sir."

"He couldn't remember."

"Yes, sir, that's what he said. He couldn't remember."

"Did you try to *prod* his memory?"

"Yes, sir, we spent an hour, maybe more, talking to him. His statement's in the file."

"He could hardly speak English," Brown said. "He's from the Middle East someplace."

"Talk to him again," Byrnes said. "Go back to the beginning."

The beginning was the dead girl.

Blue eyes open. Throat slit. Face repeatedly slashed. Nineteen, twenty years old, long blonde hair and startling blue eyes, wide open. Young beautiful body under the slashed black kimono with poppies the color of blood.

They were in the penthouse apartment again, just as they'd been on the night of July seventeenth, standing in the same room where the girl had lain before the coffee table—martini on the table, lemon twist curled on the bottom of the glass, paring knife on the floor beside her, blade covered with blood—bleeding from what appeared to be a hundred cuts and gashes.

This time the doorman was with them.

His name was Ahmad Something. Carella had written down the last name, but he couldn't pronounce it. Short and squat and dust-colored, narrow mustache over his upper lip, looking like a member of the palace guard in his gray uniform with its red trim. Squinting, straining hard to understand what they were saying.

"Did you let anyone into the apartment?"

"Dunn remembah," he said.

Thick Middle Eastern accent. They had not asked him where he was from. Carella was wondering if they'd need a translator here.

"*Try* to remember," he said.

"Many peckages always," he said, and shrugged helplessly.

"This would've been sometime in the late afternoon, early evening."

The medical examiner had set the postmortem interval at two to three hours. That would've put the stabbing at sometime between five and six o'clock. The doorman looked only puzzled. Carella guessed he was unfamiliar with the words "afternoon" and "evening."

"Five o'clock," he said. "Six o'clock. Were you working then?"

"Yes, working," the doorman said.

"Okay, did anyone come to the door and ask for Miss Brauer?"

"Dunn remembah."

"This is important," Brown said.

"Yes."

"This woman was killed."

"Yes."

"We're trying to find whoever killed her."

"Yes."

"So will you help us, please? Will you try to remember whether you let anyone go up?"

There was something in his eyes. Carella caught it first, Brown caught it a split second later.

"What are you afraid of?" Carella asked.

The doorman shook his head.

"Tell us."

"Saw nobody," he said.

But he had. They knew he had.

"What is it?" Carella asked.

The doorman shook his head again.

"You want to come to the station house with us?" Brown said.

"Hold off a second, Artie," Carella said.

Good Cop/Bad Cop. No need to signal for the curtain to go up, they both knew the act by heart.

"Hold off, *sheeee*-it," Brown said, doing his Big Bad Leroy imitation. "The man here is lying in his teeth."

"The man's afraid, is all," Carella said. "Isn't that right, sir?"

The doorman nodded. Then he shook his head. Then he nodded again.

"Let's go, mister," Brown said, and reached for the handcuffs hanging from his belt.

"Hold off, Artie," Carella said. "What is it, sir?" he asked gently. "Please tell me why you're so afraid."

The doorman looked as if he might burst into tears at any moment. His little mustache quivered, his brown eyes moistened.

"Sit down, sir," Carella said. "Artie, put those goddamn cuffs away!"

The doorman sat on the black leather sofa. Carella sat beside him. Brown scowled and hung the cuffs on his belt again.

"Now tell me," Carella said gently. "Please."

What it was, the doorman was an illegal alien. He had purchased a phony green card and social-security card for twenty bucks each, and he was scared to death that if he got involved in any of this, the authorities would find out about him and send him back home. Back home was Iran. He knew how Americans felt about Iranians. If he got involved in this, they would start blaming him for what had happened to the girl. He just didn't want to get involved. All of this in a broken English on the edge of tears. Carella was thinking that for an illegal alien, Ahmad was learning very fast; *nobody* in this city wanted to get involved.

"So tell me," he said, "*did* you send someone up to Miss Brauer's apartment?"

Ahmad had said everything he was going to say. Now he stared off into space like a mystic.

"We won't bother you about the green card," Carella said. "You don't have to worry about the green card. Just tell us what happened that afternoon, okay?"

Ahmad kept staring.

"Okay, you little shit," Brown said, "off we go," and he reached for the cuffs again.

"Well, I did my best," Carella said, and sighed heavily. "He's all yours, Artie."

"Vittoria," Ahmad said.

"What?" Carella said.

"Her name," Ahmad said.

"Whose name?"

"The woman who comes."

"What woman who comes?" Brown asked.

"That day."

"A woman came that day?"

"Yes."

"Say her name again."

"Vittoria."

"Are you saying Victoria?"

"Yes. Vittoria."

"Her name was Victoria?"

"Yes."

"Victoria *what?*"

"Seegah."

"What?"

"Seegah."

"How are you spelling that?"

Ahmad looked at them blankly.

"How's he spelling that, Steve?"

"Is that an *S?*" Carella asked.

Ahmad shrugged. "Seegah," he said.

"What'd she look like?"

"Tall," Ahmad said. "Tin."

"Thin?"

"Tin, yes."

"White or black?"

"White?"

"What color hair?"

"I dunn know. She is wearing . . ."

He searched for the word, gave up, mimed pulling a kerchief over his head and tying it under his chin.

"A scarf?" Brown asked.

"Yes."

"What color eyes?" Carella asked.

"She has glasses."

"She was wearing glasses?"

"Yes."

"Well, couldn't you see the color of . . . ?"

"Dark glasses."

"Sunglasses? She was wearing sunglasses?"

"Yes."

"What else was she wearing?"

"Pants. Shirt."

"What color?"

"Sand color."

"What'd she say?"

"Says Vittoria Seegah. Tell Miss Brauer."

"Tell her what?"

"Vittoria Seegah here."

"*Did* you tell her?"

"Tell her, yes."

"Then what?"

"She tell me send up."

"And *did* she go up?"

"Yes. Go elevator."

"How are you spelling that?" Brown asked again. "S-E-E-G?"

"Seegah," Ahmad said.

"What time was this?" Carella asked. "That she went upstairs?"

"Five. Little more."

"A little past five?"

"Yes. Little past."

"Did you see her when she came down?"

"Yes."

"When was that?"

"Six."

"Exactly six?"

"Little past."

"So she was up there a full hour, huh?"

Ahmad went blank.

"Did you look at your watch?"

"No."

"You're just estimating?"

The blank look.

"Any blood on her clothes?"

"No."

"What else do you remember about her?"

"Bag. Market bag."

"She was carrying a bag?"

"Yes."

"A *what* bag?" Brown asked.

"Market bag."

"You mean a shopping bag?"

"Yes. Shopping bag."

"Did you see what was in the bag?"

"No."

"Went upstairs with it?"

"Yes."

"Came back down with it?"

"Yes."

"Can you try spelling that name for us?" Carella asked.

Ahmad went blank again.

Brown shook his head. "Seeger," he said.

Which was close, but—as they say—no see-gah.

There were thirty-eight Seegers, Seigers, and Siegers listed in the tele-phone directories for all five sections of the city, but none of them was a Victoria. There were eight Seagers and eleven Seagrams. Again, no Victorias. There were hundreds and hundreds of Seegals and Segals and Segels and Seigals and Seigels and Siegels and Siegles and Sigals and Sigalls. One of them was a Victoria and seven of them were listed as merely V's. But the possibility existed that a Victoria might be residing at any one of the addresses listed for a Mark or a Harry or an Isabel or a Whoever.

"It'll take forty cops working round the clock for six months to track down all those people," Byrnes said. "And we don't even know if the Arab was saying the name right."

As a matter of fact, the doorman was an Iranian of the Turkic and not the Arabian ethnic stock—but people in America rarely made such fine distinctions.

They went back to the apartment again that Monday afternoon. Stood there in the living room where Susan Brauer had lain with her wounds shrieking silently to the night, slash and stab marks on her breasts and her belly and the insides of her thighs, blood everywhere, torn white flesh and bright red blood. Shrieking.

The apartment was silent now.

Early-afternoon sunlight slanted through the living room windows.

They had checked her personal address book and had found no listing for any of the Seeger or Seigel variations, Victoria or other-wise. No Seagrams, either. No nothing. No help.

They were now looking for . . .

Anything.

It had come down to that.

They'd been told to go back to the beginning, and that's exactly where they were. Square one. Zero elevation. The lockbox had been found in her bedroom closet. Twelve thousand dollars in that box. In hundred-dollar bills. Now they went back to the closet again, and searched again through the fripperies and furs, the satins and silks, the feathers and frills, the designer dresses and monogrammed suitcases, the rows of high-heeled shoes in patent and lizard and crocodile. They found nothing that Kling and Brown hadn't found the first time around.

So they went through the desk again, and the trash basket under the desk, unwrapping balled pieces of paper, studying each scrap carefully for something they might have missed, yanking a piece of paper free from where it was stuck to a wad of chewing gum, reading the scribbling on it, discarding it as unimportant.

The kitchen was still ahead of them.

The garbage was waiting for them in the pail under the sink.

It didn't smell any better than it had thirteen days ago. They dumped it out onto the open newspapers again, and they began going through it bit by bit, the whole noisome lot of it, the moldy bread and rotten bananas, the empty oat-bran box, the coffee grinds and milk container, the soup cans, the crumpled paper towels, the soft smelly melon, the rancid slab of butter, the wilted vegetables and wrinkled summer fruit, the old . . .

"What's that?" Brown asked.

"Where?"

"In the container there."

A flash of white. A piece of crumpled white paper. Lying on the bottom of a round white container that once had held yogurt. The container stank to high heaven. By proximity, so did the crumpled ball of paper, perfectly camouflaged, white on white. It was easy to see how it could have been missed on the first pass. But they weren't missing it this time around.

Carella picked it up.

White as the driven snow.

He unfolded it, smoothed out the wrinkles and creases, transformed it from the wadded ball it had been an instant earlier into a strip of paper some seven inches long and perhaps an inch-and-a-half wide. White. Nothing on it. A plain white strip of paper. He turned it over. There were narrow violet borders on each side of the strip. Printed boldly from border to border across the strip was the figure $2000, repeated some five times over at regularly spaced intervals along its length. Ink-stamped between two of these bold figures were what at first appeared to be cryptic markings:

Is. Bk. & Tr. Co., N. A.
Jeff. Ave. Br.

They were looking at what banks call a currency strap.

* * *

The manager of the Jefferson Avenue Branch of the Isola Bank &
Trust Company was a man named Avery Granville, fiftyish and balding, wearing a brown, tropical-weight suit, a beige button-down shirt,
and an outrageous green-and-orange striped tie. With all the inten-
sity of an archeologist studying a suspect papyrus scroll, he scrutinized the narrow violet-bordered strip of paper and then looked up
at last and said, "Yes, that's one of our straps," and smiled pleasantly,
as if he'd just approved a loan application.

"What does the 'N.A.' stand for?" Brown asked.

"National Association," Granville said.

"And the WL?"

"Wendell Lawton. He's one of our tellers. Each teller has his own
stamp."

"Why's that?" Brown asked.

"Why, because he's accountable for whatever's printed on the
strap," Granville said, looking surprised. "The teller's personal stamp
is saying he's counted that money and there's fifty dollars in the
strap, a hundred dollars, five hundred, whatever's printed on the
strap."

"So if this one says two thousand dollars . . ."

"Yes, that's what's printed there. And the violet border confirms
the amount. Violet is two thousand dollars."

"Then this wrapper . . ."

"Well, a strap, we call it."

"This strap at one time was wrapped around two thousand dollars."

"Yes. We've got straps for smaller amounts, of course, but this
one's a two-thousand-dollar strap."

"How high do they go? The straps?"

"That's the highest, two thousand, usually in hundred-dollar
bills. All the straps have different colors, you see. Here at IBT, a
thousand-dollar strap is yellow and a five-hundred-dollar one is red,
and so on. It varies at different banks, they all have their own color-
coding."

"And the date here . . ."

"That's stamped by the teller, too. First he puts his personal stamp
on the currency strap, and then he uses a revolving stamp to mark
the date."

"I'm assuming this means . . ."

"July ninth, yes. The straps are temporal and disposable, we just stamp in the month and the day, easier that way."

"Is Mr. Lawton here now?"

"I believe so," Granville said, and looked at his watch. "But it's getting late, you know, and he's balancing out right now."

The clock on the wall read ten minutes to four.

"What we're interested in knowing, sir," Brown said, "is just who might have withdrawn that two thousand dollars on the ninth of July. Would there be any record of such a cash transaction? Two thousand dollars withdrawn in cash?"

"Really, gentlemen . . ."

"This is very important to us," Brown said.

"It may be related to the murder of a young woman," Carella said.

"Well, believe me, I'd be happy to help. But . . ."

He looked at his watch again.

"This would mean checking Wendell's teller tape for that day, and . . ."

"What's that?" Carella asked. "A teller tape?"

"A computer printout for all the transactions at his window. It looks somewhat like an adding-machine tape."

"Would this tape show such a withdrawal? Two thousand dollars in cash?"

"Well, yes, if in fact it was made. But, you see . . ."

Another look at his watch.

"A teller can handle as many as two hundred and fifty transactions on any given day of the week. To go through all those . . ."

"Yes, but a two-thousand-dollar cash withdrawal would be unusual, wouldn't it?"

"No, not necessarily. There could be any number of those on any given day."

"Exactly two thousand dollars?" Carella said skeptically. "In cash?"

"Well . . ."

"Could we have a look at the tape, Mr. Granville?" Brown asked. "When your teller's finished with his tally?"

"His balancing out," Granville corrected, and sighed. "I suppose so, yes."

Wendell Lawton was a man in his early thirties, wearing a light-weight blue blazer, a white shirt, and a red tie that made him look like either a television news commentator or a member of the White

House staff. He confirmed that this was indeed his stamp on the two-thousand-dollar strap, but he told them that he handled many such bundles of currency every day of the week, and he couldn't possibly be expected to recall whether this particular strap had been handed over the counter to anyone in par—

"But we understand there's a teller's tape," Carella said.

"Well, a *teller* tape, yes," Lawton said, correcting him, and then looking up at the clock; Carella figured it must have been a long, hard day.

"So perhaps if we looked at that tape . . ."

"Well," he said again.

"This is a homicide we're investigating," Brown said, and fixed Lawton with a scowl that was in itself homicidal.

Lawton's teller tapes were kept in a locked drawer under the counter. His stamp was in that same locked drawer. He unlocked it now, and searched through what he called his proof sheets, looking for and finding at last the one dated the ninth of July. A tape that did indeed look like an adding-machine tape was stapled to it. Lawton had handled a hundred and thirty-seven counter transactions on that day. None of them was for an exact two-thousand-dollar withdrawal in cash. But one of the recorded transactions rang a bell.

The computer printout on the tape showed the date, and then the time, and then:

113-807-40   162   772521
SW $2400

"The first number is the account number," Lawton explained. "The next number is the number of the IBT branch here, one-sixty-two. The last number is my teller's number."

"What's the SW stand for?" Brown asked.

"Savings withdrawal. Twenty-four hundred is what the customer took out of his account. It's likely that I gave it to him in a two-thousand-dollar strap and four hundred in loose bills outside the strap."

"Can you trace that account number . . ."

"Yes."

". . . and give us the customer's name?"

"If Mr. Granville says it's okay."

Mr. Granville said it was okay to give them the customer's name. When the computer punched it up, Lawton said, "Oh yes."

"Oh yes what?" Brown asked.

"He's been withdrawing twenty-four hundred in cash every month since March."

The customer's name was Thomas Mott.

He didn't know what they were talking about.

"There must be some mistake," he said.

They always said that.

"No, there's no mistake," Carella said.

They were standing in the center aisle of his antiques shop on Drittel Avenue. A German grandfather clock bonged the hour: six P.M. again. It was always six P.M. here. Mott seemed annoyed that they'd arrived just as he was about to close. Everyone seemed annoyed at having to work a long day today. But the cops had been on the job since seven forty-five this morning.

"You *do* remember withdrawing twenty-four hundred dollars in cash on the ninth of *this* month, don't you?" Carella asked.

"Well, yes, but that was a very special circumstance. A man came to me with a rare William and Mary tankard, and he would accept only cash for it. He didn't know what he had, it was truly a steal. I went to the bank . . ."

"At twelve twenty-seven P.M.." Brown said, showing off.

"Around then," Mott said.

"That's what the teller tape says," Brown said.

"Then that's what it must have been."

"Who's this man with the rare William and Mary tankard?" Carella asked.

"I'm sure I have his name in the file somewhere."

"Then I wish you'd find it for us," Carella said. "And while you're at it, maybe you can look through your records for the withdrawals you made on June first, which was a Friday, and May first, which was a Tuesday, and April second, which was a Monday, and March . . ."

"I don't recall any of those withdrawals," Mott said.

"The teller tapes," Brown reminded him, and smiled pleasantly. "That's when the withdrawals started. In March."

"Twenty-four hundred every month."

"For a total of twelve thousand dollars."

"Remember?"

"Yes, now that you mention it . . ."

They always said that, too.

"... I do remember withdrawing that amount each month. Against just such an opportunity as the rare William and Mary."

"Ahhh," Brown said.

"Then that explains it," Carella said.

"What it *doesn't* explain," Brown said, "is how that twelve thousand dollars ended up in Susan Brauer's cash box."

Mott blinked.

"Susan Brauer," Brown said, and smiled pleasantly again.

"Remember her?" Carella asked.

"Yes, but . . ."

"She came to your shop every now and then, remember?"

"She was in here on the ninth, remember?"

"To look at a butler's table you'd told her about . . ."

"Yes, of *course* I remember."

"Do you remember giving her twenty-four hundred dollars in cash every month?"

"I never did such a thing."

"Since March," Brown said.

"Of course not. Why *would* I have done such a thing?"

"Gee, I don't know," Brown said. "Why would you?"

"The woman was a customer, why would . . . ?"

"Mr. Mott . . . we found a currency strap in her apartment . . ."

"I don't know what that is, a currency . . ."

". . . and we've traced it back to your account. The money came from your account, Mr. Mott, there's no question about that. Now do you want to tell us why you were paying Susan Brauer twenty-four hundred dollars a month?"

"For the past five months . . ."

"Two thousand in a strap . . ."

"The rest in loose hundreds . . ."

"Why, Mr. Mott?"

"I didn't kill her," Mott said.

He'd met Susan . . .

He'd called her Susan in deference to her wishes; *Nobody* calls me Suzie, she'd said.

. . . here at the shop when she came in one day in January, just browsing, she'd told him. She was renting an apartment up on Silvermine Oval, and whereas it was furnished, she missed the little touches that made a house a home, and was always on the lookout for anything that might personalize the place. He asked her what sort of things she had in mind, and she told him Oh, nothing *big*, no sideboards or dining-room tables or Welsh dressers or anything like that. But if there was a small footstool, for example, or a beautiful little lamp that she could take with her when she moved out—she was hoping to move to a bigger apartment as soon as certain arrangements had been made, she told him, but apartments were soooo expensive these days, weren't they?

He'd called her one day toward the end of the month, he'd just got a new shipment from England, this was the end of January. He and his wife had spent a week in Jamaica, he remembered calling Susan as soon as they got back because there was a beautiful set of Sheffield candlesticks in the shipment, none of the copper showing through, rare for Sheffields, and they were reasonably priced, and he thought she might like to take a look at them. She came to the shop that afternoon, and fell in love with them, of course, they *were* truly beautiful, but then expressed some doubt as to whether or not they'd fit in with the decor of the apartment, which was essentially modern, leather and stainless, you know, huge throw pillows on the floor, abstract paintings, and so on. So he said he'd be happy to lend her the candlesticks until she made up her mind, and she'd said Ohhh, *would* you? and he had them sent around the very next day.

She called him on a Saturday, this was sometime during the first week in February, and asked if he could possibly stop by to take a look at the candlesticks himself. She'd put them on the dining-room table, which was all glass and stainless, and she thought maybe the brass clashed with the steel, and she really would appreciate his opinion. So he went by at the end of the day.

She had mixed a pitcherful of martinis, she was fond of martinis.

He told her frankly that he thought the candlesticks *did* look out of place on that table, and she thanked him for his honesty and thanked him again for coming all the way uptown, and then she offered him a drink, which he accepted. It was close to six-thirty, he guessed. A very cold Saturday afternoon in February. She put on some music. They had a few drinks. They danced. That's how it started. It all seemed so natural.

Toward the end of February . . .

This was after they'd been to bed together at least half a dozen times . . .

Toward the end of the month, she told him she was having trouble meeting the rent on the apartment and that the owner was threatening to throw her out on the street. She told him the rent was twenty-four hundred a month, which he found absolutely shocking in view of the fact that the mortgage on his house in Locksdale was only *three* thousand and some change a month, and she said it would be a shame if she lost the apartment because it was such a wonderful way for the two of them to be together in such lovely surroundings. She wasn't asking him to *give* her the money . . .

"I didn't know what she meant at first," Mott said.

. . . but only to *lend* it to her, you see.

Temporarily.

The twenty-four hundred.

Just for the March rent, you see. Because she had these modeling jobs coming up, and she'd get paid for them before the April rent was due, and then she'd have enough to pay him back and then some. If he could just lend her the twenty-four hundred. Because she just *loved* being with him and doing all the things they did together, didn't he love the things they did together?

"She was so beautiful," Mott said.

So very beautiful. And remarkably . . .

"Well, in fact, *amazingly* . . ."

He could not find the word. Or perhaps he knew the word and refused to share it with the detectives.

"I gave her the money," he said. "Drew it out of a savings account, handed it over to her. She asked if I wanted a written I.O.U., and I told her of *course* not, don't be ridiculous. Then . . ."

When it came time to pay the April rent, she didn't have the money for that, either, so he'd loaned her another twenty-four hundred, and then another twenty-four in May, and when June came around, he realized this had become a regular thing, he was paying for the rent on her apartment, he was *keeping* her, she was in effect his . . .

"Well, never mind in effect," he said. "That's what she was. My mistress."

Yours and Shumacher's both, Carella thought.

"God, I loved her so much," Mott said.

In July, he and his wife went away for the Fourth . . . well, actually, they'd left the city on the thirtieth of June, which was a Saturday, and spent the whole next week in Baltimore with her sister, didn't get back until the following Sunday. Susan came into the shop the very next day, Monday. The ninth. Came in around lunchtime, wanted to know if he hadn't forgotten a little something? He didn't know what she meant at first. Oh? she said. You don't know? You really don't know? Maybe you think a girl like me just comes along every day of the week, huh? Maybe next time you want me to . . .

"Well, she made a reference to . . . to what we . . . to what we . . . well, what she . . . uh. She said I might . . . she said I ought to think about that the next time I asked her to . . . you know. Because if I was going to forget all about the *rent* coming due, then maybe she should start looking for someone who might enjoy being with her and taking advantage of her that way. She was furious. I'd never seen her like that. I hadn't really thought I was taking advantage of her, I thought she *enjoyed* it. I tried to explain . . ."

He'd tried to explain. It had been the holiday, you see, the Fourth of July, the bank would be closed on Wednesday, anyway, and he'd had to go away with his wife, she *knew* he was married, she *knew* he had a wife. She said did he know how humiliating it was for her to receive a call from the woman who was renting her the apartment, asking her where the *rent* was, did he *realize*? He'd gone to the bank while she waited in the shop . . .

"This *was* around twelve-thirty, the bank's record is correct," he said.

. . . and he'd brought the money back, and all of a sudden she was a different person, the same Susan he'd always known. In fact, right there in the shop she'd . . .

"Well," he said.

They did not ask him what she'd done right there in the shop.

Instead, Carella said, "Where were you on the night she was killed?"

"Home with my wife," Mott said.

Isabelle Mott was a woman in her mid-to-late forties, some five feet seven or eight inches tall, with long straight black hair and dark brown eyes, which combined with the silver-and-turquoise jewelry she was wearing to give her the strikingly attractive look of a native American Indian, which she was not. She was, in fact, of Scotch-Irish ancestry, go figure.

They did not tell her that her husband, Thomas, had been enjoying of late an affair with a beautiful twenty-two-year-old blonde who'd been murdered only eight days after he'd last seen her. They figured there was no sense causing more trouble than already existed. They simply asked if she knew where he'd been on the night of July seventeenth, that would've been a Tuesday night, ma'am. When she asked why they wanted to know, they said what they said to any civilian who wanted to know why certain questions were being asked: Routine investigation, ma'am.

"He was here," she said.

"How do you happen to remember that?" Carella asked.

She had not looked at a calendar, she had not consulted an appointment—

"I was sick in bed that night," she said.

"Uh-huh," Carella said.

"Sick with what, ma'am?" Brown asked.

"Actually, I was recovering from surgery," she said.

"Uh-huh," Carella said.

"What kind of surgery, ma'am?" Brown asked.

"Minor surgery," she said.

"Had you been hospitalized?" Carella asked.

"No. The surgery was done that morning, Tommy came to pick me up that afternoon."

"Where was this surgery done, ma'am?" Brown asked.

Both cops were thinking abortion. It sounded like abortion.

"At Hollingsworth," she said.

A hospital not far from here, in the Three-Two Precinct.

"And what was the nature of the surgery?" Carella asked.

"If you *must* know," Isabelle said, "I had a D and C, okay?"

"I see," Carella said, and nodded.

Brown was thinking that's what they used to call abortions before *Roe* v. *Wade*.

"What time did you get home from the hospital?" Carella asked.

"Around four, four-thirty."

"And you say your husband was with you?"

"Yes."

"Did he leave the house at any time after that?"

"That night, do you mean?"

"Yes. The night of the seventeenth. After you got home from the hospital, did he leave the house at any time?"

"No."

Firm and emphatic.

"He was home all night long?"

"Yes," she said, positively nailing it to the wall.

"Well, thank you," Carella said.

Brown nodded glumly.

The signs on the corner lamppost read respectively Meriden St and Cooper St, white lettering on green, one sign running horizontally in an east-west direction, the other running north-south. Below these, white on blue, was a larger sign that read:

```
QUIET
HOSPITAL
ZONE
```

Across the street, Farley General's huge illuminated windows glared a harsh yellow-white against a black moonless sky. It was fifteen minutes to midnight, and the street was silent and deserted. An occasional automobile passed, but for the most part the traffic was light; motorists tended to avoid this street because the speed limit here was only twenty miles an hour, and they preferred Averill as an approach to the bridge.

Standing in the shadows of the trees across the street, you could almost hear your own heartbeat, it was that still. Hand around the butt of the gun in the right-hand pocket of the long black coat, black again, wearing black again, the gun butt warm now, though it had felt cool earlier, there in the cool dark of the coat pocket. Warmer now. Palm of the hand somewhat moist on the walnut stock of the gun, but not from nervousness, you did this often enough it didn't make you nervous anymore. Moist with anticipation, the honest sweat of anticipation, expectation. Shoot her dead the moment she came through those doors. *Empty* it in her. *Kill* her.

She would be coming out at midnight.

Monday was when she worked the four-to-midnight shift, it was important to check such things, make sure you knew who would be where when. Otherwise you made mistakes. There'd been no mistakes so far. All the questions they'd asked, but no mistakes. Too smart for them, was what it was. All you had to do was show them whatever they wanted to see, tell them whatever they expected to hear, and they were satisfied. Well, sure, look what you were dealing with here. So easy to fool them, so very easy. Just play the person they *thought* you were, never mind what was inside, never mind the pain and the suffering inside, just show them the surface. Play back the image they themselves had created, the stereotype of whoever they *thought* you were, this is me, right? Isn't this who I am? Whoever you *think* I am? Whatever idea of me you had in your heads even before you met me, isn't that right? Isn't that me?

No, it's *not* me. No. I'm sorry, but no.

This is me.

This *gun* is me.

Hard and cold and wet and hot in my hand.

Five minutes to midnight.

Coming out in your starched white uniform soon, never change before you go home, do you? March right out in your whites, Madam Nurse, his first and *foremost* choice, the pattern for all the rest, how *dumb,* how essentially stupidly *dumb!* Slender, beautiful, your basic American blonde, the man has a decided weakness for blondes, *had.* But not quite so beautiful *now,* are you, Miss Nightingale? And blonde only with a little help from your friends, isn't that correct? Little help from Miss Clairol, hmm? Little help from me, too, tonight, little help from Miss *Cobra* here in my pocket, little *spit* from Miss Cobra, *empty* it in you! Bloody the image of yourself as *nurse,* confirm *my* image as whatever you *wish* me to be, whatever you've constructed in your mind as the true and only *image* of me, again all in black tonight, hidden in mourning, shrouded in black, only my face showing white in the dark, who *am* I, *tell* me!

Red light over the door across the street.

Employees entrance.

Sign says employees entrance.

Three minutes to midnight.

Door opening now.

Nurses spilling out. Orderlies. Interns. Scattering on the night. Some in uniform, some in street clothes. Dispersing. But where are *you,* Madam Nurse? You mustn't keep us waiting, you know. Miss Cobra and I become extremely irritated when . . .

There!

Coming out now. Saying goodnight to a man wearing a blue jacket over his white hospital pants. Calling something to him. See you tomorrow, voice carrying on the still night air, oh, no, you won't see *anyone* tomorrow. Turning away now. Smiling. Moving left toward the subway kiosk on the next corner. Pair of nurses ahead of her. *Now!*

Step out. Fast. Cross the street. Gun out. Move in. Fast. Behind her. Here! Here! Here! Here! Here!

Someone screaming.

Run.

Run!

11

SHE COULD NOT have appeared more fearsome had she ridden into the squadroom on a broomstick. Her blonde hair a tangled mare's nest, blue eyes flashing, lips curled back over teeth on the biting edge of anger, she flung open the gate in the slatted-rail divider and strode directly to where Brown and Carella were sitting at his desk.

"Okay, let's hear it!" she said.

Both detectives blinked. Since they'd just been looking over the report that had arrived from Ballistics not five minutes earlier, they could have told her that they now had a positive match on the .22-caliber bullets that had slain her mother last night. But she did not appear in the mood to hear that the same gun had also killed her father and stepmother. They had seen this look on indignant citizens before, but rarely quite so close to flash point. Fists clenched, it seemed as if Betsy Schumacher would at any moment strike out at either or both of the detectives. They wondered what they had done. She told them.

"Why didn't you call me?"

"We didn't have your number in Vermont," Carella said. "Your sister said she would . . ."

"Never mind my *sister!* It was *your* responsibility to inform me that my mother was dead!"

Actually, it hadn't been their responsibility at all. Nothing in the law or in any of the instructional guides required an investigating detective to notify the family of a murder victim. Moreover, in this day and age police notification was often a redundancy; in most cases, the family had already been informed by television. In a manual prepared by a former chief of detectives, family and friends ranked only sixth in importance on his suggested list of procedures:

Start worksheet . . .
Determine personnel needs . . .
Assign personnel to clerical duties . . .
Arrange for additional telephone lines . . .
Carefully question all witnesses and suspects . . .
Interview family and friends of the deceased for back-
   ground information.

Only after rounding up all the usual suspects was it considered necessary to talk to the family and friends. And then only to gather background information. But nowhere did the chief, or anyone else, insist that a detective *had* to call the family *first*, even if—in working practice—this often proved to be the case. Last night, they had notified Lois Stein at once, and had in fact asked her for Betsy's number in Vermont. She'd told them she would call her sister personally. Apparently she had. Because here was Betsy now, fuming and ranting and threatening to have them brought up on charges or hanged by their thumbs in Scotland Yard, whichever punishment most fitted their heinous crime. Carella was thinking that the *true* heinous crime was yet another murder, and he was wondering if the lady might not be protesting a bit too much about an imaginary oversight. Brown had already carried this a step further: he was wondering if Betsy hadn't boxed her own mother. Done the round-trip number from Vermont to here and back again. So long, Mama.

"We're very sorry, Miss Schumacher," he said, sounding genuinely sorry, "but it was very late when we finally got to your sister . . ."

"So many things to do at the scene . . ." Carella said.

"And we *did* ask her for your number, truly."

"She called me at four in the morning," Betsy said.

"Which was just a bit after we left her," Brown said.

Letting her know that these hardworking underpaid minions of the law had been on the job all night long, doing their crime-scene canvass, typing up re . . .

"It was still your responsibility," Betsy said petulantly, but she was beginning to soften. "Lois told me Mother was shot around midnight, and I didn't hear till . . ."

"Yes, according to the witnesses, that's when . . ."

"You mean there are witnesses?" Betsy said, surprised.

"Yes, two of them."

"People who saw the shooting?"

"Well, *heard* it, actually," Carella said. "Two nurses heading down the steps to the subway. They turned when they heard the shots, saw the killer running off."

"Then you have a description."

"Not exactly. They saw a *person*. But they couldn't tell us what that person looked like except that he . . ."

"Or she," Brown said.

"Or she," Carella repeated, nodding, "was dressed entirely in black."

"Then you don't really know . . ."

"No, Miss Schumacher, we don't," Carella said. "Not yet."

"Uh-huh, not yet," she said. "When do you think you *will* know?"

"We're doing our . . ."

"This is the fourth *one,* for Christ's sake!"

"Yes, we . . ."

"It *is* the same person, isn't it? Who killed Daddy and now . . ."

"We have good reason to believe it's the same person, yes."

"I don't give a *damn* about his bimbos, I wish someone had killed them both a long *time* ago. But if you want my opinion . . ."

Which they truly didn't.

". . . this person is after the whole family. The bimbos were a smoke screen . . ."

Which theory they had considered, too. And rejected.

". . . to hide the *real* targets, who were my mother and father. And that means maybe Lois and I are next." She hesitated for just an instant and then said, "While you do nothing."

"We're doing all we can," Carella said.

"No, I don't think so. Not if four people can get killed in the space of two weeks, three weeks, whatever the hell it is."

"It's exactly two weeks today," Brown said.

"So, sure, that's doing something. That's doing *nothing* is what it's doing. Where the hell were you last night when my mother was getting killed?"

The detectives said nothing.

"You can see there's a goddamn pattern, can't you?"

"What pattern do you see, Miss Schumacher?" Carella asked patiently.

"I see Daddy's bimbo getting killed, and then Daddy himself. So we'll think this is something that has to do exclusively with him and her. But then the *other* bimbo gets killed . . ."

"By the *other* bimbo . . ."

"*Mrs.* Schumacher, his beloved *wife*," she said mockingly. "Margaret, the very *first* bimbo. Come September, they'd have been married for two years. But isn't the irony wonderful? By last June— even before the wedding meats were cold—he'd already found himself *another* girlfriend. The point is . . ."

No, your timing is off, Brown thought.

". . . this person, whoever he is, first kills the new bimbo and then my father . . ."

He didn't start with the Brauer girl till *this* year.

". . . in an attempt to make it seem as if there's a link between them . . ."

"Well, there *was* a link," Carella said. "Your father was having an . . ."

"I *know* what he was doing, I can read the papers, thank you. My point is the killer goes after Margaret *next*, so we'll think he's after *all* my father's little dollies when instead what he's going after is the whole damn Schumacher *family*. It doesn't take a genius to recognize that. I thought you were supposed to be policemen. Who would you like to see killed next? My sister? Me?"

"You've got that wrong, by the way," Brown said.

"Oh, have I?" she said, turning to him. "Then how do *you* see it? The first three murders were . . ."

"I mean about when he started with the Brauer girl."

"I don't know when he *started* with her, whatever that means, but I know he was intimately *involved* with her last June."

"Couldn't have been."

"I'm telling you . . ."

"Miss, we've got a letter from your father saying he met her on New Year's Day . . ."

"*Her* letter is dated last June."

Both detectives looked at her.

"Whose letter?" Carella said.

"Well, who do you think? The woman he was keeping, the woman who was all over the newspapers, Little Suzie Sunshine."

"You have a letter Susan Brauer wrote to your father?"

"Yes."

"How'd you get it?"

"I found it."

"Where?"

"In Vermont."

"In the house your father gave you?"

"Not the house, the garage. A shoe box in the garage. I was cleaning out the garage when I moved in, and I . . ."

"Just that one letter in the box?"

"Yes."

"What kind of letter?" Brown asked.

"*Hi!*" she said, and put her hands alongside her face, and spread her fingers like fans. Blue eyes wide, smiling like Shirley Temple, she chirped in a tiny little voice, "I sure would love to suck your cock, baby!" and then snapped her hands shut and said in the same little voice, "*Bye!*"

Brown nodded.

"*That* kind of letter," she said.

"And you found this when?" Carella asked.

"Last July. When I moved into the house up there."

"Can't be," Brown said again. "Him and Susan . . ."

"Don't tell *me* what can't be!" Betsy said. "I know damn *well* when it was! It was the most important day of my life!"

"We have his letters to her," Carella said, "all dated this year . . ."

". . . and hers to him," Brown said.

"Well, I found that letter a year ago," Betsy insisted, "and it's dated Friday, June thirtieth."

"Has to be this year," Brown said.

"Are you telling me I don't know when I . . . look, where's a calendar?"

Carella looked at Brown, stifled a sigh, and reached into his desk drawer. He took out his appointment book, flipped through the pages till he came to the calendar for June of this year, glanced at it briefly, looked up, and said, "The thirtieth fell on a Saturday."

"See what you got for last year," Brown said softly.

At the back of the book, facing a map showing time zones and postal area codes for the entire United States, Carella found three reduced calendars printed on the same page, the current calendar flanked above and below by calendars for the preceding year and the one following. Squinting at the smaller numerals, he studied last year's calendar, looked up, and said to Brown, "She's right, June thirtieth fell on a Friday."

Brown nodded.

"You still got that letter?" he asked.

Friday, June 30

Hi!

I like this game. I'm only sorry you didn't think of it sooner. But the next time I see you, you'll have to explain the rules again. Am I allowed to write whatever *comes into my mind? Oh dear, I'll be so naughty, you won't be able to stand it.*

It's raining today. Want to go splash in the rain with me? Want me to play with you in the rain?

You always ask me what I'm wearing. Right now I have on a push-up black lace bra, cut so low it exposes my nipples. Black silk stockings, held up by a garter belt. Black crotchless panties. Black spiked heels. These silk stockings feel so smooth. I think you'd like to run your hand over them, run your hand up along my thigh until you reach the rim of the hose. Maybe then you'd like to move your hand over to my moist, eager cunt. My legs are spread so wide for you. But maybe, since you know I'm ready and aching for you, you'd just like to slide your cock inside me and start fucking me right this minute.

Do you think of me when you're fucking your wife?

I'm getting so hot sitting here, thinking of you and your big hard cock. Why aren't you here with me? What am I supposed to do without you here? Maybe I'll just put my own hand between my legs, do you think I should do that? Start rubbing my middle finger against my clitoris? Yes, that's what I'll do, I think that's just what I'll do. Just touch myself and think of you and think of your cock in my mouth. Close my eyes and see that cock in my mouth, feel it in my cunt, hear you say all those things to me, oh God I wish it was your mouth down here between my legs, wish it was your tongue licking me, licking me, licking me, this can't be me talking. I would never say to you that thinking of you makes my breasts swell and grow and ache with desire, that thinking of you fucking me makes my cunt drool a river. I love the way you caress my breasts, it makes them feel red hot with desire. My wet cunt is more than ready for you, come to me, come slip your cock inside me. Fuck me real slow at first—it's so sexy to feel a cock almost pull all the way out, and then go in again as deep as it can—faster and faster, fuck me, come fuck me, I love it, I love it, oh Jesus I'm coming and you're not even here.

What an evil man you are to make me do such things.

Stop by and I'll give you a new toy.

Bye!

The same typewriter had been used on this letter as on the letters they'd found in Arthur Schumacher's safe-deposit box; the typeface was unmistakably identical. Like the seventeen other letters, this one began with first the typewritten day of the week . . .

Friday.

Then the month . . .

June.

And then the date in numerals.

30.

June thirtieth last year had fallen on a Friday. A call to the morning newspaper's morgue confirmed that it had been raining that day. In all of the letters, there was no year following the date. There was only Wednesday, June 28, and Friday, June 30, and Tuesday, July 4, and Saturday, July 15, and so on—eighteen letters in all, including the one Betsy had found at the bottom of an otherwise empty shoe box in a dusty garage in Vermont. All of the dates corresponded to last year's calendar; there was no doubt now as to when they'd been written.

But if anyone at all . . .

Well, all the indications . . .

But still . . .

If any of the master sleuths on the 87th Squad had taken the trouble to check a calendar against the dates on the letters they'd found, *when* they found them . . .

Well, the letters seemed absolutely related to . . .

Then they'd have realized at once that none of the dates on the letters in Schumacher's box corresponded to the days in this year's calendar.

Still, it was easy to see how . . .

No, damn it, they should have checked.

"We should have checked," Brown said.

"Nobody's perfect," Carella said.

Which was true.

Nonetheless, if Arthur Schumacher had not met Susan Brauer until January of this year, then she could not have written those letters dated in June and July of last year.

Which was elementary.

In which case, who *had* written them?

None of them were signed. Each began with the salutation "Hi!" and ended with the complementary close "Bye!" The contents were

similar and so was the style—if such it could be called. Whoever had
written any one of those letters had written all of them.

"What do you think she means here?" Brown asked.

"Where?" Carella said.

"Here. About the toy."

"I don't know."

Brown looked at him.

"What is it?" Carella said.

"I don't *know*. Something just seems to be ringing some kind of
bell."

"Are you talking about the toy?"

"I don't know if it's the toy."

"Then . . ."

"Just something," Brown said.

"Stop by and I'll give you a new toy," Carella said, prompting him.
Both men looked at each other. Both men shrugged.

"Some kind of sex toy?" Carella said.

"Could be, but . . ."

"Or maybe she meant a three-way."

"Uh-huh."

"A new *toy*, you know?"

"Uh-huh."

"Another *girl*. A three-way. Stop by and I'll give you a new toy."

"Uh-huh," Brown said. "But doesn't that ring some kind of bell
with you?"

"No. The toy, you mean?"

"The *new* toy. Didn't somebody . . . wasn't there something about
new toys?"

"No, I don't . . ."

"About getting a new toy . . ."

"No . . ."

". . . or buying a new toy . . . or . . . some kind of *shipment* of
toys . . ."

"Oh God the dog!" Carella said.

The place used to be called Wally's Soul, and it still served soul food,
but the owner had renamed it the Viva Mandela Deli shortly after the
South African leader's triumphant visit to the city. At seven o'clock
that Tuesday night, it was fairly crowded. Bent was eating country
fried steak with mashed potatoes and gravy, green beans cooked with

fatback and hot buttered biscuits. Wade was eating fried chicken with mashed rutabaga, fried okra, and hot buttered corn bread. They were not here primarily to eat, but every cop in this city knew you grabbed a bite whenever you could because you never knew when the shit might hit the fan.

They were here to talk to a sixteen-year-old white girl named Dolly Simms.

"No racial bullshit about old Dolly, huh?" Wade said.

"None a'tall. Jus' no *taste* is the problem," Bent said. "Shackin' up with two crackheads from D.C."

"*If* Smiley was talkin' the Book."

Smiley was a sour-faced stoolie they sometimes used; they were holding over his head a five-and-dime for armed robbery. The Book was the Bible. Bent was wondering out loud if Smiley'd been telling them the truth when he said Dolly Simms was living with the two black dudes from Washington. Dolly was a hooker.

"You think she *really* comes in here to eat?" Bent asked.

"You heard Smiley. Every night before she heads out."

"I mean, *I* can hardly eat this shit, and I'm black."

Both men laughed.

"Fried chicken's pretty good, though," Wade said.

Bent looked over at his partner's plate.

"Changed the name, shoulda changed the food, too," he said sourly.

"Shouldn'ta changed the name, either," Wade said. "Cost two-point-nine mill to throw the man a party, he tells us to rise up and kill Whitey."

"He didn't say that," Bent said.

"His wife did. Up there in Diamondback. Said all us black Americans should join their brothers in the bush when it comes time to fight the white man in South Africa. Now what kinda shit is *that*, Charlie?"

"We got ties to Africa," Bent said.

"Oh, yeah, must be *millions* of blacks in this city got brothers all *over* the South African bush."

"Well, there are ties," Bent said again.

"You identify with some African got flies in his eyes, drinkin' goat's milk and blood?"

"Well, no, but still . . . we're talkin' roots here."

"What roots? *My* roots are in South Carolina where my Mama and Daddy were born," Wade said, "and my Gran'daddy and

WIDOWS 735

Gran'ma before 'em. And you know where *their* roots were? You know where *their* Mama and Daddy came from? Ghana—what used to be called the Gold Coast. And *that* ain't nowhere *near* South Africa."

"Plenty of slaves came from South Africa, though," Bent said.

"No, plenty of slaves did *not* come from South Africa, nossir. The slave trade was with *West* Africa, go look it up, Charlie. Places like Dahomey and the Ivory Coast and Ghana and Nigeria, all of them around the Gulf of Guinea, *that's* where the slave trade was. Or sometimes the Congo or Gambia, don't you know *nothin'* about Africa?"

"I know where those places are," Bent said, offended.

"Mandela wakes up after twenty-seven years in jail," Wade said, gathering steam, "he comes here walkin' in his sleep an' talkin' like a man who don't know the whole world's already thrown *off* Communism. An' he tells us to join hands with our black brothers in South Africa, where none of our brothers come from in the first place, what kind of dumb niggers does he think he's talkin' to?"

"I think he done some good here," Bent said.

"I think he made things worse," Wade said flatly. "We got serious problems of our own here, and parades for foreigners ain't gonna solve 'em."

"So how come you eatin' fried chicken?" Bent asked. "You so fuckin' white, whyn't you have a slice of Wonder Bread with choles-terol-free margarine on it?"

"I'm black," Wade said, nodding, "you can bet your ass on that. But I ain't South African, and you can bet your ass on *that*, too. Here she comes now."

He was facing the entrance door. Bent turned to look over his shoulder. What they both saw was a teenaged girl who looked anorexic, standing some five feet six or seven inches tall and weighing maybe a hundred pounds. She was wearing fringed, purple suede boots with a black mini and a lavender silk blouse scooped low over tiny breasts and a narrow chest. Her frizzed hair was the color of the boots. She had hooker stamped on her forehead and junkie stamped all over her face. Both cops got up and swung toward the door. They weren't going to let this one get away.

"Miss Simms?" Wade said.

Moving in on her right and stepping slightly behind her so she wouldn't go right out the door again.

Bent was on her left. "Police officers," he said, and flashed the tin.

Didn't faze her a bit. Blinked at the shield, and then looked up into Bent's face and then turned to look at Wade. They figured she was stoned out of her mind. Little past seven o'clock, a long hard night ahead of her, and she was already completely out of it.

"Few questions we'd like to ask you," Wade said.

"What about?" she asked.

Pale eyes somewhat out of focus. Faint smile on her mouth. They wondered what she was on. Bent's eyes went automatically to her naked arms. He could not see any tracks on the pale white flesh. And her skirt was short enough to have revealed any hit marks on her thighs.

"Let's have a seat," he said.

"Sure," she said.

Nothing to hide here, all very open and casual, they figured she wasn't holding. This was merely a stoned-out hooker and two cops, all of them walking the same street but on opposite sides.

They sat at a table at the back of the place. There was a steady stream of traffic to the rest rooms. Wade and Bent figured people were going in there to snort a few lines, but they were after a killer here, they didn't give a damn about arresting any penny-ante noses. That was the trouble when a city started sliding south. You couldn't bother about the little things anymore. When people were getting killed, you couldn't go chasing kids spraying graffiti on walls. You couldn't ticket a truck driver for blowing his horn. You couldn't bust people who were jumping subway turnstiles. When you had murder and rape and armed robbery to worry about, the rest was merely civilization.

"Tell us all about Sonny and Dick," Wade said.

"I don't know them," Dolly said. "Can I get something to eat? I came in here to get something to eat."

"Sure. What would you like, Dolly?"

"Ice cream," she said. "Chocolate, please."

They ordered a dish of chocolate ice cream for her. At the last minute, she decided she wanted sprinkles on it. The waiter carried the dish of ice cream to the counter and put sprinkles on it. When he came back to the table, she picked up a spoon and began eating at once.

"Yum," she said.

"Sonny and Dick," Bent said. "Two men, both black."

"I like black men," she said, and winked at them and licked her lips.

"So we've been told."

"Yum," she said, and spooned up more ice cream.

"Where are they now?" Wade asked.

"Don't know them," she said.

"Sonny what?" Bent said.

"Nope. Sorry," she said. Eating. Licking her lips. Licking the spoon.

"Dick what?" Wade asked.

"Don't know him, either."

"Remember Thursday night?"

"Nope."

"Remember where you were Thursday night?"

"Sorry, nope. Where was I?"

"Around ten o'clock, a little later?"

"Sorry."

"Remember Sloane Street?"

"Nope."

"3341 Sloane?"

"This is very good," she said. "You should try some. Want a taste?" she asked Bent and held out the spoon to him.

"Third floor," Wade said. "You and Sonny and Dick, cooking dope over a candle in a red holder."

"I don't do dope," she said. "I'm clean."

"Remember the shooting?"

"I don't remember anything like that. Could I have some more ice cream?"

They ordered another dish of chocolate ice cream with sprinkles on it.

"You really should try some of this," she told them, "it's yummy."

"One of your pals was packing a nine-millimeter Uzi," Wade said.

"Gee, what's that?" she said.

"It's a big pistol with a twenty-bullet clip in it. He fired down the stairs at us, remember?"

"I don't even know where Sloane Street is," Dolly said, and shrugged.

"Dolly, listen carefully," Wade said. "Put down your spoon and listen."

"I can listen while I'm eating," she said.

"Put down the spoon, honey."

"I told you, I can . . ."

"Or I'll break your fucking arm," he said.

She put down the spoon.

"One of your pals killed somebody," he said.

She said nothing. Just kept watching him, a sullen, angry look on her face because he wouldn't let her eat her ice cream.

"Did you know that one of your pals killed somebody?"

"No, I didn't know that."

"We think it was Sonny, but it could have been Dick. Either way . . ."

"I don't know these people, so it don't mean a fuck to me," she said.

"He killed a cop's father," Wade said.

Dolly blinked.

He leaned in closer to her, giving her a good look at the knife scar that stretched tight and pink over his left eye. You dig black men, honey? Okay, how you feel about *this* one with his bad-ass scar?

"A *cop's* father," he repeated, coming down hard on the word.

She may have been stoned senseless not ten minutes ago, and maybe she was still flying, it was hard to tell. But now there was a faint flicker in those pale dead eyes. She was allowing the words to register, allowing the key words to penetrate, they were talking about a cop's father getting killed.

"You know what that means?" Bent asked. "Somebody killing a cop's father?"

"I don't know anybody named Sonny."

"It means every cop in this city's gonna be trackin' the man till they catch him. An' then he be lucky he makes it alive to jail."

"Don't matter shit to me," she said, "I don't know anybody named Sonny."

"That's good," Wade said, "because if you *do* know him . . ."

"I told you I don't."

". . . and it turns out you were *protecting* him . . ."

"Nor Diz neither."

"Diz?" Wade asked at once. "Is *that* his name? *Diz?*"

Dolly still didn't realize she'd tripped herself.

"Diz *what?*" Bent asked.

"If I don't know him, how would I know Diz what?"

"But you *do* know him, don't you, Dolly?"

"No, I . . ."

"You know *both* of them, don't you?"

And now they came at her from either side, hurling words at her, not waiting for answers, battering her with words, Wade on her right and Bent on her left, Dolly sitting between them with her spoon on the table and her chocolate ice cream melting fast.

"Sonny and Diz."

"Two black killers from D.C."

"What're their last names, Dolly?"

"Tell us their last names."

"Sonny what?"

"Diz what?"

"They killed a cop's father!"

"You want to go down with them?"

"You want to keep on protecting two strangers?"

"Two killers?"

"You want every cop in this city on your ass?"

"You won't be able to breathe."

"You'll go down with them, Dolly."

"A cop's father, Dolly!"

"You want that on your back for the rest of your life?"

"I . . ."

They both shut up.

Waiting.

She was staring down at the melting ice cream.

They kept waiting.

"I don't know anything about them," she said.

"Okay," Wade said, nodding.

"That's the only time I ever saw them, Thursday night."

"Uh-huh."

"I haven't seen them since. I don't know any . . ."

"Honey, you want big trouble, don't you?" Wade said.

"But I'm telling you the *truth!*"

"No, you're shitting us!" Bent said. "We know you're living with them . . ."

"I'm not!"

"Okay, have it your way," Bent said, and shoved back his chair. "Let's go, Randy."

"Expect heat, baby," Wade said, and got up. "Lots of heat. From every cop walkin' this city. Heat till you die. This is *cop* business you're messin' with, this is a cop's *father.*"

"Sleep tight," Bent said, and they started walking out.

"Hold it," she said.

They stopped, turned to her again.

"Could I have some more ice cream?" she said.

* * *

They were waiting for her when she got back to the shop that night. They were standing near a tankful of tropical fish. Water bubbling behind them. Fish gliding. They were talking about a James Bond movie where a tank of fish explodes or something. They were trying to remember the name of the movie.

They'd called first and spoken to Pauline Weed's assistant, a young girl who'd told them she was out getting something to eat, expected her back in half an hour or so. They'd driven directly downtown to Bide-A-Wee Pets on Jefferson, where they'd learned that the girl's name was Hannah Kemp, that she was sixteen years old and wanted to be a veterinarian when she grew up, and that she worked here after school every Tuesday and Friday, when the shop was open till eight o'clock. She was with a customer up front when Pauline walked in some five minutes later. She pointed to where the detectives were standing near the gliding tropical fish, and said something they couldn't hear. Pauline looked up the aisle at them in surprise, and then walked to where they stood trying to remember the name of that movie.

"Hey, hi," she said.

"Hello, Miss Weed," Carella said.

"Can I sell you some fish?" she asked, and smiled.

Blonde and beautiful and blue-eyed, the type the man favored. Smile a bit wavering, though.

"Miss Weed," Carella said, "when we called here earlier tonight, your assistant . . ."

"Hannah," she said. "Great girl."

"Yes, she told us you were out getting something to eat . . ."

"Uh-huh."

"And you'd be back in half an hour or so."

"And here I am," she said, and grinned.

"Miss Weed, have you ever been married?" Brown asked.

"No, I haven't," she said, looking surprised.

"I thought the middle name might be . . ."

"Oh. No, that was my mother's maiden name. It's where I got the name of the shop, actually. The Bide and the Wee. From my middle name and my last name."

"Byerly and Weed," Brown said.

"Yes. Bide-A-Wee."

"Miss Weed," Carella said, "when we called here, we asked to speak to you, and Hannah said . . ."

"Great girl," she said again.

But she looked nervous now.

"She said . . . these are her exact words . . . she said, 'Bye's out getting something to eat.' "

"Uh-huh."

"She called you Bye."

"Uh-huh."

"Do a lot of people call you that?"

"Fair amount, I guess."

"Short for Byerly, is that it?"

"Well, my first name's Pauline, that's not such great shakes, is it?"

"Do *you* call yourself Bye?"

"Yes."

"How do you *sign* yourself?"

"Pauline Byerly Weed."

"You sign all your . . . ?"

"I sign everything Pauline Byerly Weed, yes."

"How about personal correspondence?" Brown asked.

She turned to him.

"Yes," she said. "That, too. Everything."

"You call yourself Bye, but you sign yourself Pauline Byerly Weed."

"Yes."

"Miss Weed," Carella said, "do you own a typewriter?"

Her eyes flashed. Danger. Careful. That's what her eyes were saying.

"We can get a search warrant," Brown said.

"I own a typewriter," she said, "yes."

"Did you own this same typewriter in June of last year?"

"Yes."

"July of last year?"

"Yes."

"May we see it, please?"

"Why?"

"Because we think you wrote some letters to Arthur Schumacher," Brown said.

"I may very well have written . . ."

"Erotic letters," Carella said.

"Can we see that typewriter, please?" Brown said.

"I didn't kill him," she said.

* * *

"What it was," Dolly said, "they started out as tricks, you know? I was working Casper . . . you know Casper and the Fields, up there near the old cemetery? St. Augustus Cemetery? Where there used to be like this little stone building got knocked down? Just inside the gates? Well, a lot of girls line up there at night because cars come through to pick up the Expressway, the Casper Avenue entrance, you know where I mean? Anyway, that's where I met them, they came walkin' up the street, lookin' over the merchandise, there's lot of girls along that cemetery stretch, well, I guess I don't have to tell you. I'm tryin' explain I don't want to take a rap for a cop's old man got killed. I hardly *know* these guys, they started out as tricks."

"When was this?" Wade asked.

"Last Sunday night."

"Almost a week ago."

"Almost."

"What does that make it, Charlie?"

Bent took a little celluloid bank calendar from his notebook.

"The twenty-second," he said.

Five days after Carella's father got killed.

"So they came up to you . . ."

"Yeah, and they told me they kind of liked my looks," she said, and shrugged modestly, "and would I be interested in a three-way. So I told them I usually get more for a three-way, and they asked me how much, and I told them a hun' fifty and they said that sounded okay, and we went to this little hot-bed place the girls use, it's near that big hall on Casper, where they cater weddings and things? Right next door to it? So that's how it started," she said, and shrugged again.

"How'd you end up in an abandoned building on Sloane?"

"Well, it turns out these guys were loaded . . ."

There'd been twelve hundred dollars in Tony Carella's cash register.

". . . and they liked crack as much as I do. Well, I mean, who don't? I had my way, I'd *marry* crack. So we had a nice little arrangement, you know what I mean? I'd do whatever they wanted me to do, and they supplied me with crack."

A simple business arrangement. Basic barter. A usual arrangement at that. Sex for dope. And because everyone was stoned or about to *get* stoned, it was rarely if ever safe sex. When crack's on the scene, nobody's worrying about a rubber. Which is why you had a lot of crack addicts getting pregnant. Which is why you had a lot of tormented crack babies crying for cocaine. What goes around comes around.

"I don't know where they got all that money . . ." she said.

Killed a man for it, Wade thought.

". . . but listen, who cares?"

Twelve hundred dollars, he thought.

"I do you, you do me, one hand washes the other, am I right? No questions asked, just beam me up, Scottie."

Just beam you up, he thought.

"How'd you end up on Sloane Street?" he asked.

"I think they were on the run."

"What do you mean?"

"I think they done a job that night. They called me up, told me they didn't want to come home. They were afraid . . ."

"Which is where?"

"So we like went to this crack house, you know, but the guy on the door looks at us through the peephole, he says 'How the fuck *I* know who you are?' Like we're *cops*, right?" she said sarcastically. "I been hookin' since I was thirteen, I suddenly look like I'm undercover, right? Sonny and Diz, too, you ain't gonna mistake either one of them for nothing but an ex-con. So the guy at the door gives us all this bullshit and we're forced to score on the street. Which is no big deal, I mean I do it all the time, you can buy crack on any street corner, look who I'm tellin'. But it would've been easier we could've smoked there in private without having to find a place to go. 'Cause we couldn't go back to the pad, you know. 'Cause Sonny and Diz thought the cops would come lookin' for them there."

"And where's that?" Bent asked.

"So that's how we ended up on Sloane, in that building, Jesus, what a place! Rats the size of alligators, I swear to God. So that was you guys, huh?"

"Yeah, that was us," Wade said.

"Scared the shit out of us," Dolly said, and giggled the way she had that night. "We went down the fire escape."

"We figured."

"I almost broke my neck."

"Where're Sonny and Diz now?"

"I already told you everything I know about them."

"Except where they are."

"I don't know where they are."

"You said you were living together . . ."

"But not no more."

"You said you had a pad . . ."

"Yeah, that was then."

"Dolly . . ." Wade said warningly.

"I mean it," she said. "I don't know."

"Okay," he said, "let's go up the station house, okay?"

"No, wait a minute," she said. "Please."

The Q&A took place in Lieutenant Byrnes's office at twenty minutes to ten that night. That was how long it took everyone to assemble. Nellie Brand had to come all the way uptown from her apartment on Everetts. The police stenographer with his video camera had to come all the way uptown, too, from the Headquarters Building on High Street. Pauline Weed's attorney, a man named Henry Kahn, had to come all the way crosstown from his office on Stockton. Brown, Carella, and Byrnes were the only ones who'd just had to walk down the hall from the squadroom to the Interrogation Room.

Nellie was here to find out if this was real meat. It had sounded that way when they'd filled her in on the initial interrogation, but you never knew. She was wearing a lightweight beige suit with a straw-colored handbag and pumps. She still wore her tawny hair in a wedge that gave an impression of speed, someone on the move, windswept, almost airborne. She knew that as assistant D.A. she'd be asking most of the questions unless she needed Carella or Brown to fill in something specific. She wasn't expecting any problems; Pauline's lawyer looked like a dip—but, again, you never knew. Tall and thin and wearing a wrinkled brown suit that matched his watery eyes, he sat alongside Pauline at the far end of the long table, whispering something Nellie couldn't hear. The stack of steamy letters were on the table in front of her. She had read them when she'd got here. *Some* letters. From a woman who looked as if butter wouldn't melt.

Carella started to read Pauline her rights again, but Kahn interrupted with a curt, "We've been through all that already, Detective," to which Carella replied, "Just for the record, Counselor," each of them using the respective titles in a way that made them sound derogative and somewhat dishonorable. Kahn gave his permission with an impatient patting of his hand on the air, and Pauline listened and affirmed that she knew her rights and that she was willing to answer the questions about to be put to her.

Carella looked up at the clock, and—for the videotape and the stenographer—announced that it was now nine-fifty P.M. Nellie began her questioning:

Q: Can you tell me your name, please?
A: Pauline Weed.
Q: Is that your full name?
A: Yes.
Q: What I'm asking you, Miss Weed . . .
A: (from Mr. Kahn) She's answered the question.
Q: I don't believe she has. I'm asking if that's the name on her birth certificate.
A: (from Mr. Kahn) All right, go ahead then.
Q: Is that the name on your birth certificate? Pauline Weed?
A: No.
Q: What *is* the name on your birth certificate?
A: Pauline Byerly Weed.
Q: Then *that's* your full name?
A: Yes.
Q: Thank you. Where does the Byerly come from?
A: It was my mother's maiden . . .
A: (from Mr. Kahn) Excuse me, but what's any of this got to do with . . . ?
Q: I think you'll see where I'm going, Mr. Kahn.
A: Well, I wish I knew where you were going *now*. You drag my client down here in the middle of the night . . .
Q: Excuse me, Mr. Kahn. If your client doesn't want to answer my questions, all she has to do is . . .
A: Oh, please, spare me First-Year Law, will you please?
Q: Just tell me what you want to do, Mr. Kahn. Do you want the questions stopped? That's your prerogative, your client said she understood her rights. Does she wish me to stop? If not, please let me ask my questions, okay?
A: Go ahead, go ahead, it's always the same old story.
Q: Miss Weed, are you ever known by the nickname Bye?
A: Sometimes.
Q: Wouldn't you say it's more than just sometimes?
A: Occasionally. I would say occasionally.

Q: Well, do you *answer* to that name? Bye?

A: Yes.

Q: If I called you Bye, you'd answer to it, wouldn't you?

A: Yes.

Q. What does that stand for? Bye?

A: Byerly.

Q: Which, of course, is your middle name.

A: Yes.

Q: So it's really a common thing, isn't it? Your being called Bye, your answering to the name Bye.

A: I sometimes use the name Bye. But I'm also called Pauline. And Byerly, too, sometimes.

Q: Do you ever sign your letters with that name?

A: Byerly, do you mean?

Q: No, I mean *Bye*. Do you ever sign your letters with the name Bye?

A: Sometimes.

Q: Miss Weed, I show you copies of letters . . .

A: (from Mr. Kahn) May I see those, please?

Q: They're copies of letters Detectives Brown and Carella recovered from Arthur Schumacher's safe-deposit box. We don't want the originals handled any more than they've already been.

A: Let me see them, please.

Q: Sure. Don't burn your fingers

(Questioning resumed at 10:05 P.M.)

Q: Miss Weed, did you write these letters?

A: No.

Q: You did not sign the name Bye to these letters?

A: *Nobody* signed a name to those letters.

Q: Yes, excuse me, you're absolutely right. Did you *type* the name Bye to these letters?

A: No, I didn't. I didn't write those letters.

Q: We have a typewriter the detectives recovered at your shop . . .

A: (from Mr. Kahn) What typewriter? I don't see any typewriter.

Q: It's on the way to the lab, Mr. Kahn. It was recovered at Bide-A-Wee Pets at 602 Jefferson Avenue and is now being examined as possible evidence . . .

A: Evidence? Of *what*?

Q: Evidence in the crime of murder.

A: I don't see the connection, Ms. Brand, I'm sorry. Even if Miss Weed *did* write those letters . . . and I certainly hope you have proof of that since the letters in themselves would appear damaging to her reputation . . .

Q: That's why the typewriter's at the lab, Mr. Kahn. But if you'll excuse me, we're not trying a case here, we're simply trying to question a suspect, aren't we? So may I be permitted to do that? Or, as I suggested earlier, do you want me to stop the questioning right now?

A: (from Miss Weed) I have nothing to hide.

Q: Mr. Kahn? May I take that as permission to continue?

A: Sure, go ahead, it's always the same old story.

Q: Miss Weed, when did you first meet Arthur Schumacher?

A: January a year ago.

Q: That would've been . . . what's this?

A: (from Mr. Carella) July thirty-first.

Q: So that would've been . . . what does that come to? Eighteen, nineteen months?

A: (from Mr. Carella) Eighteen.

Q: Is that right, Miss Weed?

A: A bit more.

Q: How did you happen to meet him?

A: His wife bought a dog from me. For a Christmas present. He came in a month later to ask about a collar.

Q: And that was the start of your relationship.

A: I didn't have a *relationship* with him. He was a *customer*.

Q: Nothing more than that.

A: Nothing.

Q: Then how do you explain these letters?

A: I didn't write those letters.

Q: You do know, do you not, that under the Miranda guidelines . . .

A: (from Mr. Kahn) Here comes First-Year Law again!

Q: We are permitted to take your fingerprints, for example . . .

A: (from Mr. Kahn) I would strenuously object to that.

Q: Yes, but it wouldn't change the law. Are you aware of that, Miss Weed?

A: If you say that's the law . . .

Q: I say so.

A: Then I guess it's the law.

Q: Are you also aware that whereas a great many people have already handled the originals of these letters . . .

A: I didn't write those letters.

Q: *Whoever* wrote them, the writer's fingerprints may still be on the originals, are you aware of that?

A: I don't know anything about those letters. I don't know whose fingerprints are on those letters.

Q: Have you ever *seen* the originals of these letters?

A: No.

Q: You're sure about that.

A: (Silence)

Q: Miss Weed?

A: Yes. I'm sure I never saw them.

Q: Then your fingerprints couldn't *possibly* be on them, isn't that so?

A: They couldn't.

Q: What if they *are?* What if we find fingerprints on the letters and they match yours? How would you explain that, Miss Weed?

A: (Silence)

Q: Miss Weed?

A: (Silence)

Q: Miss Weed? Would you please answer my question?

A: (Silence)

Q: Lieutenant, I'd like this prisoner's fingerprints taken, please.

A: (from Mr. Kahn) Hey now, wait just a minute. There's nothing in Miranda that says you can . . .

Q: Can someone please get him a copy of the guidelines?

A: (from Mr. Kahn) Now wait just a minute!

A: (from Lt. Byrnes) Somebody go down to the desk, see if there's a copy of the Miranda book behind it. Miss, you want to come along now? Steve, take her prints for me, will you?

A: (from Mr. Carella) Let's go, Miss.

Q: (from Ms. Brand) Miss Weed?

A: (Silence)

Q: Miss Weed?

A: I loved him so much.

I didn't know he'd found someone else. I thought he'd just lost interest. That happens, you know. People fall out of love. And I was willing to accept that. If a person doesn't love you anymore, then he just doesn't. It had been a year—well a little less than a year, actually. He came into the shop that first time on the twenty-third, that was our anniversary, the twenty-third of January. So we'd had a good run. Nowadays, a year is a long time, believe me. I have girl-friends, if a man stays with them for six months they consider themselves lucky. This was almost a year. The day he told me he wanted to end it was the fifteenth of January. I'm good on dates. That was almost a year. So . . .

You know.

I . . .

I said okay.

I mean, what can you do? If a man doesn't love you anymore, you just have to let him go, don't you?

I kept remembering the things we did together.

The letters were fun, but that only lasted a little while, it was a hot summer.

Every now and then I'd get this other girl for him. Well, for us. I used to go to college with her. Marian. A blonde, like me . . . well, he liked blondes. But that was when I was still sure of him. I mean, it was the *three* of us, sure, but it was still really just the *two* of us, do you know what I mean? It was him and me calling the tune. Marian was just there to please us.

We had good times together.

But when something's over, it's over, am I right? I mean, I'm not a child, I know when to call it a day. And even though I was lonely . . .

I was very lonely.

I loved him so much.

Still I . . . I figured I could live with it. I had the shop, I love animals, you know. I kept myself busy. And I guess I would have been able to manage if I hadn't . . .

It was one of those things where I thought I was looking at myself in a mirror, a younger version of myself, walking up the street toward me, hanging on Arthur's arm, head thrown back in a laugh, long blonde hair and blue eyes, it was me and Arthur all over again. Only it wasn't me. It was another woman, a girl really, she couldn't have been older than twenty, reaching up to kiss him on the cheek, I turned away before he could see me. Turned my back. Started to cross the street against traffic. Horns blowing, it was terrible. When I turned back again, they were gone. Lost in the crowd. Lost.

I thought Well well.

I thought The son of a bitch already has somebody new.

It's only a month . . .

This was February the twelfth, I'm very good on dates . . .

It was only a month and already he had himself a new woman, a new *girl*, really, she looked so young. And then I wondered if . . .

I mean, was it possible he could have found someone else so *fast*? I mean, only a month after we'd said goodbye? Wasn't that awfully fast? And then it occurred to me that he'd maybe had her all along, maybe he'd had her *before* he called it quits with me. And that bothered me. It really did. I guess I should have said the hell with it, but it really bothered me. You know how some things can just *eat* at you? Well, that's what this did to me. It just *ate* at my insides.

I mean, all the things we did together.

Jesus.

So I . . .

I guess I began following him. Because I wanted to find out how long this had been going on, you see. I mean, had he been making a fool of me all along? Did he have this girl on the side while I was writing all those letters to him, and getting other women for him . . . well, just Marian, but we did it a lot with her, we must have done it a dozen times with her at least. Had he been making a goddamn fool of me all along?

She lived in this fancy apartment building on Silvermine Oval . . . well, you know where she lived. He would go to see her maybe two, three times a week. I followed him up there. One day I asked one of the doormen, not the Saudi, whatever he is, the little one who can't speak English, this was another doorman. I told him I was sure I knew the girl who'd just gone in, a girl named Helen King, I was sure I used to work with her, and he said no, that wasn't her name, and I said I'm sure that was her, can you tell me her name, please, and he gave me that look doormen always give you, as if you're going to go in and kill somebody in their precious fucking building, and he said, No, I can't give out names, so you see it wasn't so easy getting her name.

I began following her around, too. Not just when he was with her, Arthur, but when she was alone. Trying to find out her name, you know. It's not easy to find out somebody's name in this city, everybody's so suspicious. I finally got it at the supermarket. From following her around I knew she got all her groceries from the Food Emporium up on The Stem, filled out this little slip to have the stuff delivered. So I just made sure I got in line at the checkout behind her, and I watched while she wrote down her name and the address on the order pad, Susan Brauer, 301 Silvermine Oval, PH, bingo.

Not that I was planning to do anything. I just wanted to know about her.

Because it kept eating at me that maybe he'd been seeing her at the same time he was telling me how much he loved me.

And then one day, I saw the other man.

Saw her and this other man together.

This was right after Easter, the eighteenth of April, it was raining. It was the daytime. Raining hard. They came out of the building together, he'd obviously been up there with her. He had white hair, I thought he was an old man at first. I couldn't understand what she saw in him. After Arthur? This skinny little bullfighter?

They went to lunch together in an Italian restaurant on Culver. Then they went back to the apartment. They were up there all afternoon. Arthur went there later that night. She was seeing *both* of them, I couldn't believe it! Mott, his name was. Thomas Mott. I followed him to an antiques shop he owns on Drittel. I went in the shop one day, just to see him up close. He was younger than I'd thought, in his fifties, I guessed. Dark brown eyes in a very pale face. I told him I was interested in a Tiffany lamp. He seemed pleasant.

But you see, she'd made her one big mistake.

This was how I could get Arthur back. By telling him she was cheating on him. I mean, in all the time I knew Arthur—it was almost a year, don't forget—I never once cheated on him. Never. But here was someone he'd known since . . . well, I really didn't *know* how long because it could have been going on forever, for all I knew . . . but it had to have been since January at least, and here it was only April, and she was already cheating on him. So I thought I'd go talk to her. Tell her I was going to blow the whistle unless she quit seeing Arthur. Reason with her. She had one man, why did she need two? Talk to her. Reason with her. The day I went there . . .

The weather on Tuesday, the seventeenth of July, is swelteringly hot, the three horsemen of haze, heat, and humidity riding roughshod over a city already trampled into submission. She is going there only to talk to her. She has called first to say she is holding some lingerie here for delivery, would it be all right if one of the girls stopped by with it later this afternoon? He *had* to have gifted her with sexy lingerie in the past, no? The whole garter-belt-and-panties routine? The bra with the cutout nipple holes? Oh sure.

Little Suzie says, "Oh, yes, please, just leave it with the doorman, please."

Little Minnie Mouse voice. First time she's ever heard the voice.

"The gentleman asked us to make sure you got it personally," she says into the phone. "The gentleman insisted that you sign for delivery."

"What gentleman?" Little Suzie asks in her little Minnie Mouse voice. "May I have his name, please?"

"Arthur Schumacher," she says.

"Oh well then all right," Suzie says in the same rushed, breathless voice, "can you send it by at the end of the day?"

"What time would be most convenient for you, Miss?"

"I just *said* the end of the *day*, didn't I? The end of the day is five o'*clock!*"

Q: How'd you feel about that? The way she answered you?

A: I thought what a little bitch she was.

Q: Yes, but did her response have anything to do with what happened later? The impatience of her response?

A: No, I just thought what a bitch she was, but I was still planning to go up there only to talk to her.

Q: All right, what happened next?

A: There was a doorman to contend with, but I knew there'd be a doorman. I was wearing . . .

She is wearing a beige silk scarf to hide her blonde hair, dark glasses to hide the color of her eyes, dressed entirely in the same indeterminate beige, a color—or *lack* of color—she hates and rarely wears. She is wearing it today only because it matches the color of the store's shopping bag. She wants to pass for someone delivering from the store. Beige polyester slacks and a beige cotton blouse, gold leather belt, the temperature hovering in the high eighties, approaching the doorman in his gray uniform with its red trim, carrying in her right hand the big beige shopping bag with its gold lettering. She has spoken to this doorman before, he is the short, fat one with the accent. She tells him now . . .

Q: When was that?

A: I'm sorry?

Q: That you'd spoken to him?

A: Oh. When I was still trying to find out her name. But he can barely speak English, so I naturally gave up on him. He was the one on duty that day. I stated my business . . .

"Miss Brauer, please."

"You are who, please?"

Looking her up and down, she *hates* when they do that.

"Just tell her Victoria's Secret is here," she says.

"Moment," he says, and buzzes the apartment upstairs.

"Yes?"

Her voice on the intercom.

"Lady?" he says.

"Yes, Ahmad?"

"Vittoria Seegah here," he says.

"Yes, send it right up, please."

Bingo.

Still wanting only to talk to her.

But, of course, there is no talking to some people.

Little Suzie is annoyed that she's been tricked. Two black leather sofas in the living room, one on the long wall opposite the door that led into it, the other on the shorter window wall at the far end of the room. Glass-topped coffee table in front of the closest sofa, martini glass sitting on it, lemon twist floating, the little lady has been drinking. She stands before the sofa, all annoyed and utterly beautiful, all blonde and blue-eyed in a black silk kimono that has itself probably come from Victoria's Secret, patterned with red poppies, naked beneath it judging from the angry pucker of her nipples.

"You had no right coming here," she says.

"I only want to talk to you."

"I'm going to call him right this minute, tell him you're here."

"Go ahead, call him."

"I will," she says.

"It'll take him at least half an hour to get here. By then, we'll be finished."

"By then *you'll* be finished."

"I really would like to talk to you. Can't we please talk?"

"No."

"Please. Please, Susan."

Perhaps it is the note of entreaty in her voice. Whatever it is, it stops Little Suzie cold on her way to the phone and brings her back to the coffee table, where she picks up her martini glass and drains it. She goes back to the bar then, bare feet padding on the thick pile rug, and—charming hostess that she is—pours herself and only herself another drink. There is a whole lemon sitting on the bartop, so yellow.

There is a walnut-handled bottle opener. There is a paring knife with a matching walnut handle. Late-afternoon sunlight streams through the sheer white drapes behind the black leather sofa on the far wall. Little Suzie Doll walks back to the coffee table, stands posed and pretty beside it, barefoot and petulant, the kimono loosely belted at her waist. There is a hint of blonde pubic hair.

"What is it you want?" she asks.

"I want you to stop seeing him."

"No."

"Hear me out."

"No."

"Listen to me, Suzie . . ."

"Don't call me Suzie. No one calls me Suzie."

"Do you want me to tell him?"

"Tell him what?"

"I think you know what."

"No, I don't. And, anyway, I don't care. I'd like you to go now."

"You want me to tell him, right?"

"I want you to get out of here," Suzie says, and turns to put the martini glass on the table behind her, as if in dismissal—end of the party, sister, no more cocktails, even though I haven't yet offered you a drink.

"Okay, fine, I'll tell him what's been going on between you and . . ."

"So tell him," Suzie says, and turns again to face her, grinning now, hands on her hips, legs widespread, pubic patch blatantly defiant. "He won't believe you," she says, and the grin widens, mocking her.

Which is only the truth. He will not believe her, that is the plain truth. He will think this is something she's invented. A lie to break them apart. And facing the truth, feeling helpless in the cruel and bitter glare of the truth, she becomes suddenly furious. She does not know what she says in the very next instant, perhaps she says nothing at all, or perhaps she says something so softly that it isn't even heard. She knows only that the paring knife is suddenly in her hand.

Q: Did you stab and kill Susan Brauer?
A: Yes.
Q: How many times did you stab her?
A: I don't remember.
O: Do you know there were thirty-two stab and slash wounds?
A: Good.

Q: Miss Weed . . .

A: My clothes were covered with blood. I took a raincoat from her closet and put it on. So the doorman wouldn't see all that blood when I was going out.

Q: Miss Weed, did you also kill Arthur Schumacher?

A: Yes. I shouldn't have, it was a dumb move. I wasn't thinking properly.

O: How do you mean?

A: Well, she was gone, you see. I had him all to myself again.

Q: I see.

A: But, of course, I didn't, did I?

Q: Didn't what, Miss Weed?

A: Didn't have him all to myself again. Not really. Because he was the one who'd ended it, you see, not me. And if he'd found somebody else so quickly, well, he'd just find somebody again, it was as simple as that, wasn't it? He was finished with me, he'd never come back to me, it was as simple as that. He'd find himself another little cutie, maybe even younger this time—he'd once asked me to set up something with Hannah from the shop, can you believe it? She was fifteen at the time, he asked me to set up a three-way with her. So I . . . I guess I realized I'd lost him forever. And that was when I began getting angry all over again. About what he'd done. About leaving me like that and then starting up with her. About *using* me. I don't like to be used. It infuriates me to be used. So I . . . he'd given me this gun as a gift. I went up there and waited outside . . .

Q: Up where, Miss Weed?

Nellie's voice almost hushed. Wanting to pin down the address for later, for when this thing came to trial. Getting all her ducks in a row in this day and age when even videotaped confessions sometimes didn't mean a thing to a jury.

A: His apartment. On Selby Place.

Q: When was this, can you remember?

A: Yes, it was the twentieth. A Friday night.

Q: And you say you went there and waited outside his building . . .

A: Yes, and shot him.

Q: How many times did you shoot him? Do you remember?

A: Four.

Q: Did you also shoot the dog?

A: Yes. I was sorry about that. But the dog was a gift from her, you see.

Q: From . . . ?

A: Margaret. His wife. I knew all about Margaret, of course, Margaret was no secret, we talked about Margaret all the time.

Q: Did you kill her, too?

A: Yes.

Q: Why?

A: All of them.

Q: I'm sorry, what . . . ?

A: Any woman he'd ever had anything to do with.

Q: Are you saying . . . ?

A: All of them, yes. Did you see his will? The *insult* of it!

Q: No, I haven't seen it. Tell me what . . .

A: Well, you should take a look at it. I was never so insulted in my life! Ten thousand dollars! Is that a slap in the face, or what is it? After all we meant to each other, after all we *did* together? He left the same amount to his fucking veterinarian! Jesus, that was *infuriating!* What did he leave the *other* ones, that was the question? How much did he leave his beloved Margaret, or his *first* wife, who by the way used to go with him to bars to pick up hookers, he told me they'd once had three of them in the apartment at the same time, three black hookers, this was when his precious daughters were away at camp one summer. Or how about *them?* The Goody-Two-Shoes dentist's wife and the stupid hippie he gave that house in Vermont to? How much did he leave *them* in his will? Oh, Jesus, I was furious! Did he take me for a fool? I'm no fool, you know. I showed him.

Q: How did you show him?

A: I went after all of them. I wanted to get all of them. To show him.

Q: When you say "all of them . . ."

A: All of them. Margaret and the first wife and the two darling daughters, *all* of them, what do you think all of them means? His *women!* His fucking *women!*

Q: Did you, in fact, kill Gloria Sanders?

A: Yes, I did. I said so, didn't I?

Q: No, not until this . . .

A: Well, I did. Yes. And I'm not sorry, either. Not for her, not for any of them. Unless . . . well, I suppose maybe . . .

Q: Yes?

A: No, never mind.

Q: Please tell me.

A: I guess I'm sorry about . . . about hurting . . .

Q: Yes?

A: Hurting Arthur.

Q: Why is that?

A: He was such a wonderful person.

A knock sounded on the door.

"Busy in here!" Byrnes shouted.

"Excuse me, sir, but . . ."

"I said we're *busy* in here!"

The door opened cautiously. Miscolo from the Clerical Office poked his head into the room.

"I'm sorry, sir," he said, "but this is urgent."

"What is it?" Byrnes snapped.

"It's for you, Steve," Miscolo said. "Detective Wade from the Four-Five."

12

THE CARS nosed through the night like surfaced submarines, two big sedans with five detectives in each of them. The detectives were all wearing bulletproof vests. Carella was riding in the lead car, with Wade and Bent and two cops they'd introduced as Tonto and the Lone Ranger. Tonto didn't look the slightest bit Indian. Carella had suited up with the others at the Four-Five, and was sitting on the backseat between Wade and Bent. They were all big men. Wearing the vests made them even bigger. The car felt crowded.

"The one done the shooting is named Sonny Cole," Wade said. "He's packing a nine-millimeter for sure, and from the way the girl described it, it's the Uzi we're looking for."

"Okay," Carella said, and nodded. Sonny Cole, he thought. Who killed my father.

"The other one's named Diz Whittaker. I think his square handle is Desmond, we're running computer checks on both of them right this minute. From what she told us, Diz is the brains of the operation."

"Some brains," Bent said sourly.

"Anyway, he's the one planned the holdup in your father's shop and also another one last Thursday night, when we almost got them."

"A liquor store," Bent said. "This is how they keep themselves in dope, they do these shitty little holdups."

Wade looked at him sharply.

Carella was thinking A shitty little holdup. My father got killed for twelve hundred dollars. He was thinking he was going to enjoy meeting these two punks. He was going to enjoy it a lot.

"Girl's been living with them a coupla weeks now, they picked her up on Cemetery Row one night, she's a hooker," Wade said.

"A junkie, too," Bent said.

"An all-around straight arrow," Wade said.

"The house is on Talley Road, in the Four-Six, mostly black and Hispanic, they're renting a room on the second floor. Two-family house, wide open, bulldozed lots on either side of it, getting ready for another project."

"Means they can see us coming a mile away."

"Yeah, well, that's life," Bent said.

The house was a two-story clapboard building with an asphalt shingle roof. Empty sandlots on either side of it, looked like somebody had built it in the middle of a desert. New low-cost housing project just up the street, not a block away, looking as though it had already been taken over by a marauding army, graffiti all over the brick walls, benches torn up, windows broken.

There were eight detectives waiting across the street under the trees, all of them from the Four-Six, all of them wearing bulletproof vests. This was a big one; a cop's father had been shot. A slender moon hung over the trees, casting a silvery glow on the scraggly lawn in front of the house. Night insects were singing. It was almost midnight. There was not a police vehicle in sight yet. They were all up the street in the project's parking lot, out of sight and just a radio call away; nobody wanted to spook the perps. The two cars from the Four-Five dropped eight of the ten detectives into the silent dark and moved off into the night. Under the trees, the sixteen detectives huddled, whispering like summer insects, planning their strategy.

"I want the door," Carella said.

"No," Wade said.

"He was *my* . . ."

"The door's mine."

None of the other cops argued with him. What they were discussing here was something called taking the door, and that meant they were discussing sudden death. Taking the door was the most dangerous thirty seconds in any policeman's life. Whoever was the point of the attacking wedge could be next in line for a halo and a harp because you never knew what was inside any apartment, and with today's weaponry bullets could come flying through even a metal-clad door. In this case, they *knew* what was inside that house across the street. What was in there was a killer with a nine-millimeter semiautomatic weapon. Nobody in his right mind wanted to take that door. Except Carella. And Wade.

"We'll take it together," Carella said.

"Can't but one man kick in a door," Wade said, and grinned in the moonlight. "It's mine, Carella. Be nice."

The hands on Carella's watch were standing straight up. Tonto put in a call to the patrol sergeant waiting in his car in the project's parking lot. There were six other cars with him. He told the sergeant they were going in. The sergeant said, "Ten-four."

The detectives all looked at each other.

Wade nodded and they started across the street.

The eight detectives from the Four-Six and four of the detectives from the Four-Five split into teams of six each and headed around to cover the sides and back of the house. Carella and Wade started up the walkway with the Lone Ranger and Tonto close behind them.

There was a low, virtually flat flight of steps leading up to a railed porch on the front of the house. This looked like a house on the prairie someplace. You expected to see tumbleweeds rolling by. Dolly had told them they were renting a room on the second floor front, right-hand side of the house. But there were no lights showing anywhere. Four black windows on the upper level, two black windows to the left of the blue entrance door. The walkway was dark, too, except for pale moonlight; someone had knocked out the street lamp. The walkway was covered with gravel.

They'd have preferred sand or snow or even mud; the goddamn gravel went off like firecrackers under their feet. They moved up the walk two abreast, swiftly, silently except for the crunching of the gravel, wincing at each rattle of stone, heading in a straight line for that blue front door. Wade and Carella had just gained the porch steps when the shots came.

They went flying off the steps like startled bats, throwing themselves into the low bushes on either side, one to the left, one to the right, three more shots on the night, the Lone Ranger and Tonto hurling themselves off the path and rolling away onto the patchy lawn, bracing themselves for whatever might come next.

The next shot came almost at once, but this time they saw where it was coming from, a yellow flash in one of the pitch-black windows on the left-hand side of the porch, followed by the immediate roar of a high-powered pistol slamming slugs into the night, and then yellow and *bam,* and yellow and *bam,* and four and five—and silence again.

Either Dolly had been wrong about which room she and her pals were renting, or Sonny and Diz had moved downstairs to another room.

That's what they were thinking.

It never crossed their minds that Dolly might have—

"Don't shoot!" she yelled. "They got me in here!"

"Shit," Wade said.

Three minutes into the job and they already had a hostage situation.

The people from the nearby project all came out to watch the Late Night Show. This was either *Die Hard* or *Die Harder* on a summer's night at the very top of August. Except that this wasn't a high rise in L.A. or an airport in D.C. What this was here was a shitty little house scheduled for the bulldozer to make room for another project exactly like the one these people lived in. And there weren't thousands of trapped airport people involved here or even hundreds of trapped skyscraper people, there were only two punks from the nation's capital—which had the highest per capita murder rate in the entire world—and a sixteen-year-old hostage who happened to be both a Cemetery Row hooker and a certified crackhead. Whose life was at stake. Carella knew that. Dolly Simms hadn't killed his father. Sonny Cole and Diz Whittaker, acting in concert, had done that. But because Dolly was in there now with the two killers—how the hell had she managed to get herself in there, damn it!—the police couldn't just go in and bust up the place.

It was amazing how the crowd grew. This might turn out to be merely *Little House on the Prairie,* but who could tell? Meanwhile, it was better being out here on the street, where there was at least the semblance of a breeze, than inside a sweltering brick tower eighteen stories high. By one o'clock that morning of the first day of August, the house was surrounded on all four sides and police barricades had been thrown up in a haphazard rectangle in a vain attempt to keep some order among the spectators. Both Emergency Service trucks were on the scene, and there were some three dozen blue-and-white patrol cars arranged like war chariots around the besieged building, with uniformed cops and detectives behind each car. A generator had been set up and spotlights illuminated all four sides of the house, but particularly the front of it, where Inspector Brady's fourth hostage negotiator crouched low behind the bushes lining the porch and tried to talk to either of the two men inside the room. Brady had used up three negotiators so far. The first two had almost had their heads blown off. None of them had dared venture onto the porch.

Dolly Simms sat in one of the windows, staring straight out at the glaring lights.

She was all you could see.

The two men were deep inside the room, far from the window.

Getting them to the window would be the first job.

It was Dolly who kept telling the negotiators that nobody better start shooting. She didn't look scared at all. One of the negotiators reported that she seemed stoned—which was not a surprise.

The Preacher was in the streets already, doing what he did best, doing in fact the only thing he knew how to do, which was to agitate people into a frenzy. Pacing behind the barricades, long hair slicked back, gold chains gleaming in the reflected light of the spots, bullhorn in hand, he kept telling the crowd that whenever a *white* girl yelled rape, then the nearest African-American males were always accused of it . . .

"But take a pure innocent young virgin like Tawana Brawley, who gets raped by a screaming mob of white men who then scrawl the word *nigger* . . ."

Yuh, yuh, from the handful of men in dark suits and red ties standing behind him.

". . . on her body, scrawl this word in *excrement* on her young violated body, and of course the white system of justice finds these rapists and bigots innocent of any crime and labels young Tawana a liar and a whore!"

The police could hardly hear themselves talking over the blare of the bullhorn.

"Well, brothers and sisters, what we've got in there tonight is a *true* whore, a bona fide and verified one-hundred-percent white purveyor of flesh who has enticed two young African-American brothers into a situation not of their own making! And that is why we have the whole mighty police force of this great city out here tonight, that is why we have this circus out here tonight, it is to once again persecute and pillory the youth of male black America!"

Young kids bobbed in and out of television-camera range, angling for a shot, big grins on their faces, this was the big chance to be on tee-vee, wow, see myself on the news tomorrow morning. The Preacher had been right in that respect, there *was* a circus atmosphere out here tonight, but not because anyone wanted to see a pair

of killers safely apprehended. Instead, the air was charged with an
excitement akin to what might have been felt in the Roman arena
where nobody had a chance but the lions. Nobody in these mean
streets believed that anybody in that building was coming out of
there alive, not with the cops lined up out here like an army. Black or
white, whoever was in there was already dead meat, that's what all
these people in the streets were thinking, whatever their color or religion, whatever their stripe or persuasion. The only pertinent question was *when* it was going to happen. And so, like Roman spectators
waiting for a lion or a tiger to bite off someone's arm or preferably
his head, the crowd milled about patiently behind the sawhorses,
hoping to be in on the moment of the kill, hoping to see all those
fake die hard/die harder fireworks erupting here in real life on their
tired tawdry turf. Hardly anybody was listening to The Preacher
ranting and raving except the guys in the suits and red ties who stood
behind him yuh-yuhing his every word. Everyone's eyes were on the
woman crouched in the bushes, talking to the girl with the purple
hair who sat in the window with the glare of the spotlights on her.

The problem here was that nobody could establish contact with
the takers. There was no telephone in the room, and so the police
couldn't ask the phone company to seize the line and give them control of it, which would have allowed them—and them alone—to talk
with either Sonny or Diz or whoever was calling the tune in there.
The further problem was that this was what the hostage team called a
two-and-one, which meant there were two takers and only one
hostage, which was a hell of a lot better than a four-and-twelve, but
which still meant you were dealing with group dynamics, however
small the group. Nobody knew who was in charge inside that house.
Dolly had told Wade and Bent that Diz was the brains of the outfit, a
supposition belied by his nickname, which they guessed was short for
Dizzy. But since neither of the two were willing to talk to anyone, the
negotiators had no idea who was running the show. A gun—or perhaps several guns—had so far done all the talking, with shots ringing
out from somewhere deep in the room whenever a negotiator so
much as lifted his head above the porch's floorboards. Four negotiators thus far. None of them making so much as a dent.

The Tac Team observers with their night-vision binocs couldn't see
far enough into the room to determine whether there was just that
single nine-millimeter gun in there or other weaponry as well. There
were five observers in all, one each on the back and both sides of the

building, two at the front, where all the action was. The observers had reported that all the windows on the sides of the house were boarded over: Sonny and Diz had been expecting company.

This was the first bit of important news Georgia Mobry got out of Dolly sitting there in the window.

Georgia was Brady's top female negotiator, back from her vacation only yesterday, and right in the thick of it now. She was the fourth one working the window, or working the porch perhaps, or more accurately working the bushes, because that's where she was crouched some six feet from the window in which Dolly sat all pale and purple in the lights. They'd all been wondering how Dolly had allowed herself to get into a situation like this one. She had told the detectives where they could find Sonny and Diz and so it would have seemed only sensible for her to stay as far away from there as possible.

But she now revealed to Georgia—who was truly expert at milking cream even from a toad—that she'd begun feeling guilty right after the two black cops left her, and so she'd come back here and told Sonny and Diz what was about to come down, and instead of getting out of there, they gave her some crack to smoke and told her she was their ticket to Jamaica. That was the *second* bit of important information.

"So please don't do any shooting," she said, "because they'll kill me, they told me they'd kill me."

Which is what she'd said many times before to the other three negotiators who'd been pulled out of the ball game. But now Georgia knew that Dolly herself had caused her present predicament, and the price of her release was a ticket to the Caribbean.

"Do they want to go to Jamaica?" she asked, checking it. "Is that it, honey?"

Accent as gentle and as thick as her name and her native state.

"Well, I'm only telling you what they said."

"That you were their ticket to Jamaica?"

"Yeah."

"Gee, I wish I could talk to them personally," Georgia said.

"Yeah, but they don't wanna."

" 'Cause I'm thinking maybe we can work something out here."

Like getting you out of there and then blowing these suckers away, Georgia was thinking. To her mind—and she'd been trained by Brady—what they were looking at here was a nonnegotiable hostage situation. Sooner or later, somebody was going to order an assault. The computer make on Sonny Cole had come in not ten minutes ago, and it revealed that he'd done some time on the West Coast for killing a man during the commission of a grocery-store holdup in Pasadena. So what they had here was not only a man who'd *maybe* killed a cop's father, but a man who'd been convicted once of having taken a life and who was now armed with a weapon and firing indiscriminately through an open window whenever the spirit moved him.

Desmond Whittaker was no sweetheart, either. In Louisiana, he'd done five years at hard labor for the crime of manslaughter, which would have been murder under subdivision (1) of Article 30 in the state's Criminal Code, except that it was committed "in sudden passion or heat of blood." How the pair had come together in D.C. was a mystery. So was how they'd ended up here in this city. But they were both extremely dangerous, and if they showed no signs soon of willingness to enter even the earliest stages of negotiation, then somebody was going to ask for a green light for either a direct assault or the use of chemical agents. A sharpshooter was out of the question; nobody could see where the hell they *were* in that room. The only target was the girl in the window. And she was the one they wanted to save.

So Georgia didn't have much hope of success here.

"Why don't you ask one of them to talk to me directly?" she said.

"Well, they don't wanna," Dolly said again.

"Ask them, okay?"

"They'll shoot me," she said.

"Just for asking them? No, they wouldn't do that, would they?"

"Yes, they would," Dolly said. "I think they might."

No two hostage situations were alike, but a hostage serving as mediator was something Georgia had come across at least a dozen times before. Sometimes the taker even gave one of his hostages safe passage to go outside and talk to the police, with the understanding that if he or she didn't come back, somebody else would be going out of the building—*dead*. Georgia didn't want that to happen here. The pathetic little creature mediating in the window seemed stoned enough not to realize that there were hordes of policemen out here ready and in fact aching to storm that house and shoot anything in there that moved. But she wasn't so stoned that she couldn't smell the immediate danger behind her in that room, an armed man, or perhaps two armed men, threatening to kill her unless—

Unless *what?*

"You see," Georgia said, "we're not sure what the problem is here."

You never defined the problem for them. You let them do that.

"If we knew what the problem was, I'm sure we could work something out. We'd like to help here, but nobody wants to talk to us."

You always suggested help. The taker or takers were usually panicked in there. The political terrorists, the trapped criminals, even the psychotics, were usually panicked. If you told them you wanted to help . . .

"So why don't you ask them how we can help?" Georgia said.

"Well . . ."

"Go ahead. Just ask them, okay? Maybe we can work this out right away. Give it a try, okay?"

"Well . . ."

"Go ahead."

Dolly turned her head from the window. Georgia couldn't hear what she was saying. Nor could she hear what someone in the room behind her said. She heard only the deep rumble of a masculine voice. Dolly turned back again.

"He said he ain't got no problem, *you* got the problem."

"Who's that? Who told you that?"

"Diz."

Okay, Diz was the honcho, Diz was the one they wanted to reach.

"What does he say our problem is?" Georgia asked. "Maybe we can help him with it."

Dolly turned away from the window again.

In the distance, beyond the barricades that defined the outer perimeter, Georgia could hear The Preacher's voice extolling the merits of Tawana Brawley, "a priestess of honor and truth," he was calling her, "in an age of political lies and paramilitary deceit. And we have the same thing here tonight, we have a fierce and mighty demonstration of white police power against two young African-Americans as innocent as were the Scottsboro . . ."

Dolly turned back to the window.

"He says the problem is getting a chopper to the airport and a jet to Jamaica, that's the problem."

"Is that what he wants? Look, can't he come to the window? He's got the gun, I'm unarmed, nobody's going to hurt him if he comes to the window. Ask him to come to the window, okay?"

Georgia was truly unarmed. She was wearing light body armor, but that was a nine-millimeter gun in there. Red cotton T-shirt. Blue jacket with the word POLICE on it in white letters across the back. Walkie-talkie hanging on her belt.

"Dolly?"

"Mm?"

"Ask him, okay, honey? Nobody's gonna hurt him, I promise him."

Dolly turned away again. The deep rumble of the voice inside again. She turned back to the window.

"He says you're full of shit, they killed a man," Dolly said.

"That was then, this is now. Let's see if we can work out the problem we got now, okay? Just ask him to . . ."

He appeared at the window suddenly, huge and black in the glare of the spotlights. It was like that scene in *Jaws* where Roy Scheider was throwing the bait off the back of the boat and the great white suddenly came up with his jaws wide, it was as heart-stopping as that. Georgia ducked. She had spotted an AK-47 in his hand.

"Who're you?" he said.

"My name's Georgia Mobry," she said, "I'm a Police Department negotiator. Who are you?"

Negotiator was the word you used. You were here to *deal,* get the people out before anybody got hurt. You never used the word *hostage* to define the people any taker had in there with him. You never used the word *surrender,* either. You asked a taker to send the people out, come on out yourself, let us help you, nobody's gonna hurt you, soothing words, neutral words. *Hostage* was a word that gave the taker even bigger ideas, made him think he was the Ayatollah Khomeini. *Surrender* was an insulting kill word that only triggered further defiance.

"I'm Diz Whittaker," he said, "an' there's nothin' to negotiate here. Georgia, huh?"

She was looking up toward the window, eyes barely showing above the deck. She saw a big muscular man with a close-shaved skull, wearing a white T-shirt, that was all she could see of him in the window frame. AK-47 in his right hand. Just the sight of that gun always sent a shiver up her spine. The illegal, Chinese-made assault rifle—a replica of the gun used by the Viet Cong—was a semiautomatic, which meant that it required a separate pull of the trigger for each shot. But it could fire up to seventy-five shots without reloading, and its curved clip gave it the lethal look of a weapon of *war,* no matter *how* many claims the National Rifle Association made for its legitimate use as a hunting rifle.

"Stan' up, Georgia," he said.

She didn't like the way he was saying her name. Almost a snarl. Georgia. Like she was Georgia the whole damn state instead of Georgia the person. Made her nervous the way he was saying the name.

"I don't want to get hurt," she said.

"Lemmee see you, Georgia." Snarling it again. "You fum Georgia? That where you fum?"

"Yes," she said.

"Stan' up lemmee see you, Georgia."

"First promise me you won't hurt me."

"You strapped?"

"Nossir."

"How do I know that?"

"Because I'm telling you. And I don't lie."

"Be the firs' cop *I* ever met dinn lie like a thief," he said. "Stan' up an' lemmee see you ain't strapped."

"I can't do that, Mr. Whittaker. Not till you promise . . ."

"Don't give me no *Mr.* Whittaker shit," he said. "How much you know about me, Georgia?"

"My superior told me who you and your friend are, I know a little bit about both of you. I can't help you without knowing something about . . ."

"What'd your boss tell you *exactly*, Georgia?"

You always told them you weren't in this alone, you didn't have sole authority to do whatever it was they wanted you to do, you had to check first with your superior, or your boss, or your people, whatever you chose to call the person above you. You wanted them to believe you were their partner in working this out. You and them against this vague controller offstage, this unseen person who had the power to say yea or nay to their requests. Most people had bosses. Even criminals understood how bosses worked.

"He said you'd done some time."

"Uh-huh."

"You and your friend both."

"Uh-huh. He tell you Sonny killed that man in the bak'ry shop?"

"He said that's what they're thinking, yeah."

"An' I was with him, he tell you that, Georgia?"

"Yes."

"Makes me a 'complice, doan it?"

"It looks that way. But why don't we talk about the problem we have right now, Mr. Whittaker? I'd like to help you, but unless we . . ."

He suddenly opened fire.

The semiautomatic weapon trimmed the bushes over her head as effectively as a hedge-clipper might have. She hugged the ground and prayed he wouldn't fire through the wooden deck of the porch because then one of those high-powered slugs might somehow find her; eyes closed, she hugged the ground and prayed for the first time since she was fifteen, the bullets raging over her head.

The firing stopped.

She waited.

"Tell yo' boss send me somebody ain't a lyin' redneck bitch," Whittaker said. "You go tell him *that*, Georgia."

She waited.

She was afraid to move.

She took the walkie-talkie from her belt, pressed the Talk button.

"Observer Two," she said, "what've you . . . what've you got at the window?"

Her voice was shaking. She cursed her traitor voice.

There was a long pause.

"Hello, Observ . . ."

"Shooter's gone," a man's voice said. "Just the girl in it."

"You sure?"

"Got my glasses on it. Window's clear."

"Inspector?" she said.

"Yeah, Georgia?"

"I think I'd better come in. I'm not gonna do any more good here."

"Come on in," he said.

From where Mike Goodman stood with Brady and the assorted brass, he saw the Tac Team come up into firing position behind the inner-perimeter cars, saw Georgia sprinting back like a broken field runner toward the cover of Truck One, which Brady had set up as his command post. She was clearly frightened. Her face was a pasty white, and her hands were trembling. One of the E.S. cops handed her a cup of coffee when what she really needed was a swig of bourbon, and she sipped it with the cup shaking in her hands, and told Brady and the E.S. commander and the chief of detectives and the chief of patrol that there were now at least two weapons in there, the nine-millimeter and an AK-47 that had almost taken off her head. She also told them the takers wanted a chopper and a jet to Jamaica . . .

"Jamaica?" Brady said.

. . . and that Whittaker didn't appreciate Southern belles doing the police negotiating, witness him having called her a redneck when her mother was a librarian and her father a doctor in Macon. The brass listened gravely and then talked quietly among themselves about the use of force. Georgia merely listened; she was out of it now.

Di Santis was of the opinion that they had probable cause for an assault. Given the priors on both perps and the strong possibility that they were the men who'd murdered the bakery-shop owner, he was willing to take his chances with a grand jury and a coroner's inquest if either of the perps got killed. Brady was concerned about the girl in there. So was Brogan.

Curran thought they should try a chemical assault, there being no gas-carrying vents to worry about the way there'd be in an apartment building, and anyway who cared if a fire started in an already con-demned building? Brady and Brogan were still worried about the girl in there. Suppose those two punks began shooting the minute they let loose with the gas? Two assault weapons in there? The girl would be a dead duck. They decided to try another negotiator in the bushes there, see if they couldn't get somebody on that porch, talk some sense into those bastards.

Trouble was, Brady had already used up all his skilled negotiators who weren't on vacation, and the only people he had left were him-self and his trainees. Ever ready to step into the role of fearless leader, Brady was willing to risk the AK-47 and whatever else they might throw at him, but Di Santis pointed out that the three negotia-tors who'd made the least headway there in the bushes had all been men and that it might be advisable to try another woman. Georgia agreed that a woman might have better luck with the young girl up there who, like it or not, was the mediator of choice until the two shitheads came around. That left either Martha Halsted or Eileen Burke. And since Eileen, through no choice of her own, had had pre-vious experience on the door, it was decided they'd let her have another go at it. Brady sent Goodman over to Truck Two to fetch her.

"Inspector wants to talk to you," he said.

"Okay," she said.

"You blowing him or what?" Martha asked.

"Stick it," Eileen said.

But as she walked away, she could hear Martha and the other trainees whispering. It didn't bother her anymore. Cops had been whispering behind her back ever since the rape. Whispering cops were more dangerous than The Preacher and his bullhorn.

The crowd was silent now, waiting for the next technical effect, this here movie was beginning to sag a little, ho-hum.

Even The Preacher seemed bored. He kept rattling his gold chains and scowling.

Brady and all the brass looked extremely solemn.

"Hello, Burke," he said.

"Sir."

"Feel like working?" he asked, and smiled.

"No, sir," Eileen said.

The smile dropped from his mouth.

"Why not?" he said.

"Personal matter, sir."

"Are you a goddamn police officer, or what are you?" Brady said, flaring.

"Steve Carella's a personal friend," she said. "I know him . . ."

"What the hell . . . ?"

". . . I know his wife, I know his . . ."

"What the hell has *that* got to . . . ?"

"I'm afraid I'll screw up, sir. If those men get away . . ."

"Inspector?"

They all turned.

Carella and Wade were standing there.

"Sir," Carella said, "we have an idea."

The crowd had begun chanting, "Do the hook-er, do the hook-er, do the hook-er," breaking the word in two, "Do the hook-er, do the hook-er, do the hook-er," urging the two men trapped in that house to break Dolly in half the way they'd broken the word, "Do the hook-er, do the hook-er, do the hook-er."

If Dolly heard what the crowd was chanting, she showed no sign of it. She sat in the window like some pale and distant Lily Maid of Astolat, waiting for a knight to come carry her away. There were no knights out here tonight, there were no blue centurions, either. There was only a group of trained policemen hoping that their organization, discipline, teamwork—and above all patience—would resolve the situation before somebody inside that house exploded.

The two men in there were criminals, and in Brady's experience criminal takers were easier to handle than either political terrorists or psychotics. Criminals understood the art of the deal; their entire lives were premised on trade-offs. Criminals knew that if you said you couldn't trade for weapons, you meant it. If the taker had a .45 in there, for example, he knew you weren't going to trade him an MP83 for one of the hostages. And if you told him you'd never let him have *another* hostage, he knew you meant that, too. If he said, for example, he wouldn't hurt anybody if only you'd send somebody in to cook his meals or wash his clothes, he knew you wouldn't do that. There was a bottom line, and he knew exactly what it was, and he knew he'd look stupid or unprofessional if he tried to trade beyond that line. A criminal could even understand why his request for beer or wine or whiskey would be refused; he knew as well as you did that this was a dangerous situation here, and alcohol never made a bad situation better. A criminal understood all this.

And probably, somewhere deep inside, he also knew this wasn't going to end on a desert island with native girls playing ukeleles and stringing flowers in his hair. He knew this was going to end with him either dead or apprehended. Those were the only two choices open to him. Deep down, he knew this. So the longer a negotiation dragged on, the better the chances were that a criminal's common sense would eventually prevail. Make the deal, go back to the joint, it was better than being carried out in a body bag. But the situation here was volatile, and Brady had no real conviction that the men inside there would *ever* be ready to talk sense. The best he was hoping for was that Eileen would be able to make a little more progress than any of the other negotiators had.

"Dolly?"

Blank stare, looking out at the lights as if hypnotized by them, the chanting wafting on the night air from across the street, "Do the hook-er, do the hook-er, do the hook-er," urging men who needed no urging at all.

"My name is Eileen Burke, I'm a Police Department negotiator," she said.

No answer.

"Dolly? Could you please tell Mr. Whittaker I'd like to talk to him?"

"He don't wanna," Dolly said.

"Yes, but that was when the other negotiator was here. Tell him there's a new . . ."

"He still don't wanna."

"If you could please tell him . . ."

"Tell me yourself."

Looming in the window again. Tall and glowering, the white T-shirt stained with sweat, the AK-47 in his hands.

"Mr. Whittaker," she said, "I'm Eileen Burke, a Police De . . ."

"The fuck you want, Burke?"

"You were talking earlier about a helicopter . . ."

"Tha's right. Stan' up an' lemmee see you. Can't see nothin' but the top of your head and your eyes."

"You know I can't do that, Mr. Whittaker."

"How come I know that, huh?"

"Well, you've been shooting at anything that moves out here . . ."

"You got somebody trainin' in on me?" he asked, and suddenly ducked behind the window frame.

On the walkie-talkie to Brady, a sharpshooter in position said, "Lost him."

"You wanna talk some more," Whittaker said, "you come up here on the porch, stan' here front of the winnder."

"Maybe later," she said.

" 'Cause I ain't givin' nobody a clear shot at me, tha's for sure."

"Nobody's going to hurt you, I can promise you that," Eileen said.

"You can promise me *shit,* Red."

"I don't like being called Red," she said.

"Tough *shit* what you like or don't like."

She wondered if she'd made a mistake. She decided to pursue it. At least they were talking. At least there was the beginning of a dialogue.

"When I was a kid, everybody called me Red," she said.

He said nothing. Face half-hidden behind the window frame. Dolly sitting there all eyes and all ears, this was the first interesting story she'd heard all night long.

"One day, I cut off all my hair and went to school that way . . ."

"Oh Jeez!" Dolly said, and brought her hand to her mouth.

"Told the kids to call me Baldy," Eileen said, "told them I preferred that to Red."

Behind the window frame, she could hear Whittaker chuckling. The story was a true one, she hadn't made it up. Cut off all her goddamn red hair, wrapped it in newspaper, her mother was shocked, Eileen, what have you *done?*

"Cut off all my hair," she said now, just as she'd said all those years ago.

"You must've looked somethin'," Dolly said.

"I just didn't like being called Red," she said reasonably.

"Cut off all your hair, wow."

"Cut it all off."

"Boy oh boy," Dolly said.

Whittaker still hadn't said anything. She figured she'd lost him. Got a few chuckles from him, and then it was right back to business.

"So whut you *like* bein' called?" he asked suddenly, surprising her.

"Eileen," she said, "how about you? What shall I call you?"

"You can call me a chopper," he said, and burst out laughing.

Good, he'd made his own joke. Variation on the old "You can call me a taxi" line, but at least he hadn't said "You can call me anything you like so long as you don't call me late for dinner." And they were back to the chopper again. Good. Trade-off time. Maybe.

"A chopper's possible," she said, "but I'd have to talk to my boss about it."

"Then you go talk to him, Eileen."

"I feel pretty sure he can arrange it . . ."

"I sure hope so, Eileen."

"But I know he'd expect . . ."

" 'Cause I'm gettin' pretty goddamn impatient here . . ."

"Well, this is really the first time . . ."

". . . an' I'd hate to see anythin' happen to this little girl here, hmm?"

"I'd hate to see anything happen to *anybody*, believe me. But this is the first time you and I have really talked, you know, and . . ."

"Why don't you come up here on the porch?" he said.

"You think I'm crazy?" she said.

He laughed again.

"No, come on, I won't hurt you. I mean it, come on."

"Well . . ."

"Come on."

"How about I just stand up first?"

"Okay."

"But you'll have to show me your hands. Show me there's nothing in your hands, and I'll stand up."

"How I know what you got in *your* hands?"

"I'll show you my hands, too. Here, see?" she said, and raised both hands above the porch deck and waggled all the fingers. "Nothing in my hands, okay?"

"How you know I won't show you my hands and then dust you anyway? Jus' pick up the piece again an' . . ."

"Well, I don't think you'd do that. Not if you promise me."

The first time she'd heard this in class, she'd thought it was ridiculous. You asked a terrorist to promise he wouldn't blow you away? You asked some nut just out of the loony bin to promise he wouldn't hurt you? She had been assured over and over again that it worked. If they *really* promised you, if you got them to say the words "I promise you," then they really wouldn't hurt you.

"So can I see your hands?" she asked.

"Here's my hands," he said, and stepped around the window frame for just an instant, waggling his fingers the way she just had, and then ducking back out of sight again. She thought she'd seen a grin, too. "Now stan' up," he said.

"If I stand up, will you promise you won't hurt me?"

"I promise."

"You won't hurt me?"

"I promise I won't hurt you."

"All right," she said, and stood up.

He was silent for a moment, looking her over. Fine, she thought, look me over. But this isn't the old man all over again, you aren't eighty-four years old and senile, you're a killer. So look me over all you like but . . .

"Put your hands on the windowsill where I can see them, okay?" she said.

"Matter, don't trust me?" he said.

"I trust you, yes, because you promised me. But I'd feel a lot better if I could see your hands. You can see mine," she said, holding them out in front of her and turning them this way and that like a model for Revlon nail polish, "so you know I'm not going to hurt you, isn't that right?"

"It is."

Still not stepping out from where he was hidden.

"So how about showing me the same consideration?" she said.

"Okay, here's my hands," he said, and moved into the window frame beside Dolly and grabbed the sill with both huge hands.

"Clear shot," the sharpshooter said into his walkie-talkie. "Shall I take him out?"

"Negative," Brady told him.

"What I'd like to do now," Eileen said, "is go back to my boss and ask him about that helicopter."

"Sure is *red*," Whittaker said, grinning.

"Yeah, I know," Eileen said, shaking her head and smiling back at him. "I'm pretty sure he can get you what you want, but it might take some time. And I know he'll expect something from you in return."

"Whutchoo mean?"

"I'm just saying I know what he's like. He'll get you that helicopter, but one hand washes the other is what he's going to tell me. But let me go talk to him, okay? See what he says."

"If he s'pects me to let go Dolly, he's dreamin'. Dolly stayin' with us till we on that jet."

"What jet?"

"Dolly tole you we . . ."

"No, not me. Maybe she told the other negotiator."

"We want a jet to take us to Jamaica."

Eileen was thinking he'd been standing there in the window for the past three, four minutes now, a clean shot for any of the Tac Team sharpshooters. But Sonny was still somewhere in the darkness of that room. And Sonny was strapped with a nine-millimeter auto.

"Why Jamaica?" she asked.

"Nice down there," he said vaguely.

"Well, let me talk to him, okay? You're asking for *two* things in a row now, and that's gonna make it a little harder for me. Let me see what I can do, okay?"

"Yeah, go ahead. An' tell him we ain't foolin' aroun' here."

"I will. Now Mr. Whittaker, I'm gonna turn my back on you and walk over to the truck there. Do I still have your promise?"

"You have my promise."

"You won't hurt me."

"I won't hurt you."

"I have your promise then," she said, and nodded. "I'll be back as soon as I talk to him."

"Go ahead."

She turned away, giving him no reason to believe she was frightened or even apprehensive, turned and began walking swiftly and deliberately toward the emergency service truck, the word

POLICE in white across the back of her blue poplin jacket, trying not to pull her head into her shoulders, thinking nonetheless that any minute now a spray of bullets would come crashing into her spine.

But Whittaker kept his promise.

It was Carella who'd realized the perps had blindsided themselves. Boarded up the windows on three sides of the house. And if all those windows were boarded, they couldn't see out. Which meant that three sides of the house were accessible to the police. This was what he'd told Brady.

They had finally got a floor plan from the realty company that had sold the house to a Mr. and Mrs. Borden some twelve years ago, long before a housing development had been planned for the area. It looked like this:

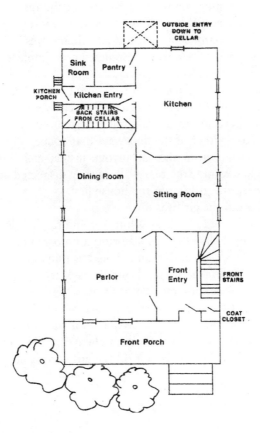

According to Dolly, when the owners of the house converted from a private residence to a rooming house, the living room and dining room were both refurnished as bedrooms, and what had once been the sitting room was now a sort of public room with a sofa, two easy chairs, and a television set on a stand. The kitchen and its adjoining pantry and laundry room—what had originally been called the sink room—were the only rooms on this floor of the house that remained as they'd been since its construction back before the turn of the century. There was only one large bathroom in the house, on the second floor.

At the rear of the house, there was an outside entry that led down to the cellar.

Carella pointed this out, too.

One of those sloping things that kids just loved to slide down, two doors on it that opened upward and outward like wings. Observer number four, working the inner perimeter at the rear of the house, reported that whereas the window to the left—*his* left—of the cellar doors had been boarded over, the doors themselves seemed not to have been touched. They were fastened by a simple padlock in a hasp.

It was Carella's thought that if they could get into that cellar, they could then come up the stairs to the kitchen entry and move through the house to where Sonny and Whittaker were holding the girl in the front room. From either of the doorways that opened into that room, they would have a clean shot at anyone inside, including whoever might be backed against the rear wall, as they suspected Sonny was.

Brady wanted the girl out of the house first.

No assault until the girl was out.

He told Eileen to go back to Whittaker and tell him they couldn't get him a chopper, but they could bring a limo around to the back door if he let the girl go at the same time. His thinking was to split up the pair. Get Whittaker to send Sonny back to the kitchen entry while the girl was coming out the front door. Time it so that Carella and Wade would be at the top of the cellar stairs when Sonny came back to check on the limo. No assault until they knew for certain Dolly was out of the house. Position themselves in the cellar, get themselves in place, but no assault till the girl was clear.

It could work.

Maybe.

*　*　*

"I'm sorry," Eileen said, "but he can't get a chopper for you."

"You tole me . . ."

"I know, but . . ."

"Tell him I'll kill the fuckin' girl! He wants to play games here, I'll kill the fuckin' girl!"

"Can I come up there on the porch?" Eileen asked.

You always asked for permission to approach. You always asked for assurances that there'd be no accidents, no slipups. You didn't want anyone to get hurt here. Not you, not him, not anyone.

"Okay?" she said. "Can I come up?"

"No," Whittaker said. "What'd you do, Red? Pick up a gun while you were back there with your pals?"

"No, I didn't. I'm not armed, I'll show you if you like. Is it okay to stand up?"

"You got to be crazy, you know that? You come back with *shit* from him, and you 'spect me to . . ."

"You promised you wouldn't hurt me. Have I still got your promise?"

"Why should I promise you anything?"

" 'Cause I think I've got a way out of this. If we can just talk it over . . ."

"I'm not givin' him anythin' till he gives *me* somethin'!"

"That's just what I want to talk about. Can I stand up? Will you promise not to hurt me if I stand up?"

"Go on, stan' up," he said.

"I didn't hear your promise."

"You got my fuckin' *promise*, okay?"

She wondered if she should ask to see his hands again. She decided that would be pushing it. He'd given her his promise, and she had to trust him. Pretending a confidence she didn't quite feel, she stood up, opened her jacket wide, and said, "Nothing under it, Mr. Whittaker. I'm unarmed."

"Turn aroun', liff up the back of the jacket."

She turned to show her back to him and the assault rifle in his hands. Lifted the jacket, showed him the back of the yellow shirt under it. Nothing strapped to her. No gun and holster. Nothing.

"Okay?" she said.

"What's that on your belt?" he asked.

"A walkie-talkie. Don't worry, it isn't some kind of trick gun or anything."

"Throw it up here on the porch."

"No, I can't do that. I have to stay in touch. In case they want me to pass on a message. Okay?"

"Yeah, okay."

"Okay to put my jacket down now?"

"Yeah, go on, Red."

"You want me to cut off all my hair again?"

She thought she heard a chuckle in there.

"So stop calling me Red, okay?"

No answer.

"Okay for me to turn around again?" she asked.

"Yeah, okay."

She turned to face the window again. She still could not see him. Only Dolly sat in the window. Blank stare on her face.

"Can I come up on the porch?"

"Why?"

"So we can talk without having to yell."

"Come on up."

"Do I still have your promise?"

"I ain't shot you yet, have I?"

"I'd like your promise that you won't."

"I won't. I promise you."

"Okay, so I'm coming up there, right?"

"I said okay."

"I just don't want any accidents. I want you to know what I'm doing, so there won't be any slipups."

"Yeah, come on up."

She went up the low flat steps that led to the front door of the house, and then she moved left toward the nearest window and was moving along the porch toward . . .

"Hold it right there," he said.

"Okay."

"That's fine right where you are."

"Okay."

"So what's your idea?"

"He says no chopper, he can't get one. There's been a big accident on the Harb . . ."

"The *what?*"

"The Harb, the river, don't you—that's right, you're from Washington."

"How you know that?"

"Well, we have your . . ."

"Yeah, what kine a accident?"

"A pleasure boat hit the ferry to Bethtown. We've got all our chop-pers out in a big rescue operation."

A flat-out lie. But the game had changed. Two men with a bolt cut-ter would soon be dancing around back to that cellar door. And once the girl was clear—

"So tell your boss t'get me a *commercial* chopper."

"I'll ask him, if you want me to. But you know what I think?"

"Whut?"

"I think you'd be better off with a limo. Time the jet gets out there . . ."

"What jet? He gettin' me a jet?"

"I thought I told you. A jet's being fueled right this minute."

"No, all you said was no chopper."

"It'll be ready in . . ."

"Be ready *where?*"

"Spindlerift. In an hour or so. If I can get him to send a limo for you, you'd be there in plenty of time. Might be *quicker* than a chop-per, matter of fact, the way air-traffic control is out there."

She could see his face now. She had lured him closer to the win-dow. He was thinking it over.

"I'll ask my boss to give you a motorcycle escort," she said, "get you to the airport in forty minutes."

The idea was beginning to appeal to him. Big-shot ambassador from Washington, D.C., in his own stretch limo with a motorcycle escort taking him to his private jet plane. She could almost hear the wheels grinding in the dark there inside the house and inside his head.

"I'll let go the girl when we're inside the jet," he said.

"Aw, come on, Mr. Whittaker, how can I tell my boss that?"

"I don't give a shit *whut* you tell him . . ."

Easy now, she thought.

". . . I'm the one got a gun pointin' at her *head!*"

"I know that," she said. Her heart was pounding. "And I don't want her to get hurt, Mr. Whittaker, I don't want *anybody* to get hurt. But I've got to go back to him with something reasonable, I'm sure you can understand that. He's giving you a limo and a jet, I've got to tell him you're willing to give him something in return."

Talking a mile a minute now, dazzling him with the brilliance of her logic. "I *know* I can get the limo for you, I've already discussed that with him. And he's got the jet being fueled right this minute, he's getting you everything you asked for, he's being cooperative all the way down the line, isn't he? It's just a chopper's out of the question because of that freak accident on the river, which was something none of us could control, am I right? So if I can go to him and say, Look, Mr. Whittaker'll let the girl go, but he wants certain assurances, whatever those may be, you tell me what you want and I'll pass it on. And if we can work it out, get you what you want, make sure the girl's safe and you're safe, we can have you on your way in five, ten minutes, be there in time to meet the jet, what do you say?"

"How do I know this ain't a *trick* is whut I say."

"That's why I asked you to tell me what assurances you want for your safety. Just tell me what guarantees you want, and I'll pass them on. We don't want any slipups here. You tell us what you want, we'll tell you what we're going to do. That way *you'll* know what we're doing and *we'll* know what you're doing and nobody'll get hurt, what do you say?"

Come *on,* she thought.

"How do I know there'll even *be* a limo. I let the girl go, you come in here with a fuckin' army . . ."

"No, we'll bring the limo up before you send the girl out. You can check to see it's there."

"Where?"

"Wherever you want it. I thought outside the door on the left side of the house. Where there's that little porch there. Would that be okay?"

"Tell your boss I want whiskey in the limo."

Good, she thought, he's ready to cut a deal.

"No," she said, "I can't get you whiskey."

"Why not?" he said.

"Well, we don't want anybody getting hurt. I know you'll keep *your* promise, Mr. Whittaker, but whiskey doesn't know how to keep promises."

Inside the house, she thought she heard him chuckle again.

"So what shall I tell him?" she asked. "If I get you the limo, will you send the girl out?"

"Suppose I see the limo out there . . ."

"We'll bring it right up to the door there. All you have to do is step down from the porch there, and get right in the car."

"But suppose I *see* the car out there, and I let the girl go, like you said, and you blow me away 'fore I even get a chance to climb *in* that car?"

Working out all the details. Knowing in his heart of hearts that no one was going to let him board a jet to Jamaica, no one was going to let him sip piña coladas in the sun on a tropical beach. But bargaining anyway. Hoping against hope that maybe this *would* be the big pay-off, after all. Let the girl go, climb in the limo . . .

"Well, how would you *like* us to work it?" she asked. "The bottom line is my boss is going to want to make sure the girl's safe before he lets that limo . . ."

"Ain't no way a limo's gonna be safe," he said. "I get in that limo, you blow me *an'* Sonny *an'* the car to hell and gone. No way, Red. Tell your fuckin' boss I want a chopper. I don't care where he gets it, but that's what I want. Tell him the girl comes out with me to the chopper, I let her go *after* Sonny's inside an' I'm climbin' in. That's when you get the girl. Tell your boss he's got five minutes to make up his mind. Otherwise he gets the girl, all right, but he gets her *dead.* Five minutes. Tell him."

On the street outside, the crowd behind the barricade was getting restless. This was already three o'clock in the morning, but no one was thinking of sleep. The only thing on anyone's mind was Showdown at the O.K. Corral. Toward that end, and with the seem-ing purpose of rattling everyone in sight so that the only possible out-come *would* be a loss of blood, a loss of life, further fuel for the inevitable fire to come, The Preacher took up his bullhorn yet another time and started a catchy little chant that had nothing what-ever to do with the circumstances at hand.

"No More Jogger Justice!" he shouted in a voice worn and ragged and hoarse. "No More Jogger Justice!"

He was referring to the raped and brutally beaten young woman who had captured the attention of the entire world. He was referring to the guilty verdicts brought in against her attackers. It didn't matter that the young white hooker and the two black killers inside that house could not by the remotest stretch of anyone's imagination, least of all The Preacher's, be identified with the jogger and her brutal assailants. What mattered to The Preacher was that he place himself at the heart of wherever the action was, creating action if there didn't happen to be any, and presenting himself on television as the lone and lonely voice of black sensibility—whereas in reality most black people knew he was nothing but a rabble-rouser dedicated exclusively to self-promotion.

"No More Jogger Justice!" he shouted into the bullhorn. "No More Jogger Justice!"

And the crowd—not a moment earlier lulled almost to sleep by this endless chess game with its black and white pieces being maneuvered on a black-and-white board that seemed to stretch off to a vanishing point somewhere all too far in the infinite distance—the crowd picked up the catchy little chant, "No More Jogger Justice!" and amplified it without benefit of bullhorns, "No More Jogger Justice!," beating out the words in a four-four tempo that all but cried for footstomping, "No More Jogger Justice!," the litany spilling out over the barricades to cascade onto the front porch of the house where Dolly Simms sat white-faced and stunned at the window.

She could hear the subtle rhythm of the chant under the steady roar of the police chopper circling overhead. Sonny and Diz were deep inside the room now, whispering, Sonny with the nine-millimeter pointed at her head where she sat in silhouette against the glare of the lights. Dolly figured they were talking about killing her. She knew they were crazy enough to kill her. Somehow, she didn't seem to care anymore.

"Mr. Whittaker?"

The redhead. Out there in the bushes again, some people never gave up. Imagine her cutting off all her hair. Maybe *she* was crazy, too. Maybe the whole world was crazy except Dolly herself, who would be dead in five, ten minutes, the way she figured it, which would probably be an easier life after all was said and done.

"Mr. Whittaker? It's me again. Eil . . ."

"They can't hear you," Dolly said.

"What?"

"They can't hear you," she repeated. "The chopper's too loud."

"Go back and tell Mr. Whittaker I have to talk to him."

"He'll shoot me if I move from this window."

"Just tell him we have to talk some more."

"I can't."

Eileen reached for her walkie-talkie.

"Inspector?" she said.

"Here," Brady said.

"Lose the goddamn chopper, I can't hear myself think."

"Ten-four," he said.

From where Wade worked with the bolt cutter, he could hear the chopper moving off, the steady clatter of its blades succumbing to the chant that rose now as if to call the aircraft back, insistent voices reaching to the blackness of the sky overhead, "No More Jogger Justice! No More Jogger Justice!"

"Dumb assholes," he said, and closed the jaws of the cutter onto the steel shackle of the padlock. The steel snapped. He tossed the cutter aside and yanked the lock free of its hasp. In three seconds flat, Carella had both cellar doors raised and was starting down the steps, Wade behind him. The sound of the chopper was all but gone now. There was only the sound of the chanting.

It was pitch-black in the cellar.

There was the smell of coal and the smell of dust.

They figured the steps were straight ahead and slightly to their left.

They dared not turn on a light.

"Where's it going?" Sonny asked.

"Shut up," Whittaker said.

"It's *leavin'*, man, can't you hear it?"

"I hear it, shut up," Whittaker said, and went to the window. "Red!" he yelled. "The hell are you?"

"Right here," she said.

"Where? Stan' up so I can see you."

"Nope," she said.

"Whutchoo mean *nope?* You want me to . . ."

"Mr. Whittaker, it's time we talked turkey here. You know there's a . . ."

"Don't you tell me whut I gotta talk, woman! I'm the one got the girl in here. You ain't got . . ."

"Okay, you want to stay in there forever with her? Is that what you want? Or do you want to settle this thing, get on your way to the airport, which is it? The chopper's here, I got the damn chopper for you, so how about lending me a hand here? I've been busting my ass for you, Mr. Whittaker . . ."

She heard him chuckling.

"Yeah, very funny," she said. "And you're making me look like a fool in front of my boss. Do you want that chopper to land, or do you want to keep me running back and forth all night? I've got the walkie-talkie right here, look at it," she said, and held her hand up over her head, over the porch deck so he could see her hand and the walkie-talkie sticking up out of the bushes. "Just tell me what you want and I'll call him. I'm trying to facilitate this operation, I'm trying to get you on that chopper and the girl outside that house without anybody getting hurt. So will you help me do that, Mr. Whittaker? I'm trying my best here, really, I am. All I need is a little help from you."

There was a deep silence inside there.

At last, he said, "Okay, here's the deal."

They had found the cellar steps.

The walkie-talkie volume control was at its lowest setting, and they were listening to what Eileen was relaying back to the inspector. The way they understood the deal, the chopper would land in the vacant lot on the left-hand side of the house, some fifty feet from what was marked on the floor plan as the kitchen porch. The pilot of the helicopter would be alone, and he would step out of the aircraft and down onto the ground and raise his hands above his head before they came out of the house. Whittaker would come out of the house first, with Sonny remaining behind in the kitchen entry, his pistol to the girl's head. When Whittaker was safely behind the pilot, the muzzle of the AK-47 angled up against the pilot's neck, he would signal for Sonny to let the girl loose. As the girl began her run back to the E.S. truck, Eileen would be waiting to lead her in. By that time, Sonny should have reached the helicopter. If anyone tried to harm Sonny as he ran over from the house, Whittaker would kill the pilot.

"Sounds to me like they're making an exchange," Wade whispered. "The girl for the pilot."

"They don't make exchanges," Carella said. "That's one of their rules."

"Then what does it sound like to you?"

"It sounds like an exchange," Carella said. "But the pilot is a cop."

"Does that make it okay to kill him?"

"No, but . . ."

"What's the plan once they get to the airport?"

"I don't know," Carella said. "I just work here."

They listened outside the door at the top of the steps. In just a little while, if all went well, Sonny and Whittaker would be coming down the hallway outside that door. The minute Sonny turned the girl loose, Carella would be face to face with the man who'd killed his father.

The sharpshooter crouched low in the cabin on the right-hand side of the aircraft. Below, a lone police officer wearing luminous orange trousers and jacket was running out from the inner police perimeter.

"Who's that?" Whittaker asked at once.

"He's unarmed," Eileen assured him. "He'll be signaling to the pilot, telling him where to put the ship down. We don't want any mistakes."

"I want him out of there as soon as it lands."

"Inspector?" Eileen said into the walkie-talkie.

"Here," Brady said.

"He wants that man out of there as soon as the chopper touches down."

"He's got it," Brady said.

"Did you hear that?" she asked Whittaker.

"No."

"He'll get out of there as soon as the ship lands."

"He better."

Dolly was still sitting alone in the open window. The other two were somewhere in the darkness of the room beyond. Eileen was talking to no one she could see. But she was certain Whittaker could see out of the room; he had spotted the man in orange running toward the cleared sandlot on the side of the house.

"Ain't nobody leavin' this house till that man's back where he belongs," he said from out of the blackness.

"Don't worry about it. He's signaling now," she said. "You can't see him from where you are, but he's signaling to the chopper."

The sharpshooter could see the man below swinging a red torchlight in a circle over his head. The sliding door on the right-hand side of the ship was open. The pilot would bring the ship down with that side facing the house. The moment Whittaker was in place, using the pilot as a shield, facing the police line out there, the sharpshooter should have a clean shot at the back of his head. The pilot *hoped*.

"Hedgehog, this is Firefly, over," the pilot said.

"Come in, Firefly."

"We've got your man sighted, ready to take her down."

"Take her down, Firefly."

"Ten-four."

A police code sign-off, even though this was air-to-ground radio traffic and a wilco might have been more appropriate. Neither the pilot up there preparing to land and be seized by an armed killer whose head the sharpshooter might or might not succeed in blowing from his body, nor Chief of Patrol Curran, talking to him from the ground, had exchanged anything but landing instructions. These days, nobody knew who was listening on what frequency, and there was still a sixteen-year-old girl in that house.

"Coming in," Eileen said.

"I'm sending Sonny back to the kitchen with the girl," Whittaker said. "He yells loud enough, I can hear him from back there. Minute he tells me the chopper's down, I'm headin' back myself. Ress is up to you whether anybody gets hurt or not."

"Just about down," she said.

"You hear me?"

"I heard you."

"Move it on out, Sonny."

The leaves on the bushes outside the house shook violently as the chopper skids came closer to the ground. Over the roar of the ship and the rush of the wind, Eileen said into her walkie-talkie, "Sonny's heading toward the kitchen now." With all that clamor, she hadn't expected Whittaker to hear her, but he had.

"Why you tellin' him that?" Whittaker shouted over the noise.

"We don't want any mistakes, you know that." Into the walkie-talkie, she said, "Chopper's down, Inspector, better get that man out of there," but this was really for the benefit of Carella and Wade, who were standing on the landing just inside the cellar door.

"Diz!"

Jesus!

His voice sounded as if it was right at Carella's elbow, just outside the door!

"*Move* it, bitch!"

Running by in the corridor now, past the door.

"Ow!"

The girl's voice.

"I said *move* it! Diz! Can you hear me, Diz?"

"You don't have to poke me with the damn . . ."

"Diz!"

A bit further away now. Yelling from the kitchen, Carella guessed. Visualizing the floor plan in his head, the narrow corridor running from the outside porch to the kitchen. Sonny Cole, his father's murderer, standing in the kitchen, yelling to his partner at the front of the house.

"Diz! It's down, I can see it! It's on the ground! Diz, can you hear me?"

They could not hear anyone answering him.

But there were footsteps again, coming back toward them in the corridor outside. Carella kept the walkie-talkie pressed to his ear, fearful of a sound leak that would give away their position. There was sudden laughter just outside the door, startling him again.

"We goin' to *Ja*maica," Sonny told the girl, laughing, his voice high and shrill.

That's what you think, Carella thought.

"That was Sonny jus' then," Whittaker said. "He says the chopper's down."

"He's right, it is," Eileen said.

"So I'm headin' back there now." He sounded almost sad to be leaving. "You sure you got this all straight in your head?"

"I hope so," Eileen said.

"Me, too," Whittaker said, "otherwise somebody goan *die,* you know? Minute I see the pilot standin' out there, I'm headin' for the chopper. You know the ress."

"I do."

"Better be no tricks."

"There won't be," she said.

"No surprises," he said, and suddenly appeared in the window. "So long, Red," he said, and grinned, and was gone into the darkness again.

"It's *Eileen,*" she muttered under her breath, and then, immediately, into the walkie-talkie, "Whittaker's moving back."

Carella would have been blind without Eileen's voice coming over the walkie-talkie. The voice of a good cop and a good friend filling him in, giving him updates on when it would be all right to come out and say hello to his father's killer.

"Chopper's down . . ."

And then:

"Whittaker's moving back . . ."

And now:

"Pilot's out of the ship . . ."

Carella waited. Wade stood tensely beside him, his ear pressed to the cellar door, listening for any sound from outside there in the corridor.

Both of them had drawn their guns long ago.

Now they simply waited.

"Putting his hands up over his head . . ." Eileen said.

She was standing midway between Truck One and the helicopter, the flaps of her blue jacket dancing in the wind produced by the whirling blades, watching the pilot as he came to a stop just beyond the ladder leading down from the ship, sliding door open above him and behind him, his hair flapping wildly, his hands high over his head. She could not see anyone inside the ship.

"Kitchen door's opening," she said into the walkie-talkie.

She caught her breath.

"Whittaker's poking his head out, looking around . . ."

She waved to him. Let him know she was here. Everything according to plan, right? Soon as you've got the pilot, you let the girl go, and I'm waiting here for her. He did not wave back. Come on, she thought, acknowledge my presence. Let me know you see me. She waved again, bigger movements this time, more exaggerated. He still did not wave back. Just took a last look all around to make sure nobody was waiting out here to ambush him, and then began running for the helicopter.

"He's on his way to the chopper!" she shouted into the walkie-talkie. "Girl's still inside the house, hold steady. Inspector?"

"Yes."

"Who calls the play?"

"I do. Just tell me when the girl is clear."

"Yes, sir."

Silence.

"He's just about there now."

More silence.

"He's behind the pilot now. Signaling to the door. The girl's out! *Dolly!*" she yelled. "This way! Over here!"

"Assault One, *go!*" Brady shouted.

They would later, in a diner near Headquarters downtown, over coffee and doughnuts as another hot day dawned over the city, try to piece together what had happened next, assemble it as they might have a jigsaw puzzle, pulling in separate pieces of the action from various perspectives, trying to make a comprehensive whole out of what seemed at first to be merely a scattering of confused and jagged pieces.

The girl was running toward her.

Purple hair like a beacon in the night.

"Dolly!" she shouted again.

"Hey! Red!"

She was startled for a moment, his voice coming out of the darkness near the helicopter where he stood behind the pilot. She turned to locate his voice, taking her eyes off the girl for just an instant.

"I *lied!*" he shouted.

And the girl exploded in blood.

They broke out of the cellar the instant Brady gave them the green light. Sonny had just released the girl and was poised for flight inside the side door, like a runner toeing his mark while waiting for the starting gun. The starting gun came from behind him, a shot fired from Wade's .38, catching Sonny in the right leg and knocking him off his feet before he could step out onto the porch. They were all over him in the next ten seconds, Wade kicking the nine-millimeter out of his hand as Sonny tried to sit up and raise the gun into a firing position, Carella kneeing him under the chin and slamming him onto his back on the linoleum-covered floor in the narrow corridor. Green linoleum, he would remember later. Yellow flowers in the pattern. Green and yellow and Sonny's wide-open brown eyes as Carella put the muzzle of his gun in the hollow of his throat. Jagged pink knife scar down one side of his face.

"Do it," Wade whispered.

The girl came stumbling forward, rosebud breasts in the lavender blouse erupting in larger red flowers as the slugs from the assault rifle ripped into her back and exited in a shower of lung and blood and gristle and tissue, spattering Eileen in gore as the girl fell forward into her arms.

"Oh dear God," Eileen murmured, and heard the shots from inside the helicopter as the sharpshooter fired twice and only twice, but twice was more than enough. The first bullet took Whittaker at the back of his neck, ripping out his trachea as it exited. The second shot caught him just above his right cheek as the force of the first bullet spun him around and away from the pilot. He was dead even before the shattered cheek sent slivers of bone ricocheting up into his brain.

Behind the barricades, even The Preacher stopped chanting.

"Do it!" Wade whispered urgently.

There was sweat in that narrow corridor, and fear, and anger, and every sweet thought Carella had ever had for his father, every emotion he'd ever felt for him, all of these burning his eyes and causing his gun hand to shake violently, the muzzle of the Police Special trembling in the hollow of Sonny's throat, great gobs of sweat oozing on Sonny's face, Wade's face close to Carella's now, all three of them sweating in that suffocating corridor where murder was just the tick of an instant away. "Do it," Wade whispered again, "we all *alone* here."

He almost did it.

Almost squeezed the trigger, almost pulled off the shot that would have ended it for Sonny and might have ended it for himself as well, all the anger, all the sorrow, all the hatred.

But he knew that if he heeded those whispered words *Do it*—and oh how easy to do it here in this secret place—he would be doing it not only to Sonny, he would be doing it to himself as well. And to anyone in this city who had ever hoped for justice under law.

He swung himself off the man who had killed his father.

"Up!" he said.

"You *shot* me, you mother-fucker!" Sonny yelled at Wade.

"*Up!*" Carella said again, and yanked him to his feet and clamped the cuffs onto his wrists, squeezing them shut hard and tight. Wade was looking at him, a puzzled expression on his face.

"I'm gonna bring charges," Sonny said. "*Shootin'* me, you mother-fucker."

"Yeah, you bring charges," Wade said. He was still looking at Carella. "I don't understand you," he said.

"Well," Carella said, and let it go at that.

13

HE CALLED his brother-in-law from the diner and told him he'd be picking him up on the way home. When Tommy asked why, he said, "Because you have twin daughters, and I think you ought to go see them."

Tommy said Wow, gee, twin *girls*, holy moley, wow.

In the car on the way to the hospital, Carella told him he knew Tommy was doing cocaine.

Tommy said Wow, gee, cocaine, holy moley, wow, where'd you get *that* idea?

Carella said he'd got the idea by following him to a house on Laramie Street, which incidentally the police had under camera surveillance, *that's* how he'd got the idea.

Tommy was about to do the wow-gee number a third time, but Carella cut him short by asking, "Who's the woman?"

Tommy debated lying. The car was moving slowly through heavy early-morning traffic, Carella at the wheel, Tommy beside him. He took a long time to answer. Trying to decide whether he should wow-gee it through or come clean. He knew his brother-in-law was a detective. This wasn't going to be easy.

"She works in the bank with me," he said at last.

"I'm listening."

"It goes back a couple of months."

"We've got time."

Tommy wanted him to understand straight off that there wasn't any sex involved here, this wasn't any kind of an affair, Angela had been wrong about that, although she'd been right about there being another woman. The other woman's name was Fran Harrington, and this all started when they'd traveled out to Minneapolis together, this must've been shortly after Labor Day last year . . .

"I thought you said a couple of months," Carella said, turning from the wheel.

"Well, yeah."

"Labor Day is the beginning of September. That isn't a couple of months. That's almost a *year.*"

"Well, yeah."

"You've been doing coke for almost a year."

"Yeah."

"You goddamn jackass."

"I'm sorry."

"You ought to be, you jackass."

He was furious. He gripped the wheel tightly and concentrated on the traffic ahead. The automobiles were moving through a shimmering miragelike haze. The first day of August, and summer seemed intent on proving that July hadn't been just a fluke. Tommy was telling him how he and Fran had gone out there to deal with a customer who was on the edge of defaulting and how they'd been able to work out a method of payment that was satisfactory to both him and the bank. This was a huge loan; the man leased snow-removal equipment, which in the state of Minnesota was as essential as bread. So both he and Fran were tickled they'd been able to work it out, and Tommy suggested they go have a drink in celebration. Fran said she didn't drink, but maybe they could scare up something better. He didn't know what she meant at first.

You wouldn't think you could get cocaine in Minneapolis, Minnesota, which Tommy had always thought of as some kind of hick city in the middle of nowhere. But Fran knew a place they could go to, and it wasn't the kind of sleazy joint you saw on television where the cops are knocking down doors and yelling freeze. The one thing Tommy had learned since last September . . . well, yeah, that's right, it *had* been almost a year now . . . was that it wasn't only black kids doing crack in the ghettos, it was white people, too, doing coke *uptown*—coke didn't know about racial inequality, coke was the great emancipator. Just the way you used to have slum kids rolling marijuana joints on the street while rich people out in Malibu were offering you tailor-mades in silver cigarette boxes, it was the same thing now with cocaine. You didn't have to go smoke a five-dollar vial of crack in some shitty tenement apartment, there were places

where people just like yourself could sit around in pleasant, sometimes luxurious surroundings, snorting really terrific stuff, socializing
at the same time . . ."

"You stupid jackass," Carella said.

"Anyway, that's how it started," Tommy said. "In Minnesota that
time. And we've been doing it together since. She travels with me a
lot, she knows all the places. The dangerous thing is getting caught
with it, you know . . ."

Tell me about it, Carella thought.

". . . so if you don't make a buy and *carry* the stuff away, if instead
you go to where the stuff *is*, one of these upscale apartments with
people just like yourself . . ."

Noses just like yourself, Carella thought.

". . . like the one here on Laramie, for example, is really nice, we
go there a lot."

"You better *quit* going there," Carella said. "You're already a
movie star."

"Do you think you could . . . ?"

"Don't even ask. Just stay away from that place. Or anyplace like it."

"I'll try."

"Never mind *trying*, you dumb jackass. You quit or I'll bust you
myself, I promise you."

Tommy nodded.

"You hear me? You get psychiatric help, and you *quit*. Period."

"Yeah." He was silent for a moment. Then he said, "Does . . . did
you tell Angela?"

"No."

"Are you going to?"

"That's your job."

"How do I . . . what do I . . . ?"

"That's entirely up to you. You got yourself into this, you get yourself out."

"I just want you to understand," Tommy said again, "this had
nothing to do with sex. Angela was wrong. This isn't like sex at all."

Yes it is, Carella thought.

Sitting here by the river, waiting for him to arrive, Eileen looked out
over the water at the tugs moving slowly under the distant bridge.
The place she'd chosen was a plain, unadorned seafood joint perched
somewhat precariously on the end of the dock, all brown shingles

and blue shutters and walls and floors that weren't plumb. Brown sheets of wrapping paper served as tablecloths, and waiters ran around frantically in stained white aprons. At dinnertime, the place was a madhouse. She was only meeting him for a drink, but even now, at ten past five, there was a sense of hyperkinetic preparation.

She sat at a table on the deck and breathed in deeply of air that smelled vaguely of the sea, activity swarming behind her, the river roiling below. She was feeling pretty good about herself. The minutes passed serenely.

At a quarter past five, Kling came rushing out onto the deck.

"I'm sorry I'm late," he said, "we had a . . ."

"I just got here myself," she said.

"Gee, I really *am* late," he said, looking at his watch. "I'm sorry, have you ordered yet?"

"I was waiting for you."

"So what would you like?" he asked, and turned to signal to one of the peripatetic waiters.

"A white wine, please," she said.

"I saw you on television," Kling said, grinning. "We'll have a white wine and a Dewar's on the rocks, please, with a twist," he told the waiter.

"White wine, Dewar's rocks, a twist," the waiter said and went off.

"You look a little tired," he said.

"It was a long night."

"Worked out okay, though."

"Yeah, it went pretty . . ."

"The girl getting killed wasn't your fault," he said quickly.

"I know it wasn't," she said.

In fact, until this very moment, she thought she'd handled the situation in a completely pro . . .

"It was the bad guy . . . what was his name, Whitman . . . ?"

"Whittaker," she said.

"Whittaker, who killed the girl, you had nothing to do with it, Eileen. Even that guy interviewing you on television mentioned right on the air that the girl was within minutes of safety when she got shot in the back. So don't start blaming yourself for . . ."

"But I'm not," she said.

"Good, for something you didn't do. Otherwise you'll mess up a real opportunity here to start a whole new line of police work you might be very good at."

She looked at him.

"I *am* good at it," she said.

"I'm sure you are."

"I'm *already* good at it."

Who needs this? she thought.

"Bert," she said, "let's end it once and for all, okay?"

The Monday-night poker game was composed of off-duty detectives from precincts all over the city. There were usually seven players in the game, but in any case there were never fewer than six or more than eight. Eight made the game unwieldy. Also, with eight players and only fifty-two cards, you couldn't play a lot of the wild-card games the detectives favored. Playing poker was a form of release for them. The stakes weren't high—if you had bad luck all night long, you could maybe lose fifty, sixty dollars—and the sense of gambling in a situation where the risks weren't frightening had a certain appeal for men who sometimes had to put their lives on the line.

Meyer Meyer was debating whether or not to bet into what looked like a straight flush, but which might be only a seven-high straight, if it was a straight at all.

He decided to take the risk.

"See the buck and raise it a buck," he said.

Morris Goldstein, a detective from the Seven-Three, raised his eyebrows and puffed on his pipe. He was the one sitting there with a three, four, five, and six of clubs in front of him and maybe a deuce or a seven of clubs in the hole. He seemed surprised now that Meyer had not only seen his bet but raised it as well.

There were only three players still in the pot. Meyer, who had a full house composed of three kings and a pair of aces; Goldstein with what appeared to be a straight flush but which perhaps wasn't; and Rudy Gonsowski from the One-Oh-Three, a sure loser even if he'd tripped one of his low pairs. Goldstein puffed on his pipe and casually raised the ante another buck. He was a lousy poker player, and Meyer figured he was still trying to bluff his phony straight flush. Gonsowski dropped out, no big surprise. Meyer thought it over.

"Let's go, ladies," Parker said, "this ain't mah-jongg night."

They were playing in his apartment tonight. The two other players in the game were a detective named Henry Flannery from Headquarters Command downtown and Leo Palladino from Midtown South. They were both very good players who usually went home winners. Tonight, though, both of them were suffering losing streaks. They sat back with the impatient, bored looks of losers on their faces, waiting for Meyer to make up his mind.

"One more time," Meyer said, and threw four fifty-cent chips into the pot.

Goldstein raised his eyebrows yet again.

He puffed solemnly on his pipe.

"And again," he said, and threw another two bucks into the pot.

Meyer figured it was time to start believing him.

"See you," he said.

Goldstein showed his deuce of clubs.

"Yeah," Meyer said, and tossed in his cards.

"You should'a known all along he had it," Parker said, sweeping in the cards and beginning to shuffle.

"He didn't start raising till the fourth card," Meyer said in defense.

"What the hell were *you* doing in the game, Gonsowski?"

This from Flannery, who was so far losing thirty bucks.

"I had two pair in the first four cards," Gonsowski said.

"You can shove two pair up your ass, a straight flush," Palladino said.

"He coulda been bluffing," Gonsowski said.

"You're still looking at aces over kings," Flannery said. "Meyer had you beat on the board."

"This is called Widows," Parker said, and began dealing.

"What the hell's Widows?" Palladino asked.

"A new game."

"Another crazy new game," Flannery said.

Neither of them enjoyed losing.

"What I do, I deal two extra hands . . ."

"I hate these dumb crazy games," Flannery said.

". . . facedown. One of them has three cards in it, the other has five cards. Facedown. Two hands, facedown."

"Is this a five-card game?" Gonsowski asked.

"What the hell you think it is?" Palladino said.

"It could be a seven-card game, how do I know what it is? I never played it in my life. I never even *heard* of it till tonight."

"It stinks already," Flannery said.

"Two hands facedown," Parker said. "They're called widows, the hands. One, two, three," he said, dealing, "that's the first widow . . . and one, two, three, four, five," still dealing, "that's the second widow."

"Why're they called widows?"

"I don't know why. That's what they're called, and that's the name of the game. Widows."

"I still don't get it," Gonsowski said. "What's the basic game here?"

"Five-card stud," Parker said, dealing all around the table now. "One card down, four up, we bet after each card."

"Then what?" Meyer asked.

"After the third card, if you don't like your hand, you can bid on the three-card widow. Whoever bids highest, the money goes in the pot, and he tosses in his hand and gets a whole *new* hand, those three cards in the widow."

"Sounds shittier and shittier every minute," Palladino said.

"It's a good game," Parker said, "wait and see."

"What about that other hand?" Goldstein asked. "The five-card hand?"

"Well," Parker said, beaming like a magician about to pull a rabbit from a hat, "after the *fifth* card is dealt, if you *still* don't like your hand, you can bid on that second widow, and if you're the highest bidder, you get a whole new *five*-card hand."

"You serving drinks here?" Flannery asked, "or did Prohibition come back?"

"Help yourself, it's in the kitchen," Parker said. "Rudy, you're high."

Gonsowski looked around the table, surprised that his eight of diamonds was high on the board.

"I need *both* those other hands," Meyer said.

"Widows," Palladino said sourly.

"Another dumb game," Flannery said.

"Relax," Goldstein said. "It'll come and go in the night."

"Like all the others," Palladino said sourly.

"Bet fifty cents," Gonsowski said.